A LOG ACROSS THE ROAD

SHEILA ROSS

A Log Across the Road

Every stream must join a river
before it can flow to the sea
MALAY PROVERB

COLLINS
ST JAMES'S PLACE, LONDON
1971

William Collins Sons & Co Ltd

London . Glasgow . Sydney . Auckland

Toronto . Johannesburg

First published 1971
© Sheila Ross

ISBN 0 00 221481 4

Set in Monotype Plantin
Made and Printed in Great Britain by
William Collins Sons & Co Ltd Glasgow

For all those who lost their lives during
the Malayan Emergency, 1948–1960.
And to those who were left behind.

My thanks are due to Group Captain Paul Gomez, CBE, RAF, for his help and advice and to wife, Jean, for plodding through my original script with such patience and care. They are also due to my husband and daughter, without whose co-operation this book could not have been written.

CONTENTS

BOOK III

IN WHICH THE RIVER FLOWS DOWN TO THE SEA

Kuala Jelang

'. . . Communist Terrorists attacked a vehicle carrying a number of civilians and members of the Security Forces in the Ulu Kuala Jelang area yesterday. Altogether ten persons are missing. Security Forces are following up . . .'

Typical Malayan Press report, circa 1952

THE TEN

James Weatherby District Officer, Kuala Jelang
Philip Morrison Officer-in-Charge, Police District, Kuala Jelang
Stanislaus Olshewski Medical Officer, Kuala Jelang
Donald Thom Forestry Officer, Kuala Jelang
Sharif Ahmat Senior Inspector, Malayan Police
Jogindar Singh Sergeant-major, Malayan Police
Vincent Lee Chee Min Detective-sergeant, Malayan Police
Omar Corporal, Malayan Police
Abdul Karim Constable, Malayan Police
Ramakrishnan Clerk, Bukit Merah Estate, Kuala Jelang

PROLOGUE

In the heat and haze of full noon, a heavy black truck nosed its cumbersome way along a Malayan jungle road. Heavily treed slopes sheered steeply to its left and to its right the vegetation fell away sharply into a ravine.

To the insect life of the jungle, it was just another large, black beetle creeping along the winding contour path. The grinding noise, which nearly deafened the vehicle's passengers, was drowned by their own shrill song and the roar and crash of the yellow river which plunged along the floor of the valley, far below.

To the occupants of the truck, eight standing, swaying and staggering with the movement of the vehicle over the rough road, and two sitting, the homeward journey seemed interminable.

Ten men of diverse race and background and from several different lands; a Scot, a Canadian and a Pole; three Malays, a Sikh, an Englishman, a Chinese and a Tamil. Ten men, thrown together in circumstances wholly unpredictable but a short time before. Ten men, each busy with his own thoughts. But no thoughts could stray far from the present for long; this was the year 1952 and, after nearly four years of Emergency, it was not possible to travel along such a road without being constantly alert to its potential hazards. Thus, a shadow or a falling leaf, the cry of an animal or bird call too oft repeated, caused muscles to tense and eyes to scan surroundings with added care and apprehension.

'I'll prepare the yellow rice, yellow rice, yellow rice,' went the wheels of the truck. 'I'll prepare the yellow rice, yellow rice, yellow rice,' went through the head of Senior Inspector Sharif Ahmat, as the heavy armoured vehicle lurched and swayed along the jungle road.

He thought with humiliation of the scene that morning, his wife's strident abuse still ringing in his ears. There had never been a divorce in his family, yet, but by God, if things did not improve, there would be soon. But, even as he thought these thoughts, he knew that he would never divorce her. The truth was that, after nearly a year of marriage on stormy seas, he was still as infatuated with his wife as he had ever been. And she? She was bored. Perhaps it was his own fault; he had not allowed for boredom when extolling the advantages of being an inspector's wife. It seemed that status was not enough.

Allahumma! He took off his floppy jungle-green hat and ran a hand through his damp hair. You know I will put up with almost anything from you, but not these awful scenes.

His thoughts travelled back to the party of the night before; the platform set up in the middle of the parade ground and the four professional dancing girls, swaying and jogging to the rhythm of the ronggeng, as the violin wailed and the men went up in turn to dance. Some were sedate, some clowns, but all enjoyed the simple dance. He had not danced – not with the knowledge that his wife's foot would be tapping and her hips swaying as her eyes bored into the back of his head. The Europeans had danced and their wives had laughed, for they sat with their husbands as was their custom, and his own officer's wife had suggested that his wife should join them. He had been cross, because she should have known better, but politely refused. The wives of the men sat demurely in the shadows, watching but taking no part, as Malay adat dictated. He would have liked to have had his own wife there, to have danced with her, but this could never be and he had done the next best thing by setting a chair for her on the verandah, where she would have a good view, and taking over satay and a bottle of orange crush. But she had only screamed at him and thrown the bottle at his head before turning petulantly into the inner room.

She was still screaming this morning and, as he left the house to answer an early call, his hat and jungle boots had whistled past his ear.

'Stay there,' she had yelled, 'and don't come back. I hope the bandits get you. I hope they kill you. Don't expect me to mourn.'

The memory of the dreadful words piercing the quiet morning air would smart for a long time. And the humiliation, as the eyes from every barrack-room had followed him across the compound. He had ignored her though, marching straight ahead and sending an orderly back to retrieve his boots and hat – he had retained *some* pride.

'When I hear you're dead, I'll celebrate,' she had shrieked, 'I'll prepare the yellow rice. Yes, I'll prepare the yellow rice.'

He saw the obstacle on the road with dull eyes. Was it a log? Who cares? he thought. If I die, it is the will of Allah and, if I live, that too is His will.

Ugly scene that, this morning, Philip Morrison was thinking. He was Officer-in-Charge of the Police District of Kuala Jelang and Sharif Ahmat was his best inspector. More than his best inspector; he had been a tower of strength on numerous occasions; an instructor and a friend. But why, oh why, hadn't he married some decent country girl, instead of that sophisticated tart? Surely there must be girls queuing up to marry a chap like Ahmat?

He stiffened suddenly and his eyes narrowed as he searched the roadsides, trying to ascertain the difference from when they had travelled along it earlier that morning. Perhaps it was imagination; there had never been an ambush here, but it was a perfect ambush area. This road gave him the creeps – but then any road gave you the creeps when you were due for leave.

Then he saw the log. Or was it a log? Not worth taking a chance. He raised his hand to bang on the roof of the driver's cabin.

Morrison's involuntarily tautening biceps had nudged James Weatherby, the District Officer, out of his reverie. They saw the object at the same time. Oh God, he prayed, not now. Please don't let me be killed now. For James's mind had at last turned to happier thoughts.

All the way out he had been worrying about this land. It was a problem which he had tried to shelve, but it had been nagging at the back of his mind for some time and when it had come up for discussion at the last meeting of the District War Executive Committee, he had been able to shelve it no longer.

Why didn't the manager want to sell now? It was an excellent site for a Resettlement Area and, in fact, old Wotherspoon himself had suggested it. 'No use to me,' he had said, 'estate's already too large for me to cope with single-handed – be glad for Government to take it off my hands.' Government had offered a good price – far more than they need have – so what had happened to make him suddenly change his mind?

He was no nearer a solution than when they had started out, but thrashing it out in the open had eased his mind and, on the return journey, he had deliberately turned his thoughts to more pleasant things.

At that moment he had been thinking of his old Nannie, who would soon be joining them to care for his own children. 'Of course, if you have the name of Weatherby, you have to be called James,' she had once told him, when he was tiny, and all along the road the nursery jingle had been running through his head. James, James, Morrison, Morrison, Weatherby George Dupree . . . in fact, unconsciously, he had been tapping it out on the side of the truck with his one good hand.

What was Philip staring at? No, God, please not now. Only a month or so ago they had come to the decision that this was no longer the life for them – his old wounds had been giving him hell and he knew he could not face the heat of the tropics much longer. Then, out of the blue, had come an old wartime friend, who suggested going into partnership in an Australian farm and now it was all arranged. Next month old Nannie would be joining them.

It couldn't happen to him now, not when everything was only just settled. Perhaps a tree had fallen across the road; perhaps there were prohibited timber cutters in the area; perhaps . . .

Detective-sergeant Vincent Lee Chee Min was dreaming of his new motor bike.

Blessed with a wealthy father, Chee Min had never wanted for much, until the day he had married without paternal consent. He had not really believed that the old man would cut off his allowance, but he had, and, for the first time, he had learned what it was like to live on a sergeant's pay. Just as he had been promised a car too. Oh well, hand it to Rose – she was the one who had insisted that they cut down and save. She had made him stick to it too and now that great, gleaming machine, because he had paid for it himself, meant more to him than a hundred cars.

He hummed gently, 'Rose, Rose I love you . . .' It was his day off to-morrow; he would take her to the cinema in town – wish his old man could see them.

He stopped humming abruptly, blinked, shut his eyes and opened them again. Damn, it *was* something on the road.

Sergeant-major Jogindar Singh stroked his beard thoughtfully as he looked around the truck. He was still young to be a sergeant-major and, as he examined the back of the European officer, he wondered how long it would be before he held the same rank. He knew that Tuan Morrison had recommended his promotion to sub-inspector – the clerk had told him so – and for a man of ambition that was but the first rung of the ladder. It had paid him to remain loyal to the British, but it had cost his father his head. Ah, but that was a long time ago and he had more than fulfilled his father's hopes for him.

Next his eyes travelled to Sharif Ahmat and his mouth curled with derision as he thought of the morning's incident. Emancipation for women indeed! The local representative of the Kaum Ibu, the women's section of the main political party, was forever in the barracks harping on the subject. No wonder her listeners looked so smug – every single one of them had their husbands right under their thumbs! Imagine his Suvindar behaving as that bitch had this morning. Sikh women knew their place.

Doe-eyed, submissive little Suvindar Kaur, who might already be in labour with his fourth child. Perhaps it would be another son, then next time a daughter. Women for children . . . the proverb ran and he thought with amusement of Karim, the driver; a fair, slender Malay youth whom he had tried to convert to his ways of pleasure. So far he had been terrified, but give him time, give him time – they all owed him money anyway.

16

'There's a boy across the river . . .' he began to hum in a high-pitched, nasal whine. That doctor, some foreign European, he did not appear to have a wife around, perhaps he – ? The amusement left Jogindar's face.

Was that a log across the road?

Stanislaus Olshewski surveyed the assembled company with a cynical half-smile not unlike that of Jogindar Singh's. He expected to die that day. Why? He shrugged at his own self-question. Philip was the Scot, he was the one who should be fey – and yet he had had that strange feeling ever since climbing into the truck; the same feeling that he had had on New Year's Eve. The possibility of imminent death troubled him not at all. It was not only that he was a fatalist, but a realisation that, although he enjoyed life, there was nothing that he would really miss.

He had no business to be in the truck anyway and, if an agitated little constable had not dashed up to him and begged him to return with them to Kuala Jelang to help his wife, he would not have been. But it was the girl's first baby and she had been in labour for thirty-six hours already; besides, he had already spent several days of his local leave on the estate and it had been enough.

A student of human nature, Olshewski had for the past half-hour been analysing each of his companions in turn. What trick of fate had brought these men, including himself, together to-day? What made them tick?

He wondered how much at least two members of the party knew about their wives. But one doesn't say to a man, on shaking hands, 'See that scar? Your wife's teeth did that!' Nor do you ask another if his wife had ever had that mole removed from her left breast that she hated so. He pondered on these facts and laughed mirthlessly to himself.

Yes, what made them tick? Look at Donald – something must have happened during the last decade to be turning what should be a normal young man into an embittered, maudlin, drunken sot.

He looked at whatever it was on the road for a second, then shrugged and closed his eyes. Taking a deep breath, he leaned back against the side of the truck with casually folded arms, to await the inevitable.

Donald Thom was peering into the forest with a professional eye. No wonder the old devil's being so cagey over selling this land, he thought; it has some damned good timber on it.

The Police had read some very unsavoury motives into the manager's sudden excuses for not wanting to sell, after urging Government to buy, and the District Officer, hoping to find some less sinister

17

reason for his change of heart, was exploring all channels and had asked him, the Forestry Officer, to come and give his opinion.

It could be timber, yes indeed, Thom was thinking, when he was interrupted by the corporal Bren gunner.

'Please move a little to the left, tuan,' he asked, 'I must have room to aim.'

He followed the corporal's eye along the barrel of the Bren – timber indeed.

Corporal Omar, the oldest occupant of the vehicle, did not want to die and he wanted passionately to save his officer, the one who had given him trust and understanding when he had needed it most. He slipped his hand inside his shirt to feel the scar across his chest. Tuan Morrison had carried him out of the jungle on his back when he had been shot and later given him his blood – how could a man forget that? And besides, with his wife and children gone, whom else had he to love?

His thoughts drifted back to a court-room and the terrible words, disloyalty, treachery and ignominious conduct, still echoed in his brain. He, a sergeant-major, with nearly twenty years' service, had been discharged. The memory could never be erased, but gratitude had softened it; gratitude to the Federation Police who had accepted him as a constable – to be watched, but accepted none the less; gratitude to Tuan Morrison. How hopeless it had been, trying to explain to somebody who did not want to understand. 'Untrust-worthy' he had been labelled and left at that. But Tuan Morrison, he had listened quietly, not understanding very well because his Malay had still been poor then, but the Mem had been there and she too had listened and smiled and helped him with the difficult words and sympathised over the loss of his wife. He had felt himself liked and trusted again. And then there were these – he fingered his corporal's stripes – they were the doing of Tuan Morrison too.

On the whole it had been a happy year; he did not want it to end. Was it just a shadow that traversed the width of the road: Like the doctor, Omar drew a deep breath, and prepared to open fire.

The movement of the Bren gunner, whose weapon was mounted on top of the cabin, above his head, sent Ramakrishnan, the Tamil clerk, into a fit of the shakes. He kept his head still, but his eyes rolled end-lessly from left to right and back again and he licked his lips nervously as each bend came in sight.

Ramakrishnan had betrayed his employers, his country, his family and all the men in the truck with him now. Their wrath would be awful if they knew, but nothing to the wrath of the terrorists if they discovered that he was about to betray them as well. What if they were to set an ambush for to-day? He moistened his lips yet again and began to wish that he was sitting somewhere where he did not have quite such a good view of the road ahead.

He heard the driver's sharp intake of breath and closed his eyes.

Abdul Karim was tired. He loved driving, in fact, being accepted into the police as a driver/mechanic had fulfilled a desire long dreamed of, but pulling the heavy vehicle round hairpin bend after hairpin bend on the deeply rutted road was exhausting. The glare hit his eyes and his arms ached.

It was a relief to know that he was carrying the doctor back to his wife. He thought of the long straight road to come and the long, cool drink at the end of it. Rokiah would soon have help, but would they be in time? He put his foot down and went as fast as he dared.

He was almost upon the thing before he saw it.

The insects could have told them it was only a branch. They had heard it crack, severed at last by some vibration – that of the outward bound vehicle perhaps – from an aged, rotting tree, struck by lightning many moons ago. A great number of their kind had been made homeless by the fall.

They could have told them too of many others of their brethren being made homeless by the felling of a whole tree, which even now was being dragged across the road; an obstacle specially devised to block a beetle's path. But that was several miles ahead – even as an insect travels on a bird's wing – the beetle's antennae would no doubt warn it of the danger long before; it could deviate. And if it didn't, who cared? One beetle more or less.

The road was narrow; impossible to turn. Morrison still had his hand raised to strike the cabin roof and his mouth open to shout the order to debus, when he saw that his fears were unfounded. The dreaded log was only a rotten bough.

'Better tell Wotherspoon,' he said, looking up, 'that tree will fall any day; it could decimate one of his lorries.' And muttered, *sotto voce*, to Weatherby, 'or his Land-Rover – with him in it with any luck.'

Every face, even Sharif Ahmat's, wore a shamefaced grin of relief and several half-stifled giggles could be imagined if not actually heard.

They were entering a temporarily more even stretch of road, where the trees grew further from the verge and they were in full sun. Everyone relaxed on the moment and it was pleasant to hear the Polish doctor's laugh. The smoother road made individual voices audible for the first time.

'That is the sort of moment when one has a horrid flashback of one's past,' Olshewski remarked, 'when you feel that Judgment Day is just around the corner and wonder if you will have time to atone for your sins.'

The other Europeans glanced at him curiously. It had never occurred to them that he might be a religious man. He interpreted their looks correctly.

'Oh yes,' he said, 'people change, but ten years ago I would have been on my knees by now. Scared bloody stiff!'

'Ten years ago?'

'Yes. Cast your mind back ten years.' He had seen the agonised expression crossing Weatherby's face when they first saw the branch and, realising that some private anguish was tormenting him, picked deliberately on him to take his mind off it. 'Where were you ten years ago, James?'

'Ten years ago? I was in the desert. Seven hundred miles from Cairo, seven hundred miles from the sea. I forget the name of the oasis now; Kifra or Kufra, or something. I was happy there.'

'Ten years ago was a bad year, Sahib. The year the Japanese came.'

Jogindar Singh had spoken in Malay and Karim, the driver, who understood for the first time what they were talking about, thought, who cares what happened ten years ago – is that or is that not a log? He had not been able to see the expressions of relief on the faces of the men above and behind him, but he felt the sweat break out on his own face as the truck rumbled over the rotten wood, crumbling it to dust.

'You *liked* it?' Morrison, who had hated his own short spell in the desert, was amazed.

'I loved it. The colours – and the peace. Not like this – too green, too lush. Flamboyant – and so noisy.' His English-speaking Asian listeners were puzzled; at least one of them had been thinking how quiet it was. 'Here, there are always cicadas or frogs or birds, but in the desert . . . Wind perhaps, drifting sand. Soft sounds, peaceful sounds. And the colours. The other chaps would be off to Cairo at the drop of a hat, but when I had any time off I would hitch a ride with some chums in the Long Range Desert Group, or take a jeep out by myself. The tops of the dunes are white or yellow, or sometimes pink, depending on the time of day and where you are, but the depths – every hue that a dove has on its breast and then some, ochre, blue, mauve, purple, sometimes a silvery green. Soft colours, never harsh.'

There was a strange, quiet moment while everyone looked at the speaker. Those able to understand him, surprised at a man they had thought insensitive and hard; those not able to understand, nevertheless interested in the unusual tone of voice.

It seemed as though time lay suspended. The road continued to unwind and, for everyone, as the truck lumbered slowly towards its destiny, there came, as in a dream, the fleeting memories of the past ten years.

Cast your mind back. Where were you ten years ago? Yes, where were *you*?

Through the deep green treetop sea, splashed here and there with flaming orange, scarlet, and deep, burning yellow, the beetle crawled, warning signals flashing to its enemies as the sun struck some burnished plane of its armoured shell.

Deep in the ravine the river dashed on, lost to the sunlit world above in impenetrable gloom, only its voice rising through the shadows and the trees. In the distance, the blue, eternal mountains slept, oblivious of human frailties and problems, harbouring their own insect life.

BOOK I

IN WHICH THE STREAMS LEAVE THE WATERSHED

Part 1. *Wars within wars*

1. THE BARMAID AT THE DOG AND DUCK

James Weatherby

'I don't want to join the air force, I don't want to go to war. I'd rather hang around Piccadilly Underground, living off the earnings of a high-born lady – '

The scene was the Dog and Duck, *circa* January, 1940; but it could have been any pub 'somewhere in England'. Of course it was monopolised by the bomber squadrons operating from the station near by – which was hardly surprising, seeing that it was no distance from the nearest dispersal point, if you went through the gorse and under the wire – but a few pongoes crept in occasionally and then it became a case of who could make the most noise. It usually ended in a rough-house, depending on booze and mood, and, on this particular night, there were all the makings of one.

It was still the time of the phoney war, long before the first thousand-bomber raid and long, long before the great armadas filled the sky in the daytime as well as at night. The crew of C for Charlie were not likely to be called out and they comprised the group with leanings towards the life of a pimp.

Thinking back, those songs, even the clean versions, were roared out with extraordinary gusto.

The pongoes were there that night and the fact that they had captured the rickety, upright piano and were bellowing their guts out, was making the already truculent RAF sing all the louder.

The landlord was looking dismal. 'There's going to be a fight,' he wailed, 'I know there's going to be a fight.'

'Keep your hair on, duck,' Elsie consoled him, 'you're making money out of them don't forget.'

'Bless 'em all, bless 'em all, the long and the short – '

Christ, you couldn't let those brown jobs get away with it. 'When you're flying bloody Ansons at five hundred bloody feet – '

'Nah then, don't you start the dirty words. No dirty words in 'ere, or out you go, the blooming lot o' you.'

' – bless all the corporals and their bleeding sons.'

' – as you find out when you end up in the Firth of bloody Forth!'

'Don't know why I don't move into the bleedin' NAAFI,' grumbled the landlord and sighed with relief as the clock struck the third

24

quarter. 'Time in fifteen minutes, gentlemen, time in fifteen minutes. Thank Gawd.'

Singing round the bar stopped as elbows were raised and mugs passed across for a last pint.

'Who's having the barmaid?' yelled Charlie's navigator, Chris Holloway, daring the pongoes to horn in. There had to be *some* excuse to start a scrap.

'We'll toss for her.' And one of the air gunners flipped a halfpenny on to the bar. 'Coins out everyone, heads toss again, tails are out.' And to the barmaid, 'We're tossing for you, Else.'

'That's all right, love,' Elsie stood complacently behind her barricade of glasses, 'no telling what the flip of a coin will do for you, eh?'

They tossed and the captain won.

'Time, gentlemen, please.'

As the pub closed, Flight-Lieutenant James Weatherby, rather flushed and somewhat in his cups, claimed his prize. Taking Elsie solemnly by the arm, he led her outside where, meeting a rush of cold night air, he was promptly sick.

'What do we do now?' he asked, swaying slightly and trying hard to focus. All he really wanted to do was to lie down somewhere in the dark and hold on to his head. God, why had he let the others go back to the station without him. Something to do with heads and tails. Thinking of tails . . . 'Well, Elsie?'

She gave a small, nervous laugh. 'Well, love, the pubs are closed, the flicks are closed; not much you can do but walk me home, is there?'

It was not long before he had to dive for the ditch again and the second bout of vomiting cleared his head sufficiently for him to appreciate the sight of Elsie sitting on a stile a few yards down the road, clear cut in the pale, cold moonlight.

'Sorry about that.' To his surprise he was sweating. 'Had too much to drink.'

'Feeling better, love?' She patted the stile and moved over to make room for him. 'Come and sit quietly for a minute, then you'll be all right.'

He sat beside her, grateful for her sympathy and after a while she turned and wrapped her arms about his neck.

In a sudden burst of passion, James had her on the ground. His weight pressed through her and into the grass, his head went round and the earth spun.

When finally he did walk Elsie home, a cold, grey dawn was breaking.

It was a cold, grey dawn all right; in more ways than one.

Allow me to introduce myself: James Weatherby, the biggest

25

bloody mug in the whole of His Majesty's Royal Air Force. Squadron Leader Weatherby now, I'm pleased to say, and that is all I've achieved since that sordid little incident.

It was two years ago that the squadron left England and we've been in Libya ever since, but now we're posted home again – at least we're posted to South Africa and that usually means home in the end – and I've been sitting alone in my tent, trying to put my thoughts in order.

Outside, the wind is howling across the desert and the night is as cold as a January night can be. Inside, I watch the shadows thrown by the hurricane lamp and they are all familiar. Shadows thrown by my few possessions in this, my own tent, which I share with nobody. I have been happy here; it is all that I want and now that I have to leave it, I find myself clinging desperately to these small, mundane things.

It has been easy to put the whole episode of my marriage into a mental 'pending' file while we have been in the desert. There is a calmness of the soul in the very monotony and a strange fascination in the rolling dunes – the same fascination as watching the sea from the deck of a ship, or looking into a fire, I suppose. It didn't take me long to understand how men like Lawrence had fallen under its spell. I'm not much good at putting thoughts into words, but I've often wished that I had a wife to whom I could write and tell these things, how the grandeur has affected me, and of the unfathomable, indeterminate peace within the cauldron of war. But no use writing to Elsie, she'd wonder what I was talking about. I write to my mother instead.

We didn't see much more of the Dog and Duck. Within a very short time the real war started and C for Charlie became my passion, my love and my main responsibility in life; C for Charlie and her crew, that is.

Larger formations were crossing the coast every day and we were usually with them. I suppose a father with eight children must feel as I felt in those early days, and I was a young father. It wasn't only the joy of flying – and that, after all, is what I had always wanted to do – but the sense of achievement when we all, and I say again, *all*, walked in to debriefing. And then, through the steam that rose from those enormous mugs of scalding cocoa, I would look at each face – some older and some younger than my own – at each pair of eyes, and know that we nine, together, as a team, had brought each other through. Love for a woman is one thing, but the love of a man for other men, compounded of affection, comradeship and dependence, is something that I doubt if a woman could understand.

Not many left of the crew now. Chris, the one who called the toss that night, Ken, and old Norman Parkes.

When we did visit the pub it was usually the same; a lot of noise, a lot of laughter, the landlord moaning and Elsie consoling.

It was the night our posting came through that the trouble started.

26

Extraordinary how the locals always knew when a squadron was on the move before we knew ourselves. The news had come through that afternoon; we were all packed up and ready to go on leave and were having a final do in the old D and D when Elsie spoke to me.

'Going away, Jimmy love?'

All of a sudden there was a deathly hush and the 'walls have ears' and 'careless talk costs lives' posters loomed from the walls. I looked at my crew, all of whom had been talking nineteen to the dozen, but were now looking expectantly at me – wondering how I was going to get out of it, I suppose.

I heard my own voice, very clear and distinct, say, 'I'm going on leave.'

And that was that. Everyone started talking again and I lifted my glass to Elsie, but already my stomach was doing a loop – there had been something in the tone of her voice.

'Seeing as how you're going away, Jimmy love,' she spoke very quietly, but the menace was there, 'there's something I'll have to tell you. Perhaps you'll see me home?'

Cold dread settled on me like a blanket of crushed ice and, when I heard the familiar 'Time, gentlemen, please', it sounded like the knell of doom.

Elsie did not beat about the bush.

'I'm going to have a baby. That's what I had to tell you.'

Her voice grated like a saw on metal and was just about as hard. When I was silent she grabbed my arm and shook it until I was afraid she was going to have a fit of hysterics.

'I'm going to have a baby,' she fairly screeched at me, 'I'm going to have a baby, d'you hear – and for God's sake don't ask me if I'm sure.'

Well, I wasn't the first man it had happened to. And for what? Oh Christ, why wasn't I shot down when so many others went on that raid last week? Then I remembered my crew. Christ, I thought again, oh Christ.

We had walked quite a long way when I stopped to look at her in the dim beam of a blacked out street light. Small, dark, neat, attractive in a common sort of way. I had only made love to her once. It wasn't her fault.

The flip of a coin and too many beers.

'Will you marry me?' I asked.

The tent flapped in a sudden gust of wind that made me shiver. Ghost walking over my grave? But no ghost I'm afraid. I pulled the polo neck of my sweater up over my ears.

The wind had howled across the Lincolnshire flats too, that day we were married by special licence.

My family had behaved splendidly. I must admit that I funked it

27

at first; I had sent them a telegram, but, by the time the Cornish Riviera reached Exeter, I had such cold feet that I left Elsie in a Torquay hotel and went on to Kingsbridge on my own. There my father met me in his battered old Ford and made no comment on my non-existent wife.

Instead, he took me to the local and it was not before we were behind two double Scotches and he had his pipe going to his satisfaction – what a useful addiction that is – that he even mentioned her.

'I expect you'd like to tell me all about it before you see your mother,' and the old man settled back to wait for it.

My father is getting on in years; an overworked country doctor. He'd been in the RAMC in the first world war and was peeved as hell because his offer to rejoin had been rejected in this one. As it was, he had a little petrol, a great deal of respect and the ability to get hold of a Scotch when the pubs were officially serving only gin or rum. We had never had much money to spare and with five sons it must have been a pretty hard struggle for him at times. I am the youngest and when I stopped to think what it must have cost him to put four boys through university, then me through Cranwell, it made everything that much worse.

I told him the bare truth.

What his private thoughts were, I could not tell. He sat sucking his pipe and looking into space for a while, then, very deliberately, turned back his cuff and looked at his watch.

'At least you've done the right thing by the girl,' was his only comment, and then, 'better get back, or your mother'll be wondering what's happened to us. I'll tell her as much as I think fit and you'd better fetch the lass to-morrow. And now I think we both need another drink.'

From my mother's strained face the next morning, it was not difficult to divine that he had told her everything, but she welcomed Elsie with open arms and, if she was not the daughter-in-law that she would have chosen no one ever would have known it.

Nannie was the only snag. There never was a greater snob than Nannie and she made no effort whatsoever to conceal her feelings. Poor old dear; it was her one sorrow that Mother had never produced a daughter, whose household she could tyrannise one day. For some years she had helped my mother in the house and my father in his surgery, but I think she still hoped that one day she would have more small Weatherbys to dominate.

There was a guest night a couple of evenings after our return from leave and I took the bull by the horns and introduced the new Mrs Weatherby to the Mess. It may have been a foolish move, but I thought it would be the easiest one in the long run.

God, what an evening. The Wingco Ops, who was also the PMC,

raised his eyebrows when he saw Elsie come in, but at least had the grace not to comment. But when I took her over to where the commissioned members of my crew were gathered and made my rehearsed announcement, the sudden silence was so awful that I thought she would cut and run. I must admit I felt so sorry for her that it alleviated some of my own forlorness.

When everyone came to, the false heartiness and vacuous platitudes were almost worse than if they had all said what they thought – and certainly worse than the silence.

Not that I was left in any doubt as to what they thought for long. Somehow we got through the evening and, relieved when it was over and I had taken Elsie back to her digs in the village, I returned to my room in the Mess to find what appeared to be a tribunal awaiting me.

The door was hardly shut before I was greeted by a chorus of, 'For God's sake, Jimmy, what made you do it?'

I told them. And then it came, fast and thick, a verbal bombardment from all sides.

'But how do you know you're the father?'

'It could have been any one of us.'

'Any member of the squadron for that matter.'

'Any member of the station more likely.'

'If you hadn't been so bloody secretive, we'd have put you right before it was too late.'

I had not said a single word and what I did utter then must have sounded trite and priggish in the extreme. 'Well someone has to give a name to the child.'

'*If* she's pregnant.'

'What do you mean?'

'My dear old chap,' it was the slow drawl of Norman Parkes, 'your Elsie is the most talented tart in the whole of East Anglia.'

I hit Norman then, square on the mouth, although God knew he was telling the truth, as I was to find out in time.

We glared at each other, blood pouring from my knuckles and Norman's lip. He held out his hand, but it was too much; I dashed from the room, down the corridor and out into the winter night and walked until dawn. As a child sobs and shouts, 'It's not fair,' I stamped around the perim, muttering to myself of the injustice I had been done. As I saw my dreams of the right marriage to someone I loved and a brilliant career fade, the hot tears gushed down my cheeks until I was exhausted and numb.

I didn't touch Elsie again and, when the squadron embarked a few days later, I hoped that I would never see her or England's shores again.

Talk of the devil – or think of him at least. The tent flapped again,

29

but this time it opened properly to admit Norman Parkes, the only one left of my original crew members, the only one who had been with the squadron longer than I.

'Good God, old man, what are you sitting in the dark for?'

It was only when he mentioned it that I realised my light had gone out, so deep in thought had I been. When I had dug out my spare lamp and it was turned up, Norman sank on to my camp bed and lit a cigarette. He had a way of looking at one that made you feel he was reading your thoughts even when he wasn't. But, as usual, he was right.

'Thinking of home?'

I nodded.

'What are you going to do about her, James?'

'Try and make a go of it.' I shook my head at his raised eyebrows. 'I've given it a lot of thought. It's unlikely that Elsie would give me a divorce and, if I ever managed to divorce her, it would hardly do my career any good.'

'Very Cranwellian of you, old man.' Norman was strictly a wartime flyer. 'Like a drink? I've got a bottle in my tent.'

'No thanks. I've got some letters to write.'

'I'll leave you to it then. Good night.'

'Good night.'

There had been a time when Norman and the rest had urged me to go into Cairo, urged me to go on leave, to find a girl friend, pick up a whore, go on a blind; but they knew better now and left me alone.

I stuck up the envelopes of the letters I had written and pulled out a snapshot from the one just received from Elsie, for better or for worse, my wife. At least she was not bad looking and she dressed reasonably well. Despite Norman's opinion, she did not look a tart.

Of course there had been no child and, once I had got over the bitterness engendered by that piece of information, I became more or less resigned to my fate. But now that the squadron was on the move and the evil day was fast approaching, the sugar coating on the pill was beginning to show some very thin patches.

2. WELCOME TO OUR NEWLY COMING FRIENDS

Ramakrishnan

I am watching through window with disgust as my father and mother bow and scrape to Big White Chief.

Estate Manager is being all most bountiful lord and inspecting labour lines for last time – saying good-bye only, he is telling us. The next place he will be inspecting is inside of Japanese gaol, I am glad to say.

I am taking last look at banner, newly prepared by yours truly. 'Welcome to our newly coming friends' is boldly printed in red paint on sheet taken from white pig's dhobi basket. I am feeling brightness of smile in mouth and eyes and my heart is beating with excitement most gleeful as I peruse said banner, before secreting it in hiding-place below sleeping-platform. Soon Japanese soldiers will be chasing white pigs from shores of Malaya and I, Ramakrishnan son of Ramasamy, will be standing here with my banner to greet them.

My father is kangani of Bukit Puteh Estate, very important Malayan rubber estate, I am telling you, and is holding responsible position. And yet all the time he is saying, 'Yes, master,' and, 'No, master,' and giggling with hand held in front of mouth, and my mother is just as bad.

And now, when I am telling them that we are to be free at last of the tyranny we have been suffering from so long, they are standing with faces wet with tears.

Truly, old people are stupid.

'Why do you kow-tow to him?' I ask, as I join my parents in long line of farewelling labourers.

'Hush,' my father is whispering. 'Master will hear you.'

'I am not caring if any white bastard is hearing me,' I shout in English, for I am attending estate English school.

I laugh and am spitting in direction of retreating manager and am looking with disgust at all fawning, cringing men and women, when my father catches me most abusing clout across ear. But I laugh all the louder.

I am fifteen years old and when I am being as old as my father I shall not be the slave in bondage that he is. I am tired of hearing how we Tamils were untouchables in India and how we are having better life on rubber estates and railways of Malaya. It is just showing how stupid are the old folk; truly believing their life is good. Everybody knows that we were brought here from India in chains – that is why the Malays call us Kelings, because of the kling-kling sound of the chains round necks and ankles. It is no use my father laughing and ridiculing and informing all that I was not even babe in womb at time. He is not believing when I tell him how he came from India – he is wishing to believe only white pigs' fabrications – he is forever shaking head and saying he is remembering well and I was not born. Truly he is most obstinate fellow.

The chains are breaking, I am telling you; the tyranny is ending. Truly I am seeing future most glorious as members of new Japanese Co-prosperity Sphere.

Soon I shall be joining glorious Indian National Army, when

formed in Malaya in co-operation with newly coming friends. Asia for the Asiatics. Welcome to our Nipponese friends who will be forever saving us. I, Ramakrishnan son of Ramasamy, am saluting you.

3. A DESCENDANT OF THE PROPHET RE-ENLISTS

Sharif Ahmat

My name is Sharif Ahmat bin Haji Sharif Ismail and I come from the leading family of one of the nine provinces of the State of Negri Sembilan in Malaya. We are Menangkerbau Malays, that is to say that our ancestors came from Sumatra a century and a half ago and we are proud of our race and heritage.

My prename Sharif denotes that I am descended from the Prophet; my father and mother have the titles of Haji and Hajjah because they have made the pilgrimage to Mecca and my mother, Sharifa Meriam, also has the courtesy title of Puan. In our state we have matriarchal law; I will not bore you with the details – it is mostly a matter of land titles and inheritance – but it means that my mother has the last word on matters concerning marriage and it also means that we, her children, obey her without question.

We are a police family, going back to 1874, when my great-grandfather enlisted in the Sungei Ujong and Jelebu Force. We number five in the force at present: my father, who is Chief Inspector at the Depot, three brothers senior to me, and one who is still a recruit. I am still a PC, but I expect to enter the inspectorate in due course – at least I did. I have two young brothers still at school and two sisters as well, one at school and one married to a sergeant-major.

I tell you all this about my family because I want you to understand that I am a proud man and, although I have been brought up to serve and to be loyal to those whom I respect, I find it difficult to be humble. And to be humble to the Japanese is well-nigh beyond what any man can endure.

I stand five foot seven inches in my stockinged feet, which is tall for a Malay, and when I have my boots on I am a great deal taller than our yellow conquerors. In a way it has its advantages; I can look over their heads on parade and do not have to meet their eyes – in this way it is easier to hide the scorn that they must see there – but it also earns me more slaps than my compatriots. For of course it is humiliating for the master race to have to address anyone above them.

I was serving, in fact still am, in Batu Rimau, a smallish district headquarter station, in Perak, and I went off duty one evening under the impression that the enemy were still far to the north. In the middle of the night I awoke to a great commotion and, before I was fully awake, I found myself, along with most of my comrades, herded into the charge room and facing a Japanese officer.

This officer had every man's record sheet laid out on the desk in front of him and he informed us, without preamble, that he expected every one of us to re-enlist in the service of the Emperor of Nippon.

'Of course you are free to choose,' he told us; he spoke in English, which was translated into Malay by our Sikh inspector, 'but here I have the details not only of you yourselves, but of your families and your villages and I can assure you that the families of those who do not choose to serve will suffer for their foolishness.'

He then went into a long and flowery propaganda speech, based on the favourite Japanese theme of the Co-Prosperity Sphere and Asia for the Asiatics – we had heard it often enough on the radio – most of which our inspector did not bother to translate, but I had been to English school and understood. I agreed with Ram Singh, in view of the previous threats, it was hardly worth the trouble.

There was dead silence after the officer had finished speaking and then Inspector Ram Singh advised us, 'Best to swear. When the British return they will know that you were forced and it can only bring hardship to your families if you don't.'

So then and there, most of us clad only in sarongs and singlets, we raised our hands and swore an oath to Dai Nippon and later signed in confirmation.

I understand that my father also advised the recruits still at the Depot to swear. I know that he must have had their lives and the lives of their families at heart, but what it must have cost his pride I dread to think.

Only my eldest brother forswore the Japanese and it would have stood him in good stead had he lived. He fled south with the British and where he is now I have no idea. He was the only one of us whom my father felt he could not influence for, although still a sergeant, Hassan was earmarked for commissioned rank – or gazetted rank as we say in the Police – and as such, my father said, must make his own decisions. I would like to know what has happened to him, but we been confined to barracks ever since our new masters took over and now we are forbidden to communicate with our families.

Everything is done to humiliate us.

We have to eat our meals in the canteen and on the second day of the new rule pork was served. We Malays are not fanatical in our religion and like most young men – I am twenty – I am pretty lax when my parents are not around. But to even the laziest Muslim, the thought of pork is repellent.

None of us ate.

For the evening meal the pork appeared again and again none of us touched it. On the next day and the next it was the only food until, finally, through sheer hunger, we were forced to eat it. Murmurs of, 'Haram,' were heard all over the canteen. It could not have been worse had we been made to eat our own excreta.

I am told that the smoked bacon that the Europeans eat is palatable, but the great gobs of white fat that were forced on us almost made one vomit to look at it and there was not one man who ate without gagging.

Perhaps it will not be for long though. It is true that the Japanese have broken through the Muar-Mersing line and several times each day we see enemy aircraft formations heading south, but Singapore, we know, is impregnable, and it can only be a matter of months before the British are pushing north again.

Meanwhile, we can only resign ourselves and pray that Tuan Allah will look down upon our human frailties with compassion and grant us his blessed dispensation for actions done under duress.

4. FRIDAY THE THIRTEENTH

Sally Gunn

My name is, or was, Sally Gunn, and I am involved because I loved two men and phases of my life have become entangled with theirs.

It is not difficult to know when my part of the story began, because all of us have punctuation points in our lives and, for me, it was a Friday the thirteenth; 13th February, 1942 to be exact.

My family had been in Malaya for many years and when the war in Europe began in 1939 I was spending my winter holidays with my father. Little did he realise what was ahead when he kept me back from school that fatal year, and never did he dream that, at the age of sixteen, I would be cast adrift in the blazing, oily holocaust that was Singapore in its last days of freedom. For his peace of mind, better by far had I returned to my Australian boarding school, but I was an only child and ever since my mother had died I had been able to wind the old man round my little finger – I was partly responsible for my own present predicament.

The lines of straggling, dragging, disconsolate men, the sirens, and the strains of 'Land of Hope and Glory' – played every hour by Radio Singapore – cut suddenly short when the radio station was captured, were behind us. The roaring inferno of the oil islands, deliberately set on fire, were all around us.

'Blimey, wot wouldn't 'Ollywood give for this lot?' muttered an old soldier by my side. 'Dunkirk were mucking awful, but nothing to this. Christ, 'ere the bleeders come again.'

34

I closed my eyes and put my hands over my ears. I suppose I prayed. I don't know. I only know that I was frightened.

At sixteen, war can be fun and I suppose I should be ashamed of having enjoyed the excitement. But now, as the ship swayed and the dotted lines of tracer lacerated the already crimson shadows, I knew that terrible fear that makes one want to vomit and dries the saliva in the throat.

There was silence for a second or two – if one can call the roaring of several acres of fire silence – and I peered hopefully from under the rim of my tin hat. But not for long. It was back again; the high-pitched, screaming whine and the quick, staccato thuds of machine-gun bullets hitting the deck. I closed my eyes again and opened them a moment later to see the woodwork opening up in front of me, as though a knife had cut a jagged wound through the pine and pitch. My shoulder gave under the weight of the soldier sitting beside me, whose body, dead or unconscious, had slumped against mine. He must have been sitting further forward than I and with his legs stretched out; my knees had been hunched up and the line of bullets which had opened up the deck in front of us had ripped across his lower abdomen. Blood spurted in great jets from beneath his clutching hands and he was not yet dead. He gurgled something and I leaned close, to catch what he said. 'Dunkirk were a mucking awful do. . . .' And then the blood filled his mouth and trickled down his unshaven chin, making rivulets through the grey-white stubble. I had to turn away from him then, and I'm afraid I was sick.

I barely had time to recover my wits, before a series of resounding explosions caused the ship to shudder and lurch madly. Like a porpoise with a crab on its back, it corkscrewed, only to pause at a seemingly impossible angle.

'Jump,' yelled a voice from above and there was no mistaking the authority in it, 'jump from the starboard side, jump, jump.'

There was no volition in our movements. The vessel keeled over and I, along with a scrambling mass of would-be survivors, slid the width of the deck, to be catapulted over the railing and into the sea.

'Christ, she's little more than a child.'

I heard the voice from far away. I was afraid to open my eyes. Then something touched me and they snapped open of their own accord. It was night time, but not black night and I could see two figures looking down at me from a great height. They were strangers and I did not feel like talking to strangers, so I shut my eyes again.

'I had two like her.' It was an older voice this time. 'Twins.' A long pause and the quietest of sighs. 'Both killed in the first raid on Liverpool.'

'Christ,' repeated the younger voice. It seemed to be the extent of his vocabulary.

I shivered; not entirely because I was cold, but something in the old man's voice had sent a cold tingle down my spine. Curiosity was getting the better of my fear and, when I opened my eyes for the second time, it coincided with the younger man bending to touch my hair. He was peering at me closely. He had a thick, black beard and the rest of his face looked very white in contrast. A strange light shone on him, making him appear a ghostly green. I was frightened and I wished he would go away.

'Don't be scared, I was just pushing the hair out of your eyes.' The voice was younger than the metallic green face. 'You're cold; we saw you shiver. The captain's gone to get something to cover you with.'

I could not think of anything to say, so I shut my eyes again.

It was not long before a muffled tread and heavy breathing announced the return of the older man and soon he too was bending over me, wheezing as he stooped, and covering me with an old woollen dressing-gown. Never did a mother tuck up her child with more tenderness and, in the same way that a child gives a mother its trust, so I put my hand into the captain's and trusted him.

'Poor little thing,' he murmured, 'poor little thing.' And kissed my forehead.

Perhaps I slept. I don't remember. I only know that when I finally did come to properly, everything seemed a great effort. I lay in the dark for a long time and tried to think, but my thoughts were muzzy and incoherent. My head hurt and the only concrete conclusion I came to was that I was hungry.

I touched the rough wood and raised ridges and listened to the dreamy sound of the sea swishing past. So I was lying on a deck; perhaps the water had been a dream, or a nightmare. Perhaps, if I sat up and looked around, I would find my soldier friend still sitting beside me. But there was no one there. My body was dry but felt itchy and sticky. I drew a strand of hair into my mouth and it tasted salt. No dream.

Then I really came awake and, jolted by a moment of near panic, tried to spring up, but my strength had deserted me and I came to rest, panting, on one elbow. It did not take me long to ascertain that I was on the outer part of the bridge. A sailor held the wheel and in every available space there were sleeping bodies. The captain leaned over the far railing, looking out to sea and the young man with the beard sat on the deck not far away with his back propped against a ventilator, dozing. His head jerked every so often and his mouth fell open. The eerie light glinted on a filling in a back tooth and made a scar on his neck appear snakelike, silvery grey. He was not a very attractive sight. I rolled over on to my other side so that I would not be able to see him and came up hard against the railing. Below, the sea crept by, a mass of green; brilliant, illuminating green. I forgot my head and my empty stomach; down below was a world of wonderment. I held my breath, in case this sudden beauty in the midst of horror should vanish.

The captain must have heard me move and seen my struggles to rise. He helped me to my feet and held on to me as I clutched the railing and continued to gaze down at the giddily dancing light, myriad stars of ice and viridian.

'How do you feel, lass?'

'I'm hungry.'

He sighed. 'That's one thing I can't help you with – not a scrap to eat in the whole ship.'

I sensed, rather than saw, the unhappy expression in the old man's eyes and felt guilty for having spoken my thoughts aloud.

'It doesn't matter. I don't think I'm really hungry.'

The rasp of stubble as he rubbed his hand over his chin crackled like a sound track for the phosphorescence. Then he sighed again. 'Well I know I am and I doubt if I have the healthy young appetite that you should have at your age.'

'Is this your ship?' I asked, mainly to change the subject.

'Aye.'

'How did I get here?'

'Picked you up, along with a number of other survivors from the *Tanjong*. You have him to thank for your being here at all.' He indicated the bearded young man, who I now saw wore the badges of rank of a RNVR Lieutenant. 'He saw you hit some floating debris and hung on to you until we came along – must have been quite some time.'

There is something very personal about someone who has saved your life and I looked with a new interest at the sleeping man. His shirt was torn and soiled and his hair straggled over his eyes, but his mouth was shut now and he didn't look quite as bad after all.

'His name's George Farelly,' the captain told me. 'He was in *Repulse* when she went down.'

I thought about this for a minute, but my brain was hardly its scintillating best and I gave it up. Instead, I asked, 'Where are we, and what is the date?'

'We should get into Tanjong Priok, that's the port for Batavia, by to-morrow evening, God and the Nips willing. To-day is Sunday, the fifteenth.'

'The fifteenth? But it was only the thirteenth when the *Tanjong* sank – I know, because I was thinking of just that, when someone yelled at us to jump.'

'That's right. You've been out for two days.'

37

'Two days! Gosh, we're moving pretty slowly, aren't we?' I could have bitten off my tongue as soon as the words were out. The last thing I wanted to do to the kind old man was insult his ship. He did not take offence though and smiled tolerantly at the child, me.

'Aye, we're limping a little. We were bombed too, you know, and anyway, I don't want to stir up the water any more than I have to.' He jerked his head in the direction of the phosphorescence, 'That stuff will show us up for miles if there are any Japs around.'

There was no sun the day we reached Java and a grey silence hung over the port that boded of worse happenings than the weather. Not a smile or a wave greeted us as we came slowly alongside. True, we were only a small and unimportant cargo ship, but the absence of usual dockside clang and clatter was ominous. A small party of Dutch officials moved lethargically towards the lowering gangway and posted a guard. We watched the captain greet them from where George and I hung over the railing on the deck above. They shook hands and saluted each other, but there was no emotion and, after a moment's conversation, which we could not hear, we saw the colour drain from the old man's face.

'Whatever can have happened?' I whispered. 'Oh George, do go and find out.'

He returned within a very short time and I could see before he spoke that the news was bad.

'Singapore's fallen. I'm sorry, Sally.' He knew my father was there 'But even the Japs will have to stick by the Geneva Convention, you know, and your father will be a prisoner of war. Come on, cheer up, you can't help him or anyone else by crying.'

It was true and I brushed the tears away. Unbelievable that we had left our home up country such a short time ago, expecting to be back in a matter of weeks. Then that nightmare journey and now, no Singapore any more.

'The Dutch say they will make a last stand in Java. They're not allowing any of their own people to leave and that bastard – ' George pointed at the tallest of the three Dutch officers, ' – is so keen to pour scorn on the British, that he suggested the captain should not wait here for rations, in case there was an air raid, but take his ship straight on to Ceylon.'

'Will he?'

'Not on your life. He's already negotiating to have us put ashore so that he can turn back for Singapore and see how many others he can pick up.'

'Look after that child, George.' The captain gripped his shoulder, then turned to me, 'Good-bye, Sally. Look after yourself.' He bent to kiss my cheek and I felt the tears spurt and roll down my face and that time they went unchecked. The old dear.

'About turn, Sally.' George pushed me firmly into line as the passengers, mainly RAF and navy, the latter twice times survivors, filed down the gangway. 'Now you see why I didn't join the army – they're expendable, but we have to be preserved!'

I did my best to muster a weak smile for his flippancy. I was grateful for his presence, but my heart was too full with thoughts of two old men; the captain, about to turn back to the inferno, and my father, still in it.

We pressed forward, nobody speaking, and at the bottom of the gangway turned to look back at the bridge. The captain waved once and a second later the ship's hooter sounded and, as the last man set foot on shore, the gangway began to ascend.

'Don't look back.'

I didn't.

Like so many sheep, we were herded through the large open doors of a wharfside godown, the Dutch guards shouting and pushing as though we were a chain gang. Finally we were all inside and the heavy doors clanged to, a Javanese soldier taking up his position before the large, double bolt.

Light filtered through slats high in the walls, showing that there were already several hundred occupants. The stench of stale sweat and urine was overpowering and I felt at once that the open deck with machine-gun bullets was preferable to this Black Hole. After a while my eyes became accustomed to the gloom and I was able to see that there were a few women and children dotted amongst the men, most of whom were khaki clad, with here and there the soiled white of a sailor who had managed to retain his uniform.

A sparse covering of straw was strewn over the cement floor and everywhere bodies reclined in attitudes of apathy and exhaustion. There was very little talk among the survivors and the only sound to penetrate was the childish laughter of a section of Javanese soldiers, who were bathing from a large jar in one corner of the godown. Used to the modesty of Malays, I could hardly believe my eyes at the antics of these men, their racial cousins. Several lay propped against a great mound of rotting cabbages – which added their gases to the general stink – hurling taunts and questioning the manhood of one of their number who stood, mother naked, pouring buckets of water over himself. Others were relieving themselves, dropping their trousers and squatting wherever the urge took them. Water and urine spread through the straw and added to our discomfort. The men laughed uproariously every time someone moved to get out of the way and often sent the buckets splashing in the direction of some inert form deliberately.

39

After a few days of waiting, scratching, and swallowing the nauseating rice gruel, for which we queued twice a day, and no new arrivals had joined us, the monotony was broken by the entrance of a Dutch officer, who clapped his hands for attention.

'Singapore has fallen,' he announced, as though no one knew, 'but Java will not fall. We shall never leave the Indies. But we cannot accept more mouths to feed, therefore we are giving you a ship to take you to India, together with some of our wounded.' Applause. He unbent a little then, as his gaze roamed over the motley mass, and, in a kinder voice, he said, 'God speed, and may we win this war.'

From the limpid green of the pre-dawn sky, Venus shone in tranquillity.

'I shall never forget that star as long as I live.'

'It's a planet.'

'Who cares? It means we're through another night.'

The Dutch had been as good as their word and we sat on the deck of a KPM ship, bound for Ceylon. We had started off in the hold, but once away from Java, the hatches had been opened and bodies erupted in all directions to seek some square that was to be jealously guarded for the remainder of the voyage. George and I sat, huddled between two ventilators, our backs against a locker. It would have been uncomfortable at the best of times, but a diet of rice gruel had reduced us to bags of bones, whose every contact with the hard, hard deck, was torture. Nevertheless, it was preferable to the mass of sweaty humanity in the saloon and, as Venus rose once again, it became every day a new covenant, like Noah's rainbow.

'What are you going to do when we get out of this, Sally?'

George was a dear. It was the first time he had asked this question and yet I knew that the responsibility of having me on his hands must be worrying him. His wife was in Ceylon and he must have wondered what on earth he was going to do with me when we arrived there. In the circumstances, I felt that a decisive answer was necessary, although in truth I merely said the first thing that came into my head.

'Join up.'

'But you're too young.'

'Who's to know? I was born in Malaya and I don't think I have any documents in England – they will have to take my word. I shall join the RAF.'

'WAAF you mean; but why them?' George did not hold a high opinion of the air force and I had said it partly to tease.

'Oh, I don't know. Nicest colour, I think. Besides, my father was RFC in the last war.'

'Why not the WRNS?'

'Those awful hats!'

'For your information, young lady, I have it on good authority that those awful hats are going to be changed for something far snappier than the other two. My sister's a Wren and she's had a preview.'

'Um,' I wasn't really interested, but repeated an odd titbit of information I had heard somewhere, 'but they're not really a proper service, are they? I mean they don't hold the King's Commission.'

'King's Commission!' George exploded, and was told by several other occupants of the deck to shut up. 'I suppose this is the sort of conversation one normally holds in the early hours of the morning in the middle of the Indian Ocean, with probably half the Japanese fleet around us! Oh Sally, you slay me – King's Commission indeed!'

I didn't think it was all that wildly funny. But it made me dig my heels in and what had, a few minutes before, been a vague idea and something that I had said for the sake of speaking, became a definite possibility.

'Certainly,' I replied, with all the dignity I could muster, 'I don't expect to get a commission straight away and anyway, I think it's a good thing for an officer to go through the ranks.' Is it possible to sound pompous at sixteen? 'Did you go through the ranks?'

He shook his head. 'Oh, what a shock you're going to get.' He was almost sobbing with laughter and our neighbours had given up any ideas they may have had of dozing through the dawn. 'I'd love to see you a year from now.'

He looked at me in the most paternal manner, which infuriated me, and, had he but known it, was the cause of a singular determination on my part to do what I had said I would.

The whole deck was soon astir and people were beginning to form the morning queue for rations.

I stood up and stretched and tried to ignore the usual morning taste in my mouth. 'What wouldn't I give for a toothbrush,' I sighed and the glamour of my intended commission receded into the dream-like quality of the night, and a world without water rationing resumed its position of number one goal in my wishful thinking.

'That's it.' George had borrowed a pair of binoculars from one of the ship's officers.

'That's what?'

'Ceylon of course, you ninny. Look.' He handed me the glasses and pointed. All I could see was a grey line on the horizon which did not appear very promising. 'Be in before dark, I reckon.'

We crept up on the slumberous island in the early dusk. From my earliest childhood I had loved coming into Colombo harbour. When my mother was alive, we all used to go out to Mount Lavinia and swim and then my father would add another minute ebony elephant

41

to my collection and we would have a scrumptious tea. The tall, thin waiters in their dhotis, high-collared jackets and crescent-shaped tortoishell combs, were quite different from Malays, but I believe that half the thrill had been that it was the last stop before home.

The claws of the harbour extended into the ocean like a huge, welcoming lobster and we could see the crows rising in flocks and alighting on their individual buoys. Then, suddenly, we stopped.

'What the hell?' George was as excited as I, but for a different reason. 'I suppose we're on the edge of the minefield – so long since I was here.'

We waited and waited and the first stars began to appear. It was Saturday evening.

Suddenly I felt very much alone. I had relied on my father and I had relied on George; to-morrow I was to be cast ashore in the great wide world.

Not to-morrow.

'Look,' George caught my arm and pointed to where an aldis lamp had begun to flash from the bridge. 'We're calling for the pilot and requesting permission to enter harbour before dark.'

After a long pause an answering lamp flashed from the shore.

George let out a great guffaw. 'Listen to this – you'll never believe it. "Berth Monday," they say. Oh brother, this is war!'

5. PROMOTION FOR A SUBALTERN

Helen Watson

I too, Helen Watson, have my place in this narrative because my life has become involved with others. But I am not one of the ten; I am only complementary to them.

The day that threw me into this involvement was that of my promotion and it was, on the whole, an amusing day.

I was a second subaltern in the ATS at the time and had just spent the first six, dreary months of my commissioned life as dogsbody to the PA of a Very Important General at the War Office. The general was all right, in fact he was a poppet, but one more day of following Florrie around was going to mean the end of my short-lived career, or me. In fact I had just rolled the application for a posting from my typewriter and was on my way to the general's office with it, when the old man himself opened the door and we almost had a head on collision.

'Ah, Helen,' he peered at me over the top of his bifocals in a way which always made me smile, 'I was just about to ring for you.

Confirmation of your promotion to subaltern is through and, if you play your cards right, it won't be long before you're junior commander.'

I fingered the paper in my hand, wondering whether to tell him or tear it up.

'Well, girl,' he rapped, 'aren't you going to ask me how and why?'

'How and why, sir?'

The general looked pointedly at Florrie who, as usual, had gone into a positive hurricane of work at sight of the old man. I too looked, not without malice, in the direction of my favourite, stuffed, female officer.

'Florrie won't be with us very much longer and I must have a PA who knows my ways when I go to Pretoria next month.'

'Oh sir, careless talk,' simpered Florrie, from behind her clacking keys. Then, turning bright scarlet, she leapt from her seat and fled through the outer door.

'Bloody woman'll drive me mad,' muttered the general into his beard, 'man deserves a medal.' And slammed the door.

Mystified, I followed Florrie into the outer office, where she was leafing through files as though her life depended on finding the minute she wanted.

'Well?' I asked. 'What's happened to you?'

She turned white, then red, then white again, dropped the file she was perusing and wailed dramatically, 'I'm pregnant. That's what's happened!'

If she was hoping for sympathy, she had picked the wrong listener. 'You're married, aren't you, so what's so tragic about that?'

With a flurry of indignation she swept up the file and, clutching it to her bosom as though it were already her baby – as indeed it was – lowered her eyes. She spoke so low that I had to lean towards her to hear.

'But on our honeymoon. It doesn't seem decent somehow!'

I honestly didn't mean to laugh. Florrie was a pain in the neck and it was a never ending source of surprise that anyone had married her, but she was rather pathetic too. I should have been kinder, but I wasn't.

'Well, what did you expect to do on your honeymoon – swop files?'

'But the general,' she wailed, 'I've been with the general since the very beginning of the war. What will he *do* without me?'

'Have some peace,' thundered the Old Man from his inner sanctum. 'Will you bloody women shut up and let me get on with some work.'

'Is our Florrie really pregnant?' It was the smooth voice of David Langham, the general's ADC, who stood, nonchalantly filing his nails, in the doorway. 'By Jove, chap deserves a medal!'

Florrie whipped round as though stung by a wasp.

'How long have you been standing there? Oh you, you, you, – beast!'

And back she swept, a ballooning figure in mirror bright Sam Browne and good, sensible, woollen stockings, dropping files and nearly sending David flying.

He laughed and bent to retrieve a fallen file.

'Helen darling, you'll be coming to South Africa with us.'

He was rather gorgeous and, despite his languid appearance, could be as quick as a snake when he wanted. He stood for a moment, propping up the doorpost, and mentally undressed me.

'Not if you're going, lover boy!'

All this was sideplay of course, because David was as queer as a coot, but we all pretended he was a great ladies' man.

'For Christ's sake, David,' roared the general, 'are you pregnant too? Will someone come and give me a little attention this afternoon?'

David shrugged and sauntered off. He was as fond of the old boy as I was.

6. A CHICK HATCHES OUT

Philip Morrison

I am Philip Morrison and there is no doubt that the present phase of my life began the day I left the RMC. It was a raw, frosty day at the beginning of March, 1942, and there was very little hint of spring in the air. Not that I cared; I was London bound. The roughness of my father's kilt against my thighs, the softened leather of his Sam Browne across my chest, and my own, brand new pips, burning holes in my shoulders all served to make it an eventful day.

Coincidentally, it was also my twentieth birthday and the mess sergeant had produced a bottle of champagne from some hidden, pre-war store. There was scant chance of eight of us – seven rather, one wasn't drinking – getting drunk on the one bottle, but we were behaving as though we were. Conduct unbecoming, no doubt, but hell, when I thought of the fight I had had to get into the army – probably never would have done if it hadn't been for the war – I had cause to celebrate.

The fight had been put up by my dear mama, who wanted me to be an accountant, a doctor, a lawyer, a bus driver, anything but a soldier. I suppose you couldn't really blame her; at only forty-eight she's already been a widow for some years and lost two of her three children. Trouble is she's fey – or so she says – believes in life circles and all that sort of thing. Father was born in India and killed on the North-West Frontier; my sister, the only one of the tribe to be born in

44

Scotland, was killed in a car crash on the A1, and my brother, born in Singapore, went down in the *Prince of Wales* earlier this year. All coincidence of course, but try and tell her that. God help me if the regiment is posted to India, I was born in Quetta.

I groaned inwardly at the thought of leave and wished I could have gone straight to the Depot. Fourteen days of dramatics lay ahead of me, I had no doubt. Well, any nonsense and I'd point out that if she had let my brother go into the regiment, as he should have done, he might be alive now.

But I didn't give my mother much more thought that day. We had reached the seventeenth verse of the 'Ball o' Kirriemuir' and the train was slowing down. I adjusted my glengarry to a more rakish angle, heaved down my suitcase and fell, as the train gave a sudden jolt, into the lap of the man opposite. Needless to say this gave rise to a spate of ribald comment from all but my victim, who merely pushed me off and suggested we stopped behaving like a kindergarten at break time, at least until the train pulled into the station, which it was unlikely to do for another ten minutes.

Well, that damped us down all right. Actually, this particular chap had been a bit of a puzzle to us for some time. A good ten years older than any of us, he had suddenly appeared about a month before, after the weeding out process had taken place and those RTUed had left us. And here he was, only a second lieutenant like the rest of us, but with the air of having gone through it all before. Rumours had been rife, naturally; one sinister one was that he had been cashiered and reduced to the ranks and now, because of the war, was being given a second chance, but it seemed unlikely. Some said he had fought in Spain with the International Brigade and others that he had been pro-Franco. He was also reputed to have been with the French Foreign Legion, mixed up with the Italians in Abyssinia, and goodness knows what else. Of course it was all speculation; he was as tight as a clam and there was something about him that defied questioning anyway. We talked about him a good deal, but I'm sure no one actually asked him about himself outright. No doubt he was an interesting personality, but I couldn't help wishing he hadn't been commissioned into *my* regiment. Well, he could remain an enigma for all I cared. London lay before us; we had the whole day before I and two chums caught the night train to Edinburgh and we had every intention of enjoying it.

War or no war, the anteroom of the Officers' Mess at the Regimental depot of the Inverness-shire Highlanders still shone with silver and polished oak, and the armchairs looked fit to accommodate old generals reminiscing over past wars with the aid of a good glass of port.

Acutely conscious of my one pip, which only a fortnight earlier had seemed to mark the height of achievement, I cast around for a kindred soul. No sign of Bill Matheson, with whom I should have arrived, nor David MacKay, but the next time the door opened, who should walk in but Dougal MacPherson, the elderly colleague about whom I was telling you. It just goes to show, any port in a storm. I found myself walking eagerly towards him, as though we had been bosom pals for years.

'My God, it's good to see a familiar – ' I stopped and gaped, and MacPherson laughed outright.

'Just put it down to previous experience, laddie. Come and have a drink.'

He slapped my shoulder in a somewhat avuncular manner and I followed him meekly to the bar. No doubt he had the right to be patronising for, besides the difference in our ages, in place of the solitary pip he had worn when I had seen him last, there were now three. I was torn between envy and admiration at his easy manner with the steward and agog to see the expressions on my other companions' faces when they should arrive.

He handed me a glass and raised his own. '*Slainte mhath*. Heard any rumours?'

I shook my head. 'Have you?'

'Middle East I gather – and hope.'

'Hope? Have you been there?'

'Aye. I know it pretty well.'

My burning curiosity remained unassuaged, because at that moment an elderly major came over, introduced himself and offered to take us round to meet some of the other members of the Mess.

Our spell at the Depot had been short but, as far as I was concerned, not particularly sweet. As a junior platoon commander I was at the beck and call of every officer in the battalion, or so it seemed, and most of the senior NCOs as well. I was not sorry when, after a couple of days in a transit camp and endless documentation, inoculations, and rekitting, we embarked for parts unknown and set sail.

It was a dreary voyage. Unseasonally cold and wet, we seemed to spend our time on submarine and aircraft watches – no fun on a streaming deck – or else routine chores on the troopdecks. From the time we left the comparative shelter of the Irish Channel until we rounded the bulge of West Africa, there were continual alerts. The Jocks moaned and groaned, the bar ran out of whisky, and we were all relieved to be round the Cape and on our way to Suez.

Beyond the fact that he seemed at home in the desert and appeared to be pretty fluent in both French and Arabic, we found out no more

46

about Dougal MacPherson. We had the odd beer together and he was always quite friendly, but it was not until I mentioned him to Bill Matheson one day that it occurred to us that he was no longer with us.

With the war hotting up again in Africa, and Rommel, reinforced, launching a new, powerful Axis drive, we had more things to think about than the past history of one of our brother officers and I doubt if I gave him another thought.

The battalion went into action before we had had time to become even moderately acclimatised and the world became, for me at any rate, a dirty trial of sand, heat, and sweat. Sand in one's eyes, sand in one's clothes, sand in one's food. Sand in every crack and crevice of the body. Give me forest or jungle any day. What luxury England had been, how clean, how unreal. Even the troopdeck seemed pleasant in comparison.

Sand and noise and silence and then we were in it. Heat and cold, the time of day etched sharply into our minds by the sudden contrasts. The boom, boom, boom of the big guns – their big guns – and the tanks – their tanks. So much has been written about desert warfare and it is now ancient history. But to me, one of the smallest ants in the hill, it was grit that I remember most. Sand and sweat equal grit and that piece of shrapnel flying past, or the whining bullet became in comparison mere irritations, minimal hazards in a world of sand.

Sand and noise and silence. Heat and cold. Was it possible that the desert could be termed monotonous? Perhaps, in so far that the privations occurred in monotonous rotation.

7. DEATH OF A SERGEANT-MAJOR

Jogindar Singh

Thwack! The head of Sergeant-major Pritam Singh fell to the ground and a great spurt of blood gushed from the severed neck. The body twitched and appeared to hesitate for a second, before it slumped and rolled over.

Not a sign of emotion passed over the faces of the assembled crowd, nor a gasp escaped a single throat, as Lieutenant Yamashuki straightened up and looked about him.

With slow, silent steps on the soft, now soiled grass, he walked over to the head and, impaling it on the point of his samurai sword, held it aloft for the crowd to see. The eyes were wide and glassy but the teeth shone through the black beard in a fixed smile, as though the sergeant-major had had the last laugh on his executioner.

47

'Look you, look all,' called Yamashuki in his clipped, staccato English, 'this miserable, misguided dog chose his vile white masters instead of you. We have come to liberate you from the red-haired ones. We have chased out the stinking British and made Singapore another island, another jewel to be added to the crown of Dai Nippon. Asia for the Asiatics. The white men have gone, never to return. You want to eat? You must obey. For those who help the soldiers of the emperor, there will be full bellies. For those traitors – like this one here – who do not co-operate, there will be death.' He paused to pivot on his heel and swing the head round for all to see, then, 'Death, death, death,' he screamed on a note of sudden hysteria, 'death. Do you hear me? Men such as this are not fit to live.' And he flung the head of Sergeant-major Pritam Singh from the point of his sword high into the air.

As the head rolled towards the crowd, a soldier began interpreting the officer's speech into Malay and a middle-aged Sikh woman gently shook the arm of a youth standing in front of her.

'Go, my son, you have a duty to perform.' She spoke clearly and the heads of several onlookers turned in her direction.

Jogindar Singh, a tall, thin, gangling youth with the first hairs of his beard lying along the jaw line, who had watched his father's execution with staring eyes and a dry mouth, blinked once, touched his mother's shoulder and marched smartly towards Lieutenant Yamashuki.

He wore a torn shirt and faded khaki shorts belonging to his father and his feet were bare, but with the proud bearing of his soldier ancestors, he marched straight across the padang to halt before and salute the Japanese officer.

'Permission to take the body of my father for cremation, sir.' He saluted again and waited.

A gasp feathered over the crowd, like wind in a wheatfield, and a Japanese soldier stepped forward to deal with the offender. But the lieutenant waved him back.

Yamashuki was twenty-one years of age, Jogindar Singh nineteen. For a long moment the two young men looked appraisingly at each other and it seemed possible that the latter's request might be granted. Then Yamashuki's eyes clouded over. He was taller than the average Japanese, but he still had to look up to the Sikh who, still growing, was already six foot one.

Quite suddenly he leaned forward and slapped Jogindar on both cheeks and spat full in his face. 'You are a brave man,' he hissed, 'but go, before your head joins that of your father.' Aloud, he shouted, 'This body stays where it is, so that the stench of his rotting remains will serve to remind you all of what will happen to the next one to defy the authority of Dai Nippon.'

48

As the crowd melted silently away, Jogindar Singh, bearing still impeccably erect, marched back to where his mother stood, a solitary figure at the edge of the field. Her pride and her sorrow shone in her eyes as, silently, they returned together to their house in the senior NCOs' compound of the police barracks.

Lieutenant Yamashuki regarded the bottle in front of him with distaste and wondered why Europeans were so fond of whisky.

When the nearby town had surrendered and the Europeans rounded up and marched off to the local gaol, their liquor had been brought in and issued to the officers. He had read in so many English novels of people drinking to forget and drinking to gain courage, that he had been tempted to try it before this afternoon's execution. Not that he had needed courage to carry out his orders, but it was the first time he had killed a man in cold blood and felt better now that it was over.

He pushed the whisky away from him, lit a cigarette, and picked up his pen to make the entry of the day in his personal diary.

'In camp near Mering, Johore,' he wrote. 'Singapore has fallen and to-day the last of the Indies fell. I too this day, have undergone an emotional experience of some magnitude. To my father and to my honoured ancestors, I am able to say that my sword has been baptised, for, this day, for the first time, I used it at a ceremony to end the life of a traitor and an enemy. The head fell with one blow and I was afterwards congratulated by my superior for my handiwork and for my speech. My superior was not pleased however with the behaviour of a young Indian, the son of the traitor, who, without deference to my rank or position, asked that he should be allowed to take the traitor's body. The captain has reprimanded me for not at once making a further example of this youngster by uniting him with his father. But, my ancestors, the son of the traitor was a brave man and it would have been to soil your sword to use it in such a way. This sword, which has been carried by brave men and used with honour through the generations, was used only with honour to-day. Many of these bearded Indians have realised that we are the true saviours of Asia and have voluntarily offered their services for the further glorification of Nippon and all Asia, but all of them I do not trust. This youth, whose life I spared this afternoon, a youth with such loyalty and respect for his father, would make a sound leader in our cause and I shall take pains to win him to our side.'

He stubbed out his cigarette and got up. The room he was sitting in had, only a short time ago, housed an Australian gunner officer, and Yamashuki wondered about him as he idly fingered his belongings. He picked up a photograph in a leather, folding frame, which had been standing on the desk before him as he wrote. The picture showed a blonde young woman with a baby in her arms and, holding on to her skirt, was another fair child of three or four. Just about the age of my little sister, he mused, and put the frame back on the desk. Duty done or not, his thoughts and the whisky had depressed him and, feeling the need of company, he turned down the light and went outside.

Rooms branched off from a long verandah and at the end, in what had once been the anteroom of the Australian Mess, a number of his brother officers were noisily entertaining a batch of local girls. Tarts presumably; no other girls would come voluntarily to the officers' mess. Perhaps, if there was one who was attractive and willing. . . .

Screams interrupted his reverie and, attracted by the male laughter and pleading female voice, Yamashuki walked the length of the verandah, to stand with a feeling of disgust in the open doorway.

A young Chinese girl lay naked on the floor, her hands and feet held by four of his colleagues, whilst a fifth amused himself. This individual looked up and grinned when he saw Yamashuki watching him. 'Want a turn, brother?' He did not even bother to stop his twisting and turning while he talked. 'Not that there'll be much left when I've finished with her.'

The girl gave a sudden, convulsive shudder and lay still. The man withdrew and looked at her with disappointment. 'Dead,' he stated flatly, 'or perhaps only unconscious. Who cares? Plenty more where she came from.'

From the corner of his eye, Yamashuki watched three small Malay girls creeping down the anteroom steps while no one was paying attention. He watched them go and made no move to prevent their escape.

'Pigs,' he muttered to himself as he turned and walked back to his room.

He opened his diary to make a further entry before going to bed.

'It is a regrettable statement of fact,' he wrote, 'that there are officers in the Imperial Forces who should not be officers at all.'

While Yamashuki was writing in his diary, the Sikh constables were holding a meeting in the barracks.

Young Jogindar Singh was a danger and must be taken in hand. Several among those present held the view that they were mercenaries, employed by a British-controlled Malayan Government which, until now, had paid them an adequate wage for their services. The government as such no longer existed and the wages would cease; it was reasonable to assume therefore that their services should cease also. The aspect of loyalty did not come into it. They were loyal to their families, their clans, their ancestors' homes in the Punjab, and whomever happened to be paying them at the time. The fact that many of their compatriots in the army had switched sides at an opportune moment was an added incentive to offer their services to the new masters.

Two of their number had reported for duty to the Japanese commander as soon as the surrender of the town had been announced and were even now acting as prison guards to the Europeans in the local gaol. Old Pritam Singh had bellowed invective at them as they marched past the police station with their white captives and it was their denunciation that had cost their erstwhile sergeant-major his head.

'Remember what happened after the Singapore mutiny?' Pritam Singh had thundered. 'Mark my words, the British will return and serve you right if *your* heads are blown from cannons.'

The two constables had laughed and it was Pritam's head that now lay rotting on the padang.

Some of them were for going over openly to the enemy, whilst others argued that it would be better to do nothing, but take what came. But all agreed that Pritam Singh's family should be kept out of the limelight and young Jogindar prevented, at all costs, from making a fool of himself and jeopardising their future. Now that the sergeant-major was dead there was no reason why the family should continue to occupy police quarters and, once they were evicted, it would be easier to deal with them.

One of the younger men unrolled his turban and removed the circular blade secreted in its folds. He held the weapon balanced lightly on the palm of his outstretched hand and looked for the nod of approval from the senior man present, Corporal Rajah Singh. But there was no nod. All the Sikhs lowered their eyes, for they were brave men and often brutal men but not one amongst them would condone the killing of one of their own kind. In silence, they began to rise and file out, leaving the young man, bareheaded, on his own.

On the third night after the execution of my father, I, Jogindar Singh, left our house by the back window. I carried a pair of wire cutters and a sack tied bandolier fashion across my body.

Only the boots of the sentry were to be heard as I lay listening in the monsoon drain and, in the distance, jazz records from the Japanese officers' mess.

Carefully cutting through the barbed wire, I eased myself into the drain on the further side and waited again. A dusk-till-dawn curfew had been imposed and the penalty for being caught abroad during the hours of darkness was death.

I did not have to look for my father. The sickly sweet stench of his corpse guided me to the spot where the trunk lay and, I regret to

51

admit it, choking with nausea, I hastily undid the sack from around my chest and bundled the pathetic remains inside. The head, I remember, was at least ten feet away from the body and, taking a line on the silhouette of the district office, and dragging the now heavy sack behind me, I crawled on hands and knees across the dew-dampened grass. My daylight planning had not been wasted and soon, for the last time, the head and body of my father were united.

He had been a large man and it was no easy task to carry him. It must have been a good three hours before I stopped under our window and called softly to my mother to help me haul him through.

My mother had not been idle while I was away and seated round the floor of our living-room were several elders of our community, waiting to say the last prayers over my father's remains.

By the light of a single candle, a fragile ancient with a long, untied, white beard, read softly from the Holy Book. He barely lifted his eyes as I entered the room, then, seeing my burden, rose slowly to his feet. All the others did likewise and made a passage for me to enter the circle.

'All is ready, my son.' The old man stood, frail as a reed swayed by the eddies of the river, resting his hand gently on the sack.

The sickly sweet smell pervaded the room, but not a nostril twitched nor muscle moved as the gathered elders, one by one, paid their last respects to the dead man.

'Go, brethren,' it was barely a whisper from the throat of the ancient. 'The pyre is ready. Light it and depart.'

Without a word to my mother or myself, the elders slipped into the night in single file and I followed with my father.

Someone had worked well and the funeral pyre had been prepared behind a high wall, where the flames would not be seen until most of their work had been done. I laid the sack on the faggots and took the lighted torch, held ready by one of the elders.

My mother was not present, for it is not our custom for women to attend cremations and, as the eldest son, it was my duty to thrust the flaming branch deep into the pyre and ignite my father's remains in order that his soul might be freed from his earthly body.

I paused for only a moment, while one of the elders poured kerosene on the pyre and then the flames sprang high with a great hiss, as though some giant serpent was ascending through the smoke to the stars.

'Go, go, go, go.' It was only a whisper, but already the field was empty.

My mother and I had spent many hours discussing my future. Word had already been passed that I was an embarrassment to the Sikhs in barracks, and as such, should be disposed of. It would save everyone a lot of trouble if I just vanished and, once I was out of the way, no one of our race would molest my mother or the younger children. In time she would be helped to make her way back to Perak, where her family still lived, and I would seize whatever opportunity came my way.

I looked neither at the pyre nor at the building where I knew my mother would be waiting, but set off down the road, travelling south, with the intention of putting as much mileage as possible between my family and myself before daylight.

8. THE RAPE OF ZAITUN

Omar

My name is Omar bin Mohamed Rais and I am a corporal in the Straits Settlement Police.

My home is in the state of Malacca, but I was serving in Penang at the time of the invasion and it is still not quite clear to me why I should be seconded to Johore, which is not part of the Straits Settlements.

Of course, had you been in Penang, you would understand that the muddle was terrible, terrible. Many places were bombed and shelled, but an island is always worse, because you cannot get away. It seemed to me that every bullet was aimed at my family. And then, all of a sudden, we found ourselves on board one of the ferries which used to ply between Penang Island and the mainland, and we were on our way to Singapore.

Wah! I can tell you, man, I didn't think much of putting to sea in that flat-bottomed craft and with so many wailing women and children aboard, the latter running here, there and everywhere and quite without parental discipline. I was hoping that they would put in to Port Dickson or Malacca and give us a chance to disembark, but one of the Europeans on board told me that no one knew what was happening on the mainland and best to make for Singapore.

But I am a dunderhead if ever there was one. Too many years of discipline behind me and not enough initiative perhaps, but I went straight to Police Headquarters in Singapore when we arrived and reported for duty. Of course times had changed and there was no barrack accommodation for my family so, when I was told that men were needed in Johore, I meekly accepted a ticket for Mering and that is where my tragedy began.

I think perhaps a bomb must have hit me, or else I have too many children, but all I could think of when we left Singapore was finding

53

somewhere for my family to live. I come from a large family myself and so, in a way, this posting was a lucky one, because my wife's second cousin lives quite near Mering and I was able to settle in with him.

Of course the Australians were still there when we arrived, but if I thought I had seen all the war in Penang I was quite wrong and, before I knew what had happened, there I was, caught, and signing allegiance to the Japanese.

Most days since have been bad, but the day they executed the Sikh sergeant-major was the worst one of all and one I shall never be able to forget.

We were ordered to parade on the padang in open square formation, little guessing what deed of horror we were about to witness. It was some three hours that we stood there before the sergeant-major was led out, stripped to his underwear and with his hands tied behind his back.

I am a soft man and have never been able to watch the slaughter of a buffalo and when I saw that large Sikh being taken on to the field by his apelike guards, a trembling started up in me that I thought would never be stilled.

But that is not all. While I had been away, Japanese soldiers had been combing the nearby kampongs for girls and my Zaitun and Zainab had been taken.

My wife was wailing and had pulled her hair down over her eyes and was beating her breast and tearing her clothes. It was some time before I could get anything coherent out of her.

It did not take many guesses to reach the conclusion that the children would have been taken to the officers' mess, for that was always their destination these days, and, picking up my parang, I hurried straight there. What I would do with my parang I did not know, because I do not pretend to be a brave man, but there are times when even men like me become so incensed that we are capable of deeds normally beyond us.

The officers' mess had originally been the Rest House and, like most of these buildings, was made of wood and atap, and stood on pillars some four feet from the ground. Long, open verandahs with bedrooms on the inner side, ran off at right angles from either side of a large, square room, normally used for eating and sitting in.

But what it was being used for now made me want to vomit.

My Zaitun was spreadeagled on the floor, naked, and held down by four of the filthy yellow pigs. From where I stood I could see the bare buttocks of a fifth as he behaved like an animal in rut.

My little Zaitun, only eleven years old. The hot tears of shame and humiliation ran down my cheeks as I looked at the parang, dangling uselessly in my hand. What good could I do against five of them?

A sudden movement caught my eye and out of the shadows materialised three little girls. I raised my hand and beckoned them to come to me, holding a finger to my lips for silence.

An officer had emerged from one of the rooms and I recognised him as the one who had dispatched Sergeant-major Pritam Singh that afternoon. My heart stopped beating as he looked in the direction of the three small shadows, one of them, I was sure, my Zainab. He must have seen them, but perhaps even Japanese can have hearts, for he did nothing and I prayed to Tuan Allah not to let him change his mind.

A cry from Zaitun, a jerk of the head of the officer, who was watching his comrades with a look which I dared to hope was disgust, and the arrival of the three little ones at my side, all happened at once.

I found it difficult to stifle a cry myself when I heard the man utter the word that I was sure meant 'dead', and hastily pushed Zainab – I had been right – and the other two children beneath the floor of the Rest House.

Thanks be to Allah the men soon lost interest and went off to the bar, although they were all already drunk.

I was about to creep up the steps when a soldier walked over to Zaitun and after only a cursory look, picked her up by one leg and one arm and flung her poor little body out on to the grass, as though it were a bundle of dirty washing. He walked off without a single glance and I was able to run to her unseen.

Poor little mite. She had fallen starfish fashion, in the position in which she must have been held for many hours. Blood ran down her pale legs and her face and chest were already puffy and discoloured with bruising.

I laid my ear to her heart. She was not dead. I quickly tore off my shirt to wrap her in and carried her back to her waiting companions, then we all crept as fast as we could away from that dreadful place.

Zaitun is not my own daughter. I can never remember exactly how many children my wife has had and how many are adopted. Some are grown up and married now, but we still have several little ones.

The Chinese still sometimes throw out their girl babies and we Malays, who believe that every child is a gift from God, adopt them, love them and bring them up in our religion. After all, when one has so many children already, what is one more?

Zaitun had been thrown from a passing car as it sped through our kampong, a tiny bundle, so well wrapped that at first my wife thought it was a biscuit carton. Imagine that! And what a noisy biscuit she had been! She was well clothed and fed, so her parents must have been quite well to do, but did not want her because she was a female. Adohi! They are a hard race, the Chinese.

And now, here was my poor little Zaitun, as much loved as Zainab, who is, I think, my own, and all the others.

My wife bathed the little body and kept sentinel all night, rocking back and forth on her heels, all the time moaning and issuing such threats as I never expected to hear from any woman.

I did not report for duty the next day, nor the next, and when they came to find me, they found only elderly women in the house. My wife's cousin and I, with all the little ones, were well hidden in the jungle nearby.

When the Japanese had gone, the women joined us, carrying the rest of our clothes and food and we all turned our backs to the east and began the journey back to our kampong, we men taking it in turns to carry the still unconscious child.

We had to cross the whole peninsula and, travelling through jungle with so many little children and carrying one, it took us several weeks to reach the state border. And not by so much as the flicker of an eyelid had Zaitun shown any signs of being alive.

We forced water between her teeth and kept her warm, but I felt that her spirit had departed with that terrible small cry – and time proved that I was right.

My kampong is named Tanjong Mas, the golden cape; it is beautiful and, even in our fugitive state and carrying our sorry burden, our spirits rose as we saw the outlines of its dear houses.

Leaving the women and children concealed in the undergrowth, my wife's cousin, who is named Yahya by the way, and I crept forward to scout out the land.

The rice was high and we were able to skirt the edge of the *padi* fields in its protective shadow. Imagine our surprise when a voice startled us nearly out of our wits and there was a man, fishing from the bund, and over whom we should have no doubt fallen headlong. 'You would do well to walk upright and look less furtive. Anyone would know you were fugitives from a mile off!'

He spoke rudely and without the proper address, but no doubt he had been startled too and we were happy to recognise one of our neighbours.

From him we learned that we were indeed fortunate. The military were registering every kampong for potential labour, but ours had not yet been visited, nor a list of the inhabitants compiled.

My house stands a chain from the beach, surrounded by hibiscus and bougainvillaea and fruit trees, amidst the coconut palms. Ripening rambutans on the bushes bore witness to the continuing prosperity of the village and, looking up, I saw with pleasure, the full nuts and feathery fronds swaying in the breeze.

The house was as we had left it. The chairs still suspended from the ceiling – for this is a sign to all who pass that the owner is away and no one would dream of abusing his home – and the cooking-pots stacked in the lean-to kitchen beyond.

As I stood and looked at my home and listened to the sea breaking on the shingle, I heard the muffled beat of the mosque drum. It was time for the evening prayer.

Normally the women do not pray with the men, but this time, I ordered my whole family to put down their belongings and, there and then, to wash and give thanks to Tuan Allah for our deliverance.

With our womenfolk behind us, Yahya and I turned our faces towards Mecca and, with upturned palms and the dying sun in our eyes, we led the prayers, with hearts full of gratitude and limbs full of weariness.

9. FACES IN A MIRROR

James Weatherby

I was correct in my assumption that South Africa would mean home. The relief squadron brought in their new kites and we flew our old faithfuls down to Rhodesia for other mugs to train on.

A few days there – sufficient to start off a drinking recruit on the road to DTs – then Cape Town. A week in a transit camp and on to the boat.

Boy, what a city that is. I was sorry to leave the desert and had no wish to see the white cliffs of Dover and if someone had offered me a transfer to the South African Air Force, I'd have taken it like a shot. Change my name after the war and disappear, given half a chance.

But of course that's just whimsy. I have music to face, and short of being run over by a bus or falling overboard, there's nothing I can do to avert it. Still, it's a month away still, at the very least; I've made my resolutions and now I can shelve them until the day of reckoning.

Oh, Helen Watson, I keep telling myself, what luck for you that Florrie had to leave the service when she did. Otherwise I would never have seen South Africa.

Pretoria was a real swan. Not that we didn't work. We did. Those interminable conferences. Whew! Thank goodness the general allowed me to précis my notes – some of those old boys certainly could waffle!

South Africa was gorgeous. The climate and the flowers, and the people were wonderful to us. I was heart whole and fancy free and there's something to be said for having a pansy as an escort – no passes to fend off and David was good company. He was able too. The general moved heaven and earth to hang on to him, but eventually, when the time came for him to go back to his battalion, he put up a pretty good show and was awarded the MC later on during the war.

Once the delegates had risen from the last conference and I had piled up my notebooks and pencils, the general lost no time in returning to London. But, however many strings he tried to pull to take us with him, there wasn't a hope. Aircraft were few and far between and unless one was a VIP there was scant chance of obtaining a seat. No use the general ranting and roaring and saying we were important members of his staff – there just weren't any seats.

We saw him off, still fuming, and informing all and sundry of what he was going to say to the Air Ministry on his arrival in London. Then, for us, the first train to Cape Town, to wait for a troopship home.

I had mixed feelings about that voyage. I hope I'm not a coward, and being able to see a little more of South Africa suited me fine, but I was not over keen on a sojourn in the Atlantic – 1942 was not the best time to be there, if you remember.

'Wish I could find an eligible South African and marry him,' I kept saying. 'What a wonderful place to live. Everything's so clean and gay and that mountain – '

'Provincial.'

'Oh David.' Well *I* thought it was all wonderful and even he was impressed by the hospitality lavished on us by the locals. Provincial? Who cared?

The summons to embark came all too soon for me. There was a hint of frost in the air as we stood in the long queue in the dockside warehouse, waiting to go through the formalities.

'Oh my God, the place is lousy with blue,' David remarked with disdain. He had the most off-putting drawl – if you didn't know him – and several heads turned in his direction, murderous intent written on all their faces. I pretended not to know him.

RAF jargon floated over our heads, meaning very little to us. Surely we never had such stupid nonsense in the army? David was filled with gloom at the prospect of goodness knew how long in a RAF troopship.

'My dear girl, we won't be speaking English by the end of this voyage. Just listen to them. Everything's goodo or whacko and every-one goes for a burton or gets buttoned up, or has a wizard prang! And then you're told the whole thing's a piece of cake! Really, it's too bad of the old boy to let us in for this. I shall need at least fourteen days leave to recuperate when I get back!'

By this time we were ensconced in deep armchairs in a fairly plush saloon and appeared to be the only people not making a good deal of noise.

58

'If that's what the desert does to one, thank God I'm not with the battalion.' He was still flogging his dead horse. 'Perhaps it would be better if our ships were dry like the Americans'. What's it to be, old girl? *If* I can elbow a passage to the bar.'

I smiled. David talked an awful lot of nonsense but, as I've said, he was good value. I knew too that he would be joining them at the first opportunity and made a mental note to have an early bed. Meanwhile I was enjoying looking around me. I had never been out of England before and this was the first time I'd been on board a liner, even if it was a trooper. David might find it a bore, but for me it was all rather thrilling.

It was easy to look round the saloon without craning my neck, because a mirror ran the whole length of one wall. There were not many women on board, a handful of RAF nursing sisters and a couple of WAAF. A few civilians and a very few army and navy, otherwise it was all air force.

At that moment, in the mirror, I caught the eye of an upside down face that was peering out from between someone else's knees, in the midst of what appeared to be a rugger scrum.

The face grinned and I grinned back, involuntarily tilting my own head to one side to see it better. There was a great heaving and it disappeared for a moment, then it disentangled itself and, throwing off a couple of bodies, stood up.

It was a stocky figure, slightly pugnacious, in a James Cagney sort of way, as it stood there, hands on hips, hair awry and collar coming adrift. It continued to grin for a moment, then wrinkled its nose and turned away.

I turned away too and by that time David was back with the drinks.

'Who're your friends?' he asked some ten minutes later, 'they're raising their glasses to you.'

The face was back, washed and brushed up, and clinking glasses with a lot of other faces. We raised ours in turn.

'I wonder who he is,' I remarked, 'he certainly has a most infectious smile.'

David raised his eyebrows. 'Interested in a Brylcreem boy? I thought better of you, my sweet. Which one?'

'The squadron leader with the round face and curly hair.'

'Want me to find out?'

'Please.' David was a past master at finding out things.

He idled towards the bar and returned after a very few minutes conversation.

'Name of Weatherby. Much liked. Much married. Hands off!'

'Oh. That puts *me* in my place!'

On a serious note for David, he said quietly, 'The four blokes at that table are what remain of the original members of a bomber

59

squadron. One can hardly blame them for celebrating their survival.'

It was a couple of days later, when I was leaning over the rail, admiring the beauty of Cape Town from the sea, that I suddenly became aware of someone standing beside me.

'Hallo Face!'

'Oh, it's you. Hallo yourself.'

The face held out its hand, then gave me a mock salute. 'James Weatherby at your service, ma'am.'

'Much married. Hands off. I know all about you.'

We both laughed, then I said, 'I'm Helen Watson.'

'Age twenty-four, fair hair, blue eyes, height five foot seven, unmarried, born in Newcastle on 7th December – ' I opened my mouth in surprise, but he stopped me with a gesture and went on: 'You see, I know all about you. I've been busy with your passport.'

'But I don't have a passport.'

'Ah, quick. Are you an IO, Miss Watson? No, of course you're not. PA to some doddering general. And what, might I ask, have you done with your general?'

I explained.

'And so I have to compete with the ADC?'

'Much married?'

'Touché!'

It was the first of many silly conversations. James would join me soon after breakfast and we would talk or play deck games and drink until lunchtime, when we had to separate to our respective tables. But in the afternoon we were together again, and the evening.

David joined us at the rail one day and James promptly waddled off – there wasn't much love lost between them – but even so, there was no doubt as to whom he was taking off. He was a wonderful mimic and had the chief engineer off to a tee. He was funny in everything he did.

I wiped the tears of laughter from my eyes. 'Oh David, he's such a clown. I haven't laughed so much for years.'

'Maybe.' David did not sound enthusiastic. 'But I've been warned by his friends to warn you to keep off.'

I was aghast. 'But we've done nothing. It isn't as if we'd been snogging on the boat deck. Good Lord, if you can't even play quoits with someone without someone else becoming suspicious, I don't know what things are coming to. I take a pretty poor view and you can tell them so.'

He listened patiently, then sighed. 'Look, honey, it's clear to everyone on this ship that you've fallen hook, line, and sinker for that chap. And his friends think that he's fallen for you. They say they haven't seen him so happy since before he was married – not a good sign apparently.'

I was silent for quite a long time. Of course I was indignant, and with reason, but they were right. I ended up by telling David what I had not dared to admit to myself.

'I have fallen terribly, terribly in love with him. But I know he's married. They don't have to worry.'

He was not convinced. 'It's just that they don't want to see him hurt. And *I* don't want to see *you* hurt, either.'

Of course I had been behaving like the proverbial ostrich, not only burying my head in the sand, but keeping my eyes tight shut as well. But we were blameless. We had never joined the giggling couples on the boat deck. We had never been alone together; even our conversation was fatuous – I intended keeping it that way.

Of course the night came when we did go on the boat deck, but even then it was pretty platonic. At least it started that way. All the male officers were on a roster for submarine watch and when James was on duty one evening, he suggested that I should go up and watch with him.

Standing beside him at the rail and watching the sea lit by a brassy sun was bearable, but locked in the velvet night, with stars hard as diamonds and a breeze as soft as the fur of a passing cat, was not. He laughed and joked, as he always did, but I could not respond. I stood silent, gazing out to sea, wanting him to touch me and dreading that he should, not really listening to his prattle.

He too fell silent after a while and we stood there, together but apart, he with his elbows on the rail and night glasses to his eyes and I rigid as Lot's wife.

'Do you know' – I tried to sound flippant – 'that some of your fans have warned me off?'

'The squadron?' He did not turn round.

'Yes. Apparently they're afraid that I might be falling in love with you. Isn't it ridiculous?'

He shook me gently with one arm, his eyes never leaving the sea. 'Is it so ridiculous?' And when I didn't reply, 'Tell me, is it so ridiculous?'

There was nothing to say and I wished then that I had not brought the matter up. We returned to silence, which was easier all round, and I thought the subject had been dropped.

But I was wrong.

'Could you love me, Helen?'

'Very easily.' My voice was husky and I was finding it difficult to control. 'But no one has mentioned the possibility of you falling in love with me.'

He put an arm round my shoulders and his lips brushed my hair.

'Oh my darling,' he said, 'my darling. If only you knew.'

Then he pushed me away.

61

'Go down and order a drink for us, sweetie, my relief will be here in five minutes.'

After that a lot of the laughter left us. Our conversation became more serious and we spent long periods saying nothing, but sometimes sighing and gazing at the sea – never at each other. Eyes are such tell-tale things.

James never mentioned his wife and I often wondered if she were as faithful to him as he was to her. We spent many hours locked in each other's arms in the darkness, until the deep tropic nights gave way to the long northern twilights. But there was never more than a kiss between us and many, many unspoken words.

Once in Cape Town we had all relaxed and even I, who did not want to return home, had been infected with funnel happiness.

Perhaps I relaxed too much.

Do you believe in love at first sight? No, nor did I. That is to say I didn't until I met that girl in the mirror and all of a sudden, wham, I'd had it.

She was as tall and slim as a madonna lily and as fair. Her colouring was pure Saxon and she was the most poised and polished creature I had ever set eyes upon. She was drinking with an equally polished lounge lizard – to whom I took an immediate dislike – and even seen from upside down she was elegance plus. And what better position to admire a pair of legs like those, that even khaki stockings couldn't mar?

In my opinion, uniform can make most women look frowsy, especially khaki, but not this one – she'd look the works dressed in an old sack. I wasn't the only one of our mob to let out a wolf whistle, I can tell you. She was real recruiting poster stuff – even if it were only to bring in the men!

It was funny how my chums, who had done everything in their power to make me go over the rails in Cairo, now watched over me like a gaggle of nannies. Within ten minutes of the most casual conversation with Helen, one of them would appear, and you'd think they were rhinos the way my hints to get weaving rolled off them.

Helen's a wonderful girl. God, what a wife she'd make. No high heels though, or she'd top me, and we couldn't have that. But we'd make quite a striking pair – Beauty and the Beast. I could just see her as Mrs Station Master; by which time of course I'd have my scrambled eggs. Group Captain and Mrs Weatherby. Group Captain Weatherby and his lady wife. But not for you, boy – dream by all means, but this is only a romantic interlude in the best tradition of sea voyages. And when the voyage is over – good-bye Helen.

By the time we reached Glasgow my self-control was badly overtaxed. It had been a longer journey than any of us had bargained for. For a start, we hung around Cape Town harbour for several days while rumours of magnetic mines wafted round, then we crept up to Freetown and wasted a good ten days there waiting for the convoy to form. I say wasted, because it was so bloody hot that I became edgy even with my love-in-life. And then zigzagging for God alone knows how long, until we ended up amidst the sponges, or weed, or whatever it is, of the Sargasso Sea. Another wait in Trinidad, where no one was allowed ashore, then up to Halifax to pick up Canadian troops and in convoy again, back across the Atlantic.

Some of those late spring evenings, as the ship ploughed north, were nearly my undoing. Helen in the tropics was beautiful, but Helen against those golden green, twilight skies, was a goddess. This was her setting and I told her often enough that she must have Viking blood.

But her blood was warmer than any Viking I had known and, although I never made love to her, I could feel it pulsing through her as strongly as mine did through me.

I had meant to say a final farewell to her on board, but while the Canadian commander made a long-winded speech in Gaelic, I managed to slip ashore and send a telegram to Elsie, telling her to meet me in London in a couple of days' time. She only had to come from the Midlands, so I knew I wouldn't be able to put her off for long, but it would give me one night in London with Helen.

Cowardly? Selfish? Unkind? All of those perhaps. Maybe it would have been better if she had refused, but of course she didn't. She had told me that she messed in some all-female hennery in London, but I persuaded her to take a room in a hotel for a couple of nights and she agreed.

Helen had to report for duty the next day, so she was off on the first train south, with that milksop ADC in tow – the worst kind of homo – I don't know how she stuck him. I hitched a ride on a kite the next night and arrived at her hotel just as dawn was breaking.

London at first light is a bleak place, but there was nothing bleak about Helen's welcome. She had left her door ajar after I'd telephoned her from the reception desk and there she was, warm, sleepy, and utterly inviting.

I stretched out beside her for a moment and, I can tell you, it took me all my willpower not to get in with her. And she was no help. 'Love me, James,' she implored, and there was nothing in this whole wide world that I wanted to do more than just that.

'Up with you, wench,' I scolded, 'you've got to go off to your general and I have to be at AM by ten thirty.' Of course we had oodles of time, but this was the only course to take. 'Let's have some breakfast and I'll meet you for lunch.'

She got her own back – for all that I *sounded* indifferent.

'Better have a cold shower first then,' she said, and not without malice, 'you can't go into breakfast like that!'

'Down, Fido. Women have all the advantages,' I grumbled.

I picked up a woman's magazine that Helen had been reading on the train and leafed through it idly while she splashed away in the bath and sang as though we had all our lives before us, instead of this one day.

I honestly had not realised that the door was open when I wandered over to talk to her, but there she was, in one of those attitudes you only expect to find in soap adverts; one knee drawn up and the other leg stretched out while she soaped it with both hands. Her hair was pinned up on top of her head, but a few tendrils had escaped and were hanging damply against her neck.

'You've got soap on your hair,' I said.

She turned round to protest and I called, 'Stop, hold it, don't move.' I wanted to remember her just as she was in that instant.

I went into the bathroom then and kissed each wet, pink tipped breast and her wet, passionate mouth.

'Good-bye my darling,' I whispered into her steam-filled hair, 'Good-bye, good-bye.'

After that I went down and ordered our breakfast.

I could not have had a warmer welcome from the general.

'You got back just in time,' he positively beamed. 'Bloody awful girl they sent me in your place – couldn't read my writing and, when I dictated, silly ass left all the swear words in! Glad to have you back m'dear.'

He patted my hand and then we really got down to work. He must have been saving it up for me and by the end of the morning I was suffering from writers' cramp and not a single page typed.

I had a quick lunch with James in our canteen and afterwards took him upstairs to see my office and introduced him to the general. Perhaps I wished him to remember more of me than how I looked in the bath and I wanted him to see where I worked.

The general was amiability itself and told me I could leave at four o'clock, but I could see he was impatient and, as soon as James had gone, he called me into his inner sanctum, where he was fairly hopping with excitement.

'I've got news for you – hush hush and burn before reading – but we're off again. I mustn't tell you where though; you might tell your young man.' The general could look very arch. 'Haven't been there since I was a young man myself and I don't mind telling you, I'm rearing to go. David won't be coming; got to go back to his battalion. New fellah, I suppose. Thank God you don't have a battalion to go

64

back to – must have one permanent fixture on my staff. Be away some months, I wouldn't wonder.'

Having imparted this tantalising snippet of information, the old boy dictated the remainder of his report and I sat down to type until James arrived, as I had expected, on the dot of four.

'I spent the afternoon scouting round Soho,' he told me, 'and I've found a restaurant that is reputed still to have reasonable food. We have a table for eight – suit you?'

I said that it did, provided I could go back to my hotel and have a wash and brush up first. I was surprised when he shook his head.

'No, darling. I said good-bye to you this morning; I don't want to go back there again. You can come to mine.'

He had taken a room at one of the big, impersonal, station hotels, but there was nothing impersonal about the double bed. I looked at it and my stomach felt as it does in a dentist's waiting-room.

James was very casual. 'Yes,' he said, intercepting my glance, 'my wife arrives to-morrow. We shall stay here for a few days, before going down to Devon. Try and get into the odd show. She's working in a munitions factory up north – must be pretty dull.'

'You've never told me anything about your wife.'

He shrugged. 'Nothing to tell. Complete opposite from you – short and dark.'

I don't think I really wanted to know about her anyway. I couldn't keep my eyes off that wretched bed and the thought of James in it with another woman was beginning to poison my evening.

'Let's get out of here and go for a walk or something,' I suggested.

'Not so hasty. I've got a job for you to do first.'

From one of his patch pockets he pulled a length of braid and, from a small parcel on the dressing table, a pair of scissors, packet of needles and a reel of black thread.

'Wing Commander Weatherby to you. They told me at AM this morning, but I wanted to wait to tell you when we were alone. D'you think you could just sew the thicker braid over the thin one without too much trouble?'

Men! Those little jobs that they think you can do in five minutes! I nearly said that he might as well leave it for his wife, but really I wanted to do it myself.

The scissors were those old-fashioned kind, shaped like a stork and beautifully worked. When I had finished sewing and handed him back his tunic, he presented them to me on bended knee, held on an imaginary velvet cushion.

'Not a very romantic present, but at least a practical one, and perhaps you'll remember me when you use them. I found them in a secondhand shop this afternoon.'

I wanted to throw myself into his arms and kiss him all over and tell him that I would never forget him anyway, but I knew I mustn't. I took the scissors and put them in my pocket and I have them to this day.

We ate an inferior meal in superior surroundings and drank toasts to James's promotion and my next swan. It was all rather strained and I wasn't too sorry when he beckoned the waiter for the bill.

Afterwards we walked slowly back to my hotel and stood for a while in each other's arms in the kindly blackout. But if I had still hoped that he would come up, I was to be disappointed.

'No future in this,' he said briskly, 'time you were in bed.' And when we had walked to the main entrance, 'No, Helen, I'm not coming in.'

I tried to be brisk too, but my heart was breaking. I clung to him, but he pushed me off and, kissing me lightly on the cheek, walked away.

Helen no doubt thought me a callous bastard, but it was for her good as much as mine.

If I had gone up to her room with her, we would have made love, that's for sure. And then it would have been that much worse for both of us.

What she did not know was that I spent the rest of the night sitting on a bench in Green Park, because I couldn't bear the thought of going back to that cold double bed on my own – particularly with the additional knowledge that Elsie would be sharing it with me the next night. I had breakfast in a Lyons Corner House, went back to the hotel to wash and shave and was just in time to see Elsie step off the train and walk down the platform towards me.

My first reaction was one of relief. She had wanted to carry on at the Dog and Duck after I was posted overseas, but I had put my foot down about that and there was nothing barmaidy in her looks now. She wore a plain black suit, her hair was well done and she was using less make-up than I remembered.

She walked jauntily, on very high heels, and I let her get right up to the barrier before going forward to take her bag.

'Well, Jimmy love, you're back at last.' Oh, that flat, East Anglian twang.

'Come along,' I said, 'I've got a room at the Station Hotel. Thought we'd spend a couple of days in town before going down to Devon. Do a show or two maybe.'

It was when she was taking off her hat in front of the mirror that my resolutions nearly deserted me. She was watching me carefully in the glass and she jerked her chin towards the bed.

'Hope you slept in there by yourself last night, love.' And the final straw was the leer and wink.

'I find that remark more becoming to the barmaid of the Dog and Duck than to the wife of a wing commander,' I said coldly.

If I had intended to hurt her, I had failed.

'Sorry, love. Seems like being married to you is going to need some getting used to.'

'Now look, Elsie,' I warned, 'there's no point in going into the reasons for our marriage, but I've thought this whole thing out very carefully. I'm prepared to make a go of it, but on my terms.'

'Terms, love?'

'And if you don't agree with them, I'll make it easy for you to divorce me.'

She went very white. She was sitting on the edge of the bed, hands in lap and straight-backed. For a moment I felt sorry for her, but then I thought, why should I? She's got her officer husband, the least I can ask for is an officer's wife.

'I don't care what you've done during the past couple of years,' I went on, 'as far as I'm concerned, our marriage starts from now. Although it might interest you to know that I have in fact been faithful for my part.'

'Chance is always a fine thing, love.'

I ignored that.

She was beginning to look bored and I was conscious of sounding pompous.

'The fact is,' I burst out, 'that the air force means more to me than anything. I'm not in this just for the duration – it's my career, my whole life. Are you, or are you not, prepared to help me further that career?'

She shrugged. 'What do you want me to do, Jimmy love?'

'Stop calling me "Jimmy love" for a start.'

That time I had hurt her and I hadn't meant to. I brought my voice down and tried to sound kinder.

'I'm sorry, Elsie. I didn't mean to be unkind. It's just that – well, I wonder if you couldn't try and improve your speech. Take elocution lessons, or something.'

'You mean you want me to talk all lah-di-dah?'

'I want you to speak like a lady.'

'Like all them WAAF officers what you used to bring into the pub?'

I counted ten. 'They were quite good examples. Yes.'

She was looking a little doubtful, but I was going to press my point, once and for all.

'Think it over,' I told her, 'it's your choice. Just give me an answer before the end of my leave.'

'No need to think it over, Jimmy love – oops, sorry – I want to be your wife, I really do, and I'll do my best to do what you ask. If you're going to be in England for a bit, you can teach me yourself and then, if you go off again, you can arrange for them whatchemacallit lessons.'

It had gone better than I had expected and I heaved a mental sigh of relief.

'Come on, Elsie, let's find somewhere for lunch and then this afternoon we'll see what tickets are available for to-night.'

10. FAILTE DHA ALBHA!

Donald Thom

'*Failte dha Albha!*' The resonant voice of the Provost of the City of Glasgow rang out over the water, before the ship had berthed. 'Welcome to Scotland!'

'*Brathren, tha sinn a tilleadh,*' replied the Canadian colonel. 'We are brothers, now returning.'

A pipe band played on the dockside and a great burst of sentimental pride swelled in my breast, as it must have in many others on board.

I am Donald Thom, sergeant, Canadian Army, but Scottish by ancestry and, as the band about-turned, the skirl of the pipes and the swing of the kilts brought all the pride of my heritage to a head. Of course, like most transatlantic visitors, I can find plenty in the British to criticise, in fact I wouldn't be anything other than Canadian and I'd suffer from acute claustrophobia if I had to live in a country this size, but that doesn't lessen the pride in my forbears.

All the way up the Clyde we had been watching the banks and exclaiming at the beauty of what many of us considered to be our native land. For we wear the kilt too, and I've heard it said that we have more Gaelic than the Scots themselves – which is hardly surprising because I've yet to meet a Scot who could speak a word! Of course I'm a good mixture – a cocktail my father calls me – and my son David is a greater mixture still. He's fourth generation Canadian on my side and further back still on his mother's, but I still tell him he's a Scot – not that he's old enough to understand yet, but he will, one day.

I must admit the Glasgow docks did little to entice anyone to Scotland's shores that day, and the drab greyness sure was an anti-climax after the lower banks of the Clyde, all dressed in its early summer green, with so many wild flowers; the patches of pink and white and yellow were dazzling.

But this was just the gateway, the beginning of a long, sentimental journey for Donald Thom.

First to see my father's home, Scotland; then my mother's, Holland

– yeah, I know there's a war on, but I reckon before I've finished I'll have seen a bit of the Continent – then my wife's, France. Not that Monica's ever seen France; in fact she's proud of telling me that her forbears had already been settled in Montreal when La Salle began his journeys in search of the Mississippi, but her family still like to call themselves French.

'Keep your men back, Sergeant. It seems there's to be a fair amount of speechifying before we can disembark.' The company commander passed along the deck, repeating his message and interrupting my thoughts.

A microphone had been set up on the hatch cover before the bridge, and, the Provost having finished his speech of welcome on behalf of the people of the City of Glasgow, our colonel was now giving tongue.

'Well, good for him,' I remarked to a soldier standing beside me as I realised that the old boy was replying in the Gaelic. 'Not that I can understand a word myself.'

'Can you not?' And the private interpreted as the colonel spoke. I was a wee bitty ashamed of myself, I can tell you.

But I wasn't the only one. Along the dockside lines of faces showed expressions ranging from pleasure to amazement, bashful smiles and gaping mouths, some enthusiastic, some indifferent.

At last our CO handed over to his British counterpart, a Scottish brigadier, wearing the kilt with battledress top and plain hose. He saluted the men – at least, if he'd had a drink in his hand, I'd say he was about to say 'Cheers' – it was a sort of a wave and his words proved that he was thinking the same thing.

'If I had a drink in my hand, I'd say, "*slainte mhath*" – because that is all the Gaelic I have!' Loud laughter and cheers from some. He looked a good guy. 'Well, lads, I had a speech of welcome pre-pared, but I must confess that your colonel has so taken the wind out of my sails, that I'm left at a loss. You're not the first Canadians by any manner of means to reach our shores during this war, but you are the first to arrive speaking what we fondly believe to be *our* language and, it's quite obvious that the citizens of Glasgow – ' (he waved his arm to include his listeners ashore) ' – are as impressed as I am. I have no doubt that the English speakers among you – ' (more laughter) ' – will understand the word "waffle", something which I do not intend to do any longer. And so, all I wish to say is welcome – indeed, welcome home – and may you enjoy this country until you reach your final destination, wherever that may be.'

The time had come to disembark and slowly we got the men fell in and, shouldering our kit bags and with full packs, we filed down the gang plank and into the waiting trucks.

There was some glamour about our actual arrival, but it soon wore off when we hit that transit camp. Judas Priest! We'd been sleeping fully clothed the whole way across the Atlantic and then, what do you know, not a single goldarned hot shower.

The march through Glasgow from the transit camp to the railway station, behind our own pipe band, had been rewarding though and the views from the train windows, as we sped northwards into the Highlands, had given us plenty of material for letters home, but now, at our lochside training camp, with nature showering her beauty all around us, prospects were distinctly gloomy.

No beds, iron rations, draw water from the loch. At the double, over hills, under boats, across the loch and through drainage pipes. Up trees and down holes. Jesus! anybody would think there was a war on!

'You know, I guess I must've been getting kinda fat.' I was talking to myself in the mirror – Monica would never believe how loose my battledress had become.

'Sergeant Thom.'

Do you feel a fool when you're caught talking to yourself? But it was okay, it was only the Adj, calling from his office window.

I marched over, crashed to attention and saluted in a manner to put a guardsman to shame – that's what a month in Britain had done. Besides, the old geezer liked a bit of spit and polish.

'CO told me to tell you that he's recommended that you be allowed to attend OCTU in this country, as your commission didn't come through before we left.'

'Gee, that's great.'

'I thought you'd be pleased. You'll stay in this battalion – unusual, but we're short of officers. Always providing you make the grade, of course.'

I suddenly came to. I wasn't even at OCTU yet, let alone passed out. In my mind I had already had at least a major's crowns up and was leading the invasion, single-handed!

'Well, thanks, sir. When do I go?'

'*If* you go, it will be at the end of this course.' Couldn't resist that, the old bastard. He wasn't a bad old codger really, just old.

'Is that all, sir?'

'Just one thing, Thom. Doing well on this course should hold you in good stead.'

'*Yes, sir.*' I was away at the double. I could hardly wait to write to Monica and tell her the good news. She had been so disappointed when I left home still a sergeant, and my brother a captain already.

I took a deep breath and threw my arms wide to the loch. This was what I had been waiting for. Life was good. Sunlight shimmered on the water and put lights of Prussian blue on the farthest hills. White dots of sheep moved slowly as they grazed, and everywhere patches of young grass, as yet uncropped, showed a tender green to the beholder. This was my country; I'd show it to Monica one day.

The peace was shattered by the sudden call of the bugle to eat and I found myself in the midst of a throng of khaki, sweating in the midday sun. I'm sure I stood there beaming at them all. My men. After the first week, grumbling had more or less stopped; cold showers had been accepted and now the topic was where to spend the first pass at the end of the course. Glasgow? London? Why not Paris? We were that optimistic. I was glad the Adj had said I'd be returned to my own battalion, *if* I made the grade! Silly old buzzard, I thought, I'll show him. And I whistled all the way to the sergeants' mess.

11. THE WISDOM OF ARJAN SINGH

Jogindar Singh

I had never examined my feelings towards the British. They were just there, that's all. That was how most of my compatriots reasoned: we work for the government in power. The British are in power, obey them; the Japanese are in power, obey *them*. But I was damned if I was going to work for, or obey, any race that had killed my father.

Normally, I would already have entered the Depot at my age, but, besides being the eldest son, I was held back because of various family affairs and missed my intake, and then it was too late. But I'm glad now. After what happened, I could not have taken that oath, even if it had meant losing my head as well.

I did odd jobs for a couple of months while I wended my way south to Singapore. Heaved sacks of rice off lorries for a few cents and a few meals, herded cattle and goats for food only, and stacked pineapple for even less. But I hitched a ride from my last employer, a Chinese pineapple-grower in South Johore, and so I was able to enter Singapore Island unchallenged, sitting atop a pile of ripe fruit. It was by then May of 1942.

I did not remain unchallenged for long though. Singapore – or Syonan as it now has to be called – seemed to contain more Japanese than Japan itself. At every road junction the driver had to stop and get out; I would climb down from my fruity seat and we would both bow to the soldiers on duty – this hardly made for a speedy entry into the city. I learned my lessons fast. At the first road junction I had remained where I was and had had several slaps and kicks to remind me of the fact that I was an inferior being. It was all I could do to hold my temper and I had to keep telling myself, many times over, that, if I were to avenge my father, I must remain alive.

Our destination was well outside the city limits and the driver warned me, 'Keep moving and don't stare at anyone, especially a Jap. You must be a shadow here, if you are to survive.'

I took his advice and made my way into the city, hardly daring to look at the many other pedestrians and especially not at the gangs of white prisoners, carrying out the menial chores of cleaning the streets and drains.

The streets were filthy, despite these gangs; great heaps of refuse being piled up on the five foot way and the stench from the public latrines overriding all other smells.

I soon discovered that, by taking the less-used back streets, I could avoid most of the Japs, but at every bridge and cross roads I had to stop and bow.

I went straight to the Hongkong and Shanghai Bank building, in the heart of the city and not far from the sea front, where my uncle, Arjan Singh, a police pensioner, had been a jaga, or night watchman. No one seemed to know the name of the present watchman and, as I did not wish to make myself conspicuous, I sat quietly on the charpoy by the main entrance and waited for the late afternoon, when I knew he would come on duty.

To my amazement, while I was waiting, I saw an army van draw up and several Europeans get out under Jap escort and enter the bank. These men were thin but clean and were treated very differently from the half-naked white soldiers I had seen working in the streets. I must have still been staring open-mouthed at them and was so far away in my thoughts that I did not hear my uncle approach.

Of course my first duty was to inform him of the fate of my father, his younger brother, but when that was done we talked of other matters and during this time the Europeans were brought out again.

'Bank officials,' said my uncle, 'they've been bringing them for a few hours each day for the past week. Handing over the books to their Japanese counterparts. Of course it is in the interest of international banking that they should co-operate.'

This may sound odd coming from a night watchman, but it is not. We Sikhs have an excellent money sense and it is a well-known fact that, throughout South-East Asia, the Sikh night watchmen run a most public spirited moneylending service. But you don't lend money to a man without going into his assets first – unless you're a soft-hearted fool, and we are not fools. That is why so much of the commerce is in the hands of us Sikhs and why we have our fingers always on the financial pulse.

'Not a bad bunch,' remarked my uncle, as we watched the men climbing back into the van. 'I'd like to help them. Better them than these – ' he cleared his throat and aimed a most accurate gob to fall just behind a strolling Japanese soldier.

'My father always said the European officers were fair and just.'

'It's true. You knew where you stood with them. Many fools amongst them of course, but they're predictable. And on the whole they're incorruptible, or were.'

'I wonder if I shall ever reach your rank, Uncle.' Arjan Singh had been a sergeant-major too.

He shrugged. 'Who knows?' And stretching out on his charpoy, he pulled a fold of his turban over his eyes. 'I'm going to get forty winks before I'm officially on duty. I've some food; come back later and we'll share it.'

I was hungry and welcomed his offer, but I wasn't too keen on wandering around, in case I found myself pressed into some sort of service, so I pulled my own turban over my eyes and lay down under his bed.

'You know what I'd do, if I were still a young man?' my uncle asked later that evening, as he folded his chapatti and dipped it into the meagre curry sauce. 'I'd become a warder in one of the gaols where they're putting the Europeans.'

I was horrified. 'But my father lost his head because of the taunts he hurled at some of our compatriots who had become warders. I could never do that.'

'Pritam was always impetuous,' my father was dismissed with a mouthful of chapatti. 'But he should have thought things out first. Oh, don't think I'm belittling your father, boy. We have never been considered cowards, but think – what better position could one be in to help the Europeans? Yes, if I were a young man still, I'd become the Europeans' favourite warder – give them news when I could, perhaps sneak in a little food or tobacco; give them sympathy and never beat them up. There are many ways of helping prisoners and then, after the war – and mark my words, young Jogindar, this war *will* end; the whole of Asia isn't going to tolerate these apes for ever – I'd remind my former prisoners of what I'd done. There'd be promotion for me, you'd see.'

I pondered his words far into the night. And the more I thought about it, the more I realised that here indeed would be a chance to vindicate my father's death. It would further my own future too – if Arjan Singh were right – and, into the bargain, I would be fed.

In the morning I thanked my uncle for his advice and began the long walk across the island to the gaol where I had heard that most of the Europeans were being interned.

73

Philip Morrison

Well, Tobruk had fallen once again and to most of us, jolting along in the high Fiat truck under an even higher sun, it made very little difference whether it had been defeat or victory, and for whom.

To be honest, I don't remember much about the final stages of the battle. I remember going in all right and I knew that a lot of people had been killed, but after that everything was hazy, except for the sudden searing pain in my thigh, which told me I had been hit, and then the RSM heaving me over his shoulder like a sack of coal and running with me to cover. Then there had been the most almighty explosion, which had lifted us off our feet and thrown us to the ground. A short-arsed little bugger, the RSM – I must be a good eight inches taller – but square, and strong as an ox. He picked me up again like a rag doll, but before we'd gone more than a couple of yards, we were knocked down by another explosion and the next thing I knew was coming to on the floor of a truck.

A splint was strapped to my thigh, with some sort of makeshift dressing, and the blood that had oozed through seemed to be providing a meal for a multitude of flies. A spasm of nausea swept over me, whether through loss of blood or the sight of those disgusting blue-bottles, gorging themselves on what remained, I don't know. I clutched the leg of a Jock sitting near my head and he helped me to heave myself on to the seat. His head was swathed in bandages and was attracting nearly as many flies as my leg. I turned my face away and looked round the rest of the truck.

It was filled mostly with men from my own battalion, plus a few odds and sods. Impossible, without recognising a face, to know what units the others belonged to, when their khaki drill was stained and dirty and tin hats were the order of the day. Not that many had any headgear at all. In the corner, a Guards officer dozed, hat still im-maculate, but that was the only thing about him that was. Both arms were bandaged to the elbow and his shirt was in rags. Beside him sat a Jock who had retained a recognisable balmoral, which he now held to his wounded face like an ice bag as he stared, placid and cowlike, ahead.

I wondered who our captors were. The nonchalant guard, swinging his legs from the cabin roof, was a German, but the trucks were Italian. I couldn't see the driver. At any rate, whoever they were, at least they believed in some sort of medical attention, for the com-mon factor amongst the occupants of the vehicle was that each and every one of us sported a bandage or dressing of some description.

The sun beat down on us as the truck jolted and bounced and the

74

sand flew, causing our eyes to sting and forming a sandwich filling between sweaty skin and sodden cloth. As I've said before, for me the desert was just grit.

Both behind and ahead were lorries full of prisoners, some heavily guarded – these I surmised correctly carrying able-bodied men – and others, like ours, with but a casual guard. With the dust rising in a solid cloud around each truck, it was difficult to assess how many vehicles there were, but it was obviously a fairly lengthy convoy.

I had just been dozing off when the suddenly halting truck jerked me awake.

'*Aus, aus,*' shouted the guard and prodded the nearest man with his rifle.

'Ye'll no' lay yer dirrty hands on me,' and the belligerent little Jock raised two bandaged fists and glared at the German from his one unbandaged eye.

It cheered me immensely to see the wee cock sparrow standing up to the Hun and, for the first time since before the battle, I wanted to laugh. But it was hardly politic under the circumstances, so I said instead, 'Shut up, Innes, no point in giving him cause to belt you one.'

The man subsided, muttering, and the Guards officer, who I now saw was a major, nodded approval.

The occupants of the truck struggled and fell or jumped, according to their injuries, over the tailboard and relieved themselves where they stood.

Shortly afterwards, two German soldiers came round with buckets of water. A mugful each and they passed on.

'Cor, wait till the Geneva Convention 'ears about this lark!'

'Eh, Fritz, didn't your muvver never teach you 'ow to mike a proper cup o' char?'

'Two of yours?' I inquired.

The major nodded. 'By the way,' he introduced himself, 'my name's Hamilton, Reggie Hamilton. It looks as though we shall be seeing quite a lot of each other.' He stopped to listen for a moment, then added, 'There's your lot starting up now.'

I opened my mouth to cope, but Hamilton laid a restraining hand on my arm and shook his head. 'Leave them,' he said, 'I like to hear them grumbling – means they're alive. When a BOR's quiet, there's something wrong!'

There was a shouted order from the head of the convoy and, pushing and shoving, the German guards went up and down the line until we were all back in our trucks.

Some time during the early hours of the morning we arrived at what we presumed was a camp. The guards were taking no chances that anyone would slip away in the dark; the lorries were driven inside and no one was allowed to get down.

At first light we were ordered to debus and a general groan went up as men began to massage stiff and aching limbs. We were inside what appeared to be an enormous cage and to me it looked as though it were already full.

Once rid of their cargo, the trucks moved off and the guards walked back and forth, chivvying us into line. There were calls for news and questions about the fighting from the earlier inmates, but most of us newcomers were still too tired and sore to be anything other than apathetic as we stood there, shivering, in the early morning light.

A routine search followed and then something vaguely akin to porridge was doled out. At least it was food, the first we had had for many hours, warm; even the most persistent grumblers ate in silence. 'Where have you come from? What unit? Any news of the Fusiliers?' from the older inhabitants and, 'How long have you been here? What are they going to do with us? What's the grub like? And, where are we?' from the newcomers.

I believe we were somewhere near Derna, but I'm not sure to this day.

That they would have to do something about us soon, was obvious. The bodies were nearly as numerous as the flies and, all that day and night and the following day, trucks continued to arrive with fresh batches of human cargo. Water was rationed for drinking only; there was very little food and no blankets. If we found the heat bad during the day, it was nothing to the cold at night.

My wound began to fester and soon I could not move my right leg at all. Reggie Hamilton's hands were no better and we entered a partnership of hands and legs which proved to be the foundation of a long-standing friendship. It was very much a case of God helps those who help themselves.

On the third day of our captivity we were sitting together, backs to the fence, when an officer from another Highland Regiment came over.

'Just had a good tip,' he told us in a low voice, 'and I'm passing it round. They're going to move us in a couple of days – trucks to the coast, then by sea to Italy. Good chance to escape.'

Reggie was looking at his hands. 'For whom?' he asked, a trifle ungraciously.

'Sorry, old man. I was just making a comment of general interest. Thought I'd have a go.'

I had been giving the idea considerable thought myself, but had not mentioned it to anyone.

'As a matter of fact,' I said, 'I might stand a better chance in Italy itself. My father was attached to their Staff College for a time and did two tours as military attaché in Rome; I went to school there during that time. Of course I was only prep school age, but I've studied Italian since – with a bit of practice it should get by.'

If I had hoped to gain importance in the eyes of these two, both older and senior to me, I certainly achieved my aim. They looked at me with interest.

'I think I should keep quiet about that if I were you,' advised Reggie, 'it might come in useful to be able to understand what they are saying, without them being aware of it.'

I hadn't given it much thought, but of course he was right.

The news had been correct. We were moved two days later, the wounded going first, Reggie and I amongst them. Which port we went to I have no idea, but general opinion was Benghazi. We travelled in covered vehicles this time and were embarked during the night. By the time it was light again we were inside the hold of a ship and had seen nothing.

Two days and two nights at sea, then we waited to disembark, again at night. Once again we had no idea where we were, but from what I could pick up from the guards' conversation, I deduced that we must be somewhere south of Naples.

The next day we were herded into cattle trucks and set off into the unknown yet again.

'If we do many journeys like this, escape shouldn't be too difficult,' I commented, prodding at a loose board with my foot. 'If we were fit, we could all be out of here within half an hour.'

'Napoli, Napoli.' The train chugged to a halt. Reggie had his eye glued to a crack in the wagon wall. 'It's Naples all right,' he said, 'I can see the board, but it doesn't look as though we're getting off here.'

As he spoke, there was a tremendous jerk and we were off again. It cannot have been more than half an hour before we stopped once more and this time we were offloaded. Back into trucks and, after a drive of about three quarters of an hour, we found ourselves inside what appeared to be a permanent camp.

'I was right about the language,' Reggie told me after we had been there for a few days, 'I've been making a few inquiries, with an eye to escaping once my hands have healed. Bribery seems to be the best bet to get out, then take one's chances outside. But there are a couple of Maltese in the camp who tell me they are watched like hawks and only have to *look* suspicious to be thrown into solitary. And another thing I've learned, that young 2 i/c who appears to have only a smattering of English, actually went to school in England – so watch out what you say when he's around.'

'If we escape together, language shouldn't be too much of a problem, and by the time we're both fit we should have something worked out.'

We had decided all along to stick together, but my opportunity came much sooner than expected, and in no way as I had planned.

The commandant was, taken by and large, a fair man, and no prisoner was sent out on a working-party until pronounced fit by the MO. Mine was only a flesh wound, but it did give me a fair amount of pain, and no one could say whether or not there might be a bullet or a splinter still inside. The day came, therefore, when I was sent to the nearby hospital to have it X-rayed and checked.

As we, my guard and I, arrived, a whole company of men were wheeled in, stripping their shirts off and dumping them on a bench as they filed past.

'Routine chest X-rays,' explained the guard, 'we shall be here for hours and I shall miss my dinner.'

He looked as gloomy as only an Italian can. This was one of the men on whom I had been practising my Italian which, with the help of several Red Cross bars of chocolate and cigarettes, had gone unreported.

'Have a fag,' I said.

He pointed to the notice on the opposite wall, as I was hoping he would. 'It is not permitted.'

'Why don't you go outside,' I suggested, 'you said yourself we would be here for hours and I can sit down here; my leg is hurting.'

'You are right. I shall stand just outside the door.'

He watched me lower myself on to the bench and wandered off.

Scarcely able to believe my good luck, I counted ten slowly then peered round the door. He was already engrossed in conversation with a driver from one of the trucks which had brought the men for their chest X-rays. None of the other drivers was in sight.

Now that my chance had come, I hesitated, but only for a second. Then, seizing one of the cast-off shirts and a field service cap, and wishing they had left their trousers as well, I flung them on and strolled, as nonchalantly as I could make myself, away from the chatting men.

The place appeared to be deserted and I was suspicious until I glanced at the overhead sun. Of course, it was lunchtime; then there would be the siesta. Blessing my good luck – what better time and place to attempt an escape than a hot summer's afternoon in Southern Italy – I started on my way.

There was a fence right round the hospital grounds; only two strands of wire and easy enough to get through, but undoubtedly I would be challenged if seen. I propped myself against the wall of an outhouse for a few moments, debating whether it would be tempting providence more to walk through the main gate than to risk being seen getting under the wire.

I came to the conclusion that the latter course would be best and, having made up my mind, didn't waste any more time. After a quick glance in all directions, I walked straight to the fence, slipped through and continued on my way. What that way should be, I had no idea, but I couldn't risk hesitation, so, guessing my direction, I pressed on.

The only thing I felt bad about was leaving Reggie. But we had decided from the start that, although we intended making the break together, if the opportunity for one to go should arise, it should be seized. And what an opportunity – presented to me on a platter. No one would have thought much of me if I had not made the attempt. And – and this was an important point – if I did end up back in the camp, which was more than likely, I should be able to give them a very good idea of the terrain outside.

Having thus absolved my conscience, I stretched out to rest while the going was good.

Lying in the shade of a few sparse shrubs, I tried to work out in which direction the railway lay. Escape had naturally been a major topic of conversation in the camp and most of us had come to the conclusion that our best bet lay in jumping trains throughout the length of the peninsula, in the hope of reaching Switzerland.

One item of information that we had obtained, was that the camp lay between two railways, both leading to Rome. How far between, I had no idea, but I reasoned that, if I went westwards, towards the coast, the chances were that sooner or later I would find myself in a more heavily-populated area than if I moved inland. With that in mind, I waited where I was until the sun lowered sufficiently to give me an idea of my position, then moved off in what I hoped was an easterly direction.

I walked steadily through fairly bare countryside, avoiding farms or any other signs of human habitation, until sunset, a good three hours, and, although I had twice crossed streams and had been able to drink, I had not come across a single thing to eat. There seemed little point in carrying on in the dark, so, as soon as I found a thickish hazel hedge, I made myself as comfortable as I could and settled down to sleep. I didn't sleep much, but at least I blessed the fact that, although it was chilly during the early hours, it was not the bitter cold of the desert.

Next morning, still tired and by this time very hungry, I set off again in the same direction, stopping to drink whenever there was water to be had and resting every so often. By the early afternoon I saw in the distance what appeared to be a railway station.

I turned north, keeping parallel with the embankment until such time as I should find a suitable place, but by this time I was beginning to feel dizzy from lack of food and was only making very slow progress. The spasms of nausea, the gnawing pain in my stomach and the light-headed, drunken feeling that accompanies acute hunger, were marring my judgment and I was afraid to go on.

There was a farm about half a mile away and I sat down with my back against a rock and tried to make up my mind whether to give myself up to the farmer and hope that, even if he should hand me over to the authorities, he might give me something to eat first, or to continue as I was.

In the end I compromised. I would search the farmer's fields for food and, if by dusk I had not had any success, I would risk the house and possible hostility. My only find was a pile of sugar beet, many of which were already beginning to rot, and the stench was foul. Nevertheless, it did not take me long to decide that I would rather have something, anything, in my stomach and risk the consequences, than remain empty any longer.

I set to work to chew one of the beets, but it was hard going. The flesh, if one could call the hard, woody pulp flesh, was stringy and tasteless, but the very act of swallowing was a relief. I finished half a root and put three or four more inside my shirt – I'd find out soon enough whether they were worth carrying or not.

It was almost dusk when I found what I was looking for. I can say that casually now, but at the time I could hardly believe my good luck, for there, ahead of me, silhouetted on the embankment, was a stationary train. I could see at once that it was a goods train and stood some hundred yards beyond the platform of a small country station. I didn't trust my judgment all that much, but I guessed it must be nearly a mile away. And then I was seized with panic. What if it moved off before I reached it? The station was between me and the train; I could not risk being seen, although there did not appear to be anyone about.

I hurried as fast as I could, almost crying with frustration at the way in which I was hindered by my stiffening leg. Oh hurry, I sobbed, help me; oh please train, don't go.

But my luck was holding. I reached it, panting and exhausted, and there was still not a soul in sight.

I crawled along the line, keeping within the shadow of the train, trying every door until I found one that was unlocked. I slipped inside and lay gratefully on the floor, fighting for breath and trying desperately not to be sick. It was completely empty. That, and the fact that the door was open, did not bode well. What if it were waiting to be loaded?

After half an hour of indecision, I ventured outside again. Still nobody. It was almost dark and I felt I would be safe in trying a few more doors.

Strangely enough, quite a few doors were unlatched at this end of the train and, before the night settled down, I had become blasé enough to take my pick. The van I chose was full of furniture, trunks and suitcases and other personal effects. Some official going on transfer, perhaps. I did not ask. I wished him joy of his new post and meanwhile made myself comfortable on a badly done up, sacking-covered pile of rugs and braced my back against a rolled-up mattress. And then, for the first time in forty-eight hours, I really slept.

When I woke up it was still dark, but we were on the move. The train pulled slowly into Rome early the next morning and stopped. If we were in the station proper, and the contents of my wagon were to be unloaded there, I might as well give myself up. I wouldn't get very far in my queer mixture of uniform on a major city station, where there were bound to be both civil and military police.

I wondered if I were important enough to be listed as a wanted man. Was the news of an escape, even of someone as junior as I, flashed to all police stations? I tried to think if they were in Britain and simply did not know.

There were no nearby sounds and, after waiting for what I considered a long enough time, I cautiously slid the door ajar and peered out.

We were halted on the outskirts of the station, which we appeared to have passed through. There was some shunting going on further along the line and I could hear voices shouting in the distance. By the shadows, I judged the time to be about six o'clock, which would account for the lack of activity.

As I jumped down from the wagon, an overwhelming spell of dizziness came over me and I collapsed by the rails. It was not surprising – I had had nothing to eat, except the beets, since leaving the prison camp and had been without water as well for a good many hours.

I was just beginning to wonder if it were all worth while, when I saw the name 'Bologna' chalked on the side of my van. That decided me. I should be able to hold out for another day if I could get hold of a drink from somewhere, and it was well worth going hungry to take the opportunity of reaching a point further north. After a few more minutes of the cool, fresh air, I crawled back inside my wagon to await events.

I have no idea how long we stayed on the outskirts of Rome, because, once back on my rugs, I fell fast asleep again and only woke for the second time when we were already in motion. I don't think I cared much where we were. All I could think of was my nigh unendurable thirst and the heat from the sun beating down on the roof of the wagon.

It occurred to me, after a while, that we must be travelling very slowly uphill. I cast my mind back to the days of my boyhood – not so long ago really – when we had often travelled between Rome and

Florence on this line. Where was there such a long, slow incline? I was too light-headed to think very deeply, but after some deliberation I decided that perhaps we were going over the Futa Pass. We could not have reached Bologna or I would not still be here, and I could think of no reason why we should travel so slowly between Rome and Florence. And if Florence were already past, we did not have far to go.

That did register. Good grief, what was I going to do when we reached Bologna?

Easing the door ajar very gently, I looked out. We were crawling at a snail's pace up a steepish gradient and, a few hundred yards ahead, loomed the black mouth of a tunnel. There were only a few minutes in which to think out the alternatives. If I succeeded in leaving the train at Bologna, I would be in the right place to catch another going north, but – and it was a large but – I would not only have to make sure of leaving the wagon before it was unloaded, but I would also have to find somewhere to hide on the station. And there were food and drink and the other essentials of life to ponder over. The chances of begging food in a town would be infinitely less than in the country.

It was the thought of food that made up my mind.

In the panoramic scene laid out below for my inspection, I could see scattered farms dotting the landscape, one of which might perhaps give me shelter and a meal. My wagon was near the end of the train; if I waited until the front half was inside the tunnel before I jumped, I would not be seen by anyone ahead. I had to risk the possibility of there being a guard at the rear, but with any luck he would be asleep.

I plumped up the mattress and smoothed the rugs – no point in advertising the fact that someone had been in there, in case a search was being made. I looked at the steep embankment, down which I would have to roll – worse than debussing from a moving truck – hesitated, but not for long, closed my eyes and jumped.

I hit the ground with a sickening jar on my left shoulder and rolled down the agonisingly hard, sharp slope until something stopped me, and there I lay, still, listening. The only sound was the tired chugging of the train as it wended its slow way into the tunnel. No shouts, no sound of brakes being applied. I looked after it with affection.

Idling in the camp while my wound healed had not been good training for the past few days. Coupled with the lack of food and drink, it made me incredibly weak and I lay still for a long time, not only afraid to move, but trying to muster the necessary energy to do so. But I did at last sit up and take stock of my surroundings.

From that height I had a good view of the road, railway and valley. It was rough land, with only sparse cultivation in isolated areas. I judged the nearest farmhouse to be some three miles away and without more ado made my way towards it.

Whether I had misjudged the distance, or was even weaker than I had thought, I don't know, but the sun had been high overhead when I had thrown away the stalk of the last beet and it was low on the horizon when at last I reached the low stone wall that was the boundary of the farm.

A dog barked and three small children ran out at my approach. I must have looked a disreputable sight. I didn't care whether they handed me over to the nearest police station or not, as long as they gave me a drink first. I called imploringly after them, but they ran back into the house.

I could go no further. It seemed that my willpower had deserted me at the wall. I sat down, with my back propped against it, and waited for the children to reappear, as I was sure they would.

I was not wrong. In a matter of minutes they were back, chirping and gesticulating in my direction and behind them came a woman.

I don't have to guess what an angel looks like; I know. She is red-faced, middle-aged and of ample form, attired in a black dress with thick black stockings and boots upon her feet. She has doughy hands and an apron, which once might have been white, and an expression of the most infinite compassion in the world.

My angel wiped her hands on the apron and pushed a sweaty lock of hair from her hot, red, perspiring face.

Then her mouth opened wide and her hands went first up to her face then down to me. 'Mamma mia, he's dying,' she yelled, 'Alessandro, Pietro, come quick.'

Two youths in their early teens came out of the house at her cry and joined the smaller children. Then the largest boy and his mother, supporting me one on either side, dragged and heaved me to the house.

How cool the flagstones felt. How blessed the wet rag wiping my face and the water trickling down my throat. I looked up at the coarse face of the solid woman in black and thought that the Madonna could not have looked more beautiful.

As there seemed little point in trying to disguise the truth, I told them straight away that I was an escaped British prisoner. None of them seemed particularly surprised and the woman just nodded.

'Show him Enrico's letter,' she commanded her eldest son.

The boy went into the other room – the only other room, as I was to find out – and emerged a few minutes later with a page torn from a child's exercise book, which he handed to me.

The writing was childish, unformed, but the spelling was correct and I saw at a glance that the figures had been written by no Continental. I read: 'This is to certify that I, 8432147 Pte. Henry Edward Bowden, was fed and clothed and looked after by Mrs Bianchi and her family for more than a month. They were good to me and I would like to reward them after the war.' It ended with a flourishing signature.

'What happened to him?' I asked.

'He wanted to go north – like you all do – so when another man came along, they went off together. He helped me fetch water from the well and the boys with the ploughing. He was a good man; we did not want him to go.'

'I too wish to go north, it is true,' I told her, handing back the letter, which was carefully folded and put away. 'If I can reach Switzerland, perhaps I shall get back to my own country.'

Signora Bianchi nodded again. 'It should not be so difficult for you. You speak like a Roman, and yet you are not Italian. How is it that you speak our language so well?'

I explained. They were not surprised. Like most peasants, they took most things for granted.

The boys began to laugh and recalled anecdotes of Enrico's stay.

While they chattered, I became overwhelmingly aware of that most wonderful of all scents – even to a man not hungry by normal standards – that of newly-baked bread. I was practically drooling, but she shook her head.

The loaves were round and fairly flat and one was given to each child and, with a handful of olives and a small portion of goats' milk cheese, comprised their meal. But I was given some corn gruel.

It was wonderful to have a full stomach, but I still looked longingly at the remaining loaves – like a small boy who is not allowed a sweet, I suppose. The good lady smiled at me and waved an admonishing finger.

'Bread to-morrow, yes. But on the empty stomach, new bread is not good.'

Kind, wise angel.

The older boys had gone outside. Signora Bianchi pulled a chair to the window, to catch the last of the light, and started to sew a patch on an ancient shirt, while the younger members of her brood played round her feet, like puppies.

'We will give you something to wear which will make you look less English,' she said after a while, 'if you will give us your thick British trousers – that is good, warm cloth, good for working on the farm in winter time.'

I agreed, of course, but looking down at the tatty remains of my battledress trousers, I wondered if it was safe to wear them in the open. In answer to my question, she shrugged.

'We're too far from the road for many people to visit us,' she said, 'and if they do, I shall say the boys found them on the railway line – everyone knows they send prisoners by rail.'

84

It was so peaceful in the pale evening light, so cool inside the thick walls, so soothing to watch the motherly figure sewing, head bent to get the most of the light that filtered through the window. The three tots had fallen asleep on the rush mat and from outside occasional laughter from the boys floated in.

My eyelids were beginning to droop, when she spoke again.

'You will want to go,' she gave a sigh of resignation – I could see that it would indeed be a help to her to have a man around to cope with the heavy work on the farm, 'so you had better go with Giuseppe when he takes the eggs next week.'

'Giuseppe?'

She pointed her needle in the vague direction of the window. 'He's our nearest neighbour and the only one who owns a cart these days. He is the only man too – he has a crippled leg, so did not have to go into the army like my man – so he collects all our eggs and vegetables and takes them to the market in Bologna once a fortnight.' I had been falling asleep, but now I was wide awake. She must have seen the doubt in my face though, because she gave an impatient little gesture and went on, 'You need not worry about Giuseppe; he's helped many prisoners already. We all hate this war, but he more than any of us. Do you know why?' Of course I couldn't know, but I shook my head. 'Before the war he had a business, a little shop in the city, and when he would not become a member of the party and pay a percentage of his profits to them, the Fascisti wrecked his shop and beat him up. It is to them that he owes his leg and now he can't fight for them, and that, he says, is the Lord's judgment.' A look of peasant cunning and cruelty crossed her face, 'He has snatched many prisoners from under their hands, and killed – that is the Lord's judgment too.'

Judging by her expression, some private vendetta had been settled at the Fascists' expense, but I was more interested in this Scarlet Pimpernel's efforts on behalf of Allied prisoners.

I waited with Alessandro and his mother at the end of the track. I suppose it was ungrateful of me to look forward to Giuseppe's arrival so much. A week with the Bianchi family had put me on my feet and I would have liked to be able to help them in some way – other than by staying – but I was young and fit and Switzerland was my goal.

I was well pleased with my disguise. Signora Bianchi had given me an old pair of patched, olive green corduroys, a rough jacket and a cap of the type worn by most of the peasants. Only my shoes were my own and they were so mud-caked that no one would know.

Giuseppe proved to be a keen-eyed man in his early forties, with a caustic wit and ribald sense of humour. However, I only found that out later. At that moment I was undergoing a close scrutiny, the older man walking round and looking at me and my clothes from every angle.

'Take your cap off,' he ordered and I obeyed. 'Hm, not bad.' He seemed quite pleased and I realised why Signora Bianchi had insisted that she should cut my hair, as she cut her husband's and her sons'. 'Better limp, I think – like me. Pretend a war wound.'

I told him that pretence was not necessary. Although healed and no longer troubling me, my wound was still red and raw looking enough, if anyone asked to see it.

'Excellent!' He jumped on to the cart with difficulty, his right knee being almost completely stiff, and held down a hand to me. 'You'll do. Your Italian is nearly perfect – lucky for both of us – but you'll have to lose some of your refinements if you want to be taken for one of us. Those pigs – ' he spat, accurately hitting a dandelion full in the face, ' – those pigs have even coarsened the language. Well, we must be off before the sun gets too hot and turns the milk.'

Like my predecessor, Enrico, alias Private Henry Bowden, I had left a note testifying to the help afforded me by the Bianchi family, but, as I looked into the good-natured faces of all three, I knew that it was totally inadequate. I shook hands with Alessandro and Pietro and kissed their mother on both cheeks, wishing that I could promise more than to send the boys some English stamps when the war was over.

Dear, dear Signora Bianchi hugged me to her, tears streaming down her already red face. 'You are like a son,' she wept, 'all you boys are like my sons.'

'Your heart is too big, Luisa,' Giuseppe mocked, 'lucky for you there is plenty to support it!'

She shook her fist at him, but smiled, the emotion of the moment eased, fixed her eyes on her apron and clasped her hands.

'May God go with you and may the blessed Madonna watch over you,' she blessed, and waved as the ancient mule moved off.

I learned a lot about escaping and escapees from Giuseppe, as we swayed along first the winding track, then the main, but equally winding road to Bologna.

With the peace of the early morning all around us and over the quiet countryside, it was difficult to believe that I was I, Philip Andrew Morrison, subaltern in the Inverness-shire Highlanders, escaped prisoner of war, and not an Italian farm labourer on his way to market. I said as much to Giuseppe.

'But that is good. Excellent,' he said. 'If you can think yourself completely into the part, then half the battle is won. It is that haunted, hunted look that points to the escaped prisoner every time. Ah, I have seen so many caught. Sometimes through lack of language, yes, but more often because they couldn't relax, just looked so suspicious without even opening their mouths. But it should not be difficult for you – you have a slight foreign accent, it is true, and some of your words are out of date, but if, in the north, you say you are from the south and vice versa, you'll pass.'

We reached the city shortly before eight o'clock and Giuseppe made straight for the market to offload his produce.

'You stay here,' he instructed firmly, as I began to get down from the cart, 'and mind the mule. I'll be back presently.'

'But you have already done enough for me,' I protested, 'you and the Bianchis. I have no wish to put you in any more danger on my account.'

'Be quiet then,' he hissed, 'this is *my* war – you do not understand – and I have plans for you. Wait here.' He patted my leg in a kindly way and sauntered off.

I waited, slightly apprehensive in case there was a trap and ashamed of myself for even considering it.

Giuseppe wasted no time. 'Allora, and now, I have a plan. But first we must go to my friends – where I always spend the night – and explain, because we shall need their help. And then we shall take some food to an open place, where we can discuss with safety, and we shall eat.'

He flicked the bony mule on the rump and we trundled out of the market square and into the main street, then several side streets, until at last we stopped in a narrow alley with high, overhanging houses on both sides.

Jumping down, Giuseppe hobbled the mule and told me to follow him. We went through the nearest door and into a small house, cavernously quiet and cool. Beyond the narrow passage and tiny main room, there was a small square of green courtyard, with a few boxes of geraniums hanging from the walls. Oblong tomatoes were spread on the paving stones to dry in the sun and their pungent odour stung my nostrils.

Four men and a young girl rose as we appeared.

'This,' said Giuseppe, taking me by the arm, 'is Tenente Filippo. He is an officer of the Scottish Army and has escaped from the Germans, so of course we must help him.'

They all murmured assent, nodding as they held out their hands to shake mine, one by one.

The young girl was dispatched to fetch wine and soon returned, a carafe of yellow liquid in one hand and a tray with six glasses in the other.

'This is poor stuff,' apologised her father, who had introduced himself as Barbero, 'the Germans take most of the vintage, but luckily they can't tell wine from ass's pee, so we still have the best for ourselves!'

We all laughed and raised our glasses and, amidst their rough good humour, I tasted my first glass of wine since leaving Africa.

'It is dangerous for us to stay here,' Giuseppe said, after he had outlined his plans for my next move. 'If you, Barbero, can find out the usual and you, Luigi, can pass a message to Matteo, I shall take Filippo to see the station and then, if Maria can let us have a little bread, we shall stay away until dark.'

Everyone rose and we all shook hands again, then Giuseppe and I returned to the waiting mule.

In silence he steered the cart along another side street, then turned left under an archway and into a blacksmith's yard. A German soldier stood by while the blacksmith, who was also a mechanic, fixed some fault with his motor-cycle.

'Have a look at the mule's rear off,' Giuseppe said loudly to the smith, 'I don't want to lose a shoe on my way home.'

The smith nodded, without looking up from the machine on which he was working, and Giuseppe guided me back under the arch, across the street and through a shop. On the further side, a number of black, greasy coats were hanging from pegs in the wall and a couple of bicycles were propped near by.

He looked at me and grinned. 'Didn't think we were so well organised, did you?'

I shook my head. I was still wondering what it was all about. 'My luck has never been so good,' I told him, 'to fall off a train and walk straight to the right house – it seems incredible, too good to last.'

He coughed and slapped me on the back in his gruff way. 'Not really so coincidental, my friend. Most of us country people are out to help – we don't want this war. Just your bad luck if you had picked one of the few who are pro-Fascist. Not many of them though, if you keep out of the towns – wasn't us peasants who made all the noise, party this and party that.'

While he had been talking, Giuseppe had taken a couple of coats from the pegs and now handed one to me.

'Stroke of luck that chap being in the blacksmith's,' he remarked, 'gives us the excuse to leave the mule for longer than usual, without any suspicions being aroused. You can be sure that Carlo won't hurry with that bike – probably make it worse. We're railway workers for the next couple of hours.'

He passed me a cap and began pushing out one of the bicycles, motioning me to do likewise.

We parked the bicycles, with a lot of others, outside the main goods shed of the railway station and went inside. There was not much activity, no trains being in, but a few men – and I recognised Barbero amongst them – were stacking bales in the corner of a shed, while a tally clerk ticked them off.

Giuseppe handed me a crowbar from the tool store, choosing a large hammer and a spanner for himself. He lifted the spanner in greeting as we passed the tally clerk and I followed him on to the main line.

Having ascertained that there was no one within hearing distance, he beckoned to me and pointed to a spot some two hundred yards away down the northern line.

'When we reach that curve,' he instructed, 'I shall bend over a nut with my spanner; it will be on the outside of the rail and you must pretend to lever from the other side. While we are there, take a good look round. Memorise the distances, both from the station and from the road below – it will depend on circumstances at the time, which way you will come, so it is important that you know both ways.'

He stopped talking and walked on. As he had instructed me, I began counting my paces from the station limits.

'Five hundred and eighty-two,' he said, as he bent over the rail; 'further than I thought.'

I slipped my crowbar under the rail and began to heave as Giuseppe played with the nut on the other side, using first his hammer then the spanner.

'Steady,' he said, 'or you'll really move it – we don't want a derailment on our hands! Now, pay close attention to what I am about to say. You can't board a train in the station before it leaves because they are searched, but quite often a long goods train is shunted out to this point to wait for an engine. Barbero will find out when there is to be such a train and will tell us to-night, if he can. You know the distance and how long it would take you to walk from the station; now, in a minute, you must slip and let your crowbar fall in such a way that it will roll over the side. You will then be able to clamber down the bank to retrieve it and measure the distance as you climb back, in case you have to come from the road. Remember, it will be dark. Now.'

I gave what I hoped appeared to be a realistic heave, tripped and sent my crowbar sailing over the edge. To any onlooker it would have then appeared that Giuseppe, by word and gesture, was berating his stupid assistant for his clumsiness, finishing up by pointing down the bank and, with a final gesture of futility, turning back to his own work.

Like so many Italians, he was a born actor. I found it hard not to laugh, but only in appreciation at his professional manner. He was a professional all right and, as I slid down the bank, I wondered how many men this group had passed northwards. We had heard, rather

89

vaguely, of escape organisations, in the prison camp, but it had never occurred to me that they would be so efficient; that there would be so many people willing to help in a game which was, after all, as far as their government was concerned, treachery; nor that I should have the good fortune to fall so easily into the hands of such dedicated men.

'Thirty-four,' I puffed as I reached the line again, 'that should not be difficult.'

Giuseppe nodded and made another rude gesture.

'It should not be difficult,' he agreed, 'but it must be sure. Timing is all important. From Bologna to Piacenza it is almost a straight line and even the goods trains travel at speed. There are only two stops on the way and this is your only possible chance of boarding it.'

We continued our working act for a little longer, then Giuseppe straightened up, looked at his section of line with satisfaction and, beckoning me to follow, shouldered his tools and made his way back to the goods shed.

Following the same procedure in reverse, we returned to the blacksmith's shop, collected the waiting mule and ambled out of town at a leisurely gait.

It was not long before Giuseppe turned the cart into a side lane and stopped at a pleasant, shady spot, where he let the mule loose to crop the grass and took down the bundle that the girl had given us. 'Brava Maria,' he exclaimed, as he opened it up, and with reason. Besides a loaf of bread and the inevitable olives, it contained a couple of slices of home-made salami, two ripe peaches, and several plums. There was also a small carafe, corked with a wad of cloth.

While we ate, he went through the rest of his plan.

'First of all,' he said, 'much will of course depend on what Barbero has managed to find out and timing will depend on his advice. But, sooner or later, there will be a goods train of the type we want and once you are on it, you will stay on it – with luck – until it is past Piacenza. They do not normally stop before Lodi, and there it slows down about half a mile before the station, sometimes sooner. Sometimes it even stops and waits – that of course would be ideal, but you can't bank on it. You *must* get off at this point, it is imperative. If you don't, it will not stop again until it reaches Milan and there the searching is far too thorough to risk. Do you follow me so far?' I recapped.

'Good. Now, the next part will depend on when there is a train and whether or not it is possible to pass a message down the line before you leave. But, assuming that luck is with us, this is your next move, once you are off the train: Keeping the railway on your right and away from the houses, you will walk until you reach a secondary road for Pavia – it is the only road going into the country on your left, so you cannot miss it. Try not to ask the way unless you have to, but, if you do get lost, remember that an air of confidence and purpose will be your greatest asset. At about five kilometres down this road you will cross the new autostrada, which is still under construction. There is to be a flyover at this point and there are many men working on it. You will stop and watch them, resting on the roadside. You will stretch like this – ' he clasped his hands above his head, stretched and yawned. 'If, after about a quarter of an hour, no one has approached you, move on and continue to the first village. Ask for the house of Matteo Boschi. If all goes according to plan, one of the workmen will come up to you while you are resting and ask if you have a cigarette to spare – it will be Matteo himself. After that you are in his hands.'

Once again I repeated the instructions back to him.

'And now it is siesta time.'

While Giuseppe snored softly and the mule demolished the grass, I lay on my back, staring up at the intense blue sky and thought about my friends, still incarcerated in the camp near Naples.

That evening we congregated again in the small courtyard and I saw at once from their faces that the news was satisfactory.

'There will be a train in three days' time,' Barbero announced. 'It couldn't be better. There is a wagon-load of empty gas cylinders to be sent to Milan for refilling. Unless there is a change of schedule, it will be best if you proceed from the road. Once you are inside, I shall slide down the bank and take back the bicycle which you will have ridden. Do you understand?'

Once again I repeated back my instructions and added, 'I have so much to thank you for and can see no way of repaying you.'

They waved that aside.

'And I,' said Giuseppe, 'must return to my farm to-morrow. My family expect me to stay in Bologna for the night, but if I am away for longer, they might start making a fuss, which could have awkward consequences. Can he stay with you, Barbero?'

'For to-night, yes. But to-morrow it will be best if he goes with Luigi; he should not remain in the city any longer than he has to.'

Seldom can three days have passed so slowly. But the time came and it was with a mixture of excitement and relief that I mounted Luigi's bicycle, just as it was getting dark, and rode off in the direction of the railway.

The train was already there. I could see it, silhouetted against the fast darkening sky, and thought of the first train I had jumped, less than two weeks ago. That one had been silhouetted too, but then I had not known where I was going, nor had there been a helping hand. I hid the bike in a clump of bushes at the bottom of the bank and began, very cautiously, to climb.

I paused at the top, still flat on my stomach, to make sure there were no guards in sight, then edged my way slowly along the line towards the waiting trucks. I would have yelped with surprise a second later if a hand had not been slammed hard over my mouth. The man had emerged from between two wagons. I heard my own sharp intake of breath, then relaxed with relief; it was Barbero.

'This one,' he whispered, and pushed me up. 'The train won't move for another hour. Good luck, Tenente.'

He cut short my thanks and with a quick handshake was away down the bank, slithering over the rough shale and making enough noise to raise the dead. Or so it seemed to me.

The cylinders were stacked exactly as Barbero had said they would be and I had no difficulty in finding the space provided. My thoughts drifted and, despite my hard bed, I dozed off and only came to when the train started.

I didn't dare risk falling asleep again and kept myself awake by going over the plans in my head; thinking of something quite different, then going over them again. In this way I hoped to keep my mind fresh.

A pity there were no rugs or mattresses this time; it was not the most comfortable position to be in, squeezed between the stacked cylinders and the carriage wall. But there I sat, without moving, until the early hours of the morning, when we pulled into a station. This could not be Lodi, it was too soon, and Barbero had told me that occasionally the train did stop if the line was not clear.

There was much shunting and, with each jolt, I half expected the empty cylinders to topple over me; but they had been stacked by expert hands. Nevertheless, it was a relief when we finally came to a stop. I waited for it to start again, but gradually daylight began to creep through the cracks and we were still stationary. There were no sounds near my wagon and, after listening intently for a few minutes, I scrambled over to the door and eased it open an inch or two – and quickly shut it!

I sat back on my heels, shaking. My heart was thumping so hard I thought it must burst. Not only had I discerned, in that fractional space of time, that we were in fact in the middle of a station, but also that there was a railway official standing not more than two feet away from my door. I waited, still as a statue, for what seemed an eternity, but thank goodness nothing happened. He could not have seen the door move.

The hours dragged by and I ate half the bread and salami that Maria had provided and drank some water. The heat became intense as the morning wore on and I squatted in my cubby hole, not daring to move again. The sweat poured down me and my bladder was bursting. I had no idea of either the time or where we were, but two things were certain, one, that I would have to relieve myself soon and, two, that this delay had not been allowed for in Barbero's and Giuseppe's planning.

I had just reached the stage where I knew I would have to risk the sound and sight of liquid trickling through the floorboards, when I had a bright idea. What better use for an empty cylinder?

My morale did not remain high for long though. Within a short time I heard the sound of a long train pulling in to the opposite side of the platform and the guard shouting, 'Modena, Modena, Modena,' as he traversed the length of what must be a passenger train.

Modena? But that was only forty kilometres from Bologna. The next thing I heard deflated me still further. It was a clear, high, woman's voice and she was asking the guard how long the train would be stopping for. I didn't hear his reply, but I heard her exclamation clearly enough. 'Twenty minutes? But that means we shan't be leaving here before three o'clock.'

Twenty to three! Good God almighty! I had expected to be off the train and well on my way by this time.

On my way to where? You will be in good hands, Barbero had said of the mythical Matteo. But there was little chance of my contacting him with this delay. It occurred to me that I had not thought further ahead than making contact with Matteo once I had left the train before Lodi. There was nothing urgent about empty cylinders, half of which were rusty and must have been left lying around for months already, and I had no idea what the other wagons contained. For all I knew, we might wait here for days.

So, back to debating whether or not to leave the train and, luckily for me, the decision was taken out of my hands. Before I had made up my mind, a whistle blew and within seconds a fearsome jolt threw me head first against the wall.

After crawling out of the station, we got up reasonable speed, stayed a short while in one station, speeded through another and stopped.

There was a great commotion on the platform, doors banging and a good deal of shouting in both Italian and German. I held my breath as I heard the door of the wagon immediately preceding mine being slammed to, then my own rasping open – I could have done with that cylinder again! A torch shone in, flickered over walls and ceiling, a cursory kick at the nearest cylinder and it was heaved to again. A finger of light still pierced the gloom and, when I had heard the door of the next wagon being opened and shut, I stood up and looked to see the cause. The door had been left about an inch ajar and the dim light from the platform relieved the utter blackness of the interior. After hesitating for a few more seconds, I slid over the cylinders and glanced out. I couldn't see the whole word, but what I could see with one eye pressed against the crack, painted on the back of a station bench, I took to be the ending of the word 'Parma'.

I was bloody hungry. I tossed up whether or not to eat and, coming to the conclusion that I would risk further delay, I polished off the remains of my food and left only an inch of water.

It was well into the afternoon before we were on the move again. 'Now,' I said aloud as we pulled into Piacenza, 'a half to three quarters of an hour, Barbero said.'

For once the train behaved according to plan and, after what I judged to be about forty minutes, began to slow down.

The saliva rose in my mouth and my heart beat wildly as I contemplated the next quarter of an hour. Jumping off on a near deserted pass and getting on at night had been easy enough, but leaving the train in broad daylight on a flat, straight section of line, so near a town, was a very different matter.

The train crawled for a further half mile, then stopped. Taking a deep breath and hoping I had sufficient courage to appear nonchalant, I climbed down on to the line, crossed the tracks and walked towards a path which I could see running along the edge of a field.

So far so good. Resisting the temptation to hurry, I idled along the path until I came to a small clump of trees, where I sat down.

A few hundred yards away I could see a figure on a bicycle. It must be the road. Five kilometres, Giuseppe had said. I looked at the sun and began to walk as fast as I dared without attracting attention.

The road was deserted and when I reached the autostrada under construction, that was deserted too. There was a vague movement and I looked again; about ten to fifteen men, taking a break presumably, were resting in the shade beneath the new flyover.

What now? I wondered. No harm to go through the antics, even if it were the wrong day. I chose a small circle of shade, thrown by a single poplar at the road's edge and sat down to wait. I made enough movement to make sure that I was seen by anyone sufficiently awake to notice, then, first taking off my jacket and rolling it into a pillow, I stretched elaborately in the prescribed manner and lay down. I watched carefully through my half-closed lids, but not a soul stirred.

After about half an hour, convinced that the plans had gone awry, I got up and walked down the road, my jacket thrown carelessly over one shoulder, as Giuseppe had told me.

It was not long before I reached a cross-roads. This was something that had not been mentioned and there was no sign to guide me. I was still pausing, wondering which direction to take, when I heard a voice behind me say, 'Keep straight on and don't turn round.'

It was only then that I noticed the tread of soft-soled shoes behind me – he must have been walking on the grass. We must have covered the best part of a mile before my unseen companion spoke again.

'You will soon come to a small river,' he said, 'stop and rest on the bridge.'

I obeyed gratefully.

'Do you have a cigarette to spare?'

A tall, sun-tanned man, wearing workman's clothes, came to lean on the rail beside me.

'I'm sorry,' I said, as I had been told to, 'I smoked my last half an hour ago.'

He smiled then and held out his hand. 'I'm sorry if I made you sweat – I had to be sure. I was watching you by the flyover, but you were so late that I couldn't discount the possibility of the real man having been caught and a stooge planted in his place.'

From Matteo to Angelo, from Angelo to Giovanni, and from Giovanni to Davido, I was passed, until, some three weeks later, I found myself entering a tall, narrow house on a neck of land jutting out into a small, sombre lake.

'This is the house of Signora Marissa. She does not stay here the whole time, but she is expecting you and will arrive later. Do not go out.'

Davido, my latest helper, shook hands and withdrew, leaving me standing in a dark, tiled hall. I heard the key turning in the lock – he wasn't giving me a chance to go out.

Once through the hall, the house broadened out, with rooms on both sides and a loggia bordering the lake. It was well appointed, with some good furniture, paintings on the walls and handwoven rugs on the red-tiled floors. From the loggia french windows led on to a small courtyard, bounded by the house on two sides and the lake on the third.

With nothing else to do, I had been lounging in the early autumn sunshine when I heard a key turn in the lock again and a door open somewhere inside the house. I made no move, standing in the shadow of one wall, terrified in case it was a trap.

'Tenente Filippo?' It was a woman's voice.

I turned back into the house with relief and found a tall, middle-aged woman, removing her hat and gloves in the dim hallway.

I don't quite know what I had expected – a peasant woman, I suppose – anyway, I can well remember my surprise at seeing the tailored suit and well set hair. But I was even more surprised when she turned to me with outstretched hand and asked, in accentless English, 'How do you do?'

I took her hand, but found myself completely tongue-tied. I must have looked a real country bumpkin and was not surprised to hear her laugh. She had a lovely laugh, good-natured and rippling; it is a laugh I shall never forget.

95

'I'm sorry,' she said, 'I have the same effect on all of you. I'm afraid it affords me some amusement in this rather dreary world.'

'But –' I was still too astonished to make a coherent remark.

'Oh yes,' she said, reading my thoughts, 'I *am* English. But come – I wish I could offer you a cup of tea, but that's something we haven't seen for many moons. I have some inferior wine, though.'

After five weeks of trains and attics and peasant homes, it seemed incredibly civilised to be sitting in comfortable basket chairs, the carafe of wine between us, watching the dying sun staining the lake outside.

Marissa stretched and sighed. 'I always love this time of day, despite the melancholy soon to come.' She paused and watched the lake, a small, sad smile on her face. 'When my husband was alive, he would sit where you are sitting, waiting for the lake to become silver after the setting sun. Then he would get up and draw the curtains and light the lamps and the maid would bring in the sherry. He would tell me about his day in the office and I would tell him what the children had done – all very domestic, very commonplace, but I have been happy in this house.'

I could see that she must have been very beautiful when she was young. She was still attractive, poised and serene, but her eyes were sad and too much frowning had caused creases to form on her forehead and around her mouth. We sat in silence, watching the last rays of the sun sink into the water and then I asked, a shade impertinently I fear, 'I would love to hear how you came to live here in the first place.' Anyone's curiosity would have been aroused.

'And so you shall,' she replied, leaning over to refill my glass. 'It's not so complicated really.'

She told me how they had lived a gay life in Milan – where her husband worked pre-war – and used this lakeside villa as a quiet week-end retreat. They had loved it so much that eventually they had lived here semi-permanently, her husband commuting to Milan. Their life had still been gay, she said, and, as she spoke, I did not find it difficult to people the room with lively figures, with a buzz of chatter and music in the background.

But that had been the happy part.

Her husband had taken to the hills on Italy's entry into the war, forming the first partisan group in the area. The Germans had caught and shot him, but treated his wife as a respected enemy. The local commander – whom she considered to be at heart no more a Nazi than her husband had been a Fascist – had asked her to help with the convalescent soldiers at the nearby military hospital and, because of his friendship, her house was now never searched and she was able to move around unmolested.

The thought of her consorting with the enemy, who had destroyed her own husband, was not pleasant and I wished she had not said that she did not mind – I was still very young then, but I grew up fast. Marissa was a fine woman and there were surprises still to come.

'What exactly do you do?' I asked her.

'In the hospital? Just occupational therapy – mixed with the right propaganda, of course! Not that they believe it, even when it is the truth – they were caught too young. Or did you mean here?'

'Here.'

'Oh, well now, that's a difficult question. I pass people through and look after them *en route* – like you – and sometimes I hide a wanted man, or nurse a sick one. I'm a sort of sanctuary-cum-transit camp, I suppose.'

I was to find out in time that she was far more than that.

She rose to pull the heavy curtains and switched on a solitary light.

'What the Germans don't know,' she added, as she carefully adjusted the blackout, 'is that I have two sons.'

'Where?'

'One, I hope, is in England – he was still at school when war broke out – and the other brought you here to-day.'

'Davido?' I heard my own voice, sounding high pitched with astonishment. Davido, that rough and ready, coarse, good-natured peasant youth? I saw the amusement on her face and knew that she was enjoying the effect. She must be teasing. Incredulously, I asked again, 'Davido? Your son?'

Her bell-like laugh pealed out. 'You wouldn't think he was the product of an English school and university, would you?'

'I can't believe it!'

Marissa became serious. 'I like the odd British person to know, but not one of his band knows who he is, not one, and that is why he is so good. He was dropped in soon after Italy entered the war and has been doing sterling work ever since. I'm very proud of him.'

'I should think you are.'

I thought for a moment of my own mother, buried in our West Highland home, in a village more off the map than this, and, much as I loved her, I'm afraid my thoughts were not very complimentary.

'To-morrow,' she said, breaking into my thoughts, 'I have a friend coming – to see you, not me – and, if your Italian is as good as I have heard, he may be very interested in you.'

'Who is he?'

'A British Army officer.' She changed to Italian, 'He is coming to collect you, with the intention of getting you across the border – as he has so many others – but, tell me, if there was a worthwhile job to be done here, would you be prepared to stay instead?'

My whole aim had been to escape. I had never considered any

other course, so I asked, a little warily perhaps, 'What sort of job?'

'An army officer's job.'

'In which army?'

She laughed then and returned to English too. 'That's another difficult question to answer – I'll let him explain – it was only a notion I had. Your Italian's good though, better than I had expected – if you don't pretend to be a local, you will pass quite well. At any rate, the Germans would never know. Well now,' she got up, smoothing her skirt and plumping up the cushion against which she had been leaning, 'you've had a long day and so have I, and, once this electric bulb burns out, I'm unlikely to get a replacement for a long time – all good reasons for going to bed.'

It was wonderful sleeping in a proper bed again. I had thought my mind too full to sleep, but it didn't take long to prove me wrong – about five minutes, I should think. Marissa had put out a pair of pyjamas for me – her husband's, I supposed – but they were too small, and an old-fashioned cut throat razor and a towel.

She was already up when I woke and, leaning out of the window, I saw her hanging strings of tomatoes across the courtyard to dry in the sun – as I had seen them in Barbero's courtyard in Bologna.

'Good morning,' I called.

She turned quickly and I could see her frown before the slight shake of her head.

'*Buon giorno*,' she returned and immediately I realised my mistake. I had not used a word of English for weeks and yet after only one evening's conversation, I had relapsed and by doing so could endanger both her and myself. I felt myself colouring as I bit my lip. 'You'll find our visitor in the kitchen; I'll be in in a minute.'

I hurried down, hoping the visitor had not heard. A figure in workman's clothes rose to greet me and we looked at each other in such amazement that all other thoughts must have been wiped from both our minds.

'MacPherson, Dougal MacPherson,' I gasped.

'Aye,' he was remarkably calm, 'and you're one of the babies from OCTU. I never could remember names, but you're Morrison – am I right?'

'Quite right.'

'If I'd known you had an Italian background I'd have asked to take you with me a year ago. But to business. Marissa has an idea and I think it's a good one. The laddie in charge of the group to the north of here was killed a month ago and to date there's been no replacement for him. Would you like the job?'

'Forgive me, but I'm in a daze. What group? What job?'

'Ah, you're quite right, boy. We're such a small part of a large

98

set-up here, that one tends to forget that others have no idea what we're talking about.'

He went on to explain that there were partisan groups operating throughout Italy, many of them led by British officers, who carried on a liaison with base headquarters.

'We may not achieve much,' he said, 'but there's always the odd bit of sabotage and hindering to be done and we have an already formidable list of prisoners who have been helped through to Switzerland – and it'll be much longer before the war is over. Several of our chaps started off as escapers, like yourself, then decided to stay instead and help others through. It's all part of the war. Well – what d'you say?'

'Yes, if you think I'm suitable.'

'You speak Italian, man – the prime requirement, and some don't even have that – what could be more suitable? And anyway, I'm desperate for a couple of bodies.'

'Yes, then.'

'Good. I suppose I should get approval first, before putting you in charge, but there's no one else, so I don't think I need worry. I have to go to Milan to-morrow – you lie low here for a couple of days and I'll pick you up on my way back. Is that all right with you, Signora?'

Marissa nodded. 'Perfectly all right. I thought you'd be pleased with him.'

When MacPherson returned, he took me, first by bicycle and then on foot, up several long, winding tracks into the forest. We changed direction so often that I began to wonder if he'd lost his way. I wasn't quite tactless enough to suggest it, but I did comment on the complexity of the route.

'Ah, that's the beauty of it,' he said, 'Gianna Maria, whom you'll meet presently, knew of it as a child. Like many families from Milan and Turin, hers used to have a lakeside villa which they used during the hot summer months. One summer, so she tells me, the children went deeper into the forest than usual and came across these charcoal-burners. Of course that was high adventure for a child, and after that she visited them every summer. I'm not sure how she came to be mixed up with the partisans in the first place, but I do know that both her parents died during the first winter of the war and she was left with a town house on her hands and the villa on the lake, up here. The town house was requisitioned by the Germans and she moved to the country. It was her suggestion that the charcoal-burners' clearing would be an ideal spot for the partisans to operate from. Well – to cut a long story short – she moved the old couple out from the forest and into the villa and the partisans took up residence here,

Gianna Maria with them. Marissa's husband started this group, you know.'

'Yes,' I said, 'she told me. Your Gianna Maria sounds quite a girl.'

'Aye, she's all of that.'

'*Buon giorno*, Signor Maggiore!' The greeting floated out from a point high to the left of the track, where a man stood atop a rock. Dougal waved. 'Ciao, Enrico.'

'Are we there? Sir?' I had been a bit shattered by that Signor Maggiore.

He grinned. 'Another half-mile. That's the furthest lookout post. No need to call me "Sir".'

Under present circumstances, I didn't think he'd mind if I asked him the question which had puzzled us all a year ago, and which had not crossed my mind since.

'I had no idea you were a major, sir,' (it was all very well saying no need to call him 'Sir,' but he was years older than I and I had only recently received my second pip) 'but you were quite a talking-point when you suddenly appeared on the course, and then, when you arrived at the Depot with three pips up. There were all sorts of rumours flying around – that you'd fought in the Spanish Civil War and had been with the French Foreign Legion.' I gave what I hoped was a nonchalant little laugh, giving the impression that of course I had not believed these ridiculous stories.

'Both correct.'

'Gosh!' As soon as the silly, schoolboyish exclamation was out, I realised that I must sound like a junior Boy Scout to Dougal – who had insisted that I use his Christian name – and wondered if he would, after all, be so keen to put me in charge of a group of men.

'You make me feel very old when you speak like that,' he said with a tolerant smile. 'There's no great mystery about my quick promotion. I went back to UK and joined up in thirty-nine and was taken prisoner at Dunkirk. It wasn't difficult to escape at the very beginning, but few did – too tired and dazed, most of them – but perhaps I was a bit harder than the younger men. Anyway, I got away. With the years I'd spent in the Legion, I had no difficulty in passing as a Frenchman and I ended up leading a band of Maquis. We weren't too well organised in the early days, but gradually, arms and equipment, and what have you became part of our everyday life and then, one day, a British captain was parachuted in to take over the section – I was still a private, mark you – and with orders for me to get out if I could and report to the War Office. I got over the Pyrenees and through Spain – I wasn't so keen on that, I can tell you, for, as far as the present government is concerned, I fought on the wrong side. Anyway, I got through and was flown home from Gib. Well, to cut another long story short, I was asked if I would like to run a similar set-up in Italy. Then, just to make things regular, I was sent to OCTU for a token period – the rest you know. I was given my crowns before leaving Africa.'

I was terribly impressed. 'And now?' I asked.

'Now I'm CO of the three groups in this area, each of which has, or had, at least one British officer with it. You will take over the one that hasn't.'

By the time he had finished telling his intriguing story, we had arrived at the end of a long moss-grown glade, with boulder-strewn walls on either side.

'What a perfect place for an ambush,' I remarked.

'Exactly. But you'll see in a moment why Gianna Maria knew it was *the* place for us.'

The glade appeared to end in a hillside cul-de-sac and it was only after I had taken it for granted that we must soon start climbing, that I saw the sudden right-hand bend. We turned into a natural clearing, where a long, low, stone building nestled under the over-hanging rock on one side and a series of peat-covered mounds dotted the other, where the forest began.

'Stores,' explained Dougal, pointing at the small hillocks, 'but they would pass as charcoal mounds to the layman, or from the air.'

As we neared the building, a tall, dark girl came out and walked to meet us. She held her hand out to Dougal and raised her eyebrows at the sight of me.

'Andy's replacement?' she asked.

'I hope so. Philip, this is Gianna Maria.'

We shook hands and I took in the clear olive skin, grey eyes, and cynical mouth. She would be in her late twenties, I guessed, and no fool. She tossed a heavy mane of glistening black hair in the direction of a group of men, who had materialised while we were speaking and now watched with interest.

'You had better meet the rest of your loyal followers, the *élite* of the partigiani.' She said the last word with such scorn that it sounded like a cat spitting. She called the men forward and introduced them with a general sweep of the hand. She mentioned one or two who were absent and ended with, 'And Enrico's on guard.'

As the men came and shook my hand then stood aside, she included them once more in a sweeping gesture that I was to come to associate very much with her. 'Scum of the Milan gaols,' she said, with a derisive quirk to her lips. 'It's true,' she went on, as I opened my mouth to protest, 'they're not patriots; they've only taken to the hills because it's a better life than being behind bars!'

At the time, I was horrified by the way she spoke to and of them, but it was not long before I realised that 'Scum' was a term of affection for the motley band and I never thought of them as anything else.

Most of the men smirked and one laughed outright. It was obviously an old joke and I could see at once that there was a strong bond between them and the girl. After the weeks I had spent with my many peasant helpers, I did not think I would find it hard to get along with them – I only hoped that they would accept me.

I listened, without understanding much, to the conversation between Dougal and Gianna Maria and then the former nodded his head in my direction and said, 'This will concern you. I'll be sending you a VIP in a few days. Bit of a problem child – you know about him, Gianna, Tom di Lucio, but for Philip's benefit: he's a Triestino, Jug/Italian, regular officer in the Italian Army, doing a course in England in thirty-nine – promptly gets himself into a British unit, God alone knows how, and is dropped in. Taken out and dropped in again. He's got an MC from us, but he's very much *persona non grata* here – "Wanted as a Traitor" posters up on every barracks and police station.'

'I've seen them,' I interrupted.

'And this time,' Dougal went on, 'he's got himself well and truly cut up. He's convalescing all right, but he's got to lie low and this is a better spot for him than with me. Besides, he will be a help to Philip and can bring my spare radio over too.'

'If I'm to be in charge here, I'd be delighted to have him,' I said, and really meant it. It's all very well to say quite happily that you'll take on a job, without knowing what it entails. I was getting cold feet. Dougal, Gianna Maria, the Scum – all years older and more experienced – I couldn't blame any of them if they resented me.

'Aye,' said Dougal, 'you should get on well. He's a good scout – apt to get a wee bitty sorry for himself, but a good scout none the less. I'll send him over as soon as he's fit enough to climb yon hill.'

Dougal left next day, taking a couple of chaps with him to collect some stores and to bring back the promised radio.

'I think after all that it would be better to let Gianna Maria continue giving the orders until I get permission to put you officially in charge,' he had said, and that suited me. I had a lot to learn and did not desire to make a fool of myself at this stage.

I listened to her shrill voice detailing the men, then I prepared to settle in.

13. 'TUESDAY TWO-FOUR'

Stanislaus Olshewski

For us Polish people there were so many events during the early days of the war, that it would be difficult to choose any particular one as the starting point of a story. But, if I am to start in 1942, then it is easy.

Like so many of my compatriots, who had reached England, via one route or another, I, Stanislaus Olshewski, was flying. And on that particular night, in the early summer of 1942, we were returning from a raid on the Brest peninsula. I had reached that state of anticlimax and disinterest when all I wanted was my bed – and alone at that.

'What do you think of, Tzadek?' I asked my navigator-cum-radar-operator – although we had not yet begun to call it radar in those days.

'Hot, strong black coffee and a treble vodka!'

'Where are we?'

'Crossing the coast. You should be able to see the surf-line.'

I looked down and there it was, a moving shimmer on the edge of the dark sea.

'God, I'm tired.'

We droned on and every time I looked at my watch only a few minutes, or sometimes seconds, had passed. It seemed an eternity.

'Tired, Tzadek?'

'Tired, Stan.'

We fell silent again. On the ground, Tzadek and I were good friends, but 3 a.m. in a Beaufighter is not the best time and place to chat.

I banked to peer below and there, once more, was the white frill of surf.

'We seem to be recrossing the coast,' I remarked, 'do you know exactly where we are?'

'Where we should be, I know, but. . . . Can you climb, Stan, and call base?'

I circled higher and higher, making it easier for the radar to pick us up. We should be pinpointed on the operations room table at Sector by now. I called base.

To me, the first impression of a fighter operations room was as though I had stumbled in a dream, like Alice in Wonderland, down a tunnel and into some secret animal or insect kingdom. It was busy, but not with the comings and goings of an anthill; rather everyone seemed to be hovering – and hovering in an erratic sort of way. Only arms and heads were moving and everywhere people – or animals or insects, what you will – were getting up and sitting down, peering over, under and to their sides, and speaking into telephones or headsets, or to each other. Long metal rods hovered over the plotting-tables, like slim-necked, mechanical giraffes, extensions of the dumpier torsos controlling them. In the background, the hum and buzz of plots told over a dozen lines and information being passed over as many telephones and, high above the outsize maps, the clacking of metal on wood as the tote operators maintained their panels of up to the minute data. And over all, the hoverer-in-chief, the controller, like some giant praying mantis, held sway.

The moods of an ops room could be as diverse as those of a temperamental Celt; dour and bleak when the weather permitted only scant flying, or bright and active as a beehive. From the day I finished my basic training and was posted to a fighter station, the infectious excitement had caught me in its grip and it was still an increasing pleasure to drift down to the ops room on a quiet, cloudless night, to be met by the live, electric atmosphere inside.

It was a long way from Malaya, a long way from Singapore, Java, and Ceylon. A long way from the deck of that ship on which I had made the sudden decision to join the air force – but it was a decision I knew I would never regret. I was young enough to enjoy the excitement of war – and what better place than a fighter station for that?

It was on a clear, cloudless night that some instinct led me to concentrate on the behaviour of one particular set of plots.

My post that night was at the foot of the main plotting-table, around which eight of us, airmen and WAAF, hovered and swayed, wielding our magnet-tipped rods to the rhythm of the plots pouring through headsets, which, by that time of night, had become a pair of extensile ears, heavy, cumbersome, and clinging. I was keeping track of nine aircraft over the English Channel, some of which were acting in a straightforward manner and some not.

I cannot say why I was worried, but, at the first pause in telling, I waved my longest rod to gain the controller's attention; then I had to give my own to a homing bomber, meandering across the sea in a series of drunken lurches.

'Yes, Gunn. What is it?'

'This track, sir. It's behaving in a very odd way.'

'What's odd about it?' he called down.

'It's one of ours and it's going the wrong way.'

The watch sergeant gave me a peculiar look, but this controller, an ageing squadron leader with RFC wings, was one who listened and seldom pooh-poohed other people's hunches.

All he asked was, 'What makes you think so?'

'It's Tuesday two-four, sir. I plotted him out on an intruder patrol at the beginning of the evening and it's the right time and place for him to be returning; but he's turned round – he's heading back for France.'

As was so often the case, the preceding hour of hectic activity had come to an abrupt close. Three of my tracks had crossed the coast and been taken over by another plotter and four were off our map. That left me with Tuesday two-four and the drunken bomber.

I flexed my fingers and stretched back, ostensibly to ease my shoulders, but really to listen to what the controller was going to say to Group.

'Get your filterers cracking on that X-raid, will you?' He gave the map reference, 'it may be one of ours.'

The easy spell did not last long and soon I was only able to give an occasional glance at the controller, standing rocklike before his chorus of R/T operators; girls with enormous lambskin earphones – grasshoppers with waving antennae – tuning dials and flicking switches and all the time calling and answering aircraft in their high-pitched, monotonous, plainsong chant. He held the receiver cupped between ear and shoulder, scribbling as he relayed the relevant facts from the tote.

'Tuesday two-four, Beaufighter, airborne on a low-flying raid, target: marshalling yards near Brest. Right. Keep an eye on it, will you?'

He looked pensive as I placed the latest plot, still hugging the French coast, then he nodded in my direction. 'You could be right.'

To the controller's left stood his Polish colleague – this was an almost international station – and to his right, the Czech.

'Whose is Tuesday two-four?' he asked.

'Mine,' answered the Pole, 'Flight Lieutenant Olshewski.'

'Unidentified aircraft now at angels ten, sir,' I called out.

'Good.' The controller grabbed the radio telephone. 'Hallo, Tuesday two-four, Tuesday two-four, Alligator calling. Are you receiving me? Over.'

No reply.

'Did you hear, Tzadek?'

'I hear nothing.'

'Hallo, Tuesday two-four, Tuesday two-four, this is Alligator. Are you receiving me? Over.'

That was a relief; I had not been wrong. 'Alligator, Alligator, this is Tuesday two-four. Receiving you strength two. Over.'

'Increase angels,' ordered Alligator.

I complied.

'Now we'll try again,' muttered the controller. 'Tuesday two-four, vector zero-nine-zero for base. Zero-nine-zero. Over.'

'Zero-nine-zero. Out.'

That should put him right. We all waited and the controller leaned eagerly over the dais railing, scanning the table for the next plot. It was coming now, but no, surely there was something wrong? I waited for the repeat. He was heading south-south-west instead of north-north-east.

'Sir – ' It was the watch sergeant, who had been standing over my shoulder.

'Yes, yes. I've seen.' And grabbing the R/T again, 'Zero-nine-zero, Tuesday two-four, zero-nine-zero. Out.'

The fool. What the hell was he doing? Unless his compass was u/s and was showing a reciprocal bearing. Heavens, he'd be over the Channel Islands in a minute.

The next plot was slap over Jersey and losing height.

'Hallo, Tuesday two-four. Alligator calling. Are you receiving me? Over.'

No reply.

The silence was dreadful; it seemed that all other aircraft had come to a standstill.

The controller tried again, but without success. Still no reply.

'Keep calling,' he instructed the R/T operator in the cabin behind him and fixed his attention on the table.

'Hallo, Tuesday two-four, Tuesday two-four. This is Alligator. Pancake, pancake. Out.'

Thank God for that. I could not understand why I had lost base when I had been given the new vector so clearly. A new voice had called up – suppose the controllers had been changing over, which would account for the delay. Oh, for my bed. Not long now. I put the stick forward and circled, preparatory to landing.

All of a sudden the perimeter lights blazed. I had landed on this runway so many times, countless times, and yet there was something slightly unfamiliar. Must be more tired than I realised. Nothing to worry about, maybe some new lights. I began to land.

The lights slid past; this was terrible; never had I felt so fatigued. We were going in too fast. I shook my head, pulled back the stick and rose to circle again before going in for a second attempt.

Flying Control sounded justifiably peeved. 'Pancake, Tuesday two-four. Pancake, I say.'

'Roger. Out.'

I turned in to land, switching on my own powerful lights and gasped, for, what had been hidden behind the staring blaze of the main runway lights, now stood revealed.

'God in heaven,' I could barely breathe, 'it's a trap.'

I placed a circling plot over Jersey. Just one plot and then no more.

I looked inquiringly at the sergeant of the watch, who shrugged his shoulders. 'Must have landed – couldn't have been ours after all. Filter must have got their tracks mucked up – unless he's gone in to strafe something. Anyway, he'd be out of our range once he dropped below five thou.'

'Well, that's that, I'm afraid.' The controller sat down.

Another plot was being told. Still over Jersey, but pointing north-east.

'It's unidentified still,' I called out, 'but it must be him.'

The track continued north-east to the Cherbourg peninsula; veered south, then west. Back over Jersey again, then north-west. A unanimous sigh went up.

'Font hiss possition at last.' The poor Polish controller sat down and mopped his forehead with a gorgeous red and white bandanna.

'Sir,' even in the well of the ops room we could hear the urgency in the R/T operator's voice, 'There's a Mayday. Listen.'

The controller switched on the amplifier and the whole ops room heard the pathetically faint SOS call.

'Tuesday two-four calling. Mayday, mayday, mayday. Have wounded. Mayday, mayday.'

There was only the fraction of a second's silence before the controller roared out, 'Direct something in the area to search. Tell them angels ten and transmit for fix.'

A dozen wires began to buzz and a babble of voices initiated air-sea rescue procedure.

'Fixer stations,' the controller bellowed, 'can't you get a fix on him?'

The watch sergeant shook his head, 'Bearing's too faint, sir.'

It was awful. Just as everything had seemed all right. I couldn't swallow the lump in my throat and gave an involuntary sob, which attracted the attention of the sergeant, who came over.

'Belt up, Gunn,' he said, but not unkindly. 'First aircraft you've seen go down?'

I just nodded; I couldn't speak.

'Boy friend?'

I shook my head, but I felt that I really did know that pilot.

'Well, it won't be the last, I'm afraid. Here, I'll relieve you for a minute – go outside and have a fag.'

As I had come in to land, our headlights had shone straight on the figures standing to the side of the flarepath; figures in German helmets and standing by a vehicle with a large black cross painted on its side.

Thank God that, despite the tiredness, my reactions had not been too slow and we had barely touched down before we were off again, soaring at an angle of sixty degrees on full throttle.

'If the Germans, better we die, Tzadek. No?'

'Yes.'

It was two years since I had last seen those hated uniforms and in a split second the whole panoramic picture of my last days in Poland and subsequent escape swept through my mind. Two and a half years since my home had become part of Russia and two since I had arrived at the French coast, hungry and humble, to join a multitude of others waiting to cross the Channel.

With all the effort I could muster, I heaved the old Beau over to starboard as a stream of bullets hit the port wing. The port engine was on fire now and, as we curved in a great arc, I saw the coast and frothing surf ahead.

'Tzadek,' I yelled, 'climb forward. Too late to bale out. I will try and flatten her, then you must jump.'

With one last heave I pulled the aircraft up, and, when we had gained as much height as I knew we ever would, pressed button 'B' and called 'Mayday'. If they were to hear my SOS that was the only chance we would have. Then I let her dive until we were over the sea and flattened out. The fire was raging all along the port side of the fuselage now. There was no sound from Tzadek and he had not moved; I got out of my seat and grabbed his unconscious body to me.

He had a bloody wound on his forehead, but he was breathing. Holding him with one arm, I forced the hood back with the other and, during the short second that the aircraft skimmed along the surface of the water before plunging down, managed to struggle free.

At last we surfaced and, Mae West inflated and hugging Tzadek to me, I said a prayer of gratitude to the Holy Virgin and resigned myself, shivering, to wait for the dawn.

'Take a look at those.' The outgoing controller tossed a sheaf of large, square aerial photographs at his relief. They had been passed round the ops room and we had all whistled in much the same way as the new controller did when he studied the prints.

'Tuesday two-four?'

'The same.'

'What's that exactly?' A rather blurred print showed the dark outline of an aircraft with what appeared to be a large, lightish panel, suspended from it. Some distance away was a vague dark blob. In the background a cliff, squared off in a manner which could be a concealed gun emplacement.

'That's a Wimpy, dropping an airborne lifeboat to them and that, in the background, is the shore battery at Corbière.'

'Lucky chaps.'

'Bloody lucky. The sea's been like a millpond all day and scarcely any cloud. If only they weren't so damned near the shore, a Walrus could have landed and picked them up by now. They found them without too much difficulty soon after first light – but look at these.'

He passed over three more prints, still wet and pegged to a frame.

'Wow! When were those taken?'

'Late this afternoon.'

We had not seen those prints, so I was more than ever interested in the conversation, but they were passed round as soon as they were dry. One of the prints showed two figures in the lifeboat, one paddling, only a matter of yards from the nearest rocks; the second, a close-up of the gun emplacements that we had seen in the earlier prints and, the third was a view of the beach. A line of German soldiers stood watching the aircraft and one was shaking his fist at it. To their right there appeared to be the nose of a launch peeking out from a camouflaged boathouse.

'The bastards. They could pick them up as easily as anything.'

'I do not zink Olshewski would wish to be a prisoner of war,' the high voice of the Polish controller remarked dryly, 'ass far ass we Poles are concerned, the Germans do not belief the Geneva Convention need apply.'

'Nevertheless. . . .'

How long would they play cat and mouse with me?

It was three days since the lifeboat had been dropped and the miraculous feelings when we were first seen were beginning to fade. Only at high tide was there any relief from that grinning, jeering mob who lined the shore.

I had assembled the sail, but each time I attempted to raise it, I was greeted with a fusillade from the beach. It seemed that I was condemned to drift.

Tzadek's body was beginning to smell too. He had probably been dead already by the time we were first seen, but I wouldn't admit it then and it had taken me all my effort to pull him into the lifeboat. Not once had he moved and soon his corpse had become puffed and bloated beyond recognition in the warm sun – better for him and for me that I had not hung on to him in the first place, for the Tzadek who was my friend had been gone a long time. Every time I tried to heave his body over the side, one of the men from the shore would take a pot shot at me and I was condemned to continuous paddling to keep the corpse to windward.

I made frequent inventories of my ship's supplies and it seemed to me that I could last out almost indefinitely, God and weather willing. There was ample water in the tanks and a considerable number of 'dog' biscuits, bars of concentrated chocolate, dried fruit and vitamin pills. There was a fishing-line too, but I was pretty sure that, although it would give me something else to concentrate on, the first time I threw it over the side would be the last.

We Polish people are a mixture of hardness and sentimentality and in my hand I held a symbol of the latter, and cherished it for what it was – a symbol of one man's goodness. I cannot recall how many days and nights I had spent in the lifeboat when the incident took place, but it was during the partially dark hours of the brief summer night. I had been dozing when something hit me. I leaped up, thinking that I had been shot after all, to find that it was high tide and my boat was a mere matter of feet from an overhanging rock, on which a sentry stood. At my feet, rolling gently with the motion of the craft, was an apple. Clearly, the sentry had saved me from running aground and, as I picked up the apple and looked at him, he turned away, but I swear that as he did so, he gave the 'thumbs up' sign.

An aircraft circled high in the distance and flew off. Every day I would see it somewhere in the sky and knew that they were keeping an eye on me. But what could they do? A Walrus or a launch would be shot up immediately, or intercepted. There was no other way. And the Germans? They would either pick me up eventually, or just leave me where I was, to die when my rations gave out.

It was nine days before Tuesday two-four was rescued and then it was not only through skill and daring, but a great deal of luck as well.

The Air-Sea Rescue Unit had waited for a storm and in the lull following it, mercifully during the murky half-light of pre-dawn, a Walrus had landed a few yards away from the lifeboat, beckoned him to paddle towards them, heaved him aboard and taxied off, just as the first gun opened up.

Our watch had been on duty for part of every day or night of those nine days and I suppose, because we had been the watch on duty the night he ditched, the determination to see him rescued became almost personal. Of course there was nothing we could do, but as long as his position was shown on the plotting-table, we felt that he was in our care. The day the controller announced that the marooned man was now safely tucked up in Station Sick Bay, suffering from nothing worse than exposure, we had all sung a mental Te Deum. But, as he so rightly said, there were other pilots airborne, so drink to Tuesday two-four when next the in Red Lion and, meanwhile, get on with the job.

'There's an airwoman waiting to see you, sir.'

'Tell her to come on sick parade to-morrow morning.' The MO was just leaving his office.

It was bad enough having been chosen to represent the watch anyway, but now, as I twiddled the bunch of wild flowers which we had picked for him, I began to feel more of a BF than ever.

The MO too was eyeing my posy, as he pulled on his gloves. 'For me?' he asked.

I went a little pink. 'Oh no, sir. For Tuesday two-four. Can I see him?'

'Tuesday two-four?'

'The pilot who was rescued off the Channel Islands last week.'

'Provided you're just a girl friend and not from Int, yes. But if you're going to ask him a lot of questions, I won't have it. Poor chap's still in a state of exhaustion.'

'I'm not his girl friend.' I glowered at the MO who shrugged.

'You can't go in, then.'

'Oh well, I *am* his girl friend.'

'Oh, go on, then.'

I opened the door which the medical orderly had pointed to as quietly as I could and crept in, expecting to see a wan figure, swathed in bandages, prone on the high, hospital bed.

What I did see was a tall and sunburned young man in pale blue silk pyjamas, looking very far from a state of exhaustion. Nor was he prone; he was sitting on the edge of his bed, meticulously removing the skin from a hot-house peach and dropping the pieces in a small pile on the floor.

'Now don't fuss because I'm making a mess, Mather. You know you like cleaning up after me!' He did not even glance up until after I had closed the door.

'I'm not Mather.'

'Well,' he grinned and looked me up and down and up again, 'what an improvement. Who are you?'

'I'm Sally Gunn.' I was suddenly so overcome with shyness that I couldn't get another word out. If only I could turn on a dazzling smile, or hold out my hand, or light a cigarette. Anything. As it was, I stood stock-still, conscious that the beast was laughing at me and of the crimson blush shading my neck and swamping my ears, while he cocked his head first on one side and then the other and finally walked over and leaned towards me.

'Boo!'

I jumped so hard that I hit my funny bone on a piece of furniture, but the shock of the momentary pain made me able to glare at him and to bring out my rehearsed speech pat after all.

'I was the RDF plotter on duty the night you were shot down. I've come on behalf of "A" watch, to tell you that we are all very glad that you are all right and – and the girls picked these for you.' I held out my now rather wilted offering of bee orchids, campion, and wood anemones.

He took a deep breath for me and accepted the flowers. For a long moment he said nothing, but sat back on his bed looking at the small, pale blossoms and, when he raised his head, there was a smile of great tenderness lighting his face. Then he got up and, filling his tooth-glass from the washbasin tap, set the flowers on the table beside him.

'For Tzadek,' he said, and at my look of inquiry, 'my navigator.'

He was like mercury and the solemn moment was gone in a flash.

'Now come,' he said, patting the bed beside him, 'this is all I can offer you in return.'

I perched rather gingerly and took a small bite of the proffered peach.

He was sitting terribly close and I was just wondering how I should behave if he made a pass at me, when he sprang to his feet, sent the peach stone in an accurate arc to fall with a small plop in the metal waste-paper basket, washed his hands, and walked over to the door.

'And now, my dear,' he said, 'you must go. Or else I shall be had up for rape!'

I could not have leaped up quicker if a wasp had stung me and once again I felt that awful, uncontrollable colour enveloping me.

'Remind me to startle you often.' The corners of his mouth were turned down in a mocking grin and his thick-lashed eyes travelled unashamedly up my grey lisle legs, my blue issue uniform, and my very red throat. 'That is the most exquisite shade of – ? Forgive me, my English fails me!'

'Tomato, I should think.' And I made a dash for the door. He held it open for me, bowing as I swished past and clicking his bare heels. 'Oh, you Poles!' I could think of nothing more original to say and I heard his laugh as I sped down the corridor.

'Is that him?'

I felt the prod from my neighbour as I leaned forward to remove some old plots. Of course I knew perfectly well who it was, but I had no intention of looking up.

'Who?'

'Tuesday two-four, of course. Oh Sally, do stop making work and have a look.'

It was true; there was really nothing to do. Outside the rain hissed on the tarmac, hot still from the morning sun. The natural crash of thunder sent relieved ARP wardens off duty and, inside the ops room, there was an animated air of domesticity as knitting and embroidery appeared. A shred of tapestry jerked over the South Devon coast and an intricate piece of Fair Isle pancaked on Cherbourg, as its owner used both hands to take a mug of tea from a proffered 'In' tray. It was the sort of watch that caused the controller to be frightfully jolly with the WAAF, calling us by our Christian names, while the airmen became 'you chaps'.

'Oh Sally, do – '

I had to look up. He was there, looking straight at me, the same cynical expression drawing down one corner of his mouth. He smiled and waved. I bared my teeth in return. I am going to be cool, calm, and collected, I ordered myself, but it was no good.

'Sally, you're blushing! Why – '

'Oh shut up; I'm just hot, that's all.'

How long is it going to take me to grow up?

The controller's clapping hands interrupted both my thoughts and my knitting.

'Flight Lieutenant Olshewski is now out of Sick Bay, as you can see for yourselves, and has come to thank . . .' he droned on and on, spreading one cliché on top of another, but no one was taking much notice of him, there was no doubt as to whose show it was.

'Boudoir eyes,' murmured the girl on my right. 'I bet he's wonderful in bed.'

'Ruddy Poles,' remarked an airman, 'all they do is look and those silly WAAF fall down and worship. What's he got that I haven't?'

'Wings for a start!'

'Turn it up there,' it was the watch sergeant, 'next voice I hear goes on a charge.'

The controller finished at last and Tuesday two-four leaned over the dais to look down into the well of the ops room.

'Sank you all vairy much for watching for me. I haf nevair been in zis Opairations Room before, alzough I haf had plenty of opportunities – I shall cairtainly come again. Sank you.'

A sigh went up from all the WAAF. All the WAAF bar me, that is.

'It's as good as when David Niven came – '

'Smooth bugger!'

'But that phoney accent,' I gasped, 'why, his English is very nearly perfect. He does have an accent, but nothing like that.'

'I thought he was gorgeous.'

'Well I think he's just a ham actor.' I did too. 'I wouldn't want anything to do with him; I hate phoneys.'

At that moment, the duty runner, an Australian girl who had been more than openly appraising our visitor, flipped a piece of paper at me. 'Old two-four asked me to give you this – my, don't some people have all the bloody luck!'

The note read: 'Meet you outside when you come off watch – it has stopped raining,' in a slanting, Continental scrawl.

My neighbour was reading it over my shoulder. 'You won't want to go out with a phoney, will you, ducky?'

Reluctant pleasure soared through me. 'Oh, he's probably not so bad!' I replied.

He was leaning against a tree a few yards from the entrance of the ops room and I hung back while the rest of the watch filed past the guard.

There were sixty of us, airmen and WAAF, on our watch and it gave me plenty of time to inspect my date. There was something feline about him and something rather spectacular too. He was an unusual shape for a Pole, tall and rather angular. Of course his shoulders were overpadded, as the Poles' always were, but his own were obviously strong and square and his legs were long. But it was his colouring that was most striking; Scandinavian, but for the dark brown eyes. His hair was almost silver, it was so fair, and, topping brown-skinned Slav features, high cheekbones and eyes with an inner Mongolian fold, it made a strange contrast.

He chatted with several people, but every now and then he looked down the line and then impatiently at his watch, and it occurred to me that he did not like being kept waiting.

Nevertheless, I did not hurry and by the time I stood before him we were alone but for the guard. I did not apologise and I don't think he expected me to.

He said nothing and did not smile, but looked straight into my eyes as he slowly stubbed out his cigarette against the tree. I don't know how long we stood there, but I was aware of the chatter of the watch going down the road fading into silence. I felt my nipples harden and my stomach contract and knew for the first time what it was like to want a man.

I lowered my eyes, because I was afraid and did not want him to read what I knew must be in them; but when I raised them again there was a mocking smile on his lips and the spell was broken.

'And what was going through your head in that so serious moment?' he asked, and I could hear the laughter in his voice.

For once my wits were with me and, instead of blurting out anything too childish, I was able to match his mood and retort, 'That I should be painting whiskers on you – tom cat!'

Stanislaus, as I was to find out, was a person who really laughed. 'Oh, zat is vairy good,' he roared, meanwhile giving my shoulders a hug which melted me completely, 'I like zat vairy much. And now, zere is a good film on in town, *Ze vay to ze stars*, and, if you like, we must hurry to catch ze bus. You like?'

I nodded. Any suggestion would have been perfect at that moment and, as my demi-god started down the road at a furious pace, I almost running to keep up with him, my heart soared and I felt that I was indeed on my way to the stars.

I am told it was a good film, but I don't remember. Stan bought me ice cream, which I didn't like, and held my hand, which I did. When the lights went on for the interval and the multi-hued organ rose in front of the screen, I looked at his hand caressing mine and saw that it was both beautiful and well cared-for. It was bony and well shaped, the fingers long and strong, with the cuticles well pushed back to give a squarish base to otherwise oval nails. I had seen hands like them before.

'You have hands like a Malay,' I told him.

'And what do you know about the hands of the Malays?' The mocking tone was in his voice again and, in my childish fear that he would think I was merely trying to sound clever, I could not prevent the indignation from entering my own.

'I've spent most of my life in Malaya.'

He turned round to look at me then and the real interest in his face made my tum do a double somersault with pleasure.

'I know nozzing about ze Far East – you will teach me.'

And as he settled back into his seat, he lifted my hand, palm up-wards, and kissed it and I wished that it had exuded some exotic scent, instead of merely being rather sticky from the ersatz ice cream.

It was late when we left the cinema and, as we stood on the kerb, accustoming our eyes to the dark, it occurred to me that my Malayan child most probably had not eaten since breakfast. I myself wanted a drink and was wondering where the hell we could go, because the only two decent pubs left standing after the bombing had this silly 'officers only' rule and we were both in uniform. For my part I couldn't have cared less and would have ignored any barman's objections, but I knew that Sally would be self-conscious and I was right.

It was she who suggested The Cellar and there we went, after a pint at a pretty sordid joint *en route*.

The Cellar was what remained under the debris of what had once been a fashionable restaurant, in a provincial way, which had not survived the bombing. They had cleverly made the best of things by shoring up the walls and covering them with the bottom ends of green bottles. Old cider casks lined one end of the cavern and the atmosphere was made gay by red-and-white checked tablecloths. Crystal and silver had given way to earthenware and, even if they did sell only fish and chips and similar plebby meals, their clientele had most probably doubled since they had opened below ground.

Sally had been right; she was certainly not the only ACW2 with an officer escort and, although it seemed to me that the whole air force was present, no one paid us any attention.

I was not particularly hungry but Sally was clearly ravenous and I sat and watched her as she downed first her own enormous helping of fish and chips, then finished off mine.

Here, I thought, am I, a fairly well-to-do, well set up male of twenty-seven attracted to this child. Young, naive, totally lacking in guile or sophistication. Why? She was physically attractive, it was true, in so far that her figure was good and she had pleasant colouring. Her eyes were wide and clear and her mouth held a hint of passion unawakened. Should I wake her up?

Steady, Stan, I told myself, she's the kind you marry, not make your mistress – and yet I believed I could do just that.

It was mean, I know, because I had no intention of leaving the station, but I wanted to test her reactions. 'I'm going on fourteen days' leave to-morrow,' I told her.

'Oh. Where will you spend it?'

The disappointment on her face was so clear that I felt a pig, but I had to go on. 'London, perhaps.'

'Oh.'

'You would like to come with me?'

'Oh yes! No, I mean. Oh no! Of course not.'

The crimson blush spread up from her collar, just as it had the day I had shocked her in sick bay. I longed to take her in my arms and tell her not to be a goose and make her laugh, but she was already standing up and pulling on her gloves and, sod that I am, I let it lie.

It was ridiculous really, I had only known him a matter of hours and I should have realised that he was bound to be given leave before going back on ops. And anyway, it was perfectly obvious that he had only taken me out because I had plotted him that day.

I looked at him out of the corner of my eye. He really was terribly good-looking. There were so many girls for him to choose from – on my watch alone I could name several who were better-looking than I, older, wittier and more intelligent. There was no reason in the world why he should have anything more to do with me. I had no idea what Stan's background was, but had deduced from the exceptional fluency of his English that he was no uneducated peasant. Nor was I for that matter, but I was a gauche, giggling, seventeen-year-old and I knew that I could never match his poise, however hard I tried.

On the way back in the bus he played with my hand and asked me about my work. I answered as politely as I could, but all the time I was imagining him laughing with the WAAF officers in the mess and telling them how he had taken out one of their chicks and held her hand in the flicks.

'Well, and then?'

He had given my hand a tug and I realised that I had been answering mechanically, without really listening to what he was saying.

'I said, and then?'

'And then what?'

'You've told me that you've just started a week on watch from eight till four and then a week of night duty and I asked you what then?'

'A week of four until midnight.' Who cared?

'But zat is fine,' he exclaimed and the genuine pleasure in his voice both brought out his accent and arrested my attention. 'Ven I am back on night ops, you too vill have a week of days off – so, ve go svim in ze river, no?'

'Oh yes, please!'

The weather had improved by the following day and it seemed that the whole world was airborne. Luckily I had had no time to think about Stan and his leave until we went off watch and then, there he was, leaning against the same tree as he had been the day before.

As soon as he saw me he pushed his cap on straight and, with a wide smile, lacking the cynicism for once, he walked towards me.

My heart beat so hard with happiness that I felt sure everyone must hear it! It was all I could do to keep myself from running.

'I thought you were on leave,' I said, as casually as I could – and knew that it did not sound casual at all.

'I am.'

He was looking at me with the same expression that he had bestowed on the flowers and I know I was beaming like a great moon.

'Well, then?'

'Well. As I am always on ops at night and you have two weeks of evenings off, it seemed a waste to spend my leave away from you.'

'Oh Stan, I *am* flattered. And happy too. But – ' My face fell as I remembered. ' – there's hot water on camp to-day and I wanted to have a bath!'

He threw up his hands in a gesture of mock tragedy, the habitual smirk back in place.

'Oh my leave. I am ze fool. I should haf gone to London, where ze girls do not bathe!'

He put his arms round me in a bear hug and swung me in a circle, right off my feet.

'Stan, put me down.' I broke away in panic. 'Everyone will see you.'

He couldn't stop laughing at my agitation and of course really I was too proud for words and wanted everyone to see.

'I'll walk back to camp with you and wait while you scrape off the grime.'

'Oh no, you wouldn't get past the guard.'

'Is zat so, ACW2 Gunn?' He blew an imaginary speck of dust from his rings.

'Zat iss so,' I mimicked. 'We ops types lead secluded lives, you know – vairy special – only a plotter is allowed to hear another plotter telling plots in her sleep!'

'And do you tell plots in your sleep?'

'Most of us do actually, especially after a heavy evening watch. I have nightmares.' As soon as I said it, I wished I hadn't.

'About the ops room?'

I shook my head. 'Forget it.'

As I was to find out in time, Stan never pressed. 'I'll go to the Red Lion,' he said. 'Come when you're clean.'

'Okay.' I waved as I danced off up the path to camp. We watch bods were housed in a separate huddle of Nissen huts, a mile or so from the main camp and within walking distance of the ops room.

'Wotcher, Sal,' one of the airmen had caught up with me.

'Wotcher, Taff.'

'That your boy friend?'

'Hm.'

'Bet he sets his hair at night!'

'Bet he does not.' I was indignant.

The malicious Taffy was triumphant and I guessed what he was thinking: always thought themselves a cut above the airmen, these ops girls did. 'Friend of mine's a batman in the officers' mess,' he went on silkily, 'says you see them Poles walking along the corridors at night and every one of them with a hairnet on!'

'What do they walk along the corridors for?'

'Looking for the women officers I 'spect!' An evil gleam came into his eye. 'Bet you're not the only one.'

I took a swipe at his head with my pint-sized issue mug. 'Who cares if he does go to bed in curlers?'

Taffy ducked. 'And they use scent!'

'Well that's something you could do with, Taff – I swear you haven't changed those plimsolls since I was posted here.' That time I caught him a wallop full over the ear.

'Nah then, wot's going on 'ere?' We had reached the guardroom.

'He's trying to molest me, Corporal.' I beamed at the SP, not normally my favourite breed.

'Nah then, Evans, you leave the airwoman alone.'

'Crikey,' said Taff, nursing an ear, 'he's welcome to her!'

It was a lovely day!

The Red Lion was what every foreigner expects an English pub to be, even if the locals had given way in part to the air force.

Stan was playing darts with two Australians when I arrived.

'Order yourself a drink,' he called, but I said I'd wait.

A Czech and a Rhodesian played shove-halfpenny, while three Canadians, a Norwegian and two Free Frenchmen drank at the bar.

'I just 'eard news, miss.' The landlord had followed my look and beckoned me over to the bar. 'Top secret and 'ush 'ush – they're going to send a *British* squadron to the station!' He stood back and roared at his own joke, one frequently heard these days.

I smiled and turned to watch the darts players.

'Got yourself a roight beaut, Snowy!'

'Sank you, I zink so too.'

Good heavens, I thought, looking round to make sure that I was indeed the only girl in the bar, they must be talking about me – I'd never thought of myself as a 'roight beaut' in any language!

I wandered outside and sat on a stone bench, still warm from the lingering sun. Moth-wing shadows played against the ochre walls as the gentlest of breezes stirred scented fronds of honeysuckle from their slumberous droop. The bees hummed in the wild roses, growing rampant over the old building and, at my feet, a blackbird stole crumbs from his smaller brethren. It was a very English scene and England was at war. Was it to preserve this that men from many nations flew? Or was this peaceful haven the sanctuary to which we homed, looking towards the shores of our forbears in those dark days?

The day I joined up I decided that memories belonged to the past and that, patriotism apart, it was my duty to myself to throw myself heart and soul into my new life. On the whole I had succeeded, but there were moments, in the quiet of the night or peaceful interludes of vacuity such as this, when I was not so sure. Voices speaking in three different languages floated from the bar and the sharp thud of each dart, followed by laughter, exclamations of admiration or derision, belonged to another world. I looked at the roses and saw the honolulu creeping over the porch; I looked at the blackbird and saw a raucous bulbul and the fir tree by the gate became a stately casuarina bending in the breeze, its unwanted ivy guest a swathe of bougainvillaea.

'Sally, what's wrong?' Stan squatted before me and took hold of both my hands. The look of consternation on his face released my tears.

I scrubbed at my eyes with the back of my hand and tried not to sniff. 'Nothing really – just a bit homesick. I expect you all are sometimes.'

He handed me a blue monogrammed handkerchief and moved to shield me from the view of the rest of the darts team, as they filed into the courtyard. He could be a very gentle person. I wiped my eyes and tucked his handkerchief into my sleeve and kept it for many years.

'Got any friends, Sal? Why don't we make it a party?'

'That's a bonzer idea, Joe – could you ring some of your pals, Sal?'

'All right.' It did seem a good idea; I would make a poor companion for anyone on my own, so I walked inside to phone.

It was a noisy party, no different from most evenings at the Red Lion and before long we were all a little high on the pernicious mixture of gin and local cider. Only Stan was quiet, the native wit of the antipodeans incomprehensible to him.

At the call of 'Time,' one of the Rhodesian pilots put two fingers to his mouth and in answer to his whistle a fifteen-hundredweight truck materialised from a side lane.

'I took the precaution of organising the squadron truck,' he grinned. 'All aboard who's coming aboard – ops camp first, Pratt.'

There was a mad scramble as we WAAF in our tight skirts were heaved over the tailboard, much slapping of hands and much bawdy laughter. The men sat where they could, the girls being passed from one lap to another; but Stan held fast to me and I would have been happy for the journey to last forever.

Being a member of a night fighter squadron gave me little chance of going out in the evenings and I had seldom joined the raucous parties at the Red Lion.

Truth to tell, I would have preferred to have taken Sally to the cinema again, but a bigger and better party had been arranged the night before. Sally was keen to go, so I went along too.

We were all very gay and the repartee flew fast and thick. Sally was in great form, right out of her shell. It was difficult to recall the tongue-tied youngster who had visited me in sick bay. But then most of these boys were only a few years older than her – at twenty-seven, I considered myself a great age then! Old enough at any rate to grow a little bored, and after a while I wandered away.

It was not only that the English was so quick and the accents so varied that I sometimes found it difficult to follow; I could not be bothered with the childish horseplay. One of the Free French pilots was standing by the bar and with him a man from the Seychelles and a couple of Canadians. It was a relief to speak French and to hold a conversation a little above the mental age of seventeen.

Besides, standing with my back against the bar, I could watch Sally without her knowing, and watching her gave me a great deal of pleasure.

If the air force had hoped to disguise the feminine form under bulgy tunics, they had reckoned without summer days. It was a warm evening; most of us had discarded our jackets and the short, tight skirts and masculine shirts did more for the girls – and for us – than Air Ministry ever intended. Sally was squealing, as one of the Rhodesians tried to cut the end off her tie – an incredibly silly custom, I always thought, and tucked my own firmly inside my shirt before it could be added to the row of black snippets adorning the Red Lion walls. At that moment she pivoted on the hand holding her tie, breasts tightly outlined as her arms were flung back and a sudden urge to make love to her rose in me like an overwhelming tide.

There was no truck that night and when the pub closed we drifted down the road in a disorderly blue surge, making patterns in the dusk as couples paired off or parted and formed groups again.

I suppose, like myself, few of the men had honourable intentions. It was less than a mile to the camp and the whole way I wondered how far Sally would let me go with her, and no doubt a dozen other heads held similar thoughts.

We walked hand in hand, saying nothing until within the precincts of the guardroom, and then I asked, very quietly, if she could get out of camp again.

It was still light enough to read the fright in her eyes and I knew that I would have to tread very carefully with this one.

'I won't do anything,' I whispered. 'I promise.'

She didn't answer for some time and, when she did, it was in such a low whisper that I could barely catch what she said but I followed the herd to the point in the wire where she had told me to wait.

The way those girls slid under the barbed wire entanglements made us all laugh and we wondered why it was only men who were sent on assault courses!

Sally herself was laughing too. She was breathless and warm in the warm dark and I soon knew that I had been right when I guessed that that mouth had the promise of passion.

I was right too when I sensed the need for caution. Although, when I unbuttoned her tunic and slipped my hand inside her shirt, she had pressed towards me and the nipples had sprung hard to my fingertips, she quickly drew away and made it plain that nothing further was allowed.

'You know you like it.'

'Too much. I am afraid.'

'Do not be afraid, little animal, I will never hurt you.'

'Take me back.'

We walked slowly across the meadow, arm in arm.

'To-morrow, Sally – will you come with me again to-morrow?'

'I have to.'

And then I spoilt it all. I might still have had her, but for my own dormant sentimentalism – or perhaps time had passed too quickly. I had held her in a long, long embrace, sensing that she had not been kissed like that before and was enjoying it and then, when she broke away from me, she made a silly remark.

'Now I know what the Victorian novelists meant by "swooning in his embrace". I could easily swoon in your arms, Stan; I could die in them.' Of course it was said in all innocence. I stiffened involuntarily, but she went on, not understanding – and after all, why should she? 'Don't you feel as though we're going down, down, down, and then rising with a great burst to the surface?'

'Don't say that. Don't say that.' I knew I was shaking her and could hear my voice coming in a harsh whisper, which I could not control. Then I let her go and crossed myself.

Sally stared at me in horror. How could I tell her? It was too recently that I had held Tzadek – probably only the corpse of Tzadek – in my arms as we sank into the depths of the Channel, to rise on the sleek, dappled surface of the summer sea. Perhaps reaction was only now setting in; it was awful to feel myself trembling uncontrollably and to remember, so vividly, the sinister blackness of the cliffs looming over us and the frightening sound of high seas breaking on the treacherous rocks.

She leaned away from me, a hand over her mouth. I knew then that she had understood; there was a communion between us that did not need words.

'Oh, it was unpardonable of me,' she gasped. 'I was being so selfish in my happiness that I forgot the shock you had had recently. And your friend, your navigator, you were holding him, I suppose?'

It was all right. The ghost was laid.

I stroked Sally's hair and told her she was not selfish, but perceptive and then she put her arms fleetingly round my neck and was gone, slithering on her stomach like an eel under the barbs.

I'm sure it was written all over my face and, although I had tried to straighten myself out a bit, there is not much one can do with long hair falling out of its roll and smeared lipstick.

A gust of laughter greeted me from the more ribald occupants of the hut and a strident voice sang out, 'I do believe Little Red Riding Hood has lost her hood at last!'

As usual, I felt that tell-tale blush creeping up my neck. Of course it wasn't true, but it was true that Stan had awakened feelings in me that I had not known I possessed.

Of course I had been kissed by plenty of men and only last week I had had to have a real battle with a Canadian squadron leader, who did not believe me when I said no. But I had always shied away from men when they came too close. I had thought that tongue to tongue thing rather horrid and kept my mouth tightly closed before, but with Stan my lips parted of their own accord and I wanted him closer and closer and closer. And when his hands held my breasts – gosh, just to think of the number of hands I've slapped away – I wanted them all over me; to touch and feel and want, as I wanted him.

I was innocent, but I was not ignorant. The first few days at the basic Training Depot, in a hut with thirty-one other girls, from all walks of life, had opened my eyes with astonishing speed. Good heavens, to think that only six months ago I hadn't even known that such things as queers and Lesbians existed, let alone the hundred and one other kinds of pervert. I remember when I was feeling a bit miz once, the girl in the bunk below had said, 'Cheer up, duck. I'm going through all this for the third time and I've survived.' And when I asked her why, she just winked and clicked her tongue at me and said, 'Barmaid in the officers' mess!' It had taken me a long time to work that one out.

In my present hut, there were fifteen of us, all Special Duties and on the same watch and, although most of the girls kept their love life to themselves, there were always a few who revelled in describing every sexual encounter in the minutest detail and some relish. Some, of course, just became boring after a while and no one listened to them, but a few were so amusing that they were never in want of an audience. We had one girl who specialised in elderly men and when she told us about the acrobatic feats she – but that had nothing to do with my feelings for Stan, he wasn't old, or in need of help. We had a Lesbian too, but she had found an officer who was similarly inclined, so she was virtually off our hands, which was a great relief because we were all terrified of her – although we always wanted to ask her what Lesbians actually *did*.

I ignored the cracks from the other end of the hut and went straight to my own bedspace. But Mary O'Connell, who was my best friend and slept in the next bed, surveyed me with a look which was far from salubrious.

'So you've woken up, have you?' she commented in a dry voice. 'Well, I wish it could have been someone other than a randy Pole.'

I was a bit peeved with Mary. After all, Pole or not, Stan *was* aircrew. There was a great deal of snobbery over boy friends and it was not so much the rank as the job that counted. Of course the number one conquest was a pilot with RAF wings, but the Poles – who had more than proved themselves – Czechs and Commonwealth pilots all rated pretty high, followed down the scale by the Fleet Air Arm and Americans. Next came any other aircrew and the army – provided they were infantry or cavalry – and sea-going navy were acceptable. Gunners rated pretty low, mainly because of the association we had with the ack-ack battery in the adjoining field, and ground crew, corps, and shore-based navy were just not on. In the circumstances, I didn't think there was much wrong with Stan.

Mary herself was engaged to a captain in the Marines and kept herself very much for him. She never came out on parties if there was the slightest possibility of any hanky-panky – which was nearly always – and hardly drank at all. But I didn't see why she had to be such a wet blanket with me.

To hell with Mary. I pulled the sheet over my head and fell asleep with my whole body atingle at the imagined touch of Stan's finger tips.

Bent on seduction, after a week of promise and frustration, I succeeded in hiring a punt. The weather had not yet made up its mind and the sky was an indeterminate shade, halfway between blue and grey. I glared at it from time to time while I shaved.

I felt my face carefully and, once satisfied with its smoothness, put my razor away. Next my hands. Sally liked my hands and to-day, if she would only relax a bit, they were going to give her pleasure. I have always been rather vain about my hands and, as I made sure there were no nicotine stains and the cuticles were well pushed back, I looked at them critically and thought perhaps I should have been a surgeon, or a pianist – then I remembered a famous pianist from my own home town, a beaky little man with soft pudgy hands and a belly which made it difficult for his short arms to reach the keyboard! I laughed aloud and saw the batman, who had just come in, smiling at me in the mirror.

'Sound 'appy, sir.'

'I am.' He had told me that there had been two air raids during the night, but I had slept right through them and felt fine. I stretched and picked up my watch. Time to go. After attending early Mass, there would still be time to make a couple of trips to the river with my carefully organised paraphernalia and be back at the ops room by the time Sally came off watch.

The outgoing watch were silent. Some wore tin hats and others carried them languidly. The WAAF normally enjoyed wearing tin hats, which they could push on the backs of their heads halo fashion, and were more becoming than their issue caps. Indeed, I had laughed one evening when taking Sally on watch during a raid, to see all the WAAF filing past the guard with their hats on the backs of their heads and the sergeant pushing each one down in turn, only to have them pushed back again the minute his head was turned. But there was nothing jaunty about these girls; they looked dead beat and then I saw Sally.

She stood, blinking, in the early sunlight, her face without make-up and hair straggling untidily down her back, saying nothing, the marks of strain showing clearly round her eyes and mouth. Her shoulders were covered with a fine white powder and as I looked around I saw that it was on everyone.

'I must sleep, Stan. We've had a terrible watch – I've been on the busiest plotting point all night without a relief and my legs are killing me.' She could not possibly know that a black cloud of disappointment had settled on me, making me feel thwarted and peevish. 'We had a couple of bombs too – a great chunk of plaster fell on me – jolly lucky I was wearing my tin hat. Look – ' She brushed impatiently at her shoulders, but the sticky powder did not budge.

'If you can keep awake long enough to get to the river, I have a very comfortable place for you to sleep – and we have all day.'

She looked doubtful. 'We're not allowed off camp before midday after night watch and I daren't go under the wire in daylight – if I were caught, it would ruin it for everyone.'

'You don't have to go back to camp. I've borrowed a bike for you.'

'We-ll,' she looked down at her trousered legs, 'we're not supposed to go out in battledress.'

'Oh, come on, Sally, who cares?' All I wanted was that she should sleep it off and be herself again – this niggly, querulous Sally was not the one I had looked forward to spending the day with. 'We're only going down country lanes; no one need see you.'

'Well, all right. Let's go then – if I keep moving I'll be okay, but once I lie down, I've had it.'

'That is what I have been hoping for the past week!' But if she heard, it did not sink in and there was no retort.

'Ee looks proper sleepy, ee do,' remarked the lock-keeper's wife, as we piled our bits and pieces into the punt. She pointed at Sally and gave me a severe look. 'That young woman needs sleep, she do, not gallivantin' on river.'

'And zat, Mrs Jenkins, is just what she will have.' A sudden thought occurred to me and I asked, 'Do you have a fishing-rod I could hire? I could fish while she sleeps.'

The old lady looked thoughtful. 'Not for hoire there baint,' she said at last and I realised that Sally had woken up sufficiently to regard me with some amusement – why had I found the Colonial accents difficult to follow? 'But moi Willy gone and left his when he went to join army; Oi could get it shipshape for ee boy to-morrow. Oi'll only lend it to ee, moind.'

'I've not been on this stretch of river before, do you hire out many punts?' Sally had come to my rescue.

'Not now, dear.' She pointed at a boathouse, stacked high with punts, 'Put away for the duration, they be; wasn't till this young gentleman axed me, thet I'd a-thought of hoiring 'em out again.'

While they were talking I had been sorting out our clobber and Mrs Jenkins now added some faded cushions. 'Well, Oi'll leave ee to it, then,' and the old dear, her dropsical girth swaying under a heavily-flowered apron, made her slow way back to her cottage.

Sally had perked up but there was no doubt that she was all in.

'Sit down a minute,' I told her, 'while I blow this up.' And taking hold of the much patched Li-lo I had managed to borrow, I began to puff.

The river was deserted, peaceful, barely moving. There should have been fishermen lining the banks. other punts and even, possibly, a pleasure steamer. Sally should have been wearing a flowery summer frock and I – if I were to anglicise myself into the scene – should be sporting white flannels and one of those atrocious blazers so beloved of the otherwise conservative English.

As it was, the silence was only interrupted by the suck and plop of my pole and the staccato notes of a distant cuckoo. Sally's legs protruding from rather scruffy blue trousers, and our uniform caps and battledress blouses flung in the bows, prevented me from forgetting the war; a section of Spitfires racing overhead were a further reminder. On one side, a meadow thick with clover, sloped gently up to a low, tree-crested hill, an old Roman burial mound – reminder of past battles and successful invasions – and an ancient oak stood by the bank, witness to many human frailties and squabbles.

Sally stirred. 'Why don't you take off your collar and tie?' I called, but she was sound asleep.

I smiled down at my appealing urchin and thought back to the last time I had been on a river; thirty-eight, I suppose. It had been a tributary of the Oder, which ran through our University town; a very different river from this. I had been racing with my twin sister, Anna. Poor Anna. Better not to think where she might be now, nor what had happened since those last uneasy months of peace.

It was not long before I spotted an ideal place on the far bank. A smooth, grassy meadow, ending in a low cliff where a clump of willows leaned far out over the water, their feathery tips trailing in the current and arched branches forming a hollow dome of shade.

Manoeuvring the punt to port, I tied up to one of the trees and left Sally to sleep in the filtered half-light, while I stretched out in the sun.

It was wonderful to throw off my uniform and feel the warm breeze on my skin. I looked at Sally and wondered what her reaction would be if she should suddenly awake to find me starkers. I could guess and, sighing, pulled on my bathing trunks – there was no use in tempting providence. Sally's innocence was a difficult hurdle to clear.

It seemed that she was set for a good long sleep. I took the bottle of wine, which I had wheedled out of the Free French, and secured it in the shallow water to cool. Then I leaned back against a tree and settled down to read the Sunday papers.

I had long since finished with the newspapers and fallen into a doze myself, when I was aroused by a noise from the punt.

Sally was leaning over the edge, her face only a few inches from the water and her eyes wide with terror. For a second or two I sat, rooted to the spot with fascination, then she made that strange, strangled sound again, almost as though she were about to be sick; and then she screamed.

There is something horrible about a real scream of terror – and who should know better than us? I had heard some screams before I left Poland. This, undoubtedly, was one of the nightmares she had once fleetingly referred to. One leap took me into the punt beside her.

I woke her up as gently as I could, calling her name and stroking her hair, but she still struggled out of my arms and leaned over the side of the punt again, staring at the water as though she could see some picture emerging from the trailing weeds and muddy depths and, when she spoke, it was to the river and not to me.

'Those awful eyes, and he was smiling – he was smiling when he pulled the trigger and then his guts spilled out, all over me.'

'Whose guts? Sally, what are you talking about?'

'The man next to me, of course.' She looked into my eyes as though I should know all about it and I saw that she was still only half awake. I shook her and was about to tell her to forget all this nonsense, when some inner sense told me that it was better to let her talk.

'It was his eyes; every time I could see his eyes and every time he pulled the trigger, he smiled.'

'Who smiled?'

'The pilot.'

'Which pilot?'

'The Jap pilot, of course.'

'He would have been wearing goggles.'

'No he wasn't. I'm sure he wasn't.'

'Was there only one aircraft?'

'Oh no, there were hundreds of them – at least it seemed like hundreds.'

I pounced on the small note of uncertainty which had crept into her voice. 'Well, you wouldn't have seen the same pilot the whole time and at least some of them would have been wearing goggles.' It was a small point to niggle on, but I thought it worthwhile. 'And you couldn't have seen him smile, because his oxygen mask would have covered the lower part of his face.'

'At that height?'

She sounded really indignant now and I was beginning to think myself something of a psychologist. But it was true – I myself always felt my facial muscles contort into an involuntary grin when I pressed the tit. Nervous reaction, presumably. And I knew too that fleeting look which, when I had been on day fighters, I had seen on my opponents' faces as they flashed past or we came towards each other – but that was the last thing I was going to admit to Sally.

'You're letting your imagination run away with you,' I said instead, 'You are making your dreams worse because your imagination is stronger than your memory.'

'There was nothing imaginary about that –.' She traced a line across the bottom of the punt and it did not need much perception to realise that her eyes were seeing the boards of a deck beneath her. 'The bullets perforated him, right across the middle, just like a postage stamp. At first there were only little fountains of blood and that was not so bad; besides, he was still alive. He was looking at himself. But then he sort of opened up – everything came out, snaky, all pink and white, and he fell over me and emptied them on to me. Oh, it was horrible – .' She gave a violent heave, leaned over the side of the punt and was sick.

I felt a wave of nausea rise in my own throat. I had seen as much as most people needed to harden their senses and sometimes there would be a brief and gory account before we left dispersal point and then the subject was closed. Heaven alone knows, our own women had suffered in a way that few English women could visualise and not so long ago I had put thoughts of Anna resolutely out of my mind, but nevertheless, hearing this young girl's description of a very recent event, was somehow utterly sickening.

The current quickly carried the vomit away and I pushed her firmly to the other side of the punt, where she washed her face.

'I'm sorry. That was horrid for you – I just couldn't help it.'

I wrapped my arms tight about her, feeling an infinite tenderness towards this child, and a pity – which she would no doubt have resented. I held her quietly until the sobs died down and asked, 'Is it always the same dream?'

She shook her head. 'Mostly this one, but sometimes it is only a quick slap, as I feel myself falling towards the water – I must have been going into that one just now, and the shock of waking and seeing water so close, pulled me out of it. I was probably going to be sick anyway – I expect it was that disgusting citric acid that the NAAFI call lemonade. It was such a stuffy night in the ops room and the electric kettle burned out, so there was no tea or coffee, and people kept handing me glasses of it all night – I don't blame my stomach if it rebelled!'

I squeezed her but said nothing, feeling that it was important to let her go on.

'You know we were carrying a lot of wounded in that ship, many of them plaster cases who couldn't move – they were in one of the holds and of course the hatch was kept open because of the heat and one of the incendiaries fell straight in. I shall never forget those men's screams as long as I live – that is one of the worst ones. And then, sometimes, I dream about burials at sea – despite the Japs, the captain stopped the ship and read the burial service over each corpse before it was tipped over. They had been lying under a tatty flag and, when it came to the last one's turn, the captain had the flag released as well and it fluttered down after them. Then he saluted and we all sang "Abide with me". It was awful.'

Tears had formed in her eyes and I was silent as she shook her head impatiently and knuckled her eyes. There was nothing to say; only time could help.

'Let's forget it, shall we?' She gave me a wan little smile. 'This is spoiling a beautiful day.'

I smiled too and kissed each eyelid. Then I pulled her to her feet – I was about to deliver my psychological trump.

'Now for your surprise.'

The blessed resilience of youth. Her eyes lit up with childish curiosity as I produced the parcel from behind my back. I was feeling positively avuncular!

'Oh, oh!' There was no mistaking the genuine pleasure as she held up the bathing suit. 'Oh, Stan!'

She flung her arms round my neck and practically swung me off the ground, then kissed me hard. I was probably deriving as much pleasure from the gift as she was.

'I didn't want to get you a black one, but there was very little choice. First, I had to find a shop that would take service coupons and then, find something your size – I think it's your size.'

'Oh Stan – you couldn't possibly have known, but it's identical with one I bought years, no, months, ago and those beastly Japs walked in before I was even able to wear it.' The costume was a well-cut one-piece, made of velvety elasticised material with a low, square neck and she regarded it almost lovingly. 'I thought it made me look frightfully *femme fatale* – Daddy didn't really approve.' She giggled.

'Well, put it on.'

She retired behind a bush and emerged in less than a minute doing full justice to the suit. I must admit I had thought it pretty glam myself and the spiel about service coupons was not strictly true.

'Whee-ow!' I gave the wolf howl that I thought was expected of me and found myself in the river for my pains!

'Race you to the other side.' And she dived in over me. Sally was a strong swimmer, far stronger than I would have expected, and won easily. But this was no competition as far as I was concerned and I paddled casually after her, only to be jumped on and ducked as soon as I reached the further bank. It was difficult to believe it was the same girl of half an hour before. She hugged me briefly, kissed my wet face and was back across the river before I had time to duck her.

'I'm hungry, Stan. Do we have any grub?'

'Of course and – *if* you can wait until I reach that side – ' When I got there I dug triumphantly under the stones, ' – and this.'

'Ooh, vino! Goodo! Wherever did you get it?'

'Influence, my dear, just influence!'

'Chicken sandwiches, yum! Stan, how *do* you do it?'

'Made love to the mess sergeant.'

'WAAF, I hope!'

'Of course – nothing wrong with Olshewski!'

It was a silly joke, current at the time, and we both went into paroxysms of helpless laughter – it had, thank goodness, turned into that kind of day – and Sally bit into the first of many sandwiches. For a small girl, she had a prodigious appetite.

When half the bottle had disappeared I corked it firmly. 'Shall we keep the other half for to-morrow?' I asked.

'To-morrow?'

'I've hired the punt for the whole week.'

'Oh Stan, how wonderful. I shall take the bathing-suit on watch with me to-night, and a skirt and a toothbrush.'

'And I shall borrow the fishing rod, to amuse myself while you sleep.'

'Are you going to cure me of my nightmares, Stan?'

Looking back, it occurs to me that that day on the river was the one on which I first thought of becoming a doctor – one day, war and circumstances permitting. I had been pleased with myself for the way I had handled Sally, soothed her and calmed her down, but the word 'cure' was something more.

I can see her now, hands on my shoulders, face gone suddenly grave and her eyes full of trust. 'Are you going to cure me?' she had asked, and I had replied, 'I shall do my best, my darling.' And quite suddenly I knew that I did want to help her, to cure her of the nightmares that were tormenting her sleeping hours, but not only Sally. Perhaps, one day, justice would decree that I should give life back in the same number that I had taken it.

I had kissed Sally on the forehead, as one kisses a child, and made a private pact with myself.

I had been awake for some time, but it was so peaceful lying in the bottom of the punt, that I did not move.

Dragonflies chased each other overhead and the boat rocked lazily with the motion of the river. On the bank nearby, Stan sat and fished. He might have been carved from wood, he was so immobile. There was scarcely a breeze, but a very slight movement of air caused the willow fronds to cast their shadows over him and he looked like some woodland creature, with the moving sunlight and shade dappling his brown, silken body. Perhaps it was the light, but his cheekbones appeared higher than ever, coupling with the tilted eyes and clear cut nose and chin to give him an elusive, fly-away look. I do believe that even his ears were slightly pointed! I love you, Great God Pan, but you will never be mine. It was true. I had thought him wonderful from the very start, but it was his gentleness during the past few days that had really won me. It was wonderful to be able to pour out all my doubts and fears and loneliness to someone as kind as Stan. Wonderful to wake from bad dreams to look into those eyes; deep, compassionate and very tender.

'Stanislaus,' I called softly, and instantly he was alert, muscles moving like those of a well-conditioned cat.

'Darling, you're awake. No nightmare to-day?'

I shook my head and held out my arms to him.

He came and stretched beside me and I felt myself engulfed in a wave of warmth and love.

'Oh Stan, if I could only be close to you like this forever.'

He did not answer, but his mouth left mine and his lips travelled down my throat. His hands were pulling down the top of my bathing suit and I did not resist. I could not.

Looking at his fair head, while those hands cupped my breasts and he kissed each one in turn, I could have died of love then and there. I pulled his hair gently and ran my own hands down his neck and back. He was warm and glossy smooth; wonderful to touch.

Instinctively I rolled over on top of him and buried my mouth deep in the hollow at the base of his throat. I could feel the pulse beating and his whole body tensing.

'Sally, for God's sake!'

'Don't you like that?'

For answer, he groaned and grabbed my hand. 'Don't you know what you're doing to me? Sally, I'm a passionate man – it's cruel to play with me like this.'

I had never touched a man like that before. It was somehow thrilling and at the same time embarrassing. I wanted to feel him and yet I was relieved when he let my hand go.

'Sally, Sally. Are you ever going to let me make love to you?'

'But isn't that what we're doing?'

I held my mouth up for his kiss, my questing tongue ready for his. Just when I thought I must surely drown, he drew back and looked at me.

'Sally,' his voice was tender and soft and my eyes were so misty I could hardly see him. 'Sally, you do not kiss a man like that unless you want him to go the whole way.'

'You must think I'm terribly young and stupid, Stan; you see I haven't – , I've never – ' I implored him with my eyes to save me from having to say more.

'You would enjoy it, Sally.'

Oh God, as if I didn't know it. My willpower was fast running out. He looked at me from under those fringed lids of his and I wanted to melt.

'You would enjoy it, Sally.'

131

He was caressing me with his eyes, his lips, his hands. Stroking until my whole body became alive in quivering anticipation; every sense alert to his touch, every nerve ready to respond.

'Oh Stan. Your hands – they're wicked!'

'I wish I were an octopus, with eight hands to give you pleasure!'

He had pulled my bathing dress down still further and when his hands reached my thighs, forcing them gently apart, it was too much for this mere mortal. I went overboard.

I had not fallen asleep until after lunch. The sun was low and the water had turned cold. I swam vigorously to the other side of the river and back.

'You're bad,' I yelled at him, 'bad, bad, bad – d'you hear?'

'I know,' he said, 'and you love it.'

'I hate you!'

'I know you do.'

'Don't come near me or I'll – ' He dived in, straight on top of me and I only had time to gurgle before I went under.

'What'll you do?'

'You are a scoundrel.'

'Why? Because you *know* you would enjoy it?'

'Oh, Stan,' I kissed his wet, laughing face as we trod water, 'I love you and I hate you; I want you and, and – you're utterly repellent!'

It was freezing and I scrambled out, grabbed my towel and dashed behind a bush to change while he was still laughing.

'Oh my God, my trousers.' I looked with dismay at my battledress. The top was all right, but I'd flung the trousers down early that morning and dumped everything else on top of them, and they really looked like a dog's dinner. It would be bad enough trying to get my hair dry, but I'd never get past the watch sergeant wearing those.

'Give them to me and I'll see when I can do with some hot stones and the bottle.'

I handed them to him gratefully, but as I did so he burst out laughing again.

'Only someone as innocent as you, Sally, would so uninhibitedly step out of their trousers and stand there, like a character from a bad musical comedy, in pants and shirt-tails.'

I ignored him and scrubbed away madly at my hair. It seemed hopeless.

'Don't worry, we've got bags of time.'

'I must be in by ten,' I told him. 'They call the roll before supper now, to stop people going on watch without eating, and there'll only be about ten minutes of darkness before that when I can get under the wire.'

'You take your job very seriously, don't you, Sally?' He was not entirely laughing at me.

'Yes, I do – we all do. That's why it's generally acknowledged that girls are better in the ops room than men. We have more conscience.'

'Oh come now, that's a bit hard.'

I shook my head vigorously, partly to dry it. 'No. In the first place, we're all volunteers, whereas the men have mostly been called up. You see, if you volunteer, you can choose your trade, provided you pass the initial tests, but the call-ups are just sent where they're needed – there are always plenty of volunteers for ops, so they haven't needed to use conscripts yet.'

'Why did you volunteer?'

'My family always volunteer!' How pompous I must have sounded. Needless to say this brought forth another gale of mirth from my best beloved. 'Oh, you are a little prig!'

'Your English bewilders me – I didn't think you'd know that word. Where did you learn it – English, I mean?'

'A little from my parents, some at school, then I read modern languages at University – French, English, and German. At least I began to, then I switched – changing horses in mid-stream I believe is the expression? – to aeronautical engineering.'

'But why?'

'Because most of my generation realised that war was inevitable and it seemed a more useful subject – besides, I was able to learn to fly at the same time.' He gave a rueful grin, 'I'm sure I'm more acceptable in England at the moment as a pilot than as anything else.'

'Possibly, but it seems a pity to forgo the languages.'

He shrugged. 'A language isn't difficult to learn. No one speaks Polish outside Poland, so, if we want to travel, we must know other languages. This week has been good for me, speaking English with you the whole time, I already feel more fluent. The accent is difficult though and I don't believe I shall ever conquer it.'

'You know, I don't notice that you have an accent any more.'

'You have become used to it, that is all.'

'Can you really get to know someone so well in just a week? Is it possible, Stan?'

'Of course – if they are compatible.'

'Now you're showing off! Come on, by the time we've got back to Mrs Jenkins, stowed the punt and ridden back it'll be almost dark. Shall I try and scrounge something from the cookhouse to-morrow?'

He shook his head. 'No need, all fixed.'

I hardly touched Sally the next day. Playing cat and mouse with me was all very well, but I didn't trust myself after yesterday.

She had had an easy watch and was not particularly tired. I could not have been fishing for more than an hour when I heard her call out, 'Any luck?'

'Not a sausage.'

'I'll change and come across.' I was trying out the far bank that day.

'Roger.'

She was soon stretched out beside me in the sun, glistening wet and squinting up at the clear blue sky.

'England would be a bearable place to live in if every summer was guaranteed to be like this one.'

'Stan? About yesterday – '

'Um?'

'Well, you did achieve your aim – at least as far as making me want you. I did, terribly. I couldn't think of anything else all night.'

'I spent most of the night pole-vaulting too.'

'What a dreadful pun!'

'Please?'

'No matter. But please, Stan, be serious for a minute.'

'I am – and I think I've got a bite.' I pulled and pulled and eventually a large chunk of weed came up. I might as well give up fishing and I put my rod away with a sigh. 'Well Sally, if you want me to – '

'Oh no, no Stan. You see, what I wanted to tell you was that, thinking about you all night, I also listened to my conscience, and my conscience tells me that what we are doing, at least what we want to do, is wrong.'

'It's a God-given pleasure.'

'But it's wrong.'

I turned to face her and tried to lift her chin, but her eyes were on the grass and it would appear that all her concentration was devoted on a blade which she was systematically tearing to ribbons.

'It's only wrong where there is no love. Prostitution is morally wrong because it is loveless – except that it appeases a man's hunger – and it *is* a hunger, Sally.' I forced her to look at me. 'I sometimes think that, for a woman, it is a pleasure only when she wants it, but for a man it is a necessity. I may be wrong, but if God had meant us to unite only for procreation, He would have made women seasonal, like animals. If two people love each other, nothing they do to give each other pleasure can be wrong. It is not only the immediate pleasure – which is of course only a pleasure of the senses – but the contentment that follows, and the warmth. I can tell you, my navigator would be a far safer man if I were not so tense.'

She was silent and I was afraid I had gone beyond her and then, at last, somewhat tentatively I thought, she made a suggestion which made it very hard for me to keep my patience.

'You've often said that all the bars are full of tarts – couldn't you pick one up and have me as a, a companion?'

'You've missed the point completely.' I flung my rod and line down on the ground and stood up. I didn't want to show my irritation, but she was being either remarkably obtuse or perhaps just naive. When I sat down again I saw that she was looking miserable, so I did my best to keep the impatience from my voice. I put my hands on her shoulders and held her eyes. 'I don't want a tart. To me it would be sordid – just sordid. Sally, dear Sally, you enjoyed yesterday – it *was* a pleasant day, wasn't it?' She nodded and I let go of her. 'You slept, I read the newspapers, we swam, we enjoyed our lunch, we enjoyed the wine and then afterwards, in the punt, you had a taste of love; just a taste, but you enjoyed that too, didn't you?' She nodded again, but her eyes had fallen. 'You wanted me, Sally – no need to flatter myself – you wanted me as much as I wanted you, and that is nothing to be ashamed of. When your senses are aroused and as excited as that, there is only one conclusion, a delicious conclusion, when you melt together in the climax. And then, a lazy contentment, a happiness where there is no room for tension and frustration and bitterness.'

'At risk of sounding an awful prude, I have been brought up to regard that as something sacred to marriage.'

'Oh, in peacetime, yes. I was brought up the same way, believe it or not. But now – to-morrow you may have another bomb on the ops room and bang – no Sally. I go back on ops next Monday; perhaps I'll be shot down next time and bang – no Stan. And look what we would have missed. Oh Sally,' I lifted her face again, 'there is nothing more beautiful than making love with someone you love.'

I turned to pick up my rod.

'Do you really love me, Stan? Just a little bit?'

'Of course I do,' I roared at her, 'or why the hell do you think I'm behaving as I am? If I were out for only one thing, I could find plenty of willing partners.' I flung the bait in with a vicious slap. 'But I'm not going to marry you – I want to make that quite clear.'

'But – '

'No. What sort of a bastard do you think I am? I could be shot down again at any time and next time I might not be so lucky. Who wants to leave a seventeen-year-old widow?'

'But – '

I shook my head firmly. 'No buts. Besides, when you're older, you'll look back and be glad that you didn't marry me – a foreigner and a Catholic.'

'Well, I don't think I mind about you being foreign.'

She stopped dead and her thoughts were so transparent that I couldn't help letting out a great guffaw.

'There you are, you see – you Protestants are far more bigoted than we are!'

'Oh, I don't know. We had some very good friends among the priests at home and my best friend here is Mary O'Connell, and she's a Catholic if ever there was one.'

'Little chance of your marrying either a Catholic priest or Mary O'Connell.'

At last she laughed.

I would have liked to have let the matter rest, but there was no point in hurting her and I wanted her to know my more practical reasons. As a matter of fact, had she been a little older and the circumstances different, I might well have married her.

'Another reason why I won't marry you – nor anyone else for that matter – is that, until this war is over, I have no idea what position we Polish people will be in, let alone what I myself might have to offer.'

'But you have your engineering degree.'

'No. Unfortunately I hadn't sat my finals when the Germans arrived – you see I had spent too much time on languages first. I'm afraid I'm completely unqualified.'

'But you have your land.'

'Do you know where the city of Lvov is, Sally?'

'I think so. It's in the eastern "boot" part, isn't it?'

'Exactly. Well, my home is, or was, to the east of Lvov. It's now deep in the heart of Russia – and likely to remain so, I fear.'

'But the Russians are our allies.'

I raised my eyebrows but tried not to sound too sceptical, 'Your allies perhaps – for as long as it suits them. But not ours. Not now, nor ever. We hate the Russians far more than we hate the Germans.'

'This is a puzzling war. After all, the Germans were the ones who marched into Poland.'

'In the west, yes. And what a heyday the Russians had in the east. I am only here now because I had just returned to study in Breslau when the Russians moved in. My sister should have followed, but she was caught.'

'What happened to her?'

'She and my mother were taken to Siberia. My father was sent to a forced labour camp. Our lands confiscated.' I paused for a second and crossed myself, although I knew it was a gesture that embarrassed her. 'My mother died on the way.'

'Oh, Stan. How awful.'

'No. It is a blessing. They treat women like cattle. I wish my sister could have died too.'

'Do you know if she's alive?'

I shrugged. 'Sometimes there is news of people. There are rare escapes from Siberia, you know, and occasionally – when the camps are becoming too full – they just open the gates and let a certain number go. We are a tough race – we have had to be for centuries – more and more are reaching India and they have set up camps for them in Kenya too.'

'Do any women ever survive the journey?'

'Oh yes. I think our women are tougher than the men – at least the peasants are.'

'Perhaps your sister will appear one day. What is her name?'

'Anna. Perhaps she will. Oh well,' I put out a hand to touch her cheek; she looked like a young animal, curled up and listening. 'I have my Russians and you have your Japs and meanwhile we have each other – *and* some lunch!'

She took my hand and rubbed her cheek against it.

'I love you too, Stan, very much. And if I ever do let anyone make love to me, it will be you, only – ' she looked pensively at my hand, tracing the lines with her finger, ' – what I am going to say will make you laugh at me, I know, and make you think me even younger and sillier than you do already, but, if we ever do, please, do you think we could wait until it is dark?'

She gave me the most imploring, apprehensive look. I couldn't have laughed at her even if I had wanted to.

'Oh, my little one, my shy little English animal, how I adore you.'

'As a matter of fact I'm not really English at all.'

'Oh. Malay?' I *was* laughing at her now.

'Don't be an ass. Gunn is a very old Scottish name. My full name is Sarah Catriona MacCallum Gunn.'

'Good heavens. I'm sure that deserves some sort of tribal salute! Pass the bottle!'

During the last of Sally's night watches, the ops room and camp were strafed. By that time I had come to know her well – I had set myself to cure her of her nightmares and knew only too well that the most oft-recurring episode involved machine-gunning. Of course she had been in several air raids, even since I had known her, in fact she told me that she had actually arrived on the station during the worst raid of all, when most of the town was flattened and she, along with everyone else, had spent long off-duty hours digging in the debris for bodies; but being strafed was different and I was worried about her reactions.

I need not have been. She came off duty simply bubbling with excitement and far more awake than usual.

'If I'd been in bed I'd have copped it,' she fairly crowed, 'there's a row of bullet-holes straight along our hut and just at bed level. And do you know what day it is? Friday the thirteenth! You see, I told you it was my lucky day. I'm jolly well not going to waste it sleeping – no watch to-night, anyway.'

' "By God's mercy, danger shall only excite the soul and we shall fear nought until the eagle owls have wrought vengeance and brought justice to the land. But, woe be to any man who kills in wanton hate; for him fear shall stalk and his soul shall quake in the night".'

'Who are you quoting?'

'Our squadron priest – it was part of his blessing when we changed from day to night fighters. There was a ceremony in the hangar, all the new aircraft lined up, with crews beside them, and as the holy water was sprinkled on the nose of each machine, the chaplain gave his blessing. He was a very fine man; his words imprinted themselves on my mind and they must have on other peoples' as well, because, when he died, one of the airmen – a skilled engraver in civilian life – put it down in illuminated lettering and we have it in our dispersal point.'

'Why did he die?'

'Why, I don't know, but how was an unfortunate tragedy.'

I told her the story of how the young priest, working with others amongst the wreckage left by the bombing, had come across a dying man, his legs trapped and lying beside a tottering wall. It was obvious that he would not survive the time it would take to dig him out. The priest stayed with him and, on finding that he was a Catholic, administered the last rites. Several calls had warned him of the imminent collapse of the wall, but the man to whom he ministered was still alive and the priest refused to leave him. They tried to drag him away, but it was useless and when the wall gave way, both men died together.

I could see that the tale had affected Sally, who was apt to be emotional. She was thoughtful for a long time, and we parked our bicycles and got out the punt in silence.

'I was afraid for you last night,' I told her, as we let the punt glide gently downstream.

'And I was afraid of being afraid – do you know what I mean?'

'Oh yes.'

'I was on relief when they came over – they were too low for the radar to pick them up, so the first news was when the Observer Corps spotted them crossing the coast – and I was walking up and down outside, when one of the RAF Regiment guards shouted, "The camp's being strafed and they're coming this way." I had a terrible feeling in my stomach – like going down in Swan and Edgar's lift – for a second, and then they were overhead; so low that, in the moonlight even their camouflage markings were clearly visible and those black crosses – gosh, how they stood out – and then I was thrilled and excited and when the ack-ack opened up I was shouting and shaking my fist with the guards. I remember it was the same in Singapore – I had often wondered how I would behave when the war proper hit us and, when it did, I knew that the fear had been in anticipating

138

horrors; when they actually happened it was exhilarating – of course I was never physically hurt, that must be different, I don't think I've ever known really terrible pain. But your priest was right – excitement is a mercy.' She was silent for a little while, then asked, 'Have you ever been afraid, Stan?'

'Many times. Only a few weeks ago, when I started to land on that German airfield and saw those soldiers and the trucks – as you say, how those black crosses stand out – I had a sickening moment of fear. But it passed, luckily, as it usually does, long before we were actually shot down and when I was in the lifeboat I didn't really feel anything, except frustration.'

'I hope I never feel afraid again.'

'You will. We all feel afraid at times, throughout our lives – I'm sure we must.'

We took the punt as far downstream as we could go, until a weir blocked our passage, then poled back to our favourite place and swam until the sun was high overhead.

Sally accused me of fussing over the lunch preparations like an old hen, and although I didn't think the simile very apt, it was rather special. I banished her until all was ready and I must say that when I called her, her look of pleased surprise was gratifying. Not without reason mind you, for the mess sergeant had done us proud. An enormous veal and ham pie nestled in a positive garden of lettuce, tomatoes and cucumber; a freshly baked *white* loaf, butter, and a crock of cottage cheese. I had wangled a bottle of *vin rosé* out of my usual chums – I often wondered where they got it from – and we had long, thin-stemmed wine glasses instead of the usual unbreakable tumblers.

'My dear Stan, wherever did all this come from?'

'Courtesy of the mess – or, at least, the messing sergeant. Look at the pie, Sally.'

Amid Tudor roses and curly leaves, a large figure 13 stood out. She looked puzzled. 'To-day's date. But why?'

'It's for you.'

'But I don't understand.'

'The sergeant's a motherly old duck and, when she knew who was to share my picnics, she went out of her way to make them nice.'

'But I still don't understand – after all, she doesn't know me.'

'Nevertheless, she has a soft spot for you. It seems she read some newspaper articles about you. I must admit I didn't see them myself, but she says you had quite a write up when you first joined up – the little waif who got out of Singapore on Friday the thirteenth – and her RAF son is a prisoner there.'

'I didn't read them myself.'

'You didn't?' I was amazed, I thought every young girl would enjoy seeing her name in print. 'Why ever not?'

'I just didn't want to – I can't exactly tell you why. Anyway, I offended the Press, so I expect they were rather rude. I suppose I did behave stupidly – it seems silly now.'

'What did you do?'

'Let's eat first and then I'll tell you.' She took the knife and cut the pie, while I filled our glasses. 'Gosh, real eggs.' We drank to each other and when she had devoured a large chunk of pie, she told me the story.

'All those reporters were frightfully nice to me and when the interviews were over, they arranged a dinner for me at Quaglinos, and to go on to the ballet afterwards. I only had one dress and a coat which the Red Cross had given me in India. Everyone was so kind, so sympathetic and made such a great play of the fact that we had lost everything, only the clothes I stood up in, etcetera. One of them slipped me some clothing coupons, to buy something nice to wear for the dinner – but it never occurred to anyone that I didn't have any money! I joined up as soon as I arrived in London, but I had five days to wait before the next intake of recruits for the training depot –'

'Whatever did you do?' I couldn't help interrupting.

'Lived, slept and ate on Waterloo Station!'

'What?'

'Honestly. It was quite an education! One of the reporters, a woman, said she'd pick me up and take me to the party and asked me where I was staying. I told her the Cumberland.'

'Why?'

Sally shrugged and bit into a tomato. 'Pride, I suppose. I was afraid that if they knew the truth someone would offer to put me up and look after me. I didn't want that. I wanted to stand on my own two feet. Anyway, when I reported back to Adastral House, the recruiting officer was furious with me – said the reporter had told her that they had never heard of me at the Cumberland and, after waiting hours for me at Quags, decided I was a phoney and had made fools of them. She ordered me to write letters of apology to them all and to the RAF Public Relations Officer – I should have done, I know, but I didn't. Of course she didn't know the truth either.'

'Where did you eat?'

She made a small expression of disgust. 'For the first couple of days off scraps from the station restaurant – you know it's surprising how many half-eaten sandwiches and rock cakes get left on plates when a passenger suddenly realises he might miss a train. Daddy would have been horrified, but you see I had to keep enough to pay the fare on the tube to Kingsway – if I'd missed the intake it really would have been the end of the world. My undoing, or my luck, came on the third day. There is a small café, just round the corner from Waterloo, and, when I ambled past, the smell was too tantalising for words – it was quite early and I suppose they were cooking for lunch – I just couldn't move on; just stopped and gaped through the open door and sniffed. It was run by a dear old lady and when I told her that I was hungry but didn't have any money, she let me have the rest of my meals there for free – I helped peel vegetables and did some of the washing-up – but she was so kind. When I reached the Depot, I got one of the NAAFI girls to sell my civilian clothes for me and I sent her the money – I hope she got it, although it wasn't very much.'

I looked at Sally in a new light. Innocent and naive, maybe, but able to look after herself, it would appear. I raised my glass, 'To you, Sally. May you go far.'

She smiled and drank to me in turn. 'Is it really our last day?'

'Afraid so. Back on ops on Monday night. New kite, new navigator – don't even know who it is yet. Which just goes to show how much interest I've been taking in other things.'

'Monday?' Her face clouded. 'It's so easy to forget that we are personally involved in the war when we're like this. I shall be on duty when you go out. I hope I'm not plotting. Oh! Plotting – Stan, I didn't tell you. . . .'

She jumped up in a flurry of excitement and raced over to her pile of clothes. After rummaging in her battledress pockets, she held up a pair of embroidered propellers, a wide, triumphant smile on her face.

'My props! We had a trade test last week and I came out on top, with a hundred per cent. Think, Stan – *a hundred per cent*! So, no ACW1, I've gone straight up to LACW – *Leading* Aircraftswoman to you, Olshewski!'

I no doubt smiled indulgently, but I was proud of her all the same and I loved her for her enthusiasm.

'What better excuse for drinking the rest of the wine?' I asked.

'Stan – tragedy I shan't see you for a whole week.'

'I'll take you out to lunch.'

'But you need to sleep until midday and I have to be on camp by 1400.'

'I shan't fly every night – unless there's a flap on, I'll take you out then.'

'Promise?'

'Promise.'

Replete, she quite suddenly curled up and went to sleep. My darling little animal, I thought, as I packed the lunch things away, I wonder how long this idyll can last.

My new navigator was a squat, placid peasant from Silesia, one Sergeant Zgoda. He reminded me of my father's farm hands; unimaginative, dependable. I was glad to have an NCO – Tzadek being my off-duty friend as well as my operational partner had made it that much worse.

Our first mission together was to strafe a road convoy between Caen and Rouen. It was good to be in the air again, the sky clear and only just dark, the early moon already playing on the ripples of the Channel below. I thought briefly of Sally and wondered if she was plotting us, but she belonged to another world.

It seemed no time at all before the French coast was before us and it soon became evident that, either the pinpoint we had been given at the briefing was wrong, or else the convoy had left before or after the appointed time. Zgoda checked our position. We patrolled up and down the empty road, shining chalk white in the moonlight between the darker fields, the rows of poplar trees, like black exclamation marks, marching beside it for mile after mile.

We had just about given up hope when I saw the convoy creeping out of the shelter of a wood near Lisieux. Crafty sods, I thought, think they can escape along a side road, do they? Well, I can play the same game. I continued my patrol of the main road, pretending to ignore them, until sixteen huge trucks, headed and tailed by smaller vehicles, were rolling down the open road. Once again down the main road, then a quick slew to the right and dip. The crimson of the tracer turning the scene into an annotated black and white photograph. I had been briefed to make absolutely sure of my target and to make it one run if I could and I soon knew the reason why. Boom! No doubt what *they* were carrying. We rocked in the explosion as the first truck went up, but not enough to prevent my finishing the run and then up in a sharp climb.

Below, a sheet of flame was quickly spreading along the road and, for the first time, the ack-ack was opening up. 'Too late,' I sang out, as though the guns could hear me, 'too late. I'm going home.'

Elated, I shot up a couple of coastal guns on the way back and landed smoothly in the calm, warm night. Zgoda and I looked at each other and smiled; I punched him on the shoulder and he gave me the 'thumbs up' sign. It had been a good beginning and I went happy to bed.

Three new aircraft were to be blessed the following week, including Stan's, and having told me about the ceremony, he asked me if I would like to attend.

I had not been inside the main hangar before. It was vast and the three little Beaus looked like toys lined up along one side. Even smaller, was a tiny, pale blue Spitfire, a high-flying 'Foto Freddie' who had run out of fuel and limped in the night before; he was parked by himself at the far end and looked such an orphan, that I rather hoped the priest would bless him too.

I had brought Mary with me and we arrived early because, although I wanted to stay at the back during the actual ceremony, I did want to have a good look at Stan's aircraft first. All the Beaus were painted a dark, dull grey, with black patches and the RAF roundels standing out in dramatic relief. Below the cockpit on Stan's plane, three tiny trucks, a gun and a train had already been painted and I quickly inspected the others to make sure that he had scored the most hits – he had and my heart soared with pride. I stared long at the cockpit, memorising its every detail, so that next time he was airborne I would be able to visualise him in it. Mary made a few sceptical remarks to the effect that it was lucky I didn't have to visualise the whole interior of an aircraft-carrier – her Marine was in a carrier – and then we went to the back of the hangar to wait for the ceremony to begin.

The hangar was soon full, not only with members of the squadron concerned, but men and women from the other Polish squadrons on the station and various interested spectators, from the station commander down.

Candles were placed on the wings of the aircraft – which were beginning to remind me uncomfortably of goats at the start of a Hindu ritual sacrifice – and soon the scent of incense was heavy on the air. The summer days were drawing in and outside the huge doors, the dusk was slowly deepening into dark.

The chaplain blessed each Beaufighter in turn, holding his right hand high while his medals clanked against his cassock. There had never been much church-going in my family, but what there had been was Presbyterian and it was not long before the whole ceremony was beginning to smack of hocus-pocus to me and, as each aircraft was pushed out to be prepared for the night's work, the unpleasant feeling that they were being led out to the slaughter still persisted. I was glad after all to see the little 'Foto Freddie' left on his own, without candles, but somehow with his life.

The blessing ceremony was followed by a pre-take-off Mass and Mary went forward to take part. I remained where I was, one amongst many other Protestants, but feeling strangely alien and alone. The aircrew knelt before the portable altar as the priest intoned, the bells rang, and a small, chilly breeze, first herald of autumn, threatened to blow the candles out.

As the service droned on, not understanding, I wondered idly if God were equally invoked by the other side. There had been something uncomfortably pagan about the ceremony which I had not liked; not the harmless animism of the yule-tree and the mistletoe, but something intangible, wrathful, made obscene by the hidden guns and the undertone of hate.

I was just wishing I could go home when the spoken part of the Mass ended. The men rose and their voices soared in a hymn, reaching crescendo after crescendo, until it seemed that the hangar must burst with sound. The deep, often melancholy, Slav voices rose again and stopped to let a tenor break through. I felt the gooseflesh rise on my arms and down my spine; the emotion in the hymn must surely communicate itself to even the most insensitive ear. The voices harmonised, being led from one hymn to another by the solo tenor, alternatively rising to a stirring, martial rhythm and dying away to a mournful lament.

When the singing ended, the aircrew marched out. Stanislaus, bulky in his flying suit and swinging his helmet in his hand, walked straight past me, into the night. His eyes, as did the eyes of all his companions, looked far out beyond the horizon. The candlelight shone on his fair hair and his eyes and mouth were slits, the cheekbones in between seeming more tightly stretched and Oriental than ever.

I gave an involuntary shudder as the men tramped past; quite suddenly Stan had become an alien thing. It was difficult to associate him with the eager, loving, down-to-earth Stan that I knew, alternately cynical and tender, practical and indolent.

The candles were snuffed and the main lights switched on and I came back to earth and looked around for Mary. It was a relief to hear the chatter of the ordinary erks as they got down to their normal work. The big doors had been shut and the mysticism of the night remained outside; the hangar was light, alive, normal, and the little 'Foto Freddie' was being attended to with loving hands.

We cycled back to our own camp in silence. I, who valued my friend's opinion highly, had wanted Mary to see Stan at his best, but when asked what she thought of the ceremony, she confessed that she simply did not know what to say. The latter part she had enjoyed.

' "The muttered Mass"?' she replied in answer to my question. 'It's something that is part of us, a comfort, which you would not understand – don't try. But the men? That singing was terrific, I could feel tears of pride and sadness pricking my eyes and the lump in my throat was as big as an egg. But there was an element of hysteria in it – they're very *foreign*, Sally. Those expressions of fervour and exultation as they marched out, and the absolute silence except for the tramping feet – can you imagine a British squadron behaving in the same dedicated, dramatic way?'

She had voiced my own feelings exactly. I shook my head. 'I wonder how long it lasts?'

'Not much further than the hangar doors, one hopes. Still, God help any Huns they meet to-night!'

The summer came to a close and the sad beauty of autumn engulfed the land.

We took the punt on the river only once more before it become too cold, but, although we started off in high spirits and enjoyed the sumptuous tea of scones and strawberry jam provided by Mrs Jenkins, it was not the same.

Before five o'clock, a damp, cold mist had begun to rise and the swans glided past like wraiths returning to the grave. Stan was moody and silent and even I, who am always being accused of talking too much, could find little to say. I looked at him and loved him, and didn't love him, and was undecided.

The aircraft-blessing ceremony was never mentioned by either of us – for which I was glad, because I am too transparent to tell a successful lie, and I would have ended up by saying what I really thought of it and then his feelings would have been hurt – and I doubted if he even remembered that I had been there. Perhaps it was only in my mind, but it seemed to have raised a tiny barrier between us, imperceptible and undefined, but it was there.

The drinking parties at the Red Lion still went on, inside, now that the nights were cold, and there was usually much merriment over the fire as hot chestnuts were tossed around and mulled cider downed in some quantity. There was seldom room for all of us and, in the crush, Stan would stand close to me and be as gay as the rest. He never let me go and yet there was no contact between us any more. During the summer he had never come back from an op without telling me how it had gone and what sage remark the good Sergeant Zgoda – who was renowned for stating the obvious – had made on their return. But now he seldom mentioned his work; just shrugging off questions with casual references to Cherbourg or Brest or Rouen, and our conversations had become a matter of question and answer. I don't think he wanted to be alone with me any more; when the pub emptied, we would walk back to camp, four or six or more of us together, and at the entrance he would hug me briefly – I often wondered why he continued to spend his off-duty time with me at all.

It was not long before the colours of autumn gave way to a dark November with an early frost and iron grey skies. The war was going badly and a depression hung over the whole station. There had been so many accidents on the airfield that sabotage was suspected and everyone was nervy and on edge.

Early one morning, when we were still on night watch, Stan suddenly appeared on the controller's deck. He had been flying most of the night, I knew, and his unshaven face looked grey and haggard and his hair, surprisingly enough, was darkened with streaks of sweat. There was no mistaking the look of dumb misery in his eyes as he looked down and I wished that I was able to go to him. He made signs to me to meet him outside – I was busy, but once satisfied that I had understood, he sat down beside the Polish controller to wait for the watch to be relieved.

He was so tense and so silent that I followed him, without asking questions, through the cold, frosty park until we came to the woods and there, in the shelter of the evergreens, he took me in his arms and held me hard against him. I could feel his whole body quivering and quite suddenly, as though a dam had been released, the tears poured down his face and on to mine. I tried to put my hands up, but he only held me tighter, pressing my head against his chest until my hair was saturated with his tears.

'Stan, what is it? Whatever's happened?'

But he only shook his head dumbly and I stood quietly until the great, wracking sobs died down.

'We were on an intruder patrol,' he blurted out, and it seemed that he would say no more.

'I know. I was on the R/T – didn't you recognise my voice?'

'Was it you? You sounded different, but I thought there was something familiar about it. As you will already know, our destination was Le Mans, first the airfield and then a train just to the south. It was a troop train for Marseilles – reinforcements for North Africa I expect – they were loading at a small country station. There's a big army depot near there, I've done it before – in fact nearly pranged near there once.'

There didn't seem anything very special about all this, but he put his hands up to his face and stood there with bent head for what seemed an eternity. After a while I succeeded in pulling his hands away and said, as gently as I could, 'Go on. It'll be better if you get whatever it is off your chest – like listening to my dreams.'

'We were carrying bombs and drop tanks – a long range patrol. Our mission was to bomb the transport aircraft on the field, then strafe the troop train. My bombs had gone and as I went in for my first run over the station, all the lights suddenly went on. The Resistance, I presume, lighting up the target for us. And what a target – the longest troop train I've ever seen. Those lights showed a milling mass of men – and women. *Women*, Sally.' He grabbed my shoulders and shook me, all the time staring hard into my eyes. 'Women. Wives and mothers and sweethearts, saying good-bye to their men. And I killed them. I killed them.'

Once again he was shaken by uncontrollable sobs.

'I doubt if the pilots who strafed our ship worried very much about the women on board,' I remarked dryly.

If I had known then what I know now, I would have kept quiet. I was very young and, despite my *naïveté*, very hard, I think. I realise now that Stan was on the point of collapse – lack of moral fibre was the air force term; a cruel, ruthless judgment of a mind that had taken too much, but we were cruel and ruthless in 1942. I was not exactly unsympathetic with Stan, but I had never seen a man cry before – I have seen several since – and I was a bit embarrassed by it and, in my own mind, thought him a bit soft. If I had been older and had more sense, I should have led him quietly back to camp and reported it to someone, before he cracked up. As it was, I would have been too ashamed of him to report it and didn't really know what to do. But I loved him still, so I remained quiet and comforted him as best I could, encouraging him to talk.

'In the split second before I pressed the tit, I saw a young couple standing at the edge of the crowd. The girl was like you, Sally, and about your age. She stood with her arms round the soldier's neck and looked up at the sky. There was an overwhelming look of surprise on her face – and then she was gone. I aimed at her – I couldn't help myself. I aimed at her and all the time I knew I was killing you.'

'Oh, don't be so ridiculous. How could you aim at any one person when you were shooting up a station? Pull yourself together Stan – you were only doing your job.'

He ignored my outburst and went on as though I had not spoken. 'The lights went out before I had gained height. I *had* to go back and see what I had done – at risk to the aircraft and Zgoda, I had to go. I had to see. I went in low and before I reached the station, I did an unforgivable thing – I switched on my own landing lights. She was there, Sally, she was there – covered in blood, on her back on the platform, the man's body sprawled on top of her. She was dead and I had killed her. It was as though I had killed you. All those women – there may have been children too, although I didn't see any. How can I ever hope to gain an immortal soul with so much blood on my hands?'

His eyelids began to flicker and soon he slumped against me. I was not sure whether he had fainted or fallen asleep, but he made no resistance as I freed myself and so, holding him against a tree, I let him slide to the ground. He started to mumble and I sat beside him, trying to hear what he was saying, but it was mostly in Polish and unintelligible to me. What does one do with a semi-conscious man in the woods on a cold, wet day? I did the only thing possible in the circumstances – made myself as comfortable as I could with my back to the tree and pulled his head on to my lap, to wait for him to become normal again.

I cannot think of any more depressing place than those woods that day. In the early summer they had been carpeted with daffodils and bluebells and through the fresh green leaves the sky had shone, a clear, pure blue. How many hours Stan and I had spent there, sometimes talking, but more often lying silent, listening to the myriad summer sounds. But now, how drear. Nothing moved, not a bird sang and the sky showed dull grey through the gaunt bare branches of the oaks. All about me was the decay of autumn ended and the only sound was the continuous dripping, as the evergreens shed their surplus store of last night's rain. I was tired and hungry, for I had been up all night and had had nothing to eat since the evening before, but I could not sleep and soon my legs became so cramped under Stan's weight that my own discomfort was uppermost in my mind.

Stan moaned and his head rolled from side to side in my lap; otherwise he did not move, but it was hardly a restful sleep. The awful whiteness of his face was accentuated by his beard which, although his hair was so fair, was coming through dark, shadowing his mouth and painting gaunt hollows on the pallor of his cheeks. Poor darling, what could have happened to cause this sudden guilt complex, I had no idea.

We seemed to have been sitting there all morning, although by my watch it was in fact less than an hour, when it started to snow. Gentle, wet snow that lingered white for a moment then, as I watched, changed into a dark patch. I turned up my greatcoat collar and pulled down my cap as far as it would go, but it didn't prevent the icy slush from seeping down my neck and into my shoes. Stan was without a coat, but he still had on his flying boots and was wearing a thick, polo necked jersey under his battledress blouse. I searched for his cap, trying to remember whether or not he had been wearing it when we left the ops room, but, if he had, it must be somewhere underneath us. I tried my best to protect his head, but his hair was soon wet through and the moisture collected in drops by his eyes and the corners of his mouth. It came to me, with a flip of the stomach, that that was how he must have looked when he climbed from the sea half a year ago.

I was so cold and stiff and mentally numb that, when he woke up, I was caught completely unawares. I was vaguely conscious of his eyes opening, red, sunken and totally unrefreshed, and then he grabbed me, forcing me under him into the mass of slimy, dead leaves; ripping at the neck of my greatcoat and kicking my legs apart with vicious jerks. I tried to cry out, but he closed my mouth with his own, his bristly chin rasping my cold skin like sandpaper. His breathing was heavy, but otherwise he made not a sound and it was only when I finally succeeded in freeing my arms and pushing his face away, that he appeared to be aware of what he was doing.

'No, Stan,' I cried, 'no, no, no – *not* like this.'

'I've got to have you.' It was a strange, hoarse, croaking voice, the mouth hardly moving and his eyes closed. 'All summer I've been wanting you, dreaming of you, masturbating because of you. Your nearness has been torture – I can't fly, I can't sleep, I can't eat. I can't go on any longer – this is a hunger, Sally – '

With both hands he gripped the collar of my coat and the tortured look of his face aroused a great wave of compassion in me. I put my arms round his neck and pressed him close while I whispered in his ear. 'Wait Stan,' I implored, 'however much I wanted you to make love to me now, I couldn't. It's the wrong time – please try and understand.'

The meaning of my words slowly sank in and with a sigh he released my collar. 'Well help me then,' he begged, 'help me.'

When his inert form finally collapsed against me and I felt his relaxed weight pressing me further into the wet ground, I believe I felt more tenderness for him than I had ever felt before.

'I'm sorry,' he said after a while, and it was a relief to hear his voice sounding normal again, 'can you ever love me again after the way I've behaved to-day?'

I said nothing, but kissed his forehead and smoothed his hair and I think he knew that I could.

The early dark was almost upon us when I stood up and retrieved the remains of Stan's cap from the leaves. 'Hope to hell there's some hot water, I could do with a bath – but it'll need more than that to cope with this.' I handed it to him.

'And I could do with a shave.' He was feeling his chin with one hand and turning his cap in the other. He looked ruefully at me and touched my face. 'Sally, I hurt you.'

'Yes, you did,' I admonished, 'don't you ever do it again.'

We walked back to camp arm in arm and on the way, trying to sound as casual as I could, I remarked, 'You know, Stan, when we were helping to dig people out of the ruins after the bombing, I kicked something which I thought was a sausage – it had been a grocer's shop – and then I saw it was a baby's arm. I must admit I was sick. But you see, what you did last night was exactly the same as they do to us. Think of the women and children who were killed in the blitz. But the German pilots were only doing their job – you are doing yours.'

He was silent and we were almost at the camp before I spoke again. 'Are you flying to-night?'

'Yes. 0200 take off, unless it's been altered.'

'What's the target?'

'I don't know yet.'

'Well, whatever it is, for God's sake don't let your conscience prick. Just try and remember that whatever you do, they are doing the same.'

'Thank you, Sally.' We had reached the wire. 'Shall I see you to-morrow?'

'Not too early. I've got to have some sleep after to-day – and so have you.'

'I shall sleep until midnight. Let's have lunch in town – I'll meet you in Kimberley's at noon. Okay?'

149

'Okay.'

He helped me under the wire.

The red hot stove pulsated with heat and our Nissen hut was almost cosy as, dripping, I slipped through the blackout curtain and thankfully began to shed my clothes.

'Wherever have you been?' Mary put down her book and regarded me with a stern, matronly air. She was the sole occupant of the hut and I must say I was grateful. I wanted so much to tell her about the awful day.

Mary was five years older than I and she had taken it on herself to mother me from the start. She was a dedicated sort of person, dedicated to Peter, her fiancé, and dedicated to her job – so dedicated in fact that, although she had been on a fighter station since the beginning of the war, she had consistently refused a commission rather than leave it. Needless to say, there was no hot water, but while I rubbed myself down and put on some dry clothes, I told her everything – and what a relief it was.

'That poor man,' she said at length, 'I think, Sally, that you should report this – either to his flight commander or the MO. It's clearly time he had a rest from ops.'

'Do you think he's a bit unhinged – sexually, I mean?' I asked.

'Unhinged?' She was high-pitched with incredulity. 'My dear girl, that poor man is thoroughly normal. Frankly, Sally, it amazes me that this hasn't happened before. You've been working and playing in close proximity for months – it isn't as if he's in Burma or the Western Desert, where there probably aren't any women to hand. You've led him on until it's a wonder to me he's sane at all. Canoodling in the woods, holding hands in the pub and gazing into his eyes with a promise that isn't there – '

'Okay, okay. You've made your point.' I could feel the prick of tears.

'I'm sorry,' she put an arm round my shoulders as I sat in front of the stove, trying to get warm, and her voice was kind, 'but you've hardly been fair. If you'd ever asked my advice, I would have told you ages ago to keep your distance and let him cool off a bit.'

'I love him so. I wanted to be close.'

'I know you did. I've seen you positively wasting away these past few months. Quite honestly, I thought it was frustration on your part as much as his.'

I shook my head; it was far more simple than that. 'I was afraid of losing him,' I said.

One more night like last night and I'll be off ops, I told myself firmly, as I walked across the tarmac.

The dumpy form of Zgoda stood by the aircraft, nattering to one of the armourers. No highly-strung nonsense about him, I thought, not without gratitude. The square face lit up in a welcoming smile and he climbed up into the Beau. I grinned in return, gave the thumbs up sign to the armourer and climbed in in turn.

Thank God it wasn't another train; at least not a specific one. The marshalling yards at Cherbourg and certainly not for the first time. I made myself comfortable, turned to see that my navigator was settled, a last quick check and a glance at my watch. 0200 dead on.

'Tuesday two-four airborne.'

I turned to look at my opposite number when I heard the voice of flying control over the Tannoy. A large red spot appeared; there he was, circling over base. If I went on my favourite point I would just be in time to pick him up as he crossed the coast.

I had taken an early relief in order to be back by 0200; I couldn't bear anyone else plotting him out. Soon the controller was giving him a vector for Cherbourg and, a matter of seconds later, the first radar plot was told as he crossed the coast. I listened for an erratic course, prepared to plot inaccurately if the worst came to the worst, but I need not have worried – he crossed the Channel as straight as a die until he disappeared into France.

It was a busy, but routine and uneventful night. I plotted Stan back in the hour before dawn, knowing that he would be home and in bed before it was light. Then I went off watch, ate a hearty breakfast, and set my alarm for 10 am.

Sally was late, but I didn't really mind. Knowing how it filled up for lunch, I had deliberately arrived early at our rendezvous.

Kimberley's was an Olde Englishe type of café in the Cathedral Close, a small haven of genuine Elizabethan architecture in one of the few unbombed areas of the city. An early fall of snow had melted away and a thin shaft of watery sunlight lit a small green patch of grass by the main door of the Cathedral. This was my favourite patch because someone, to do with the church I presume, always put out scraps for the birds and their arguments and scuffles never failed to amuse me.

The Cathedral clock struck the half-hour; my God, she *was* late. For an awful moment I was afraid that she might not come; then the door opened and there she was. In my eagerness and relief I jumped up, almost knocking the table for six and hitting my head on one of ye olde oak beams. I saw Sally laugh and went forward to help her with her coat.

As soon as I saw the expression on Stan's face when he bumped his head, I knew that all was well.

'Hope you're not too hungry,' he said. The menu advertised a light lunch and that is exactly what it was. 'Luckily I remembered it was Kimberley's and took the precaution of having a sandwich in the mess before coming out.'

'I had an enormous breakfast – I'm all right.'

He gave the order and leaned back in his chair. He looked content, more like the old Stan than he had been for months. His eyes were clear, uniform immaculate and smile back in its usual place – it was difficult to associate him with the dishevelled creature of twenty-four hours earlier. I said a silent prayer of thanks.

'I have the rest of the day mapped out,' he announced. 'We have a leisurely lunch, dawdle over our coffee; go for a walk – river or park – until three, when the first house of the flicks starts – that is where you make the only decision of the day.' He handed me the local paper and I chose, *The Way Ahead*. 'Then drinks at the Mont Blanc – and I don't care if you are in uniform, the barman can say what he bloody well likes – and fish and chips at the Cellar.'

'And back to camp in time for supper – what a stuffing day!'

'You could do with it,' he looked at me critically. 'I've only just noticed how thin you've become. Aren't you well?'

I shrugged, remembering Mary. 'I'm all right.'

'Worry? Nightmares? Do you still have those nightmares, Sally?'

'Sometimes. Not so often now. Time is supposed to heal, isn't it? No, that all seems very far away now. As a matter of fact, Stan, I think it's you.'

'Me?'

'Loving you so and being so inadequate.'

'Inadequate? It is a word I don't think I quite understand.'

'Less than enough. I realised yesterday – with Mary's help – what a selfish little prig I've been.'

'Yesterday I behaved like a swine and I'm ashamed of myself – I ask your forgiveness, Sally. Besides everything else, it's a wonder you haven't caught pneumonia.'

'No need to ask forgiveness. You opened my eyes. But it was Mary who made me see what my petty morality is driving you to.'

Stan said nothing and we looked deep into each other's eyes for a long time, in fact until the waitress put the soup down in front of us. Then we drank the soup – well diluted Heinz tomato, I remember – in silence. It was not until we were half way through the dehydrated scrambled eggs on toast that either of us spoke. When Stan did, his voice was very soft.

'Sally, will you – one day – come away with me?'

Tenderness, pity, love, and desire all welled up in me at the same time. It was something I had never considered, but, after yesterday, I did not think I had any right to hesitate.

'Yes,' I said, 'one day, I will.'

He leaned across the table and took my hand and for a second I saw the tortured look in his eyes that had been there the day before. He shut them quickly and when he opened them again they were shining. 'Thank you, my love,' he said and kissed my palm.

'Two coffees did you say, sir? Black or white?' The voice could not have been more disapproving.

'She's jealous,' Stan remarked as the waitress moved away. 'Perhaps she can guess what I'm worth!'

'Give me a little time to think about this,' I asked. 'After next week we're reverting to our old watch system of working like beavers for four days and nights, then having seventy-two hours off – to sleep, of course!'

'You won't get much sleep – I promise you that!'

I hadn't blushed for ages, but there it was, that hot, red, tell-tale shadow, starting somewhere around the base of my neck and working up over my face and ears.

'Stan, really. I love you and I want you, but I'm not in the habit of jumping into bed with every Tom, Dick, and Harry – '

'My dear, I am not asking you to jump into bed – what a horrid expression that is – with Tom, Dick *or* Harry, but with me, Stanislaus Olshewski, and – '

'Two coffees, one black, one white – sir!'

'You're drunk and your lipstick's all over your face,' said Mary disapprovingly.

I grabbed my friend and whirled her round and round, then collapsed in a laughing heap on my bed.

'I'm not drunk – at least not on alc; I'm more in love than I've ever been before and I don't care a damn where my lipstick is! Oh Mary, I'm so happy – it's all right again.'

Having once come to the decision to stop being a bitch to Stan, I felt free and elated and I wanted her to understand, but, if I had hoped for her approval, I was to be sadly disappointed. As I told her about our wonderful day, how happy Stan had been and where we were going on my first seventy-two, a little frown settled itself firmly between her brows.

'I wish you wouldn't, Sal,' she said, when I had finished.

'But you were the one who said I'd been cruel to lead him on.'

'I know. But Sally,' she was thoughtful for a minute or two, wondering how best to convince me I suppose; she always treated me like a child, 'have you ever thought of what the consequences might be – becoming pregnant, or getting VD, or anything like that?'

I think my indignation was justified. 'You can't possibly imagine that Stan has VD,' I said hotly. 'He's so clean – in every way. And as far as becoming pregnant is concerned, he says it will be all right.'

'Even the most careful people slip up sometimes, you know.'

'But, Mary, he might be shot down again. Think how awful I would feel if, having promised him, he went up one night and didn't come back. It could happen any time – it could happen to-night.'

'Oh God, Sally, if we all slept with every pilot who looked at us with imploring eyes and said he might never come back, we'd never have any time to go on watch at all!'

I sighed and put my head in my hands. I was cross with my friend. All the happiness and elation of the day was being swept away and it was all the worse because, although I couldn't and wouldn't break with Stan, in my heart of hearts I knew she was right. 'I want him, too,' I said through my fingers.

'Sally, look at me.' I let her take my hands away from my eyes. 'Sally, you're only seventeen. This sort of thing can become a habit you know – Stan could be posted away without warning, or you could be, and then, having had Stan, you might have acquired the taste, so to speak, and want other men. It's the beginning of the end.' She paused long enough to let this sink in and then went on, 'Catherine Thomas on "B" watch was discharged last week – do you know why?'

'Preggers?'

She nodded. 'And Kathleen Lumley was as big as a house when she got married in February – reluctantly at that, she didn't *want* to marry him. However careful one is, it's too much of a risk.' But I wasn't going to be convinced. She gave an impatient sigh and I'm sure she wanted to shake me. 'Anyone can see that Stan is a passionate man – a damned attractive one too – and I'm sure he would be a wonderful lover, but it wouldn't be just once, would it?' I shrugged, but Mary's words were boomeranging – the thought of Stan loving me sent a pleasurable thrill down my spine and I smiled at her, *not* the reaction she wanted. That time she did shake me, quite hard. 'Sally, will you listen, and for Christ's sake stop looking so bloody smug.' I had never heard her swear before and was so surprised that I did begin to pay her a little more attention. 'You yourself tell the story of the waitress who was at training depot for the third time – we've all laughed at it and it's very funny, but when you really think about it, isn't it pretty sordid? Two kids sitting in an orphanage somewhere, who needn't have been born at all.' I had never looked at it that way before, but I suddenly saw that it was so. 'And then Betty – '

'Oh no, not another one!'

'Yes, another one. Betty – who has been in on all those squadron parties with you. Not long before you were posted here, she woke us all up in the early hours of one morning, screaming; said she had the curse so badly she couldn't stand the pain. There was blood everywhere. Diana went for the medical orderly and they carted her off to sick bay. When we cleaned up the floor the next morning, we found a blood-stained knitting-needle under her bed.'

If Mary's intention had been to turn the glamorous into the sordid, she had certainly succeeded. I suppose the expression on my face must have told her so, because she suddenly announced that she was off to have a bath and left me alone with my thoughts.

I finally came to a compromise with myself.

Just once, I decided, just once. The first seventy-two of our new watch system had come and gone and I had hardly seen Stan; it had been full moon and good weather and he was flying every night, so that put paid to any arrangements that time. But I would go away with him when our next time off coincided and after that – well, that would be a problem to face later; apply for a posting perhaps. Never me to underestimate my own will-power! Mary's tirade had certainly dampened the possibilities of any permanent liaison and if I viewed the forthcoming honeymoon, for want of a better word, with tingling thrills of anticipation, I was also a little frightened.

Stan had become more openly possessive and this scared me too. Some streak of Puritanism in me made me shrink from too affectionate gestures in public, and this would make me turn away from him, and sometimes I would feel some sense akin to an electric shock shoot through me and raise my eyes to find his, literally burning into me – it's a silly phrase, but it's true. At such moments I would melt and shiver alternately, wondering what I had let myself in for and how I could possibly wait. Stan's fringed eyes were always upon me, his mouth ready and his hands near – I was no longer sure of whom I was afraid, him or myself. It seemed that he knew what was going on inside me and sometimes he would smile at me and there was a hint of cruelty in it. Of all these things, I was afraid.

It was a colder than usual December, with biting winds and occasional flurries of snow. Thick sea fogs rolled in without warning, grounding aircraft on both sides of the Channel and bringing work, both on the airfield and in the ops room, to a virtual standstill.

At a time when I wanted, more than anything, long hours of hard work to occupy my mind, half the watches were being stood down and there was more time off than we had ever had before.

I too, although at 'Standby', had time on my hands. There was no night flying and, although as many aircrew as possible had been sent on leave, even for those of us remaining on the station, there was little work.

Without my job to think about, of course my attention was focused more and more on Sally. I took to paying frequent visits to the ops room when she was on duty, so that I could watch her. Sometimes she was on the R/T where, in this weather, she would have nothing to do but listen out for SOS calls, in case an aircraft from another sector should call for help. The R/T point was on the top deck, near the Polish controller, so we could sit and chat. But mostly I did not want to talk.

I liked it best when she was plotting, for then I could stand on the top deck and look down, unobserved, to where she worked in the well of the big square room. Not that there was much to watch when the weather was really non-op; most of the girls had bits of knitting or sewing lying around and one, who was embroidering a tablecloth, usually became the focus of attention. Sally would put down an occasional plot and then I could watch her every movement as she rose, swung round for the appropriate symbol and, if it were far enough away, reach for her eight foot rod, draw back to place the magnetic head on metal arrow, then swing forward and stretch and back. To be a really good plotter, she had told me, you had to work up a rhythm.

It was on one of those days, when the clouds had lifted sufficiently to allow a few aircraft to fly, that I wandered in to the ops room, partly because I was bored and partly because I had the afternoon off anyway and thought I might take Sally out to tea somewhere when she came off watch.

She was keeping tabs on half a dozen tracks; not enough to keep her really busy, but sufficient to keep her on her feet. Back and swing, turn and swing, back and stretch. The slow, easy rhythm and the graceful movements of her young body were exciting me to fever pitch when my compatriot spoke.

'Sexy, isn't it? The English controller thinks they should be kept in battledress on the day watches as well as at night, but I'm all for sweaters!'

His remark pulled me back to earth and, although I disliked anyone else watching Sally in the same way as I was watching her, it was better to laugh and chat. I watched him watching the WAAF for a few minutes and his thoughts were not difficult to read; he turned to me with a grin and sent a mock shiver through his frame.

'You can keep your little shrimp – for me, the big one on the right!'

In fact my little shrimp did not have a bad figure; not up to Betty Grable maybe and a bit on the thin side, but uniform suited her. All the girls wore air force blue pullovers of various shapes and designs, but none of them sloppy. Perhaps the Chinese opinion that a high collar and short skirt are more enticing than our Western *décolleté* had something; Sally had a long neck, still brown from the summer, and rising from the severe, starched, pale blue collar and black tie, in turn vee'ed by the pullover, it excited me as much or more than when it rose from a bathing-suit. I let my eyes travel along her arms and down her body, lazily, perhaps greedily, over the short, tight skirt and down the long legs to where the feet performed their ritual dance. Swing on the right heel, weight on the left, right foot back and swing across, weight on the right, and back on the left. She was like a caged lion; always the same place and always the same tread and the same turn. But I was the caged lion. I suddenly realised that I couldn't bear it another minute and would have to go, when I saw a girl approaching Sally, headset on, who stopped and plugged in beside her. She watched for a moment and then she began to swing and sway and Sally unplugged and dropped her headset to her shoulders. Taking her jacket from the back of her chair, she slipped down from the platform and started walking towards the door; I jumped up to intercept her.

We met on the stairs, where she had paused to light a cigarette. 'Hallo, Stan. I didn't see you in there.'

'I've been watching you for over two hours.'

'Good heavens, haven't you anything better to do?'

'I like watching you.' I had wanted to have an ordinary, friendly conversation with her, to laugh with her and ask her if the girls knew what effect they had on male watchers from above and if they put in a few extra movements of their own to tease. But you couldn't hold any sort of conversation with this cool, distant, withdrawn girl, who was avoiding my eyes. 'Sally, why do we have to wait? Now that you've promised, it's so much worse. I *can't* wait.'

I saw the warning flicker of fear pass across her eyes and it only made me the more desperate. I wanted to grab her, to shake her, and to hurt her. Instead my fingers went to the top button of my tunic and I twisted and turned until it came off in my hand.

Sally looked at the button but not at me. She threw her half-smoked cigarette into a sand bucket and held her hand out for the button.

'We can't talk here,' she said, 'I'm only off for a ten-minute break. Give me your tunic and I'll sew the button on – someone in the rest room is bound to have a needle and thread.'

I watched her walk down the corridor to the Other Ranks' Rest Room, then turned left into our own. It was empty except for one WAAF section officer, who was just in the act of filling the electric kettle when I went in.

I didn't feel like conversation, so I picked up a magazine and in a very few minutes there was a knock on the door. The section officer opened it and I heard Sally's voice say, 'Please ma'am, would you give this to Flight-Lieutenant Olshewski – I've been sewing on a button for him. And tell him I've left the needle in the top left-hand pocket.'

'All right, Gunn.'

She handed me the tunic with a smirk. 'Present from your girl friend, Stan.'

I wonder why I had thought that no one knew about Sally and I. Not that I cared; I suppose everyone knew everything about everyone else, particularly in a closed section like ops.

I found the note in the pocket; she had written: 'Must go back to camp first, but will meet you at main gate shortly after. S.'

Better if I didn't go back to the ops room; in my mind's eye I could already see her walking along the corridor, putting her headset on, plugging in and starting her ritual dance.

'Busy, Babs?' I asked my sole companion.

She shrugged. 'Not much to do in this weather, unless there's a sudden flap. Cuppa?'

'Thanks.'

I watched her reach for the cups; she was a plump, pretty little thing. Why couldn't I work up some feeling for her? Why couldn't I work up some feeling for anyone other than Sally? And what was so special about her anyway? Just one of the WAAF who was playing hard to get. Playing hard to get? Christ, that was the understatement of the century – she'd had me running round in circles for months. Little bitch; she had become an obsession, a disease.

I hurried back to camp and found the hut empty, everyone having tea. In a way I was glad to be on my own and yet I wished that Mary had been there. For the first time in my life I was scared stiff. Why didn't I have the courage just to say, 'No, Stan, I've changed my mind'? Why didn't I have the courage to call the whole thing off, be finished with him? The trouble was that Stan's magnetism for me had never waned; even when I was frightened of him, I was attracted. But there had been something about him that afternoon that I did not understand; he was so tense and I'd never known his hands to be fidgety before. I looked down at the Polish button in my hand. I had kept the button, moving one from a place that wouldn't show to the top and replacing it with an RAF one from my own tunic. You see? Even when I was scared of meeting him, and wishing that I had the guts to cry off, I still wanted to keep him.

Sensing that in his present mood he would probably want to walk – he never seemed to feel the cold – I flung on my thick issue vest and a pair of blue woollen bloomers – passion-killers. Passion-killers? I stopped to ponder. There was a point – if I were uncomfortable enough, it might knock any weak ideas out of my head and, if there was any nonsense with Stan, they would soon put him off too. Better make doubly sure; I put on two pairs. Then, as an afterthought, I stripped off my narrow suspender belt and hooked myself into my issue corset. It was as unglamorous a garment as I could have wished for and sagged in odd places where I had removed the bones – as we all did – to improve my cap; nevertheless, as chastity belts went, it should serve its purpose.

Complete at last, I waddled out of the hut and rolled towards the gate. The cold air hit me and I was thankful at least for the warmth afforded by my chaste protection – perhaps the air force had not been so unkind when they issued us with these hideous undergarments. It would soon be dark and I hurried to where I could see Stan, pacing backwards and forwards, on the track beyond the guardroom. Hands in pockets and greatcoat collar turned up, he looked as cold and as miserable as the landscape.

'Ah, there you are at last,' he said, taking my arm and clearly impatient, 'What do you want to do – have tea in town?'

'All right.'

Once settled in the bus, he looked at me critically, 'You know, Sally, you've put on weight – and yet I thought you looked so thin in the ops room this afternoon.'

'It's all the clothes I've got on,' I laughed, trying not to sound nervous. 'I'm not used to English winters yet.'

Tea was an almost formal meal, with conversation as strained and polite as though we had only just met, and I found myself looking at my plate, out of the window and at the other occupants of the café; anywhere except at Stan. And Stan – he looked at me; his eyes never left my face throughout the hour we were there.

It was dark when we came out and a light drizzle had set in. I jammed my cap on hard and turned up my coat collar.

'Cold?' he asked and slipped a warm hand round my neck. Involuntarily I shivered. 'Do you find my touch so repulsive?' he asked in a cold, hard voice.

'Repulsive? Oh, no. Of course not.'

He appeared not to have heard. We walked for a few yards and then, dragging me into an alleyway, he crushed his mouth down so hard on mine that I felt the warm blood as my lip split.

'Stan, you hurt me,' I complained and heard my own small voice, plaintive with nerves.

'You liked me well enough in the summer.' His voice was even harder than before. 'You wanted me then – my hands couldn't touch you enough – but now you shudder.'

'I don't, Stan. That's not so. You're imagining things.'

He pulled me after him, back into the main street, and strode towards the bus stop.

He bought two tickets to the village and we sat in silence the whole way out. I was feeling sick with fear. What had happened to turn him into this brutal stranger all of a sudden? I tried hard to remember the pleasant times we had spent together and all I could bring to mind was his face as he left the hangar after his aircraft had been blessed. I stole a sideways look at him, but it was difficult to make out his expression in the dim light of the bus; his mouth was set and his eyes were hard – impossible to guess what his thoughts might be.

When we entered the light and warmth of the pub, he appeared to notice the blood on my mouth for the first time.

'Better go and wash that off,' he said gruffly, and handed me a handkerchief.

I stayed in the 'Ladies' for some time, not wishing to return, but when I did, Stan turned from the bar, where he had been talking to a friend, and I saw that the hard look had gone.

When we were seated he looked at my swollen lip and took my hand. 'Forgive me, Sally,' he shook his head, 'I just don't know what gets into me at times. I love you so much and yet I want to hurt you.' My heart melted, as it always did, and I longed to pull his head down on to my breast and cradle it, as I had during that nightmare morning in the woods. 'I think I'm going mad.'

'Oh, Stan, please don't say that.'

'It's not just you,' he paused for a long time, gazing into the fire. 'I don't want to fly any more – I'm afraid to fly.' I sensed that this was not the time for briskness. I held his hand, kneading the fingers, until he spoke again. 'We haven't flown at all this week, but the weather's beginning to improve. In a few days there'll be night flying again and I don't want to go up.'

He tossed off his drink in a single gulp and rose to replenish it.

'Help me, Sally.' His eyes implored me and his hands, lying palm up in his lap, were the very emblems of supplication.

'How can I help you?'

'Stay with me, be with me. I don't want to be alone. You won't go back on your promise, will you? You will come away with me? Oh, Sally, do you understand? It isn't just the sexual act, it's having someone to hold, someone to love, someone to wake up with in the morning, not just anyone, but *someone* – in my case, you.'

'I promise, Stan. Next week. I've got three days – perhaps we could go to Torquay or somewhere.'

'Anywhere, my darling. Anywhere.'

'But not in the fields or alleyways or woods. Please not. Sometimes, when I'm with you, I can feel your impatience and I'm frightened.'

'Sally.' I saw his breath come fast and his nostrils dilate as he got up to get himself another drink.

'Don't drink too much,' I begged, as he sat down.

He gave a short laugh. 'What is this to me – reared on vodka?'

The warmth of the fire, the easy chit-chat going on around us and the alcohol soon relaxed us both and it was not long before we were talking about all the things we used to talk about. I quite forgot the time and jumped when the landlord gave the first warning.

'Oh gosh, I mustn't be too late,' I told him, 'I haven't got a late pass.'

'Plenty of time. Another drink?'

'No thanks.'

'Nonsense – do you good. You haven't got to work to-night.'

A happy smile lit his face when he returned with our refills. 'We'll find a pub like this next week, shall we, Sally? Then we can enjoy a pleasant evening before I take you up to bed and – in the words of the locals – do ee proper!'

'You've got it just right.' I couldn't help laughing. 'Been taking lessons from Mrs Jenkins? Stan – it *was* a lovely summer, wasn't it? The days on the river especially.'

He nodded. 'You were a little devil though – leading me up the garden path. In the nicest possible way, of course.'

'Oh, I didn't.'

'Of course you did – in your maidenly innocence. And now at last I am to be rewarded. I promised I'd never force you and I've kept my promise, haven't I?'

'Yes, you have.'

Leaning his elbow on the table, he traced the outline of my mouth with the back of a finger. 'I want those lips all over me, everywhere.' I lowered my mouth to kiss his palm. 'Sally, you're asking for trouble.'

'Stan?'

'Hm?'

'I have a confession to make. When I said I only looked fat because of all the clothes I was wearing, I was telling the truth. You were in such a frightening mood earlier on that I was scared of you – so scared that I put on my issue chastity belt *and* both pairs of passion-killers – thought that would dampen your ardour!'

Stan roared and slapped his hands on the table. He laughed until the tears ran down his cheeks and a couple of members of his squadron turned round from where they were standing at the bar to look at us.

'Oh, just wait until I tell them all about this,' he wheezed.

'Don't you dare, or I'll never speak to you again.'

'Oh, my God. No wonder you've been waddling around like a pregnant duck all evening. This calls for another drink.'

I jumped up as I saw the time. 'No, Stan. I must go.'

The cold air hit us and we staggered slightly. Stan sang at the top of his voice, in Polish luckily, and I shushed him the whole length of the village street.

It had been a far better evening than I had expected when we started out and I sighed with content as he put his arm round my shoulders, as he always used to, and we started on the mile long walk back to camp.

We stopped once or twice and kissed and then, as the road entered a tree lined hollow a few hundred yards from the camp, his mood suddenly changed again and, grabbing my arm, he flung me into the ditch and threw himself on top of me.

'Why the bloody hell should I wait any longer?' he shouted at the top of his voice.

'Stan, be quiet.' I struggled to free myself.

I don't care who hears me. You've led me a dance long enough. There are a few names for girls like you in English, but this one in Polish fits and it's a pity you can't understand.'

'Stan, you're drunk.'

'Drunk or sober, what's the difference?'

He thrust an iron-like arm up my skirt and ripped at the wool. The resistance infuriated him and he tugged with all his might, tearing my stockings and scratching my flesh.

'You little bitch,' he hissed, 'so you really did wear all those clothes.'

'Stan – '

'Shut up.' He took hold of my head in both hands and banged it against the hard earth, then holding my mouth shut with one hand, he used the other to pull and tear. After a few seconds he gave it up. 'Take them off,' he hissed in a menacing whisper, 'take them off, or I'll kill you.'

But I was too petrified to do anything but lie still and remain silent. I stared at him, a grotesque, hunched shape in the dark. I was too terrified to scream, although he had removed his hand from my mouth, too terrified to resist.

'So you won't help, eh?' He jammed his knee down cruelly on my chest and thrusting both hands inside my coat he started to tear again.

I felt my skirt rip and then, just at that moment, the blessed sound of footsteps.

He heard them too and, in the second that he paused, I regained my wits and brought my knee up with all my strength into his groin. He moaned and fell back and before he could recover I sank my teeth into his hand. He snatched it away with a screech of pain and I was up and away, running over the hill as though all the demons of hell were after me.

I ran until I reached the darker shadow of the guardroom and then, panting and sobbing, I stopped, half expecting to hear him behind me, but there was no sound.

I walked to the back of the hut and sat down, trying to pull myself together before I had to face the guard. My whole body was shivering and shaking and it took me a few minutes to calm down, then, in the glimmer of light from a faulty blackout, I took stock of myself. Thank goodness my greatcoat appeared to be unharmed; one stocking dropped round my ankle and the other was a bloody mess – I could always blame that on the barbed wire at the gate, not having a torch with me. Pulling a rubber band from my pocket, I fixed the torn stocking as best I could, rolled up my hair, straightened my coat and walked into the guardroom.

'Gunn?'

'Yes, Corporal.'

'There's a message for you from Station HQ – you're posted. Course starts at 1700 on the 31st; here's your railway warrant and you'll have to be clear of the station by noon to-morrow if you're going to make it. Better get a jildy on.'

'Where am I posted to?'

'OCTU.'

I reached the hut to find Mary already laying out my kit; it seemed that everyone else had known about my posting before I had myself.

'I thought I'd help, in case you were late – ' Mary stopped short and I suppose I must have been a sight. There was an awful silence as everyone stopped chatting, sewing, or whatever they had been doing, and turned to stare.

Slowly I removed my cap and greatcoat and hung them up, revealing my torn skirt and stocking. 'It's nothing,' I told them, 'I just had a fight with Stan.' And to Mary I added quietly, 'I think he's gone mad.'

Soon everyone returned to what they had been doing before I came in and I started to undress. Mary was not amused by the state of my uniform, but when I removed first one pair of torn, bloody bloomers and then another, followed by the corsets and my heavy woollen vest, she suddenly burst out laughing.

'Oh, Sally – did you really put on all those clothes to avoid rape?'

I nodded dumbly. I too had thought it funny in the pub, but it was no longer so.

'And were you raped?'

'No. But I should have been – I deserved it.' And I burst into tears.

I got up and sucked my hand. Damn her, I thought, it throbbed agonisingly and the pain in my groin was still sharp.

The footsteps, which I had not noticed coming slowly but steadily down the road, suddenly came to a halt and the torch, which had been casting a small pool of light in front of them swung in my direction.

'I'm sure I 'eard a cry from 'ere.' It was a girl's cockney voice. Normally I would have ducked under the beam, but I was so incensed with women in general, that I lunged towards it. 'Cor, Vera — a Pole!'

The sight of their retreating figures as they drew away from me did me good, and I stood up straight and bowed over the edge of the ditch. 'Mesdames,' I addressed them in my most gallant manner, 'I can assure you, you were never safer!'

The sound of their running steps however only served to remind me of Sally and a red hot haze of anger swept over me. I'd show her she wasn't the only fish in the sea and, pulling my greatcoat into true and jamming on my cap, I started off on the long walk back into town.

The wound in my hand bled freely and as the moon rose I could see the blood spattering to right and left as I walked. Approaching the first shops, I threw away my blood-soaked handkerchief and entered an all-night chemist.

'I've cut my hand.'

I thrust it across the counter at a balding, middle-aged man who was busily totting up a column of figures. He looked as though he were about to make some frivolous remark, so I scowled at him.

But he had the last word anyway. Having cleansed the wound, bound it with a pad and accepted payment, he waited until I had my other hand on the door before asking, 'Your anti-tetanus shots up to date?'

'Yes, I think so. Why?'

'Human bites are frequently the most poisonous of the lot.'

I scowled again and banged the door.

The night club half of the Mont Blanc was just opening up and I said a mental prayer of thanks that at least there was still one place open where I could get a drink. Several couples were already ensconced on cushioned seats around the wall, while another sleep-walked round the minute dance floor and three unattached women propped up the bar. Two were conversing in low tones over their drinks, and the third played liar dice with the barman.

She looked such an obvious tart that I immediately decided that she could not possibly be one. A tight, shiny, black satin dress outlined her ample bosom, hips, and thighs; and high, ankle-strap shoes encased her feet. The hair was dyed and brassy, and a strong wave of a cheap scent, currently popular among the WAAF waitresses in the mess, emanated from her. A large, red, artificial rose held my eyes in fascination as it bounced upon her breast.

'Something, sir?' the barman asked.

'A double Scotch.' I smiled at the woman.

'Thanks, dear,' she said, 'I'll have a gin and lime.'

Oh, the blessings of a hot bath. I scrubbed myself until my skin tingled and the bloody patches were reduced to the mere scratches that they actually were. My mouth too had been full of blood and, on finding that all my teeth were still firm, I realised that I must have given Stan the most almighty bite and that it was his blood which had spurted on my face and hair. Thank God the guard hadn't noticed it.

I dashed back through the cold night to my hut and climbed gratefully into pyjamas which Mary had warmed in front of the stove for me. What a friend was Mary; I gave her a grateful hug as I saw that, not only was all my kit now neatly laid out ready for inspection, but that it included brand new bloomers, stockings and corset and that one of my other friends was mending my skirt.

'Donated by Sutherland, Howard, and Rose,' Mary said. 'I know that corporal in Equipment quite well; she'll change your damaged things, I know – though how a pair of passion-killers could become like that through fair wear and tear will take a bit of explaining. Still, take these, it isn't as if anyone ever wears them and you can't afford not to have your things in order.'

'Thank you, everyone,' I said, 'you've all been marvellous. It's funny to think that when you come off watch to-morrow I shall be gone.'

'Seargeant Goodbody came in while you were in the bath and said the WAAF Admin officer will be inspecting the camp to-morrow and she'll come early to do your kit inspection before she starts.' As she talked, my practical friend was systematically removing the kit from my bed and helping me in. 'And that new ASO on the main camp, the assistant Adj, who is newly commissioned herself, says that if you can spare a few minutes when you're clearing to-morrow morning, she'll give you what tips on OCTU she can.'

'Everyone is so kind.'

'Taken by and large, people are.'

Everyone was in bed now bar Mary, who sat on the end of mine. 'I'm glad you're going,' she said. 'I think you'll make a good officer in time – it's a good thing to have gone through the ranks and experiences like to-night's will make you more tolerant of other people's weaknesses. I hope it will put that poor man out of his misery too.'

'Mary, this sudden fear of flying he's got – do you think it's anything to do with me?'

She shook her head. 'It can happen to any of them at any time and I should think he's pretty highly-strung,' she said, 'though no doubt frustration and those nine days in the drink played their part.'

'I'll miss you all,' I told her and I really meant it. 'I've had such good friends here. Do you think, if I'm RTU'd, I'll be sent back to the same station?'

'You won't be RTU'd, Sally,' she patted my knee, 'not unless you give away your real age that is, and anyway, if you are, I shan't be here.'

'Why not?'

'Because I'm pregnant.' She said it so calmly, but I almost fell out of bed with the shock.

'Mary! *You?*'

'I told you, didn't I, that even the most careful people slip up – not that I knew it then. Don't look so upset – it's Peter's and we were going to be married on our next leave anyway. Just jumped the gun, that's all. We hadn't planned it quite like this, but it's brought one thing to light which is a good thing.'

'What's that?'

'That Peter, who, as you know, is a Black Protestant, was only turning RC to please me and our families, who were bent on a large wedding in Dublin next leave – we couldn't be married in Ireland otherwise. As it is, we shall be married quietly here next week – with a perfect excuse too, because he's already standing by to go overseas – and he won't have to change after all.'

'Oh, Mary. I'm stunned. I do hope it will be all right.'

She leaned forward and kissed me in her most motherly fashion on the cheek. 'You know, Sally, I really believe that, generally, things do work out for the best.'

'Good luck, Mary.'

'And to you, Sally. God speed.'

I ran my tongue round my mouth and withdrew it in disgust. The proverbial birdcage had nothing on me that morning. My next experiment was to open my eyes a fraction, but the white hot, searing pain that that caused was just not on and after one more effort I kept them closed.

I remained supine for a long time, trying to think what had hit me. Beyond the fact that I had the great-grandparents of a hangover, my thoughts simply would not go. A further eye-opening venture assured me that I was in fact in my own room and, as various bits of uniform were strewn all over the floor, presumably I had undressed. But how the hell I had got in this state remained a mystery.

When I turned my head to the left my nostrils were assailed by a scent; there was something familiar about it but I could not place it. Ah yes, the one that came in with the soup and again with the meat and veg. Good God. I sat up abruptly and wished I hadn't. Don't tell me I'd had one of the waitresses up here – I must be crazy.

I lay down again and, after a few more experiments with my eyes, let them follow my nose until they reached a rather nasty looking handkerchief beside my pillow. I picked it up and looked at it and saw with distaste that it was indeed mine and that it was smeared all over with a good many bright orange smudges. Lipstick? What else? But Sally never used that shade. Sally. Oh, my God. At the same time as the name struck me, I noticed for the first time my bandaged hand, and then it all came back to me.

That time I sat up and stayed sitting and when I was able finally to focus my eyes on the dial of my watch, discovered to my horror that it was already two o'clock. She would be on watch.

I must have sat on the edge of the bed for a good twenty minutes or more, holding my head, and the sinking feeling in the pit of my stomach told me that something was very wrong. I pushed the handkerchief out of sight, but the scent had already recalled the picture of a room, sordid in the extreme, which we had reached after climbing several flights of stairs. I remembered it well because, drunk as I was, the sight of the unmade bed and none too clean sheets had put me off. And then I remembered the woman undressing and the unpleasant white bulges where she wasn't boned in. How old had she been? Twice Sally's age without a doubt.

But it was the thought of Sally herself that was really worrying me. What had I done to her? That part wasn't clear – I regarded my bandaged hand and beat my forehead, trying to remember, but it would not come. I must think. I *must* remember.

Crawling from my bed, I lurched across the room and rang the bell. It seemed an age before the batman appeared.

'Do you think you could get me a cup of coffee – very black?'

The batman grinned. He was a good bod, that Russell, and used to the sore heads of off-duty aircrew. 'Better than that, sir,' he said. 'Shan't be a tick.'

The rain outside matched my mood exactly and I lay back again, waiting for the coffee, and tried once more to think. The immediate problem was to decide whether I should or should not go over to the ops room. I wanted desperately to see her, but the thought of the hurt I would see in her eyes made me hesitate.

The door opened and Russell came in, bearing a tray on which reposed a glass of water with a tube of Alka Seltzer, a plate of cheese sandwiches – for which I was *not* grateful – and a large cup of coffee.

'Good man,' I said and drank off the effervescent brew.

Then I had a bright idea. 'Russell, would you do me a favour?'

'If I can, sir.'

'Well, you see, I have a girl friend in ops' – curse the man, did he have to grin so knowingly? – 'we had a bit of a tiff last night and I'm not too sure that she'll be so pleased to see me to-day. If I knew whereabouts she was working, I could go and have a look before I try and speak to her – not going to risk having my face slapped as she comes off watch, if I meet her by the main door.'

'What do you want me to do, sir?'

'If you would ring the guard post and ask them to ask one of the girls which point LACW Gunn is on.'

'Okay, sir. Do you want another cup of coffee?'

'Please.'

He took the empty cup and went out and, once I had pushed the cheese sandwiches well out of sight, I lay down again and closed my eyes, well pleased with my plan.

In no time at all Russell was back and handing me my second cup. 'She's not on watch, sir.'

'Not on watch? But she must be.'

A feeling of horror swept over me. Had I hurt her? Hurt her so badly that she wasn't fit to work? I remembered, with a wave of nausea, kneeling on her chest – she was so small and I was no light-weight, I might have broken her ribs. I had not hit her, I was sure of that, quite sure. Oh, God. I was stone cold sober now.

'Just a minute, Russell,' I called, as he was about to leave the room. 'Do you know anyone on the ops camp?'

'I know one of the NAAFI girls, sir.'

'Do you think you could ring her and ask if she could find out if LACW Gunn is on camp – her hut is number eight.'

'All right.' He was looking a bit queer; something must be up. Oh, God, I breathed, for about the fiftieth time.

By the time he returned I was washed, shaved, and fully dressed. 'Any luck?'

'Not there, sir. Not on camp.'

I was now genuinely alarmed. Perhaps she had not returned to camp. Could she have been upset enough to have committed suicide? Oh, God, surely not. She wasn't the type.

I pushed past Russell and made straight for the anteroom phone. I rang the ops camp guardroom; they would know if she were missing. I drummed my fingers impatiently against the bar. What was wrong with that bloody PBX? Wouldn't I ever get through?

'Hallo, yes?'

'LACW Gunn is no longer stationed here.'

'Has anything happened to her?'

'Not as far as I know,' the man sounded surprised. 'She's just no longer shown on the board here as being on strength.'

'Do you know where she's gone?'

'Sorry. Couldn't say.'

'I wonder if you would get Corporal O'Connell to ring me when she comes off watch; Flight Lieutenant – oh, on second thoughts, it doesn't matter.'

While I was holding the receiver a light had suddenly dawned. Of course she was there – just briefed everyone to say she wasn't, in case I rang. Well, if that's the way she wanted it . . . she'd come round, given time.

It never occurred to me for one moment that it might be true.

168

14. THE COURIER

Philip Morrison

'Should be a drop in a couple of days,' mused Gianna Maria, as she looked up at the moon, 'twenty-second was the date Tom had, before the radio broke down.'

'What do they drop?' I still felt very new at this game.

'Stores, arms and ammo if we've asked for them, bodies, food, sometimes money,' her teeth glinted in the moonlight, 'that's when the trouble starts – when there's money – you make sure the Scum don't know about it; too many have ideas of caching it away for the future – there'll be people digging under every marked tree after the war, mark my words!'

She smiled. It was a very attractive smile; she was a very attractive girl.

'There's a courier coming this time – we haven't had one for a few months.'

'How will we know when they're coming,' I asked, 'if the radio's not working?'

She shrugged. 'We won't, until they arrive. Just be prepared to expect them any day now – day after to-morrow is my guess.'

'But I thought drops were made during the dark of the moon.'

'Not here. It wouldn't be possible, not with the mountains so close at hand – they actually fly along the valleys sometimes – and anyway, there's no German opposition anywhere near here.'

I had just got to sleep a couple of nights later when I felt someone shaking me. It was one of the Scum.

'Come,' he said, and was off before I had time to ask him where and why. I was already dressed and it was not difficult to follow him in the moonlight, although he was some way ahead. By the time we reached the dropping zone, I could already hear the sound of an engine.

Gianna Maria was signalling with a torch from the edge of the clearing. The plane came in low and dropped a string of containers, circled and came in for a second run; not so low this time. A parachute flowered in the moonlight, opening like some gigantic lily in the night. The aircraft dipped its wings and was gone.

Slowly, slowly, down the great flower came. It was the first time I had watched a parachute descending at such close quarters. All faces were upturned towards it and, as it neared the ground, the Scum leaped forward as one man to release its burden.

'That's a small chap,' I remarked. Even in his bulky clothing he looked little over five feet tall.

'No chap,' answered Gianna Maria, who had been following the course of the 'chute intently, 'that'll be Wendy.'

'Wendy? A woman – here?'

'Well, I'm a woman, aren't I?'

Perhaps it was as well that she was gone before the involuntary exclamation, 'That's different,' had left my mouth. I would have to learn some tact.

In no time at all the parachute was folded and a smallish girl in air force blue battledress stood brushing herself down and talking nineteen to the dozen to the Scum.

By the time we reached the group, the girl had already pulled off her uniform. Underneath she had on a turtle necked sweater, bloomers and green woollen stockings. One of the men made some comment, inaudible to me, but I saw her turn quickly and, whatever she said, made the others laugh. This appeared to be another one who could hold her own with the Scum. She dived into her pack and pulled out a woollen skirt, with a wide waist and deep, zipped pockets – Italian made without a doubt. She was pulling this on as we arrived, but did not stop to greet us until she had removed the badges of rank – one higher than mine, I noticed with chagrin – from the epaulettes of her battledress blouse and zipped them inside one of the skirt pockets. Whether all this show of efficiency was for my benefit or not I didn't know, but, for no reason that I could think of, I was finding her precise act rather irritating.

Only when she had rolled up the discarded uniform and stowed it in her pack, did she straighten up, give her hair a shake and hold out a hand to Gianna Maria, who, I had just noticed, was looking slightly amused.

Gianna took the proffered hand, then the two girls kissed each other on both cheeks and turned to me.

'Wendy, this is Philip.'

'How do you do?' I asked formally, feeling slightly foolish under the circumstances, then, because I couldn't think of anything else to say, 'do you do this for a living?'

'Well, yes, don't you?'

I forgot that I was an officer in the Regular Army, that I had Sandhurst and Tobruk behind me, that I had been wounded, taken prisoner and escaped, that I had jumped trains and gone hungry. All I could think of was the fact that I had not volunteered for the parachute course when I had had the chance and, for the first time, was bitterly regretting it. I would so like to have had a few operational jumps to my credit, something to put this self-assured young woman in her place. She looked altogether too professional and, although I would never have admitted to jealousy, my pride was a little put out.

'I suppose so,' I answered as nonchalantly as I could. Then, to change the subject, although, if I had thought, I would have known better, asked, 'Wendy what?'

She frowned and replied, a little tartly, 'Hill. Flight Officer Hill. But we don't normally use surnames in this job, you know.'

God, I could have kicked myself – of course I had already discovered that. Rebuked, and unable to do anything but bow to her superior knowledge, I asked her, 'Have you any instructions for me, ma'am?'

If she noticed the irony in my voice, she chose to ignore it.

'Oh, yes. Oodles and oodles of bumph in here,' she patted her pack. 'You've been put officially in command of this group, so I'll hand them all over to you when we get back to the hut. But the most important thing is to contact Dougal as soon as possible.'

She sounded so good-natured that my feathers could not remain ruffled for long. And anyway, it appeared that Gianna Maria was still in command of us all. 'Sleep,' she stated in an authoritative tone, 'It is late and there will be much to do to-morrow.'

I awoke to the sound of girlish laughter and emerged to find them stirring a large pot full of a yellowish mixture over the fire.

'What's that?' I asked. It had a vaguely familiar and not altogether pleasant smell.

'Dehydrated egg,' Wendy told me, 'it was dropped in with the stores last night.'

In a flash I was back with my mother. Funny, I had thought more about her during the past week or two than I had for months. It did not seem so long ago that I had stood beside her as she too stood and stirred the tasteless egg over her stove, looking out over the Atlantic and mourning for the men who died in crossing it to bring Britain her rations.

Gianna Maria's strident voice raised me from my reverie.

'Wendy suggests you go over to Dougal with her, to-day. You haven't been there yet and I think it is a good idea.'

'And it will save me passing on the same verbal instructions twice,' Wendy added.

I had never been impressed with my mama's cooking – one of her main moans about the war was that she was having to learn to cook for the first time – but after tasting the concoction produced by these two, I came to the conclusion that she was not too bad!

'God help the man who marries either of you,' I remarked and was amused to notice that not one of the Scum even deigned to try it. They were wise.

Wendy disappeared behind the hut for a moment and returned carrying two olive green packs. They were square, canvas, and appeared to be heavy. I went forward to take them from her but she waved me away – they were independent all right, those girls.

'Our latest toys,' she dumped them at my feet. 'We'll christen them to-day – better bring a spanner with you.'

Immediate interest lit up the faces of the Scum, and soon Wendy was the centre of a circle of childishly gesticulating men. They had more clues than I had, obviously.

'What are they?' I asked.

'Portable bicycles. We'll assemble them nearer the road, though.' The Scum looked disappointed. 'You ready?' And without waiting for my reply, led the way down the hill.

It was not a difficult journey, but I was terribly impressed by my companion's sang-froid. Once the bicycles were assembled, we had hidden the packs and marked the place, we set off along the main road and you would have thought Wendy was on her way to the shops in some English village. She waved to the odd acquaintance working in the fields, flirted with a German soldier who was guarding a bridge which we had to cross and behaved with almost regal dignity to another who cheeked her. I was sweating, but she only laughed at my discomfiture, wretched girl.

I had been surprised when Gianna Maria had told me that the couriers were usually girls, but I soon began to see why. As Wendy herself remarked, whereas able-bodied young men would undoubtedly be stopped and questioned, able-bodied young women could usually get away with it.

By mid-afternoon, having hidden our bikes when it became easier to walk than ride, and we had been climbing pretty steadily for more than an hour, Wendy stopped and pointed to a farm track a few hundred yards ahead.

'Dougal has his HQ at the end of that track,' she told me. 'There are two houses; the original tenant farmer still lives in the first and Dougal's men help him farm the whole area. They keep quiet and are pretty well fed; Dougal has a cover and his men are kept busy. It's an ideal set-up.'

Ideal maybe, but hardly what I had expected. 'Sabotage and enemy harassment, I thought was the aim,' I remarked dryly.

But Wendy was not to be goaded. Instead she asked, 'Did you see how the Scum crowded round when I brought out those bikes this morning?'

'Yes, I saw them; but they were only interested – we all were.'

'Interested maybe,' she retorted, 'but they also get bored, bored stiff. That's the trouble with this job – for every day you spend being really active, you spend at least a dozen sitting on your bottom. Now Dougal's men are always at hand for any job, but they still work on the farm. Of course they moan and groan, just like BORs, but I'm sure they're happier in the long run, and they're very healthy.'

'Any bright ideas as to how our group might be kept occupied?'

172

I asked. I had the impression that she had deliberately initiated this conversation, so I might as well find out why. 'They do seem to chop quite a bit of firewood,' I added as an afterthought.

'Well, if it were my group,' I had been right and she lost no time in seizing the opportunity, 'I'd rebuild the hut before winter sets in – it'll start getting cold in a month, you know. You can't cook inside because of the smoke; in fact you can't do anything inside bar freeze and it gets damned cold up here.'

'And yet the charcoal-burners used to live there,' I remarked.

'Only two of them and not always through the whole winter. There are often twenty of us.'

The weather had been warm enough to spend most of our time outside and I had not thought about what it must be like in winter – which would be with us very soon. And as for being occupied, although I had not yet taken part in any operation, I had been so busy learning about the radio, cyphering, etcetera, from Tom, and the local countryside from Gianna Maria, and localising my Italian with the Scum, that I hadn't thought about that either. But this was to be my group and I remembered one of my father's favourite remarks, that the only creature more difficult to handle than a Jock in peacetime was a bored Jock in peacetime. Looked at objectively, there was not all that much basic difference between Jocks and the Scum and I would have to handle them.

I thought about what Wendy had said, but there was one thing that worried me. 'Surely it would be asking for trouble, erecting a new building? The Germans might notice it and at least the present one is authentic.'

She guffawed at that suggestion. 'The Germans? Do you really think that they would climb all that way, single file, through some of the most perfect ambush positions that exist, just in the faint hope that they might surprise a handful of partisans? Don't make me laugh!'

I wished she hadn't the knack of making me feel such a fool. I was grateful to her for advice and of course there was a lot that I could learn from her, but I did wish I had thought of improving conditions myself. If only she weren't so damping, so damned superior. A woman too, older than me, senior in age *and* rank – what an irksome thought! She had told me that she was not the only courier; well, I hoped the next one would be a brand new second lieutenant half my age! I was getting a bit tired of being the youngest and most junior person around.

While I had been thinking these thoughts, we had reached the wall surrounding the first farmhouse. A couple of mangy dogs rushed out to bark at us, scattering chickens on their way, and were soon followed by a plump woman, dressed in the inevitable peasant black, her broad face perspiring freely as though she had been bending over a hot stove, as indeed she had. She smiled at Wendy and wiped first her hands and then her face on her apron.

I blinked and wondered if I were dreaming. It was all so like my arrival at the Bianchi farm, when I had first escaped. It was rather like seeing a film for the second time.

'Ah, Paolina,' she called out, smiling as she came towards us, 'we haven't seen you for such a long time.'

Wendy did not appear surprised and took both the woman's hands in hers. 'I don't get away from college very often,' she said, and indicating me, 'this is my cousin, Filippo; he has been with the army in North Africa and is now on leave.'

The woman at once looked ill at ease and Wendy bent to whisper something in her ear.

'I'm sorry,' she said quietly, taking my hand, 'of course your secret is safe with us.'

I gave her what I hoped was a friendly smile and shook hands. Then I followed Wendy quickly up the hill.

'What the hell did you tell her?' I hissed, as soon as we were out of earshot, 'and what's all this Paolina business?'

'I told her that you had been accused of cowardice by the Germans and beaten up – Gianna Maria says you have a newish scar on your thigh which you could show if it came to it – and so you had deserted and are going to help Dougal fight the bastards.' She gave me a quick, sideways look, but I decided not to comment until she had finished. 'As for Paolina – you can't translate Wendy and they have no idea that I am not fully Italian and don't live in Rome. They think I am Dougal's fiancée and run errands for him – which is true – when I'm on vacation from the University of Turin. It's best that the old couple don't know the entire truth, then they can't split inadvertently.'

'But did you *have* to say I was a deserter?' I hadn't cared for that!

She laughed. 'Oh, male pride – forget it. You're in Italy now and, as their own son *is* a deserter and working for Dougal – though not in this group – it was the best way to ensure both her sympathy and her silence.'

Right again. Infuriating woman!

'And how about Dougal himself? Do they think he's Italian?' I asked.

'Oh, no. They know he's a British officer. They know that there are others too, but the less they know about each individual the better it is – for them and for us.'

It was a steepish climb to the second house and we both stopped talking until we reached a flat-topped stone and I was glad to follow Wendy's example and sit down.

'I'll tell you something,' she said, and it was advice I was to remember, 'if you ever have to have a cover, it's best to go for the half-truth – you're less liable to slip up than you would with a completely new personality. In my case, Pauline is my second name, my family did live in Rome before the war and I did, for a very short time, attend lectures at Turin University. Beautiful though the view is from here, shall we go on now?'

Dougal was out when we reached the house, but Wendy introduced me to his second-in-command, Johnny Fielding, a flying officer in the RAF, and left us.

Fielding had a similar history to mine – escaped from a working party, train-jumping, through Marissa's hands to Dougal and, like myself, elected to stay on with him.

'I have the technical know-how, you see,' he told me, 'messing around with detonators and explosives and machines comes easy. Dougal says he'll keep me on just as long as I don't open my mouth!' He pulled a long face. 'You know the set-up, I suppose? Pat Tindale has the most westerly group, you now have the easterly one, I'm pig in the middle and Dougal's over the lot.'

'I see you two are getting together. That's good.' We both turned at the sound of Dougal's voice. He shook hands with me. 'How's it going in the Near East? Pat Tindale should be here soon – I sent a message to him as soon as I heard that Wendy was on her way. Big job, Wendy?'

'Biggest yet.'

'Aye.' Fielding and I had both looked up when we heard the enthusiasm in her voice, but it took more than that to ruffle Dougal's habitual calm. 'We'll just wait for Pat if it's to be a three-group show,' he said.

He started filling a home made pipe and soon a foul stench was polluting the air.

'Hm.' It was the only sound in the room, except for the rather revolting sucking noises Dougal made with his pipe. 'Hm.'

He had listened to Wendy without comment and we sat in silence, watching his expression, while he waded through the written details and instructions. Then he got up and disappeared into the inner room.

No one said a word, but we all looked at each other. Wendy appeared deflated – it did not need a clairvoyant to see that Dougal was far from enthusiastic.

When he returned, he was carrying a rough clay model. From Wendy's description and the two oblique, aerial photographs which had been passed round, it was undoubtedly the target in question.

He turned the model round for everyone to see. 'This the one?' Wendy nodded. 'Aye. It's one of many targets that I've had up my sleeve – one of the ones I'd discarded.' He mumbled on, between sucks, about Cairo, backroom boys and being able to select one's own targets, while we all had a good look at his model dam.

'That's a job for the air force,' Johnny remarked, 'medium bombers or torpedoes. Surely they're not expecting *us* to breach that lot?'

Dougal shook his head. He was clearly impatient, but whether with Johnny or HQ, I didn't know. 'I've already made a pretty thorough recce of yon dam. Too many guards for my liking and the main camp, where the Germans are quartered, is too near – reinforcements could be there in a matter of minutes. We'd have to work in absolute silence and use every man we have. But we're not being asked to hole it, merely to put it out of action.' He sat silent for a few minutes, stroking his chin, sucking and staring broodily at the model, but the sarcasm of his last words still floated over the room. 'Only one thing we can do,' he said at last, 'sabotage the machinery; put the turbines out of action. Six men, with Johnny in charge, on the actual dam; the rest to cope with the guards and give cover. We haven't much time – next month at the very latest – may even have an early freeze this year, who knows?'

Whether Dougal liked the prospect or not, if he was going to do a job he did it properly and, in what seemed a miraculously short time to me, he had the detailed instructions for each group worked out. By the time we had finished, there was not much of the night left and, after a short rest, we broke up to return to our respective territories.

It had been arranged that I was to take seven men and meet Dougal, at the appointed time, below the dam.

We were all in high spirits when the day came, despite our earlier misgivings, as we set off in single file down the glade.

We left a sullen Wendy behind. She had wanted to take part, but Dougal had waved her protests aside impatiently. 'This is a tricky enough job at the best of times,' he had said, 'without having women around. You stay behind, miss; you have your own job to do.' She hadn't liked that, but I was glad he had been firm.

We had left enough time to be able to bivouac in the woods, as near the dam as we could without losing the shelter of the forest, the night before. We had a few hours of fitful sleep – I speak for myself; the Scum went out like lights – and then we were on our way again.

The dam nestled high in the mountains, not far from the Swiss border. Like a crucible of hydrochloric acid, it shone, pure, vivid, electric blue, against the grey-green countryside. As we came out on to the higher slopes and looked down, I halted for a moment, startled by the sudden patch of colour in an otherwise grim landscape. Bordered on three sides by the bare, grey, natural stone, it presented its flat, man-made face to the world. Along the rim were squat, square, concrete structures, with a few, heavily-barred, windows; it was in there that Johnny and his saboteurs would be working. Not far away was the powerhouse and below it, disappearing into the trees, the path that led to the German camp. It was our job to give cover and support the men of Dougal's group, who would be doing the actual sabotage.

We began the descent, keeping just within the trees, until we were on a level with the dam. I emerged cautiously from the woods, preparatory to taking up position, and stopped dead on seeing a white handkerchief waving at me from the middle distance.

'It is all right, Tenente,' Angelo whispered, 'he is one of us – I do not know his name, but I recognise him.'

Ordering the men to remain where they were, I went forward to meet the waving figure. It turned out to be Archie Albright, Pat Tindale's number two, whom I had not yet met.

'Dougal told me to intercept you,' he said, 'he has an alternative plan, in case the original doesn't succeed. He's behind there.' he jerked his head in the direction of the main buildings of the dam. 'Johnny's already inside.'

He was standing outside the secondary powerhouse which, from the purring sound that came from inside, must have housed much of the machinery for the dam. It occurred to me that, in different circumstances, I would have enjoyed going on a guided tour of the installations.

'What's your role in this?' he asked.

'Support. And yours?'

'Guards. We've already dealt with them.' He grinned and jerked his head again, this time in the direction of the building immediately behind him. 'We're just on the *qui vive* now, to deal with any unexpected visitors.'

I noticed then that several men were in the vicinity. One lolled in the doorway behind him, low voices told me that there were at least two more round the corner of the building and three had taken up positions behind boulders, covering the path to the camp.

It was nearly time to rendezvous. I said so to Archie and made my way to where I was to meet Dougal.

The sudden burst of fire split the fresh morning air.

I leaped forward and, as I did so, saw Johnny and a couple of partisans dash from the main powerhouse and make for the only available cover, a rocky outcrop some fifty yards away. They were halfway across the open expanse when a figure rose from behind a clump of bushes on their left. I saw his arm swing back and took aim, but, before I had fired, heard a report from the opposite direction and saw him fall. Not soon enough though. The grenade had found its mark. One of the men fell flat and I saw Johnny's body arch high in the air and descend in a motionless heap.

A fraction of a second later, the man beside me gave a gasp and fell. It seemed that there was a second occupant of the bushes. Dougal and I were upon him at the same moment, but not before one of the Scum had lunged ahead and made short work of him with an evil-looking knife.

I turned away and swallowed.

'Quick,' Dougal called, 'get your men down to Archie's post. Give them what help you can.'

Before we reached the powerhouse, we were met by a torn, bloody figure, who stopped us with a gesture at once both urgent and hopeless.

'It's no use,' he cried, 'the Tenente is dead. They are all dead. There are many more Germans. . . .'

'Get back,' Dougal had caught up with us, 'I'm damned if I'll fight it out; sacrifice the wounded. We've too few able-bodied men left. Johnny's alive, I'm getting him back. Take your wounded and scat.' I noticed then that he was clasping the upper part of his left arm with his right hand. Blood was gushing through his fingers. 'Only a flesh wound,' he said impatiently, 'nothing to worry about. But see if you can make a tourniquet, will you?' And, as I grabbed up a long, thin stone and my handkerchief, 'now get the hell out of here.'

Two of the Scum carried a third between them, while I supported another. Three men were gone; their bodies left unburied under the early sun.

Obeying Dougal's orders, we had put as much distance between us and the dam before stopping to rest. What a fiasco, what a disappointment – and for me, I felt, a dim beginning as commander of a group. No doubt in due course we would find out what went wrong, but, for the present, suffice to say that I had started out with seven men and was returning with only four, one of whom might never walk again. What casualties the other groups had suffered, I had no idea and, to be honest, at that moment, did not care.

I could hardly bear to face Gianna Maria and the eyes of those who had remained behind and, as they came forward to relieve us of our burdens, their silence was worse than any comment they could have made.

Dougal arrived at our group some three weeks later, the day before Wendy was due to be picked up and guided to the coast. It was only then that the story of the abortive operation was made known to us.

'Disobedience to orders invariably costs lives,' he said bitterly, 'and in this case, Archie's own as well. I gave orders that the guards were to be killed, but instead, Lieutenant Albright thought he knew better and only had them knocked out and bound – it would appear

178

not very efficiently at that. There were eight guards, two of whom must have crept up to those bushes, where Johnny nearly bought it; at least one must have dashed off to the camp for reinforcements and, I presume, the others were the ones who opened fire. All I can say is that it's lucky you scarpered – we couldn't move fast enough, carrying four wounded, and hid. They came pounding up the path at the double and, strewth, the amount of ammunition they wasted – you must have heard them?' I nodded. We had only been just inside the woods ourselves and did not stop. 'A good achievement, making them use all those rounds, and all for the price of sixteen men.'

But his bitterness was not against the young subaltern, whose disobedience and lack of attention to detail had been the cause of things going wrong, but with the chairborne staff on the other side of the Med, who had demanded that he do the job, against his will, in the first place. Archie should not have been on the op, it was only because Pat was sick that he was there at all, but Dougal was too big a person to cry against Fate. 'Destiny's one thing,' I heard him say on several occasions, 'but it's those chair-polishing bastards in Cairo that I'd like to fix!'

Dougal was edgy. He had asked permission to go himself, but it had been refused, so he had come over with the express purpose of instructing Wendy what she was to say when she reached the other side. Normally, I gathered, she would not be returning for some months, but Dougal – having had his own request to go turned down – had demanded that someone should argue on his behalf.

Johnny was a further aggravation. Although healthy enough, his wounds would not mend and the only doctor in the area who had been friendly towards the partisans, had gone south some weeks before. Pat, too, still had his 'bug', lying feverish and shivering for most of the time. Poor Dougal; he certainly had his troubles.

Wendy's escort arrived, dead on time. A small, weasly man, he looked to me as though he were more likely to murder her for her few possessions, than deliver her safely to the MTB, or whatever it was, that was going to pick her up. But Wendy herself, who had done the journey with him once before, seemed quite pleased to see him.

Dougal took her by the shoulders, just as she was ready to leave, and shook her to emphasise his point. 'Tell them one more balls-up and I resign!'

'Anyone else?' the guide asked, obviously keen to get away.

'Not this time,' he was told.

He sniffed the air and shrugged. 'Shan't be back this way again this winter. Shouldn't think you'll have any more drops before the spring either – cold weather's not far away.'

They were off. It had seemed only a matter of minutes between the guide's arrival and their departure. Once they were out of sight, Dougal brightened up.

'Well, I'm glad Wendy's away,' he said, 'Wish she could have taken the broken radio with her though. Must have been a vessel coming in anyway or they probably wouldn't have agreed to her going. I can trust yon lass and I couldn't have gone, not with Johnny and Pat ill and Archie gone and the groups depleted as they are.' He was silent for a while, his eyes still following the path where the two figures had so recently disappeared from view. There was a wistful look on his face. 'In some ways it was much easier in France,' he said at length, 'when someone had to be got out, more often than not a Lysander would come in – like great, roosting storks, I used to think they looked – and Bob's your uncle, they were off and away and broken radios and suchlike with them. It's a pity we're not within their range here. When Wendy comes in next time, I doubt if she'll go back again.'

It was very quiet after the sound of their footsteps had died away. We stood together at the edge of the clearing, saying nothing, but looking towards the mountains. The guide had been right when he sniffed the air; the higher slopes were already white and there was more snow in the offing. Dougal remarked that he had best be on his way.

'I know one thing,' he added, as we walked back to the hut, 'and that is that I should have insisted on Johnny going with that lass. I tried to persuade him, but he was adamant – afraid he'd not get back here, and I doubt if he would. There's loyalty for you.'

'What will you do with him?' I asked.

'Get him to Marissa, I think. She has a better chance of getting hold of drugs – but she'll have him for the whole winter, I'm afraid.'

As he spoke, I felt the first soft flakes dampen my hair.

'Can we do much in winter?'

'Very little up here. Even when we're not cut off, tracks in the snow are too much risk for the little we could achieve. Lie low and lick our wounds and prepare for next year. Wendy will ask them to drop in what they can while there's still time – weather permitting. You've got the best dropping-zone, so we may send a foraging party over in a week or two.'

A week later we did receive a drop. Among other things, it contained enough tinned food to see us through the worst of the winter, medical supplies and, best of all, a new radio. It was a comforting thought that we would not be entirely cut off during the months to come.

The following day I dispatched two of the Scum with supplies for Dougal and Pat and that was the last time that any of us emerged from the clearing until the following spring.

Stanislaus Olshewski

The turn of the year 1942-3 was a busy time. It was a hard winter, but with little cloud or rain, and the cold, clear, frost-bitten nights were ideal for our low-flying sorties. Only twice did we suffer from icing and then because we were flying at higher altitudes than usual and, as far as Zgoda and I were concerned, those two occasions were the only times we missed our target.

It was a good thing that I did have plenty to keep my mind occupied, because it did not take me long to find out that I missed Sally more than I would ever have believed possible.

I never visited the ops room again and it must have been more than a month before I discovered that she had in fact left the station. And then it was only by chance. I bumped into her friend, Mary O'Connell, one day in town – only she was Mary something else by then, having recently been married – and she told me.

That's a nice girl, that Mary. We were both at a loose end, so I took her to tea at Kimberley's – trying hard to forget the last time I had been there – and it wasn't long before I understood why Sally had been so fond of her. We talked about Sally – of course – and it seems that the liking was mutual; a spoilt, only child, Mary said of her, but with plenty of guts, and I echoed that. I don't know if she knew what had happened that last night, and of course I couldn't mention it, but, my God, I felt bad – I did tell her that I had something to apologise to Sally for and would write to her now that I knew where she was, but she was adamant that that would be a bad thing. 'I'm convinced it's better for both of you this way,' she told me. 'I gather she's finding that OCTU needs all her concentration and it's just what she needs – and you, you're hardly idle these days, are you?'

So there it was. I had spent a month of utter misery – worse by far than my previous frustrations – sure that Sally was so near and yet so far away, always hoping to catch a glimpse of her, to bump into her accidentally perhaps, and all the time I had been torturing myself for nothing. Perhaps Mary was right – she knew my address; had she wanted to, she could have written to me.

The strange thing was that, having been driven nearly crazy by Sally, my interest in women disappeared. I did make the effort to go to the Red Lion parties occasionally, but it was an effort and I never had the slightest desire to pick up anyone else; soon I stopped going altogether. I found myself drifting more and more towards my own compatriots, lending a more interested ear to Zgoda's complicated domestic affairs and spending more time with my own men. I took to wandering down to dispersal and giving a hand with the rearming and refuelling and helping the chaplain in his welfare work. Some of the men, like Zgoda, had their families with them and some had married local girls, but mostly they were, like me, on their own, with no idea what fates their families had suffered. Not that Zgoda didn't have his problems – not only he and his wife had got out of Poland, but both their mothers as well, and there they were, with both mothers-in-law with them, living in the one-room flat he had rented. Who could blame him if he sometimes sighed with relief when we were airborne and said the best part of flying was the lack of women's chatter! Poor Zgoda, he was a good scout.

As a matter of fact, if it hadn't been for Zgoda, I would not be alive to-day – not that he saved my life, but because of him I saved my own, if you get my meaning. I may have succeeded in fooling others that I was throwing myself, heart and soul, into my work to get over a broken love affair, but I wasn't fooling myself. I realised more and more that I had clung to Sally as someone, something tangible outside my work and that she had kept me sane. The plain fact was that I was becoming sick of killing, sick of flying, sick of the whole bloody war. Every time I started up I hoped that the engines would fail to respond – but they did, they always did.

I did my best to avoid sorties involving trains – a repetition of that Le Mans incident would have been the end for both of us – but, of course, there was no choice and I would go into briefing, telling myself that if I didn't kill the other man first he would kill me, and then go and carry out the slaughter as though I enjoyed it. We had successes too – none more zealous than I at killing my fellow men – and I was put up for the DFC after we had sorted out the docks at Le Havre one night; a DFM for Zgoda too. What the rest of the squadron did not know was that it had very nearly been curtains for Zgoda. We were hit on that raid and I found myself in a spinning dive right over the harbour – suddenly the sea was coming up to meet us and I thought, this is justice – I cheated the sea last time and now it is coming to claim me. And I was glad. *Glad*, do you understand? No more worries, no more fears, no more death. Down, down, down we went, and I was smiling to myself, and then suddenly a shrieking in my ears, a voice that told me I was killing Zgoda. I don't know to this day how I got out of that dive; all I do know is that it left me with two convictions: one, that I was not meant to die in the air and, the other, that if I went on flying I would be the end of Zgoda – Zgoda with a wife and an unborn child.

We went on many more raids; Cherbourg, Rouen, Brest, and then, one night – we were destined for Brest that night, I remember – I looked at Zgoda as we walked across the tarmac and thought, 'No. I will *not* fly to Brest to-night.' I looked around me and there, right in my path, was a chock, which some careless airman had left lying there. Under normal circumstances, I would have cursed and sworn and had the culprit found and reprimanded, but on this occasion it seemed providential.

What more natural than, talking as I was to Zgoda, and wearing clumsy flying boots, to trip. I might sprain my ankle, or better still break a leg, and in any event, I could feign sufficient pain to prevent our take-off.

I entered into an animated conversation, all the time keeping the chock in the corner of my eye and then, when I was less than a metre from it, an airman dashed from under the wing and hauled it out of my path.

'Sorry, sir,' the oaf was actually grinning, 'nearly tripped you up.'

My swearing certainly was not feigned.

What next? As I walked round the nose a sergeant slid to the ground; unusual for him to be near my aircraft; I thought with a ray of hope, 'Perhaps something's wrong.' But no.

'All ready and shipshape, sir. Engines are purring like cats.'

That was out.

The compass, that would be the thing. After all, they did go wrong. And who should know better than I? I had been travelling on a reciprocal bearing when that phoney station in the Channel Islands picked me up last May.

Feeling happier, I settled myself at the controls and set myself on course for Brest. But once over the coast I veered to port and held a course up Channel.

I could imagine the scene in the ops room – at least Sally was not there to witness my defeat – as the plots appeared and our destination was checked. It was not long before my headset crackled.

'Tuesday two-four, Tuesday two-four. This is Alligator. You are off course. Over.'

As if I didn't know! I don't know what Zgoda was thinking, but I did not reply.

They called me up a couple of times after that. I veered south – put them at their ease for a while – then I did a wide U-turn and headed north again.

It was not long before they were on the air again and that time, it having occurred to me that the radio would be checked on my return and found in working order, I thought it politic to respond.

'Receiving you strength half.' Let them chew on that.

Group Captain Tillworth, DSO and Bar, DFC and Bar, Station Commander, and one of 'The Few,' stood, gloved hands behind his back and cap still on, behind the controller and listened to the R/T exchange.

The duty controller was new, young, wingless, and inclined to flap. He also angered easily and was becoming increasingly vexed by Tuesday two-four. Why the hell, he thought, does the Old Man have to pay one of his rare visits to the ops room at a time like this? Standing up, he turned to greet his superior.

'Good evening, sir. Clear case of LMF I'm afraid – fellow's made up his mind he's not going to France to-night.'

Tillworth's eyes narrowed. 'Isn't that the chap who spent nine days in the drink last summer?'

'I wasn't here then, sir, but I believe it is.'

The Polish controller nodded confirmation.

'Bring him back.'

'But, sir, he's only been airborne eighteen minutes.'

'Bring him back, I said.'

'Very good.' Reluctantly he flicked the switch of the R/T over to 'Send'. 'Hallo, Tuesday two-four. This is Alligator. Are you receiving me? Over.'

And the same reply, 'Receiving you strength half.'

He turned to the Station Commander with a shrug, 'You see?'

'Give me the phone. Tuesday two-four, this is Pinhead. I repeat, Pinhead. Over.'

No reply.

'Listen, Tuesday two-four. This is Pinhead. Operation cancelled. I say again, operation cancelled. Return to base and pancake. Over.'

Still no reply, but he could imagine the sigh at the other end and the wary man on the alert, suspecting a trap. He sighed himself and turned to the Polish controller.

'How long has Olshewski been on ops?'

'Since the beginning, sir.'

Tillworth nodded. He himself had been grounded six months before. Every man has his breaking-point, but it comes to different people at different times and in different ways – or, if lucky, not at all. 'Give me a course,' he said to the British controller, who promptly handed him a slip of paper. 'We'll try again.'

'Hallo, Tuesday two-four. This is Pinhead for Alligator. Vector zero-eight-five and pancake. Over.'

'Hallo, Pinhead. Tuesday two-four. Receiving you loud and clear. Wilco. Out.'

Handing back the receiver with a thoughtful look, the Station Commander quietly left the room.

Providence really had stepped in. Imagine – all the ways and means I had been exploring to avoid that flight and then the op was aborted. What luck.

To my surprise, I was met on landing by the squadron MO.

'Hallo, Stan. The Old Man has decided it's time you had a rest from ops.' He flung an arm round my shoulders in a brotherly manner and we walked together to dispersal point.

The MO climbed into his jeep, but, before leaving, he handed me an envelope containing a couple of white tablets. 'Take these,' he ordered, 'and get a good night's sleep. Then to-morrow morning pack a bag and come and see me. Good night, old boy.'

'Good night.'

I looked at the tablets and wondered.

16. THE FILLING IN THE OMELETTE

Donald Thom

Honey heart, [I wrote] I've made it. The last batch were weeded out to-day – I've made the grade. One thing, I may have had a lot of flab when I left you in Quebec, but I'm the fittest man here now.

This must have been quite a spot in peacetime. The lights are not lit up now, of course, but I've been counting the bulbs from my bedroom window and I can see 1,044!

Less than a month to go now and I'll be all set for the real war. The battalion is housed in what I hear is a real swell camp, 'somewhere in England' and not too far from what they call 'the smoke'. Get me? There's another fellow here who'll be coming with me – he was over in thirty-nine and joined the British Army, but now he's transferring to our mob. Don't blame him, those British get the lousiest pay ever.

How's David? I miss you both, but being so busy has been a help. Did you get the job with the Red Cross? A Canadian Red Cross girl welcomed us in Glasgow when we finished the course – tried to imagine what you'd look like in that uniform, pretty fetching, I guess!

The bell has gone for the next lecture. So long, honey – my love as always.

Don.

I licked the flap and stuck up the envelope, putting it in my pocket to post at the first opportunity. Monica sure would be pleased. Second Lieutenant Thom – it'd look better on an envelope than Sergeant Thom.

Well, I started listening to that lecture with only one ear. My thoughts were with my wife, but they didn't stay there long. The subject was strategy and that guy was the best instructor ever. Kind of childish, I guess – like playing trains – but as soon as that enormous relief map came out, the tin soldiers entrenched and Battalion HQ planted, I could almost hear the toy tanks rumbling along. It was always the same. Guess I should have chosen the army as a career instead of Forestry.

The troops were all deployed. The instructor held a handful of parachutists. 'Now,' he asked, 'where do we drop these? Stevens?'

Hell. Why didn't he ask me? Stevens was a first-class clot.

When Stevens boobed – as I knew he would – the instructor turned to me. I sure was pleased with myself when I was held up as a strategist to the rest of the course. Thom the General – you won't be putting Second Lieutenant on the envelope for long, my girl!

I spent most of that night lying awake and wondering what real action would be like. I wasn't so darned cocksure of myself that I didn't realise that dropping parachutists over a papier maché landscape was a little different from the real thing. Judas Priest, I remember my dad telling me a thing or two about the first world war. I seemed to have spent the last God alone knows how many months going somewhere – always a bell or a bugle or a shout. Going to a lecture, going for grub, going on parade, going to PT, going for a bath. Physical fitness, assault, unarmed combat, how to build a field kitchen, how to dig a deep trench latrine, strategy, tactics, a legal question under the Army Act. Theory, theory, theory. I had good gradings here and good gradings from the course in Scotland. But what gradings would I get in the practical, the real job of war?

What an anti-climax I was in for. I passed out from OCTU okay and arrived at Battalion HQ, 'somewhere in England' – which turned out to be Surrey – full of enthusiasm and fighting fit and I certainly wasn't prepared for the lethargy that greeted me.

I reported to the Adj and he was hardly brimming over with *joie de vivre* either. 'We all expected action,' he remarked, 'and what do we get? A camp which at least we can't complain about; running water, hot and cold showers, film show twice a week. Grub's good – and morale couldn't be lower.'

It was true. Fights broke out at the least provocation; men grumbled, read their letters from home, went to the movies, went to the village hop, argued and fought. Why can't we be sent to the Middle East or Burma, they asked each other at first and then, slowly, came the insidious thought, why should we move anywhere – everything is too much effort.

I stood just a month of that depressing idleness and then volunteered for a course in mountain warfare in the Cairngorms.

It was a long course and a tough one, but used to the cold of Winnipeg, it was no real hardship for me and it was great to be doing something again – even if it was still a long way from the real war. But it didn't last. By the time spring came round again, there I was, back in beautiful Surrey, listening – or trying not to listen – to the same old groans. Nothing had moved, but nothing; even the camp looked a bit scruffy and the colonel began to go down in my estimation – not that there was much he could do; you can't really start your own private invasion without at least a little co-operation.

Well, I couldn't cope with it, that was for sure and I sat and twiddled my thumbs and waited for the next course to appear on orders. Just as I had given up hope of anything coming my way, up popped a parachutists' course. And the first person to volunteer? Well, need you ask – Thom of course. Actually that wasn't difficult – I was the only volunteer.

I can't say it was quite the sweet potato this time. Not that I didn't enjoy the course – and I didn't do too badly on it either – it was just wondering if it wasn't all a waste of time. By the time the second front did materialise, I would probably be a grandfather, and the thought of returning to unit again was enough to put anyone off. Before the end of the course I had tried to pull every possible string to get myself transferred to another outfit. But nothing doing – there never is when you really want it.

But – it's an ill wind, don't they say? I had only been back in camp a few days, philosophically putting all thoughts of action behind me, when a miracle happened – nothing to do with action, mind you, but a miracle just the same.

It happened this way. The phone rang in my office and a cryptic message was passed for me to be at a certain number in Grosvenor Square at five pm the following day. Well that wasn't difficult – I was free at five pm every day.

I made my way to the given address and rang the bell. Before the door opened a gruffish voice commanded me to turn round and face the street. I turned like a lamb, didn't even hesitate, and then a couple of hands were placed over my eyes and a familiar voice asked, 'Guess who?'

'Monica!'

Wow! Could I believe it? There she was, large as life and laughing with childish delight at the success of her trick.

'You never told me – '

'I wanted it to be a surprise.'

'Oh, honey, what a difference this is going to make to my life.'

Well, that was a couple of months ago and it made a difference all right. I just carried on with my routine job, but our whole humdrum life ceased to matter – come five o'clock, unless I was orderly officer, I was racing to catch the first bus. What matter how the day goes when you have a girl like Monica to meet at the end of it?

Soon after her arrival I put in for a couple of weeks leave and took her off to Scotland. As you've probably gathered by now, I'm a great ancestor worshipper – must have been a Chinee in my last life, I wouldn't doubt – and I guess I must have bored her to tears with tales of this ancestor at Culloden and that one at Glencoe. Another had helped hoist the standard at Loch Shiel and yet another had stolen sheep with Rob Roy. I could tell that she had had enough when she reminded me that my father had told her that, as far as he knew, none of them had ever moved out of Galloway – a bit below the belt that, I thought – but on the whole she was a patient listener. And whether she listened or not mattered little, because what can be more beautiful than Scotland in October?

She soon found out that the purple o' the heather was no myth. 'Oh, Don, just look at that – ' she would say and whether I was with Bonnie Prince Charlie or Rabbie Burns at that moment, I too had to stop to admire the splendour.

The gold of sunset on the turning bracken as we sat together in the fields on the east coast; the misty glens when we made our way further inland; all the breathtaking beauty of the North was ours, and at night we would laugh as we sank into the huge feather beds and love each other anew.

I was getting ready to go out and making my bawdiest lyric echo across the shower-room when I heard the batman call, 'Mr Thom.' I peeked from behind the curtain, because it always amused me to see his pursed lips tut-tutting at the waste of water, and waited for him to draw my attention to the poster which announced to all and sundry that even King George VI only had five inches of water in his bath. But I didn't stop, I was enjoying my shower, as I always did. He never let slip a chance to point out how wasteful we Canadians were – never mentioning the pounds of Canadian butter and soap he took home on each pass – so I decided he could wait a little longer.

'Mr Thom, sir,' he positively bellowed, and I decided that the time had come to acknowledge his presence. 'Adjutant wants you. And you're wasting water – sir!'

'Never stops raining in England anyway,' I informed him and picked up my towel.

It seemed an odd time for the Adj to send for me. I soon found out why.

'I understand that you are half Dutch, Thom.' The Adj made it sound like a question, but he was merely stating a fact.

'That's right, sir,' I told him, but a tiny alarm bell was sounding in my sub-conscious and I was already beginning to wonder where this was going to lead. 'My mother emigrated from Holland as a young girl.'

'And you speak Dutch.' It was a statement again.

'Yeah, I speak Dutch.' It was on my records anyway.

Perhaps I sounded as wary as I felt, because the old buzzard took off his reading-glasses and studied me for so long that eventually I asked him what he was thinking about.

'Your colouring. Sandy hair, freckles, blue eyes – just wondering if it was Scottish colouring or Dutch colouring. You could pass for either.'

'So?'

And then came the claptrap. I should have guessed.

'As you know, Thom, the dark times have to pass, we are bound to invade the mainland of Europe soon and there is much preparation to be done on the other side. Our Allies are doing a wonderful job in the field of resistance, but they could do much more with more men who know both sides of the coin, so to speak, men who are trained in the use of radio, men who can drop from the sky to their aid –'

Pompous old bastard, I was thinking. I knew all right where it was leading now and I knew equally well that I didn't want to go. Why the hell did I ever volunteer for all those courses? Crikey, Fate must be having a good laugh.

I let him waffle on until I couldn't stand it any longer, then I interrupted. 'Okay, sir, I've heard all that before. That's the egg part of the omelette – what's the filling?'

I must say he looked gratifyingly surprised.

'The filling, Thom, is that units have been asked to recommend suitable men urgently; men with suitable backgrounds. I have to signal back by return. I'm recommending you and the CO agrees that you're an obvious choice. You have to be a volunteer, of course.'

So that's it, I thought. Aloud I asked, 'And if I don't volunteer?'

'Good lord, man –' I guess he was about to read me a further lecture and point out that I had been nagging for action throughout the past year, but perhaps he does have a spark of humanity, or maybe he could read the pleading in my eyes. He carried on, but at least the pomposity had gone from his voice. 'Well, what is it? This is an honour, man; a chance to really do something, instead of hanging around here, putting up with the jeers of the locals and the "what's happened to my hero?" letters from home. You'll probably get a medal. Your wife would like that, wouldn't she? Good-looking young woman, your wife.'

'That's just it, sir. My wife's in London.'

'Your wife in *London*? What the blazes is she doing here?'

He was actually on his feet and prodding viciously at the blotter with a ruler. I'd never seen the old geezer so worked up before. I reckoned the time had come for a spot of comic relief, so I backed up with hands raised, in an attitude of mock surrender.

'Okay, okay. Keep your hair on, sir!' The Adj was British-trained and I guess he was thinking, these young officers, etcetera, etcetera. 'She came over under her own steam. She's working for the Canadian Red Cross.'

He slumped down in his chair then and put his head in his hands. There was dead silence for so long that I began to wonder if he'd had a stroke. I could hear vague parade ground commands in the distance and as I looked through the frosty window at the toy soldiers drilling, I thought a few thoughts. Drilling, manoeuvres, exercises, gradings, more drill. What did it all amount to? Monica was constantly talking of Red Cross parcels and POWs, of writing letters for men who had lost their sight or the use of their hands, of occupational therapy for victims of shell-shock. It was just that it was so wonderful having her near by – still, she wouldn't think much of me and, as the Adj said, I was an obvious choice.

'Okay,' I said, 'when do I go?'

You know, that fellow had aged. He'd never been young, but he looked real old all of a sudden.

'What did you do before the war?' he asked. I was taken completely by surprise.

'Why, I was at university still. Studying forestry. My wife was there too; she's a botanist. We married during our first year – quite a furore it caused – then, when war broke out in thirty-nine, I left to join up and she stayed on to graduate. I've been sitting around ever since – I should have joined the air force.'

He smiled tolerantly and addressed me by my Christian name, first time ever outside the mess. 'You know, Donald, I'm an old regular and I've been eating my heart out here. I was over in the first world war and my wife did the same thing – came over as a VAD. I never saw her, but somehow it was a comfort knowing that she was here, and we needed a bit of comfort in that war. She was killed in thirty-eight in a car accident; our only son too. I would have gone crazy if the war hadn't come the next year and I thought it was my call to join her – and here we all are, 1943 and the nearest to the front we've been is Surrey.' He paused for a moment, a sad little smile on his lips that made me feel a cur for all the uncharitable thoughts I had had about him, then he assumed his normal briskness. 'Training starts in about two weeks, I believe. We shall have to think of a plausible tale to tell your wife – can't tell her where you're going, you know.'

17. TO ELSIE, A SON

James Weatherby

'Elsie, Elsie. It's me, James.'

Very slowly Elsie turned her head and opened her eyes. I looked down at her small white face, the eyes shadowed with heavy, grey-blue rings and hair still damp with exhaustion and for the first time in our married life I felt that I really loved her.

She gave a tired smile, but her eyes were luminous. 'I've given you a son, Jimmy love.'

'Yes, darling, you have. What shall we call him?'

'You choose, love. I'm not much good at names.'

'I had thought of Christopher, but – it may sound silly – but I would really like to call him Toby.'

'Call him both then,' her voice was faint with weariness.

'Tobias Christopher, known as Toby – sounds a bit pompous, doesn't it?'

I wanted to tell her why I wanted to call our first son Toby. When I had first started on operational flying, as a very young and junior pilot officer, our skipper had been RC and St Tobias was his saint. The aircraft had the name St Toby painted on its side and it was the luckiest kite in the whole wing. Old Mac – he was a good deal older than any of us – had survived to be posted to Rhodesia as an instructor and I had inherited St Toby. I'd flown many different aircraft since then, but they were always named St Toby and, good God, out of all the squadron, look who were still alive. I wanted him to be lucky too.

It was whimsy and Elsie was a hundred per cent practical. Of a sudden I didn't want her to laugh at me. I was wondering how best to put it, when I noticed that her eyes were closed.

'Elsie,' I called softly. I had not been aware of the nurse standing by my side, until she spoke.

'You'd better leave her now. She's had a hard time and needs her sleep.' She took me by the elbow and guided me firmly towards the door.

Thank God, I sighed with relief; I had thought for a terrible moment that she was dead. I paused by the door to look back at my sleeping wife, happy for the first time, happy that I was married to her and that she was still alive.

'May I see the baby?' I asked the nurse.

He was red and wrinkled, with a mop of black hair. I wanted to pick him up, to cuddle him, and love him. I looked at the nurse, but she shook her head. I suppose babies are hideous, but to me he was beautiful, as beautiful as his mother had just become, and very precious.

It was a cold February day, but I left the hospital feeling that it was midsummer. The miracle of life had happened to me. I wanted to go back and have another look at them, but no, I mustn't be a tiresome father. I saw a church and wondered if I should go in and give thanks to God, but that would be hypocrisy – I went into a pub and had a drink instead!

When I reached the station I found that Elsie's mother had already arrived and was installed in our quarters. I had done my best to persuade old Nannie to come and look after the baby, but, after one excuse had followed another, I realised that nothing would make her come and gave it up as a bad job. I hadn't been keen on having Mrs Beckett, whom I had only met once, but I was flying most nights and we were too short-handed to put in for leave; there had to be someone in the house with Elsie and the babe for the first week or so, so there was really no choice.

Mrs Beckett was as big and blowzy as her daughter was small and neat. She's the one who looks like the barmaid, I thought, instead of an East Anglian farmer's wife. But the contrast didn't end there. It was when she spoke that I realised what strides Elsie had made.

Regrets were useless and once I had made my bargain with Elsie, I did my best to stick by it and so had she. I can't say that she was ever really at home with the other wives – a lot of them were no great shakes either – but she dressed well now, had gained poise and, provided one didn't have to listen for too long, spoke in a clear, usually accentless voice. But I couldn't say the same for mum.

It was a relief for me to have a bona fide excuse for getting out of the house each evening.

We had a fairly uneventful week, mainly bombing targets on the Dutch/German border and with remarkably little resistance, but the night before Elsie was due to return home, Q for Queenie, alias St Toby, got a pasting.

Thank God it was on the way home. We'd gone in practically without opposition and then whoof, everything opened up. Our port engine was knocked out at the first burst and after that it seemed that we were a sitting target.

'For Christ's sake keep your finger on the tit,' I yelled at the rear gunner, as I did my best to manoeuvre the heavy craft away from an ME 109 on our tail.

'Rear's gone, sir.' It was the voice of the other gunner, who was also the wireless op.

'Well, do your best, Tim. We've got to get away from this bastard.'

Tim chose that moment to get himself hit. Christ, I thought, who'd be a Wop AG – I always did think it the worst job of the lot.

'He's only wounded,' reported the navigator, 'but he's bleeding like a stuck pig.'

It could have been worse. The radio was undamaged and by the time we limped into base, several hours after the last of the rest of the squadron had landed, the ambulance was ready to whisk Tim off to hospital, and blood of the right group was waiting for him.

It was a relief when the ambulance doors were shut, but then we had to turn to the grisly job of removing what remained of the rear gunner.

It was midday before I arrived home. I had written to the rear gunner's wife and ascertained that our other casualty, Tim, was out of danger, and I was sticky and dirty, and my eyes felt as though salt had been rubbed into them with a red-hot poker. I meant to have a bath, but I was too tired even for that. I kicked off my boots and flung myself on my bed and must have fallen asleep on the instant.

Not for long though.

'You can't sleep in there.' I thought I was dreaming, but I wasn't. It was the authoritative voice of Mrs Beckett. 'Elsie'll be home soon and she's going to have this room – you'll have to sleep on a camp bed downstairs until I go home.'

I rolled over, looked at my mother-in-law, and closed my eyes again. 'Go away,' I said.

She shook my shoulder. 'Are you listening to me, young man?'

I took no notice, but the old cow went on shaking until I was properly awake, then she repeated what she'd said before. Even so, I didn't really take it in. I sat up and she must have seen the blood and dirt on my chest for the first time.

'How dare you come in here like that,' she shouted. 'Have you no feeling for your wife and child?'

I hadn't meant to be rude to her, but that blood belonged to a good man.

'Oh, shut up, and leave me alone, you silly old bitch,' I mumbled. 'Can't I have some peace in my own bed? I'm tired.'

'Don't you speak to me like that, young man,' she was off again, 'and it isn't your bed any longer. Elsie wants me to tell you that she has no intention of sharing a room with you again.'

What a time to hammer *that* nail in.

'So that's the way it is?'

'That's the way it is.'

'In which case, I shall go to the mess and you can go to hell!'

And with that I got up, flung a few clothes and my shaving kit into a grip and stamped out. I went to the room of a friend who was on leave and passed out cold for the next twelve hours.

When I woke up I went to see the Mess Secretary.

'I'm sorry, old boy,' he told me, 'Mess is absolutely full. No harm in your using Maddison's room while he's on leave but, even if we had the space, I couldn't give you a room yourself while your wife is occupying married quarters on the station.'

'Well, I shall send her off the station then.' I really meant it at that moment. 'She can go home with mother for all I care. I shall go and see her now.'

I've no doubt he was sceptical of my bravado, but was tactful enough not to say so.

It was difficult to recapture the feeling that I had felt towards Elsie while she was in hospital.

The two women must have been watching my progress from the window and by the time I opened the front door I found myself confronted by both of them. Mrs Beckett hands on hips and Elsie holding the baby in a 'don't you touch my child' attitude.

'Where are the rolling-pins?' I asked caustically, and walked straight past them and on up to my room.

'You can't go in there.' Elsie had overtaken me on the stairs and stood barring the door.

'Don't flatter yourself,' I said, 'I'm not going to rape you, I'm only – '

'It's a bit late for that.' That was Mother.

I turned and looked at those two stupid women, and wondered what I had done to deserve it.

Trying hard to suppress my growing irritation, I said to Mrs B, 'What I was about to say was that I am only fetching some clothes to take back to the mess. Fourteen days should be sufficient time to have Elsie on her feet again. That is as long as I can stay in the mess. After that I shall come home and I don't want to find you here. Oh, and another thing,' I had my hand on the door by that time, 'as far as Elsie and I and bedrooms are concerned, that's entirely our own affair and has nothing to do with you.'

I walked inside and slammed the door. And then I did a despicable thing; I listened.

'How dare he speak to you like that?'

'Ah, that's all right, Else girl.' Mrs Beckett was a good-natured woman at heart – I had already realised that – but she was ambitious. Ambitious for her daughter, that is, and she was coping with the situation in the only way she knew how. 'You wanted to marry an officer; you've done it and we're proud of you, girl, but up to now I've not been sure of how long it would last. But you've got the whip hand now. Refuse to sleep with him. You just be firm and he'll do anything to make you change your mind – and he won't divorce you, because you've got his son.'

'He won't divorce me anyway – it'd upset his precious career.'

194

Well, *that* couldn't have been more sarcastic. The couple of scheming bitches. 'But what about you, Mum?'

'I hadn't planned to stay longer anyway. Father's all on his own and we can't have them land-girls running the farm *and* Father, can we, love?'

Elsie gave a coarse laugh; it didn't take her long to revert. 'You know, Mum, sometimes I'd give a lot to be back in the old Dog and Duck. We had fun there.'

'Maybe you did, love, but you're Mrs Wing Commander Weatherby now and don't you forget it.'

The baby crying downstairs interrupted them and I peered through the keyhole to see if either woman was going to move.

Elsie began to unbutton her blouse. 'Better feed the little bugger I suppose,' she said. 'One thing's for sure though, I'm not going to have any more of them.'

Despite the conversation to which I had listened so shamelessly, Elsie was a good mother. She thawed and bloomed and the baby thrived and really things weren't so bad. Playing on a rug in front of the fire with Toby was as relaxing a way as any to spend my off-duty evenings and Elsie would bring in our supper on a tray and we would smile at each other. It's true what they say about mothers-in-law – we wouldn't have been smiling if that old bag were still in the house.

'You've done a good job, love,' I told Elsie one evening, mimicking her old speech – she could take that now, 'how about another couple?'

She stiffened immediately and I could have kicked myself. 'I'll never have another,' she snapped. 'You men don't know what it's like.'

'Oh, come on, Elsie. I know you had a bad time and anyway, I wasn't really serious. He'll do me fine.' I held my hand out to her but she didn't take it – not then nor at any other time.

Eight weeks, the doctor had said, and I had settled myself patiently in the spare room. But far more than eight weeks had gone by and she showed no signs of relenting. We had a humdinger of a row one evening; I can't remember what we said and anyway the exact exchange of words is not important, but it ended up with my leaving the room.

Quite deliberately, I made a good deal of noise opening the door of the hall cupboard and sliding the chain of my greatcoat against the hanger.

'Where are you going?' she asked querulously from the door of the sitting-room.

'I'm going over to the mess to have a drink.'

'You never take me anywhere for a drink.' A note of self-pity had crept into her voice.

'And you never take me into your bed,' I retorted, and slammed the front door.

As the months went by I found myself spending less and less time at home. Not that we had much off-duty time anyway; we were penetrating further and further into Germany and were airborne for longer and longer spells each week.

I spent most of my free time, at least in the evenings, in the mess, playing snooker or bridge, or just drinking. The raids went on, there were new faces in the squadron and in the mess, and at home Elsie cooked and looked after Toby and was cheerful enough during the day.

I only tried once more to resume my previous relations with her, but she was adamant.

'We could take precautions,' I suggested, 'if it's only having another child that you're afraid of.'

'I'm just not having anything more to do with *you*,' she said, and added nastily, 'You're not much cop in bed anyhow.'

'Well, you knew before you married me,' I retorted, but no man likes having his virility belittled and I was hurt all the same.

I didn't try again after that. She could stew in her own juice.

It came as something of a relief, in what was becoming an almost humdrum existence, when my posting came through.

'Your own station,' the CO told me. 'Congratulations, James. You must be one of our youngest Group Captains.'

'Group Captain? Already? I hadn't hoped – '

'Dead men's shoes, I'm afraid. But don't think about that – someone had to get them and I'm glad it's you.'

I had one pang though. 'I suppose that's good-bye to the squadron?'

'Afraid so. Most of your work will be administrative from now on, but there's nothing to stop you flying when you want to. You've still got to clock up sufficient hours each month to remain operational anyway – it'll sort itself out.'

'Thank you, sir.' I was overwhelmed.

Elsie would be pleased. Another feather for her prestige, I thought bitterly; Mum's ambitions for her little girl were being realised at quite a speed. It would be further from her home, but nearer London.

It was late when I got home that evening but there was still a light showing under her bedroom door, so I knocked.

'Who is it?' she called.

'Me, James.'

'Just a minute, love.'

Could I possibly be hearing all right? Scuffling and giggling and the sound of a window being opened? Surely not. I resisted the temptation to look through the keyhole that time – not that it would have done me any good, there was always a key in it these days, usually turned.

'All right, love, you can come in now.'

She was lying diagonally across the wide bed, the pillows side by side, leaning awkwardly on her elbow on one of them. The blackout curtain moved slightly in the current from the open window and from an ashtray on a table beside the bed, the smoke curled up from a newly-lighted cigarette.

'But you don't smoke, Elsie,' I remarked naively, and remembered afterwards hearing the incredulity in my own voice.

'No, I don't, do I, love?' There was no mistaking the note of triumph and her eyes shone with malice.

'You slut,' was all I could say, 'you filthy little slut.'

I know I fled from the room and I know I cried. Then I went out and walked all night, just as I had on that night so long ago.

'My dear old chap,' I had not seen Norman Parkes for over a year, but I could hear his voice as clearly as though he walked beside me, 'your Elsie is the most talented tart in the whole of East Anglia.' I had been a flight lieutenant then.

Why, I asked myself on and off throughout the night, why should I mind so much? It wasn't Elsie's blatant infidelity that had upset me so much, but the injustice of it all.

18. HOME IS NOT WHAT IT USED TO BE

Abdul Karim

My name is Abdul Karim bin Abdul Ghani and my home is in Trengganu, on the east coast of Malaya.

My teacher says that, although Trengganu is not a very important state and one of the most backward, we do have the three Ts: Tigers, Turtles, and, of course, Trengganu himself. Of course we have beautiful beaches – my village is called Pasir Perak, which means Silver Sands – and an iron mine, a little rice and a little rubber, but not much else.

But home is not what it used to be. It is the middle of 1943 now and the war that I thought was going to be such fun had turned out to be no fun at all.

We were in Kelantan – that's the state to the north of us, on the Siamese border – when the Japanese first invaded. It was on the same day as Pearl Harbour, my father says, only we didn't get so much publicity. It was exciting. Wah! Such a noise. Air raid sirens going, bombs dropping, guns from all the ships, and guns from the shore. It was really thrilling.

My father – I call him Pak – is a turtle fisherman and we were in Kelantan because so many families were fishing off the Trengganu coast that he thought we might do better there. We had a small hut, which Pak built himself, on a famous beach; translated, the name means the Beach of Passionate Love, but Pak says that unfortunately the turtles didn't understand that and he had to look for them in deep waters instead, which was not nearly so profitable.

At the sound of the first gun Mak – that is what I call my mother – became anxious and would not leave Pak alone until he agreed to come home. It was easy then. We put our few belongings into Pak's boat and stole down the coast in the middle of all the confusion.

I thought the whole war was going to be like that – much more fun than going to school – but it isn't. I'm hungry. I'm always hungry.

I am ten years old and I can climb a coconut tree faster than my father and I can swim nearly as well too. But when I go up a tree now I soon begin to feel all dizzy and sick and Inche Yacob, our headmaster, says it is because we do not have enough food inside us.

We're all hungry at school and I think that Inche Yacob is hungry too, because he doesn't get cross any more when we don't work. He just says we use up too much energy anyway and it's better that we rest. He never used to say things like that.

Almost everyone is bad-tempered these days. It's no use calling out, 'Mak, can I take a cake?' as I used to, because there aren't any cakes. And if I do steal some little titbit from the side of her cooking place, she slaps me and screams at me. It's awful.

And my father. He tried to sneak out to sea once or twice, but, although we've only seen the Japanese once in our kampong, three of Pak's friends have had their boats confiscated. He says it just isn't worth risking the loss of his boat. So he sits. Just sits. Sometimes, when the season is right and the night is dark enough, he goes off in search of turtles' eggs and that is the only time we have a proper meal.

It wasn't so bad at first, when we usually had fish to eat, but when the Japanese put a ban on fishing we had to rely on the eggs and the few vegetables Mak manages to grow in our sandy soil. I've always wanted brothers and sisters – it's not that I'm lonely being an only child, but Mak fusses over me so – but now Mak says it's a good thing we're such a small family, or we might not survive at all.

Ai-ee. I don't think this war is any fun at all.

We used to have lots of fun in Kelantan. My father was always happy and smiling in those days; my mother was always singing, and when I came home from school there were always wonderful smells coming from the kitchen. I could hardly wait to take my shoes off at the front door, the scent was so tantalising! And when I rushed in, there would be Mak, tendrils of hair falling over her hot face, and she would brush them back and laugh and ask me what sort of morning

I had had at school. I would go and wash and by the time I came back my father would be home and soon Mak would be laying out all the good things to eat and then we would all be silent while we ate.

Adohi! Those were wonderful days. Plenty to eat and my parents always laughing and chatting and singing. And sometimes, when there was a Malay film showing at the local cinema, my father would feel in his pockets. My mother loved the wayang and so did I and she would pretend to become cross with Pak for his teasing. Often he would feel in each pocket, looking glummer and glummer as he turned each one out in turn. Then he would shake his head and turn down the corners of his mouth and Mak would jump up and down and say, 'Oh, Ghani, you're teasing. You know you have some money.' And Pak would answer, 'No, not a cent. No wayang to-night I'm afraid.' Then he would sigh and presently his eyes would light up and he would say, 'Aha! I've just remembered,' and feel in yet another pocket, and out would come just the right money for the film show!

All this was show of course. My father was a great tease. But it's difficult to remember him like that now. He doesn't tease any more and he seldom laughs. And he's so thin – like one of the scarecrows we put in the padi fields to scare the birds away. Sometimes I see him look at my mother and sigh and she looks at him and sighs too.

We're all hungry, Mak says, but I don't think grown-ups feel as hungry as we do. How can they get hungry doing nothing? Looking doesn't require much food and that's all they ever do – look into space and sigh.

No one laughs these days. Even the mangosteen trees haven't had any fruit this year and my parents won't allow me to pick the rambutans – fancy rationing rambutans! – and the durians cost too much to buy. Adohi, I don't think this war is any fun after all.

19. A POSTING EAST

Stanislaus Olshewski

I don't really remember just how long I spent in hospital. It seemed ridiculous that I should be in hospital at all – it wasn't as though I were sick. But I must admit it was wonderful just to lie back and sleep and do as I was told. No decisions, no initiative needed; just 'Yes, Sister' and 'No, Sister'; wonderful. According to one of the nurses I had been ordered 'rest and sedation' and I suppose that is just about what I had. I know I slept an awful lot and there seemed to be eternal pills and injections.

And then the pills and injections became fewer and I became the victim of a pretty therapist. I made a basket, I learned to knit and I even went as far as doing a bit of embroidery. Imagine me, of all people, in the psycho ward, but that's where I was all right – no doubt about it.

My future worried me. I began to wonder how I would be received back in the squadron – would people like Zgoda still be happy to fly with me? When the time came, I made up my mind to request a transfer to one of the day fighter squadrons – I didn't care much what happened to me, but I was damned if I'd take anyone else with me, should I crack up again.

I tried talking about this to a couple of the MOs, but like so many doctors, they immediately withdrew into defensive shells and muttered such nonsensical phrases as, 'There there, old chap, everything will turn out all right' and 'You don't want to think about the future yet', and 'You mustn't worry' – always, 'You mustn't worry.'

I noticed that every time I questioned a doctor on this subject, the number of injections would be increased, so I gave it up and just waited. As they kept telling me, why worry, after all, there were plenty of important things to do, such as jigsaw puzzles and waste-paper baskets – I never have been able to look at a raffia waste-paper basket since then without wondering who made it, where and why.

But the time did come when I put my puzzles and baskets away and went before a medical board.

I puffed and blew, hopped on one foot and divided green wool from red. I listened to an orderly whispering 'biscuits' behind my head; I was X-rayed, measured, weighed, and had my teeth counted. And then I stood before the CMO.

'We've found you fit to fly,' he told me. 'Return to the hospital now; your posting will no doubt come through within the next few days.'

It did, too, the very next day. I was posted to Transport Command.

At first I was furious. Having only just succeeded in working myself up into the right frame of mind to return to my squadron and then, wham, not just out of the squadron, but right out of the Wing, out of Fighter Command.

But it wasn't so bad. It took me time to adjust, of course, but, once I accepted the fact that fighters had seen the last of me and I buckled down to my new job, I began to enjoy it. Being on night fighters could hardly have been called monotonous, because every sortie was different and we never knew what to expect once we were over the other side, but the area was basically the same. How many times, I wondered, had I crossed the Channel? I had the map of Normandy and Brittany etched in my brain for all time.

Once away from the training unit, I flew as second pilot for a spell from a base in southern England, mostly to Gib and Malta, and sometimes to Cairo. We were ferrying at that time; stores, bodies – both ordinary and VIP – and once we flew a whole team of doctors and nurses to join a hospital ship in West Africa. Then I was upgraded and took over my own kite and crew, based on Cairo.

It seemed that from that day on I never looked back. I had inherited a good crew, all British but for the Australian co-pilot, Harry Ames, and myself and, with the exception of us two, all noncommissioned. Harry and I became good friends and when we were off duty usually managed to pick up a couple of popsies and do the town.

A lot of people moaned about Cairo, but we didn't find it a bad base. When we weren't flying, there was always plenty to do and when we were, it was over completely new territory as far as I was concerned. South and East Africa, Belgian Congo, Aden, and Palestine. I don't think Harry ever noticed what he was flying over but I, who had always wanted to travel, was delighting in the newness, the difference.

The time came when the gay and fickle Harry fell head over heels in love with one of the WAAF cypher officers and then, tragedy, the girl was posted to Delhi. We put up with a month of his moping – and seldom have I come across a more lost and miserable man – when he burst in on me one evening, waving a sheet of paper and yelling that we were off to India.

I thought for an awful moment he was going to kiss me, he was so happy! Then he calmed down. In fact we were not off to India at all, but reinforcement crews were wanted and they had asked for volunteers.

I did not need much persuading. I liked Cairo well enough, but I had itchy feet; what the hell – India was a new place and I might as well stick to my cobber. So down went our names and up went the hopes of one juvenile Australian!

We were scheduled to fly a party of VIPs to Delhi and then take ourselves on to Calcutta, for points east, but before then the kite had to be overhauled and a few modifications carried out. That left us with time on our hands, so I volunteered to take another kite back to UK, which was going to be left there for some reason or another, and find my own way back.

Coincidentally, I returned to Cairo, as a passenger, in the aircraft carrying a general and his entourage who were to be my passengers to Delhi in a few days' time.

The general's wife had been there to see him off – how she wangled herself on to an RAF Station I'd like to know – and he had been followed to the aircraft by his ADC and PA, carrying everything but the kitchen sink. There were a couple of not so senior army bods also travelling and we had stood by, grinning, while this circus got itself stowed.

I had not realised at that time that these were my future load and the grin left my face when I discovered who the old codger was. Remembering how much clobber Harry and I had ourselves, I introduced myself to the general and told him, as politely as I could, that he would be proceeding from Cairo to Delhi in a smaller wagon than this – we were in a Liberator at the time – and I'd be grateful if he would keep his baggage down to the minimum.

Later I noticed both the ADC and the PA regarding me with some amusement and I went to sit with them. There was a hold-up before take-off, and we had to wait in the stationary aircraft for nearly twenty minutes. In that time I found out that the general had a most charming PA – Helen her name was – and I offered to show her, and of course the ADC, who wasn't a bad chap, round Cairo. They both groaned and grimaced and said, many thanks and that, in the unlikely possibility that they had any time off, they would take me up on my offer. Listening to them, I came to the conclusion that being nursemaid to a general was no picnic!

Yes, it was my general, and that poor pilot had every right to comment on his baggage.

What a performance it had been getting him, let alone ourselves, organised. But, of course, this was to be a much longer trip than our swan to Pretoria last year.

The long awaited Indian trip – as you will by now have gathered – had at last materialised, following one postponement after another. And, as is so often the way, when I had quite given up hope of it ever coming off, the general had suddenly announced that it was definite.

David had returned to his battalion since our last trip abroad and the general now had a new ADC, one Mark Elliot. He was quite reasonable and madly keen, but not up to David in any way. This meant, of course, that a lot of the ADC's work fell on me. Not that I minded really – I knew the old boy so well by this time – there were times when I could happily have strangled him, but he was immensely kind and could be immensely patient.

The red-letter day came when I typed out the final fair copy of our itinerary, and formidable it was too. I should say his itinerary though, because I was to be left behind in Delhi, while he went off to Burma, and then Mark would jolly well have to pull his weight for a change.

'I wonder what generals do when they retire,' I remarked as Mark and I walked towards the aircraft which was to take us to Cairo, clearly objects of mirth to our fellow passengers. And no wonder; we were like a couple of walking Christmas trees, festooned with cameras, water bottles, binoculars and files. On top of those, Mark carried the general's favourite walking-stick and I his golf umbrella. 'No ADCs or PAs to wait on them hand and foot.'

'I suppose their wives and children take over.'

'It must be terrible being married to a retired general. I shall marry someone with no rank at all and then he won't expect VIP treatment.'

It so happened that the general's staff did have some time off in Cairo and, as I had promised, Harry and I showed them the sights. All the sights that we were expected to show them that is – you know, the pyramids, Tutankhamen's mask and so on. I had been round all those hackneyed places countless times and yet some of them still didn't pall.

Harry thought that Helen was 'too cool by half' – I'm quoting his words – and did his best to upset her dignity by making the jeep back-fire just behind her camel – a trick I never could master, that, making a jeep backfire on purpose. But she was quite a girl. The camel went off at full gallop with Harry yelling in the jeep beside it, but she clung on and came back laughing.

'Well, good on you,' he shouted as he helped her down. She couldn't do anything wrong after that and we quite enjoyed our couple of days as professional guides.

The war didn't seem just around the corner.

The general had said, 'Helen, go and see the sights,' so I stood on the pavement of the wide, white street and tried to drink in all the hard sunlight, smells and noises.

I don't quite know how I had visualised India – elephants and maharajahs perhaps – all jewels and turbans and mysterious music. I thought everything would be slow and stately and courteous. I wasn't prepared for the hustle and bustle, so many black faces in such white clothes, so many uniforms and being jostled by such a crowd. It was all too much. Music was wailing out from the shop behind me, but it wasn't music and there was nothing mysterious about it – it sounded like a couple of cats fighting to me!

'Tonga, Miss-sahiba?'

I shook my head, but sucked in my breath at the sight of the miserable little pony, all ribs and mange.

'No, don't,' I cried as the driver raised his whip to flick the poor creature. He looked at me and grinned and I could have taken the whip to him with pleasure.

I felt a tug at my skirt and looked down into the eyes of a gnomelike child, scudding along on calloused pads that were actually knees, the lower part of the legs and feet bent up behind the shoulders. I tried not to shudder but, ugh, it was horrible – and I'd been told that mothers here crippled their children on purpose to beg. I was beginning to hate this place.

I looked at my watch. Time to go back to the hotel, have a bath and change. And then what?

Truth to tell, I was bored. Bored and lonely. The daytime was all right, because the general kept both Mark and me on the hop the whole time during office hours; meetings, conferences, arrangements to be made for this visit and that inspection. In fact the first week I had had so much work that I had had to take my portable typewriter up to my bedroom and carry on during the evenings. But now there wasn't enough to keep me busy overtime and, when I was off duty, I was at a bit of a loss.

In Pretoria I had been something of a novelty as an ATS officer and had been asked to most of the official functions, but here they were two a penny and with WAC(I)s as well. It would not have been so bad if I had been put in a mess, but being only on temporary duty and not posted, we were staying at a hotel, and a hotel can be a pretty lonely place.

I took as long as I could bathing and changing that evening, but there was still a good hour before dinner. I didn't like going into the lounge on my own – I always felt that it looked as though I were there to be picked up – but on the other hand I couldn't spend every evening in my bedroom.

Plucking up courage, I found myself a magazine and went downstairs. An air force trio, two men and a girl, sat up at the bar, but otherwise the lounge was empty. I had just settled myself at a table in the far corner and beckoned to the waiter, when one of the men turned round and I saw it was one of the pilots who had flown us from Cairo.

He recognised me at the same time and nudged his companion. They both turned round and waved, then the tall thin one, the Pole, came over and asked me to join them.

Seldom have I been so glad of company.

'Come and save me from being odd man out,' he said. 'These two have just got themselves engaged and are trying to persuade me to join them in a celebration dinner.'

'Say, that's a bonzer idea, Stan. Let's make it a foursome. You game, Helen?'

I was game all right, never more so. Harry introduced his fiancée, Una, and after a couple of drinks at the bar we went on to a very cosmopolitan restaurant, complete with a minute London night-club type of dance floor.

I don't think it was a particularly memorable evening, but I know I enjoyed myself.

Stan, the Pole, was both a good dancer and an easy conversationalist.

They were to be there for two days before returning to Calcutta and, when they asked me to join them again on the following evening, I eagerly accepted.

The next morning the general announced that all was now set for his tour of units in Burma and that he and Mark would be leaving the following Tuesday.

'Sorry you can't come too,' he said, 'I've told GHQ you'll help out there, but frankly, the secretaries are so thick on the ground they're falling over each other – if you want to take some time off and see what you can of India, I should. See if one of your RAF boy friends can't wangle the odd lift for you.'

It occurred to me, certainly not for the first time, that the old boy missed very little.

There were a few hectic days before his departure, then very little to do indeed. It wasn't quite as bad as before, because Una occasionally invited me over to her mess for the odd game of tennis and a meal and I made one or two casual friends, but she was on a watch system, so her off-duty hours seldom coincided with mine.

The general must have been gone about a week when Stan and Harry breezed in out of the blue again. They arrived during the lunch hour and Harry made straight for the phone.

'To tell Una to try and get someone to stand in for her this evening,' Stan told me, 'we're only here for the night. You'll come out with us, won't you?'

'Thanks, I'd love to. But I would have thought Una and Harry would want to be on their own.'

'They'll probably drift off later. If you'll put up with me, I'd like you to come.'

It was not until we had finished dinner and Una and Harry were dancing, that Stan mentioned – oh, so casually – 'By the way, I gave your boss a lift yesterday. He said to tell you that he expects to be away at least a month and will have a lot of work to catch up on when he returns, so it wouldn't be a bad idea if you took your leave while he's away.'

'He did, did he?' Making sure no doubt that he wouldn't be left for a fortnight when we got back to England. He knew I was long overdue leave and still moaned about the time he had to do with whoever was available when I was stuck in South Africa.

'My leave's been piling up as well and it's just been approved. A friend of mine has a flat in Bombay, which will be empty while he goes off to Karachi for a month, and he's offered it to me. You could come too.'

The invitation was so casual, so totally unexpected, that I blinked a couple of times, then thought it over – but only for a moment.

The lights were dim and a coloured spotlight shone on one of those many-faceted glass orbs, suspended from the centre of the ceiling. I watched it for a few minutes, not really thinking of anything, as the sequined light and shadow dappled the faces of the dancers. Una and Harry moved slowly round in a world of their own, silent and cheek to cheek.

Stan was lighting a cigarette with a nonchalant air. It occurred to me that his response would probably be exactly the same whether I said yes or no.

I said, 'Yes.'

'Good. That's fixed then. Let's dance.'

Well!

Our companions had not returned to the table at the end of the dance and we sat down again on our own.

'Whew!' Stan mopped mock sweat from his brow. 'One never knows how English girls will react. You see that – ' he held out his hand and there, stark white against the brown skin, was a fine, crescent-shaped scar. 'A dear, innocent, little seventeen-year-old WAAF was responsible for that. You don't bite, do you?'

'I haven't to date.'

'Good. Where the hell's Harry? Take off at first light; it's time we were in bed.' He scribbled his leave dates and address on the back of the menu and handed it to me. 'Think you'll have any difficulty?'

'I don't see why I should. At the moment I'm only relieving other people to go on leave. They can't object to me taking some myself.'

We walked back to the hotel and at my door Stan clicked his heels and kissed my hand. It was the first time that it had really struck me that he was a Continental.

'Oh, by the way,' he had already left me and stood with one foot on the stairs, 'it wasn't the general's idea that you should take your leave now – it was mine.'

We took off next morning, loaded to the gunwales with stores for Burma.

I hadn't flown over Burma yet, but it was my destination after leave. We had spent our time ferrying bodies and freight and the CO had suggested we take our leave while we were temporarily over strength – a rare occurrence. The whole crew were due and it suited me all right.

It was really Harry who had been offered the flat, for his honeymoon, but Una couldn't get any leave, so he would be staying in Delhi and the owner, an elderly civilian, had said that any of us were welcome to it. I'd only met him once, when Harry introduced me on the only occasion we had landed at Bombay, and thought it pretty decent of him, but my first reaction had been, what the hell would I do with a flat on my own? And then, quite on the spur of the moment, it occurred to me that here was this girl, on her own and with virtually nothing to do, and I couldn't get anything worse than a slapped face. Of course the leave hadn't been my idea – I only said that to give her something to think about – women are so much more amenable if they think you're in love with them! She had guessed correctly that her boss didn't want her deserting him when they got back to UK – those were almost his exact words. It seemed to suit everybody.

Delhi had been pleasantly cool compared with Calcutta. We landed in a whirl of hot dust and as I stepped down, I could feel the heat from the tarmac burning through the soles of my shoes. That was a place I never did learn to care for and I wasn't sorry when the CO told us that, by the time we returned from leave, we might well find ourselves moving further east.

Harry raised his eyebrows when I told him about my leave plans.

We were settled in the marquee, which served as a temporary mess, over two long and, I'm thankful to say, very cold, beers. He regarded me over the top of his, then deliberately blew off the froth.

'Well, you're pretty cool,' he remarked at length, 'you hardly know the girl.'

'I soon shall.'

He raised his tankard to me then. 'Trust a bloody Pole! Remind me to tell them in Canberra that that's one lot of immigrants we shall be able to do without after the war. Not the men at any rate – if your women as as hot as you lot, we could do with a few of them!'

I laughed. In fact Harry was always urging me to emigrate – he saw no future for Poland and nor did I. And, if I remembered correctly, he hadn't done so badly for himself before Una appeared on the scene. I told him so.

'What do you see in an English girl, Stan?'

'The same as you, I imagine!'

Travelling to Bombay by train was not half as bad as I had expected. We sat on cane chairs in a compartment to ourselves and Stan had brought a sort of zinc haybox thing, full of ice, with beer and ham sandwiches and fruit. He had also brought a pile of magazines, a couple of packs of cards and a small battery radio, which wouldn't work.

I wasn't going to miss Delhi one jot. And as I watched him flipping over the pages of a glossy, out-of-date journal, while he munched a sandwich and a rather tired lettuce leaf, I was glad that the general, or Stan, or whoever it was, had suggested that I take my leave.

The flat was large, airy and only just across the road from the sea. And that, large and airy, was just about how I felt the first morning I woke up and joined Stan on the balcony.

He was pouring out a cup of tea, very English, which he handed to me, then slowly peeled himself a banana.

And the way he peeled that banana, all the time looking at me with those deep, brown, bedroom eyes, I felt he was peeling me. And I didn't mind a bit!

I was not all that experienced with men but – well, hell, I wasn't a virgin either – and when Stan had invited me to spend my leave with him, I hadn't expected it to be a platonic fourteen days, with separate bedrooms. I knew what I was letting myself in for.

There had been no preliminaries, but I could have told you from the time of our first meeting that he would be pretty capable. But capable was not the word – he was expert.

I finished my tea and stretched luxuriously, holding out my arms to him.

'Do we have to go out to-day?'

'Greedy!'

Then he took me back to bed and we made love again before breakfast and, by the time I heard the servants rattling around in the kitchen and the smell of frying bacon, I was purring like a cat.

We were waited on by the same thin, very black Indian who had welcomed us the evening before. Immaculate, in high-collared white suit and silent, barefeet, he served us soundlessly and efficiently.

Iced papaya, bacon and eggs, mountains of toast and marmalade, and foamy hot coffee. Never had breakfast tasted so good.

'Breach Kandi,' I told the driver and the taxi took a murderous turn and swept along the sea front as though the Japs were right behind us.

'Where are we going?' Helen asked.

'Wait and see. It's a heavenly place for swimming. I think we can get lunch there too. Then this evening we'll go out and dance and have a super-duper dinner somewhere.'

That was more or less the pattern of our leave – we swam and sunbathed and lazed during the day, danced and dined in the evening and home to bed.

I doubt if we would have mentioned a single serious thing if it hadn't been for one morning when we woke up to hear the rain pelting down, and the sky a dull, angry grey.

The owner of the flat had wanted his servants to have a semiholiday while he was away and had asked if we would agree to them coming in at nine in the morning and leaving at the same time at night. In fact this suited me very well. I liked to potter in the kitchen and usually brought Helen her breakfast in bed. After the first day, I had told the servants that they need not come in until ten and could leave at six in the evening. We ate out most nights, but when we didn't, I cooked the dinner.

'No point in hurrying to get up,' I told Helen as I carried in her breakfast tray that particular day. 'It's a filthy morning.'

I went back to fetch my own tray and a pile of English newspapers I had found in the study. There must have been at least a couple of dozen, ranging over the past six months. Helen had a penchant for crosswords, so I sorted out the *Daily Telegraphs* and passed them over to her. Then I settled down with my coffee and a cigarette to read some rag or other.

I looked up as Helen made a small, startled sound and saw her turning the paper over to see the date; she was counting on her fingers.

'Anything wrong?'

She shook her head, but her face had gone dead white under the tan. 'Just thinking that promotion, a son, and a gong are fair achievements for one man in only nine months.'

She passed me the folded paper, indicating an entry in the Births column.

I read aloud, 'To Elsie, wife of Wing Commander J. M. Weatherby, DSO, DFC, RAF, a son, Toby.' It was a superfluous question of course, but I asked, 'Old boy friend?'

'Sort of – in so far that a married man, who has no intention of being unfaithful to his wife and tells you so, can be a boy friend. No. Just a shipboard casualty. Let's forget him.'

But she was depressed all day and the weather was no help. If it hadn't been for that wretched newspaper, we could still have been quite happy in the flat, but Helen was restless and moody and eventually we braved the deluge and went to a flick.

It was a terribly old film that we had both seen before, but at least we didn't have to try and converse with each other and when we came out the rain had lessened.

'Where shall we eat?' I asked.

'Home.'

I stepped into the road to hail a taxi, but Helen grabbed my arm and shook her head violently. It was becoming heavier again and her hair was already soaked.

'Let's walk,' she yelled through the downpour. 'We can't get any wetter.'

It was a long way back to the flat and I wasn't enjoying the water running down my neck and squelching in my shoes, but she laughed and was almost dancing along by the time we reached the sea front.

She made straight for the bathroom and I listened to her, singing above the splash of the running taps, as I went to mix us a couple of stiff drinks. God, what a day. I took a good swig from the whisky bottle before taking the two glasses into the bathroom. As if we hadn't had enough water for one day.

'Stan.' Helen had gulped her drink down in one swallow and was holding out the glass, her arm straight in an imperious gesture, for a refill.

When I came back from the living-room she was out of the bath and stood watching me, naked and only half dry.

'Do we have to eat?' She took the glasses from my hands and stood them on the edge of the bath, then pushed me back into the bedroom, wet as I still was.

She was like a lioness, an angry, hungry lioness. We loved and hated and hurt each other until we were both exhausted and then I no longer wanted to eat.

Stan was marvellous.

Seeing that entry in the 'hatches and matches' had turned a knife in a wound which I had thought healed. Well, it had been – now.

I got the breakfast the next morning and no newspapers!

I thought Stan looked a little wary when I carried in the tray and who could blame him? I'd been in a vile mood the whole of the day before and it was his leave as well as mine.

'Back to normal?' he inquired, and I kissed him demurely on the forehead for reply.

When I had exorcised James from my system, once and for all, I really was back to normal. We still had half our leave ahead of us – why spoil it? The answer to that is that we didn't and the anticlimax only came when I had to return to Delhi.

I only saw Stan once more during the rest of my stay in India. He and Harry had cadged a ride while they were off for a couple of days and he spent that night with me. After that I only had odd messages and heard from one of his friends that he was back on operational flying and would be unlikely to visit Delhi again. The same friend also gave me a message from the general, saying that he would be back in a few days' time, and I was not sorry.

Three days later I was back in the centre of the whirlwind. Mark looked exhausted, but the old boy was as boisterous as ever and I realised at once how much I had missed him. He dumped the most enormous pile of foolscap, covered with his worst scrawl, on my desk and I didn't wilt in the least.

'Just sort it out,' he told me, 'you can begin typing when we're back in the War Box.'

He was ranting to get home and, in less than a week, we were on our way.

I left my address with Una to give to Stan, but I never really expected to see him again.

I glanced out of the window and drew Harry's attention to a speck of red in the distance.

It was our first airdrop and it had been so long since I had had to pinpoint myself on a target, that it was a relief to realise that the hill ahead was indeed the one that should be there, with the DZ a few hundred yards to the left of it.

The aircraft had been cleared of seats and all other cumbersome paraphernalia and now, behind me in the new space, the dispatchers were getting ready for the drop. I reduced speed and height and went in carefully. Round the hill and there was the clearing. Newly-felled timber and cloth laid out to form the letter Z on the ground.

Four times we went in before all the cargo was away and, as we gained height after the final drop, a forest of arms rose to wave us on our way.

'Thank Christ we can go home for a shower and a beer,' Harry shouted. 'Who'd join the PBI?'

A strange feeling came over me during that first mission. A feeling that I'm not sure I can explain – a sort of lump in the throat feeling. One that I would keep to myself, but, because sometimes I need to bare my soul, I will say it – a sort of dedication to my fellow men. I can just hear Harry saying, 'Chee-rist!' and changing the subject with embarrassment.

For Harry I'm sure it was just another routine flight. He'd done his job, now he wanted to get back to base for a beer and to put through a long distance call to his girl friend. If he could read my thoughts, he would think I was due to go back to the nuthouse.

I did not want to kill any more and, for that reason, was glad to have left Fighter Command, but I didn't want to be out of the war either. Seeing those upturned faces around the perimeter of the DZ made me feel that my aim must be to help them. I wanted to help them. If we were to believe what we heard, service in Burma must have been hellish. Every drop had to be successful.

I sang to myself on the way back to base. I was glad to be back in harness again.

We had moved further east, as predicted, to a temporary airfield, where we lived under canvas. It was a different world from the other India I had seen and there were no doubts in my mind that it was the preferable of the two.

Flying over Burma was different too. Quite different from any other terrain I had been over. The jungle, green, dark and infinite, threaded by broad yellow rivers rushing through the land, to spill themselves in great fan-shaped swirls of sediment into the dark blue tropical sea. The occasional road, mine, and village, and splodges of brilliant creeper, red, yellow and orange, adorning the treetops, were the only other punctuation marks in an otherwise limitless expanse of blue-green hills and valleys. It was difficult to believe that battles could be in progress down there, hidden by the dense canopy of leaves. It looked a silent world, unmoving but for the rivers, and uninhabited.

But, my God, it was hot. Never had I known such humid heat. I downed my second beer while I waited for Harry to join me and wondered if there had been cans of beer in the stores we had dropped. God knew, those poor sods could do with the odd pint.

Harry was counting small change in the palm of his hand as he walked into the mess tent, a rueful look on his face.

'Lucky we've left the fleshpots, Snow,' he remarked. 'I'm dead broke. Lucky the phone calls go on my mess bill.'

He wasn't the only one. We had lived it up in Cairo and on our few jaunts to Delhi. And on leave we hadn't exactly stinted ourselves. 'What the hell,' I said, 'you can't take it with you.'

20. THE UNINVITED WEDDING GUESTS

Sharif Ahmat

I shall never forget the year 1943 and most especially June, because that was the month in which my father ran amok.

After more than a year of working for the Japanese, we had all discovered that there were both good and bad amongst them – as there are in all races. But one thing applied to all of them without fail – they were inconsistent. Completely unpredictable. One day you'd be beaten up for some minor offence and the next a similar misdemeanour would be condoned. We never knew where we stood with them.

There had been a terrible first few months under the new régime. Wholesale massacres for no reason whatsoever, road blocks everywhere, and restriction of all movement. Many is the time I have had to man a road block and many is the time I've seen both men and women hauled from their vehicles and beaten up and sometimes even shot, and for no worse crime than a wish or a need to travel. It was the Chinese who suffered worst, on the whole, and I frequently saw my own compatriots behaving in a manner most shaming. It is terrible what authority can do to some men – men who would never have had it in the ordinary way. Brought up as I was to be obedient to those in authority, but to kowtow to no man for base reasons, much of what I see these days goes against the grain. The only thing to do is to shut one's eyes.

Once they had made their point, our masters relaxed – at least they did in our particular station – and life wasn't so bad, provided you did not think about it too much, or delve into affairs that were not one's own. It was only when we were sent out to arrest one of our own people for sedition, or on similar charges, or to collect rice and taxes from the kampongs, that I was really ashamed of my uniform.

But, as I have said, they were unpredictable, and when my father sent word by a recruit who was posted to us from the Depot, to say that my sister's marriage had been arranged for the following month and I should apply for leave in order to be present, I had little hope of it being granted. But granted it was, without a single question being asked either.

My sister was only fourteen and would not normally have been married for another two or three years. But quite often the Japs would enter a village and demand all the unmarried girls, but would respect a married woman. Not always, of course, and many a young wife was raped, but in some instances it was a preventive and most of the girls were being married off as soon as they attained the age of puberty.

My sister's betrothed was our second cousin and they had been intended for each other since childhood, so there was no element of surprise in the match and, as far as Maznah was concerned, it was merely a case of accepting the inevitable sooner than expected.

There was not much of a feast by peacetime standards and most of the ceremonies had been curtailed. Nor were there many fine clothes about either. Normally the women of my family wear costly wedding garments of gold and silver threadwork, with an elaborate head-dress of gold filigree. These weigh so much that by the time the purification ceremonies have been carried out, the marriage contract signed, the nails hennaed, and the bride and groom are ready for the bersanding ceremony, where they sit, straight-faced and emotionless, on a gilded platform, the bride has to be carried to her seat.

Maznah wore a flowered silk baju kurong, a kind of long tunic over a skirt, or sarong, which the women of my kampong usually wear. She had been saving this one for a special occasion and with it she wore the ceremonial head-dress. The rest of the regalia had been hidden away and my mother refused to bring it out at any cost.

A few rice cakes and a quantity of paper flowers adorned the mats and a little watered-down coffee from our own few bushes was passed around. No buffalo had been slaughtered, nor a single chicken or goat, and no painted hard-boiled eggs, symbols of fertility, were handed to the departing guests.

Nevertheless, despite the austerity, a goodly throng was present, for we Malays love a wedding more than any other ceremony. This was to be a double event too – as there was little chance of a similar assembly twice in one year in these troubled times – and the feast, if one could call it such, was to mark not only my sister Maznah's wedding, but also my youngest brother's circumcision.

My young brother and sister were well surrounded by their kin and only my eldest brother, Sharif Hassan, was absent, who knows where?

My mother had been directing the cleaning and polishing since dawn the previous day and, by the time the tambourines heralded the arrival of the bridegroom, the whole house shone as though it were new.

We men of the family, all but young Hussein, who was lying in a back room, feeling as sorry for himself no doubt as I had done a few years before, stood in the entrance porch, waiting to receive the bridegroom's chair as it was lifted from the shoulders of his friends and relatives. He and my father were the only men present in full dress; rich, embroidered sarongs over silk bajus – Malay type shirts – and trousers, with gold studs at throat and silver-sheathed ceremonial kerises tucked into waistband folds.

Sharif Razali alighted from his chair and stood with solemn dignity while the tambourines were jangled, tapped, and shaken high above the bearers' heads. Everyone rose as he walked with stately grace to his throne, for a Malay bridegroom is King for the day and his bride the Queen. Then Maznah, face powdered white and with lowered eyes, was escorted by two elderly crones, one supporting each elbow, to her throne beside him and her sarong arranged in becoming folds about her ankles.

The rice was scattered at the feet of the bridal pair and the guests reclined to partake of the make-do kenduri.

Except for the austerity of the meal and the lack of regalia, it was such a normal celebration that soon the guests were chatting animatedly, the drabness of their clothes and lack of food forgotten.

How could anyone have guessed what an ill-fated day this was to be?

Quite suddenly, and with soundless approach, two Japanese soldiers stood in the doorway. Our house is large and square, standing on pillars some four feet from the ground and with a wide verandah running along two sides. There are two entrances, one by broad, ornamental steps to the apex of the triangle formed by the two verandahs, where most of the wedding guests were seated, and one by a wooden ladder to the kitchen, at the rear of the house. No Muslim would dream of entering a dwelling house without first removing his shoes and I saw my mother's eyes go first to the rubber-shod feet of the two squat and grinning, apelike barbarians.

Motioning my father to be still, she rose with slow dignity and spoke in clear, basic Malay to the soldiers.

'If you wish to join the guests at the celebration of my daughter's wedding, I bid you welcome. But please first remove your footwear.'

The soldier nearest her took a step forward and pushed my mother hard in the chest, so that she fell back and tripped over one of the seated guests.

At that my father sprang to his feet, but my elder brother and one of my uncles grabbed his arms and held him. The intake of breath by many throats was audible across the room and I know I held my own. It was one of those moments when everything stands still, like a film that breaks down and suddenly starts again.

The soldiers continued grinning and the silence was broken by one of them, who said, in slow, precise Malay, 'We have come for the bride.'

At that moment a scream, followed by laughter, was heard from the room behind. The bersanding dais, where Maznah and Razali still sat, fingers spread on knees, like stuffed dummies, was near the back of the main room where the more important guests were seated, and behind them the kitchen and bedrooms were full of womenfolk, near relatives and friends of the family.

Soon there were seven soldiers standing beside the dais, each with a woman held before him.

The two soldiers who had entered the house from the front now drew their pistols and, still grinning, began firing at the decorations. 'The bride,' they demanded. 'If the bride is not handed over by the time the last flower falls, our bullets will be for the men.'

Suddenly my father threw off the restraining hands and, drawing his keris, leaped across the room and plunged the blade straight into the chest of the soldier who had spoken. There was a moment's stunned silence, only broken by the next shot, aimed at my father by the dead man's companion. He missed, because my second brother, Ghazali, leaped on him from behind, knocking the pistol from his grasp.

It was as though that last shot had been the signal for a general uprising. Ghazali somersaulted over the soldier and, seizing the pistol from the floor, shot him at point blank range.

By this time the other soldiers had dropped the women and rushed through to the front room. The bersanding dais, with its silken canopy, had been overturned and everywhere chairs and tables, bottles and plates flew. Only Razali and my father carried kerises and none of the other men were armed, but broken bottles and china became weapons, together with chair legs, long pins pulled from the women's hair, and wire from the paper flowers.

A whistle from the back had brought more soldiers. Bullets flew, bottles stabbed, and the women screamed. And over all, my father, wild-eyed and screeching religious slogans, reddened his keris again and again.

My mother stood, silent and still, a small pinnacle of rocklike sanity, as a lighthouse stands in the midst of a storm-tossed sea. Tight-lipped, eyes flashing, not a move escaped her.

It was not long before the last Japanese fell, garrotted, stabbed, or shot. But my father was mad.

'Amok!' The clear, high, blood-chilling scream flew from my mother's lips as though her spirit went with it – as indeed it did. But she was too late.

Perhaps it was the pistol waving in Ghazali's hand that caught my father's eye and misled the inflamed, unhinged mind. All I know is that one minute Ghazali was standing beside my mother, panting, the pistol in his hand still, and the next my father was upon him, plunging the blade of his keris into him. Three times he stabbed before the awful act registered. And then, letting out a howl like a dying animal, he bounded away into the dusk, followed by my other brothers and myself and half the men of the kampong.

We never found him.

The jungle comes to within a couple of chains of our house and it was already dark under the trees. It is my belief that he took his own life. But to us Muslims, suicide is the most heinous of crimes, the murder of a soul bequeathed by God. And so we like to think he died of starvation, or became the victim of a predatory beast. Men who run amok seldom live and it was the will of Tuan Allah that he should die.

When we returned, my mother was sitting on the verandah, cross-legged and cradling Ghazali's head in her lap. Her eyes were opaque and she said not a word, but nodded when I told her that my father had gone.

The bodies of seventeen Japanese were laid out on the ground and a party of men were already digging a communal grave within the jungle limit.

On the verandah beside my mother, lay the bodies of Ghazali, a woman who had been killed by a stray shot and little Hussein.

I gasped when I saw him.

In the general mêlée no one had given a thought to the boy lying in the back room, in whose honour part of the celebration was being held. But someone had gone to work on him with a bayonet and he was not a pretty sight.

'Go,' my mother hissed. 'Go. And take Mahmood with you. You are now my eldest son.'

'But the burial – ' I could hear the sound of changkols from the jungle's edge; the enemy would soon be disposed of, then it would be the turn of our own kin.

'Do as I command.' She barely opened her mouth, but her words were clear-cut and decisive and her eyes hard as diamonds. 'Your uncles and I will take care of the rites. There will be reprisals; I do not wish to lose any more sons.'

Silently we obeyed my mother's command. We went before her to receive her blessing. She touched our foreheads and in our turn we touched the foreheads of Ghazali and Hussein. Then, taking coins from our pockets, Mahmood and I laid them on the eyelids of our dead brothers, as is our custom.

My other brother, Sardon, had already been dispatched to the home of one of our relatives by the time we had donned our uniforms and were ready to go. Only my new brother-in-law remained. He my mother could not command, for it was his duty to stay and protect his bride.

The floorboards were already being removed for the washing ceremony of my brothers' bodies and the corpses of the dead Japanese and their arms had already disappeared. My mother stood alone, her tiny figure as erect as ever, dry-eyed and tight-lipped. Whatever emotions were racking her mind were for herself alone. I knew that pride would never let her break down while there were watchers, but my heart went out to her, knowing what the night to come must be like

'*Selamat jalan*,' she intoned the age old farewell, 'safety in your going.'

'*Selamat tinggal*,' we returned, 'safety in your staying.'

And then, as though returning from leave in the normal way, we laced our boots and tramped down the road from Daun Chempaka, our beloved kampong, to the railway station, to wait for a train to take us to Kuala Lumpur.

Mahmood had still been a recruit when war broke out, but his training had been cut short and he was soon posted to one of the large police stations in the capital, Kuala Lumpur.

We had talked little in the train. For one thing the hard wooden seats had been crammed full and there were too many ears all around us and, for another, we were both deep in our own thoughts. He left me in KL. We shook hands and touched our hearts and as I watched him walk along the platform to the exit gate, I wondered if I should ever see him again.

Yesterday I had had four brothers, possibly five – we still liked to think that Hassan might be alive, although we had heard nothing of him since he fled south with the British some eighteen months before – to-day I had maybe three. What had started out as a day of celebration had ended in an evening of mourning. My mother had lost a husband and two sons; I had lost a father and two brothers.

Such were my thoughts as I watched Mahmood march towards the barrier. Soon he was through, bowing to the Japanese guards as he presented his leave pass and, shouldering his small case, he was lost to me among the crowd. I sighed with relief. Soon he would be back in barracks, safe at least until the investigations started, and I had warned him to be always on the *qui vive* from now on. It was bad enough losing two brothers – or so I thought, but in fact I was wrong.

I had been back at Batu Rimau, lying low and expecting to be called out at any time, for many months before the dreadful news trickled through.

There had been reprisals all right. It had taken the Japs less than twenty-four hours to discover the grave of their compatriots and to find out their fate. Every man has his price and torture is a persuasive means to cope with the most incorruptible – I know, I have seen and heard things during this past year which I do not wish to think about, only they had not touched me personally before.

By the time Mahmood and I had taken leave of each other in Kuala Lumpur and I was settling down on the platform to wait for a north-bound train, amongst many others, my new brother-in-law, three of my uncles and cousins and my younger brother, Sardon – who had never reached our relatives' house – had been put to death. My mother and younger sister were mercifully untouched – the latter because she was well hidden – and my elder sister and her husband had left in time. Seventeen Japanese had been killed; seventy-one Malays were executed by the Kempeitai, some of whom knew neither my family nor my kampong and had never heard of the wedding feast. But that is justice, Japanese style.

With the news came a message from my mother. 'Do not return while Malaya is Maraiee.' It was a command.

21. THE EMPEROR'S TALLEST SOLDIER

Jogindar Singh

Adams, Ainsworth, Beck, Graham, Gunn, Hall, Innes, MacIntosh, Parkinson, Wise.

I ticked the names off the list, but I didn't have to read them out, I knew them by heart.

I tried not to meet the eyes of the ten old men. I did not *know* what their ends would be, but I had seen many deaths since that of my father and I knew that when men entered the cells of the Kempeitai, they seldom emerged the same. It was Singapore; the middle of 1943.

It had not taken me long to grow fond of my charges and I never regretted my uncle's advice. It was very silent, very still, as we waited in the early morning for the Jap officer, who was to read out the formal charges against these criminals. None of them spoke and neither did I. Instead we waited, matching each other's calmness. Only they were older than I; older and more composed. I had thought my hands to be relaxed round my notebook until the chink of my steel bangle against a button made me conscious that I was tugging at my beard – a habit I have when I am not at ease. I brought my hand down at once, but not before I had caught the eye and the quiet smile of one of the men. I returned the smile, wishing I could give them some word of en-couragement. It seemed that we were in for a long wait and I cast my mind back to some of the happier events since I had become a prison warder.

That I became a warder purely to avenge my father and to further my own ends, I readily admit. At first, the welfare of my prisoners was merely a means to an end as far as I was concerned. I never dreamed that I would become so attached to so many of them.

My uncle, Arjan Singh, was right when he said there were innumerable ways of helping prisoners. Of course food is the obvious one, but I can't help much there, I'm afraid. Too scarce for all of us. The warders fare little better than the prisoners and the Japs themselves are hardly feasting.

Of course we Sikhs don't drink or smoke – at least we are not supposed to – but I don't mind helping people who are used to it and need the stuff. The old men in my block have a still and the things they ask me to collect you wouldn't believe – old fruit skins, bark, leaves. And sugar when I can get it – not that it's ever more than the odd bit of cane. The stuff that comes out is perfectly revolting – I've tasted it – but it makes them happy! They call it jungle juice and say that one of these days they'll get all the Japs drunk on it and then they'll escape. Not that there is anywhere to escape to, unless you're a pretty good swimmer, and even then it would be almost hopeless. The Japanese Co-Prosperity Sphere covers a lot of ground.

Once a fortnight I get a night off. Then I go to stay with my uncle and aunt. How they laugh when I tell them about the inmates of 'B' Block and the things they get up to. You'd never think so many men in their sixties could behave like primary school boys! Playing practical jokes on us is one thing, but playing them on the Japs – whew! they don't half ask for trouble. However, even some of those little sods have a sense of humour – not many, mind, but the odd one.

Sometimes Arjan Singh manages to get hold of some cigarettes. He doesn't smoke himself, but he saves them for me and I take them back to my charges. Not that they ever smoke a cigarette as such. The paper is unrolled carefully, put away, and the tobacco mixed with the various leaves and grasses they collect, then rolled back into a cylinder and wrapped in a leaf. I am sure they enjoy these homemade fags they call cigarettes far more than any they smoked before they were interned, or that they will smoke in the future – if any of them have a future, that is.

If the news is bad I tell them I haven't heard anything – and it has usually been bad of late – but if I hear any item that I think will cheer them up, I lay it on thick. It's pathetic to see how they grab at any straw, enlarge and embroider it, until a major victory has been achieved. Still, if it keeps them happy there is no harm done.

I've found another way of helping my charges too, and this one will make you laugh. To keep flies down, the commandant has ordered that each prisoner must catch ten flies before each meal. The flies are counted and thrown into a bin before the men are fed. It's not difficult to empty that bin into a piece of banana leaf and hand it back to the prisoners. And so the same flies come up time after time again; they're getting a little dried out by now though and I really must tell my lot that it's time they caught some fresh ones.

That of course is the lighter side. Seeing old men, white-haired and arthritic, their skin hanging in folds like that of ancient elephants, putting up with some of the humiliations that those little bastards can devise, is awful. Making them kneel for hours on end with a strip of sharp bamboo behind their knees is one of their favourite amusements and another is to make them kneel on grains of rice – it may not sound much, but you should see some of those old chaps after a few hours of one of these ordeals.

Several have died and one or two have gone blind and almost all of them have legs like gourds, but soft and puffy, from beri-beri.

Sometimes I can get hold of odd things from the Jews – eggs and a few jars of yeast extract and suchlike – but they demand payment, and payment in full. Signet rings, watches, gold cigarette-cases – all the little things the prisoners managed to secrete when first interned – all gone now and as often as not to people who *asked* to be interned for their own protection. It makes you spit.

A murmur from one of the old men pulled me back to the present. The Jap officer was approaching and we all bowed low and then an NCO gave each man a slap across the face, just to put them in the right frame of mind to listen to the charges.

The gist of the charge was incivility to the Emperor, but of course Japanese can never be written down, nor read out, in as few words as those. Everything has to be couched in the most flowery language once it's committed to paper – even the death sentence. Strange really, when you think how tersely they bark out the spoken word.

All ten listened without betraying the slightest emotion. I believe they are becoming too tired to be worried very much more.

Their crime had been their height, and their inability to bend with the agility of young men. On the Emperor's birthday, the tallest Japanese soldier to be stationed locally was paraded with the internees and the Great Sahib help those who were taller than the Emperor's tallest. Of course many were. Next they must be able to bow lower than the soldier. Few could. And from those incivil enough to bow only so low to the Emperor's chosen soldier, ten were chosen from each block to represent their bad-mannered compatriots and to learn manners on their behalf.

'A – W'. I looked with wonder at the returning figures, but I dared not smile, for the Jap NCO was watching me closely. Instead I administered a slap to each, saying gruffly that really the Japanese were too merciful to allow them back.

Next day Ainsworth died. And the following evening, Wise. They never spoke about what they had gone through in the Kempeitai special prison in the city. And I never asked. Better that all had died. Old men made older. Those who had had teeth when they left me a month before, no longer had them. They seemed deaf and blinked at the slightest glare.

The following week Beck sat down, the look of an animal who could go no further upon his face, and never got up again.

Seven old men remained; none taller than the Emperor's soldier now. And all able to bow lower, much lower. Seven old men who had been given a lesson in manners.

As I write this, my mind goes back to the smoking lamps in my mother's room and the faces of the elders as they intoned the last prayers above the sack that contained what had once been my father. I was only a boy then, nineteen; I am not twenty-one yet, but I am a man. I have reached my full height – a good deal taller than the Emperor's tallest soldier – and look down on many of my compatriots. If I were eating as we used to eat, I would be a big man. My beard will be full one day and I swear that, by the time I have reached my father's stature, I will have avenged his death.

22. A SUBSTITUTE FOR WENDY

Philip Morrison

'But it's not Wendy.'

It seemed that we were doomed to receive every female in uniform except the one I wanted.

The aircraft had arrived as expected, the containers had been dropped, the flower blossomed over the strip and Gianna Maria and I had been among the first to free the small figure from its cumbersome harness. And then it had pulled off its helmet – and it wasn't Wendy.

Remembering Dougal's exhortations, I certainly was not going to cause another scene – what could I do anyway? – but the whole clearing must have heard the disappointment in my voice.

I stood in the middle of the clearing in the warm July night watching the scene being enacted in the clear moonlight and felt myself engulfed in waves of frustration and annoyance.

The last drop had been in April and Wendy had not arrived then either. I looked back with shame to that spring night when four bodies had dropped from the sky; a wizened little Welsh captain – who should have taken over my group – a baby – young regimental eager beaver, a multi-lingual RAF type and a French girl. Trouble was we had all been expecting Wendy and I had wrought my infantile ire on the nearest thing in air force blue – no point in going into it again, but Dougal had had to separate us and had had some pretty tart things to say to me afterwards. Dougal himself had left the next day. He had picked up Johnny from Marissa, together with a demi-john of wine, and we had celebrated his recovery whilst waiting for the drop. I can recall the excitement well, and the ensuing disappointment.

It was when we had all calmed down and Dougal was wading through the mail that had been dropped that I received my consolation prize. He had opened a long buff envelope and extracted a pair of khaki drill epaulettes, the kind you slip over the button down ones on a KD shirt. Three pips were embroidered on each, but there was no regimental identification. He had looked none too pleased and muttered something about demotion, then he'd read the covering letter and tossed them over to me. I made some facetious remark, but Dougal was not amused. He scowled.

'Put them in your pocket and pipe down, I'm trying to concentrate.' He went on reading, but he cocked his head in the direction of the two new boys, both of whom now wore civilian clothes. 'You know the drill I suppose?' They nodded, but he was making sure. 'The theory is that if you're caught, you produce your badges of rank and demand to be treated as an officer. You are then supposed to be carted off to a PW camp, instead of languishing in some civvy gaol – in theory at any rate, we haven't put it into practice yet, so I can't tell you if it works.'

He finished the pile of bumph then told the newcomers their postings: the Welshman was to take over temporarily from Dougal while he was away – I raised my eyebrows at the time, but he frowned and mumbled something about Johnny not speaking Italian – the baby was a replacement for Archie Albright, killed on the dam last year, the girl and the RAF type were both for the border group; they'd both worked in Vichy France, they knew their way around. No one for me; I was both relieved and surprised, but furious too, because of course I should have had Wendy.

Next came details of what Dougal whimsically termed the 'spring offensive'; systematic destruction of bridges and viaducts, each group working separately. After he'd finished with my area, I wandered outside; I never could stand the fumes of his pipe for long.

I had been standing on a high rock – I remember it clearly – looking down the valley as it sprawled below us, cold and white in the moonlight, when I heard a footstep behind me. It was Dougal.

'Philip.' I had already turned. 'I haven't had a chance to say how pleased I am about your captaincy coming through. I must be honest with you though and tell you it was none of my doing – I merely recommended that you be put in charge of this group; it seems to have followed automatically. Anyway, I'm glad.'

'Thank you. And thank you too for asking me to stay in the first place.'

'How old are you, Philip?'

'Twenty-two.' I was surprised that he should ask; anyway, I thought he knew.

'You're doing very well for one so young. Oh yes, I've been looking about me this afternoon,' he waved a hand in the direction of the building, 'I can see you've not been idle during the winter months. The improvements are very noticeable and Gianna Maria tells me that you've worked wonders on training – even that cynic, Tom, has been singing your praises. That was my reason for altering Bill's posting – ' Bill was the Welshman. 'If your third pip had not come through so opportunely, I would have had to put him in charge of this group, which seemed a pity when you are doing so well – anyway, it's worked itself out, as things so often do, and I genuinely want a relief for Pat by the time I get back. But, pleased with you as I am, you must not let your emotions run away with you.'

'Emotions, sir?' There were times when I still called Dougal 'sir'.

'You shouldn't have caused that childish scene to-night. We all realised that you were disappointed when Wendy didn't show up – for that matter we all were – but in your case it couldn't have been clearer and, for that reason, I'm glad she didn't. We can't afford to have woman-trouble in this job. You need your energy for other things.' I started to protest, conscious of the fact that my face was growing hot and thankful that the colour would not show, but Dougal merely laughed. 'You see, I know more about your emotions than you do yourself! And now, if I can find somewhere to doss down for a few hours, I'll get some sleep. Good night.'

Dougal left us the next morning to be picked up somewhere along the coast and we have had no word of him since.

I suppose it was stupid and petty of me to be so frustrated, but Wendy had sown a seed when she suggested improving our living quarters and I had been looking forward to her seeing the results – wanted her praise, if I were to be really honest.

I was in fact pretty pleased with the quarters myself. Tom was now housed, with the radio, in a separate room at one end of the main building, then a room for me – and two others if necessary – a main room where we could all sit, eat, and cook, with one door leading straight out from it and another from the back into a hidden tunnel, and a room at the other end for the Scum. By digging into the rock at the back, we had gained extra space without altering the face of the building. One of the Scum, it transpired, had been a carpenter, and after Gianna Maria had made a trip to the villa to obtain tools, he was set to organise the making of tiered bunks in each room and a table for the radio. The other old building had been turned into a store, with a room for Gianna Maria and Wendy, when she was with us. This too had been extended into the hillside, giving a false back to the store, where our most precious and seldom-used possessions could be kept. It was also a hiding-place for the girls. Wendy would no doubt scoff at my security precautions, but I felt that even she must be a little impressed with the other improvements.

All this was going through my head as the small figure disengaged itself from the last of its trappings. I pulled myself back to the present. 'No, I'm afraid I'm not Wendy. I've taken her place.' When she was quite free, she stood up straight and held out her hand. 'I'm Gunn, Section Officer Sally Gunn – and you must be Captain Morrison.'

'We don't normally use surnames in this job,' I replied tartly. The girl sounded so damned friendly; it was like kicking a puppy and I should have been ashamed of myself. I saw Gianna Maria raise her eyebrows and tried to pull myself together. 'This is Gianna Maria,' I introduced, 'Queen of admin and organisation and general factotum. I'm Philip.'

'Sale?' asked one of the men, 'Salt? Well, that is a precious enough commodity. You are very welcome, Signorina.'

Until that moment not one of the Scum had spoken. None of the jabbering and jokes that had accompanied Wendy's arrival. They too were disappointed apparently, but at least one of them was showing more manners than I had.

'What's happened to Wendy anyway?' I asked.

'She didn't come back from leave. Everything was ready and the aircraft loaded; it couldn't be kept waiting, so – well, I came instead.'

'Good heavens! Just like that?'

'Just like that. Not so difficult really; we share a room in the mess and we're about the same size – it was just a case of taking her kit and docs and running to a waiting aeroplane.'

'Sounds dangerously easy.'

'Piece of cake!'

'But you had jumped before?'

'On the course, but this was the first time at night.' She gave a nervous little laugh, 'Actually, I was a bit scared.'

I began to forgive her when she said that; it made her more human. Much as I had looked forward to seeing Wendy, I was becoming rather tired of self-assured young women.

We had reached the buildings by that time and I was surprised when Gianna Maria asked her if she would like some hot soup. We never had soup at night in the summer. It looked as though she was trying to relax the girl. 'I was just going to heat some up anyway,' she said. 'It's a cool night and the men will be coming in soon with the stores; they could do with some.'

'It's a wonderful night and thank you, I'd love some soup. Can I help?'

Gianna shook her head. 'Sit down and talk to Philip. I shan't be long.'

Sally lifted her arms and stretched luxuriously, the battledress top coming adrift from the trousers. She smiled at me and I did my best to produce a sickly grin in return.

'Isn't this wonderful?' She took a deep breath and lowered her arms. 'I've always wanted to come to Italy and here I am.'

I could hardly believe my ears. 'What?' I tried not to shout. 'You've never been to Italy before?'

'No. I'd always lived in the Far East until eighteen months ago.'

'The Far East? Strewth! What will that crumby unit do next?' A horrid doubt crept into my mind – but perhaps she'd been on a course or something. 'I suppose you do speak Italian?'

'Not a word!' The brat even had the cheek to sound unperturbed. 'I daresay I could learn though and anyway, I'm sure Wendy will be back by next month – there's an aircraft scheduled – and some sort of surface craft is being organised to collect your Italian officer – I don't see why it can't take me back too.'

What use was she going to be to us if she couldn't even speak Italian? I ask you!

'Gianna Maria,' I called, and I didn't care if the girl heard the nastiness in my voice, 'she's useless. Can't do Wendy's job at all – can't even speak Italian.'

'Nor can Johnny,' she answered, 'but he's still Dougal's right-hand man. She can do my job and I can do Wendy's for the time being.'

Well, that squashed me. I suppose it served me right for being a sadist, but I was still peeved and it was not only pique at Wendy's non-arrival. I had had a lot of jobs stored up for her, which Gianna or I could have fitted in somehow, had we known she wasn't coming; now we'd have to reorganise. It was annoying.

'I'm not blaming *you*,' I said, still rather crossly, 'but it just seems utterly ridiculous to me that any unit should put a group like this in a position where it can receive someone so totally unsuited for the job.'

If I had expected her to lower her eyes in shame, or burst into tears or something, I had another thought coming. She whipped round like an angry swan, the moonlight glinting on her eyes, and I saw her jaw muscles tighten. Quick as lightning she flashed back at me and her voice was full of scorn.

'I am not a fool, *Captain* Morrison, and I have had access to the files on the people working in this area. If I am not mistaken, you are an ordinary – I should say *very* ordinary – infantry officer, with no intelligence background whatsoever. You are merely here through circumstance, whereas I have been trained for this type of work.'

I was so taken aback that I couldn't think of a single suitable retort – of course one never can at the time. In the circumstances I decided that discretion was the better part of valour. Without looking at her, and playing the strong silent man, I got up and walked into the hut, where Gianna Maria was heating the soup.

'Don't be so hard on her, Philip,' she said, before I had time to open my mouth – it was enough to put one off marriage for life, knowing in advance how a henpecked husband must feel. 'I rather like the look of her and there's plenty she can do here – she won't be a liability, I'm sure. And just because you're in love with Wendy and are disappointed that she isn't here, is no reason for taking it out on her.'

'I am *not* in love with Wendy. Can't women think of anything else?'

'Prove it then. Behave like a man instead of a small boy. Go out there and say something to break the silence – something ordinary.'

I scowled, but I knew she was right. We went out together, I carrying the large pot of watery soup. Thank goodness, at that moment the first of the Scum arrived back, carrying a container and was soon followed by his noisy comrades – not much tension when they were around.

I put down the soup and Gianna began ladling it out.

'Can you cook?' I asked in my most conversational tone and saw Gianna's approving nod.

'Not very well, but I'll do my best.'

'Hm. Well, we'll introduce you and give you some idea of the work to-morrow.'

Gianna Maria handed her a mug of soup and asked, 'Have you nothing else to wear?'

'Oh yes. I know all about labels and things and, as I hadn't anything Italian-made, I've done the next best thing and brought only things that I've made myself.'

As she spoke she removed her battledress blouse to reveal a thin black sweater. We nodded our approval.

'I'm sure I can pass as an Italian if I don't open my mouth.'

It was difficult to say when the moonlight made everything colourless, but I very much doubted it.

It was easy enough to say, 'I just took her place,' but of course it had not been easy at all. And when I admitted to being scared in the aircraft, I had not meant scared of jumping – I couldn't have cared less about that and wondered why people made so much fuss – but of just what I was letting myself in for.

After I had finished OCTU and then Intelligence School, I had been thrilled to bits to be sent on the parachute course. But my hopes had been dashed the minute I returned to the peculiar inter-service unit to which I had been posted, when the CO told me that they had never even considered dropping women in the Far East. Of course he was right; there was nothing that I, or any European woman, could have done, as I was to find out. I would be useful in India or Ceylon, he said, where I could liaise with the men who were dropped, and perhaps interpret and identify aerial photographs. I didn't want to go to India or Ceylon; I wanted to get into the war. And what a waste of a course. And I knew what Ceylon was like – I'd seen everyone fall flat, just because an aircraft had flown low over one of the hotels. I had been in a really bloody-minded mood, waiting for my posting to Ceylon, when a vacancy in the Middle East occurred, so I volunteered.

Wendy was my best friend – at least she was on the rare occasions that I saw her. We had got on well together from the start. Of course she spent more time in Italy than with us, but, because I knew the work she was doing and had heard so much about the people with whom she worked, I felt that I could do her job. We were not supposed to go beyond a certain radius of Cairo for our leave, but Wendy had wangled herself a trip to the Lebanon, and I was the only person who knew she was there. I knew who she was with too, and that would have caused a furore if it had leaked out. She knew the exact time and date of her next trip and it was so unlike her to be irresponsible. I tried to find out what had happened to her – she was due back a couple of days before the flight – but no luck. Then I made a crashing bloomer. The CO was becoming so agitated that I told him she was back, but busy drawing her equip, etcetera. I never dreamed she wouldn't make it, but then the great day dawned and there was still no sign of her. I went through the briefing, the documentation and drew her equipment – unquestioned, because I'd done it for her before. Zero hour came and still no Wendy. I already knew so much about the group she worked with and this time there were not many orders to be explained, because the CO of the area, Major MacPherson, had been over himself and was now in UK for a short spell; he would be dropped himself next month.

To be late from leave for normal duty was forgivable, but to be late when an aircraft was laid on and other people were depending on you, was not. At least it would be better for Wendy when she returned to find that at least the drop had not been cancelled because of her. Or so I reasoned, as I walked across the tarmac and climbed into the waiting plane.

It was only after take-off that the enormity of what I had done came home to me. How could I possibly do Wendy's job? It wasn't only the language; she knew the area, had lived there before the war – was half Italian anyway. And would she in fact be dropped next month?

Perhaps she could produce an explanation and be dropped in with Major MacPherson and I could leave with the Italian chappie. I could only hope.

Nevertheless, by the time the warning signal came I was almost praying that my parachute wouldn't open. And then that odious Philip Morrison – Wendy had said he was quite a decent type, but I thought him detestable. Anyway, at least his rudeness had made me stand up and fight and, so help me God, I'd go on fighting. As Gianna Maria said, I could always do her job while she was out. She was nice – I'd keep my end up to help her, if nothing else. And I would *not* let them down – I'd hand over to Wendy when she arrived without feeling ashamed of my efforts, or die in the attempt.

Sally's entrance next morning brought forth great merriment from the Scum and a half-smothered cry from Gianna Maria.

Personally, I could see nothing to laugh at. She looked fine to me. Everything had been black and white the night before, but as she strode out into the sunshine she was the very picture of health. Her legs and arms were bare and brown from the Egyptian sun and her hair was bright, brown and shiny. I could almost see her striding over the moors at home; her colouring and her tweed skirt would be just right for a Highland background. I didn't think much of my compatriot, but I was proud of the way she looked – and said so.

'I'm afraid this skirt's not quite right,' she was saying. 'Perhaps if I could find a piece of material somewhere I could run something up.'

I looked at Gianna and then at Sally. The latter was by far the more attractive – to me at any rate – but there was no doubt about it, she wouldn't look Italian in a hundred years. Perhaps it was the skirt.

'It's the walk.' Gianna Maria was gasping with laughter. 'Never mind the skirt, I can lend her one, but the walk! And those legs! No one but an Englishwoman walks like that!'

'Well, I think she has very nice legs,' I said primly, surprised at myself for defending her. She had, and the Scum obviously thought so too.

Gianna Maria fetched a skirt that Wendy kept there and began a lesson in walking, Italian style. 'Shorter steps,' she called. 'Swing your hips. Don't march!'

I must say she took it in very good part, laughing with us and trying her best. It didn't take her long to copy Gianna's walk, but there was still something wrong.

'I'll think about it,' Gianna said. 'Now you must come and meet your fellow criminals.'

I smiled as I listened to her introducing the Scum in much the same manner as she had to me.

'Stefano, idle but strong; Giorgio, got himself wounded to avoid work; Andreo, biggest thief in Milan; Luigi, well, at least he's a good carpenter; Mario, bone lazy; Carlo, hoodlum at the very least.' And on, until the last man had stepped forward and shaken hands. 'Sweepings of the Milan gaols – the Scum!'

'Now the only member of the group you haven't met is Tom,' I said.

'Sounds English.'

'Jug/Italian, but British Army – a long and complicated story which he will no doubt enjoy telling you himself.'

'Where is he?'

'Trying to find someone to repair our radio. Which reminds me, did you bring a battery with you?'

'Two.'

'Thank God for that. Tom thinks it might only be the battery and we haven't had any news for more than a fortnight – if last night's flight had been changed we would not have known.'

'No news for two weeks? Gosh! Haven't you heard about the invasion then?'

'What invasion?'

'Sicily. On the tenth of July. It's the turning point – '

'Hold it. Gianna Maria,' I called, 'tell the Scum to come back; Sally has some stupendous news. Go on, Sally, bit by bit, so that we can translate as you go.'

It was unbelievable; we had no inkling of it.

'First we took Pantelleria, a stepping-stone so to speak, and then launched the full-scale invasion of Sicily.'

I held up my hand and Gianna interpreted. The Scum were already hugging themselves and hopping up and down.

'Palermo fell only a couple of days ago and we've bombed Naples to smithereens, preparatory to landing on the mainland.'

Gianna did not translate the last part and told them that that was all. When they had dispersed, she said, 'Let's just stick to Sicily for the time being. Enrico is a Neapolitan – he's our best man and the most temperamental. We have a big do in a few days time and we can't afford to have him upset; the others follow his lead.'

I could see that the Scum would not be easy to handle from now on; they were already telling each other that the war was over and they wouldn't be keen on risking their lives when thoughts of reunion with their families were just over the brink. I was not as optimistic as Gianna Maria and Sally, but I never dreamed, then, that it would last nearly two more years.

'I've got it!'

We were eating our so-called supper in the still warm evening sun when Gianna Maria suddenly waved a chunk of bread in the direction of Sally's head.

'It's the hair. No Italian girl wears her hair like that.'

We had tried hard to make Sally look Italian during the past few days, but without much success. She put her hand up to the thick, heavy roll which encircled her head and said, 'I'll change the style if you think it would help.'

'Cut it off.' Gianna Maria swished her own hair, which hung loosely on her shoulders. 'No one of your age in Italy wears their hair long any more; that's what looks wrong.'

Could be. I looked through narrowed eyes; I too had tried to put my finger on the defect. It was not the colouring; her skin was sun-tanned, her eyes a sort of greenish hazel and her hair that chestnut brown quite often seen in the north of Italy. We had cured her of her striding walk. She was a bit coltish – legs and arms too long for an Italian, and skinny – still, she was quite an attractive little thing. Could be the hair.

'Enrico will cut it; he's an excellent barber. Honestly,' as Gianna saw Sally's doubtful face, 'he always cuts mine. He was put in gaol for murdering his clients and turning them into salami – like your famous barber – not for bad haircutting!'

Sally laughed, but she kept both hands firmly on her head. Then she untied a bootlace, which appeared to be the only means of holding it up, and pulled. A great cascade of hair, a real mane, fell down her back and rested on the rock where she sat.

'Mamma mia,' gasped Enrico, 'it would be a sin to cut that.' He scurried off to the hut and came back with a comb. 'With permission, Signorina.'

He lifted Sally's hair and began to comb it with an expert hand until it shone smoothly around her, burnished to copper in the last rays of the summer sun. It was very beautiful hair.

Seeing her sitting there, quiet, but as though tears were not far away, I looked at her, a young girl of my own race, and felt a lump in the throat. She had told me that she was 'officially twenty-one', but I wondered.

'How old are you really, Sally?' I asked.

'I'm just eighteen.'

'Just eighteen,' repeated Gianna Maria to Enrico.

'Just eighteen,' murmured the Scum, shaking their heads and thinking possibly of their younger sisters and some even of daughters.

'Is it possible,' Gianna asked, 'that the war is going so badly that they have to make officers out of children?' She nodded to Enrico, who was already stropping a murderous-looking cutthroat razor. And to Sally, 'You know, you'll see more of your hair when it's short. Why do you have that dreadful hairstyle anyway?'

'It's supposed to be above our collars, and it goes well under a cap. It's known as an "admin roll".'

'An admin roll? Holy Mother of God, what a name for a hairstyle! It sounds like a cross between a 1920 dance and a union of salami vendors! Come on, let's see how it looks short.'

Poor Sally; as Enrico took a great swathe of her hair and held up the spoils as though it were a head from the guillotine, she looked utterly miserable. I wished I hadn't been so beastly to her.

One of the Scum had brought a bucket of water and after Enrico had plunged her head into it, he began to cut and shape with the intense expression of the artist contorting his face. By the time he had finished, Luigi had also finished whittling some twigs into curlers. It was strange to see the Scum, usually so intent on scrounging food and arms, engrossed in a girl's hair. It had been Enrico who had disembowelled a German on the dam.

'Gianna Maria and I have to be off at first light to-morrow,' I told Sally – I was sorry I would not be there in the morning to see the result of Enrico's handiwork – 'and we may be away for more than a week. I have to get right over to the border group. Wendy took her time, but then, being a courier was her only job.'

'I'm sorry that I'm not an adequate stand-in,' she said, 'but it seemed the only solution at the time.'

I surprised myself by giving her shoulder a friendly pat as I stood up, preparatory to going to bed. She wasn't a bad little thing, only she wasn't Wendy.

'Don't worry,' I told her, 'you'll do fine. We're only taking a couple of men with us; the rest will look after you.'

Gianna Maria got up at some unearthly hour and both she and Philip had gone by the time I woke for a second time. It was late and most of the Scum were lazing round the tiny fire, enjoying the coffee that had been dropped in.

'*Buon giorno, Signorina*,' it was Enrico, brandishing his comb in one hand and a billy of something that looked like porridge in the other. '*Pettino*,' he waved his left hand, and, '*mangiate*,' handing me the billy with the right.

My education had begun. I sniffed at the polenta – I only learned what it was later – and ate obediently as he combed out my hair. From the expressions of the other men, he must have done a good job. I was hungry and anything related to corn on the cob met with my approval – it certainly didn't by the time I left Italy, but I was new then.

It was a week later that I met the famous Tom. I had been sitting with my head in my hands, I remember, trying to relax my buzzing brain. Undoubtedly it was the best way to learn a language but I had reached a straining point where I simply *had* to have someone who could speak English to explain. The afternoon sun was hot on the back of my neck and the air was filled with the drone and buzz of countless bees and flies, the snores of Enrico and the monotonous conversation of two of the men.

Suddenly there was a shout from the lookout and everyone jumped to their feet, including me.

'It is only Tenente Tom,' someone called, and a minute later I was looking into one of the most aristocratic faces I had ever seen – the sort of face that needed an Elizabethan ruff to do it justice. A long thin nose, hooded eyes, and mobile mouth.

'This is Signorina Sale,' Enrico produced me as though I were all his own work.

'Ah, one of the necessities in life,' the newcomer murmured. 'Allow me to introduce myself: Tomaso di Lucio, at your service, Signorina – or should I say Tenentessa?'

'Sally.'

One of the Scum explained that I had replaced Wendy.

'Ah.' As he clicked his heels and brushed my hand with his lips, his eyes travelled up my arm to mine, no longer amused, but bright. 'Have you brought a new battery?'

I'm afraid I went into a fit of giggles and he, reasonably, looked somewhat surprised.

'Yes, I have,' I said, 'and I'm sorry I laughed. I was thinking of the last person who kissed my hand – radio batteries were certainly not what he had in mind!' He smiled, but I don't think he was amused. To change the subject, I asked, 'Have you heard the news about Sicily?'

'From Bill and Johnny. But unlike most of my compatriots, I cannot believe that this war will end next week. The Germans *must* make a stand here – it'll be a year or more.'

How right he was.

But his mood changed a short while later and he positively danced out of his cubby-hole to sniff at the supper we were preparing.

'It works! I knew it was only the battery all along. And now, tell me all about yourself, why you are here.'

I groaned and told.

He was amused but practical. 'And have you started learning Italian yet?'

'Of course,' I waved in the direction of the Scum, 'I have all these teachers.' It was a relief to speak English again, but not for long.

'Good. Now I shall take you in hand. We speak only Italian from now on.'

I groaned again.

The foraging party returned next day with two beardless youths in tow. The Scum eyed them with cynical scorn.

'Well at least they've never been in gaol,' Gianna Maria retorted. 'It's a pity that they should be forced into a life of crime so young!'

'What a transformation.' Philip was looking at my hair. 'It suits her, doesn't it, Gianna?'

I was so pleased to see their smiling faces; so pleased to have them back. I was still hating Philip when he had left, but Tom had told me about his disappointment – with a certain amount of malice – and I had forgiven him. It occurred to me that he was really frantically attractive when he didn't wear that disagreeable frown.

23. A DINKUM AUSSIE

Vincent Lee Chee Min

I am Vincent Lee Chee Min, and to those of you who are unfamiliar with Chinese names, that means that Lee is my surname. Chee Min is my first name and, because I am a Christian, I have the extra name of Vincent.

By this time, August 1943, I am a dinkum Aussie and I cannot say that either this year nor the last have meant much to me, at least not as far as the war is concerned. Of course I knew that Malaya, my home, had been invaded by the Nips, but the first event that brought it home to me was the sudden arrival of my mother and my sister Rosalie. They had been evacuated – we were full of evacuees from South-East Asia in Aussie – and I sure was surprised when they suddenly appeared at school one day.

My three elder brothers and I had already been in Australia for some time, receiving higher education. A laugh really, because Dad can't even sign his own name! Not that he isn't a canny old devil and rich as Hades – he's in tin and he's worked for it, so good luck to him. Grandfather came from China to Malaya as a coolie and that's what Dad started out as, and he's proud of it. No airs and graces about Dad; he'd go down well in Aussie. One of my brothers has already been called to the bar in New South Wales and he'll practise law in Malaya as soon as the war's over, and I have another brother there studying engineering and another doing medicine in Melbourne, and here am I, the youngest, at High School still in Western Australia. Just like our old man to send us all to different places and map out different professions for us – or for him rather. One to look after his health, one to bring technical know-how to the mines, one to fight his lawsuits and I'm destined for the family business. The daughters of course don't count – two are married off already and it's just Rosalie's good luck that the war has given her the chance to study in Aussie too.

Rosalie began to enjoy life the moment she was enrolled at the convent. She was a day girl and lived with Mum, but she was out of Dad's clutches and it was only after I'd been here for a while that I began to realise how much girls from old-fashioned Chinese families like ours miss.

It didn't take Mum long to settle down either, although a tiny flat and having to do everything for herself was not what she was used to. Holy Cow, we had a huge old place near Ipoh, in central Malaya, far bigger than any house I've seen in Aussie. Square, with a central court and wide verandahs running right round both the ground and first floor rooms. Big rooms too – pretty poky these rooms here, but my cobbers think I'm boasting if I tell them so, so I keep quiet now – and solid. We have, or had, our own swimming-pool and that is something I've had cause to bless my Dad for here, because you know swimming is a religion to the Australians and I've been able to hold my own from the first. At the top of the house there was one extra square – you couldn't call it a room because it was open on all four sides – with railings and a bit of fancy woodwork, you know, curly, to make it look a bit like one of those old Chinese pagodas. Dad used to stand for hours up there, meditating, he used to say, but I think that really he liked to survey his property. It was pretty flat land and the tin mines were all around us; our tin mines. I suppose dredgers and palongs and those great yellow pools aren't everybody's idea of a beautiful view, but Dad found beauty in them and the thickness of his money belt testified to that beauty all right. For my father doesn't believe in banks; he has, or had, his own strong-room under the house and carried what he could on him. Of course Mum had plenty of servants to look after her at home and the only work she ever did was to tend Dad's orchids when he was away. Orchids were Dad's hobby and the high wire fence round the compound was to keep out orchid-thieves as much as anyone else. This is not as foolish as it may sound; there's a high price for orchids and many of my father's trips to Singapore and Kuala Lumpur were connected with the breeding and crossing of these plants. Of course he had second and third wives in these places too, but we weren't supposed to know about that. I think it is one of the reasons why Mum likes her little flat here so much – here she is the only Mrs Lee. She is a Christian and no number of orchid hybrids being named after her could compensate for my father's concubines – she refused to call them wives – and although I'm young still, she's confided quite a lot in me.

We've heard news of Dad once, in a roundabout way. It was via an English naval officer, one of a few who'd got out of Singapore at the end and had since been in Ceylon and India, but more latterly in Australian waters. It seems that an Aussie army officer who had been cut off up country in Malaya behind the advancing Nips and then made his way to Ceylon via Sumatra, had heard that this chappie was going on secondment to the RAN. He'd asked him, if he should ever touch West Australia, to look up Mum. Apparently some character called Lee Chee Onn – that's Dad – who had started some sort of resistance group in Perak, almost before the Nips had settled in, had wanted her to know that he was all right. Crikey, you should have seen Mum's face! It would take more than the Nips to kill *her* husband, she informed this chap – she was positively bursting with pride. Mum's right of course; he's a tough nut, my Dad.

I guess school's the same everywhere, war or no war, and we all enjoy the Aussie way of life. Mum says she wouldn't swop her little flat for all the servants and money and jewellery that she used to have, and I don't blame her. She didn't mention the word freedom – that's taboo – but even at my age I know that's what she really likes.

Well, I won't bore you with a diary of my schooldays. I guess you've all been to school – you know what goes on.

24. A WORLD OF DISILLUSIONMENT

Ramakrishnan

Truly I am living in a world of disillusionment.

It is now one and a half years over since glorious Nipponese Army are liberating Malaya. But are we liberated? I am asking myself. Of a truth any master is better than the white pig, but when I am waving banner to greet illustrious Japanese and expecting embraces and speeches of welcoming enlightenment to workers, what happens? One soldier slaps me and another is tying banner round my neck and is telling me that English is now forbidden language.

A Chinese manager is now in charge of estate and I am telling you, he treats us Tamils worse even than the white pig who was here hithertofore. Indeed, as though we are sweat beneath his armpit. But when Nipponese masters are appearing he is all smiles and bows and rubbing of fat hands. I am telling you, there is no justice. Where is expected freedom? Still we are having enslavement most vile. When are chains to be broken, man?

Japanese teacher we are having now twice weekly in school to teach glorious new language and erstwhile teacher Vanniasingham is fled. There was rumouring that he was in trouble with authorities because of disobedience regarding teachings of various subjects as laid down by newly coming friends. Verily good riddance. I am telling him that we must believe in honourable dictum of Co-Prosperity Sphere.

Now that white man has been kicked up arse and out of Netherlands East Indies, French Indo-China, American Philippines, and all British territories in Asia and glorious Indian National Army is liberating India and Ceylon both, joining hands with our Nipponese brothers, hands across land as well as sea. But he is not believing above-mentioned facts. He is saying that he is only staying so long in employment of Japanese because he is man much bewifed and bechildrenised and having need of steady job. But better to starve than be slave, he is saying. When I am telling him of true facts, he is calling me rabble rouser. I am not for asking him what he means – he is stupid man and if he is wishing to call me obscene and blasphemous names I shall be telling masters of his most devious and unillustrious intent, I am telling him. But then he is laughing and calling me junior rabble rouser. I was laying down pen and hastening to manager, but next morning the bird has flown. Birds. Mister-teacher-Vanniasing-ham and his crony Mister-medical-Ratnasingham, the estate dresser, had flitted during the night.

I am being made to look foolish indeed when soldiers are arriving at school next day, and for my taking of pains am being insulted most publicly.

My father is for laughing off stupid head and praising Vannia and Ratna both, but I am telling him soon he will no longer be *kangani* if he does not co-operate and then he is abusing me.

But these humiliations are of content most piffling compared with others, as I shall be relating forthwith.

It is because of the seductions of Muriani, daughter of Pillai the clerk, that troublesome times have fallen on me.

Indeed, this Muriani is most immoral girl and I have watched her emerging from bushes with Nipponese soldiers many times. Clearly they have been having most frolicsome times and why, I am asking myself, should Nipponese enjoy our maidens and not yours truly?

One evening, after secondly rated teacher we are now having has rapped me over knuckles with most uncomfortable ruler, because I am watching the hips of Muriani swaying towards weighing-shed instead of attending to his prattle a dozen to nineteen, I am approaching said girl as she is placing latex bucket on weighing machine and rubbing hip against hers. Truly she is surprised. I am telling her that I know of first-class secluded situation by river most opportune.

But that bad Muriani is laughing at me and telling me that I am only boy; to run away and be for trying again in ten years' time.

'I am man,' I say to her, 'come, and I am showing you.'

Muriani is bending most speculative gaze in my direction and my tongue seems to be swelling so that my whole mouth is feeling full and dry with expectations most fruitful. But then she is shrugging and walking away and I am spending night in tortures and fevers.

Twice I am being slapped at school, because next day is tuition day in glorious Japanese language and all pupils are forever slapped by illustrious teacher for even most petty of misdemeanours. Truly my head is in different world of unobtainable clouds, but when I am passing Muriani that evening, she is not laughing at me, but gives me look most come hithers and enticing.

'Is it that you are man that you are still wanting to show me?' she asks, and without further ados I am dropping schoolbooks and hurrying hugger-mugger with Muriani to most conveniently concealing bushes.

'You are in great hurry, Krishnan,' she is laughing. 'A man would take me to most secluded spot you talked of by river bank.'

Verily I am thinking river bank is too far and am not for waiting. I am not believing that Muriani is for waiting either, because as soon as we are behind first bush, she is dropping skirt and revealing herself to me. Nothing under her skirt she is wearing.

But it is too late. With shame I drop my eyes to my wetness and Muriani is protruding loins at me and telling me to hurry.

'Another time,' I say in husky voice and am walking away before she sees my shame.

'Pig, swine,' she calls after me, 'breaker of promises. And you a man!'

'To-morrow,' I say. 'No hurry. And I will show you river bank most secluded bower.'

There is no point in giving chances for heapings of scorn, so next afternoon, straight from school, before there is time for putting angry blaze in Muriani's eyes into most scorching words, I am propelling her with utmost urgency and authority in direction of trees.

This time I am ready and before she is knowing of such happenings, I am leaping on to her and soon stars are bursting like Deepavali lights in head and all around. Muriani is squealing and wriggling like eel on hook in deep waters and I am electric eel giving her shocks.

After all is over, my whole body is wet with perspiration, springing like dew from most active pores, and I know that I am man and no longer boy.

'Verily thou art a man, Krishnan.' Muriani is saying it for me and now I am understanding why cockerel leaps to summit of almighty dunghill to crow.

The sight of Muriani's damp, heaving belly and parted legs is causing my newly arriving manhood to rise again and soon I am kneeling over her, ready.

'Oh Krishnan, you are so greedy.' But she is greedy too.

Man, when I am seeing Muriani's legs parting wide and her mouth opening wide to reveal most pink tongue and teeth unstained, there is madness in me that is not for satisfaction. I am on her again and again and soon she is calling for me to stop and I see her smile is changing from enjoyings to fear.

'You are hurting me, man.' She is like whipped animal and I hurt her again. And again. And again. 'Krishnan, stop.'

I am stopping then, but I laugh, because now I know I am truly man and can do to Muriani what Nipponese soldiers are doing.

I am watching my parents that night and thinking that I am more man than my father, who only does it once and falls asleep. Verily he is not much of a fellow.

Next day I am taking pails of latex from Muriani and pouring straight into coagulating tank. She is not protesting that they are not being weighed, but merely looking at me like I am mongoose and she snake and when I beckon she is following without hesitation. This is jolly good show. Soon I am hearing her giggling behind me and I am turning round then to laugh with her and see she is no longer afraid.

Copulation is most finest thing, I am telling you. That day I am taking Muriani to secluded bower on river bank. For many months past I am knowing of this small little beach, half moon in shapings and with bushes all round.

I watch Muriani drop her skirt, then I motion her to be removing blouse also. I am liking to look at all her private parts, breasts like small papayas, rounded belly, etcetera, etcetera. Then I am like charging buffalo, throwing her to ground.

Every day for two weeks I am adulterating with Muriani.

'I will be putting ten children into you,' I boast.

'And the apothecary will be taking them out!'

We are having most gay and frolicsome time one afternoon by river, when most troublesome surprise is in store. To wit: I am just trying out new position when most painful kick is being delivered from rear. I feel pain tearing through my backside and in fear I am slowly turning head. What I am seeing is most accursed Nipponese soldier standing over us, with smile I am knowing is not for fun – our fun.

Verily, even pleasures of fornication are being torn from us. Even the white pigs did not interfere with a man's lustful inclinations. Perhaps after all my father is not such stupid fellow, I am thinking, when he is kicking me again. Forcing us apart with most dishonourable boot.

'Get up, there are peoples waiting for you.' He is smiling now in manner most malicious and of evil intent. 'There is reception committee.'

All is becoming crystallised clear. This is soldier who is emerging from bushes with Muriani hithertofore. I am hearing noises in bushes earlier and am thinking it is only animal, but it was jealous soldier seeking to humiliate yours truly.

Muriani stands up and is going to tie her skirt when dishonourable

238

Nipponese is seizing same, together with my trousers, and hanging on end of rifle like flag.

'The peoples want to see you as you are,' he is saying and smiling again. 'Start walking.'

Muriani is wearing only short blouse, ending below breasts, and whilst being full choc-a-bloc with sympathy for predicament, I am glad my shirt tails are long enough to cover nakedness of yours truly.

But Nipponese is most dishonourable production of unmarried parents. He is taking my shirt and tying hands behind back with tails, so that I do not even have hands free to protect genitals or conceal private parts.

Soon we are emerging from bushes, Muriani first, covering herself with her hands, myself uncovered and then Nipponese soldier with clothes most indecorously from rifle swinging. There are two lines of peoples and it is becoming most clear that we are entering ordeal most vile.

I hear Muriani's mother scream, then I am seeing that one side is of her family, friends and relations, and the other line is my family, friends and relations.

'Your son has seduced my child,' it is Muriani's mother screeching at my father. 'Treating her like whore, and she a virgin to this day.'

Truly Muriani's parents are stupid as mine, for it is being many years I am telling you since Muriani was virgin. Stuck up they are, because her father is clerk. But my father is kangani and I am about to speak up, to ask how many Nipponese soldiers have taken Muriani into bushes, when I am feeling blows falling on shoulders like rain. It is Muriani's father and soon my father also, beating me with bamboos.

'Run him off the estate.' Soon everyone is taking up this cry. 'Run him off the estate. Run him off the estate.'

And I am running, with stones whistling round me and blows from sticks and fists on back and head and then I hear my father's voice pleading, 'Only let him have his trousers first.'

I am spending night under weedy roadside bridge and next morning am having much pain from contusions caused by flying missiles and bruises can be felt on all parts.

At first sound of approaching vehicle I am springing into road and waving arms above head. Malay driver of lorry is looking scared but fortunately he is most helpful fellow and I am persuading him to give me lift. Verily I am in state most sad and sorry, with torn and soiled shirt and of footwear utterly devoid, neither can I pay driver when he is dropping me at estate some miles along his route. Consolation is only in patting of top pocket, wherein all papers are most permanently kept secure.

I am going straight to kangani, with whom I must make contract to labour. He is good fellow who is offering me meal before story is unfolded.

'I have tale of durances most vile,' I tell kangani, wife and family and friends, who are gathered to listen. 'Nipponese soldiers without number are fornicating with my betrothed and when I am taking her myself – for why should I wait when she is being covered by all and sundries? – these same soldiers are beating me and running me off estate in state most humilitous.'

'Goodness gracious me,' kangani is expostulating, 'where will be the end of these evils?'

'It is true,' I say, 'for everyone is knowing that our maidens are most frolicsome and easily taken by swaggering braggarts who promise riches untold and delights unsurpassed.'

'And you are after wanting job?' kangani asks. 'It is very possible that I can add you to list of tappers with facility, but from your hands you do not look like coolie.'

'I am schoolmaster,' I say, 'but I can tap to earn honest wage until vacancy for teacher is occurring.'

I have taken most wisest precaution to provide myself with credentials. Secondly rated teacher replacing Vanniasingham is also named Ramakrishnan, only son of Ramanathan, and it is easy to smudge end of said appendage on certificate. And so I am taking all necessary documents and references from desk some months past and am now intending to put to good uses.

'You look very young for teacher,' kangani is shaking head, 'and this is not large estate with own school.'

'I am only teacher just,' I say, 'and of stature small, not having grown since being sixteen.' Which is not a lie.

Manager of this estate is Japanese and passing good fellow for Nip, kangani is saying. I am therefore careful to be keeping mouth tightly closed and am accepting with grateful attitude offers of clothings and also tuition in newly found trade and am putting humilitous past behind.

25. PLAYING WITH FIRE

James Weatherby

The summer went by like lightning. Being a station master was a full-time job and, as my previous one had told me, I didn't have to worry about finding a chance to fly. There never seemed to be enough bods to go round, with the formations becoming larger, the raids more frequent and further afield. Targets were becoming more specific too, which meant more concentration and more strain. Rest became more important than ever and I could have flown every night – there was always someone who could do with a relief.

It must have been October when I first got up to London. Elsie went quite often – doing what, I haven't a clue – but she led her own life these days, and I led mine. I was ordered by Command to attend a conference, which ended after a blessedly short time, and then I had a small job to sort out with the army – their ack-ack had opened up on one of our homing kites and I was not amused. It's irrelevant here, but a tiff with their local commander had resulted in my being referred to someone in the War Office, and that is how I happened to find myself in Whitehall on that golden, autumn day.

I had spent an amicable half-hour with the type I had come to see and was just on the point of leaving the building when it occurred to me that I had been in there once before. I wondered if Helen still worked there.

'Junior Commander Watson still work here?' I asked the doorman.

'Yessir, third floor. You can telephone her if you like.'

It had taken me some time to get something resembling order out of the chaotic mess the general had left me to sort out after his Burma trip. And no sooner was that over than his attentions were focused on Europe. Of course we all knew something was impending and the general, whose main job was personnel, was going to be in the forefront of the organisation.

We were just in the midst of some rather complicated figures when the phone rang and the old boy passed it over to me.

'For you, Helen. A Group Captain Weatherby – must be that new liaison Johnnie from the Air Ministry. Anyway, he asked for you, so you'd better deal with him.'

I shook my head; the name didn't ring a bell. I was *that* engrossed.

'Junior Commander Watson speaking.'

'Helen, it's me, James.'

'James?'

'Yes, James. James Weatherby. You can't have forgotten me, have you?'

I swallowed a couple of times. 'No. It's just that I was so surprised. Where are you?'

'Downstairs, by the main entrance. When can I see you?'

'Not now. It'll be lunch-time in half an hour.'

'I'll wait here.'

I replaced the receiver, feeling thoughtful and – I don't know how I felt – very odd. 'It wasn't the liaison officer, sir. A personal call, I'm afraid.'

'Yes. Well, you look as though you'd been talking to a ghost. Now where were we?'

To say that I found it difficult to concentrate for that last half-hour would be the understatement of the year. By the time the lunch hour arrived, I was so filled with mixed emotions that I wasn't sure whether to go downstairs or not.

Of course I did go down. And when I saw him standing there, with that well-remembered grin splitting his face, I didn't know whether it was the happiest moment of my life or whether I should turn and run. I did my best to assume a flippant manner and grinned back.

'Hardly recognised you under all that braid and all that fruit salad.' We shook hands.

That laugh. It took me back with a tug of the heartstrings.

'My, my, how formal we are!' He propelled me through the door. 'Lunch. I'm starved. Come on, we'll swop all our news once we've ordered.'

Well-organised creature; he had reserved a table while waiting for me and had a taxi at the main door.

I left the ordering to James. I wanted to be able to sit back and look at him. He had aged; a year and a half since I had last seen him, but he had aged far more than that. He needed a haircut and the hair curling on the back of his neck was quite grey, I saw, and so were streaks over each ear. He had a weatherbeaten look about him that I did not remember, the skin coarsened and wrinkled about the eyes.

'Well? Am I still the same man?' When that white smile creased his face, the years fell away and indeed he was the same man.

'Why did you seek me out?' I asked. He had picked up my hand when the waiter left us and was fondling it in a casual way. But not casual enough. Even that was sufficient to give me gooseflesh. No doubt he would tell me in due course, but I was already in a tizzy of anticipation. Was he no longer married? Was he free? He would never have sought me out otherwise, I was sure.

'I've got to be honest, darling. I had to come up to the War Office for a meeting this morning and I remembered that that was where your old geezer worked, so I asked the chap on the door if you were still there and when he said you were, I couldn't resist the temptation of seeing you again – that's all.'

That's all. I felt the prick of tears behind my eyes.

'Perhaps it would have been better if you hadn't rung me,' I said.

'Oh, Helen,' he squeezed my hand hard. I ought to have taken it away, but I didn't. 'In my present job I shall be coming up to AM pretty often, certainly once a month, and I thought it would be fun if we could meet. It would be fun – wouldn't it? Come on, Helen – say it would be fun.'

I sighed. My heart was already breaking and singing with happiness at the same time. You cruel bastard, why did you have to do this? I said to myself, and to him, 'Yes, it would be fun.'

'That's settled then.'

He dropped my hand and caught a passing waiter. 'A gimlet for the lady and a beer for me. And when is this blankety blank food going to arrive? You people don't seem to appreciate the fact that I haven't eaten since breakfast!'

The down-at-the-mouth, seedy old waiter grinned as broadly as James himself and hurried off. My God, I thought, he does it to everyone. Turns on the built-in charm and they all, we all, bow down and worship. But why, oh why, does he have to do it to me?

When our drinks arrived, he raised his glass, 'Here's to my new kite.' He laughed outright at the expression I had obviously not been successful in hiding. 'I know,' he wagged a finger at me, 'you expected me to say, "to us", didn't you?' He laughed again, 'But there wouldn't be much point if my kite let me down, would there? Practical bugger, Weatherby, that's why I'm still alive – the only original member of the squadron still flying.'

I gasped. 'But what happened to the three who were on the ship with us?'

'Two in the drink and one in the bag – and he's got such a nagging wife that he'd probably be better off six feet down – ah, grub at last!' He put a hand under the table and squeezed my knee – and that time I did move away from him.

Perhaps the air force are different. Or perhaps if I'd spent my war on a RAF Station, I might have looked at these things through different eyes. But as it was, I could hardly bear to eat my food. He's grown hard, I thought, hard, hard, hard. Oh, *why* do I want to be with him?

Wanting to hurt, I asked him, 'How's your wife?'

'She's fine – spending a couple of weeks with her parents just now.'

'How convenient.' I hoped I sounded as dry as I had intended.

He looked up quickly and laughed again. 'Oh, come on, Helen, don't be such a sourpuss!' And in went another mouthful. 'This is good – aren't you eating?'

'And your son?'

'Did I tell you about him?'

'No. I saw it in the paper. I remarked to a friend at the time that you'd done rather well for yourself in nine months – Wing Co, DSO, and a son.'

'Well for heaven's sakes – how long do you think it takes to have a child? Really, Helen, I can see it's time I took you in hand.'

'No, thanks.'

'No?' He cocked his head quizzically at me – as he had once in a mirror, a hundred years ago. 'Sure?'

It was no good, I would never be able to stay on my high horse with him. I smiled, however involuntarily. James was pulling out the inevitable photograph.

'He's terrific. You must have children, Helen. I adore children – like to have a whole rugger team!'

'By how many wives?'

The white flash split his face again and his fingertips gripped my knee until it hurt. Then he leaned over and whispered in my ear, 'All by you!'

The next moment he was looking at his watch and trying to catch the waiter's eye. We were soon outside and he was looking at his watch again, an agitated frown wrinkling his forehead.

'You can find your own way back, can't you, Helen? I've got to dash, or I shall miss my train. You will have lunch with me next time, won't you?'

'I suppose so.'

And he was gone. Just like that.

And so, what began as a casual meeting, became a habit. For the next few months James appeared at regular intervals and always without warning. I never stopped to consider what his reaction would have been if I had not been available – but then, damn it, I always was available; available for him that is.

It must have been during the third or fourth lunch that I had with him that I asked, as usual, some dutiful question about his wife, and for the first time he frowned and snapped impatiently at me, 'Please, Helen, let's not talk about my wife; there's so much you don't know.'

It was little enough, but I went back to work with a light heart and hummed over my typing non-stop, until Mark protested that I was driving him mad.

'Just because your Pole's returned to the scene,' he said, 'there's no need to send us all round the bend.'

My Pole! Good heavens, I hadn't given Stan a thought in months. I did have a pang of conscience then, remembering the wonderful time he had given me in India and what good company he'd been. Here was I, going ga-ga over a fortnightly luncheon date with a character who couldn't care less about me, and I hadn't even bothered to write. I'll settle down and drop him a line this evening, I resolved, but although I always intended to, I never did.

'You're playing with fire, you're playing with fire, you're playing with fire,' went the wheels of the train.

I looked out of the window at the flat winter countryside; the trees raising skeletal limbs to the snow-laden sky, while my conscience and my desire fought a battle in my soul and in my loins. I had not meant to drop a hint to Helen that all was not well at home, but my stomach contracted again with the delicious memory of the way she had lit up when I did.

God, how I want her, I thought, at the same time mentally kicking myself for ever having contacted her again. It's not fair to her, I thought, I'm being selfish; I'm being unfair and I *could* stop myself if I really tried. She loves you too, a small voice told me. If only I were free.

'But you're not, you're not, you're not,' the train screamed through a tunnel and, 'you cannot have, you cannot have, you cannot have,' as it eased to its routine pace.

'First tea, anyone for first tea please,' echoed down the corridor. I got up. Might as well do something. It was useless day-dreaming over Helen.

I lurched into the first vacant seat and looked around the restaurant car. A couple of drab, middle-aged women with heavy shopping baskets, a young girl with a squalling baby – why in heaven's name bring it in here anyway? – and a couple of sailors. Opposite me sat an ATS private, blonde and pretty. Not bad, I thought, breasts a bit on the heavy side, mouth showed promise, wonder if the hair's natural. 'Excuse *me*!' the girl got up and gave me such a look of righteous indignation that I realised I must have been staring. Oh well, who cared? I turned my attention and my teeth on the LNER rock cake.

I wasn't in the mood for Elsie, so I went straight into the ops room to see what was on that night. The briefing for the evening raid had just begun.

'What's the target?' I asked a young pilot officer, as I slid quietly into the back row of chairs.

He began to stand up, but I pushed him back into his seat. 'Essen, sir.'

'Christ. That's the third time this week.'

The young man nodded. 'Flying, sir?'

'I think so.'

When the briefing was over, the IO had covered the maps, and the Met officer had given the weather conditions, I went up to the Wingco Ops.

'Anyone sick or absent?' I asked. 'Got to keep my hand in.'

'Oh, hallo, James, I didn't know you were back. No.'

I ran my finger down the list of names. 'Weston needs a break,' I said, 'his wife's due to pup any day. I'll stand in.'

'Right, sir. I'll advise control.'

There was a murmur of voices and a clink of glasses from the drawing-room when I got home. Elsie entertaining, I supposed. I called to her softly from outside the door; I had no wish to intrude.

'Hallo, James. Just back?'

I nodded. 'I'm flying to-night; want to get a couple of hours sleep first – do you think you could keep that mob quiet?'

'Okay.' She turned and shut the door behind her.

Ever since the day that her mother returned home, leaving her and the baby to my mercy, we had lived in a state of semi-armed truce. At first it had seemed that we might make a go of it, but, except for Toby, we had no more in common now than we had ever had and gradually we drifted apart. Except for the fact that we lived under the same roof, we might have been casual acquaintances. After her final rebuff, I had made no further attempt to get her back and found my pleasures elsewhere. At least I never gave her the satisfaction of refusing me again and I had to acknowledge the sad fact that, as one's rank increased, so did the number of girls who were only too willing to oblige.

Thank God I'd never lost the knack of being able to go to sleep at will. I set the alarm and pulled the blankets over my head.

Taking off was always a busy time, but once we were on course I was able to sit back with my thoughts for a spell. I had relieved Weston before; he had a good crowd, but it was not the same as having my own crew. I often looked back to the days when I was part of a squadron and felt a pang of nostalgia.

We were across the enemy coast and the flak came up exactly where we expected it to. Then the routine destruction took place. Perhaps it was luck that I was still alive, or perhaps it was because I was still able to review the damage with an abstract mind, remaining unmoved by what was going on down below. When men began to think, they were apt to crack up; the answer was not to think.

I was just turning in for a second run over the target when the agitated Scottish voice of the Bomb Aimer came over the intercom.

'Bombardier to Cap'n, sir. I cannae get her oot.'

I barrelled, first to port and then to starboard.

'Any luck?'

'She'll no' dislodge, sir.'

'Damned waste. Work on her, Bombardier.' And to the Navigator, 'Course for base, Bill.'

As soon as we were out of immediate danger, the whole crew set to work, trying all the tricks we knew to dislodge the offending bomb. Once across the coast, I headed for the open sea.

'I'll keep her away from the coast for as long as I can,' I told them, 'but we can't go on for ever, fuel's running low.'

As I said the word fuel, I sniffed. Was it imagination? 'Anyone smell petrol?'

There was silence, then one of the air gunners said, 'I think one of the tanks has been hit, sir. We're leaking.'

'For Christ's sake get rid of that bloody bomb then. Can't stay out here much longer and she'll only explode on landing if you don't.'

There are times when everybody's mouth goes dry.

Suddenly there was a jubilant cry, 'She's awa', sir. Oh, thank God, she's awa'.'

I swear you could *feel* the sighs of relief.

'New vector, Bill,' I said, and to the wireless operator, 'Ask base for priority; tell them we're holed.'

It was not long before we heard the voice of Flying Control, instructing us to circle once and come in.

I was already in line with the flare path when I found the undercarriage was stuck. Thank God we'd got rid of that bloody bomb. I advised Flying Control and told them to clear the circuit. Meanwhile I circled again and came in for another go.

It was no good. The landing gear was stuck fast – it could be that we were more damaged than we realised. There was nothing for it but to crash land. It wouldn't be the first time.

'Hold on, chaps, I'll have to bellyflop.'

I was at minimum speed, but the ground still appeared to rush sickeningly towards us. As I said, it was not the first crash landing I had ever made, but it never seemed any the less frightening.

Thump. We were down and I held myself tense and ready for the final jolt. But we were to have a grander finale than that.

There was a hideous lurch and a noise like a thunder crash combined with tearing paper, as the fuselage parted in the middle. I was told afterwards by onlookers that the two halves spun madly towards each other before we came to a grinding halt.

'For Christ's sake, everybody, out.' The intercom was no longer functioning, but it didn't make any difference – nobody was going to spend a second longer than they had to in what at any minute might become a flaming coffin.

I jumped free and saw at once that the tail section had caught fire. Ground crew were already fighting the flames and the ambulance and fire-wagon were on the spot.

'It's the tail gunner,' someone roared in my ear.

'Oh Christ,' I yelled to no one in particular, 'it's always the tail gunner. Poor sod.'

It was unfair that he should buy it; in the air they were the most vulnerable, but on landing should have the advantage. What bloody bad luck.

I pushed my way through the crowd to the tail. I could see the figure of the airgunner, frantically clawing at the flaming wall of the aircraft, his clothing alight and face already blackened.

'It's his legs, they're trapped.'

'Haven't you got a bloody axe?' Of course they had, but it seemed

247

to me, in that awful moment, that the poor bastard was fighting it all on his own. I lunged towards the screaming man and through the flames could see that his legs were more than trapped, they were crushed at the thighs. The smell of burning flesh caught in my throat and I tried to take a deep breath as I fought my way in. 'Oh die, damn you, die,' I sobbed and at that moment felt a searing pain flash up my own legs and something inside me seemed to explode.

I came to in a white hospital bed to find Bill, the navigator of A Able, bending over me.

'How do you feel, old boy?'

I didn't feel anything. 'What happened?' I asked.

'Your suit caught fire. Lucky someone had the sense to slash it at the waist and rip the upper half off, or you'd have been a goner.'

I looked down at my body, covered by a cradle, and had the most awful moment of panic. I didn't dare ask – they said you could still feel your toes, even when your legs had gone, but I couldn't feel anything at all.

Instead, I asked, 'How badly am I burnt?'

I suppose my apprehension must have shown, but Bill misinterpreted my fears. He looked at me and burst out laughing.

'Don't worry, you old lecher, your manhood's safe. Only your legs are burned and they could be worse; stomach too, but only superficially, I gather.'

'Don't suppose there was much saved of that other poor bugger, was there?'

Bill shook his head and his mouth was taut. 'If only he'd lost consciousness it wouldn't have been so bad – I thought he'd never go. The bomb aimer broke his arm incidentally. Well, I must be off. Glad to see you're all right, old chap; I'll be in again soon. The AOC sends his regards and said to tell you he'd be around later.'

I'd known Bill for a long time, I was sorry too see him go – even sorrier when his place was taken by a nurse, an ominous kidney tray in hand and a purposeful air about her.

Bill grimaced and fled. 'Better you than me!'

I spent the whole of that week in a dopy haze. People came and went and inquired after my health and once Elsie popped in in a nonchalant manner, flipped some cigarette ash on my bed – she had taken up smoking herself since the time I'd caught her with someone else's fag on her bedside table – and departed after five minutes.

After I had been up and walked for the first time, the Adjutant came to see me.

'Well, sir, the MO says fourteen days sick leave and light duties until you're a hundred per cent fit.' He ignored my growl. 'Do you intend spending your leave on the station, sir, or do you want to go away? If you'll let me know, I'll have the railway warrant prepared.'

I thought for a moment, then I said, 'I think I'll go home and submit myself to my mother's tender care. Could you make the warrant to Kingsbridge, South Devon?'

'Wilco, sir.'

'Just a moment, though,' he had already saluted and was turning away, 'I'd better ask my wife, in case she wants to come too.'

The Adjutant raised his eyebrows. 'Won't she be going with you anyway?' he asked, in a slightly prim voice.

Had we really put on that good a façade?

'I doubt it,' I smiled grimly at his discomfiture. 'Don't look so upset. Be a good chap and ask her to come and see me, would you?'

Elsie showed not the slightest interest in my leave. 'You go where you like, love, it doesn't worry me,' was her only comment. I thought she might at least have made some effort and said so. She only shrugged.

After a few minutes of chit-chat, during which she looked at her watch no less than three times, and I was fighting hard to keep down my irritation, I asked her, out of the blue, 'Ever considered divorcing me, Elsie?'

I was pleased to see that she did look slightly shaken, but only momentarily. Then her mouth set in a hard line and she said with firmness, 'No, and I don't intend to either.'

'A pity I didn't die, isn't it?' I hurled at her, 'you'd have had the prestige of being a group captain's widow, without the annoyance of having me around.' She gave me a dirty look and walked straight to the door. But my ire had been raised and I wasn't through. 'Better think about a divorce, Elsie,' I called after her. 'After all, I might consider divorcing you.'

She spun round then as though stung by a wasp and asked between clenched teeth, 'And why should you want a divorce all of a sudden?'

I was calm now. 'Because I should like to marry someone else.'

'Marry? Divorce? I thought your precious career was all that mattered.'

'In many ways that's still true. But things have gone beyond that.'

'I see.' Her knowing grin roused my irritation again.

'No, Elsie, you don't see,' I told her.

'And who do you want to marry? A lady, I've no doubt.' Her scathing tone was lost on me.

'It just so happens that she is.'

'One of the WAAF officers?'

'No. It's no one you know, or are ever likely to, so drop it.'

'And you'd give me grounds? With her?'

'I'd give you grounds, yes, but not with her – there are no grounds.'

'A likely story,' she flashed. 'Well, I'll not divorce you, Jimmy, so you can just forget all about it.'

She stalked towards the door, looking exceptionally smug, but I had the impression that I had rattled her. It might not be such an impossibility after all.

The next day a medical orderly escorted me up to London and saw me off on the westbound train. I think I must have slept, because it seemed no time at all before I looked out of the window and heard a voice calling, 'Exeter St David's.'

I should have changed trains there, but I didn't have to. There was my father, looking a little greyer and a little shabbier since I had last seen him, but otherwise just the same and, standing by his side, old Nannie. It was just like coming home from school.

After a week I was feeling right as rain and my father pronounced himself satisfied with the way my burns had healed. I scarcely saw him during the daytime and neither my mother nor Nannie imposed on my privacy as I sat, reading, in the glassed-in loggia with the bare barked vine climbing above my head. But I liked their company. What bliss, I thought, to be able to turn back the clock to the days when these three people were my only attachments. I hadn't seen any of my brothers since the beginning of the war and had grown away from them.

While I sat with my mother in the kitchen one day, polishing the silver while she cooked, I told her about Helen and my attempts to get a divorce from Elsie. She made little comment at the time, but later, when they thought I had fallen asleep in my chair, I heard her say to Nannie, 'Poor darling, she'll never let him go.'

'He might divorce *her*,' Nannie said darkly, 'and, much as I dislike the thought of Master James being dragged into the muck and mire of a divorce court, in this case, I would thank the Lord with all my heart.'

To which my mother responded, 'Amen.'

26. DOUGAL RETURNS

Philip Morrison

'Dougal!' I had risen at the first call from the lookout, expecting a visitor and a friend, but not Dougal. It was more than seven months since he had left us; it was nearly the end of 1943. 'My God, it's good to see you – we had no idea you were back. How did you come in?'

'Aye, a week ago I returned. Dropped in with the new OC for the border group – difficult country that – I still say this is the only place to be dropped in our area.'

I never ceased to marvel that a man who had spent so little of his life in his native land, could still have such rolling r's. I turned to call the others, but they were already there.

'So this is Wendy's replacement,' Dougal was regarding Sally with mock severity, his beetling brows drawn down, but his eyes were twinkling – the bluest eyes she'd ever seen, Sally told me a long time later. 'Young woman, you've caused quite a furore. You realise, I suppose, that you've left yourself wide open for Court Martial, leaving your job like that?'

'Yes, sir, I realised that,' she replied quietly.

'Did you say Wendy's replacement?' I interrupted, not caring whether I was rude or not.

'Aye. Yon Wendy's a very sick girl – seems she went sick on leave, but didn't tell anyone until the last minute. Sent a telegram, but it didn't arrive until an hour or two after take-off – I have to admit that Sally had not been missed until then. The brigadier was furious, I can tell you, and as for the Air Ministry – you'd have thought the army had abducted one of their precious WAAF to flog to the white slave traffic, the way they carried on. But when everyone had simmered down and a bit of soul-searching had taken place, the brig himself said that if the telegram had arrived in time, damned if he'd have known who to send.'

'So you see, they would have had to send me anyway.' Sally was jubilant.

But Dougal held up his hand to quell her enthusiasm. 'Oh no, they wouldn't have, miss.'

'How long will Wendy be out of action?' I asked.

'A long time, I'm afraid, and she certainly won't be back here. She's got TB and not in the early stages either. I gather it will mean an operation, then several months in a sanatorium.' There were sighs all round and a gasp from Sally; Wendy had been popular. 'So, Sally stays, on probation, so to speak, at least for the time being.'

'No men?'

'None available; all out.'

Well, no good flogging a dead horse. I looked at Sally and thought what a nuisance she was, but we'd just have to make the best of it. Changing the subject, I asked Dougal, 'What's the latest news on the landings?'

'Salerno? They've reached Naples, but the weather's been so unseasonable for that part – only October and already they're harassed by winter in the mountains. The Germans aren't giving in easily either, I can tell you that.'

'It's true,' Gianna Maria entered the conversation for the first time, 'you can tell it's going to be a hard winter.'

'Oh for a decent meal,' I sighed, as the two girls passed round the midday soup, 'what's this, potato again?'

I got splashed for that. 'With turnip leaves as well to-day – you're honoured, Dougal!'

After we had finished the unappetising brew, Dougal took me on one side, as I had hoped he would, for I was avid for news of the outside world and to know what our immediate future held. I wondered if he'd been able to see my mother, as he had promised he'd try, if he did get home, and if he had any news of the battalion.

He shook his head to both of these. 'I didna' see a soul from the regiment,' he said, 'and my stay in UK was confined to London – and busy I was too. But we're in the right area to be busy here. You know Philip, something's got to give in the south. The Germans are making a stand all right and no doubt they'll hold us up for the winter – but after that? You should see the preparations being made in England – the whole South Coast's one big jumping-off ground and, it's my guess, that they won't invade France until we're pretty well consolidated here. And that means they'll pour everything into Italy to make sure of victory – can't afford not to. And then, boy, and then – when the Hun feels the push, he's going to move north as fast as he can. And once they realise it's only a matter of time, they'll pour everything into France to try and make a stand there. And that's when we'll have more work to do than we've ever done. Everything will be moving up, transport, stores, equipment, men. That's when we go to work on every road and railway; bridges, viaducts, aqueducts, power stations, the lot. We must see that our groups cover exact areas, no overlapping, no accidents if it can be helped; then we'll mark off every target and attack systematically.'

It was a thrilling thought and he was the boss, but it seemed a hopeful dream to me.

'You sound very confident,' I said, and hoped I didn't sound presumptuous, 'but I wish I had more men. Reliable ones. I have the Scum, but they're apt to be a bit undisciplined these days; they were all right before the end of the war was in view, but they always went off at a tangent – they have to be led. There aren't so many left now either – four more gone since you were last here. And if anything should happen to me, what then? I can't even use Tom. Incidentally, what is his position now?'

'As far as the bulk of Italians are concerned, he's a co-belligerent, along with the rest of the army, but while Musso retains his power – which he will as long as he has German backing – he's a traitor. His picture is still up as a wanted man on every public building and that photo's too darned good, you couldn't mistake him. No, he'll have to carry on as he is. But you'll have a couple of new boys soon, I was just coming to that.'

'New boys? How new?' Not as new as I had been, I hoped.

'Well, not too new, as it happens. They've been working in the Abruzzi – originally escapers like yourself – but the main work is going to be up here, so they'll be transferred to you.'

Things were looking up. 'Sounds like a regular bus service,' I said.

'Aye, our organisation's no' so bad, when you come to think of it. I'm getting a couple myself, and an American girl who's got herself out of internment somehow. She's of Italian descent, no language problem, so I can use her to replace Anna.'

Anna had been Dougal's counterpart of Gianna Maria, but one day, nearly a year before, she had disappeared. Just went in to Turin one day and was never seen again. The whole area had been on tenterhooks for some time and Dougal had nearly moved his headquarters. Nothing had happened, but with Johnny's lack of Italian, it had been a strain on Dougal's group.

'It must be a relief for you to get someone at last,' I said.

'Aye, it was one of the things on my mind while I was at home. With Anna gone, Sally here, and that French girl with the border group getting a bit windy, it looked as though our contact service was falling apart.'

'Wendy was a loss all right. I'm not at all happy about keeping Sally, I can tell you that,' I said flatly.

But Dougal was unsympathetic. 'I'd not underestimate yon lassie, if I were you,' he said. 'It took some guts to do what she did, you know. There's some tough fibre under that English rose exterior. When I got back from UK and found out what had happened, I made it my business to find out a bit about her – I can tell you, the history of Section Officer Gunn made quite interesting reading. She's a determined little thing, mark my words – every opening, every course that might spell action for a woman, she's been on it and passed out pretty well. She's bent on making the air force her career and she jeopardised it all by taking Wendy's place that day.'

'What does she need a career for? She'll probably get married and have hordes of screaming brats before she knows what's happened to her. Anyway, she has a family, hasn't she?' I really could not see why Dougal was making such a fuss of her.

'No, she has not. At least it's unlikely that she has any longer. Mother dead, father most probably dead, only child, home gone – the lot. Didn't you know that?'

'No, I didn't. She's never mentioned it. Just told me that she had lived in Malaya, but I presumed she would have been at school when war broke out.'

'And so she should have been, but she wasn't. That young woman – I refuse to call her a child – has seen some pretty brutal war already.

She's been under shellfire and machine-gun fire; she's been short of food and sunk at sea. She's seen men killed. And I've read that she was digging bodies out after her station was blitzed, without turning a hair. She's unlikely to panic in an emergency; she's steady, and that's important.'

'She's a good enough kid, Dougal, I've nothing against her – ' in fact his discourse had put her in a somewhat different light – 'it's just this language problem.'

'Well, of course I agree there, but Tom tells me her Italian's coming on fine – she's not likely to be mistaken for one of the natives just yet, but if it's good enough to get past the Germans, I feel that in a wee while it won't matter whether the natives suspect her or not – they're mostly on our side around here anyway.'

I'm ashamed to admit that I had considered Sally to be such a temporary measure that I had taken no interest in her Italian – she seemed to spend every spare moment at it, certainly, but I thought the attraction was Tom. I'd better listen to her myself.

'Will you come back with me to-morrow? I've sent for Tony Marker and Bill to come in – we can have a real good confab and co-ordinate our plans. Johnny's been briefed pretty thoroughly from home, I gather, and although I don't understand half the things he talks about, he should be able to tell us what the RAF intend doing.'

'Who is Tony Marker?' It was a new name to me.

'Of course, you need not have heard. Pat was killed soon after I left. Bill should have taken over, but as HQ had this tame airman on hand and, as his French is as fluent as his Italian, he was an obvious choice for the border group.'

I had heard about Pat – killed when he was so sick he should have been in a hospital somewhere, instead of attempting to lead a raid. Dougal had been trying to get him out for months – it was the kind of thing that made one really bolshie.

It was a good discussion at Dougal's place. He told us that it was now the opinion at base that each group could do more harm by harassing the enemy in their individual areas and in their own way – this had been his opinion all along, I knew, and he had no doubt got them to agree – but he was the soul of tact. He instructed each of us to prepare our targets up to the end of the year, and he would act as co-ordinator to ensure that none clashed.

There was some argument about the merits of simultaneous sabotage as opposed to pockets of trouble popping up in one place after another. I was in favour of the latter, pointing out that it was more nerve-racking for the enemy never to know what was going to happen next, or where, but to be sure that something would. We grew a little heated at times, but Dougal always sorted us out.

Tony Marker turned out to be a flight lieutenant; about thirty-five, I judged, an academic, intelligence type; so once again I was the youngest and least experienced there. But times had changed since I was first in on one of Dougal's confabs and I wasn't afraid to air my views any more.

It was agreed, finally, that the border group should start the ball rolling by blowing a bridge, to be followed almost immediately by Dougal's group – which had now been taken over by Bill, allowing Dougal to remain mobile – derailing a train, and then we were to sabotage an aqueduct.

The aqueduct in question was an easy target, but well guarded. I went on a recce with just one man, Mario, and came to the conclusion that the fewer to do the job the better. And so we set out one crisp morning in early December with Stefano, the strong man, carrying the heaviest gear; Luigi, the cleverest with his hands; Mario, and myself.

We carried picks and shovels, parked our bicycles casually on the open road and began to dig a hole.

A German convoy squeezed past, the officer in charge swearing at the state of the road, and several vehicles stopped to see what we were doing, but nobody actually asked us – which was a pity, as I had thought up a long-winded rigmarole, guaranteed, I felt, to try the patience of any German, but I didn't have a chance to try it out.

As soon as the first hole was a decent size, we filled it in and moved on down the road to start a second one. And so a third and a fourth, always nearer the pipe.

The aqueduct itself commanded a first-rate view and it was natural that we should sit astride the great pipe to eat and talk when we broke off at noon. After we had finished our meal we snoozed, then set about the task of filling in the last hole.

As the early dark began to close in, we set up a roadside shelter for the night. The aqueduct guards watched us all the time and when we were settled in and ready for our evening meal, such as it was, Mario called out to them to come and share our wine.

They came gladly enough and we carried on a stilted conversation well into the night and parted the best of friends.

Next morning the *buon giornos* and *guten tags* floated across, the guards cleaned out their hut and inspected the aqueduct, and we began to dig another hole.

We followed exactly the same procedure as on the previous day and the guards took no notice when, once again, we took our midday bread to perch and eat on the great pipe.

Soon all was ready for the blast. I signalled to Mario, who nodded his head, then pushed the plunger home.

The explosion was almost instantaneous and a great fountain of water shot sky high.

The guards erupted from their hut like peas from an overripe pod, only to be knocked senseless by Stefano's fists and Mario's sten. I was glad that, in this case, it had not been necessary to kill them.

We dragged our bicycles to the road, all laughing and pleased with the results, and prepared to ride away. As we did so, a truck came down the road – the explosion had obviously been heard and it was rushing towards the gushing aqueduct.

Hoping to act as a decoy, I turned my own bike and rode off furiously in the opposite direction. The driver hesitated, but only for a second, then came after me, as I had hoped he would.

A few shots were fired, but the truck was going at a hell of a lick along a corrugated road and they all missed me. Nevertheless, I hadn't enough start on them to remain in the lead for long and had no intention of being shot if I could avoid it, so, as soon as they began to gain, I deliberately fell off the bike and lay, defenceless and unarmed, on the side of the road.

Fishing in my trouser pockets, I pulled out one of the KD epaulettes showing my badges of rank. Now, I thought, we'll see if this works.

The truck stopped and a corporal got down and ran across the road. I could see that he was covered by his mates, in case I was not as defenceless as I appeared no doubt, so I put my hands up, waving my embroidered captain's pips in the air.

'I am a British officer,' I called out – it really did sound rather ridiculous under the circumstances, 'and I shall only tell you my number, rank and name.'

The corporal stopped a yard or so from me and gaped. I decided that I was rather enjoying myself and continued, while I had the whip hand, 'I demand to be treated with the respect due to my rank and to be taken to a prisoner of war camp.'

The corporal came to his senses and the last thing I remember was him clouting me over the head.

27. A PAINFUL DISAPPOINTMENT

Donald Thom

Cra-a-ack! My legs took the full impact of landing and it hardly needed the pain shooting up my body to tell me that something was broken. I lay for a moment, while the silk of my chute folded round me, then I gritted my teeth and tried to roll over.

I guess I must have passed out for a second or two, because next thing I knew, two guys were bending over me and prodding my legs and it took me all my willpower not to scream. Judas Priest, I bit into my lips and clenched my fists while what I sure hoped were expert hands felt me all over.

I don't think they'd realised I'd come to, because when I let out a sound which I just couldn't help, the one who had been doing the prodding came quickly to my head and held it up, while the other guy poured something from a flask between my lips. Schnapps or something, I guess. But I was not at all sure at that moment that I wanted to be revived – I'd rather they just knocked me out good and cold, wrapped me in my built-in shroud and just quietly disposed of me. The pain was that bad.

The flask holder took it away and corked it. 'Radio's all right, Hans,' he commented, 'I'd better check the rest of the equipment.' I guess the radio was more important than me.

The one called Hans grunted and shook his head. 'Both legs gone – he won't be able to walk for weeks.'

A great wave of disappointment flooded over me. Once the initial decision had been taken, I'd been aiming at just this moment, keying myself up for weeks. And then, to break both legs on my first operational jump. I looked up at the two hard-faced men as they rooted among the containers that had been dropped with me – I was a disappointment to them too, no doubt – they'd wanted a man, not a wheel-chair patient.

I tried not to sound irritable as I asked them about my immediate future, but I knew that the pain and the anticlimax were putting a whine into my voice.

Neither of them answered me – barely spared me a glance if it came to that – but argued the pros and cons between themselves. This went on for several minutes – or so it seemed – until they decided to hide me nearby until such time as a doctor could be found to attend me.

'Finish me off now,' I said petulantly, 'it'd be less trouble for everyone; especially me.'

They ignored the outburst and started taking off their coats. Then began the most agonising few minutes I hope I shall ever have to spend in this life. I don't think for one moment that they were as callous as they seemed – in fact I found that out later – but if you've ever been dragged, with both legs broken, on a couple of coats and a parachute across some fifty feet of rough ground, well, I just don't have to tell you any more.

They left me then and I've no idea how long I lay under that bush and whether or not I was conscious the whole time. I only know that at one point I reached for my pistol and if it hadn't been so firmly strapped to one of my broken legs and the pain had not been sufficient deterrent to make me give up the idea, I wouldn't be telling you this now.

Quite suddenly there were several faces bending over me and one of them belonging to a slight, white-haired man, possibly in his sixties, smiled at me. He was feeling under my back for something, but in a moment he sat back on his heels, apparently satisfied.

'I'd give you a jab to stop the pain if I could, son,' he said in slightly accented English, 'but my drugs are too precious. Anyway, your spine seems all right and your legs will mend. You'll have to bear the next few minutes while I splint them, then you'll feel better. Bandage his mouth, Konrad, and you, Hans and Jan, hold him still; we can't risk being seen or heard here.'

Konrad, who turned out to be the man who was more interested in the radio than me, lifted my head and wound a crêpe bandage tightly round my mouth. He looked kinder this time and nodded and smiled as he did it, and patted my shoulder when it was done.

Prepared for the worst, the pain was not as bad as I had expected, and it was not long before I was propped up against a tree, my pins sticking out like a couple of giant sausages, straight in front of me. That time I was able to say thanks for the dollop of firewater.

'How will you move him?' the doctor asked when he was ready to go.

'We will use Jan's father's lorry. It is all arranged.' It was Hans who spoke and it was clear from his tone that he was the leader. 'When the last load of wheat is taken to the mill, he can go with it. It will be nearly dark by then and he can stay in the mill.'

'No.' The doctor did not approve of that plan. 'That is no good. He cannot be left unattended. Take him to Marijke's house; she is a good nurse and they have an attic. I will warn her. Meanwhile one of you stay with him.'

So it was arranged and all the men but Konrad pulled the branches away from their bicycles and rode off.

I felt pretty vulnerable sitting there. I guess any aircraft flying overhead would have mistaken my legs for the identification letters of a dropping zone! It seemed that Konrad thought the same and he soon covered them up with branches, same as the bikes. Then he sat down to wait for the other guys to return.

'Marijke is a good girl,' he told me, 'but you must be careful. Her mother is a garrulous woman and there will be danger, not only for you but for all of us.'

Danger, at that moment, seemed the least important of my problems.

28. DINNER AT THE ATTERY

Stanislaus Olshewski

We flew pretty solidly until the early part of 1944 when, quite suddenly, the whole squadron was posted back to UK.

I had no desire at all to return to Europe and both Harry and I grumbled a good deal during the short time we had before we were actually on the move. But it soon became clear why we were wanted – and why the remaining bods would have to carry on, under strength, and lump it.

When I had left England nearly a year before, the war seemed at a standstill and invasion but a dream of the future. In Cairo, the invasion of Italy had been predicted and of course taken place while we were in India. But in India itself, European events belonged to another world.

We landed at Cairo for the night and it didn't take us long to remember that winter was something else we had been able to forget in a very short time.

The mess was almost empty but the same barman was there and from him we learned that everybody we had known had either been sent to Italy or posted home. Major events were obviously in the offing. It was an exciting prospect.

It was sad saying good-bye to our aeroplanes. Our future was only partly revealed, but we knew that, for us at any rate, it was farewell to our dear old Daks. Meanwhile we had forty-eight hours to paint the town red before reporting to a station within the coastal security zone.

'Why don't we look up Helen?' It was Harry's suggestion.

I had only seen her once since our leave in Bombay; that had been about a fortnight later, when we had cadged a ride to Delhi for the night. We had never written. Turning up out of the blue might be an embarrassment to her.

'Do you think she'd want to see us?' I was a little dubious.

'Of course.'

We found our way to her mess without too much difficulty and ascertained that she did indeed still live there. She had booked dinner, but had not yet returned.

It was a terrifying place. Hordes of elderly, military females, and nearly all of them senior in rank as well as in age to either of us. But they were charming. By the time Helen arrived, we were sipping our second sherries and no longer feeling so male, nor so blue.

Helen was charming too and did not appear in the least surprised to see us.

259

'I knew you'd turn up one day,' she said, as she took our hands. 'It's splendid to see you both.'

There was a chorus of protest from the elderly ladies when we told Helen to hurry up and get ready, we were taking her out to dinner.

'But why don't you dine here?' asked one with a colonel's pips and crown up – whatever a female colonel may be – who appeared to be the senior member. 'There's always someone who doesn't turn up for dinner and, Watson will agree, our food is pretty good.'

'Oh, I do, ma'am. Cook's first-rate.'

I had wondered who Watson was for a moment. It always sounded odd to me, hearing women calling each other by their surnames. Helen winked at me.

'Why don't you stay,' she suggested, 'and we can go on somewhere afterwards.'

So we stayed and did justice to the food. The female colonel had been right; it was pretty good and we were hungry.

'Whew!' Harry took a deep breath as we left the mess, 'wait till I write Una and tell her I had my first proper meal in England in an Attery – that should get her applying for a posting home, *toute suite*.'

'How is Una? Still enjoying Delhi, I take it?'

'Sore point. You know I wanted to marry that girl before I left India and then we were posted at a moment's notice. If she doesn't get to England before I leave – ' I kicked him hard before he blabbed any more, ' – heaven alone knows how I'll ever get her to Aussie.'

We did the pub crawl that you would expect and ended up in some underground joint – and it was a joint – not far from Piccadilly Circus. And that was the last we saw of Harry.

With a shriek that sounded like a posse of Highlanders coming to grips with a band of dervishes, a good dozen dark blue RAAF uniforms met in a scrum. It seemed that Harry had met some long-lost cobbers.

'You two don't need me,' he yelled from the other side of the dive, 'and you can use the room. See you at sparrow's fart on Thursday!'

I looked sideways at Helen, expecting to see her blush or at least look annoyed, but she was smiling.

As I've said before, she was quite a girl.

I told her which hotel we had booked in at and she lifted her hands in horror.

'Oh no! My reputation would never stand it!'

But she came with me nevertheless.

How unfamiliar London seemed. I had forgotten the cave-dwellers of the Underground, the rush for the late night trains, and the cold, whistling wind that came in blasts down the stairways and ventilators. Muffled up in a greatcoat, Helen looked different too. Even the formality of collar and tie and uniform jacket had repressed the casual girl that I had known in India. I was glad when we were safely past the doorman and I was putting a bob in the gas meter.

Helen in bed was not unfamiliar and the cool veneer was soon put aside with her uniform. She didn't stay long though. Either the hotel was worrying her, or there was something else on her mind. She was the same old Helen, but she wasn't relaxed.

After standing on the kerb for hours, we got a taxi and I took her back to her mess and, fool that I am, I forgot to tell him to wait and spent most of the remainder of the night walking back to the hotel.

No matter. I was meeting Helen for lunch, but I could sleep in as long as I liked.

I was glad to see her again, glad to have a couple of days in London, but for choice I'd still have been back over Burma, dropping what I could, and as accurately as I could, to men who had every right to consider themselves the Forgotten Army. Helen would not have been flattered to know that those were the thoughts I went to sleep with, but those are what they were.

Why, why, why? Why, in heaven's name, couldn't I put that wretched Weatherby out of my mind? Seeing Stan again made me realise, more than ever, that he had all the qualities which James lacked.

He was kind, where James could be hard and callous; he was completely unselfish – something I could never say for dear James – and he spared my feelings.

Every month, when James came up to town for his conference, I walked on air for days. My whole me, body and soul, lit up and sang at one glance, one insinuation that could hint of love. And then what happened? He went back, leaving me as flat as a pricked balloon. And for days I'd mope; angry with myself for being such a fool and angry with him for being so unfair. Because he was unfair; no doubt about it. He knew I was in love with him; knew I always had been. He should never have sought me out again after that first break.

Well, I wasn't going to see him again. It was time I used a little strength of mind, a little willpower. What was I – a chicken, to be hypnotised? Anyone would think so. Oh come, Helen Watson, don't be so bloody stupid. When is the next conference? The seventeenth? And by the fifteenth you'll be singing at work and grinning your silly head off. Make a clean break indeed! You'd better just pray that something happens to make it for you. Oh, please God, no. Don't take him away from me – not that he's mine to take. But no, I don't want a break. Even the monthly lunches are better than nothing. I didn't mean it; I don't want a break.

And with these imbecilic thoughts whirring through my head, I eventually fell asleep. Never a thought for poor old Stan, with whom I had been making love only a few hours before.

Stan. I woke with a strong feeling of guilt and remembered that I was meeting him for lunch.

He would be off at crack of dawn the next day. I wondered if the general would let me off early so that we could really make an evening of it. And a night. I'd try and make it up to him for last night.

I suppose you will think it wrong in the circumstances – loving James, however hopelessly – that I should sleep with Stan at all. As a matter of fact I hadn't really wanted to, but he was such a good egg and I'm sure he was expecting it. After all, there had been no inhibitions in Bombay and he did give me a wonderful time.

'I shall be thoroughly extravagant this evening,' I said, 'and I'll bring my toothbrush.'

'Are you sure you want to?'

The sun was out and we were walking in St James's Park, after a snacky lunch in a crowded café.

I stopped to sniff at a clump of lily of the valley. 'Quite sure,' I told the flowers.

'I thought, maybe, last night you were – I don't know the right word. Not chilly – preoccupied perhaps?'

'Oh, Stan. It's all so *silly*.'

Dear, reliable Stan. As I walked to a vacant bench and sat down, I wondered how many people had told him their troubles. I told him mine.

'The father of Toby?'

'Yes.' I looked at him in surprise. 'Fancy you remembering that.'

'Well, it was hardly the happiest day of our leave, was it?'

I squeezed his arm. 'You were an angel, Stan – and still are. I don't remember any love for James coming into my feelings that day – just jealousy and pique. I was so sure that he had been in love with me and, to take me to the room that he was going to share with his wife the next night and then, almost nine months to the day, a son arrives. I kept seeing that double bed and imagining them together. Oh, it was horrible. I hated them, and I hated myself even more.'

'But, as you say, she was his wife.'

'And is. He's utterly worthless as far as I am concerned and brings me nothing but unhappiness. But why spoil the first sunshine we've had this year? Let's enjoy each other's company while we may – heaven knows when we shall meet again.'

Stan had not mentioned his posting and I knew next to nothing about the air force, but I had a shrewd idea that his squadron's sudden move to England must have something to do with the invasion. Despite the Official Secrets Act, maximum security zones and screenings, invasion prophets were two a penny. No one knew when or where or how, but there was an air of suppressed excitement all around us – not only in every office with which I had dealings, but even in the shops and on the streets.

I knew better than to question him, but I wondered when indeed we would meet again.

'I nearly forgot these – collected them this morning.' He was pulling a large yellow and black envelope from his pocket, bulging with photographs. He spread them out on the bench between us and we went through them one by one.

'You know, Stan, I *did* enjoy that leave – I wish I had never had to come back from India.'

There were several taken in Bombay, but they were mostly of me. 'Take any you want.'

I chose a couple showing the flat, and one of our favourite swimming place. Then I picked up one of Stan, a half portrait, taken in Cairo.

'May I have this one too?'

'If you want it, but it's the only one of me in blues and I look so solemn. Whatever made you choose that?'

'It's also the only one that shows your wings and your DFC – I like to be proud of my men, you know!'

I tucked them into my wallet and put it away.

I took Helen to a so-called Polish restaurant that evening. I can't think why, really. The food was deplorable and the atmosphere too phoney for words.

We ploughed our way through lukewarm beetroot soup and a spiced mess, which Helen called 'haggis gone wrong,' and drank vodka which must have been distilled on the premises – and what from I dread to think. It really was awful, but she was amused, imploring me to see the funny side.

My lovely Helen.

I looked into her eyes and saw, not the funny side, but an answer to the urgency that was in me.

Who cared about beetroot soup? I paid the bill.

After sneaking Helen down the fire escape as dawn was breaking, I hurried back to my room and rang for an early breakfast.

Harry was waiting at Waterloo. Bleary-eyed and worse for wear, but punctual none the less.

'How was the reunion?'

'A fair cow,' he croaked, 'I'll stick to Poles and Poms from now on. Christ, I'm crook!'

Our new aircraft turned out to be good old Daks again and I for

263

one was not sorry; I'd grown fond of them. We soon learned that training was to begin at once and our future role that of towing gliders across the Channel when the balloon went up.

I stood on the balcony of SHQ and looked at the field. Aircraft were ranged wingtip to wingtip as far as the eye could see; an airborne armada in the embryonic stage. Four years and more since I had set foot on Europe proper. I wondered what it would feel like to be flying over France again, perhaps even Poland, in time.

My only disappointment was that Harry and I were to split up. But I couldn't complain; he had flown as second pilot for long enough. Time he had his own kite.

My new crew were all British, all NCOs. A good bunch.

29. IN FOR A PENNY IN FOR A POUND

Philip Morrison

After languishing in the central gaol for three months – so much for that being treated as a POW lark – I decided that the time had come to put my escape plans into effect.

Everywhere the Germans were doing badly and Southern and Central Italy were already in Allied hands. In the circumstances, I didn't think it would be too difficult to soften up one of the warders and I picked on one of the youngest, Alessandro by name, and had been beaming my propaganda at him for the past two or three weeks. It was simple propaganda. I impressed on him how well he would be treated if he helped me to escape, and how badly it would go with him if, when the Allies marched in, they found that he, a so-called co-belligerent, was helping to hold a British officer for the Germans.

Poor Alessandro. It was unfair really and I felt quite a brute as I watched him biting his nails and squirming at the thought of what either side might do to him. He didn't know which way to turn.

I waited for the right psychological moment, a day when there had been a major German defeat. There were several, but the one I chose was a day when there had also been a bad air raid the night before. Knowing that the area was full of factories, I banked on there being more.

'Psst. Alessandro,' I hissed next time he passed my cell. 'I have thought of a way to make it easy for you. You see how buckled this door is?' I rattled the bars to emphasise my point, 'next time there's an air raid, unlock my door, then leave it open with the lock out – provided it's near enough, it will look as though the blast has opened the door. You can lie near it, pretending the blast has knocked you out too.'

264

He made no reply, but went away and, every time I saw him, he had that worried, pensive look that showed me he was still thinking it over. But he was quite bright next morning and announced that he had an even better idea.

'There is an empty cell a little way along, where the ceiling is about to fall in. I will damage the lock of this door, so that it would no longer keep you in, and move you to the other cell – it is the only one empty, because it is unsafe. Then, when there is another air raid, I will unlock your door and you must hit me – not too hard, but enough to leave a bruise – and I will tell the Chief Warder that I was afraid of what would happen if the Allies learned afterwards that a British officer was killed in an air raid because he had been confined in an unsafe cell. I will say that I was going to move you when you hit me. How's that?'

'Brilliant,' I agreed. He was beaming from ear to ear. I was glad he had seen sense at last. 'Splendid. And now, if you will give me pencil and paper, I shall write a note that you can hand to the Allies when they arrive.'

He promised to work out a plan and a few days later told me that we were in luck, as it had been ordered that the main gate should be left open during air raids. Not only that, but his sister, Emilia, would be at the Duomo at six o'clock in the evening after the very next raid, to help me. She always wore a red coat and she would supply me with food and clothing. All we had to do was wait for another raid.

Funny how the little chap changed, once he had made up his mind to help. Thoughts of getting in with the Allies from the start – as he undoubtedly had with the Germans – I suppose. He wasn't greedy – just afraid. He told me that his sister was to be at home every afternoon after four o'clock, waiting and ready with the food, in case there was a raid.

The day came and my heart palpitated at the sound of the siren. Alessandro was nearly as excited as I when he came to let me out. I'm afraid I hit him considerably harder than I said I would, just to make sure he didn't change his mind, and left his unconscious body lying on the floor outside the cell.

The prison was like a rabbit warren and it was no straightforward walk to the main gate. Thank God for the good old Latin temperament. There was such chaos; people rushing madly in every direction, arms waving and voices raised, so I started rushing and shouting myself until I reached the main gate, then walked calmly through.

I judged the time to be about three o'clock. Seeing a passengerless, gas-driven cab approaching, and blessing the fact that I had not been issued with prison uniform, I jumped into the middle of the road and flagged it down.

'Please,' I implored the driver, my hands together in an attitude of prayer and pointing to my torn and soiled clothing, 'I have no money on me, but if you are going in the direction of Cathedral Square, please take me with you. I have just had a very narrow escape from a descending bomb and wish to light a candle to Our Lady in gratitude.'

This was taking a chance of course, as there may well have been other churches nearer than the Duomo; but I could see that he was pretty shaken himself and his cab was covered with dirt and dust. Perhaps he approved my piety, wanted company, or was just a decent type. Whichever it was, my luck was in and he leaned over to unlock the passenger door.

Once inside the Cathedral, I really did look at the statues with gratitude and blessed the vaulted dimness as I sank into a pew. I sat with head bowed for what must have been nearly two hours and when the clock struck six, got up and walked towards the main door.

Most of the famous paintings had been covered or removed, but I stood admiring one while watching the door out of the corner of my eye and it was not long before a young girl, not more than thirteen or fourteen, I would think, wearing a red coat and carrying a basket over one arm, came in.

She walked slowly into the main well of the building, looking neither to right nor left, genuflected to the main altar, and moved to a pew on the right-hand side of the aisle. The Duomo was practically empty and after a moment or two, making sure that I was not being watched by one of the black-clad old crones who knelt nearer the front, I followed the girl and knelt beside her. 'Are you Emilia?'

She looked up, like a scared little mouse, and nodded silently. I smiled as reassuringly as I could and told her that Alessandro had sent me.

'I know,' she whispered back; she seemed less frightened now. 'If you will follow me, I will give you the things outside.'

It was dusk when she slipped out of a side door and I hurried, fearful of losing her, soon afterwards. She looked back once to make sure I was following her, then turned left and darted furtively into an alleyway behind the Cathedral.

'Please take them quickly,' she was still whispering, 'and give me the basket back. I'm frightened and I must get home before dark.'

I changed into the clothes she had brought, a rough pair of trousers, thick sweater and corduroy cap, in a nearby doorway.

'Perhaps you would dispose of these?' I asked, holding out the things I had taken off.

'Leave them here,' she said, 'there are many poor people in the city who will be glad if they find them.'

266

I took the food, a loaf and two hard-boiled eggs, and stuffed them into my trouser pockets.

'God bless you,' I said and, following her directions, turned and walked away.

I walked all the way to the Central Station, where, Emilia had told me, I would be able to find a bench on which to sleep for the night without being questioned. Then, very early next morning, I cadged a lift on a lorry going north.

At the junction to Turin I asked to be let off and waving good-bye to the driver, trudged off down the deserted road.

I must have been walking for the best part of half an hour when I heard a motor-bike coming up behind me – it was the first vehicle since I had left the lorry, but of course this was not the main road.

Hopefully, I held up my hand and then wished I hadn't. The rider stopped and I saw to my horror that he was a German dispatch rider.

Oh well, in for a penny in for a pound, I thought. We shan't be able to hold much of a conversation if he keeps up that speed.

It was a most exhilarating experience, clasping the German soldier round the waist and having him take me where I wanted to go. I suppose, if I had been a really keen type, I would have strangled him or something and taken his bike, but there didn't seem any point.

Once past our turning, I waited for a suitable cross roads, then asked to be put down. With a wave he was on his way again.

It could not have been much more than 10.30, but I knew where I was now and I had a good long way to go. Normally I could have made it by evening, but three months of doing nothing but sitting or lying down and the prison diet had weakened me more than I had realised. When I came to a suitable place, I dossed down and fell asleep and only woke up when it was almost dark. I was stiff and hungry, but there was no point in going further before daylight, so I ate my last hard boiled egg and the remains of the crust and lay down to wait for the dawn.

It was a long trek through rugged country, strewn with boulders and stunted trees – the type of country I had come to know well and to feel an affection for. There was no longer a bite in the air and, as I climbed, I could feel the warm sun on my back.

My homecoming had been tempered for the last mile or so with apprehension and as I walked along the familiar path, I scanned every rock and bush for signs of anything that might have happened during my absence.

And then, sooner than I had expected, from a high ridge I heard the lookout yelling wildly.

'*Il Capitano è tornato; Filippo è tornato. Ah, Filippo, Capitano*

Filippo.' And I found myself clasped in a garlicky embrace as Enrico, who had been jumping from rock to rock down the hillside and quite forgetting his duty, covered the last few yards.

God, it was good to see the old rogue. And he hadn't quite forgotten all the discipline I had tried so hard to instil in them. 'I must go back.' He gave me another hug and was off again up the hill and I walked on through the glade.

And then I saw them. All of them. They were standing like a bunch of sheep, gaping.

Then someone started running and they were all running and I was running towards them. And suddenly it was Sally running on her own, running faster than the others and then she was in my arms.

'Oh Philip, you've come back,' and she was hugging me and kissing me, laughing and crying at the same time, and I was hugging her back.

Letting us two compatriots greet each other first, the others held back, but I saw with satisfaction over Sally's head that they were all there, at least, nearly all: Mario, Carlo, Salvatore, Giorgio, Stefano, Luigi, Tom, and Gianna Maria; and behind them, the babies, Giuseppe and Francesco. Andreo was missing, and Vittore. Gianna Maria stepped forward then and gently pushed Sally aside.

'My turn now, I think,' she said, and winding her arms round my neck, she kissed me hard and long.

We had been cleaning the arms and ammo when Enrico's ecstatic cry rent the air.

I closed my eyes and said a little prayer of thanksgiving, and when I looked up he was there. In the distance still, but there was no mistaking the tall, lanky figure, approaching through the glade.

Neither Mario, Luigi, nor Stefano had known what had happened to Philip. After waiting for him to join them in vain, they had retraced their steps and come across his bicycle, lying by the side of the road. Gianna Maria had been as far as Milan itself, trying to find out news of him, but the only information she had gleaned had been that a man calling himself a British officer had been taken into Gestapo headquarters. Whether it had been Philip or not was doubtful, when there were so many prisoners of war escaping the whole time now. What had happened to the man no one knew and, whether Philip or not, we feared the worst.

We all rose, hardly daring to believe our eyes, standing still, waiting. Then someone began to run and we all ran.

But I ran fastest. I outdistanced Gianna Maria, Tom, the Scum, and then he was running too. He looked like a tall, thin scarecrow, trousers and pullover sleeves too short and arms outstretched – like some great, flapping bird.

I laughed as I ran and I saw Philip laughing too, then we met head on. I flung myself into his arms, hugging his large, bony body, and kissing every bit I could reach. And he was hugging and kissing me too and we laughed and kissed again. Then I saw him looking over my head and felt Gianna Maria pushing me away.

I don't think I remember much of what happened during the next hour or two. We hadn't much to eat, but Gianna and I did the best we could to prepare a celebration meal, while Philip talked to Tom and the Scum.

'Those are the first words of English I've heard for three months,' Sally had said when I greeted her and they had caused a niggling doubt in my mind. I knew that Tom and Gianna Maria had made a pact with her to speak only Italian, but what about Dougal and Bill, and don't tell me Johnny had suddenly blossomed into a linguist after all this time?

There were so many answers to my questions and by so many of the Scum at once, each eager to give his version of the operation, that I put my hands over my ears and waited for them to sort themselves out.

'Hush, I will tell you,' Gianna Maria called from the fire and the Scum subsided.

The bridge, I knew, was on the list for destruction, the main item after one or two smaller incidents following the aqueduct. The winter had not been as bad this year and it seemed they had been able to carry on where I left off. I was glad to hear that our efforts on the aqueduct had been successful, but I couldn't help feeling slightly envious of their greater success on the bridge. Gianna was a little hazy on the placing of explosives – she was essentially a woman really – and I heard three different versions from the Scum, but the important thing was that it had worked. They told me how half the German convoy had gone down to join the spring thaw, as the great blocks of ice hurtled downstream. They told me how Sally had attracted the sentry's attention, while Carlo crept up from behind and garotted him. They told me about a cryptic message that had been dropped with the explosives that made them think that the end of the war was near. And they told me that, because of the blowing of the bridge, there had been no further contact with Dougal. They also told me how Andreo, one of the old faithfuls, had gone down with the ice and how Vittore had just disappeared.

'Although I must admit I am surprised,' said Gianna Maria, 'that none of them have come this way. But I'm sure Dougal's all right, or I would have heard from the contadini.'

'Give me a few days and I'll be fit enough to look for a way.' Then I told them that they had indeed interpreted the message correctly and the end of the war was near. I told them how I had bribed my way out of gaol and how easy it had been to get back. 'Everyone's mind is on the advance, and I'm sure if I had stood up in one of the main squares of Milan and announced that I was an escaped Allied prisoner, no one would have paid me the slightest heed.'

We all had a lot to say and by the time we sat down to our evening meal, the sky was ablaze with stars and we were grateful for the warmth of the fire.

When we all sat down to eat round the fire, I sat next to Philip and when we had finished eating he took my hand – something he had never done before and, if he had, I would probably have snatched it away. He didn't talk to me very much; mostly to Gianna Maria on his other side, and Tom, but he played with my hand and I could feel his warmth close by.

It was a clear, starry night; I remember it very well. We talked for ages, and when Tom at last got up and stretched and announced that he was for bed, Philip and I looked at each other in the firelight and I know that there was no doubt in either of our minds.

I followed him into the woods and up to a vantage point, where we could watch the moon rise above the serrated edge of the mountains. Even on the most unromantic occasions, it was always awe-inspiring from this spot and we watched it in silence, the beauty almost hurting.

There was no holding back this time. No hesitation. No fear. I would never again do what I had done to Stan; I had grown up in a year. I sank down in Philip's arms and gave him what I had never given any man before, myself – and wholly.

The agony and the ecstasy. I didn't mind the pain – on the contrary, I welcomed it, locking me with his hard body and his gentle nature.

Afterwards we lay very quietly, for a long time. Discovering each other, loving each other. And when I heard Philip's voice saying, 'Will you marry me, Sally, when all this is over?' I had no hesitation in saying, 'Yes.'

Funny, isn't it, how someone can be there, irritating at first and unwanted, and then just there and, quite suddenly, *there*.

When I had thought of Sally while I was in prison, it was only as one of the group – on a par with Gianna Maria and Tom, less than Dougal.

And then, when I held her in my arms, something like an electric shock ran through me, fusing us together, and if Gianna Maria hadn't pushed us apart, I don't know when I would have released her.

While I talked with the Scum, watching the two girls preparing the meal, I really looked at Sally for the first time. I hadn't realised before that she was all eyes and legs. There was grace – and a wide, wide smile.

I made myself talk because it was expected of me, but all the time I could feel that little warm hand in mine and I wanted to hold her close and never let her go.

But it was all right. I knew when we stood, watching the moon rise, even before we made love, that it was going to be all right.

It was only afterwards that I remembered it had been an exhausting day and the next thing I knew, Sally was shaking me and calling, 'Philip, Philip wake up, it's nearly daylight, we must get back.'

She was right, of course. I doubt if there was a person in the group who did not know that I had been making love to her that night, but we had to keep up the pretence; maintain the façade of respectability. I picked up my new small love and brushed her down and we slipped quietly back to the clearing.

I had just stretched out on my bunk when I heard the first man stirring, and the daylight filtering through told me that morning had come.

I didn't sleep. As soon as I heard Gianna Maria getting up, I got up too. She wasn't exactly talkative that morning, in fact she was a little curt – I don't know why; as far as I knew she had no particular interest in Philip.

Early as it was, he was already up, talking to a couple of the Scum and drinking his acorn coffee. He raised his mug to me and I looked into his eyes and wanted him all over again – Stan was right, I had enjoyed it.

The day passed somehow and then it was dark again and we were alone together. Looking at the fleecy clouds scudding across the moon and feeling Philip's warmth upon me, I was blissfully happy.

'I thought you were horrid, hateful,' I whispered into his ear, 'and now I love you more than anything else in the world.'

'And I you.'

It was a wonderful feeling, to want and be wanted. We talked, but we didn't talk of the future – perhaps we didn't dare – but only of each other and the present, and just a little of the recent past.

'Lucky we're not in Jugoslavia,' Philip said. 'We would be shot for this.'

What better bed than pine needles? What better roof than the sky? Or so I thought, lying there with my love beside me, listening to the gentle breeze in the pines and her heart under my ear.

'I know I may sound old-fashioned,' I whispered, 'but I'm glad I was the first.'

'You nearly weren't.'

'Tom?'

'Oh, no. Ages before Tom.' Was it ages? Under two years to be exact.

'I must admit I was surprised – you came with me so readily.'

Even through the filtered moonlight I could see the frown creasing her brow and when she spoke it was thoughtfully, and very low.

'I once nearly drove a man insane with my Puritanical ideals. I thought I was right, but I should have left him alone. He taught me a lot though – I swore I'd never do that to any man again.'

'Did you love him?'

'Yes, very much. But I was afraid of him too. I've had lots of boy friends, Philip, and I thought I had been in love half a dozen times, but really only once before and you're the first person I've ever wanted to marry.'

'I thought, being holed up with him these past few months, that you'd be madly in love with Tom by now.'

'Oh, Tom.' Her voice was full of irritation. 'He's a good sort really, but I think self-pity is one of the worst traits I know. If I've heard about his Jugoslav mother and his Italian father and the complications arising from that union and his present position once, I've heard them fifty times. And you know, even Gianna Maria, who I think is a splendid person, sighs for the poor hard-done-by Italians. My gosh – you should have seen me waving the Union Jack! I know Britain hasn't been invaded or occupied, but I'm tired to death of hearing how everyone else in Europe has suffered bar us.'

I was amused by Sally's vehemence, but I knew that feeling well. I kissed her before I let her go on.

'You must admit, Philip, that nine-tenths of the time we do very little here. I know there have been casualties, and no doubt there will be more, but when you think that every time a bomber is shot down, eight or nine men go with it. And when I think of that wonderful old man, the captain who picked us up off Singapore, who'd lost all his family in an air raid and then went down himself. And those soldiers in Singapore – dragging themselves along the Bukit Timah road, utterly exhausted, each man blindly following the one in front – straight into prison camp – or the Siam railway. They were *British* soldiers, Philip. No, I don't feel sorry for the Italians, not one little bit. And as for Tom – I've walked with him in the woods at night; but those long, shuddering sighs – had they been passion I might have succumbed, he's very attractive – but they weren't! Many's the time I could have hit him with exasperation!'

'I take it I have nothing to worry about there, then?'

'Oh, Philip, you have nothing to worry about anywhere.'

'Oh, yes I do. Dougal. Can you visualise his reaction when he finds out?'

'Need he find out?'

'My darling, I've only been back two days, but we've hardly been discreet.'

It was well after midnight when we returned to the clearing and I was surprised to find Tom and Gianna Maria still up. They were talking in low voices over the fire and looked up with, I thought, relief, when we joined them.

Gianna came straight to the point. 'To be honest,' she said, 'I am a little worried about Dougal's group and I think we should try and make contact. You and Tom can hold the fort while the rest of us go. I think it best if we split into two groups, one to try via the north and the others by the south, and see if we can't get across the river without using too public a bridge.'

How easily she has assumed command, I thought. Besides being able to handle the Scum, her planning was worked out in detail and nothing left to chance. By the time she had finished, I was filled with admiration.

'I shall lead the northern group,' she stated, 'Stefano will take the south.' The Scum were in fact still around; I hadn't noticed them, dozing and chatting in the shadows. 'Stefano,' she called, 'divide the men into two groups like I've just been telling the Capitano. Which group will you go with, Sally?'

'Yours. I'd rather climb than drown.'

'Good. We leave at first light.'

I rose immediately, obeying orders. Then I remembered I wasn't going and thought I'd sit down again, just to show her that I would go along with her, but would not be bossed, but I remained standing. There was a sardonic grin on Tom's face; he caught my eye and shrugged. Then he got up too and we both went to bed.

I heard the morning departure, but made no effort to get up until after they had gone.

Tom was sitting in his favourite place near the fire while one of the men brewed up. There were only the four of us left, Tom and I and two of the Scum. How empty the camp seemed. I had never been left behind before, but I was glad of the respite that day.

Tom grimaced over the mug of ersatz coffee, as he had grimaced every time that I had seen him drink it. 'Dio mio, but I'm bored,' he said. 'I shall be glad when I can get some action again. Firewood's running low – what say we go and chop while these two stay on guard?'

'Might as well,' I agreed. 'Sitting for months in that bloody gaol has turned my muscles to cotton-wool. It was all I could do to scramble up the hillside the day before yesterday.'

'You seemed to have enough energy after you'd arrived,' he remarked dryly, but I chose to ignore the sarcasm in his voice.

It was not until we were well into the forest that he spoke again and then his words surprised me.

'Gianna Maria is not always as bossy as that, as you know – it is only because she is hurt.'

'Gianna Maria hurt?' I couldn't think what he was talking about.

'A kind of reflected jealousy – seeing Sally getting from you what she will never have from Dougal. It would be a pity to upset the group.'

There was no ready answer to that, so I did not reply.

I sensed that there was more to come, but we walked for another ten minutes before he stopped and looked me straight in the eye and, that time, he was unable to keep the bitterness from his voice.

'I have held Sally in these woods. I could have loved her too. She was willing, but I have nothing to give and it was not the place, nor the time. I would not let myself make love to her.'

That's one in the eye for you, I thought. Aloud, I said, 'All going well, I hope to marry her one day.' And before he could interrupt, 'And as far as the group is concerned, there will be no change. Now that I am back I shall resume command; both Gianna Maria and Sally are too sensible not to realise that emotions can have no part in an organisation of this type.'

If Tom thought differently, as his look implied, he had the sense not to say so. I could have been cross with him and told him to mind his own business, but I knew that his warning was justified.

'All right, Tom,' I said after a lengthy silence, 'message received.' And having arrived at a convenient place, we chopped wood in silence for the rest of the morning.

The southern section returned soon after midday, to say that the river was in full spate and that the only remaining bridge was seething with military traffic.

No chances were being taken since the main bridge had been blown and papers were being scrutinised most thoroughly at both sides. We had never reached the state of having documents that would stand up to anything other than a brief look. That way was hopeless.

But all was not lost. Gianna Maria arrived back late that afternoon and in good spirits. They had not actually contacted Dougal's group, but they had found a way of crossing the river farther north, up near the watershed.

'It would have been useless going on to-day,' she told us, 'we had spent too much time reconnoitring. It will take a full day at least, if we go straight to the point I have in mind, from here – and then only if the weather holds and the streams don't swell any more.'

'Give me one more day of rest,' I said, 'then I'll come with you. First light day after to-morrow, Gianna?'

In fact I was pretty sure that I was fit enough to go the next morning, but after Tom's remarks, I wanted a full day with everyone there to make it quite clear that I was still OC Group and not a moonstruck calf.

We started off at dawn of a beautiful spring day, the sort of day when you really do feel it's good to be alive. Gianna Maria carried a small sack of food and I a blanket, rolled bandolier fashion, in case we were stuck out at night.

We stood at the edge of the forest, listening to the sound of water and looking up at the mountainside. The first thaw had started rivulets meandering down every fold in the hillside, cascading from rocks and forming pools in the hollows. Everywhere there was the sound of water, trickling, falling, rushing. The mountain had come to life. Great patches of snow receded at the edges before our eyes and sometimes a sheet slid wholesale from one slope to another. Spring flowers dotted the alpine meadows; brilliant yellows, pale pinks and deep pinks, purples, white and the breathtaking blue of the alpine gentian. Great splashes of colour against the grey-green landscape.

At first the going was easy enough, but only the first mile or so was on the level. After that we began to climb. By midday we were at the watershed and Gianna suggested we stop to eat. I was thankful for the rest; my calves were throbbing and my chest hurt in the rarefied mountain air.

What was to become a great river here rushed down numerous rocky streams, none too deep to wade.

By six o'clock we were across the watershed and well down the farther bank, but dusk would be setting in soon and, having seen how trigger-happy everyone was, I was loath to approach Dougal's hideout in the dark.

'We'll spend the night here,' I said, when we came upon a cow-herd's deserted summer hut, 'I don't think we dare light a fire, but at least we'll be out of the wind.'

Gianna said nothing; she must have been as tired and cold as I was. We were still pretty high up. The remains of the snowline not far above us, and the wind whistled round as I imagine it must do in the Himalayas.

We ate our meagre rations and without more ado climbed into the one flea-infested bunk. And then, a little late, I fully appreciated what Tom had been getting at. It was not the first time I had cuddled up for warmth with Gianna Maria – or one of the Scum for that matter – but it was the first time that I thought about it being a woman beside me. I could see then that, loving Sally as I did, could play havoc with my perspective.

Neither of us slept much. The bunk was hard and itchy and the wind kept up its monotonous howl all night. We were up before daybreak and my legs were so painful I wondered if I'd ever make it – of course, especially when you're out of training, it's always worse going downhill.

It's always the same when you have had an eventful time and you meet someone who knows nothing about it – reaching Dougal's was pure anticlimax.

'Well, it's about time you found a way round that bridge,' he said. 'I'd expected you weeks ago.'

'But Dougal, he's been in gaol.' Gianna Maria was suitably indignant on my behalf.

Dougal blinked and lit his revolting pipe. 'All right,' he said, 'I apologise. Tell all.'

He did not even know how much of a success the blowing of the bridge had been, nor the aqueduct and the various other incidents. We had been out of contact for so long. Then he told us what his, or rather Bill's, group had done and the achievements of the border group.

'If you hadn't arrived within the next few days, I would have been coming over to see what had happened to you all myself soon. Marissa has quite a camp down on the lake; some who've been working with the southern groups and some escapees. We'll have to get them up to you – there'll be a drop quite soon and I've asked for as much food and medical supplies as possible. There won't be any more bodies coming in by air. I might as well come back with you to-morrow, then I'll carry on to Marissa.'

It was marvellous to see Philip coming back with Dougal and Gianna Maria. They were all laughing and talking and the sun was out – I wondered for a moment if the war was over.

Tom and I walked to meet them, although I longed to run, and we shook hands all round. Philip and I looked at each other and smiled. We were very sedate, not giving Dougal cause to suspect. But he knew. I know he knew.

'Well, Sally,' he said, 'Gianna Maria tells me you're a proper native now. Taking part in the ops too, I hear.'

And all the time he looked at me with his most penetrating gaze. Then he looked at Philip. And back to me. We all carried on small talk for a quarter of an hour at least and Dougal's eyes went back and forth to each of us in turn. He said nothing, just watching while the others talked, but he was thinking and I didn't think I liked his thoughts. The looks that sped across his face, fleetingly, but there, were varied; first a smiling 'all the world loves a lover' look, then a look of pity and compassion, and then his face became stern. I shivered as I watched his expressions change. Philip had been right, he would have no mercy on us if he thought there was to be any jeopardising of the group.

He went off to Marissa's the next day and Philip and I were alone together for the first time.

'How could he have known?' I asked. 'We said nothing, we never touched each other.'

'Oh, my darling,' Philip held me tight and kissed the top of my head, 'if you could have seen the love in your eyes. I knew it was for me and so I loved it too, but we must be careful. I don't think he will take any action unless we give him cause. It would be too difficult to replace either of us at this stage, but he'd do so if he thought it necessary.'

Dougal was away for two days and during that time we tried to school ourselves. But when we sat it was together and when we stood it was too near. Our hands would touch and our eyes meet. Even the most hardened sceptic would have known that we were in love.

Thank God he returned only for a short time, and then he was so full of the news of the stand at Monte Cassino, and so horrified by the destruction of the monastery, that we were quite outside his thoughts. He had made all arrangements with Marissa and was in a hurry to return to his own territory, in case it rained and cut him off. He left his men to pick up stores, when and if we had a drop, and then he went. For the first time ever, when Dougal departed, Philip and I heaved an almighty sigh of relief.

30. ONE VERY THICK RING

James Weatherby

As you will know, I made a few resolutions when Stan arrived in London and made me realise, more than ever, that this thing with James Weatherby just could not go on. I waited for his mid-monthly visit, determined to be strong-minded and tell him, once and for all, that I would not see him again.

But he didn't come to London that month. I was in such a tizz by midday and no sign of him, that I cajoled Mark into ringing up the Air Ministry and finding out if the conference had in fact been that day. It had. So James had been in London and not contacted me.

I did my best to throw myself heart and soul into my work and forget him, but every time that blasted phone rang and Mark or the general said, 'It's for you,' my heart jumped like a salmon from the river and sank as quickly as a stone in the same waters.

And then one day it *was* him.

'Helen?' he sounded happy and as casual as ever, 'We've something to celebrate.'

'What?' I'm sure it was only a whisper that came out.

'You'll see. 'Bye.'

My hands were shaking as I replaced the receiver and so were my knees. I sat down, feeling quite sick and a moment later felt the general's hand on my shoulder.

'You all right, Helen? You've gone quite white.'

'I'm sorry, sir. I just had a bit of a shock. I'm all right.'

I went back to my own office and tried to get on with my work. But it was no good – people like James should be had up for sabotaging the war effort.

The reason for the celebration was obvious as soon as he walked into the mess to pick me up. Circling each sleeve, glaringly new and blue, was one very thick ring, replacing the four to which I had only recently become accustomed.

'Good heavens, James,' I gasped, 'who've you killed off now?'

He was more excited than I had ever seen him; like a schoolboy who has just passed some difficult exam.

'It's more than just this,' indicating his new rank, 'I've got my own Base. That's three stations, Helen. Never in my wildest dreams did I expect to make air commodore at my age. We're a bit farther away from London of course, but I doubt if we'll be here for long anyway.' He looked round the anteroom, but there were only a couple of my colleagues, talking over their drinks at the far end of the room. 'I don't know how much you know about the big show, but you must know that we'll invade soon – ' I nodded, ' – and then we'll be part of TAF – Tactical Air Force – operating from Continental airfields directly after the invasion. This is history, Helen. My God, I've never been so thrilled in all my life.'

I felt a momentary pang. James seldom talked about his job, in fact never, now that I came to think of it, and always seeing him in London, it was difficult for me to visualise him in the role of an operational pilot.

'But will you still have to fly?' I asked. 'Surely you're becoming a bit senior for that. I imagined you'd be purely on the Admin side now.'

He shrugged. 'I could have been purely on the Admin side for the past year. I don't *have* to fly. But I relieve; I just can't send men over night after night without sharing it with them. Hell, Helen, you've no idea what it's like – once you're past the first flak it's not so bad, you're too busy, have too much to think about, but until then, that sick feeling of anticipation in the pit of the stomach – ' he shrugged again, ' – perhaps other people don't feel that way, but I do. I don't believe the man exists who is never afraid. Even when I've been in the depths of despair, when I thought I *wanted* to die, to get myself killed, I was afraid.'

I looked at him in a new light. Had he become so hard after all? Was half his callousness façade?

The anteroom had emptied. We were alone. I tiptoed over and kissed his cheek. 'I'm glad you've got your Base, James.'

In his typical way, James's mood changed instantly. The wide, white grin was there and he searched behind him and eventually produced a bottle-shaped brown paper parcel, which I had not noticed before.

'Look at this,' he said. 'Cost me a fortune – champers!'

'Oughtn't it to be on ice?' I asked, 'if we're going to drink it this evening?'

'My dear girl, you haven't been outside. It's bloody cold. Freeze the balls off any brass monkey. Come on. Hurry up. Go and get your nightie and a toothbrush, we're going to make a weekend of it.'

I raised my eyebrows, hypocrite that I am.

'Sorry, ma'am, forgot to ask permission!' He threw up a mock salute. 'I've booked you a room at my hotel – single room, no dirty work at the crossroads!'

We felt our way along the dark road, heads bent and coat collars turned up and when I'd caught my breath I asked, 'Where are we going to celebrate?'

'Wait and see. Don't think there's a hope in hell of getting a taxi; we'd better press on to the tube.'

Jammed close to him in the crowded, rocking train, I studied his ear, only a few inches from my face, and the way his hair curled under his cap. I closed my eyes and traced the line of his ear with my lips in imagination and when I opened them, he had turned and was looking straight into them. 'Oh, James,' I whispered, too quietly for him to hear, 'I love you so much.' A tiny frown appeared on his brow, but he still looked into my eyes, then turned abruptly as we jolted to a halt at a station. He didn't look at me again until we reached our stop.

As soon as he guided me into Shaftesbury Avenue I knew where we were heading.

The blackout curtain dropped behind us and we were hit by the fug as we struggled out of scarves and greatcoats. James handed the bottle to the waiter and turned to me with a triumphant grin.

'See? We've got the same table – can't beat Weatherby when it comes to organisation!' And when we were seated, 'Sherry? They'll frown at you if you ask for anything else anyway.'

'Sherry will be fine.'

It was all very romantic – something I didn't trust where he was concerned – the candlelight glinting through the stream of golden liquid, making a molten path between the bottle and the glass.

'To us.'

Helen looked so surprised that I had to laugh.

'You're getting soft,' she said, 'you wouldn't say that before.'

I twirled the glass slowly in my hand. The soft light glowed on Helen's fair skin and caught the gleam in her hair. She was a very beautiful girl.

'On the contrary,' I said, and voiced my thoughts, 'it's time I stopped being soft. I came to a decision just now, in the tube.'

'You caught me off guard.'

'I caught you with the most naked expression in your eyes – there can't have been a soul in that carriage who couldn't have read your thoughts – and I know they were for me.'

'And so?'

'And so I have decided that I have *got* to get Elsie to give me a divorce.'

We sipped our sherry in silence, looking at each other. I saw pain in Helen's face, but I don't know what she saw in mine.

'Tell me about your wife,' she said at last. 'I know nothing about her, but I always thought you were pretty devoted.'

I tried to sound nonchalant, but my laugh had a bitter ring beyond my control. 'Oh yes,' I said, 'we've put on a good show.'

'But you must have loved her once?'

'Oh, Helen, if only you knew.' And, although I had never intended to mention it, I found myself telling her the bare details of the accident of my marriage. 'I've tried, God, how I've tried. And you know, when Toby was born, I really thought we'd made the grade.' I wasn't sure whether to continue or not, but I did. 'She's never let me touch her since that day.'

'You mean she won't sleep with you?'

I nodded. I had not meant to angle for sympathy, but once I had started I seemed unable to stop. The compassion in Helen's eyes was unnerving. 'I'm certain she's having affairs, but as long as they've remained in the dark I've done my best to ignore them.'

'But why? Surely if you could prove it, you'd have your divorce handed to you?'

'And ruin my career? I'm ambitious and I'm not ashamed of it. I'm proud of being one of the youngest air commodores in the air force and I want my son to be proud of me. I wouldn't be proud of having put snoopers on my wife, nor the muddy business afterwards.'

'And have you been so faithful to her?'

'Believe it or not, yes. For a good many months after she stopped having anything to do with me. But she'd made it plain from the start that it was for keeps and I couldn't cope. It may sound weak, but I was afraid of making a mistake in the air – God, women can be unfair.'

It flashed through my mind that, since the renewal of our friendship, James had never so much as made a pass at me, who would have been such easy game. It was all very well being put on a pedestal, but I would have come down to earth and provided his grounds; it would have been a pleasure. I was so far away that he had to repeat his question.

'Do you know when I first fell in love with you?'

'Yes, I think so. In Cape Town harbour – the mirror.'

'Yes. I would have given anything to have the ship sink and us go down with her, I wanted so much to remain with you. But I put you very firmly out of my mind once I left you and every time an errant thought raised its head, I slapped it down. I would have kept it that way too, but when I found myself actually inside the building where you worked, the temptation was too great. I should no doubt have resisted it, but I didn't.'

'I'm glad you didn't – although I've cursed you often enough for disturbing my peace of mind.'

It was very late by the time we left the restaurant. Helen insisted on walking to the hotel. It wasn't very far.

I got her key from a sleepy clerk and we felt our way along fusty, dimly-lit corridors to her door and there I said good night. At least I had intended saying good night, but the pleading in her eyes was too much, so I relented, partly. I had a bottle of Scotch in my suitcase and there was no point in drinking on my own.

'We'll have a nightcap,' I told her and went up the stairs to my own room.

When I returned, bottle and toothglass in hand, she was undressed and sitting up in bed in a nightdress which was either good or bad for morale, depending on which way you looked at it.

I shook my head firmly and patted the leather sofa beside me; even old Willpower Weatherby had a breaking-point. I put her greatcoat over her shoulders and went into the bathroom to fetch her toothglass. Then I poured each of us a strong tot.

We drank and Helen kissed my ear. 'I've been wanting to do that all evening,' she said.

'And I've been wanting to do this.' I took her in my arms and kissed her gently, slowly, feeling myself melt in her response; kissed her as I had not kissed her for two years.

And then one of those things happened that sometimes makes one think that indeed there must be a Fate or someone watching, someone who takes an evil delight in causing accidents. Gremlins of the boudoir, maybe. Helen leaned against me and as she did so her hand slipped on my thigh, pinning my trouser leg and just a sliver of flesh to the sofa. A pinch can be painful at the best of times and although Helen was slim, she was quite a big girl, and of course her hand had to find the one patch of tissue that had not healed.

I let out a cry that I was ashamed of later, but the pain was so intense.

'James, whatever is the matter? What have I done?'

'Nothing.' I didn't trust my voice, but there had to be an explanation, so I rolled up my trouser leg and showed her the still red scars.

'Oh my God,' her eyes were wide and she was biting the edge of her hand, 'and I made you walk all that way when you didn't want to – teased you about being lazy. It must have been agony. Why ever didn't you tell me?'

In fact the walk had not been too bad.

'I don't like women's sympathy for one thing,' I told her, 'and for another, I've always tried to keep you quite separate from my work.'

'Oh, James, and I had hoped you would make love to me – would you have done to-night, if you could?'

'No. I wouldn't before because I wasn't free, and I'm not free now.'

'Tell me about the burns.'

'Nothing much to tell really. We came home pretty holed one night, the undercart was smashed and I had to do a belly landing. We caught fire on impact.'

'And the others?'

'Mostly all right. A few superficial burns. Except for the tail gunner. The fire broke out in the tail and he was trapped. We tried to get him out, but it was hopeless. He should have been dead, but he wouldn't die. He screamed and screamed.' Suddenly I realised what I was saying. Throughout the kaleidoscope of life our eyes register so many visions, those that lightly brush the surface of our senses and fade, and those others that stay imprinted on our minds, with a clarity and freshness that remains undimmed through the years. If we could choose, it would not be so bad, but we cannot. However much we may try to bury those unwelcome images in the forgotten past, they still recur in our mind's eye. I knew that for me, side by side with Helen in the bath, would march the memory of that air gunner, hands already claw-like, scrabbling in the flames to be freed.

'Helen, why do you get me to talk to you like this? We don't talk about our prangs in the mess, you know. Those things happen, but they're nothing to do with women – most of us lead two lives.'

'But your wives must know. You must let go sometimes, surely?'

'No. You're wrong. At least, I'm speaking for myself. The WAAF are different – they're on the station anyway and part of the job – you can open up to them if you want to, but there are two schools of thought there. Some blokes like to have a WAAF girl friend, who will understand and maybe sympathise, and others, like myself, prefer to seek companionship elsewhere.'

'And to think that all the time you were in hospital and on leave, I was worrying myself sick because I thought you'd dropped me.'

Helen's hair was so soft and smooth. I rubbed my cheek against the top of her head, then nuzzled her neck and her soft, yielding breasts.

'I love you, Helen,' I whispered, but she had fallen asleep.

The next time James came to London it was only for one of our brief lunch-time dates, but he was jubilant.

'I've asked my wife for a divorce and I really think I'll get it.'

I wasn't so enthusiastic. 'From what little I've heard of her, it sounds out of character,' I replied.

But he was undaunted. 'I had to do a bit of threatening, I must admit. I told her that I could prove her infidelity – that was just bluff – and as she had refused to have anything to do with me since the baby was born, the court would be bound to sympathise with me. I made it quite clear that I could, and would, get a divorce in three years on the grounds of desertion anyway – but, darling, I don't want to have to wait that long.'

'Nor I.'

'Anyway, to cut a long story short, I did an unprecedented thing last night – I went up to Command and asked the C-in-C for some fatherly advice. It seems that he knows far more about my private life than I would have thought possible and he's not exactly pro-Elsie.'

'And?'

'He said, and I quote, "bugger the three years, you go ahead and give her grounds for divorcing you and risk their Airships' displeasure". It's a gamble, but when so many men have been lost, perhaps they won't worry too much about my morals. Would you still marry me if I dropped right down in rank, or even had to leave the service altogether?'

'What a silly question. Anyway, as your C-in-C says, I doubt very much if it would come to that – times have changed, you know.'

'She still needs a bit of softening up, but I think it'll work. Oh, Helen, it's as though I've been crawling along a dark tunnel for goodness knows how long and, having given up hope of ever reaching the end, suddenly I can see daylight.'

'Please, James, let's not talk about it any more. I've had my hopes dashed too often.'

'By whom?'

'By you of course, you big mutt. It all seems an impossible dream.'

We ate in silence, conscious that time was pressing on and when next he spoke, I looked up, surprised by the seriousness of his tone.

'I don't think I'll be in England much longer. You know I can't tell you as much as I would like to, but . . .' he spread his hands in a helpless gesture and I smiled, a sick feeling of dread already pervading my inside. 'Now that it looks as though one day you really will be my wife, come away with me for a couple of days – just in case – '

There was no need for either of us to complete the sentence. By this time I had a very good idea of the invasion plans – far more than James realised – and no one but a fool would think that we could get away with it without heavy losses.

'All right,' I said, 'give me as much notice as you can and I'll try and get some time off. It won't be easy though, we're desperately busy at the moment.'

'Thank you, darling.' He kissed my cheek and went off to catch his train.

31. A MYSTERIOUS MESSAGE

Sharif Ahmat

It must have been getting on for a year after my sister's wedding, that I received a mysterious message.

I was preparing to go on duty early one morning and when I put my first foot into its boot, I felt a crackle of paper in the toe. It was a slip of plain white paper, typewritten and unsigned, and the message: 'On the grounds that your mother, a widow, is old and un-well, you should apply for a posting to your home state.'

I carried the paper around with me for many days, checking it whenever the opportunity arose with the typewriters in the office. But it had not been typed, as far as I could tell, by anyone in the police station.

In view of my mother's command, it seemed unlikely that she would want me near by and I made no application. Mentally shrugging my shoulders, I screwed the note into a ball and threw it into the nearest dustbin.

That same day we had an unpleasant duty to perform and by evening all thoughts of the message had left my mind.

We were stationed on the edge of the great Perak tinfields. To someone unfamiliar with the scene it would present a weird landscape. Rising from the ground at intervals are great palongs, frames of scaffolding, sometimes more than a hundred feet high, supporting trays along a gentle slope to ground level. At the high end, a revolving belt, with buckets at intervals, lifts the gravel from the earth below and empties it on to the topmost tray. Water from pipes all the way down washes the tin free, and it is collected at the foot, where the dirty water and gravel run away.

Most of the mines are owned and run by Chinese, who live in large, communal kongsi huts on the sites. The Japs had put in their own bosses to work these mines, often men who had posed as photographers, barbers, or dry cleaners before the war, but who had been watching how it was done all the time. The Chinese worked under them because of course, like us, they had no option.

Well, the day before, the day I had been checking the typewriters, the body of one of these Japanese was found on a *palong*.

There was something fishy, because a Jap patrol appeared on the scene just at first light, just as the body was found, in fact. The mineworkers said it must be the remains of a body dug up from the earth, but of course those buckets are not big enough to lift anything larger than a dog. Besides, the body, or what remained of it, had an initial inlaid on a gold front tooth and a ring, both positively identifying it as the corpse of a foreman who had been missing for more than a month.

The workers denied all knowledge – who wouldn't? – and it was our unpleasant task to make them change their minds.

People will tell you that there is no love lost between the Malays and Chinese; but that is not necessarily so. I have had many Chinese friends and I can tell you, it gave me no pleasure to wade into those mineworkers and crack heads.

The men were standing in a huddle when we arrived, armed with parangs and changkol handles, and I thought for a moment that they were going to put up a fight. But if that had been their intention, they thought better of it and just stood, docile as goats, while we laid about us with truncheons and rifle-butts. After ten minutes or so, the Jap NCO ordered us to bind them and throw them into the trucks.

Just as we were getting the men on board, I was seized by a cramp in the stomach. I had been suffering from dysentery off and on for the past year and it was not the first time I had had to dash into the bushes when on patrol. The Jap corporal made some remark and his compatriots laughed. I took no notice; I couldn't get my trousers down quick enough and anyone who has suffered those griping pains will appreciate my predicament.

While I squatted in the bushes I felt a hand on my shoulder. It was an elderly Chinese, who enjoined me to silence with a finger to his lips.

'You look a decent type,' he whispered. 'Some of your friends are enjoying their power, but I could see that you derived no pleasure from it.'

To my surprise, he lifted his singlet and from his money belt extracted a hundred-dollar note. Real money, the old Straits currency, not the new notes which the Jap government had issued recently. He handed it to me. I took it and examined it carefully, while he examined me. I could feel his bead-bright eyes on my face and the intelligence was plain in his when I handed the note back.

'Quick,' he hissed, pushing the note back at me again, 'we haven't much time. The apes are drinking up our tea in the kongsi hut, but they'll soon be finished. Take the money. And when you leave this bush, leave it alone. You haven't seen me. Understand?'

I shook my head at the proffered note. 'I haven't seen you, taukeh, but I don't want your money. My family are not poor – and what could they do with it anyway?'

'Ah,' the man drew a deep breath of satisfaction, 'I judged correctly. You are not one of the running dogs who has joined the police for greed. My life means nothing to me, my family are safe – would it surprise you to know that my wife, four sons, and a daughter are all in Australia?'

It certainly did surprise me. The man looked like an old coolie and spoke dreadful Malay.

He enjoyed my surprise and for the first time smiled. 'Yes, a doctor, a lawyer, an engineer, and one still at school. Four sons.' His pride was short-lived though; this was no time for a casual chat and he quickly changed the subject. 'You know there are underground movements? Well, I – '

I shook my head. 'Don't tell me, taukeh. I don't want to know. Better keep these things to yourself. I was forced to remain in the police; I do my duty, nothing more.'

He looked disappointed and there was a slight sneer in his voice when he spoke. 'It's a pity you Malays are so spineless. We are the ones who do the killing – and the ones who suffer the reprisals, whether we've done the killing or not.'

It was all I could do not to blurt out the whole story of the massacre in my kampong. Seventy-one men had died and all our animals slaughtered. I could have kicked him and wiped that sneer from his face. But generations of discipline came to my aid and I could have done nothing anyway, because at that moment I was overwhelmed by another attack of the trots.

'Mat, Mat,' I heard one of my friends call, 'hurry up, man, we're off.'

There were looks of interest on some of the less battered faces aboard the truck and ribald remarks from my colleagues and the Japanese NCOs. No one mentioned the missing man.

This, as it turned out, was to be one of the occasions, so frequent nowadays, of a great show of taking people in, supposedly for questioning, then shooting them out of hand. Mine after mine, squatter area after squatter area, had had their entire inhabitants murdered, men, women, and children. I was glad the man had got away. At least that was one saved from the tyrants. What happened to the rest of the men after we reached the police station I don't know. To date, thanks be to Allah, I have not been called upon to do worse than I did to-day. If I were ordered to perform some of the duties that my comrades have been forced to undertake, I am sure that, like my father's, my brain would snap.

I wondered what reprisals would be taken for the loss of that one pig. Better not to know.

A couple of weeks passed. I had forgotten all about that mysterious message until one day, when I was on beat duty and walking down the main street of the small township, a very old Malay brushed past me, nearly knocking me off the five-foot way. I have been brought up with courtesy and certainly would not have abused the old man, but the police have a bad name these days and people are frightened of us. I was not altogether surprised therefore when he bowed and, taking my hand in both of his, begged forgiveness for his carelessness. I *was* surprised though to feel something hard pressed into my palm.

I didn't look at the old man as he shuffled off, but blew my nose, returning the hard object to my pocket with my handkerchief.

I was too scared that some Jap might have seen the incident to dare look and see what had been passed to me until I was back in barracks and locked safely in the latrine.

It was a one cent piece with a note wrapped round it. Once again it was typewritten and read, 'You have not applied. Hurry up'. But this time it bore the initials SH. My elder brother, Sharif Hassan, the missing one, who had followed the British nearly two years ago and had not been heard of since. Could it possibly be?

I was eager for beat duty then. Keen to get into the public places, scan the coffee-shops and bus stops – any place where I might see the old man again. But I never did.

Our police chief had changed since the time of my sister's wedding. The present one was a squat, sullen character who seldom spoke. He grunted whenever anyone went in and his orders, unintelligible to most of us, were issued in a series of monosyllabic barks. He was not the type who was likely to be sympathetic towards a son asking for a posting to be near his mother. I wrote out the application and carried it around in my pocket, but that was as far as it got.

But, to my surprise and astonishment, I was called before the sergeant one morning, who told me to pack my kit. I was posted to Rembang, a station in Negri Sembilan. Not my own district, but close enough and in my home state.

'Headquarters posting,' he remarked. He too was from Negri and, if he knew about my father's running amok, he never mentioned it. 'You must have influence.'

I wondered.

287

James Weatherby

I have found just the place [James wrote], a delightful pub and only an hour from London. It's all fixed. The landlady is a sentimental old soul – I suspect she guesses that we are not married, but I don't think there'll be any questions asked. To-day week – can you make it? Try.

> In haste,
>
> Your James.

PS. I've never seen you in civvies. Enclosed are my supplementary coupons – use them to buy yourself something nice.

PPS. Ring me as soon as you can – I have to confirm the booking.

> X James.

Complex creature, I thought. The slightly pompous air commodore, so afraid for his career and his dignity, and then that childish X at the end of the letter.

I had waited for a month to hear from him. It was already April and we were frantically busy; it was not going to be easy to persuade the general to let me have a Saturday morning off.

As the train lurched its way to the north-west I could hardly keep still, so pent up was I with the twin emotions, apprehension, and excitement. Just outside the main station we had stopped when a doodle bug chugged overhead and everyone in the compartment except myself had bent their heads in their hands. But I hadn't. I had looked up and prayed. Oh no, I had prayed, not to-day, oh, please God, not to-day. Then it had landed and we had all started talking at once, intimate in relief. After that, every time we had lurched over a point I had expected derailment at the very least.

But we were there at last and James was there, the white grin visible even from the other end of the platform, and I felt that I had been reprieved. I ran straight into his arms and hugged him.

'Steady on, old girl,' but he was laughing as he shoved me off. 'Remember your dignity, Junior Commander Watson!'

He led me out of the station to an ancient and decrepit black Ford and threw my suitcase into the back. 'Hang on, I have to crank.'

'Yours?'

He nodded, already bent over the handle. 'Had it for ages. I managed to wangle some extra petrol to-day, so that I could drive over and pick you up. The pub's a couple of miles away.'

On the seat was a sticker, recently removed by the marks on the windscreen. 'Station Commander,' it read, 'On duty.' I picked it up and James grinned. 'Thought that would be going a bit too far,' he said.

The pub, unoriginally the Hare and Hounds, was long, low, white-washed and thatched.

'What do you think of it?' he asked me as he put my suitcase down.

'It's perfectly heavenly. You couldn't have found anywhere better.' I looked round with delight. The room was low-ceilinged and not very large. Whitewashed walls with old family cross-stitched samplers on two of the oak supports. Chintz at the window and on the only easy chair and double bed. A door led into an adjoining bathroom and there were deep cupboards at the other end.

Can my luck last, I wondered, is he really here with me? I didn't want to go downstairs again. I wanted to lock the door and stuff our ears with cotton-wool, terrified that the telephone might ring and he would be called away.

'Do we have to wait?' I asked.

'And have everyone know that we're definitely not married? No, we're going for a walk. Work up an appetite for the special dinner I've ordered and then – and then my girl you've had it!'

'Couldn't I have it now?'

'Shame on you! It's only half past five and there are some beautiful beech woods only a few hundred yards away. Look alive, Watson – walk!'

For answer I put my arms round his neck and brushed his eyes with my lips. We were almost the same height; I hardly had to reach up.

'Helen, Helen darling,' his hands were entwined in my hair, caressing the back of my neck. 'Do you know that I love you more than anything else in the world? That I've loved you all the time, ever since I saw you upside down in that mirror?'

'James?'

'Um?'

'Don't break my heart again. I want you now because, somehow, you always seem to leave me at the last minute. I want to tie you down, here and now.'

'But anticipation is part of the pleasure – didn't you know that?'

'I don't know anything any more. Only that I've never loved anyone in the way I love you; never wanted anyone in the way I want you.'

'Darling, tell me all this to-night and I'll tell you. Now,' briskly, 'we're going for that walk. Pull yourself together. Wash your face and comb your hair and make sure you have a clean handkerchief!'

'Sir!'

'By the way, did you buy a dress?'

'Oh gosh. Yes. I almost forgot.' I took the dress out of my case and held it against me. 'Do you approve?'

It was a dark cherry red of a fine woollen material and I knew very well had the effect of making my hair look fairer and my eyes darker. I was very pleased with it.

'I do indeed.'

I hung the dress up in the vast, empty cupboard and we left the room, hand in hand.

We walked fast, saying little, but it was a good day to be alive. Helen was a good walker – Elsie was one of those women who complains if she has to walk for more than a hundred yards and I'd never seen her in anything other than high heels – and swung out, cap in hand, the evening sun shining on her face.

At the top of the hill she stopped, the breeze blowing her hair out of place, and smiled at me.

'Is it right that anyone should want anyone else as much as I want you?' she asked.

And I replied, 'Quite right, my darling. May we both always want each other as we do now.'

We turned for home after that and when the pub came into view I stopped and pulled her close. I wanted to stop and look in silence, but, sensing her questioning, I said, 'Pictures are important to carry with one and this will be another memory for me to cherish.'

'James, when you go away – ' But I covered her mouth with my hand.

'Hush. Not a word to remember there's a war on. Let's forget everything but ourselves. We have two whole days and two whole nights; let nothing mar them.'

We walked very slowly back, saying nothing, Helen's gloved hand quiet in mine. But it was too precious, too tense.

'Bags first bath!'

There was no one at the reception desk and we dashed in and scrambled up the stairs in an undignified manner and arrived in a heaving, panting mess at our bedroom door.

I undressed her very slowly and if anyone thinks there is anything unromantic about taking a woman out of uniform, they're wrong. I laid each garment on the bed and all the time she just stood there, docile, yielding, her skin smooth milk and honey and I loved her, every inch of her.

I ran the bath, then I carried her to it and put her in, arranging her legs and pulling and pushing her hair to get her into the exact pose that I remembered so well. Neither of us said a word. Then I undressed and got into the bath with her.

She looked at me, a small smile on her face, and put out a gentle finger to touch my scars, which would still take some time to fade. I wondered if she had seen a man naked before, but I didn't ask her, I didn't want to know.

If we went on like this we'd never get down to dinner. I splashed her and she yelled, clutching her hair.

'James, get out. We'll have the landlady up to say water's pouring through the ceiling below.'

So I bit her and leaped out of the bath, showering the whole room.

'God, but you're slow, woman. Hurry up, I'm hungry.'

'You're always hungry.'

'So hungry I shall eat you up if you stay like that a moment longer!'

She got out then and dried and followed me into the bedroom. It was fun to watch her dress.

'You're honoured,' she told me, as she pulled on the sheerest stockings I'd seen for some time, 'this is my last pair from Delhi.'

The dress was marvellous. I stood behind her, fastening her pearls, and looking at her in the mirror at the same time.

'You're beautiful, Helen – even in khaki.'

She smiled. She knew she was and that colour flattered her just as it should. She bent to pick up a matching lipstick and I watched as she outlined her mouth and filled it in. Next came small pearl earrings and I stood, lightly caressing her shoulders as she fixed them in her ears and watched her putting compact and comb, lipstick and wallet into a small evening bag.

'God, I feel possessive,' I said, 'I look at this woman and I want to know that I'll be looking at her to-morrow and the next day and the day after that and no one else will. I want you to be mine, mine, mine. Do you hear?'

'I hear.'

We were the only occupants of the dining-room. It was a pity in a way, no one else to see Helen except the waiter, when she was looking so superb. But I didn't mind.

'I ordered our dinner especially early,' I explained, 'partly for reasons which need no elucidation and partly because I wanted to have you here to myself.'

'Why? Jealous?'

'Yes and no. The fact is that we're a bit too near Bomber Command for comfort. A lot of air force people come here and once you get a thick ring people notice you more. I don't want it getting back to the station that I was seen here with you – might jeopardise our chances.'

'But why should they think I'm not your wife, if you don't know them?'

'There may be someone who's seen me out with Elsie. Oh yes – ' I saw her eyebrows raise in surprise, I suppose she thought we were completely separated, ' – she won't sleep with me, but she creates merry hell if I go anywhere without her. These duty trips to town have been a blessing.'

I heard her sigh and wished I had not had to bring up the subject of Elsie on this of all days. But further conversation was cut short by the arrival of the waiter at our table.

He had just left us when a sharp movement of Helen's arm sent her bag flying. It landed on the floor with a splitting thud and out rolled lipstick and comb in one direction, compact in another and her wallet opened to loose a shower of stamps, identity card, money and a photograph.

'You clumsy creature,' I chided her, as I bent to retrieve the compact and wallet while she scrabbled for her comb and lipstick.

'Look alert yourself,' she hissed, 'and get that identity card closed before someone comes in and sees the name.'

'Why do women carry all this stuff around with them,' I grumbled. 'God alone knows what you'd do if you had to empty all your pockets before take-off and couldn't take your handbag with you.'

I gathered up the cash and put the stamps back into the wallet, then paused to look at the photograph. Rather a smooth type, I thought.

'Who's that?' James asked.

'Oh, one of my many boy friends.' I held out my hand for the photograph, but he did not give it back. Instead he studied it more intently.

'Those wings?' He knew perfectly well they were.

'Yes. He's a Pole.'

'A Pole? A bloody Pole? Do you mean to tell me that you've been going out with a bloody Pole?'

'Well, he's a pilot – one of the union. That at least should make you happy.' I kept all but the merest hint of sarcasm out of my voice, determined not to lose control.

'What squadron?'

'I don't think he has a squadron.'

'What do you mean – doesn't have a squadron?'

'Well,' I knew next to nothing about the air force, but I didn't want to let Stan down, 'I think he was three hundred and something when he was in fighters, but he's in Transport Command now.'

'Transport?' James shouted. 'A bus driver? Not only a Pole, but a bloody, mucking bus driver as well.'

'Well, some people have to be transport pilots, don't they? I don't expect it was his fault that he was taken off fighters.'

'I bet it wasn't,' he sneered, 'I haven't much use for fighters at the best of times, but to go to Transport – I've no doubt it was lack of moral fibre on his official report, but cowardice in plain English.'

It was all I could do to hold my temper, but I was not going to let go and say something I would regret later.

'Oh, stop being so unreasonable, James,' was all I said.

'I'm not being unreasonable – one's got to draw the line somewhere.'

292

'And what exactly do you mean by that?'

'Well – a Pole. You'll be telling me he's made love to you next.'

'And so he has.' It was no good, his tone of voice was too much to take. I shouted too.

'What?' He was on his feet, a livid red spreading over his face and neck. For a moment I thought he was going to hit me. He tore the photograph into small pieces, methodically, the cruellest expression on his face, and flung them on the floor. Then he drew himself up very straight. 'I don't expect my woman to jump into bed with every f –'

'If you say every Tom, Dick and Harry, I'll scream!' I was screaming. And then, suddenly the true import of what he had said struck me. '*Your* woman – did you say *your* woman?'

'I did.'

'I'm bloody well not your woman and I never shall be. How have you got the cheek – you, a married man, so devoted to your wife, except when it suits you – how've you got the cheek, the nerve, to speak to me like that?'

He ignored the thrust. 'Are you going to marry him?' he asked, quite quietly.

'I shouldn't think so.' We were both calmer now.

'Why not?'

'For one thing, he hasn't asked me and for another, I don't think it's ever entered either of our heads.'

'Does he love you?'

'I don't think so. In the terms of the Press, we are just good friends.'

'It sounds a mercenary enough arrangement to me – even for a Pole.' His blood was up again and I could see by the changing expression on his face, the unpleasant twist to his mouth, that he was going to say something to hurt me. 'How much does he pay you to be just good friends?'

That was the end. I jumped up and with all my strength I swung my right arm back and hit him, full across the face.

We stood for a second, glowering at each other, our chests heaving, then I bent to retrieve the remnants of Stan's photograph, thought better of it, and hurried from the room, James at my heels.

'Where are you going?' he shouted.

'Where the hell do you think I'm going?' I shrieked back, 'stop yelling – it doesn't befit your exalted rank.'

And I slammed the door.

I coughed and looked around me, embarrassed now that my temper was subsiding again, but there was only the receptionist in sight and she quickly busied herself with a card index.

Within moments Helen reappeared, back in uniform and carrying her suitcase. I tried to take it from her but she wrenched it away. Outside, she stepped into a waiting taxi and I jumped in beside her before she had time to stop me.

'No scenes,' I hissed, 'you're in uniform now.'

'Where to, miss?' the cabby asked.

'To the railway station.' She still stared straight ahead.

She had the right money ready when the taxi stopped and the right money ready for her ticket. When a woman is as independent as that, it can make you feel very foolish.

'Oh, Helen, think it over,' I tried to take her arm and used my most cajoling voice, 'I know we've said a lot of stupid things to each other, but it's only a lovers' tiff.'

'Lovers?' She turned a look of the utmost scorn on me. 'You don't know the meaning of the word.'

And with that she turned and walked down the platform and apparently out of my life.

'Helen,' I pleaded. But it was no use. She didn't falter in her step.

I took it out on the nearest object to hand, a wooden bench, and kicked it so hard that I both felt and heard my toes crack. At that I let out an oath that I very seldom use and looked up to meet the amused gaze of the ticket collector.

'A woman?' he asked sympathetically.

'Yes, a woman,' I roared back at him, 'a bloody, mucking woman.'

I walked all the way back to the pub, almost enjoying the agony of my injured toe, and kicking everything else available with the other foot.

The hallway was empty when I arrived back and the hum of voices from the dining-room told me that dinner was now in full swing. I heaved myself upstairs and stood in the open bedroom door.

'You bloody fool,' I said out loud, and hit my clenched fist against the wall, 'you stupid, bloody, bloody fool.'

I sank on to the bed, head in hands, body and brain at fever pitch of frustration with my own stupidity. I turned to look at the bed – was it I who had said that anticipation was half the pleasure and refused her when she wanted me to love her? What an oaf you are. If I had taken her when she wanted me to we would never have gone down to dinner; there wouldn't have been a handbag to knock off the table and the whole stupid incident would never have occurred. Then reason got the better of me – and even if it had, why should I have got so upset about a photograph? It wasn't as if she was trying to hide it. It's just my bloody, stupid, jealous temper. And what right had I to be jealous? I, who had had her on the end of a string for months? You idiot, Weatherby, you bloody, stupid idiot.

I looked around the room, at the whitewashed walls and the old-fashioned samplers which had so delighted her. At the kidney shaped dressing table, on which her cosmetics had stood so short a time before, and the mirror where I had watched her as I fastened her pearls. In the open cupboard two coathangers still hung, H. Watson printed on each in ink. I touched them, then closed the cupboard door.

Much as I tried to avoid it, always my eyes came back to the bed. This was to have been our coming together, our awakening in each other, our wedding night in all but legality. And I had spoilt it all by a ridiculous outburst of temper. And I hadn't even told her my most important item of news.

After an hour and a half had gone by and the lounge filled up, I went down to the reception desk and asked for notepaper and an envelope. Then I went back to the bedroom to write.

My darling [I wrote,] I'm sorry. It was all my fault and I hate myself more than I can say. I look at this room and think what I have wasted and feel positively suicidal.

I had a very important item of news to impart too and, having foolishly decided to wait until we were in bed to tell you, I never did. The news, my darling, is that my wife has at long last agreed to give me a divorce. What the next step is I am not quite sure, but all going well, I should be free one of these days and then, please Helen, forget our silly tiff, will you, please will you marry me?

Oh God, what a fool I am. I would give anything in the world to have you in my arms this moment and to be asking you in person. And it's all my own stupid fault.

I don't know when I shall see you again – even if you will see *me* – but I do not think it will be very soon.

I love you, Helen. Please say you forgive me.

Yours – and only yours,
James.

I addressed the envelope and put it in my pocket and sadly began to pack my things.

'I'm sorry,' I said to the receptionist a few minutes later, 'nothing ever seems to work out as we plan it, does it? Would you mind posting this for me, it's rather important.' I handed her the letter and saw her reading the name. She looked so sympathetic that I decided to be honest with her. 'That's the lady who was with me. I'm afraid we shan't be staying here this time, but I swear I will bring her back here one day, and then she will be my wife.'

I paid the bill and slung my suitcase into the back of the car. But I couldn't face the thought of going back to sleep under the same roof as Elsie, so I pointed the car towards the nearest town and spent the night in a rather dreary hotel.

Stanislaus Olshewski

It was now May 1944; we had had three months hard at it. Non-stop training and practice, practice, practice. Nothing must go wrong on the great day. It was a completely different type of flying. Whereas before we had flown as individuals, often with only vague timing, now it was flying in formation to a stop-watch schedule and with a glider attached.

However exciting the future might be, tempers were apt to be short, cooped up as we were and with no relaxation other than the station flea pit and the odd game of snooker in the mess. All leave had been cancelled and even the local pub was out of bounds. It was a relief therefore when we were told that we could have a long weekend away from camp and, although it was never said, we all felt it would be our last.

I missed Harry. Seeing him for the odd beer was not the same as having him to work with. We'd had some good times together and we liked each other's girls.

Thinking of my girl, I packed my bag and caught the London train.

I had never taken Helen to the theatre; in fact I had never been to an English theatre myself. I told the taxi driver to take me to the most likely agents and prepared to queue for the afternoon. After all, it was still Friday and Helen was unlikely to get back to her mess before six o'clock.

Just as I walked into the office a chap called out, 'Two cancellations for *Blithe Spirit*.' My luck was in. Pocketing the tickets, I went in to the confectioners next door and used up my sweet coupons on the lushest box of chocolates they had.

It was only three o'clock and I had nothing to do. I strolled for a time, thinking how long ago it was that my mother and twin sister used to window shop. Dressing a window in wartime must be a frustrating business. London looked very drab. Two Highlanders marched down the street, their kilts swinging and jaunty red bobbles on their berets – they and a bus were the only spots of colour on the grey scene. It was all rather depressing. I turned into a news cinema and fell fast asleep.

The box of chocolates slipping from my knees woke me up and, as I grabbed them, I remembered Helen and looked at the clock. Good grief, it was nearly nine o'clock. I had slept for more than five hours.

Snatching up my cap and gloves, I raced from the cinema and

into the nearest tube station. What a ridiculous thing to do. It was probably the last chance I would have of seeing her too.

Helen's mess was in north London and about half a mile's walk from the nearest underground. I reached the open door of the old house and could hear the babble of female voices coming from the anteroom. I couldn't just barge in, so it was a relief to see an ATS private coming out of the dining-room. I beckoned her and asked if she would find Helen for me. She disappeared through a door, but returned a moment later.

'Sorry, sir. Junior Commander Watson is away for the weekend.'

But it was only Friday. She must have a long weekend too.

Just my luck. If only I hadn't fallen asleep I might have caught her before she left.

I wondered where she had gone. Home, perhaps. Then it suddenly occurred to me that I knew nothing about her; whether she had a father and mother alive, brothers or sisters. I didn't even know where she lived. What an extraordinary thing. The relationships of war.

I was just turning away with disappointment when I saw a taxi stop at the house opposite. The mess consisted of three old houses and the one where the taxi was drawing up was the one where Helen had her room. I peered into the cab – could it be? It was.

'Helen.'

She turned, saw me, and turned away. When I had crossed the road to join her I saw why. She was carrying a heavy, old-fashioned suitcase and her eyes were red and puffy.

'Hallo, Stan.' She gave a wintry smile that pulled at my heartstrings. 'I didn't expect to find you here.'

I picked up her case and followed her into the hall. We had missed the show, but at least I could take her somewhere and buy her a strong drink. I suggested it.

'I'm afraid I won't be very good company, but, as you once said to me, if you will put up with me, I'd like to come. I'll just take my things upstairs. There are some chairs in the garden if you'll wait for me.' She sounded as though she were on her last legs.

The bomber type again, I supposed, as I watched her weary back view disappearing slowly up the stairs. There's a character I'd like to sort out.

I sat under a syringa bush and waited for a good half-hour before she came down and I was sure she had been crying again. What did that chap do to her?

I sensed that she would not want to go anywhere where she would be seen. It was the only time I had seen her looking really plain. I took her elbow and steered her gently out of the front door.

We walked in silence for nearly an hour and I was becoming ravenous. I had skipped lunch to catch the London train and it was

297

beginning to get dark; perhaps I could persuade her to have something
to eat.

I've said so often that Stan was a good egg and I'll say it again. I had
been in such a temper when I left James that I had flounced out,
really believing that I never wanted to see him again. And then, in the
train, remorse had set in. Of course he was right, it was only a lovers'
tiff, and I had spoilt it all. I dug my nails into my palms in a fury
against Fate. The light was leaving the sky; just about the time we
would have been going to bed. Was James still there? Or had he left
in a huff too – back to his wife? Oh God, *why* did I have to drop my
bag? *Why* did I put my wallet in it in the first place? If only – but here
I was, instead of climbing into that patchwork quilt-covered bed,
with the scent of honeysuckle and the late bird song coming through
the window, I was trudging along London streets with Stan, who, as I
had so recently said, was just a good friend. Well, he was a good
friend, none better – how many men would behave with the sympathy
and tact that he did?

I looked at him, profiled against the darkening sky. Physically he
was immensely attractive; mentally he was a wonderful companion. I
was terribly, terribly fond of him. But I didn't love him. And I was
pretty sure he didn't love me. He saw me looking at him and took my
arm.

'It's getting chilly and I'm hungry. Let's go and eat somewhere.'

The last thing I wanted to do was eat. I had already had dinner
and the thought of that meal brought the tears again.

'We could probably get some sandwiches in the mess,' I said dully.

'We probably could, but we're not going to. Look, darling – ' I
turned round in surprise, he seldom used endearments and he had
never called me that before, ' – I only have a couple of days and then
I don't think I shall be seeing you again for a long, long time.'

I realised suddenly that I was being a selfish pig.

'Oh, Stan, I'm sorry. By all means let's go and eat. Better hurry or
everything will be shut.'

We hopped on a bus and got off again and ate – what or where I
couldn't tell you. Stan gave me a lot to drink and gradually the sharp
pain became a dull ache. I did my best to make bright conversation,
to recall the good times we had had together and to discuss mutual
friends, but every so often I would cast my mind back a few hours and
there it was – that falling feeling in the pit of the stomach and the
bile in the mouth.

We went on to a night club, drank some more and shuffled slowly
round the floor, silent, cheek to cheek. I wished that Stan's physical
magnetism would work – usually I couldn't dance with him without
wanting him to drag me off to bed – but that night he might have

298

been a tailor's dummy for all I cared. And all the time I was dreading the hours ahead.

'Well, Helen,' it had come at last, 'it's getting pretty late. What are we going to do?'

I suppose I must have looked as unhappy as I felt. 'I don't want to leave you, Stan, but to-night I don't – I don't – '

'Want me to make love to you. I know. I had already accepted that. Just come and keep me company then.'

It was not really cold outside, but the clear air sent my head whizzing off like a rocket. I had had far too much to drink and before I knew it Stan was holding my head and forcing me to lean over the gutter. I felt better when I had been sick, but a little ashamed of myself.

'I think we had better walk for a bit.'

'More walking? Oh, Stan.'

But we did walk and by the time we reached his hotel I had sobered up.

'I suggest you have a bath and clean your teeth – I don't expect my brush will give you foot and mouth disease – you'll feel better.'

I hope the gratitude showed in my eyes. I washed my face and cleaned my teeth, but I did not have a bath and I did not undress. How many hours ago had James undressed me and we had splashed so childishly in the bath together? I should be with him now. Oh, James.

When I came out of the bathroom Stan was in his shirtsleeves, lying full length on the bed. He kicked off his shoes and held out his arms and I went into them and buried my head in his shoulder and wept as I had never wept before.

Saturday was not a bad day. I wasn't able to get evening seats for the show we'd missed, but we did manage the matinée.

It was not entirely unselfishness on my part that I did not leave her alone. I did not want to be alone myself. It was quite ridiculous, but I was beginning to suffer from that quaint malady which the English so aptly call 'butterflies in the stomach'. We had spent three months working up to a crescendo of excitement, anticipation, climax, call it what you will, and now that the time had almost come – and we all knew it was close – I was dreading it. It was the thought of crossing the Channel again. I had flown over most of Africa, the Middle East and India; had air dropped for months over Burma. But it was that strip of water that I hated so much. Not the water – I had crossed the Atlantic without giving it a thought – but *that* water. It would be all right when the time came, I did not doubt, but meanwhile – well, I just didn't want to be alone, that's all. So, once again, for diverse reasons, Helen and I were in accord.

I had supper with her in her mess and then I left her.

On Sunday morning we embarked from Westminster to see the river from the middle and to have a picnic by the Thames.

I organised some sandwiches and a Thermos flask of coffee and it should have been fun, but somehow it fell flat. To start with, the day was grey, overcast and airless. The sort of day when the rumble of thunder is always in the offing.

Walking along the tow-path at Richmond should have been gay. The Sunday crowds were there, but it seemed that they, like us, were silent, wondering too perhaps if this was a last outing, a last Sunday, a last hope. The river reflected the gunmetal sky and there was sadness in the air.

I wanted so much to make this a happy day for Stan. One that he could recall with pleasure if he was to be off so soon. But he could be moody as well as I and, hard as I tried, there appeared little I could do to alleviate his depression.

We ate our uninspiring meal sitting on a bench at the water's edge and fed the remains to the swans – they did well, neither of us were hungry.

'Only in England the swans are fed, instead of becoming food in wartime,' Stan remarked, as the last crumb disappeared. 'To me it is one of your most endearing traits as a nation.' He was silent for a time, looking at the river, then said, rather wistfully, 'If I live through this war, I think I should like to become British.'

Neither of us spoke, each busy with our own thoughts and idly watching the passers by, until an air force couple, arm in arm, strolled past. Stan's eyes followed them, then, casually selecting a blade of grass to chew, he said, 'You never told me what the trouble was the other night. I took it for granted that it was your bomber friend.'

I had not talked about James because I wanted to spare Stan's feelings and, for that reason, I could not give him a verbatim report. But I was as accurate as I could be without getting too near the bone. He just humphed.

'Haven't you ever been in love?' I asked.

His face clouded over even more and he seemed reluctant to answer. He looked at the retreating backs of the now distant air force couple and flung the blade of grass into the river, where he watched it float out of sight before he spoke.

'Yes. With a child. I reached a pitch of frustration where I didn't know whether I was standing on my head or my heels.' He stared hard into the water and an expression of such pain crossed his face and a look of such tenderness was in his eyes, that I wished I hadn't asked. 'I loved her. I adored her. I would have given her anything; done anything for her – except marry her.'

'And is that what she wanted?'

'I think it is what she thought she wanted.' He paused again and pulled another blade of grass. 'If your James, after all he has done, were to suddenly appear and say, "I'm free," you'd still marry him, wouldn't you?'

'Yes, I would. Without any hesitation.'

'There you are, you see. Women are all the same. No sex without a wedding ring.' Well, hell, I thought, he could hardly say that about me. 'But it wouldn't have worked. She would not have been happy with me – not at that time anyway. Mind you, I've changed since then. Eighteen months away from my own people – I suppose you would say I have been anglicised. Do you know I've only spoken my own language half a dozen times in more than a year? I went round the Polish camps in Kenya and India, hoping to hear news of my sister, and it was I who felt the alien. But before that I was intolerant of English ways – you would have found me very foreign, very Catholic, just as she did. Every time I crossed myself I could see her looking at me as though I were performing some superstitious rite – making a sign against the evil eye or something.'

I looked at him with interest. This was a Stan I had not known. 'I've never seen you cross yourself,' I remarked.

'Can you imagine it, after a year with Harry? You've no idea what I used to be like – miss a mass and I expected the whole squadron to disintegrate!'

'It's Sunday to-day.'

He ignored that. 'Besides, I'm not the marrying type.'

'All men say that.'

'There are places, places of the mind where a woman cannot follow.' He paused and lit our cigarettes. 'For once I am stuck in your language. It is a searching. A woman is by nature practical – always bringing you back to earth from the far places. I don't think I could be tied to another human being. To be accountable to someone else for my actions; to have to eat because she had cooked; to have a house and children. No, I don't think I would want children, not my own.'

'I have to agree that, for a man to be a great man – even a whole man – he must be part mystic. No great poet or painter or composer has yet been a woman. I suppose we are a mediocre lot.'

'And your James – does he have this mysticism?'

It was my turn to stare into the waters, searching my thoughts.

'No. He has not. But you have.' I could see that Stan could never be tied down. He was right about marriage – for him. 'Neither has he your intuition, nor compassion. Nor would he be as good a lover as you.' Of that I was sure.

He raised his eyebrows. 'And yet – ?'

'And yet I would still marry him to-morrow. Tie him down and smother him with love – and children. I would need to have his children and he would want them. But he's practical all right – no mysticism in James.' As a matter of fact I was wrong there.

Stan lifted my hand and kissed it. 'You're an incredible girl, Helen. You didn't know it, but when I asked you to join me in Bombay I was in a vacuum. I had been bitterly unhappy not long before; I had got over that, but I was lost. I needed to find myself and you helped – more than you will ever know. I asked you on the spur of the moment and you came – just like that. You've given me something very precious.'

'No more than you have me.'

'Did you never wonder that I made no mention of love or marriage to you?'

'No, I never wondered. It didn't seem necessary.'

'That's just it. You've never asked questions. Never taken me for granted. Never been demanding. You're beautiful to look at, a joy to be with, and wonderful in bed – what more could a man ask for?'

'A biting WAAF apparently!'

No sooner was it out than I regretted it. Human nature is a quirky thing; I, in love with someone else, who had had so much from Stan, was nevertheless jealous of the unknown girl to whom he had given his heart.

He clapped his other hand over the scarred one and his mouth went hard.

'That is something that I prefer not to remember.'

'Where is she now?'

'I haven't the faintest idea.' The freeze had set in.

'Oh well. As I have so often said about James, let's forget about him – and let's forget about *her* as well.'

'You're right. I wish to God England would civilise her licensing laws; I could do with a drink.'

He got up and stretched and held down a hand to me. It was still grey and stuffy, but the sun was trying to break through. We walked a few paces, then Stan suddenly stopped and, taking my shoulders in a hard grip, turned me to face him. He looked so earnest that I nearly laughed.

'Helen. Be mine to-night. Please. I want to enjoy you and being with you for the last time.'

I put up my hand to smooth the frown marks from his brow and smiled into his eyes.

'Ssh. Stop talking nonsense.'

But he was right; it was the last time.

I received James's letter some three weeks later – what the delay had been I have no idea, someone forgot to post it, I suppose – at any rate, when it did arrive, the greatest invasion in modern history was already in full swing.

I made straight for the telephone, but the reply, as I had expected, was negative.

34. THE CARE OF A GOLDEN GIRL

Donald Thom

Marijke was a real honey of a girl. And I mean honey-coloured too. A real golden girl – you know that 'Golden Girl of the West' hooey? Well, she ought to have been on an ad for a packet of corn flakes or something. She was a kind of crinkly girl – if you know what I mean. She had this corn-coloured, crinkly hair, and a kinky nose and a sort of kinky smile, and clear brown eyes. No beauty in the classical sense – Monica would knock spots off her – but she sure was attractive; and kind too.

When the doctor had made a further examination, he'd found something he didn't like too well about my spine after all. There was no X-ray to confirm or deny his suspicions, but he ordered that I be kept flat on my back, immobile, until such time as any cracks would have mended. And I was, right through the worst of the winter.

I was left alone much of the time, but, when she was free, Marijke would come and sit with me and tell me about her life and the local resistance unit which I had been sent to help. But not too often, because she was afraid her mother would suspect she had a foreigner in the attic and make a scene.

'My mother has Javanese blood and they are a hysterical race,' she told me, her voice full of contempt. 'We had a pilot from the RAF shot down near here when we were first in the war – the Germans were never able to prove that we sheltered him, but they had their suspicions and Mother has been terrified ever since.'

I looked at my nurse with renewed interest. Of course, it was the blood she so despised that accounted for the brown skin and dark eyes, which contrasted so attractively with the ripe corn hair. And her long, thin, beautiful hands and legs; they didn't look Dutch.

'And your father?' I asked.

'Oh, he was Dutch all right,' she gave a short, bitter laugh, 'real solid, heavy Dutch. He faced the Germans with their own courage though and I was proud of him.'

'What happened?' I asked. In fact Konrad had already told me that he had been shot, but it seemed wrong not to ask.

'He was shot. They took a man from each family in the village, because of the bomber crew we had helped – the pilot I mentioned

303

was one of them – and then the rest of the village were made to watch.'

'You actually saw your father shot?'

'Yes. But the Germans always do that – we were expecting it.' Not a flicker of emotion stirred her well-disciplined face. 'I was determined not to cry and I didn't. Mother behaved abominably; yelling and screaming and tearing at her clothes – just what the Germans wanted to see – I was thoroughly ashamed of her. But I looked at my father and he was ignoring her; standing there as casually as though he were waiting in a bus queue. All of them had refused to be blindfolded. When my father saw me, he gave a little smile and a nod; I nodded back and tried to tell him with my eyes and my bearing that I would carry on where he left off.'

Listening to this hard young woman – made hard by such events as these – I felt a hot surge of shame that only a short time ago I had tried to get out of doing this job. Judas Priest, all I had thought of was getting out of the office to take Monica to a movie and maybe sometimes spend the night with her.

'But how could you carry on the work of a man?'

'There are many jobs in the resistance. I am strong, healthy, twenty-three years of age, and a fully qualified nurse.'

'Three years younger than my wife.' Jesus, was it possible? She looked years older than Monica, but then nurses have that matter of factness about them which Monica certainly hadn't got.

'So? And your wife – is she qualified to do something?'

'She's a botanist,' I replied. In those surroundings it seemed a silly thing to be. 'Not much use in a war, but she's working with the Red Cross in London.'

'Well, she is doing something then and that is good.' She flashed her quick, bright, professional smile, that turned my heart more than coquetry could have done, and made for the door. 'I will be back later. Now I have two other patients to attend to and some illicit errands for Doctor Huysen.'

'Who are the others?' But she only smiled and shook her head. 'Marijke,' I called her back, just as the door was closing. 'Marijke, make me well, make me well quickly. I must help you. I *will* help.'

She shut the door.

The time came when Doctor Huysen pronounced himself satisfied with my back, but shook his head over my legs.

'You are young and you are doing well, my boy,' he said. 'Nothing but time can heal those now and you will have to be patient for a few more weeks. But we have to move you out of this room, because there is another casualty, a very sick man who needs Marijke's constant attention. Hans has a place fixed up for you, and if things go as planned, you will be able to start work there.'

The place Hans had in mind was a deserted mill, a mile or two beyond the one that I had been destined for originally. He and a couple of other guys came along that evening and told the tale. It seemed that this mill had fallen out of use over the years because it was in an inconvenient position and the surrounding woods cut off the wind. It was used now as a store for old pieces of farm equipment and as an occasional extra storage place for grain. Seems it would be ideal for me, because the farmers had reason to visit it and yet it was well protected by trees and off the beaten track.

The situation certainly was brighter and if Marijke had a real sicky on her hands, I reckoned the sooner we got moving the better. So did the others; so that was fixed.

There were three floors in that mill and, Judas Priest, I'm never likely to forget any one of them. They had been put in for storage purposes, I guess, but the top one of all had been cleared for me. When they finally had succeeded in hauling me up that near vertical ladder and I'd lain still for a few minutes, I was able to look round and take it in.

There was the couch on which I lay – a straw-filled sack really – and within reach, my code books and radio. The other side of the room there was another couch, a small primus stove, a wash basin and an ominous bucket.

Following my glance, Konrad told me, 'You will not be left alone too much. One of us will come in and cook for you and pass the radio messages, and Marijke will still nurse you. It may be necessary for one of us to sleep here from time to time and so the other couch is there. You will not be able to use a light at night, there are too many holes in the roof, but if we find this place as good as we think it will be, we will try and rig up some sort of blackout for you.'

'And now, Lieutenant Thom,' broke in Hans in his CO's voice, 'there is work for you to do. Messages have been piling up from London, because our old transmitter was destroyed and we do not understand this new model. In time you must teach us to use this machine – one never knows.'

I guess I gave that radio a real loving look. She was a honey. The newest mark, receiver and transmitter combined, and as compact as a kid's school satchel. I sure didn't need any urging to make her acquaintance.

Hans had spread his hands in a fatalistic way, but when I looked round at all those friendly, sweating faces – and they'd sweated all right getting me up those ladders – my radio, my books and the sunlight shining softly through the cobwebs, death seemed a long way away.

I saw with satisfaction that they had rigged the aerial just as I had

305

told them to and it only remained for me to connect it. That didn't take too long and in two flicks of a lamb's tail I was acknowledging messages from London and coding the ones Hans had prepared for me to send. It was just great to know that we were really in touch with the big, outside, free world, and that I was the contact.

At the end of the day I tapped out a personal message of my own, 'How's my wife?'. I sure missed Monica.

Konrad brought me a meal, already prepared in a billycan, just before it got dark and helped me with my ablutions. No one slept in the mill with me that night and, jeepers, it was eerie. I would certainly have liked to be able to have a light, but Konrad wasn't making excuses when he mentioned those holes – I could see the stars right through them – God help me when it rained. Which reminded me, I must request some sort of cover for the radio if the weather looked bad.

I tossed all night, thinking of Monica and my year-old son, safe with his grandparents back in Canada. Guess I was so proud of him, and yet I hardly knew the child. I'd already been in the army by the time he was born and I found it difficult to conjure up his face. Indeed, I found it pretty difficult to picture my home, or Canada at all for that matter. I could picture Monica all right. I only needed to remember her when she first surprised me in London to feel a warm glow all through. I could see her as clearly as daylight in my thoughts, standing there on the steps of the Red Cross office. With her sleek black hair rolled round her cap and perfect make-up, her neat figure and excited, dark eyes, she looked a trim little bird in her grey-blue uniform. 'My,' I had said, holding her at arm's length, 'you should be on a poster. You look good enough to eat.' 'Well eat me,' she had replied, and I had.

I worried about her worrying about me. I had told her that I was being sent on a hush-hush course in the south-west and would only be able to send the odd message through pals in town and she had appeared to believe me. But I wondered. She was no fool, my little bird. I guess she knew, or had a good idea.

The next afternoon I was slowly decoding the last message and spelling out the letters M-O-N-I-C-A-F-I-N-E, when Marijke came for the first time. She looked all in, tired and quiet, as she glanced over my shoulder.

'Who is Monica?' she asked, 'someone else coming to join us?'

'My wife.'

'Oh yes, of course. I am glad she is all right.' She dropped a bag of food on the floor and slumped down on the opposite couch, burying her head in her hands. She was all in all right. She just sat there, pretty quiet, for a time and then she began to talk. 'I have spent all night and this morning delivering a woman whose husband was killed some weeks ago. He was one of our best couriers. She is out of her mind; she has suddenly decided that her husband is not dead at all, that he has been taken to Germany. And now she is convinced she must go and look for him. We are very near the border here and if she is let loose she may unwittingly betray the lot of us. I have been given the job of silencing her. What am I going to do? Oh, what *am* I going to do?'

She looked at me with desperation and I was at a loss. The strong, brave Marijke. Judas Priest, what a thing to ask a girl to do.

I guess we must've sat there for fifteen minutes or more before I came to the conclusion that the best way to calm her would be to give her something to do.

'How about cooking us something, before it gets dark,' I suggested, 'and stay here for the night. Perhaps the woman will come to her senses meanwhile and there won't be any need to do anything too drastic after all. Who's looking after her now?'

'My mother – babies are more in her line than mine. I'm not even a midwife.'

As I had hoped, she pulled herself together without more ado and began busying herself with the meal. Out of the bag came a long string of sausages and I whistled appreciatively.

'They're not really sausages,' she said, 'mostly sawdust and flour and a little flavouring. But they will taste good, because Jan stole them from the German camp.'

I slept better that night. It was great having Marijke's company and since the early morning I had been chewing over her problem and thought I might have a solution. I put it to her while she was bending over the primus, heating up some ersatz coffee for our breakfast.

'How about moving the woman in here,' I suggested. 'It's far enough off the beaten track to keep her out of harm's way and, if she's agreeable, she could help look after me and I would be company for her.'

Sure, I was pretty busy with the radio and I could do all my decoding and encyphering sitting down, but I still needed a lot of help and someone had to bring me my food. This way it would be killing two birds with one stone, so to speak, so I was kind of disappointed when Marijke looked doubtful.

'I don't know,' she said, 'it might be a good idea if she were on her own, but it's the child. If he wakes in the middle of the night and wails, it might attract a German patrol and we can't risk that.' She walked over to the window and pointed. 'Look, Don – can you see those trees? Those are in Germany – we're as close as that.'

She left me soon after that and I didn't see her again for a few days, but when she did come back she had the woman with her. So my wheeze had borne fruit after all.

307

'Donald, this is Berthe.'

'Pleased to meet you, ma'am.'

I held out my hand which she barely touched before backing away. Like a cat on hot bricks, I thought, and, to see if I were right, I deliberately dropped a book. Sure I was right – she jumped a yard or so and her eyes opened so wide you could see the whites both above and below the irises. No wonder they were concerned.

'Come over here,' I said as gently as I could. I've never been told I'm good-looking, but Monica wasn't the first girl to tell me I have an open, honest face. Homely, she says. 'Look at my legs – you can see, can't you, that I still need a lot of help. Would you help me?'

'But my baby – I could not have him here. And besides – ' she walked to the window and looked out, ' – I have to go to Germany, to find Karl.'

When she turned round there was an expression of great sweetness on her face. 'I hope you will soon get better, Mynheer,' she said and slid quietly to the ground.

Marijke was over to her in a flash. 'It's my fault,' she sighed, 'I shouldn't have brought her here so soon. It's a long walk and she's only been delivered five days.'

I let my hands fall in a gesture of frustration, it didn't seem after all that it had been such a bright idea.

'Well, what do we do now?' I asked.

Marijke bit her lip. 'The more I thought over your suggestion, the more it seemed the only solution; I was hoping that she would stay here. "Dispose" I was ordered, and this would be disposal in a way – at least you'd be the only person she could blurb to.' She paused and looked imploringly into my eyes, her mouth and forehead creasing in a frown. 'I couldn't kill her, Don. Killing Germans is like killing lice, but killing one of your own – and another woman – in cold blood. I just couldn't do it.'

'Sure you couldn't, kid – I couldn't do it myself. You'd be some kind of a monster if you could,' I assured her.

A lightness of relief smoothed out her face and she looked down at the woman whom she had propped against the couch but was still holding under the arms. Neither of us had realised that she had come to.

How much she had heard was uncertain, but the look she gave each of us in turn was so filled with horror, that I guess both of us could have bitten off our tongues.

'Kill me?' she asked, her hand at her throat and the fear on her face giving way to incredulity. 'You are going to kill me?'

'Nobody's going to kill you, Berthe – '

But Marijke interrupted me. 'If you're strong enough now to stand up, Berthe, please do so, and look out of that window.'

The woman got slowly to her feet, looking puzzled now, and did as she was told.

'What do you see?'

'Trees mostly, and fields.'

'And where is that, over there?' Marijke pointed.

'Why, Germany of course.'

'Do you want to go to Germany, Berthe?'

'Oh no.' She turned quickly, her hands clasped in front of her, and shook her head violently. 'Oh no. Please don't send me to Germany. The Germans killed my husband. They killed Karl.'

'Sit down, Berthe, I have something to say to you.'

Berthe perched on the couch and listened, while Marijke told her about the past few days. She was sitting forward with her head in her hands, but when Marijke mentioned the baby, a look of wonderment dawned and she touched her breast and smiled. 'Ah, that explains the discomfort here. It must be near his feeding time.'

'Yes. I will take you back now – we must walk more slowly this time. But, if you agree, you must start to wean the child straight away – I can get tablets from Doctor Huysen to help you – and then come here and look after Don.'

I had been watching the two women carefully and tried to make up my mind about Berthe. There was a strong strain of hysteria there, but I doubted if she was play-acting. To look after me seemed the obvious solution.

It was more than a week before I saw Marijke again and when she did come she was thoughtful. I guessed the trouble was Berthe.

'The baby's dead,' she said. 'It looked like an accident, he'd rolled off the bed and pulled the pillow with him. He was suffocated. She wouldn't be the first woman – ' she looked steadily at me and I in turn looked at the floor. I couldn't bear that hard gaze. 'And I'm not yet convinced that she is entirely normal.' She picked up my earphones and glanced at them idly, turning them over and over in her hands. 'You'll have to watch her, Don. If you can talk with her and try and get her mind off her husband and the child, you'll be doing us all – and especially me – a service.'

That afternoon Berthe arrived; pale, composed and dry-eyed. If Marijke's suspicions were correct – and I surely hoped they weren't – it seemed a terrible thing to me and this was certainly some cool cookie. But I had to make allowances; I knew that. I was thankful though that I was no longer entirely dependent on other people for my needs. I was able to pull myself upright and, with the aid of the chair, propel myself across the room. I often looked at the trap door and the ladder leading down and wondered how long it would be before I would be able to play an active part in local affairs.

Not that I wasn't kept busy. Hans came in several times each day now and we had come to an arrangement whereby I nailed an old sack over half the window if I had any special news to convey.

On the morning of 6th June, 1944, I could hardly get to that window quick enough and, as soon as I heard footsteps on the floor below, I just threw caution to the winds and yelled at the top of my voice, 'Great news. Fetch everybody. Great news.'

Within half an hour an expectant throng was assembled in the mill, some still panting from running, and others, who had arrived first, fidgeting, because I was determined to keep this momentous news for all to hear at one go.

'We've invaded,' I told them. 'The Allies have invaded France.'

I had written down, word for word, the bulletin I'd got over the air that morning and I now passed this round for everyone to read.

They all talked at once and there was a lot of back-slapping and Konrad announced that this seemed the right time to broach his keg of Geneva, which he had been hoarding in the mill. What a din we must have made. Jesus, I expected the Krauts to arrive any time.

Only Berthe remained silent and unmoved and it was not until the gathering had broken up and I was left on my own again that I realised she was not there.

'Berthe,' I called softly down the ladder, and then louder, 'Berthe.' But there was no reply.

Hans had banned a party. Although he had shown as much emotion as anyone, his solid Dutch common sense soon got the upper hand. 'This is just the time the Germans would expect to find us all together,' he told us, 'and we must remain alert.'

Of course he was right, and, as he said, there would be other times to celebrate. And so the men had disappeared, one at a time, and when the last had gone I felt very much alone.

I called Berthe several times, but without response.

The light had not quite gone inside the mill and, coming up through the hatch with a string of sausages dangling over her arm, Marijke looked much as she had when she cooked my first meal for me there.

I didn't want to spoil it, but I had to.

'I'm worried,' I told her, before she was half way through the aperture, 'Berthe has disappeared.'

She put her things down slowly and straightened up.

'Disappeared?'

The light was fading fast. She picked up the torch and went down again without saying another word.

More than an hour elapsed before she returned and when she did she was tight-lipped and white-faced. There were no tears, but I knew it would have been better for her if she could have cried. She sat there, numb and white, and I dragged myself over to her.

'What is it, Marijke? What's happened?' I asked.

'She's killed herself,' she whispered, 'she cut her wrists – she's down there in the woods, in a pool of blood.' Neither of us said anything for a moment and I thought she was too upset to go on, but she did, 'I've covered her up as best I could. She's stone cold – must have been dead for hours.'

'Poor Berthe.'

'In a way it's best, with the husband and baby gone. I suppose she felt so alone, when everyone else was rejoicing, that she just wanted to join them.'

I took Marijke in my arms, my strong golden girl that nothing daunted, and soon we were making love. And then we fell asleep.

It was not until the next morning, when I woke to find Marijke in my bed, that the enormity of what had happened occurred to me.

35. D-DAY

Stanislaus Olshewski

It had come. *The* Day. D-Day. 6th June, 1944.

All the tension and excitement that had prevailed on everyone concerned had come to a climax.

It was still dark when we took off, some hours before the first troops would be put ashore. There was no fear after all, no disinclination to cross that narrow strip of sea, that I knew was below me. Only an exhilaration and a pride in being part of history. For there was no doubt in my mind that this was history, unfolding below and around me. An invasion, on a scale unknown, from island to mainland.

Gliders away. It was difficult to see much, but I watched intently as the dragonfly-like craft pirouetted and slid down to join its comrades. Then we turned and headed homeward again. How many men, I wondered, would land in France that day.

Later that morning we crossed again, the first of many trips carrying stores and equipment. Looking down on the Channel below, there was so much shipping that, from this height, it appeared as though a long, wide, flexible bridge was spanning the water from coast to coast. I looked ahead and to either side; we were forming an air bridge too.

The excitement was infectious. I sang as we took off and every face that I saw that day, however tired, seemed to be wearing an exultant grin.

Below us now, the beaches looked like antheaps that had been disturbed. Everywhere landing-craft disgorged their ants, to wade and crawl on to the alien soil. For as far as the eye could see, the ants swarmed, divided, swarmed again, and the big, lumbering tanks, like snails among the insects, heaved and roared and found a footing for themselves.

A far cry from the deep green forests and yellow rivers of Burma, but I was glad to be air-dropping again. Wave after wave after wave. Day after day after day. Absorbed in the drama that was being enacted all around me, I lost count of how many times we had landed and taken off. We flew, refuelled, ate, rested little, and were off again, and each time another load was flung into the inferno that was France.

It must have been D-plus-three when Harry bought it. We'd hardly spoken for more than a week, but he was there and, suddenly, he wasn't there. Poor sod. No wedding after all. No Una. No return to Queensland. Better that it had been I, uncaring and unattached.

But we were too busy to think for long, and too tired. The crossing, however diverse the goings on down below, became so routine that I had become indifferent to opposition. I was just about to turn for home, when a loud crumph jolted us to one side and I swung to evade the flak. That was near. Too near.

Crumph, crumph, crumph. A Dak ahead of me released its load and went down. Suddenly there was a shambles of aircraft, stores and parachutes, spinning, weaving, sliding. Some were still on course and we had not, as yet, wavered too far off, but a collision immediately ahead caused me to swerve and narrowly miss the aircraft on my starboard wing.

Pulling up, I tried to turn, but the rudder had jammed. The plane dead ahead suddenly disintegrated before my eyes, and a second later we shuddered from side to side and began to lose height.

I pulled her out of a spin just in time, but we were too low to bale out. The only thing was to hold her as best I could and come down as gently as possible. Providence appeared to have supplied some flattish, seemingly uninhabited countryside ahead and I felt no fear as the ground sped towards us.

'Hold on everybody,' I said. I had taken it for granted that the undercart would be jammed and I was right. The rain of the preceding day had left the ground soft. We dug in and our speed churned up a great furrow of mud, then slewing round, we came to a halt resting on the starboard wing tip. As we did so, I experienced the most extraordinary sensation of seeing another aeroplane carrying out a similar manoeuvre in reverse. It was like watching myself in a giant mirror.

One last shake and we were still. I glanced round to make sure that we were all right, then turned my attention to my counterpart, who neatly executed an arabesque and, like a flower opening in the spring, burst into flames.

Stunned by the sight, I hastened to free myself and, as I did so, saw the pilot from the other plane – a single-engined fighter luckily – jump, seemingly unscathed, from the flames and run towards us.

We all leaped out and met him head on.

'Wal, whadyouknow? Mr Livingstone, I presoom!'

The American held out a blackened hand, looked at it, withdrew to wipe it down his trouser leg and held it out again.

The incongruity of us two, solemnly shaking hands in that deserted field in France, while the battle raged behind and overhead, did not occur to me until much later, and with equal solemnity I introduced my crew: Stubbs, Williams, and Barnes.

But the field was not deserted for long. In the distance, down a slight rise, a dozen or so men were pouring out of a truck and running towards us. Even at that distance their fixed bayonets were clearly visible.

'Looks like them Krauts reckon we're going to be tough nuts to crack,' our new companion remarked, 'wal, I'll go easy – reckon I've earned a rest.'

I had not been afraid in the air, but the sight of those men, slowly advancing across the field, brought the bile up into my mouth and I wondered if my colleague was as calm as he appeared. It was difficult not to cut and run for it, but I told myself firmly that it was ridiculous, the war was nearly over, not worth being shot at this stage.

To my crew I said, 'Don't resist. We can't be put in the bag for all that long.'

'Say,' my companion was looking at me as though seeing me for the first time, 'all these formalities and we haven't been introduced ourselves! My name's Burnett. Samuel T. Burnett. My friends call me Sam.'

'Olshewski – Stanislaus.' We shook again.

'Polack? Say, whad'ya doing in that limey outfit?'

Before I could answer, the Germans were upon us.

'Take it easy, take it easy,' called Burnett, raising his hands above his head, 'you Krauts just remember the Geneva Convention – I don't want no bruises when I enter that cosy camp, see?'

The soldiers were pathetically young. One butted me in the back and I looked round to see a beardless boy staring nervously ahead. We were marched to the truck and shoved in without ceremony, the youths scrambling on top of us. Looking at those boys, so dispirited and underfed, made me wonder how my own people had fared in Poland. It was not a happy thought.

We stopped once when a bomb exploded near by and again when

the road was jammed with refugees. The driver hooted and honked and finally broke through and, in a short time, we stopped and were ushered inside a building which turned out to be a police station.

After listening to the conversation for some minutes, I interpreted for the benefit of the others. 'They're going to keep us here overnight and decide where we shall be sent to-morrow. It appears that we shall end up in Germany.'

'Guess so. Oh well, let's make like Bugs Bunny and unlax!'

The American was quite a tonic and although my three had little to say, they smiled every time he spoke. He sure could 'unlax' too and, without another word, dossed down on the floor of the cell and went fast asleep.

The next morning we were put in a closed truck, already occupied by half a dozen Free French soldiers, and after driving for several hours, arrived in the late afternoon at what appeared to be a temporary, sorting-out camp. There was no shelter and apparently no food.

'I'll tell the Red Cross about this when I get home,' complained Sam, 'no roof, no grub. Say, where does a guy have a pee?'

One of his compatriots pointed to the ground.

'Gee. And I always thought them Krauts was a hygienic race!'

I looked around me at the crowds of men, herded like cattle behind the wire. They were mostly army; British, American and Canadian. But there was a smattering of air force, navy, and marines and among us, besides the major Allies, Poles, Czechs, Dutch, and Free French. We were a mixed bag all right.

All that evening and the next day trucks continued to arrive and disgorge their motley load of prisoners. Then it must have been full and no more vehicles came.

Just as we had given up hope of any comfort and were settled for the night, a staff car rolled up and two soldiers carried a portable table from the rear of it. This was set up just inside the wire and in a moment a German officer stepped from the car and mounted it.

'Chentlemen,' he called, and raised his arms for silence. 'Ass you can see, zis iss only a temporary camp. To-morrow you vill be sorted out and zen transported to Chairmany – '

'How about some grub?'

The officer raised his arms again. He seemed remarkably un-annoyed. 'I vas chust coming to zat. Even now your food iss being prepared and very soon you vill eat. Zat iss all, but I vould like to speak viz ze senior American and ze senior British officers now.'

After some muttering, hesitation and looking around, an American air force colonel and a British major stepped forward. Whatever the German had to say to them did not take long and he was soon back in his staff car and away.

A few minutes later a truck drove into the camp and two soldiers began lifting urns on to the tailboard. Potato gruel was ladled into tin cans and handed to us as we filed past. There were no utensils and it was a case of coping as best we could. I drank mine down gratefully, more amused than annoyed by the continual grumble Sam kept up. There were plenty of his compatriots around, but he remained with us.

'I expect things will improve when we reach a proper camp,' I told him.

'I certainly hope so. Say, Stan, do you suppose we'll be put in the same camp – you a Pole and me a Yank?'

'I hope so.'

At that moment the American colonel stood up amongst the squatting men and banged on his tin can for attention.

'I thought you'd all like to hear what the German gentleman had to say. At first light to-morrow, we'll be sorted into four groups – seems they're not too fussy as to which service a guy belongs, but first we'll be split into two main groups, English speaking and otherwise, that is to say, British Commonwealth and Americans in number one group and the others in number two – ' Sam and I looked at each other and grimaced ' – then we'll be split into Officers and Other Ranks. He promised we'd get another meal before we go and he said that, when the war is over, he hoped we'd all be friends!'

Assorted cheers, boos, whistles and obscene comment greeted that, as you can imagine.

The gruel routine was repeated early the next morning, then tables were set up with a German NCO and a clerk behind each one. Queues formed and as each man left the table he was directed to a group.

I was well behind. I saw the 'Others', both officers and other ranks, being led off to a line of waiting trucks, while the British and Americans stood at the far side of the camp. I felt a knife twisting in my guts.

I watched Sam join the latter group and then it was my turn.

'Number, rank, name and unit,' called the NCO and the clerk held his pencil poised.

'17351 Flight Lieutenant Ol–' There was something ominous about those waiting trucks. What had Sam said? What are you doing in that limey outfit? I had a terrible moment of conflicting loyalties. 'Ol–' I gulped air and started to cough. My only parlour trick had been taking off an old man with a rich, wheezy cough; I had it down to a fine art. The clerk began writing down the particulars of the next man.

Was it my imagination, or did I hear a whisper behind me, 'He who fights and runs away, lives to fight another day'?

315

Imagination or not, it made my mind up for me. I thought quickly; badge, buttons, wings, shoulder flashes. It had been a hot day when I started out, my battledress blouse and cap were still hanging up in dispersal and I never bothered to wear my identity discs.

'17351 Flight Lieutenant Oliver, Stanley. RAF.'

As I walked across to the group of British and Americans, I looked back. Flight Sergeant Stubbs gave me the 'thumbs up' sign and the other two were standing behind him, grinning like Cheshire cats. It had not been imagination.

A German sentry had once given me the 'thumbs up' sign, after tossing an apple into my lifeboat; so had Sergeant Zgoda after our first op together; and now Flight Sergeant Stubbs. I closed my mind to the fate of the men being herded into the trucks.

'I only hope they don't take us right across to the eastern part of Germany or Poland,' I remarked to Sam, as we were loaded into trucks ourselves the following day. 'Or that will be the end of me.'

'How come?'

'I'd rather be a prisoner of the Germans than the Russians.'

'Yeah? Wal, you Polacks should know – sorry, Limey!'

Within half an hour we were out of the trucks and on to a train. The wagons were sealed and no one came near us, despite the fact that we halted several times.

Some time during the afternoon, when we had been stationary for quite a time in what sounded like a large station, we heard a voice announcing over a loudspeaker, 'Strasbourg, Strasbourg.' And then we were off again. Some little time later we heard, and felt, the un-mistakable sound and motion of a train crossing a long bridge. I made a note of the time and then I fell asleep.

I awoke with a jolt to the noise of the doors being unbarred and the tramp of boots. Once again into trucks and a short journey, until we were off-loaded in a permanent camp.

I looked at my watch. 'Only two and a half hours since we crossed the Rhine,' I told Sam, 'so we can't be all that far inside Germany. I only hope we stay here.'

36. BOTTLES AND TINS

Sharif Ahmat

I had been in my new station farther south in Malaya a month or more before the reason for my posting was made clear.

In the early hours of a still, dark morning, I was woken by a tapping on the wooden shutter above my head. We were housed in a long, low, wooden barrack room within a barbed wire compound; it was unlikely that a person would be tapping at the window – must be a ghekko or a twig.

My sleeping mat was in a corner, directly under the window, and again it came, tap-tap-tap, tap-tap-tap. There was no mistaking the rhythm of a human hand.

And then a voice called softly, 'Ahmat, Mat.'

I struggled out of my mosquito net, wide awake and slightly apprehensive.

'Who wants me?' I asked. I dared not raise my voice above a whisper, but the reply came straight away.

'Mat. It's me, Hassan. When will you be off duty to-morrow?'

I told him.

'Good. Six pm at Woo Fung's coffee-shop. Try not to look surprised or over eager when we meet – a casua coffee with a casual friend. Right?'

'Right. Hassan – '

But he was gone.

My heart beat so fast and so hard that it seemed that everyone must hear it. But no, not a soul stirred. Thankfully I climbed back under the mosquito net and lay down to think.

He was there. Thinner than he used to be and sporting a small moustache.

I obeyed his wishes and did my best to greet him in a casual manner, although I was so excited and the questions that filled my mind kept leaping over each other for priority. But my curiosity was not to be satisfied.

'Not too many questions,' he warned in a low voice, 'there will be time.'

Once cups of the revolting brew which we call coffee nowadays, and which I suspect is made from rubber seeds, were on the table before us, I had to ask the one important question which was uppermost in my mind.

'Have you been home recently?'

'Not since Sardon's circumcision.'

That had been in August, 1941. So he could know nothing.

'Sardon is no more,' I said.

Hassan raised his eyebrows, at the same time making a sign for caution.

'There is much to tell.'

He nodded.

We drank, and spoke of a recent thunderstorm, while two Japanese soldiers seated themselves at a nearby table and only relaxed when they began a loud, animated conversation with two of their colleagues

317

in the coffee-shop opposite. The shouted exchange gave excellent cover for our own conversation.

'Do you still go fishing?'

I was puzzled. I have never been a fishing enthusiast but it was clear that an affirmative answer was required.

'Not recently. Do you know of any good spots around here?'

'There is an excellent place about a mile from the police station. You take the path at the back and follow the river. You will come to a deep pool with several large rocks. I might join you there some-time.'

'When?'

'Can you borrow a rod?'

'I could make one in a day. We have a bamboo hedge with – ' in a lower voice ' – barbed wire on the inside.'

'I know.' Hassan's eyes twinkled, 'but the front gate is easier!'

He looked at his watch, which I envied him. 'I don't think we'd better stay here too long. When will you next be off duty?'

'Friday morning.'

'Say ten o'clock, with fishing rods? I'll bring the bait.'

It seemed an eternity to wait, but I busied myself with the rod while I was on standby duty and eventually the morning came.

Wearing an old pair of shorts and singlet and a pair of the rubber slippers the Japanese now issued us with, I walked straight out of the compound and towards the river, the rod over my shoulder making, I hoped, my intention quite clear.

The spot Hassan had described was easy enough to find and he was already there, squatting on a rock and smoking a homemade cigarette.

We spent a few moments baiting our hooks and making ourselves comfortable, then I saw him give a slight nod.

'We're free to talk now,' he told me, 'the lookout has signalled all clear – we were afraid you might be followed. Shut up if you see me suddenly jerk my line.'

The surprise at the mention of a lookout must have shown on my face and my brother grinned.

'There is much to tell on my side too,' he said, 'but you first. What happened to Sardon?'

I told him all about that awful day, the day of our sister's wedding, when both she and our mother had become widows.

He was silent for a long time. 'No wonder you did nothing about my first message,' he said at length. 'Allah, to think I knew nothing of all this. And to think I called Mak a widow, not knowing it was a fact. But then it's only recently that I returned to Negri. We were cut off in Johore and immediately made our way north again and we've been in Pahang ever since.'

'We?'

'I attached myself to the Inverness-shires, interpreting and so forth; when we were cut off there were seven of us, but by the time we'd finished dodging bombs there were only three left – an officer, a corporal, and myself. The corporal died of malaria last month, so now there are only two of us. Two of the originals, that is.'

'But what are you doing?'

'I don't think I can tell you any more until I'm sure that you will help us.'

I looked long and steadily at my elder brother, now grown so hard and thin. To date I had spent my time keeping out of trouble, but I had often thought of the Chinese taukeh who had offered me the hundred dollar note, and how I had smarted when he called me spineless. Now I faced facts. When all was said and done, I had been pretty spineless.

'I will help,' I said.

'I never doubted but that you would, but I had to be sure – your record is unblemished as far as the Japs are concerned – ' I smarted again at that ' – and that is to our advantage. Have you heard of Force 247?'

I shook my head. Indeed, I'd seen and heard nothing.

'Well, they're mainly British officers who've been dropped in or infiltrated one way or another. Several are police officers who joined the army and of course they're most useful because they know the country and the language already. One was put ashore from a submarine quite near Port Dickson only last week.'

My mouth flew open and Hassan grinned.

'Yes, I thought you'd be surprised. There'll be two more put in soon, we're told. We now have a nucleus in Negri of two Europeans, myself and some twenty Chinese.'

'But how can *I* help?'

'You'll see. Passing information mainly. When can you come fishing again?'

This was a difficult question to answer, because the Japs had a habit of suddenly cancelling all off-duty time and confining us to barracks, or they would mess about with the rosters at the last minute. They employed us, but they didn't trust us. The chief of police in the area was a Sikh and as pro-Japanese as they come, but it was still the Nip NCOs under him that were the real power. Then we were the mugs, who did as we were told by all and sundry.

I explained the difficulties.

'No difficulty really,' he replied, 'we always have a lookout between here and the police station. You know that great pile of tins and empty bottles behind the latrines?' I nodded. 'Leave a message for us: bottles for the day of the week and tins for the time. For instance, for to-day, Friday, at 10 am, you would have put out six bottles and ten tins. Simple, eh? It's a code we often use.'

It was wonderfully simple.

As soon as I was sure of the next time I would be able to meet my brother, I stacked up the bottles and tins accordingly.

Quite suddenly my brain was filled with excitement. Thank you, Mr Taukeh whatever-your-name-is for calling me spineless, and thank you, Hassan, for trusting me.

The next time I met him we stayed for only a few seconds at the pool, then I followed him in silence through the rubber estate to the left of the river and into the jungle. Hassan never faltered, although I could see no path, but later he showed me the signs to look for and I was able to find my own way. Our destination proved to be a small clearing with a couple of atap huts, a covered fireplace, and a net stretched across to prevent them being spotted from the air.

'So near the edge of the jungle,' I commented with wonder, 'and so near the town.'

It seemed incredible.

But this was not the main camp, I was told. The Chinese did not trust me sufficiently to allow me there and they all agreed that it was best if I did not know the exact whereabouts of their headquarters, so that I could not spill the beans if tortured. In my excitement, torture was a thought which had not entered my head and, to my shame, I began to feel a little less enthusiastic.

But any misgivings were immediately erased from my thoughts by the appearance of two Europeans, entering the clearing from the opposite side from which we had come. Both wore the drab, olive tint later to be known as jungle green and without rank or insignia. One was a stranger, but the other – Wah!

'I don't expect you'll remember my young brother, Ahmat, Dick, but he'll remember you.'

They all laughed because, clad as I was, in singlet, undershorts and rubber boots, I quite automatically came to attention and saluted!

'Tuan Richardson,' I exclaimed in wonderment, and pumped the proffered hand.

There are officers and officers – of course with a very few exceptions they were all Europeans in those days and they are the ones I am talking about. Some were dour and best kept away from, and many were just officers, neither popular nor unpopular. But every so often there was one whom we loved – yes, loved. I remember once hearing one European talking about another and saying that the men loved him and I had thought it was a silly thing to say, but then, as my English improved, I began to understand what he meant – this was the officer they had been talking about. ASP Richardson – that means Assistant Superintendent of Police and he wears the same badges of rank as a captain in the army – had been adjutant at the Depot when I was a recruit. On duty he was the strictest officer we had, but off duty he was a clown. Seeing him so unexpectedly brought back kaleidoscopic memories, hurtling helter-skelter through my mind.

What a good world it had been. What a happy life. One always realises these things too late.

'I think I remember you, Ahmat. But, to be honest, so many recruits have passed through my hands since your day. And then I've been in the army for the past couple of years. Of course I knew your father well. I'm extremely sorry to learn of his death.'

Tuan Richardson – I could only think of him as that, although I was quick to note that he and my brother and the other officer, whom they called Jock, were on first name terms – then said it was time we got down to business and put me in the picture.

Hassan carried on from what he had already told me of his own movements. He spoke in English, because the other officer and the Chinese who had slowly filtered in, did not speak much Malay and it seemed ill-mannered to use a language which excluded them – although I don't think many, if any, of the Chinese spoke that either. But for me it was hard going; I had not realised how rusty my English had become.

Hassan had been contacted by one of the Chinese guerillas in Pahang, who was in turn in contact with members of Force 247. They wanted a local man to be on the spot in Negri Sembilan, before the British officers arrived, and my brother was the obvious choice. One of their key men was already actively installed in Police Contingent Headquarters in Seremban, but it was difficult for him to make direct contact with them; he needed a go-between. And I, said my brother, was the obvious choice for that role.

'You know Corporal Wong of the CID?' he asked. 'He visits your station each week, doesn't he?'

I was aghast. Wong was a known collaborator.

'You must not trust him,' I gasped, 'he's hand in glove with the Japs. Why, he's even been known to torture people himself.'

'He's also been responsible for a lot of people *not* being tortured,' put in Richardson. 'He's also the chap who put the screws on one of the clerks in Police Headquarters to write out your posting order.'

'But – '

He held up his hand. 'No buts, Ahmat. I'm afraid you're in for a lot of surprises. Wong is our very best man and, as you've proved by your allegations, has an excellent cover. He has ready access to a number of documents and files and makes access to others and,' he paused to let it sink in, 'he speaks fluent Japanese. But very few of us know that and I hope I'm secure in trusting you.'

I assured him that he was.

'There is another surprise coming, Mat, and I'm afraid you're not going to like this one. Your great friend, Hasbullah, who talks so loudly in the canteen about the short-arsed pigs – have you ever stopped to wonder how he gets away with it? No? Well, think. Because of course he *is* hand in glove with the little monsters.'

'But I've known Hasbullah since we were recruits together.'

It was true. Hasbullah and I had been good friends at the Depot, members of the badminton team – partners in fact in the doubles – and keen competitors in the athletic meets which played such a large part in our lives at that time. I'd lost contact with him after we were posted to our respective contingents, but I'd been as pleased as anything to meet up with him again here.

'It's true, Mat,' Hassan broke into my thoughts. 'He made advances to one or two of our chaps some time ago, who, unfortunately for them, thought he'd make a good contact. That was the end of them. The whole cell had to go to ground and now that our new HQ is in the vicinity we're not too happy about him – he hasn't been here all that long and Wong has still not found out whether his posting was purely coincidental. One of your jobs will be to keep an eye on him.'

'And let us know at once if you have cause to suspect him,' added Richardson. 'But your main role is a simple one. Corporal Wong will pass messages to you and you will relay them to us. Verbally, whenever possible; it minimises risk. Use the code we've already suggested and someone will be by the fishing-pool to meet you. Keep your eyes and ears open and let us know any items of information that you can glean. Movements, postings, transport – you'd be surprised how much can be pieced together from these snippets. And don't trust a soul.'

I met my brother as often as expedient and one day I told him about the Chinese who had offered me the one hundred dollar note.

'You should have taken the opportunity of joining him,' was Hassan's curt reply, 'if he was able to slip away, it should not have been difficult for you to do likewise.'

'I was working on the policy of keeping my eyes shut to trouble.'

'Yes. You were hardly a ball of fire!'

The expression was beyond my comprehension, but his tone of voice stung and when the two Europeans laughed I was more than ever determined that they should not regret having taken me into their confidence.

37. CHE FATIMAH'S STORY

Abdul Karim

'Karim. Karim, come back here.'

It was my mother's imperative voice and I was surprised to hear her call, because I'd just left the house on my way to school. I could have pretended that I had not heard, but something in the tone made me turn back.

'Now listen,' she held my shoulders and looked down into my eyes, 'you know Che Fatimah, who lives down the road?' I nodded. 'She has been away for a long time and only just returned. She has brought a child back with her, a little girl, a white girl. She will be starting school to-day and you are not to poke fun at her – just behave as though she had always been there. Understand?'

I didn't, but I said I did.

I walked off, wondering at my mother's excitement. What was so special about a white girl? There had been plenty of European children around before the war and I had often played with them on the beach. They weren't any different from us. Their colouring was different, of course, but then so was the colouring of the Indians and the Chinese.

It was not until I was quite near school that it dawned on me what was so unusual about this new pupil – of course it was true that I had seen plenty of European children, but not since the invasion.

This might be interesting after all. Anything to break the monotony.

I could already hear the chatter from the school playground and began to walk faster.

'Karim. Karim, do hurry.'

This time it was Rokiah, one of my special friends.

She came running down the road towards me, her blue school sarong held high and her pigtails streaming out behind her.

Rokiah was a year younger than I, but brighter. I was glad we were in the same class, because she sat in front of me and when I couldn't cope with a question, I would tweak one of her plaits and she would pass me the answer on a slip of paper. Of course, Rokiah should have been a boy. She could outclimb most of us when we scaled the tall palms for coconuts, and outswam us when we raced through the surf.

'Oh hurry, Karim, do.'

She grabbed my hand and pulled and we ran the rest of the way, and while we ran she told me the reason for her excitement.

Then of course I remembered. Che Fatimah was Rokiah's mother. I often played at her house and I had forgotten that the woman who scolded us for putting too much weight on the jambu tree was not

Rokiah's mother, but her aunt. Her widowed mother worked abroad on one of the islands; I had heard my parents talking about her but I had not really listened. Now I wished I had.

We were both out of breath when we reached school and Rokiah dropped my hand and ran to the centre of a circle and took instead the hand of a little European girl, who stood on her own, looking at the ground.

'Karim, come and say hallo to Noraini. Mak says we are to be like sisters.'

Wah! How strange she looked. How different from us. And how pretty.

She wore one of Rokiah's white school bajus and blue sarong – I know it was Rokiah's because I recognised the mended tear and remembered her falling out of the jambu tree. I had had a beating because her aunt had said I pushed her and Mak said no one could afford to spoil clothes in wartime. Her hair was the colour of a new one-cent piece, sort of golden and coppery. I had never seen hair that colour before. Her skin was as white as the buffalo milk we sometimes had and her face and arms were all covered with little golden freckles. I was just trying to make up my mind whether her eyes were the blue of the plumbago flower or the sea after a storm when Rokiah nudged me.

'Don't stare so, Karim. She's just the same as us underneath!' The little girl giggled and I turned away, feeling hot and foolish. I could have killed Rokiah!

The desks were arranged in three rows in our classroom, girls in front and boys behind. Each desk was shared by two children and there were about forty pupils in our form.

I shared my desk with a boy named Musah. He was older and bigger than me and a bully; I hated him. Rokiah had had a desk to herself before, but now she shared it with Noraini and when I listened to the horrible things Musah was saying about her, I wished for the first time that they were farther away. But I stared myself. Her scalp showed pale pink where the hair was parted down the back of her head, to be pulled into two tight plaits, like all the other girls'. The golden freckles marched down and around her neck and her ears showed pink too.

Musah was preparing scratchy blotting-paper pellets to put down the little girl's neck when we both looked up, surprised. None of us can speak English, but I can recognise it when I hear it and I wondered why the teacher was addressing us. But it was to Noraini that he spoke.

She took no notice and we sniggered and Musah remarked, loudly enough for the teacher to hear, 'He only *thinks* he can speak English.'

Then he said something, which I'm sure was rude, in Chinese – he is Chinese actually, but adopted by a Malay family.

'But aren't you English?' asked the teacher.

The little girl shook her head again. 'No,' she replied, 'I am Malay.'

We all giggled again, because of course we knew she wasn't Malay. But then I felt mean because she went bright pink when we laughed and began to cry.

Rokiah put her arms round her and glared at us over her coppery head. 'Goats,' she hissed, 'leave her alone.'

My mother had been waiting for me when I came home from school, eager to hear about the little white girl. Mak couldn't wait to see her and as soon as Pak came home we went over to Che Fatimah's house.

I had not seen Rokiah's mother before. She was plump and had a kindly face which smiled easily, creasing her eyes and her mouth. She sat at the top of their steps, Noraini on one side of her and Rokiah on the other, with an arm round the shoulders of each of the girls. Only they didn't remain there for long because she used her hands a great deal when she talked.

The two girls looked bored and Rokiah told me afterwards that her mother was just starting on her story for the fourth time when we arrived.

This was her story: Fatimah had worked as a servant in the house of a rubber planter in Borneo for several years. Then her husband had died and she remained, cooking and looking after the children, until the arrival of the Japanese. The Mem had so many children, she told us, some older than Noraini and three younger. It was terrible, she said, when the Europeans were taken off to the internment camps. The men and older boys went one way and the women and children another. How could the poor woman look after four young children, the youngest but a few weeks old? Here she paused until the tut-tuttings and sighs of sympathy for the poor mother had died down. As the women were being hustled into trucks by the Japanese guards, Fatimah's mistress, two children in her arms and two clinging to her skirt, had bent swiftly and detached Noraini. 'Look after her for me, Fatimah,' she had called, 'she will be better off with you than me. If I live I will find you again.' Noraini had run to Fatimah, unnoticed by the guards, and the Malay woman had quickly snuggled her inside the extra sarong that she wore draped over her head and shoulders, and taken her to the house of a fisherman friend. For more than a year they had lived in constant fear of detection, Noraini being kept inside during the hours of daylight and smuggled from house to house when a Japanese patrol was in the area. Fatimah's own husband had been a member of the small colony of Trengganu fishermen where they hid, and when one of his former friends, and her kinsman, decided to try and reach home, she and Noraini sailed with him. And now, here they were.

Noraini's past and future were the topics of many grown-up conversations from time to time, but as far as we were concerned, we soon forgot that her hair was a different colour and that she came from a foreign land. She was quieter and not as much of a tomboy as Rokiah, but she still climbed trees with us, played hide and seek, swam and chased the crabs in the rock pools.

Soon after her arrival, the headmaster called the whole school together and told us that it was our duty to protect her and that, should the Japanese visit our kampong and ask questions, we were just to act dumb – not that that should be very difficult, he said, it would not need much acting for most of us! Inche Yacob was always saying things like that. But of course everyone in the village would have looked after her anyway, just as they would look after all the other girls – even at my age I would have had to protect my sister if I had one – and we all knew that at the first sign of a Japanese all girls and buffaloes must be hidden at once. It was rather an exciting thought, like playing hide and seek in real life.

38. IN LIMBO

Omar

Ai-ee. Malaya was not a happy place indeed in that year of 1944. Two and a half years now we have been occupied by the Japanese, and for all of us in this kampong it has been the worst two and a half years of our lives. Time passes, but only Tuan Allah knows what the outcome of these present times will be.

I have already told how we trudged across the peninsula from the east coast to the west, bearing our Zaitun in a coma, and finally came home. I was trembling for many weeks after that, and not only because of the fate of our little one and memories of that terrible day when they also decapitated our sergeant-major, but because I was a deserter.

Not that the Japanese oath meant anything to me, but I was a deserter none the less and worthless though it may be, I wanted to keep my head. Times are hard enough for my family already; what would they do without the little food I bring? And then I had a stroke of luck. I had been a police driver in my early days and, just in case I should ever want to become a taxi driver when I retired, I had taken out a civilian licence as well.

The day that licence was issued is clear to me still, because it is one of the only occasions on which I have lost my temper with anyone – I am a placid man. It was because the clerk had copied my name down back to front – I am Omar bin Mohamed Rais, as you already know, but he wrote it as Mohamed Rais bin Omar – and refused to change it. When I pointed out his error he called me an ignorant, illiterate policeman and if one of the other clerks had not stayed my hand I would have hit him. But I was cross with him no longer.

There must be many Omars in the police, it is not an uncommon name, but I was happier facing the Japanese as Mohamed Rais. I destroyed my warrant card and my notebook and a few letters that I had kept and then, with regret, my framed Commissioner's Commendation – which I had received for life-saving when a ship had gone down in the Straits – and now there is nothing to show except the licence, and this I produced when the Japanese came to register the inhabitants of the village.

All the men of Tanjong Mas are collected every morning in a lorry and taken to a rubber estate to tap the trees. None of us are tappers and there has been no instruction, so I cannot believe that we perform this task very well.

Ours is primarily a fishing village, but we cannot all be fishermen and, like so many kampongs in Malacca state, we provide men for the police and army and the shipping company whose vessels sail round the peninsula and over to Borneo. My father was a sailor, but I chose the police.

Of course the Japanese will not allow our boats to put to sea, and so they lie there, idle and rotting away on the beach, and with them goes all the loving care that we put into their fashioning – for we are all interested in the fishing fleet, all helping to build the boats and haul in the catch when we are to hand, even if we are not fishermen ourselves. We could do with some fish to eat now and I miss the salt, pungent tang of the fish drying on the creepers above the tide-line.

And so we go, every day, fishermen, soldiers, sailors and policemen, to tap the rubber trees, while the Tamil tappers are sent to remove the railway line, so that it can be sent up to Siam. We hear it is being relaid there by white prisoners and many of our own officers are amongst them. Ai-ee, I do not try to understand the Japanese; I only wish they were not here.

But work is a salve and my pity is for the women and children who have only food to think about, and who wait so eagerly for the meagre rice ration that we bring home – for the Japanese do not pay the labour gangs, only issue us with a handful of rice each day. And where does a handful go when there are eleven mouths to feed? Adohi, we did not know how well off we were before the war.

Our rice stocks were removed within the first weeks of the occupation, and then went our livestock. First the buffaloes, then the chickens and ducks; even our pigeons, which most of us kept only for pets, were taken from us and now there is not even a dog or cat to be seen. Not a bird in the tree nor fish in the river. My wife digs for roots and the sea-snails and slugs which crawl out at low tide, taking all the children with her to search under the rocks and stones. But we are not happy to see so many women and girls digging in the tidal mud, they are too vulnerable. Even now we dare not let the girls stray far from home. We have many hiding-places for them and each time the lorry comes, in the morning and evening, they are hidden, so that the soldiers will not see them and come back another time. It is a hard time for women and children, worse by far than for us. My wife has no flesh on her and her bones stick out like those of a starving horse.

Only Zaitun remains happy and unaffected by lack of food, so perhaps Allah the merciful had a reason for causing her affliction after all. Day after day she sits, smiling and playing with a hibiscus flower. She has grown beautiful as the hibiscus – and as useless. But my wife cherishes her beyond all others, caring for her as one would a baby still, for she has never progressed since the day she awoke from the coma.

Last week we were taken all the way to a river in Johore, to salvage goods which the Japanese thought the British had thrown there. All day we dived in the shallow muddy river – and we were frightened too, because that river is well-known to be full of crocodiles – but found nothing. Our captors were so annoyed that we were left without rations for three days. Allahumma. That was not funny, going home empty-handed three nights running, to all those little ones.

There is a greyness over the land. We are in limbo; greyness on the edge of dark. Maraiee the Japanese call our beloved land, a name we shall remember always as belonging to the grey times that we are going through now, for surely Tuan Allah cannot intend us to exist like this for ever?

Meanwhile we live from day to day, guarding what little we have, accepting the humiliations and privations along with the rice ration and praying always that the soldiers will leave our few tapioca plants and the little maize that we have and that our womenfolk will not again be molested.

We can only put our faith in the almighty goodness of Tuan Allah, who knows all, sees all and guides our lives accordingly – although I sometimes wonder why He made the Japanese – and hope that He will lead us out of this grey world.

We must accept our destiny. And so we turn our eyes to the trees from which we extract the sticky white latex during the day and to the sea at night, hoping that one day new sails will be seen on the horizon, the sails of friends returning.

Jogindar Singh

The Chinese festival of the Double Tenth, that is the tenth of October, invariably provided an excuse for sport of one kind or another – and by sport I don't mean athletics. And in Singapore that year it was no exception.

As I'm sure I have said before, the Japanese are as unpredictable as the monkeys they resemble and any festival, whether it be Christmas, New Year's Day, the Malay Hari Raya, or the Double Tenth, might be the occasion of a party or an execution. Mind you, the parties thrown by the Japs for local dignitaries were never very popular, because the hosts had an unpleasant habit of reading out lists of forthcoming victims and, if one of them happened to be present, there wasn't much point in his trying to make a getaway.

By late 1944 our conquerors were becoming a little desperate. Things were not going the way they had planned – oh yes, we managed to hear about the American naval successes in the Pacific and the way the British were pushing them back in Burma. We'd heard of British officers being parachuted into the mainland states of Malaya too, and all this gave us heart.

But food was becoming increasingly short. The internees of course were in a worse state than ever, but the Japs themselves weren't faring much better.

Rumours of disposal of prisoners and internees abounded and, with the knowledge that even their meagre rations would be a saving to the hungry Nips, I could not blame anyone who believed them.

Some said that the Nips intended locking the prisoners in, saturating the huts with kerosene and setting them alight. Others that they were to be buried alive in a vast grave, which they would first have to dig themselves. And others that they would be driven into the sea and machine-gunned. Subsequently it came to light that all these rumours had some foundation.

On the eve of the Double Tenth, 9th October, 1944, I was surprised when one of my elderly charges, obviously having waited for a moment when he would be unobserved, called me aside and pushed a small banana-leaf parcel into my hands.

He was a man in his early sixties, I should say, strong once, no doubt, but emaciated now to the build of a frail old man. He had been a member of the Straits Settlements Legislative Council and appeared to be the acknowledged leader of my lot. He was also one of the survivors of the Emperor's Birthday lark, more than a year ago. A tough old bird.

'Take these and hide them,' he said, with some urgency, 'they may be dangerous to you, but we want you to have them, just in case.' I took the packet and buttoned it inside my shirt. 'Who knows,' he went on, 'what will happen to-morrow – another Double Tenth.' Then he held out his hand, 'My thanks, Jogindar, and the thanks of all of us. You've been bloody good.'

He turned away then and hobbled off towards the latrine-pits and I looked round to make sure that no Jap was in sight.

Privacy was a commodity hard to come by. The permanent warders and some of the older men had individual quarters, where they lived with their families, but we young bachelors were all together in one large barrack block.

We were all Sikhs and there were several my age or a little older, but I had no real friends. Uncle Arjan had taught me to trust no one and his teaching had been proved correct too often to be ignored.

There may have been other warders who helped their charges in the same way that I did – in fact there must have been – but if there were, I didn't know who they were. We played cards and talked of money and had our own physical pleasures when we were off duty, but we never discussed the prisoners and we never discussed our masters. These subjects were taboo, and wisely so.

I could not risk opening the packet inside the barracks, nor could I take it with me when I went to bathe, for then I would only have a towel wrapped round my waist. The only place was the latrine and, ensuring that I would have good reason to remain there sufficient time without arousing suspicion, I made a great show of holding my stomach and rolling on my charpoy in supposed agony for some time first.

The package contained many sheets of writing. Some proper paper, edges from the Japanese newspaper, backs of orders, pages from ordinary books and exercise books, opened-up cigarette packets, and suchlike. They were all testimonials. Testimonials from my charges, aware that this Double Tenth might be their last.

I read each one through while I squatted there. I didn't understand English very well, but I knew what they were.

I could hear in my mind as clearly as anything the voice of my uncle when he first told me what I should do. 'There are many ways of helping prisoners and then, after the war . . . I'd remind my former prisoners of what I'd done. There'd be promotion for me, you'd see.'

Whether you will believe it or not, at that moment, the thought of promotion in such circumstances was utterly abhorrent to me. Later I came to see reason – not that I ever had to approach any of my ex-prisoners, there was no need, what I held in my hands was enough.

What premonitions had my old friends – I call them friends deliberately – had?

I went on duty at 6 am on the morning of the Double Tenth and at seven there was a special parade for all warders, a most unusual event.

We were given the usual flowery speech, which invariably ended up with someone's head parting from his body, and this one was no exception.

It seemed that this was to be just another excuse for a massacre. Ten Europeans from each gaol and camp; a hundred Chinese from each place that the Japs felt like collecting them. We had grown used to this wholesale blood-letting; after more than two and a half years as members of the co-prosperity sphere it came as no surprise.

I did not see the execution, although not to attend was courting trouble. I pleaded abdominal pain again and lay on my charpoy, my turban over my eyes.

But no turban could block my ears and at every roar from the onlookers I saw the scene clearly in my imagination.

But the Great Sahib knows it was a blessing. At least the sword falling is quick. To men who had suffered the water treatment, had chillies stuffed up their backsides, and nails and teeth extracted, this quick execution was a mercy.

My uncle Arjan was solemn when next I visited his house.

He and his wife had grown old and I saw that his gums were almost toothless and his skin grey from malnutrition.

He took my packet, gave the contents but a cursory glance and nodded.

'I'll stow them safely,' he said, 'although God knows if they'll ever be of any use to you. Things are getting worse and worse – you don't see what goes on, incarcerated at the other end of the island – but I have plenty of time to watch from the five-foot way. Fewer and fewer people leave the safety of their homes these days – if they can be called safe. Except of course those merchants who are still kowtowing to the Japs – and they'll get away with it, see if they don't.'

I pottered around, playing my uncle's old gramophone, but the only two records were so old and scratched that I soon stopped. The old couple sat in a maudlin daze until it was time for Uncle Arjan to go on duty.

'I'll walk with you,' I said, 'I have to be on duty at 6 pm myself.'

But my uncle shook his head. 'Better not to be seen strolling around, not a young man, even if you are in the employ of the Japs.

331

Anyone gets picked up these days – it's a case of grab, and ask questions afterwards. And afterwards is usually too late.'

I went back in an even more sombre frame of mind than when I had left – if that were possible – and I didn't see my relations again for nearly a year.

40. MORSE FROM AN OLD DUTCH MILL

Donald Thom

That summer of 1944 sure enough passed quickly for me. Nothing much happened in Holland immediately after the Normandy landings, but the feeling was there. A tremendous spiritual upsurge, giving, as Hans said, the whole country a glimpse of blue sky through the grey clouds of oppression.

My legs had mended pretty well and, except that I walked with a bit of a limp and couldn't run quite as fast as I could before, I was as good as new. At least *I* thought I was – it appeared that the others thought otherwise. There had never been any question of my being dropped in purely as a radio operator, so, as soon as I had regained a reasonable degree of agility, I fretted to be away from the mill – leave the radio to one of the girls or older men – and take part in the raids and sabotage. First of all Hans made excuses and then Konrad came out in the open – they were afraid that I might slow them up. Hans tried to persuade me that I was too important with the radio to risk, but I knew that that was a lot of crap.

Because of my supposed lack of speed in delivering messages, and to save someone fetching and carrying, Hans decided that one of them should sleep in the mill with me. I was glad, but disturbed when Marijke volunteered. I hadn't needed nursing for some time, but she volunteered on the double pretext of being able to collect and deliver messages while coping with her patients and that her mother, who was becoming increasingly difficult and nervy, was not safe to have too close. Both Hans and Konrad agreed and she moved in forthwith.

As I said, I was both dubious and pleased. I had never meant our relationship to be anything but platonic, but – and I admit it – I was lazy. Lazy and weak. I just lay back and resigned myself to the fact that there was no turning back. Of course there was – if I'd wanted to.

Marijke softened and bloomed and although the word was never mentioned between us, I knew that that girl was in love. Judas Priest, a woman doesn't look like that just because she's had a man. Nevertheless, I could never entirely relax – my conscience wouldn't let me. Every time I took her in my arms I felt a stab of guilt, both for the

332

infidelity to Monica, my wife, and because of the ultimate hurt that I must cause her, Marijke.

Messages concerning Monica ceased. But she was still very much on my mind.

Marijke often asked about her, acknowledging the fact that she would never be mine alone – Jesus, you had to respect that girl. Tough and soft both at the same time, and completely frank and open, always. I did my best to be frank with her too. I never pretended that Monica didn't understand me, or any of that bilge. I told her right out that I loved my wife and we didn't ought to be doing what we were.

But I suppose if you lived as they, the resistance units did, you learned to live from day to day. Take love where you find it, I guess. And Jesus knows, there wasn't much love about.

'She need never know,' Marijke shrugged my wife away, 'and what she does not know will never hurt her. Let me have you now, for when this is over you will be hers forever.'

Well, what would any guy do in the light of that philosophy? Just what I did, I guess. It was easy to lie back and enjoy Marijke's companionship. Easy to worry about her when she went out – as I did, more and more. Easy to relax when she returned. Easy to love her when she did.

It didn't take long to find out that although my feelings for Monica had not decreased, I loved my golden girl as well – and I told her so. I was married and that was that, but if I hadn't been, or our law and religion permitted us two wives, I'd certainly marry her as well. Guess man's a polygamous animal, mentally as well as physically.

As the Germans dug their heels in and more and more troops were camped in the area, our activity became less and less. We assumed the role of watchers and, at all times of the day and night, men would come in with snippets of information for me to relay to the Intelligence pundits in UK. I didn't do anything very active as far as my feet were concerned, but I sure enough tapped and received, tapped and received, hour after hour. I liked to think I was earning my keep and probably, for the first time since I'd been dropped in, I was doing my full share.

But unfortunately, during this spell, we threw too much caution to the winds and one day Jan reported that he was almost sure the mill was being watched. After that I seldom left the building and when I did, only at night. And unless she was absolutely sure the coast was clear, Marijke too would leave before dawn and only return after dark.

Autumn was setting in again and by four o'clock each afternoon Marijke would have collected all the news for me to transmit. Then she would return to the mill and cook our supper while I put it into code.

During the early days of winter nothing moved. It seemed that both the Allies and the Axis were stuck. I sent messages telling of the concentrated German might in south-east Holland and our elder statesmen, Konrad, Hans and Jan, would nod their heads while I tapped and say that we would have to drop troops in, it was the only way.

It was in the early hours of New Year's Day that Hans surprised us. He barged in and came straight to the point.

'They know we're sending messages from here,' his tone was urgent. 'Donald, you've got to get out. Destroy the radio and go.'

Of course I protested at that, suggesting that I should take the radio and hide. But he was quite emphatically against it.

'We're packing up,' he said, 'we can't do any more and quite honestly, Don, although you've been a tremendous help, you'd only be a hindrance now. Send a last message so that they won't expect any more and then deal with the radio. You must be gone before it's light. Jan will be here at five o'clock to guide you to the coast. I must go now.'

He shook hands with me and gave Marijke an inquiring look. He had completely ignored her presence until then.

'I'll leave when Don does,' she said.

He nodded and was gone.

We looked long into each other's eyes. Sufficient unto the day. But the day had come. I felt a sick feeling in the pit of my stomach as I put her aside to attend to my job. I didn't bother to put the message into code. 'Closing down stop returning home stop tell Monica' I tapped in clear.

Then I looked at my watch and took Marijke in my arms. 'We have three hours,' I said.

Soon after four I got up and dressed, ready for the journey. I had left the radio, just in case they should need to send any message in return, but nothing had come through. I pulled out wires and plugs and got busy with a knife, until a small explosion and a puff of smoke made Marijke sit up in bed.

'Let's say good-bye now,' she said. 'I don't want to see you go.' She smiled at me and said dreamily, 'Besides, Don, not all of you is going – one of these days I shall bear your child.'

I spun round and was by her side in one stride. I couldn't stop myself from shaking her. The feeling of fear and responsibility that had settled on me was like a dead weight.

'Marijke, no. You *can't* be pregnant.' I wonder why one says these things?

She just went on smiling; smiling at me. 'I had hoped, and now I am sure. Oh, Donald, can't you understand? I *want* to have your child. I can't have you, but he'll be mine. I shall never forget you and I shall be a good mother to your son.'

I bent my head and felt the hot tears spurt from my eyes. Never had I known such humility. 'Oh, Marijke,' I cried, 'what have I done?'

'Loved me – without ever knowing it,' she said.

Jan arrived punctually at five o'clock and gave me a quick, approving glance. I was wearing clothes that had belonged to Marijke's father and I didn't need a mirror to tell me that I looked the part.

He checked the contents of the mill and showed me a small sack of food he had brought.

'The truck will meet us in about ten minutes,' he said, 'it will drop us just outside Utrecht. It should not be difficult to reach the coast. Everything is in turmoil. My brother has not been allowed to fish since we were first invaded, but he has kept his boat ready all this time, for just such an emergency as this. We'll hide until dark and then set sail for England – I've never been there before.'

'You're coming too?' It was the first pleasing news I had heard.

He grinned. 'I must. I doubt if you can sail and my brother will need two pairs of hands to bring the boat back.'

Before long the truck arrived and we climbed aboard. I didn't look back. The mill was empty anyway.

The journey to the coast was uneventful. Everyone was too preoccupied with their own movements to worry about one lorry. We stuck to roads with a reasonable amount of traffic and, on the only occasion when we were stopped, our papers were given only a cursory glance. By thumbing lifts and walking a few miles we were at our destination long before nightfall and Jan led the way to his brother's house.

Judas Priest, if the Dutch aren't a solid race! Who says the English have so much phlegm? Wouldn't you think that the sight of a brother, unseen for more than two years, and a stranger, would arouse some emotion? But no. The family were in the middle of their evening meal when we arrived.

'Another one?' was the only comment as the family looked at me and I was told to sit down.

We shared out the food we had brought with us and soon the whole family were munching again, while Jan and his brother talked.

As soon as we had finished eating we followed him down to a small boathouse by the shore and set sail about an hour after dark. Jan told me that we would be able to use the inboard once we were well out to sea, but for the first few miles silence was imperative and they dared not risk the noise.

All three of us were silent, occupied with our own thoughts – and frankly I'd rather not have had mine. I sat huddled in a blanket, numb with cold, my mind darting back and forth to both sides of the Channel.

After an hour or so the two brothers began talking in low voices and soon the elder started up the engine. It made a terrible noise, even in the blowy January night, and I expected at any minute to see a German patrol boat looming out of the darkness.

We chugged along gently throughout the hours of darkness, seeing no one and apparently ourselves unseen. And then, in that spooky grey light that precedes the dawn, with the fog swirling round us like streamers of dirty cotton wool, the sound of a powerful engine came through the mirk. Jan's brother immediately switched off and we drifted, silent – if you can call three hearts beating like temple gongs silent – but of course I speak for myself – those two probably couldn't hear theirs.

In a very short time we heard the other craft slow down and I presumed it had entered the same bank of fog. Without warning, a light suddenly shone on us and a voice called out, 'Ahoy there. Stand by to show your identification.'

My gongs calmed down. Full of relief, the three of us raised our arms and I called out, 'We're friends. I'm Lieutenant Thom of the Canadian Army and these two are Dutch Allies, members of the resistance, who are helping me to reach England.'

The vessel, which turned out to be an MTB, came alongside and two sailors, armed with Sten guns, jumped aboard. Before replying to my call, a third sailor searched us three men and the ship, while we were covered by the other two.

A very young man in jersey and duffle coat leaned over the side. 'Any means of identification?' he asked.

'Sorry, none. But if you're homeward bound, perhaps you'd take me in and I can contact my unit as soon as I'm ashore.'

'Fair enough.'

I gripped the hands of my two friends and said good-bye quickly. I'd had enough of farewells that twenty-four hours.

'We'll follow you in until we're nearer the coast,' Jan said to the skipper, 'and anchor until the afternoon. We can't return before it's dark.'

Then I was helped aboard.

In what seemed a remarkably short time we were in sight of land. The fog had lifted and a grey mass loomed. We swung west as the light grew stronger and I sure was getting excited.

'Lucky for you we were off our beat,' the skipper said, 'and when we picked you up on the radar we thought we'd come and investigate before going home. It'll have saved you a lot of trouble when you get ashore. Damned brave, those Dutchmen, always coming across, but of course they're too like Germans to be let in easily.'

Jesus, did that breakfast taste good? The skipper said he'd run me into town to catch the London train, but I'd reckoned without my unit –

when I called to tell them I was back, I'd been told to sit tight where I was and they'd send a vehicle to collect me. No use ringing Monica either, I'd been told to keep my trap shut and report for interrogation and debriefing when I reached them. I wondered if they'd told her I'd be back.

I accepted another cup of coffee and a cigarette. Back in this world of British voices and British uniforms and marmalade on the ward-room table, it was easy to forget the world over the other side. Marijke was a dream.

Judas Priest, would you believe it? Four days before I was allowed to go free and I hadn't even been allowed to contact my wife. Those security guys sure make a lot of mountains out of molehills. But at last I was on my way to a phone.

I listened to the click as she lifted the receiver at the other end. 'Monica?' I yelled.

'Where are you?' she asked, and when I replied, 'Your unit told me you were coming back from wherever you've been. I'll meet the train.'

We thundered into the station and I nearly lost my balance, I was leaning so far out of the carriage window, trying to catch a first glimpse of my grey-blue bird.

I couldn't see her at first, then the round badge with the bright red cross on her sleeve caught my eye. She was well down the plat-form, not looking at the train, chatting to a Free French Naval officer.

'Monica,' I yelled, but she did not turn round. I guess there was too much noise.

Hurrying down the platform my legs hurt me for the first time in months. 'Monica.' Hey, this is a fine reception for your returning spouse. I was near enough to hear that they were speaking French before she finally turned round.

Her face was white and strained. I'd never seen her looking like that before. But it was her all right, my honey heart – probably worrying about me had caused the pallor. I hurried towards her, my arms wide – and then I stopped. Some sixth sense had warned me that all was not well. My smile faded as I caught her eye.

Monica did not smile. 'Hallo, Don.' She spoke so quietly I could hardly hear. 'This is Emil.'

She didn't actually say, 'I love him, I want to marry him, will you give me a divorce?', but I read it in her eyes.

A fortnight later I reported to my unit and asked to be sent back to Holland.

'We're not dropping people in at this stage,' I was told. 'Didn't you have a good leave?'

'No.'

337

James Weatherby

I often looked back to the day when I had been told that I was to be one of the senior officers of TAF. We had gone over in high hopes, and everything had been dimmed in the dull, Dutch mud. I rolled over and tried to work up enough energy to write to Helen, but the effort was too much. She would understand – and if she didn't, hard luck. I was long past caring about anything other than keeping what aircraft we had flying and that silly quarrel we had now seemed too petty for words. Nothing like action to put one's personal problems in their right perspective. I'd write to her to-morrow.

But the gift of sleep had left me. It was no use. I sat up with the blanket round my shoulders and lit a cigarette. I had never smoked until these past few months, but I could understand now why one became addicted. When I had finished I put on my flying-jacket and boots and wandered outside.

It was a bright night and I stood and watched my own breath for a minute or two before going over to the cluster of huts which served as SHQ. Might as well have a look at the latest sitrep.

Was that really the sound of carols coming from one of the huts? I stopped and listened, glad that at least some people's morale was higher than mine.

'Noel, Noel, Noel, No-e-e-el.' The flat, discordant voices cracking on the last syllable reminded me that it was Christmas Eve. I really should have written to Helen. I turned back to my hut.

I had received a few odd notes from James, always brief, always tired. 'You cannot imagine the exhaustion,' he wrote on one occasion, and on another, 'the worst times during the war were never as bad as this. The losses are terrible and the material coming out is raw – don't they train pilots any more these days? No time to train them ourselves, they are up – and usually down – before we have had time to get to know them. When we first came over with TAF, I don't know what I expected, but I suppose we all thought it would be over in a matter of months. Give the Huns their due, they certainly know how to hang on'. And on another, 'Oh God, I'm tired. Will this never end?'

The war dragged on on all fronts and the jubilation in people's hearts at the time of D-Day had dulled to a hope that it would not go on for another year.

It was a drab world all right.

Early in the new year of 1945 I flew operationally for the last time. The news of my divorce had come through that morning, but with long months of too little sleep and too much worry and having waited for so long, it was almost an anticlimax.

I stood in Flying Control, looking out on the bleak Dutch landscape. There was a strange silence and stillness about the airfield which contrasted oddly with the booming of field guns in the distance. It seemed to affect us all in the same way. The duty officer stood looking out of another window and the R/T operator stared idly into space, no sound coming from his headset.

'Depressing, isn't it?' It was the Flying Control officer, tapping a pencil on the pane in front of him.

The slight sound irritated me. I merely nodded.

'Are you flying to-night, sir?'

I nodded again. He had an artificial leg which creaked as he moved. It occurred to me that I had no idea how he had come by it and I had always prided myself on knowing the full history of everyone under my command. 'Get a bit of fresh air,' I said, and opened the door on to the narrow, rickety wooden balcony which surrounded the main cabin.

The cold took my breath away and I began to notice that there was activity on the airfield after all. Fitters and riggers were working at all the roughly camouflaged bays, rearming and refuelling and making sure that the aircraft were in as good a shape as one could hope for these days.

I had been debating whether or not to write a quick note to Helen. Take-off was at last light, in about an hour's time. I'll write to-morrow, I decided, and turned back into the cabin, down the stairs and across the short distance of bare earth to the Nissen hut that was my quarters.

My batman had laid out clean clothes and was already pouring hot water into the tub which served as a bath.

I stripped and stepped into the steaming water and stepped out as quickly.

'Christ, Burton,' I yelled, 'it's bad enough being burned up there without having to suffer it in my own bloody hut!'

'Sorry, sir,' he unconcernedly emptied a bucket of cold water into the tin tub, 'gets cold very quickly in here, sir.'

I was ready, with half an hour to spare, when the thought suddenly crossed my mind, what if my luck doesn't hold? What if I get shot down to-night? By the law of averages it was my turn. If I don't write to Helen now, she might never know. I gave a quick glance at my watch and pulled out my writing pad.

Helen darling [I wrote],
We are due to take off in less than half an hour. The raid in which I shall be taking part will be historic, in so far that it will

339

be one of the last of the large formation raids of this war – which *cannot* go on much longer. I do not have to fly and yet I have to – I have explained all this to you before.

The important news is that my divorce is through at last. Marry me, Helen, please marry me as soon as I get back to England – whenever that may be.

All my love for you always, darling,

James.

PS. Get rid of that Pole – I hate him!

I sealed the envelope and handed it to the batman.

'Post that for me, Burton. And make sure it goes – it's the most important letter I ever wrote in my life.'

And I walked out into the dusk and my waiting kite.

As the first aircraft revved up and prepared for take-off, Burton turned the letter over in his hand and thought it would make a nice bit of gossip for the Airmen's Dining Hall. Junior Commander H. Watson, ATS. Now who might she be? Well, she certainly wasn't Mrs Weatherby, that was for sure. The most important letter of his life, eh? Looked as though the old Commode was human after all!

There was no anticlimax for me when I received James's note. I read it, reread it, and reached for a memo pad.

Will write a proper letter later, but for now, suffice to say that I love you more than ever and of course will marry you. Until that day, my love – Helen.

I came to, choking, in the mud. My mouth and nostrils were full of the vile stuff and my legs were stuck fast. I was vaguely aware of a pull on my shoulders as gusts of wind caught at the remains of the parachute, which trailed on the marsh behind me.

But I was even more conscious of an excruciating pain in my left arm and the fact that my eyes would not focus. I lifted my right arm to my face, but it did not bear touching. There was a thick crust over most of it, which I thought must be coagulated blood, and my eyes were agony.

I knew I was in marshy land by the birds which flew over and the sound of the wind, which is different over flat land. The Fens, I supposed – once I had reached the coast of England I had set the plane on a course out to sea and baled out.

It hurt to think; hurt to move. Hurt to do anything but lie absolutely still with my eyes shut – and even that hurt in the bright light. I judged it to be about noon and I longed for the darkness.

How long I was there I never knew. Occasionally I woke to the sound of the birds and would then wonder what had happened to the rest of the crew. I had flown as close to the base as I dared, to let them bale out, but someone had stayed behind. Someone who had refused to bale out when I gave the order. Someone who had stayed until I was ready to jump myself. Someone who had jumped just before me. Who was it? Harry? Kenneth? Paul? It made me cross that I couldn't remember and I burst into angry tears. The tears hurt my eyes and I became even angrier. Who the bloody hell was it?

Next time I woke up, it was to see a nursing sister bending over me. I looked at her – my eyes still hurt, but I could see. I looked at her starched white coif and tried to place myself. Of course, my legs were burned and Elsie had not been to see me.

'Are they very badly burned?' I asked.

'No,' she told me, 'you're not burned at all, luckily.'

Silly bitch. Of course I was burnt – I remembered the fire; they were pulling old what's his name out, the tail gunner. Didn't she know a burn when she saw one?

I suppose I drifted off again.

It was dark, then it was light, then it was dark again. My eyes hurt. Dear God, how my eyes hurt.

In Holland, the survivors of R Robert had been debriefed.

The bomb-aimer and the engineer, wireless operator and two air-gunners had all returned.

'The skipper wouldn't ditch her until she was over the sea,' they told the IO, 'and the second pilot wouldn't leave because he was wounded.'

'Who was wounded? Flight Lieutenant Rowton or Air Commodore Weatherby?'

'The AC. He couldn't use one hand and there was blood all over his face. He told us to be ready, then came over the airfield as slowly as he could and ordered us to bale out.'

'We saw him.'

'Any news of him, sir?'

'Not yet. I'll let you know.'

The next time I came to there was a doctor by my bed.

'Good news for you,' he smiled down at me, 'your Air-Sea Rescue chaps picked up your second pilot. He's only very slightly hurt and will be coming to see you soon.'

'Ah,' I could hear my own rasping breath, 'what's his name?'

'Rowton, I believe. A Flight Lieutenant Rowton.'

'What's your name?' I demanded of the young officer who stood by

my bed some time later. He was vaguely familiar and I knew that it
was important that I should find out his name.

'Why, Rowton, sir. Paul Rowton.'

'Ahhh. Paul. That's it. Paul.' I knew at last. I was happy. I could
sleep.

For days he drifted in and out of coma, hovering between life and
death. Forever muttering lists of names. 'Harry, Bill, Geoff, Nick,'
he would mumble, 'Kenneth, Norman, Dick.' Names of his friends,
names of the men he had flown with perhaps. No one knew. Paul
Rowton sat by his bed for long hours at a stretch, every day until
his leave was up, but he had not known him well and could throw no
light on what was worrying him.

'Hasn't his wife arrived yet?' asked the surgeon after a few days.

'I understand they were recently divorced, sir,' the duty sister
informed him. 'There have been several friends of his – they take it
in turns to wait.'

As he entered the sister's office, two men rose. One introduced
himself as Group Captain Galbraith and the other as Flight Lieutenant Wainwright.

'I'm the Station IO on the other side,' the younger man added.
'I was sent home with pneumonia a fortnight before the crash and
now I'm on sick leave. Air Ministry suggested I should come down,
in case I could help.'

The surgeon nodded. 'I hope you can. How well do you know him?'

Two two men looked at each other. Galbraith spoke. 'Very well
indeed. I've been following in his footsteps, quite literally, for the
past couple of years.'

'If you've got the time to spare, I wish you'd sit with him for a
bit. He keeps gabbling long lists of names – you might be able to
make some sense of it. It's not helping him to mend physically, being
so mentally disturbed.'

When they reached his bedside the sister was with him again. The
surgeon told her to let the two officers remain with the patient and
asked her to tell them what he had been saying.

She did, then added, 'The nurse on duty last night said he was
also mumbling about someone called Helen. It's the first time he's
mentioned a woman's name. She said he sounded more urgent than
he had done before.'

'Helen?' The surgeon turned to the two RAF officers, 'Is that his
wife's name?'

They shook their heads. 'I've never heard of Helen,' Galbraith
said after a moment's thought, 'although I knew him so well. His
wife's name is Elsie, but they've been virtually separated for ages
and now they're divorced. I know he had girl friends, but I don't

think any of them were very serious. I'll make inquiries if you think it important.'

'I do.'

'Any luck?' the surgeon asked Galbraith a few days later.

'We've drawn a blank so far,' he said, 'but I've had a search of his personal papers authorised. He may have left something in Holland – the odd photograph or letter. No one here had ever heard him mention anyone called Helen. I'll let you know.'

Luckily Fate appeared to be on their side after all.

Having searched his personal possessions and found nothing of importance, Wainwright and a friend were discussing who the mysterious Helen might be when Burton, who was waiter as well as batman in the makeshift mess, was pouring out their tea.

'Excuse me for interrupting, sir,' he said to the IO, 'but I couldn't help hearing what you was saying to Mr Parker.' They both looked at him expectantly. 'Well, sir,' he went on, clearly embarrassed, 'just before the Air Commodore took off that last time, he handed me a letter. Told me to be sure it went, because – quite dramatic he was – he said it was the most important letter he'd ever written in his life.'

'Did you read it?'

'Only the envelope, sir,' there was a hint of outraged dignity; he hadn't even thought of opening it. 'But I can remember the name, clear as anythink. It was addressed to Junior Commander H. Watson, ATS. P'raps the H could be for Helen, sir?'

'My God, Burton, it could indeed. Do you remember the address?'

'Not exactly, sir, but there were some numbers I think, but then it had The War Office, Whitehall. But I know I got the name right, because I remember thinking, fancy the old Commode 'avin' a bit o' fluff!'

The two officers jumped to their feet and hurried out. It was not long before the 'old Commode's bit of fluff' had been contacted and was on her way north.

I arrived at the hospital the next day and was told that the surgeon wanted to see me before I went in to James. He was a bright faced, elderly man, with kind eyes; I felt that James was in good hands.

'Ah, Junior Commander Watson. Are you Helen?'

'Yes, I am.'

'If you don't mind my being rather personal,' he gave me a quizzical look, 'it is rather important that I know what relationship exists, or existed, between you and Air Commodore Weatherby.'

'Quite simple,' I replied. 'I am going to marry him.'

'That's what I thought. I must tell you that he has lost the sight in one eye and it was unfortunately necessary to amputate his arm – his left arm luckily.'

'Not luckily,' I said. 'He was left-handed. But the nurse told me.'

'And it makes no difference?'

'I cannot see why it should?'

He gave me a very long, penetrating look, then he got up and patted my shoulder. 'Good girl,' he said. 'I hope it all works out.'

I stayed with James until he had fully regained consciousness and knew who I was. Someone from the Air Ministry had convinced the general that my presence was necessary there and I had been granted compassionate leave for as long as I was needed. It was wonderful to know that he was alive, but I couldn't bear the beaten dog look in his one good eye and, to be honest, it was something of a relief when the surgeon told me he was on the mend and I was able to return to London.

As soon as he was fit enough to be moved, he was transferred to a RAF hospital not quite so far away, but it was still far enough, and it was not easy for me to get up there as often as I would have liked. I realised very soon that I had a difficult time ahead when he started to accuse me of deliberately staying away and in the end had to take a letter from the general, stating quite firmly that I could not be let off whenever I liked. That satisfied him for a time, but he would go through bouts of self-pity when he would swear that our marriage would never work. At other times he expressed relief that the war was practically over and that soon we should be able to settle down – I never knew what mood I would find him in.

The initially neglected wounds and exposure had taken their toll and the doctor said it was a miracle he was alive. His arm, taken off below the elbow originally, would not heal and had to be reamputated and then, poor lamb, he had the tedious job of having to learn to use his right hand. It would be many months, they told me, before he would be able to leave the hospital for good.

My demob group came out later that year and once out of the army, I took a secretarial job and a bed-sitter in the town near by, so that I could be near him. The war was over, but for James it was just the beginning of a long, struggling, personal battle with himself.

42. AN ALPINE INTERLUDE

Philip Morrison

It was in November that Dougal had ordered Sally out.

I had been over to discuss the position of the scores of Allied prisoners now passing through our hands on their way to the border. With the Germans moving all prisoners of war out of Italy into Austria and Germany in such numbers, escaping had become the norm. Guards no longer had their wartime zeal and, with their losses on the Russian front and in Western Europe, insufficient men could be spared for the task. Marissa's lakeside house had become a transit camp and every few days men would arrive, guided into the hills, to wait for the final lap.

'No enemy like a wounded enemy,' Dougal had said, 'and this is no time to have women on our hands.' His American girl and Blanche from the border group had left some weeks before. I agreed with him in principle, but for both Sally and me it seemed a reprieve when the man I'd dispatched to contact one of the guides returned to say it was too late; impossible to traverse the high passes before the spring.

Of course we had never expected that the war would still be dragging on. Florence had fallen in August and, optimistically, we had expected the Allies to push straight through after that. But it seemed that the area which had been such a godsend to me, the Futa Pass between Florence and Bologna, was proving to be a thorn in the flesh. The battle there had gone to and fro until it appeared that no one was going to win it. It seemed a long time since Sally had arrived with news of the Sicily landings and there had been one set-back after another.

From the time of her first arrival Dougal had never mentioned Sally to me in anything but an impersonal way, so it came as a surprise when, just as we were nearing the clearing – he had returned with me, *en route* to Marissa, as he so often did – he asked suddenly, 'Is it true that you're going to marry that girl?'

No point in pretending that I didn't know what he was talking about, so I told him it was. As a matter of fact we had thought we might be married by an army chaplain when our troops reached the area.

'You might have told me,' he sounded hurt.

'We wanted to, but I was afraid you'd move one of us to another group.'

He grinned then and clapped me on the shoulder. 'Quite right, laddie, quite right; I would have, at that. All the more reason for her leaving now.'

'She'd better go with the next batch of escapees.'

345

'Tell you what, Philip, you go too, and when you've seen them safely over the border, come back.'

We were not doing much by that time, other than shepherding escapees; nevertheless it was decent of him.

As Philip said, that had been in November, but it was March 1945 before we actually left.

All winter, escapees had been coming in and most of them bore out Dougal's news that the German fighting units were making a firm stand, while everything else moved northwards behind it. Half Italy must have gone north in those convoys; priceless art treasures from Florence and Rome, wine, brides, and prisoners.

Philip had sent over eighteen men with the last batch, but we knew it would not be long before we were full again. Food of course was our main problem and there can't have been a corn cob or a potato in the whole area that hadn't been scrounged by the Scum. No more air drops and we could never have survived without our scroungers, and Gianna Maria's organisation.

It was not all that simple getting prisoners over the border and the guides were few and far between. They were marvellous men – Philip had been terribly impressed on the one occasion when he had taken over some men himself – mostly shepherds and cowherds, but with a sprinkling of hydro-electric workers, ski instructors, and a hard core of professional smugglers. They knew every path and shelter, every danger spot and every weak link in the border patrols.

Towards the end of the month, Dino, the guide who was to take us, came to inspect his brood. By that time we had twenty men assembled and his eyebrows shot up at the thought of so many bodies in uniform to be taken across. We would have to wait for the dark of the moon, he told us, and hope that by then one of the passes would be passable. He looked doubtfully at me and I hoped for a moment that he would refuse to take me, but I burned my own boats.

'Do you think the little signorina will be able to make it?' he asked Philip. 'It'll be tough going for the men.'

I had almost burst with indignation. Me? I could outclimb the lot of them. I'm as tough as old boots!

'She's pretty agile,' was Philip's reply and I could see he was amused, but there were more important things to hand. Soon afterwards he and Dino went into a huddle and I went to bed.

The next evening I drew a map for Sally in the ash from the dying fire.

'There is a small and seldom-used pass to the east of Monte Rosa,' I explained, 'but it is guarded. We shall keep slightly to the west and will only join the track once we're on the Swiss side. It won't be easy – I'm not worried about you, but most of these chaps are pretty

346

unfit.' In fact I had seen to it that those who had been with us through the winter had exercised, but most of them were newish arrivals and none of us were exactly over-fed. 'First we shall have to get them to a high valley that one of the Scum knows, where the dam-builders had their huts, and then it will be up to Dino to guide us, but he's pointed out the worst climbs.' I showed her on my map.

When the day came for us to leave, Sally burst into tears.

'Oh Scum, I love you all,' she wailed, as each of the men in turn kissed her on both cheeks and wished her Godspeed. Quite a few tears were wiped away surreptitiously and old Enrico and Gianna Maria wept unashamedly. There's good in everyone, I'm told – anyway, I had grown pretty fond of the bunch of rogues myself. I knew how she felt.

Gianna Maria would be going off to her villa soon and Tom was hoping to make for Trieste; the group was breaking up. I felt sad too.

'Come on, Sally, we have to rendezvous before dark,' I said. It was time, I thought, to end the farewells. But half way up the hill she stopped to turn round and wave again.

'Oh Philip, it's awful,' she cried, 'like leaving home.'

We slogged all that first day over harsh but familiar terrain and arrived at the valley in the early dusk. Dino was waiting for us and he was impatient. He was like a cat, finding his way in the dark with what appeared to be the utmost ease. He allowed us a couple of hours only, then we were off again and arrived at first light at the next staging-post. Here he instructed each man to find himself a rock or a bush and to lie low during the hours of daylight. It was bitterly cold and the wind howled down the valley, whining like shells, but we couldn't risk movement in case some unseen lookout had binoculars trained in our direction.

Most of the men were so shagged that they flaked out without a word, but Sally and I had too much on our minds to sleep. We lay in the shelter of a large, overhanging rock and talked, for the first time, of our future. Not that we could plan much, but I felt sure I would be repatriated as soon as our line moved north and then it should not be too difficult to find her. I made her memorise my mother's address, then we lay in silence, trying to get what rest we could.

The second night's climb was far worse and had us all panting and gasping for breath. Two of the BORs didn't make it and I had had to leave a third with them. I said I would collect them on the way back, but in fact I never saw them again. Hardly a second went by without some oath hissing out of the darkness and time and time again Dino had to caution the men. Having escaped once, it was difficult for them to understand that here, amongst the snowswept peaks, they might still be caught again. Nerves were on edge and physically most of them were on the point of exhaustion. We were scrambling up shale most of the time, one step forward and three back, the most exhausting I know; only Dino took it in his stride.

Perhaps it was wrong of me, but I climbed away from the sleeping men on the third day's rest. I had to be alone.

We were well above the tree-line and the cold was intense, the wind blowing gale-force, but the sun shone on the hard, glistening snow and the sky was a clear, cerulean blue. I wondered if Philip was experiencing the same excitement – difficult to say, he guarded his feelings well, although I felt that by this time I knew him inside out.

There is something about the sun and wind in high places that brings both exhilaration and sadness. In different circumstances I would not have been able to stay still, having to get to the top of the serrated ridge cutting the sky above me, having to know what the world looked like on the other side. But I already knew what lay on the other side – a world without Philip, and I didn't want to go there.

We had been very practical the day before, discussing money, banks, passports, ways to get in touch. We had still been one day further from the border then.

I looked up as a flurry of late snow temporarily obscured the peaks and a shiver went through me. We were not over yet. One of us might be killed. And Philip would be going back. At that moment I hated Dougal for making me leave.

'Sally.'

The call was low, but I turned to see Philip fighting his way against the wind towards me. The urgency on his face made me contrite and I moved, the wind pushing me, to him.

'Sally, you shouldn't have gone. I've been worried stiff.'

'Nonsense. You were fast asleep.'

'Darling, if – ' But whatever he was going to say was torn from his lips by a sudden gust, stronger and colder than the monotonous, shrieking wind that we had almost grown used to. He grabbed my arm and we fought our way back to the rock-dotted slopes where Dino and the men lay huddled together for protection. Most of them were awake and it was not long before the dusk came down and we were on our way again.

This was the last lap. One man had died of exposure during the day and as soon as a meagre covering of snow had been scraped over his body, Dino called the remainder together and asked me to interpret his orders.

'The guard hut is actually on the pass,' he told us, 'and at 0200 they will change the guard. At that time, then, there are no patrols. The point where we shall cross is about ten minutes' walk from the hut, giving us a clear passage for ten minutes either side of the hour. There are nineteen of us to cross; two or three at a time with intervals in between is how we must go, and pray there are no dogs. We must be in position by 0130 at the latest and at 0150 we start across. Is it clear?'

I could hear the shallow breathing of anticipation all around me. The thought of having come so far only to be caught at the last was in all our minds. Even Dino was no longer his normal, placid self.

'From here on there must be the strictest discipline,' he said. 'No talking, no noise at all and, above all, no lagging behind. Signor Capitano, I must make it clear that any man not in position by 0130 does not cross.'

I laid it on a little thicker than that.

Sally tugged at my sleeve. 'Philip,' she whispered, 'as soon as we reach the border, will you turn back?'

That was up to Dino. As Sally has already explained, these guides had followed a number of select professions before the war; Dino was one of the smugglers. I could see the glint of his gold front tooth in the last of the light as he smiled. The laughter was only just below the surface of his voice when he answered my question.

'If the Capitano is not in a hurry, what's one day here or there? It will not be difficult for the two of us to cross, especially coming the other way; it would be a pity to return empty-handed when there are so many things in Switzerland that we have forgotten about in Italy. Perhaps a couple of days?'

I was doubtful, knowing how Dougal would disapprove, but I was in Dino's hands and I wondered if Sally had been getting at him on the sly. His next words confirmed my suspicions, but I was weak.

'After all, Capitano, it was the Signor Maggiore's wish that you should see the little signorina safely over the other side, and all the soldiers as well. Once we are on the track it is not far from civilisation, – not a real town, but big enough to have the essentials of life.'

Big enough in which to do a lucrative deal, he meant.

Sally slipped her hand into mine as we started off and I could feel her trembling. I looked at her dim white face and wondered if I would see it again in daylight, then I kissed her hard and we separated in silence.

The last climb was the most gruelling of all. Twice Dino stopped to listen and once I thought I heard a shout. We all strained our ears, but the wind howling round us camouflaged any sounds of a human source.

We reached the point just below the border in good time. I put my arm round Sally as we stood stock still, listening, and felt her heart beating at the double, whether through exertion, excitement or fear, I did not know. Mine was the same. I knew the feeling well; the fear of a sudden bark, a searchlight shining out of the darkness, the sound of gunfire.

'Hsst,' it was Dino. 'I am going now to where I can see the hut. On my return, follow me in single file. Now, absolute silence.'

He crawled away and we waited for what seemed hours before he came back. He was breathless.

'Quick. Now. The patrol on this side has just passed; they have dogs, so we must let them get farther away.' He counted, thumping on my shoulder as he did so, and the sickness of fear was suddenly in my throat. I had made two escapes, would I make a third? And there was Sally. He gave my shoulder a last, hard grip. 'Now.'

I had placed Sally immediately behind Dino, followed by the sixteen men, and myself bringing up the rear.

We crawled, scrambled and climbed and the silence seemed as loud as the noises I expected but blessedly did not hear. I paused when the man in front paused and wondered all the time how they were faring at the head of the column.

Suddenly there was a soft scrunch, the unmistakable sound of boots on snow. The man in front heard it too and came to a quivering, sudden halt. 'Go on,' I hissed, but he was paralysed with fear and remained, stiff and silent. The sound again. Impossible to tell whether they were coming or going. Had Sally got through? There had been no shots, no shouts, no lights. I jabbed the man in the back as hard as I could with my elbow, then, overtaking him, hauled him up the slope behind me.

Quite suddenly we were crawling along the level, then slithering down another steep incline. We must be over.

We must have slid and bumped our way down the rock-strewn slope for a good half-hour when I was hailed by Dino's quiet call. 'We're all over,' he whispered, 'you're the last. That was a bad moment; they must have changed guard extremely fast.'

It was strange to be laughing and talking in broad daylight. Philip was still with us – he hadn't been given much choice. We had all followed Dino blindly and here we were, swinging down a potholed track.

'Thank God for this.' Philip pulled a wad of Swiss francs from his trouser pocket that had been sent in with the last drop – as I've said, our main role in recent months had been the dispatch of prisoners to points north. 'Do you think that village is big enough to have a shop?'

A small alpine village nestled in the fold of two hills, looking as though it had come straight off a postcard. Dino had nodded to Philip's question and we all put on a spurt.

Half an hour later nineteen silent people were sitting on the grass, munching bread and jam. There was fresh butter too and I rolled a pellet of it round and round on my tongue, savouring the long-forgotten taste.

Philip had gone into the shop on his own and come out a moment later laughing. 'When I told them I was a British escapee and apologised for my poor French, the woman merely asked me how many men!'

Dino smiled. 'You are far from the first, signore.'

Then we fell to and soon everyone but Philip and I were asleep, sprawled out on the lush green grass that must so recently have been covered with snow. The alpine meadows were ablaze with flowers; cattle and goats were already enjoying the high pastures. The peace seemed unreal.

'It's time I turned back, Sally.'

'Oh Philip, no.' We had been walking for nearly an hour and had seen glimpses of the little mountain town in the valley below for some time. Now we were nearly there. 'You said a couple of days.'

Now that the excitement of our escape was over the thought of him returning was unbearable, and yet I knew he must.

'Look at that little church.' I pointed to the whitewashed square, its spire glinting in the sun, more to change the subject than anything else. It had a blue tiled roof with a burnished bronze bell and stood out against the emerald fields with the clarity of a print. 'It's like a Christmas card. I can just imagine it under snow.'

'If we are to be married in a church at all, I would like it to be one like that; knocks spots off the more ornate.'

'Philip, why don't we?'

He looked at me, aghast. 'My dear girl, you must be mad. It would never work – imagine all the formalities and – '

'Oh don't be such an old stick in the mud,' I interrupted. God, how men could make difficulties. 'We could try.'

Philip sighed. He knew that now the seed had been sown he wouldn't have any peace till he did something about it. But what that something was I hadn't the faintest idea. We walked on in silence for a while.

'Philip.' He looked at me warily. 'Only a couple of days ago we were wondering what we'd do when the war ended; where your battalion might be sent.' He grunted and gave me a sideways look. He probably guessed that I had it all worked out. 'Wherever they're sent, I doubt if wives will be able to go with them, not at first, but WAAF – ' I stopped to give him my sweetest smile, 'I might wangle a posting to be with you, but they don't post married WAAF overseas, so it would be our secret.'

'Oh for heaven's sake, Sally. Talk about jumping the gun. It's ridiculous, a chance in a million.' He stamped on, looking cross, then turned back to me. 'This is the most absurd conversation I've had in years. Of course we can't be married here, anyway.'

'We don't know yet. We can try. You know, Philip, I really might

351

get myself sent to wherever you are and then, when it paid us, we could come into the open and present them with a *fait accompli*.' He said nothing; I could see he was becoming irritated. 'You don't seem very enthusiastic. I don't believe you want to marry me at all.'

'It's not that, and you know it. Sally, I will not argue. We'll try.'

Before we had time to say any more we heard a vehicle coming up the track and next moment we were being confronted by an antique armoured car. An officer and half a dozen soldiers climbed out.

'I have to inform you, in case you do not know, that you are in Switzerland,' the officer addressed us in excellent English, 'and as we are a neutral country there are certain formalities. I regret that you cannot just go free.'

Philip stepped forward and the two men shook hands. 'I am Captain Morrison of the British Army. This is Section Officer Gunn and the others are all British soldiers except for – ' Philip glanced round but Dino had disappeared; he left the sentence unfinished.

We all stood in the road talking for a few minutes, then the Swiss officer motioned to the occupants of the armoured car, who got in and went at a snail's pace down the centre of the track. He walked with us.

'There's just one thing that I would like to ask, although I think it is impossible – ' both the Swiss and I looked at Philip with interest ' – but my fiancée will give me no peace until I do, and that is if we could get married here. We were hoping to be married by one of our chaplains when our forces arrived in the north of Italy, but – '

'You would like to be married here?' The Swiss officer interrupted, clearly delighted. 'The Mayor will love that. You are Protestants, I suppose? I myself am a Lutheran – I'll see the minister and ask if it is possible.'

I had been surprised enough by the Swiss officer's reaction – though he had held up a laughingly cautious hand to Sally's undignified excitement – but I was absolutely amazed by the lack of formality. It seemed quite incredible. I borrowed from the Swiss francs provided to pay for the civil licence, we both swore that we were free to marry, and that was that. The army did the rest.

We were married that afternoon. The army officer acted as best man and the Mayor gave Sally away. The soldiers filled the front pews of the tiny church, and that was all. Dino had not reappeared.

I was very much afraid at one point that Sally was going to get a fit of the giggles. The ceremony was in German, which neither of us understood, so we just said, 'I do,' whenever someone prodded us. I'm sure we weren't taking it nearly as seriously as we should have done. The whole scene was so incongruous. The Mayor in his Sunday black and the best man in immaculate uniform, and there was I, in corduroys and the pullover that Alessandro's sister had given me in Milan. And Sally – dear God, what a bridal dream! She had pulled out her motheaten battledress for the journey, but the idea of trousers in church had caused some tut-tutting and so, there was my bride, beautiful in a battledress top and a skirt, several times too big for her, borrowed from the Mayor's wife, and Italian Army boots!

At the end of this farce the minister held up his hand in blessing and announced surprisingly, in very stilted English, that we were now man and wife. And suddenly it wasn't a farce any longer. She was my wife. Sally had no veil, but a handkerchief-sized square of lace, also borrowed. I pushed it back and we touched cheeks.

Back at the Mayor's house, corks were pulled and cakes produced and even the unemotional Swiss entered into an hour of hilarity with us, strangers who would shortly be gone. I was embarrassed by the party; everyone had gone to so much trouble and I was not allowed to pay a penny towards it.

'We may be neutral and have enough food,' the Mayor confided in me, when I tried to tell him how overwhelmed we were, 'but even so, war is very dull.'

As soon as we decently could, Sally and I slipped away and walked up the hillside on the opposite side of the village from whence we had come.

'It's so difficult to realise that ridge is Italy,' Sally sighed, 'and that soon you'll be back there. Already Gianna Maria and the Scum seem part of another world. But I know one thing, Dougal was right. If there is any fighting, you'll stand a far better chance without me in the way.'

I pressed her hand but said nothing. What was there to say?

The Mayor had lent us his spare room for our wedding night.

'Such hospitality is overwhelming,' I said, 'and so is this bed!' And I bounced on and into the enormous feather mattress and laughed as I sank. Philip stood, naked, and watched me. I had never seen him completely naked before.

'Do you realise,' he said, 'that this will be the first time we've slept together in a bed?'

'Ssh,' I replied, 'we're supposed not to have slept together at all yet. But come on, stop wasting time.'

'Sleep has seldom been further from my mind, Mrs Morrison,' he said, and that was the end of our conversation. But we were more tired than we knew and it was not long before we were both flat out, held loosely in each other's arms.

We were woken by a shower of pebbles hitting the window pane and Philip was up in a flash.

As we had expected, Dino stood below. 'Capitano,' he called softly, 'rain is forecast. We must not delay. We leave before it gets light. I will be back in one hour's time.'

We made love then with more urgency, more bitter sweetness than we ever had before; then Philip got up to dress.

On the journey back, I was outside the realm of reality. I followed Dino blindly, unheeding and he, being an Italian, to whom passion was more important than war, was sympathetic.

'Ah, Capitano, you will see the little signorina – I mean signora – again. The war will soon be over; all is not lost and there will undoubtedly be a bambino on the way.'

'Oh Lord, I hope not,' I said in English, half to myself, then smiled and thanked him.

We were above the dam and he was to leave me here. We shook hands and I crawled into one of the empty huts for the night.

Now that I was back on familiar soil, the past few days seemed part of a dream. I was glad that Sally had had her way and that we were married now. The thought of 'a bambino on the way' had worried me for a long time. Sally had never appeared to worry, but it had become a nightmare for me. It wasn't the moral side – I've no doubt we could have got over that somehow – but the physical. The thought of her having a baby in the clearing, without help of doctor or midwife, or being taken to hospital and denounced, had caused me to wake up in a cold sweat on several occasions. It was one worry off my mind.

Gianna Maria and the Scum were indignant. Nothing would make them believe that it had not been planned. 'Why couldn't you have been married here, before you left?' they asked. 'It would have been a civil marriage and we could have found someone sympathetic in the Municipio, we're sure.'

In fact Sally would have loved it, but it was too late now.

'Perhaps there will be a bambino on the way,' they all said, by way of consolation!

43. A WASTE OF TWO LIVES

Donald Thom

'Did you have a good leave?'

'Didn't you have a good leave?'

I hit my head with my clenched fist and threw down my pen on the report I was trying to write. Judas Priest, did I have a good leave? *No, I did NOT*.

I'd rather not think about that leave – and anyway, it's past history now – but I couldn't get it out of my mind then. I hadn't seen

354

Monica for weeks, but it still felt as if that awful meeting on the railway station platform had taken place only yesterday.

I'd walked up the platform with my wife and that dapper little French guy and I'd made myself be deliberately blind. I'd asked Monica if she was all set for some leave and when she said she wasn't taking any leave, I lost my temper.

I look back in shame at the way I'd behaved – compounded of disappointment and frustration I guess – shouting at her in the station refreshment room that she was betraying our son, acting like a whore. I shouldn't have said that, because, after all, how'd I been behaving myself? Only mentally I'd stayed faithful to her all along and I could have forgiven her taking a lover, if only she'd ditched him on my return.

Then I started grovelling – Jesus, what happened to my pride that day? First, I'd been angry, then I pleaded with her to come up to Scotland with me. Told her she'd forget this Emil once we revisited our old haunts and she was back with me.

And then, that bloody Frog, with such a look of condescension on his face, had said in the most patronising way, 'Go with him, Monique. I can wait.'

Monique! I should have hit him. Well, she went with me all right.

We travelled north in silence and spent the first night in the same hotel that we'd stayed in before. She hadn't resisted when I made love to her, but she hadn't responded either. Confucius say, 'when rape inevitable, lie back and enjoy it'. Well, she had lain back, but she hadn't enjoyed it – and neither had I. Her passiveness and total lack of response sure made it feel like rape. And when it was over she had lit a cigarette and stayed there, lying flat and looking up at the ceiling.

'Well?' she had asked at last, between smoke rings, 'do you think it's going to work?'

I tore my second effort at this darned report into small pieces and studied the London rooftops instead.

Jesus, but they were buggering me about.

It was March already. Marijke would be nearly three months further on the way. Monica could have her divorce all right; I wouldn't be able to marry my golden girl before the child was born, but I'd give it my name.

The battalion, my battalion, had been in the invasion of Normandy; fulfilling the role that we had waited for for so long. And then – and this is where the real frustration begins – they had fought their way right up to the Dutch border and were in fact in Holland now. I wasn't too sure of their exact whereabouts, but Holland's such a little country, nowhere could be too far from where I wanted to be. I'd done everything I could to try and rejoin them and all people would talk to me about was leave.

Back in this phoney unit, I'd pestered everyone in sight to get back to Holland, but they all thought I was wacky. Judas Priest, maybe I should shout my personal problems aloud to someone and see if that had any effect. I'd done nothing but be interrogated and filled in forms and written reports.

Reports. They sure wouldn't let me go anywhere till I'd finished with this one. I sat down and really tried, but after about ten minutes I gave it up and lit a fag instead.

I just couldn't stand that office one minute longer and was striding down the corridor, away from it, going nowhere, when a head popped out of a door on my right.

'Ah, Thom. I was about to give you a ring.' I groaned. It was that effeminate British major with the DSO, who had first interrogated me. 'Yeah?'

'Don't sound so sour, old boy; you've got your wish. Come in.'

I didn't need to be asked twice. I was inside that office in one bound.

'Yeah?' It's amazing the number of different tones you can put into that one word!

'Your medical shows that you're not yet fit for active service, but your battalion has just occupied the area where you were working and you can be useful in another way. You've been appointed Battalion IO.'

'Gee, you mean that? When can I go?'

Guess I was pumping that guy's hand like I used to gush it out into the horse-trough on the farm, back home. Yeah, I was a farm boy all right and I guess I looked it too, with that silly grin splitting my face from ear to ear.

The major looked embarrassed and withdrew his mit.

'In such a hurry?' he asked, in that la-di-dah Oxford accent, 'Well, it shouldn't take long to arrange.'

The village sure looked different, coming at it in a jeep instead of from the air.

The CO had been pretty decent, welcoming me back to the battalion like a long lost son, and the Adj – there were a lot of faces missing though. I was the hero, dropped in to help the Resistance – it sure sounded good – but *I* knew who'd fought the real war. It made me feel kind of phoney. It seems they'd had a hard pull, right up through France, then the Ardennes and the Battle of the Bulge.

It had been the CO's suggestion I take a jeep and go and look up my old cronies before settling down, and that sure suited me fine. We weren't quite in my old area, but it wasn't far. There was another

Canadian unit here, so I suggested to the driver that we cadge some lunch off them, then I left him for the afternoon and took the jeep off on my own.

Of course I made first for Marijke's house. I saw at once that the glass had been blasted out of the windows, which were boarded against the cold with paper and cardboard. No one answered my ring, so eventually I went inside.

Marijke's mother was in the kitchen, huddled beside the stove and looking old and wizened and very brown. I don't think she recognised me.

'Marijke's not here,' she answered my query, and I felt dismissed.

It was obvious that I wasn't going to get any more out of her, so I returned to the jeep and drove in first down the village street, hoping that if I went slowly enough I might find someone I knew. I guess I must have gone up and down that one street half a dozen times before I saw the backview of old Doctor Huysen turning a corner at the far end. I hurried after him.

The doctor threw his arms round me and I really had the feeling he was pleased to see me. Then he held me at arm's length and beamed.

'You look fine,' he said. 'We wondered if you had made it.'

'But didn't Jan tell you?' I asked.

'Jan never came back,' he said. I guess he must have seen the expression on my face then, because he added, somewhat hastily I thought, 'Perhaps he stayed with his brother on the coast.'

'But his wife and family are here.'

The doctor shrugged.

'And Hans and Konrad and Marijke?' I asked.

The old man gave me a strange look. 'I must hurry,' he said, 'I have a very sick child to see, but I will direct you to Konrad's house.'

Konrad came to the door, wearing carpet slippers and with an open newspaper in his hand. He removed steel-rimmed glasses from his nose and gestured, slightly self-consciously at the paper, the American *Stars and Stripes*.

'Catching up on my English,' he explained, after he had greeted me. 'I was a schoolmaster before the war – did you know that?'

'No, I didn't.'

'Well, come in, come in.' He shuffled around like an old woman and for the first time I realised that he was quite old. Come to think of it, I'd never seen him without a cap before; he was nearly bald and what little hair he did have was greyish white. 'You'll have a cup of tea?'

He continued to bustle round, taking a packet of tea from a shelf – Canadian, he pointed out, very generous the Canadians – and sugar from another. Then he went outside to fetch the milk.

357

When at last we were seated, I came to the point. 'I'm looking for Marijke,' I said.

Konrad did not answer at once, but busied himself with pouring the tea, then lifted his cup and looked at me steadily over the rim.

'Yes,' he said at last, 'I was afraid you were. Marijke's dead.'

I did my best to control myself, but nevertheless the tea splashed from my cup. I put it down very carefully. This was something I had never even considered.

'Where? And how?' I stammered.

'The Germans shot her only a few hours after you left – at the mill.'

'But she left before I did.'

'I just don't know what happened exactly,' Konrad shrugged. 'She must have left something behind and gone back for it, I suppose. Hans saw it all. Knowing that the Germans would be coming to the mill that day – at least being pretty sure that they would – we laid an ambush for them. Hans was up a tree; he was to give the signal to the others to fire. The Germans arrived at the mill and went in, firing as they went. It was our intention to catch them as they came out again, one by one. All of a sudden, while we were waiting for them to emerge, Marijke arrived on her bicycle and leaned it by the door. Hans tried to warn her, but it was too late. As soon as the Germans heard the sound they rushed down and opened fire. She fell in the doorway from the first blast. It was instantaneous, Donald – she could not have suffered any pain. We fired too then, and killed all three.'

I longed to cry, to bury my head in my arms and weep. But in front of this man I couldn't. I clenched my fists until the knuckles showed white, and swallowed before I spoke.

'I was going to marry her,' I said.

'But we thought . . .'

I dismissed this with a wave. 'I was – I am. But it's over, finished.'

Konrad stood up and put a hand on my shoulder. 'They killed my wife too,' he said, very quietly, and in answer to my look of surprise, 'Oh yes. We did not always live here. I used to work in Rotterdam. My wife went in the bombing – and my son.'

I rose in a daze and walked towards the door.

'Won't you wait for Hans?' he asked. 'He and I share this shack.'

I shook my head. 'Not now,' I said, 'another time.'

'Where are you going?'

'To the mill.'

'Shall I come with you?'

'No,' I replied, 'I want to go alone.'

'I understand.'

The door of the mill hung drunkenly on one hinge. It was riddled with bullet holes, as were the walls and the nearby trees. Judas Priest, they'd used some ammo here.

I sat in the jeep, trying to picture Marijke as she must have been and the surprise and horror on her face as the Germans appeared. But no, most likely she would not have seen them, only heard their fire, and she was too brave a girl to register any emotion in front of the hated Hun.

What a waste of life. Two lives.

I got down from the jeep and walked towards the door. Brown stains showed on the wood and stone. Her blood or theirs?

I climbed the ladder. Both couches were still there and the remains of the radio lay on the floor. I was right about using some ammo – everything was holed.

I looked at the couch where we had spent that last night and my eyes travelled round, first to the sacking curtains that Marijke had made, then to the small stove where she had cooked, and to a bucket of water which still stood there, stagnant under a layer of dust.

Was her ghost here? Our ghosts?

I turned to go, my heart heavy but my senses mercifully numbed.

44. A WHOLE NEW WORLD

Sharif Ahmat

Contact with my brother, Hassan, had opened up a whole new world for me.

Within a couple of months, Corporal Wong had suggested that he should have a junior to do his work in each station and of course the Japs thought so highly of him that they not only agreed and let him choose his men, but promoted him to sergeant at the same time – Tuan Richardson snorted like a buffalo when I told him this and talked about Empire-building, but I didn't understand what he meant. Naturally he chose me in our station. To all intents and purposes he was a Japanese stooge, so my local appointment put me in an advantageous position, in so far that I too came to be considered a toady, but it lost me most of my friends. Wong no longer had to seek me out and once we had developed a simple code, he could ring me up at any time, ostensibly on CID matters, and pass the messages verbally. It meant too that I worked office hours and, in my new, favoured position, I was free to come and go whenever I was off duty.

The only fly in the ointment – or bean in the bed as we say – was my erstwhile friend, Hasbullah. Irrespective of whether he was a collaborator or not – and I had no proof of it – CID was always a sought-after job and, having been in the station longer than I, and with the same qualifications, he considered it should have been his. There had been several occasions when I had been aware of his following me and had had to bypass my contact. Hassan's warning had been timely and it was lucky I knew which of my colleagues I had to watch.

Two more European officers had been put into Negri and I believe a training camp had been set up, which was now more than a hundred strong. I say believe, because I had never been farther than the clearing I mentioned before, where usually there were several people living, and I was still very much in the dark. However, I too was learning to string odd bits and pieces of information together, and Hassan probably told me more than he realised.

Many people were brought in for interrogation during that year and more often than not one of us was called upon to soften up the unfortunates before our masters took over. I got hardened to dealing out slaps and kicks and shouting, '*Rei*,' which means bow, without turning a hair. But I could never have taken a knotted rope to the victims in the way that Wong could – I sometimes wondered if he was only a good actor or if he actually enjoyed his job. I had learned to appreciate his ability, but I could never like the man.

One morning, several Chinese were brought in, bound and gagged. They had obviously been beaten up before arriving at the station and the Jap sergeant gave orders that they were to be kept in the cells without food or water until his superior arrived the next day.

This was news for Hassan, for I sensed that they were more important than the usual man in the street. I set up my bottles and tins at the first opportunity and as soon as I could get away that evening, picked up my fishing tackle and set off to the meeting place.

To my surprise my brother had come half-way to meet me and I could see the urgency in his walk as soon as he came into view.

'You've got to spring Ah Keow, Mat,' he told me, 'the rest don't matter, they're only helpers and know nothing, but Ah Keow's our chief armourer. He knows exactly what weapons we have – he's been in charge of listing them as they've been dropped – and where each lot are cached outside the camp.'

I had memorised the names of the men who had been brought in, but they would of course be aliases. However, from Hassan's description, I knew exactly which one Ah Keow was and I sat down to think out a plan. But beyond a straightforward release from the cell I could think of nothing.

'That would never do.' Hassan tossed my idea aside with a shake of his head. 'He'd never get past the Jap NCO and we can't risk your being implicated.'

We both thought in silence for several minutes, then my brother got up to go.

'Sleep on it,' he advised me, 'and the rest of us will talk it over to-night. Have your tiffin in the coffee-shop to-morrow. One of our chaps will join you and let you know what we've decided.'

I lay awake most of the night trying to think of a solution, but none came and by morning I was heavy-eyed and dull with tiredness.

It was one of the few Malays, who had recently joined Hassan's set-up, who met me the next day. He was a wise choice, for we came from the same district and had reason to greet each other and talk.

He handed me an envelope with some white tablets in it and I guessed straight away what they were for.

'If you can't get Ah Keow out before the Kempeitai start on him, you're to slip these into his food. Can you manage that?' I nodded. I had frequent access to the cells when interrogations were pending. 'Don't use them unless you have to – he's a valuable man and we'd rather have him alive, but Richardson says that if you hear of his being moved and no chance of springing him, then give him the poison and let him know what it is – if you get the chance.'

Mention of the man being moved gave me an idea. Surely it would be worth the risk to wait and then arrange an ambush of the vehicle, or something similar?

Wong arrived the following afternoon and none too soon, because he had grave news. The move would take place in three days' time and the men would be taken, not to Seremban, as we had presumed, but straight to Kempeitai Headquarters in Singapore – which meant they must be fully aware of their importance.

'If I can get some sort of distraction organised in the town, perhaps he could get away as the vehicle moves off.'

'Handcuffed?'

'Wouldn't you have the key?'

'If I can bribe the escort.'

We thought for a spell and then I had an idea.

'If we could get one of us on escort duty, in the rear of the van, you could sit beside the driver and clobber him when the distraction starts.'

'Possible.'

If Ah Keow knew who I was he made no sign of recognition and when I told him, 'You're being moved on Thursday, be prepared to make a dash as the van starts up, if you see the opportunity,' he did not even appear to have heard me. But he had.

There was no chance of organising the distraction I had hoped for – which would have needed the co-operation of Hassan or one of his

361

friends – because for one reason or another I was either on duty or standby the entire time, with no chance of contacting my brother.

However, I made my preparations and it was with great relief that, when the van arrived to take away the prisoners on Thursday morning, I saw Sergeant Wong jump down from the seat beside the driver.

Two constables got down from the back, a Sikh and a Malay, both armed with shotguns. My heart sank. The Sikh was a big man and whereas a rifle butt might deal effectively with the Malay, there was scant hope of doing much damage to that turban-protected head.

Wong strode into the Charge Room in his usual authoritative manner and demanded to see the prisoners. I heard a lot of slapping and a fair number of oaths coming from the lock-up and then, one by one, the men were brought out for further interrogation.

'I'll just have a cup of coffee before we start off,' I heard Wong tell the CRO and then my door opened and he came in. 'Send the orderly for some coffee,' he said loudly, slammed the door and sat down.

'Quickly,' he whispered to me, 'there's not much time. Is your part organised?'

I nodded. 'There will be a fire and, if everything goes according to plan, there should be sufficient chaos to occupy everyone's minds. The only thing I'm worried about is the escort, that Sikh – '

'He's fixed. Moktar – the Malay escort – is one of us. I've told Ah Keow to lash out with his feet and try to get the Sikh in the crotch or the spleen. At the same time Moktar will pretend to panic and make sure the Sikh's shotgun is thrown out of reach. He has the key, but whether or not he will be able to unlock the handcuffs depends on how things go. I'll deal with the driver. Timing is all important. Once he's in the van he's stuck; you've got to do your part before the doors are closed. Unfortunately he's the only man the Kempeitai want – I had reckoned on the lot going, but with only one it will be more difficult.'

My plan was very simple. The CID office was at the corner of the building and next to the Charge Room. I had often noticed both Malay PCs and Jap soldiers when going on duty, throwing away their cigarettes just before they rounded the corner and, luckily, I had on more than one occasion called out to men to tread on the butts in case they started a fire – that's what had given me the idea.

Nature was on my side. We were in the midst of a drought and that Thursday must have been one of the hottest days of the year. My preparations had been carefully made and during the previous night I had part filled old, rusty tins with kerosene and placed them at strategic points round the compound. Two pm was the time Wong had set for his departure and during the lunch hour I had made sure that the grass outside my window was well saturated with kerosene.

362

At one-thirty, I lit a cigarette myself and chain smoked in order to have a lighted end ready, in case no one else did the job for me.

At five minutes to two exactly, Wong ordered Ah Keow to be removed from the cell. PC Moktar locked the handcuffs and put the key in his pocket and the Sikh PC prodded the man with his shotgun and motioned him towards the main door and the waiting van.

This was the moment. I flung my lighted cigarette and a couple of lighted matches on to the grass and poured on half a bottle of oil for good measure.

The result was most satisfactory. I waited just long enough for the crackle of flames to be heard then, shouting, 'Fire, fire,' at the top of my lungs, I rushed out to sound the alarm.

The flames soon caught a wooden out-building and men rushing towards them conveniently overturned most of the unobtrusive tins I had laid in their path.

I did not see Ah Keow get away, but I felt sure our plan had succeeded. I had been watching the van from my window and saw the driver slump suddenly. I guessed Wong had prevented him from starting up. The back of the van was hidden from my view and I turned away from the window, partly because I wanted to find out what was happening behind the van and also because I thought it time I did a little make-believe fire-fighting.

But I was too late.

I heard the hiss from the doorway and there, standing so as to fill the aperture, was Sergeant Akaru, our Japanese NCO i/c Station. He held a pistol in his hand and it was pointing straight at me.

'You do not try to stop fire?' he yelled at me in his abominable Malay, 'maybe you start fire. We see.'

He indicated with his pistol that I was to precede him through the open door and, just as I was about to move, I saw an arm raised behind him and a rifle butt come crashing down on the side of his head.

The Jap fell to the floor like a stunned buffalo and I jumped across his body into the room beyond.

The Charge Room was empty. I caught a glimpse of part of a back view as a figure ran out of the main door. I was not able to see who it was, nor even what race or rank.

He had dropped the weapon, a twelve bore double-barrelled shotgun, behind the Charge Room counter. There were no witnesses. I seized the gun and discharged both barrels into the prostrate form of Sergeant Akaru.

A quick glance assured me that I was still alone, and, without a further look at the dead Jap, I rushed out to join the fire-fighters.

The van still stood with doors open and engine running. I saw the body of the Sikh, sprawled in a pool of blood, beside it and no sign of the other occupants. He was weaponless and I guessed the shotgun I had used to finish off Akaru had belonged to him.

Allah, I thought, I'm a fool. Someone in this station will know who killed Akaru and if they should choose to denounce me there will certainly be a check for fingerprints on the gun. There was the possibility of blackmail too, but that didn't worry me just then.

Cursing my stupidity, I dashed back into the Charge Room. Thank goodness it was still empty – and no wonder, for the flames were already licking the main barrack block and everyone was occupied.

I seized the gun and wiped the butt and metal parts as well as I could on my shirt then, praying to Allah that my luck would hold, I once again sprinted through the main door, threw the shotgun down beside the van and raced to join the fire-fighters.

The murder of Sergeant Akaru was blamed on the missing Ah Keow and his escort, PC Moktar. Despite the fact that they had been locked up at the time, the remaining Chinese were taken from the cells and flogged publicly.

Akaru was not the first Japanese to be murdered and I knew that our masters would bide their time, then pounce for reprisals.

The damage to the station could have been worse, but the wooden walls and roof of the main barrack block were badly charred.

A lorry load of rusty kerosene tins was delivered and we were given the job of beating them out and using them to patch up the buildings. All station personnel were confined to barracks until the job was done. This may have seemed reasonable on the surface, especially as on the day the last hole was patched a sumptuous meal was served in the canteen. Fish and goat's meat, which we had not seen for more than a year, was brought in and rice was unrationed. We were also given beer and sake, the Japanese rice wine, and the new Jap sergeant congratulated us on our diligence and bade us drink up.

It was my belief that they hoped that someone in his cups would begin to boast, or let out some inadvertent remark that would lead them to Akaru's killer.

Men who have had near empty stomachs for a long time and nothing stronger to drink than peanut coffee, get drunk quickly.

I had never had anything more than the odd beer in my life and did not like it much, but I pretended to drink and kept my ears wide open. One of my colleagues knew who had killed Akaru. For a fortnight I had searched every face, seeking a sign of recognition or maybe a gloating look. But nothing.

A fortnight and no reprisals. There was something wrong and my stomach began to contract with panic every time my office door opened or my name was called.

I did my best to remain friendly with Hasbullah, even suggesting that he should come fishing with me, but I still drew a blank.

Sergeant Wong had made his usual visits and I learned from him that Ah Keow had got away. His escort, Moktar, had also disappeared.

The day the restriction was lifted, I longed to rush off to my brother and tell him what had happened and find out if Ah Keow had returned to their camp, but I thought it prudent to lie low and went to the village with Hasbullah instead.

When I did go to the fishing place again I was met by one of the Chinese, who told me that Hassan was sick. He had had malaria and succumbed to a chill before fully recovering and now the Ceylonese dresser who was with them thought he had pneumonia.

The Chinese members of this band had always treated me with caution and a certain amount of suspicion and I felt that, despite the fact that I was Hassan's brother, they did not wholly trust me. There had never been any warmth in our relations and this man, Shu Chu, had been particularly chilly.

On this occasion, however, he seized my hand as soon as I arrived and was wreathed in smiles, so I knew at once that Ah Keow's escape had been successful.

'He brought a friend with him.' Shu Chu clasped his stomach and rocked with laughter.

I had seen Ah Keow handcuffed and led out, but then I had gone back into my office to start the fire and had not seen him again. Apparently, when they reached the van, Sergeant Akaru had taken the key from Moktar, unlocked the handcuffs and recuffed escort and prisoner together. Of course this was common practice and I hit my head as I remembered that neither Wong nor I had thought of it. Anyway, it seemed that Moktar was content and had been welcomed at the main camp.

I was full of envy and told Shu Chu that I too would like to join them. In fact I would happily have gone there and then.

I didn't let on that I was scared, of course, although I expect he knew it. But my request had been anticipated and I was relieved when he told me that Richardson had said that if there was any intimation that I was suspect and likely to be blown, I was to make my way to the clearing. 'But only if you're certain you're not being followed,' Shu Chu warned me. 'Things are going too well to risk wasting all our efforts at this stage. It won't be long before we get the word and then there'll be uprisings all over the country. You wait and see.'

This was thrilling news. So far the band had only concentrated on training – even sabotage had been ruled out in case some accident should lead to them – but I knew from what Hassan had told me of Ah Keow's work that they must be well armed and well organised.

'Richardson told me to say that you are one of our most useful outside contacts and that he wishes you to remain where you are for as long as possible.'

Good for my pride maybe, but I would have preferred to have taken to the hills.

The next day I received a brief message from Sergeant Wong. In case of eavesdroppers, we had taken to using a simple code over the telephone, consisting of the information being passed in every tenth word. Of course this was only possible with a prepared message and meant writing it down beforehand, but to date it had been very satisfactory. There had been no urgency in his voice but, as I replaced the receiver and picked out the relevant words from his conversation, my throat went dry. 'Lie very low' were his instructions for me.

From that time on it seemed that every eye was upon me. Who amongst my fellow PCs had seen Akaru enter my office and whose arm had wielded the shotgun butt?

A week went by and another. Still no reprisals. Nothing. My nerves were at breaking point.

'Don't you go fishing any more these days?' asked Hasbullah, and I realised that by my very act of lying too low I had drawn attention to myself. I took the only course.

'Funny you should ask that,' I replied, 'as I was only just thinking that I hadn't been for some time and might go to-morrow. Why don't you join me?'

'Yes. I think I will.'

I lay awake most of the night, pondering on what action to take.

I could kill Hasbullah once we were away from the station and make a dash for it. But what would that achieve? My usefulness here ended, inevitable reprisals from amongst my friends and another slaying on my conscience. I washed that out, except in self-defence or as a last resort.

I could lead him on a wild-goose chase, but he was no fool.

I was tempted to take him to a completely different stretch of the river, but what if he had followed me before?

In the end I took him to the meeting pool. I had not put out my signs and therefore no one would be expecting me to come and, if there was a lookout, he would see that I was not alone.

I was on hot bricks the whole way to the pool and encouraged Hasbullah to talk as much as I could. But luck was with me and not only did he appear completely unsuspecting, but we caught two fine fish.

My companion was delighted. 'Why didn't you invite me to join you before?' he asked, and I pointed out that I had. 'We'll certainly do this again.' He was laughing and talking all the way back to the station. 'What a change this will make from the eternal tapioca and yams. What a sly fellow you are, Mat. No wonder you're always sneaking off.'

'But keep it secret,' I warned, 'it's only because no one else knows about the pool that there are any fish in it at all. I came across it quite by chance one day and have fished there ever since.'

The atmosphere improved from that day on and I was able to relax a little. On the surface Hasbullah and I again became inseparable friends and all seemed well.

Another fortnight passed and I considered it was time to contact Wong. I had legitimate business for him anyway, so I picked up the phone without a trace of apprenhesion, my message contained in a few sentences relating to the theft of a car.

A cold voice the other end informed me that Sergeant Wong had been granted indefinite compassionate leave, to be with his dying mother. He was Corporal Poong, and I would deal with him in future.

I expressed my polite regrets that Mrs Wong should be so ill and tried my best to keep any emotion out of my voice as I made my routine inquiry, but my hand was trembling when I put down the receiver.

It could mean one of two things. Either Wong had invented an excuse and flown, or else he was in the hands of the Kempeitai. If the latter, I shuddered to think what might be happening to him now.

I fingered the envelope in my pocket. The envelope containing the poison intended for Ah Keow. Ever since his escape I had kept it with me; better that than torture and I would not implicate my brother or his comrades.

I knew that I must contact Hassan without delay. This was urgent news. If Wong had been arrested, it could be but a matter of time before I was too.

Since our first fishing expedition, Hasbullah had accompanied me every time. I quickly scanned the roster to find out when he would be on duty and unable to come with me – that was the time I must go. If Hassan was still sick, someone else would come.

That evening, after I had visited the latrine, I set about arranging my rendezvous code. I had placed the bottles and was just starting on the tins when a familiar voice hailed me.

'What are you doing? Always rummaging amongst those bottles and tins.' It was Hasbullah, his voice tight with suspicion. 'I've seen you here before.'

Allahumma! And I hadn't even got the tins set up. There was no other way of contacting Hassan and it would be useless going on spec.

'Just looking for a suitable tin for bait.'

'What's wrong with this one?' Hasbullah had picked up the tin nearest him.

I took it and dropped it again. 'Too rusty. Bait's scarce; you couldn't keep it alive in that.' I hoped my voice sounded natural and I continued looking around for a better tin. I wish I had known how long he had been there. Eventually I found one slightly less rusty, 'This'll do.'

Hasbullah's eyes had not left my face for one moment and it had been impossible to arrange the tins. I *had* to remain casual; I turned to go.

'Do you want to come to-morrow?' I asked.

'You know very well that I can't.'

'Oh, I'm sorry. I didn't know.'

'Yes, you did. I saw you examining the duty roster.'

His voice had become peevish and querulous and I realised he was in a dangerous mood.

Bang went my chances of getting in touch with Hassan. I would never be able to put out the signs unless I was absolutely sure I was not being watched. And it was quite clear that Hasbullah would be watching me from now on.

I didn't have long to worry about not contacting my brother.

Only two nights after my encounter with Hasbullah, I was woken up by the sound of a truck stopping outside the police station and the noise of a great many boots hitting the ground. I heard the sentry slap his rifle butt and the CRO call the men in the Charge Room to attention. Some senior Japanese officer must be visiting the station, but at what an extraordinary hour.

All of a sudden I was wide awake, warned by some sixth sense. And not an instant too soon.

The door was kicked open at the same moment that I leaped from my sleeping mat and there was Hasbullah at the head of several Japs.

Clasping my sarong round my thighs, I snatched up my slippers and dived for the window.

'Fire!' It was a Japanese word I knew well.

A bullet nicked my upper arm, but the rest thudded harmlessly into the wood and into the air.

I dropped to the ground and ran as fast as I could to the nearest opening in the wire. They must have relied on the hour and taking me completely by surprise. Even as I ran I commented to myself that, had I been the officer, I would have surrounded the building first. I blessed his omission.

The apes were not far behind me and I could hear Hasbullah shouting hysterically, but I knew exactly where I was going. Although I lost time by zigzagging to avoid bullets, I still outstripped them with ease.

Once through the wire, I flung first one slipper then the other on to the path that led to the shops, but which also had a track, much used by hunters, into the jungle. Then I doubled back and made for the river.

Sprinting on an athlete's training diet is one thing, but tapioca, yams, hard corn, and an occasional handful of rice had scarcely improved my stamina. I knew that before long I would have to stop and hole up until morning. It was a dark night, for which I was thankful, and I was already beyond the range of their torches, but I would never be able to find my way to the sub-camp before daylight.

As soon as I was a few hundred yards into the jungle and keeping my direction by the sound of the river, I crawled into the thickest undergrowth and lay still.

I could hear the voices in the distance and knew that my simple ruse of discarding my slippers had succeeded for the time being. I was pinning my faith on the fact that Hasbullah knew that I had seen him and would not therefore head for a place which he knew. With any luck they would comb the shop-houses, expecting to find me hidden by some accomplice.

I heard voices off and on throughout the night but guessed that they would leave a jungle search until daylight, and in this I was right.

It had been a hot night when I went to bed and I only wore a sarong. The stuffiness behind the mosquito net and closed shutters had made me sweat and I had discarded even the singlet in which I usually slept. I have no idea what time it was when the Japs arrived, but I had not been lying in the undergrowth long when I found myself enveloped in a chill mist rising from the river and began to shiver. My arm too was throbbing and it seemed as though every mosquito for miles around had picked on me as its chosen victim.

Dawn filtered slowly through the tall forest trees, but as soon as I could make out the shapes of trees and bushes, I rose cautiously from my hideout and looked around.

To my horror I found that my arm had bled far more than I had realised. My arm, chest and sarong were a mass of dried blood and any tracker would have been able to follow the trail left on leaf and stone. It made it imperative that I should get away without further delay.

I was torn between caution and a need for speed. Although I had never seen them, I had heard that the Japs had tracker dogs and I was terrified lest I should suddenly hear the sound of these animals on my scent.

I found my bearings, but the sun was already rising and I was not more than a couple of chains along my path when I heard voices coming in my direction. I strained my ears but could not hear what they were saying. I felt sure that I recognised Hasbullah's voice and became panicky as it occurred to me that he might have followed me along this path at some time. Unless I gave up all hope of remaining silent and crashed through the bushes and vines, I was bound to be overtaken.

Deciding that the only course was to hide again, I slithered on my stomach under the brambles and covered myself as best I could with leaf mould.

All morning they combed the area, but the fact that no one walked directly along the marked way, reassured me that Hasbullah could not have directed them along a definite path, but only in some vague direction that he may have seen me take.

It must have been midday when I heard a whistle and the men all converged on one spot. Then I heard what sounded like orders being given and the patrol appeared to be going back along the river bank.

I remained without moving for a further half-hour or so and, when the only sounds were those of insects and small animals, I emerged from my bed of leaves and crawled on all fours along the familiar path. Every few yards I stopped to listen and, satisfied that the patrol had been called off, I had just stood upright and started to walk at a more normal pace when, on rounding a bend, I saw before me, his back turned, a Japanese soldier. I froze in my tracks and waited, hardly daring to breathe. One hand slapped at insects that were landing on his face and the other loosely held a rifle with fixed bayonet.

I melted back round the bend. There was nothing for it; I had to get away – and fast. Once more I went flat and slithered snakelike under bushes for a few feet, then went as quickly as I could, never minding the noise nor the commotion behind me. A shot was fired, but it would have been a chance in a hundred that they should get me at that range and firing blind. I carried on as far and as fast as I could until I subsided in a panting heap, sobbing with fear, fatigue and hunger.

Whether or not the search was called off I don't know. Perhaps the crashing had been put down to an animal. I didn't care. Perhaps I lost consciousness – I'm sure I didn't sleep – but all of a sudden the sun wasn't there and I knew it must be night again.

The second night was worse than the first. The cold was well-nigh unendurable and nothing I could do would stop my teeth from chattering and my whole frame from shaking. Soon every bone in my body was aching as the fever mounted. I must have lost more blood than I had at first appreciated and it was already more than twenty-four hours since I had eaten.

At dawn, the fever had abated somewhat and I fell into a sleep of exhaustion. At the time I thought that I had only slept for a short while, for it was still only half light when I awoke, once again the target for innumerable insects, but with the blessed sweat breaking out all over my skin as I waited for the sun to rise.

But the sun didn't rise and I don't know how many hours it must have been before the awful truth dawned on me. I had escaped the Japs, but escaped into the thick, virgin jungle, where no sunlight penetrated. If you have been in the depths of the Malayan jungle you will know how all sense of direction is lost, all sense of time suspended, and loneliness dominates the mind.

Peering into the entwined branches above me, I tried to pierce the leafy screen and pinpoint the life-giving, direction-pointing sun, but to no avail.

I'm afraid I panicked then, turning this way and that, lunging for any opening or hole in the undergrowth, in the hope that it might lead to a path.

I crawled, pushed and struggled, first in one direction and then another. When night fell and even the twilight faded and deepened into an opaque, dense black, still I did not stop.

I cannot tell you how long I struggled in that hellish world before I heard the sound of water. It was near, so near that I lay still, trembling with fear that I might overlook it. Then, straining my ears to bursting point, I pushed my way on, stopping every few inches and listening, to ascertain that the sound had not grown less.

There are moments of gratitude in all our lives and, whether one is religious or not, there must be that time when we give unstinted thanks to some higher being. It was one of those moments when I bent, or lay, over the small clear stream which bubbled and fell in the gloom down a gentle slope.

I slept that night. The stream was only a few inches deep and not more than a couple of feet wide, but it was wonderful really to drink and to sink my weary body into its coolness.

The stream widened with amazing rapidity and within a few hundred yards the trees began to part overhead and let in a glimmer of sunlight. I found some berries growing on a bush by the bank and risked a handful.

The monotony of weakness and hunger makes it difficult to recall exact time, but I know that in due course I reached the river and, after following it downstream, ended up at my old pool. It was an odd feeling, standing there and knowing that, after all my scrambling through the jungle, I was only a mile or so away from the police station.

I didn't worry any more whether or not there were any patrols out. Being lost in the jungle is more frightening than the thought of what other human beings can perpetrate, and my one aim was to reach the sub-camp clearing as soon as possible.

The camp was empty and it occurred to me that they must have withdrawn their lookouts. I had never been inside the huts before, but to my relief I found that they had split bamboo floors, sleeping-mats, mosquito nets, and a supply of canned food and first-aid equipment. In the corner of one stood a large earthenware jar full of water with a wooden cover, a couple of tin plates and some rudimentary cooking utensils.

I had lost count of days, but I knew that it was a long time since I had had anything to eat other than a handful of suspect berries, and I had been all day without water. I was very weak, but not too weak to be able to wield a tin-opener and that long draught of cool water seemed to come straight from heaven.

I used a little of the water to cleanse my body, but I was afraid to touch the wound in my arm in case it should start to bleed again. It was puffy, yellow and purple, and throbbed incessantly, but I decided to rest it for the night and see what I could do with the first-aid kit the next day.

By dusk no one had come near the camp. I began to worry in case they had withdrawn from the area altogether, but it was useless to go on as I had no idea of the way, or even in which direction the main camp lay.

Consoling myself with the fact that there was still ash in the fireplace although it had rained less than a week ago, I ate a few tapioca flakes and attacked a tin of pilchards. Then, curling up on one sleeping-mat and pulling the other over me, I settled down to a blissful, insect-free night.

I was woken soon after dawn by the almost inaudible slap of footsteps. I knew at once that whoever had made the sound was wearing rubber plimsolls and that there was more than one person. Lying very still, I quaked with fright and dared not think about what would happen if I found myself caught, like a rat in a trap, by a Jap patrol.

I must have moved without realising because the first voice I heard spoke sharply in Malay.

'There's someone in that hut. I heard a movement.'

'Maybe an animal.'

'We'd better see.'

Whoever spoke was taking no chances. There was no door to the hut, but they must have been standing to the side of the opening.

A hand holding a pistol appeared in silhouette and the Malay voice called out, 'Whoever you are, come out with your hands on your head.'

What to do? I had no choice.

I scrambled out from under the mosquito net. Adjusting my sarong and putting my hands on my head, I walked out of the hut to face whatever fate had in store for me.

Imagine my relief when I found myself confronted by the Malay who had met me in the coffee-shop when Ah Keow had first been captured.

'Ahmat!'

We touched hands and hearts – ludicrously formal in the circumstances – and were joined by the second man, a Chinese whom I had not seen before.

Kassim, for that was the Malay's name, looked gravely at my arm, which by this time had swollen considerably and was turning an even nastier colour than it had been the previous evening, and my bare feet. My whole body was a mass of scratches and bites and I needed a shave. I cannot have been a very prepossessing sight.

It was wonderfully comforting to squat there while Kassim and his friend boiled water for a hot drink and to clean my wound and to tell them all that had happened since the escape of Ah Keow.

I submitted to their painful ministrations, but neither were experts and after a while Kassim grunted and shook his head.

'I daren't do much to this,' he said, 'I've only washed off the surface dirt. Better leave it until we can get you to Ratnasingham.'

As I told my tale both men nodded several times.

'Your brother thought something of the kind must have occurred. It is so long since you made contact. We were on our way to Rembang to pick up what information we could about another anti-Japanese organisation that is supposed to be operating in the area and to find out about you at the same time.'

'Don't go into the town,' I implored them, 'there are Japs everywhere.'

We discussed it for some time but finally they decided that they must go ahead. They both unrolled small bundles which they had carried with them and, taking off their green uniforms, changed into clean civilian trousers and shirts.

'We'll have to try and find you a pair of shoes,' Kassim remarked, 'you'll never make the camp with your feet in that condition.'

It was true that my feet were in a bad state. I had landed on a sharp tin when first jumping from the barrack-room window and after that had trodden on some broken glass. I wasn't used to walking barefoot in the jungle either. But the pain in my arm was such that I had barely noticed my feet.

Kassim had given me some aspirin tablets from the first-aid kit and as there was nothing to do but wait for their return, I carried a sleeping mat into the dim, filtered sunlight and dozed the day away.

They came back shortly before sunset and to my surprise had two Chinese with them, both of whom I recognised. One was the owner of a small radio and cycle repair shop and the other, a woman, was a nurse from Seremban hospital.

The three men each carried a radio battery and a sack and the girl a cloth bag and a large newspaper parcel.

As I've said often before, Hassan had kept me very much in the dark and it had not occurred to me that they had so many contacts and supporters amongst the local population.

Boon Poh, the radio man, amazed me by saying that he had been supplying dry batteries and charging wet ones for Hassan's bunch for nearly a year and relaying information from his own radio when theirs was not working.

As I had surmised, the Japs had had everyone out of bed and searched each shop-house for me before combing the rubber estate and nearby jungle. Realising that it might well be his turn next, Boon Poh had sent a warning message by a lorry driver to Siew Lin, the nurse, and at once made preparations to return with the next person who came into Rembang from the camp.

From Siew Lin I learned an item of dreadful news, which confirmed what I had already been afraid of. Sergeant Wong had indeed flown – or tried to fly. His application for leave had been approved and he had set off for Kuala Lumpur. But he was seized at the railway station before he could board the train. He had been placed in the lock-up over night, awaiting escort to Kempeitai headquarters. But Wong had no intention of facing the Kempeitai and when they came to fetch him the next morning, he was found hanging, the noose made from strips torn from his shirt.

I was silent a long time after hearing this, only listening with half an ear as Siew Lin went on to tell me how she too had been passing information to Wong, gleaned both from the Japanese doctors and from patients of all races.

'I would have joined them before,' she told me. 'My nursing ability would be useful, but they're Communists and I don't like their politics.'

Kassim's Chinese companion, grinned. 'Of course we're Communists. We are fighting for freedom and a say in ruling the country. Whether it's Jap tyranny or British tyranny, it makes no difference.'

This was certainly news to me. I was quite sure Hassan wasn't a Communist. And the European officers who had been put in specially? I couldn't believe that they were Communists.

I was just opening my mouth to speak when I saw Kassim frown and give an almost imperceptible shake of his head. So I said nothing.

Before I had time to puzzle further, Siew Lin changed the subject. 'I'd better have a look at that arm,' she said in the authoritative voice nurses assume when on duty. 'It looks as though it should have had attention some time ago.'

I gritted my teeth as she washed off the dried blood and prodded and probed.

The sacks contained maize cobs and we roasted two each for our evening meal. I was content – more content than I had been for many weeks. The ministrations of Siew Lin had greatly relieved my distress and the parcel she carried had contained clothing, from which I was given a shirt and trousers. Before putting these on, Kassim had taken me to a stream a short distance from the clearing to wash. It was a wonderful feeling to remove the stale sweat and sticky blood and don clean clothes.

While at the stream I asked Kassim about the Communists. It was easy for us to converse, because the Chinese only spoke a little bazaar Malay and we Minangkerbaus have many words that even Malays from other parts of the peninsula do not understand.

'You will see for yourself,' he told me, 'that there are two distinct cliques within the band. On the one hand, the few Malays, Indians, and Europeans, and a handful of Chinese; and on the other, the Communists, all of whom are Chinese.'

'Why do they stick together?' I asked.

'Because numbers are important and we are all fighting for the same *immediate* aim – to rid Malaya of the Japs. I believe there are many bands of mixed races throughout the peninsula, but the Communists are the only properly organised ones – and the British helped organise them, believe it or not. It's no use trying to train large numbers of men without discipline and the Communists are the only ones who have any. Of course they're dogmatic in the extreme, but they're tough, dedicated, and trust no one. But you'll soon see for yourself.'

'You sound as though you're dedicated.' I knew that he had not been with them for very long.

'I'm quoting your brother,' he admitted, with a smile which made me feel at once that he was my friend; '*he's* dedicated if you like. But he looks forward to working with and under the British again and that is *not* the Communist aim. I sometimes wonder if he's completely in their confidence. I doubt it, nor Richardson – although they have to acknowledge him as their titular head if they want the Allies to drop arms and supplies.'

I had never given much thought to politics, but he had been a schoolmaster and it seemed that he was conversant with many matters beyond the confines of his native land. He was an idealist and had joined the guerillas in the first place because he refused to teach Japanese propaganda, nor would he be told how and what to teach. There were two teachers with the band, he told me, the other a Ceylonese who had taken to the hills for the same reason. To Kassim, the young mind was sacred and the pollution of it by the Japanese one of the most heinous of their crimes. He gave me much to think about, then and in the months to follow.

The hot sweet corn tasted delicious. More aspirin had made me dozy. Looking at my four companions, a difference in politics seemed immensely unimportant.

It was terrible to see the emaciation of my brother, Hassan.

The long march to the camp, shuffling in my inadequate footwear and doing my best to protect my arm, had left me exhausted. I had been placed at once in the capable hands of 'Doctor' Ratnasingham, who turned out to be a Ceylon Tamil dresser from one of the large estates, who possessed great skill and gentleness.

'Tut tut, dear me. Another Sharif,' he murmured as he dressed my arm. 'Didn't your mother ever teach you boys to look after yourselves? I never thought we'd pull your brother through.'

Hassan, who was sitting beside me while Ratna checked my wound, smiled. He had lost several teeth and the skin stretched over his gaunt bones gave his face the appearance of a skull. He was nearly as pale as a Chinese.

'Just because he has white hair, Ratna thinks he can bully us like schoolboys. Don't you, Doc?'

The old dresser wagged his head and said, 'No, no, that's not my province – I leave that to Vannia. But, of course, his politics are wrong here too.'

He indicated a compatriot – his assistant I had taken him to be – who was busy at the back of the hut, listing stores in a large ledger. Later Hassan told me that these two elderly men, dresser and teacher from an erstwhile European-run rubber estate, had left their posts within the first few months of the occupation and, after settling their wives and children with relatives, had taken to the hills on their own, in the hope of contacting one of the many anti-Japanese organisations – and, miraculously, they had. Looking back on my own feelings during the first year or so of the war, I could not help but respect men of such a mature age who were prepared to put ideals before all thought of safety and comfort.

It was clear that a great bond of affection existed between the elderly Ceylonese and the men under his care, and it was easy to see why.

I could hardly believe my eyes when I saw the camp properly the next day.

I don't quite know what I had expected but it certainly was not the well organised layout that greeted my eyes.

Well-constructed wooden huts with atap roofs ran along three sides of a square, sheltered by tall trees, and the fourth side was open on to a Sakai clearing.

Sakai is a term we use to cover the various tribes of aborigines in Malaya, and in this area we had the Jakun. They are squat men, darker than us, with broader features and curlier hair. As a boy I used to listen to their bells and wonder what their homes would be like – but I never expected to find out. They are nomads who clear an area, plant a little hill rice and tapioca and, when the patch of earth is no longer fruitful, move on. Some hillsides are patchworked with their clearings, some overgrown by belukar, or secondary jungle, but many remain scars on the slopes because of soil erosion.

It was not until Hassan showed me an aerial photograph which had been dropped with their supplies, that I realised how excellent was their camouflage. There was nothing to distinguish the clearing from several others in the area except for one building, and that, as he pointed out, had since been removed.

The Sakai had frequently collaborated with the Japanese, mainly because they did not know who they were and, anyway, they were prepared to guide anyone for a measure of tobacco and cloth. One of Hassan's initial tasks had been to win over the local Sakai and to persuade a few to return to the deserted clearing they had chosen for the training camp. Thus, any activity seen from the air would appear normal and the larger cleared area was ideal for a dropping zone.

There was constant activity in the camp. Weapon-training, map-reading, and PT classes were held every day, and Ratnasingham instructed in first-aid and held frequent medical checkups.

One day, soon after my arm and feet were sufficiently healed, Hassan took me to the top of the mountain, where they had a lookout post built in the branches of a giant tree.

The view was magnificent. Deep green valleys merged into deep blue, then purple; mauve and smoke blue hills marched in layers in every direction that the eye could see.

'Look,' he pointed to the west. 'The sea. We should have a good view of the invasion fleet from here, and it won't be long now.'

That evening in the camp the Chinese were extra regimental, lining up and singing with full throats.

'What is it that they are celebrating?' I asked Richardson, for no particular victory had been announced.

He seemed a little tight-lipped as he answered, 'May Day. It has its place in the folklore of the British Isles too, in a rather whimsical fashion, but to our comrades it's Labour Day. What you are listening to is the "International," the Communist anthem. It gives me night-mares when I wonder what we're going to do with this bunch at the end of the war.'

I found it difficult to understand how the British officers were so blatantly anti-Communist and yet had deliberately contacted them for support. Kassim had done his best to explain, but it remained an enigma to me.

45. GOOD NEWS IN BAVARIA

Stanislaus Olshewski

I was a happy man. I patted my pocket to make sure the letter was really there, as I walked back to my hut from the camp hospital, and then stopped to take it out and read it again.

In fact, the letter was not addressed to me. It was addressed to Lieutenant-Colonel J. B. MacArthur, RAMC, and it advised him that, pending a personal interview, a place would be available – when we were released – at St Andrews University for one, Flight Lieutenant S. Oliver, RAF, to study medicine.

From this you will gather that I had not been idle during my year in captivity.

It was the 1st of May, a glorious summer day already, and nearly a year since D-Day, and we were waiting for the news that the war had ended. The scent of pines was all around me, the sky above was a deep, clear blue, and every face I encountered had a smile on it. The camp notice board had its usual knot of loafers round it, waiting for news, as we all were, but the fact that they were still there and not rushing around the camp told me that nothing had come through yet.

The hut was cool and empty. I read the letter yet again, then settled down to fill in the forms which Colonel MacArthur had handed me.

The bunk above mine, bare and unoccupied, caused my only regret that day – regret that Sam was no longer there to share my triumph.

Taken prisoner as we had been, so near the end of the war – and at that time we had not expected it to last more than a couple of months at the most – very few of the officers had attempted to escape. But Sam, who as soon as the gates had finally closed behind us had announced that he was putting his feet up for a good long rest at the Krauts' expense, had nevertheless fallen into the doldrums. He became maudlin and morose, and one day, when it had rained for some hours and we had not been able to take our usual exercise, he suddenly made a dash for the wire and was shot as he hung there, in broad daylight.

The memory made me sick. In fact, I was saved from falling into a state of melancholia myself by listening to someone else's conversation one night, not long after Sam was shot. These two chaps were discussing the number of friends they had lost during the war and their own good luck, when I chipped in. I hadn't meant to intrude, but the fact that first Tzadek, then Harry, and now Sam had all been killed after they had become friendly with me had made me wonder if I

378

wasn't some kind of Jonah. After that the conversation became general and it was amazing to find out just how many of us had been labouring under the same fears. That had been a good air-clearer, and the next day I had doubled my efforts and put the picture of Sam's body, spreadeagled on the wire, firmly out of my mind.

We had been moved from one stalag to another, ending up in what had once been a German Army camp in Bavaria, with wire and towers hastily flung up around it. We weren't too badly off really and suffered few of the privations known to earlier prisoners.

As soon as we had been docketed, counted, and assigned to huts in the first permanent camp, I approached the Senior British Officer and told him my real name and what I had done. He had shaken my hand, very warmly I thought, and from that moment on I was protected on all sides. Luckily my English was by that time a hundred per cent fluent and I doubt if I had sufficient accent to be noticeable to the Germans.

On hearing that I was keen to study medicine eventually, the Canadian Army Chaplain, who was also the Camp Welfare Officer, offered to write off for books from the Red Cross, and Colonel Mac-Arthur, the senior medico in the camp, suggested I should become one of his assistants and learn a bit of the practical side.

So there I was, in the words of that delightful piece of English idiom, treading on air. I had passed my first written paper and had a place in a medical school assured. My only worry was what would happen when I got back to England and they found out that S. Oliver was, in fact, S. Olshewski and that I wasn't a British subject. 'Cross that bridge when you come to it,' was Colonel MacArthur's advice, and it was all I could do.

We were released the following month. Rumour had it that the Americans had been in the vicinity for some time and suddenly, one morning, there they were.

The lorries arrived. An American top sergeant jumped out. The German sentry quietly put down his gun and opened the gate. It was as uneventful as that.

The Americans brought fresh food and fruit juice, chocolate and cigarettes – and left us where we were. Sam would have had something to say, no doubt!

A few days later a convoy of empty trucks arrived and we were off on the first lap of our journey home.

Home? By the end of June I was officially enrolled at St Andrews, had put in my application for British naturalisation, and awaited my release from the air force. There had been no trouble over my name

379

and the British had promised us – those of us who for some reason or other could not return to Poland, or did not wish to – citizenship under certain conditions. When I went to fetch my application forms there was a queue a mile long. We no longer had a home.

46. REJOICING IN PICCADILLY

Donald Thom

Whooosh! Another rocket burst into a million stars and my head was doing the same. I watched them as they went up, one after another, whoosh, whoosh, whoosh! And each one followed by a hysterical scream from the crowd.

For this was VE-Day, 1945. Victory in Europe. But not victory for Thom. I wasn't quite sure why I was here, in the midst of this crowd, dancing round Piccadilly. Something about a course. Yeah, that's right, I'd been sent on another course – at this stage of the proceedings, Judas Priest, would you believe it? Great guy for courses, Thom. Been on more courses than any other man in the whole blankety blank army. Can't remember what this one was about – something to do with Intelligence, I guess – only I'm not feeling very intelligent just now. Anyways, it just so happens that I ended up in Piccadilly – which everyone told me was the place to be on VE-Night – and I was stinking high.

An elderly civilian and a young soldier did a double handstand on the top of Eros. Some guys really go for this. Me, I preferred it when the war was still on.

'Knees up, Mother Brown, knees up, Mother Brown – ' the noise was deafening and hands on either side swirled me along with them. I could hardly keep my head up, let alone my knees! Round and round we went in two vast circles, and then they split up into couples, sometimes men, sometimes women, sometimes one of each, no one cared. It was a relief when the circles re-formed and I found myself held up again. But they stopped too suddenly the next time and I felt myself falling.

'Careful.' A small figure was supporting me and for a dreadful moment I thought it was Monica. But when I looked again I saw, to my relief, that it was not the bluish grey of the Red Cross uniform but that of the air force.

'You look a capable young woman,' I said – at least I think I said, 'do you think you could help me across the road?'

The girl laughed and took my arm, piloting me across the street to the entrance of the Underground. I bowed ceremoniously to her and she laughed again. Then I accomplished the impossible and got down the first flight of stairs without missing a single step. At the bottom I turned – she was still there – and bowed again. She was really a very nice girl and I would like to buy her a drink.

'I am going to be sick,' I announced, 'please wait.'

I thought I had better wait. I had seen this big Canadian soldier standing on the edge of the crowd, looking just about as happy as I was, long before he'd fallen on top of me in that mad dance. I'd give him five minutes and, if he hadn't appeared, look for a porter or someone to help – I was terrified he'd break his neck. You know all those steps?

I wasn't exactly unhappy; just alone and a little sad. Philip was still in Italy – I imagined he was all right, but I'd had no news of him as yet – and the Far Eastern war was still going on. It was difficult to rejoice when my father was still imprisoned in Singapore – I presumed, I'd never had any news of him either – and, working in Far Eastern intelligence as I now was, I had a very good idea of what might happen to him if and when we invaded. I knew too that the Japs were not likely to give up just because the European members of the Axis had.

I looked at my watch – four minutes had gone by – and as I raised my eyes, there was the large Canadian coming back. He looked more sober now and had a pleasant, sheepish grin on his open, freckled face. I turned to go.

I could hear the roar of the crowd overhead, but I felt a lot better as I left the 'Gents.' Where was that little WAAF I'd found? She said she'd wait. Was that her standing at the top of the stairs? But she only had one ring – I thought she had at least three! She had seen me and was turning away.

'Hey, wait,' I called, 'the war is over – what better excuse for a guy to buy a girl a drink?'

'But you would appear to have had quite enough!' Jesus, all women are the same.

'Aw, come on, honey,' I gave her what I had always been told was my most engaging grin, 'the war's over. Just one drink.'

We fought our way up the steps and through the crowd – I recall those guys moaning about my weight when they dragged me up the ladder in the mill, but boy, it sure helps when you have to push your way through a crowd – and down to an underground bar which used to be a haunt of me and some of the boys in my early Surrey days.

It was full, but a couple got up just as we arrived and I heaved this little WAAF over the shoulder of a chap who was bending down and bagged the table before anyone else had a chance.

'Highballs,' I bellowed at the bartender, 'none of your Scotch to-night. Got any Canadian Club?'

I guess we all got pretty high. I looked at this kid – nice-looking kid she was – and wondered what sort of war she'd had.

'You ever hear a shot fired in anger?' I asked.

'Of course.' I guess she had too.

'Well, I'll tell you something, honey – I haven't.'

She looked so wide-eyed and innocent – a real nice kid – that I told her all. All about my courses and the frustration of the waiting months, being dropped, being nursed, playing with my radio set, being taken for a sail. And all without hearing a shot. Only one person I didn't mention and that was my wife – as far as I was concerned she didn't exist – but I mentioned my buddies, those who had heard shots. Yeah, I mentioned them; those whom I'd see again in a few weeks' time and those who had gone. I mentioned them all right. Good guys, every one of them. There had been a good girl too.

Some three hours later and knowing his life story back to front, I rose. We were the last occupants of the tiny bar and my Canadian friend was not only dead drunk, but fast asleep.

I looked at the bartender. 'What do I do with him?' I asked.

'Isn't he your friend?'

'Never saw him before. He was just one of the Piccadilly crowd.'

'Leave him here.' He walked round the bar and looked at the sleeping man. 'Parachutist's wings,' he pointed out, 'who knows what sort of a war he's had. Dropped into Germany, for all we know.' He sighed and shook his head. 'Over on D-Day I wouldn't doubt, fighting all the way. It's been all right for the likes of you and me, sitting at home with only the odd bomb to dodge, but look at him – all the way from Canada to help us win the war. If it hadn't been for the likes of him we'd never have won this bloody do at all.'

Shaking his head sadly, he walked over to an open door. 'Albert,' he yelled, and in answer to his call an elderly gent wearing pyjamas and a tweed cap came out, blinking and half asleep. 'Help us lift this carcass on to Ma's couch.'

The three of us heaved and pulled and eventually got him on to the couch at the side of the bar, normal perch of the port and lemon brigade.

'Rest in peace,' I said, and folded his hands on his chest over his cap.

I walked out into broad daylight. There would just be time for a cup of coffee before going to the office. The war in the Far East was still on.

47. THE BOMB IS DROPPED

Sharif Ahmat

There are milestones in our lives that remain fresh in the memory over the years, and the morning in early August 1945, when the whole camp was called out to hear an important announcement, was, for me at any rate, one of them.

When we were all assembled, Dick Richardson stood up with Goon Swee, the leader of the Chinese Communist guerillas, and told us about the dropping of the atom bomb on Hiroshima. He spoke in English and Malay and was followed, sentence by sentence, by Goon Swee in Mandarin.

The announcement was quite short and we soon broke into groups to discuss the momentous news.

I didn't understand the technicalities, but I did understand the magnitude, the fantastic square mileage of devastation. That one bomb, just one, could flatten such an area; that a few such bombs, dropped strategically, could virtually wipe Japan from the face of the map, was awe-inspiring indeed.

'I doubt if we shall see any invasion fleet after all,' Hassan said, and I thought he sounded a trifle wistful. 'The war should just end quietly now, without any fighting at all here. Surely the Japs won't hang on to see their homeland disintegrate?'

'I can't say I'm sorry,' it was Dick Richardson, who had just joined us where we sat in the shade of a wild mango tree. 'But all this seems an awful waste of time, doesn't it? All this training and so much money spent on a role never to be fulfilled. Still, a peaceful Malaya again is a wonderful thought.'

'I'd not cross your bridges before you come to them; we're not out of the woods yet,' it was the sobering voice of the Scottish officer they called Jock. He was older than the others, the only one married and with a family. He had shaken his head on hearing the news and muttered, 'Terrible, terrible.' I couldn't understand why, until he enlightened us. 'All those women and children,' he shook his head again, 'babies and old folk. It's terrible. Drop a bomb on these little blighters –' the gesture of his hand indicated the Japs who were occupying Malaya, the soldiers, ' – by all means. But to wipe out a whole city with one bomb. It could have fallen on Glasgow or Aberdeen, or Kuala Lumpur. I keep thinking of having the whole of my family wiped out like that – and wondering too how it will affect those who remain alive. Terrible, terrible.'

I doubt if any of the rest of us had had those thoughts, but it made us think a bit.

On 17th August we were told officially from Ceylon that surrender terms had been accepted by the Japanese.

There was nothing we could do then but sit and wait, but unfortunately during this time we had one very sad incident. An incident that brought the whole futility of the times to a head.

It was just bad luck that our radio should peter out shortly after the surrender announcement, and Boon Poh's last battery was becoming so worn out that reception was too faint to hear anything accurately. After a few days, Dick Richardson said that he was going down to Rembang to find out what was happening. After all, he said, there had been time enough for the Japs to lay down their arms and it was as well that a British officer should show himself publicly.

But, alas, he never reached the town.

He set off with Hassan and half a dozen Chinese at first light and by midday the others were back – carrying his body.

Before I tell the story of what happened – it is Hassan's story, of course, I was not there – I had better recount a previous incident which, as it happened, was the real cause of the tragedy.

Ever since I myself had arrived at the camp, it was seldom that anyone returned from Rembang or the sub-camp without company. Mostly these were contacts who had served their purpose, or who were becoming windy – as I had – and didn't dare remain where they were. But some had had no previous connections and were merely joining us to be with the right people at the right time – 'jumping on the bandwagon,' Dick Richardson had called it. It was not difficult to contact those who had already taken to the hills – there are few secrets in Asia. Of course, these people were unwelcome, as they could not be considered trustworthy – and ate up the meagre food supplies – but to send them back might be asking for trouble, so they were usually kept, albeit unwillingly.

It was on one of these occasions, not more than a couple of weeks before, that a young Tamil accompanied two of the Chinese back from the town. It was natural, of course, that his two compatriots should come forward to greet him, but with one accord both Ratna and Vanniasingham shouted, 'No, no, we will not have this youngster here. He is a Japanese spy, you must not let him see the camp.'

The atom bomb had already been dropped by then and we all felt that our days in the jungle were numbered anyway.

'Send him back then,' Richardson ordered, and Hassan and the other Europeans agreed with him.

Goon Swee was all for shooting him, and it would have been a good thing if he had had his way. I don't think the Europeans liked the idea of execution without trial much, but the Chinese were quite ruthless with suspected traitors, and I'm not sure that they weren't right.

'If you let him go he will heap troubles on our heads,' cried Vannia.

'Oh, Dick, you are being foolish, man. I do not hold with summary execution either, but incarceration would do the trick.'

'The war's as good as over. He can't do any harm now. Let him go. He'll have lost too much face by being rejected to broadcast the fact.'

But there Richardson was wrong. By the time anyone was going down to the sub-camp again the second bomb had been dropped, this time on Nagasaki, and the Japanese Cabinet had agreed to surrender unconditionally. I doubt if any of us spared a single thought for the young Tamil being escorted back to civilisation. Our thoughts were on other things.

'If' is a hopeless word in any language. But when we heard Hassan's account of the death of our leader, we must all have thought it a good many times.

Whether the Japs had refused to surrender, or whether in isolated areas they were still determined to hang on, I don't know. At any rate, a few were prepared to follow our rejected friend, it seemed.

Apparently they were not more than a third of the way when they walked into a perfect ambush. Richardson fell with the first shot.

Of course they had not been as alert as usual; I gathered from Hassan that they had thrown a certain amount of caution to the winds. The war was over – Richardson was walking openly into town, not skulking behind bushes. He was a police officer with several years' service in Malaya and the police station was to have been his first port of call.

Hassan and the Chinese all shouted to the Japs that the war was over; to stop firing. Suddenly, Hassan said, half a dozen Japs and the young Tamil came out on to the path. The Japs flung down their weapons and started off down the track without saying a word, but the Tamil hesitated before following them, and yelled out, in English, that they were only a small scouting party, sent to find the way, and that the main force was behind them. He ran too then, and Hassan said afterwards that he wished he had shot him. But what was the use?

Richardson must have died instantaneously. There was a bullet hole through his forehead and Ratna said it had undoubtedly entered the brain. Poor Ratna, he had looked after his flock so well and now he was helpless. It was terrible to see him holding Dick's body and crooning over him in just the same way that my mother had held Hussein.

I felt the hot tears pricking my eyes as we lowered his body into the hastily dug grave, and as I looked up I saw Hassan and the two Ceylonese weeping unashamedly. Most of the Chinese appeared unmoved, but it is difficult to tell with them – it is possible that many were as upset as we were.

As soon as the burial was over we began to make preparations in case there was indeed a large force on its way.

We waited in readiness for more than a week, but no one came. Whether they had thought better of it or whether the force had never existed outside the Tamil's imagination, we did not know.

The next party to go into Rembang returned with the news that the Japs had surrendered but the British not yet arrived. There was disturbing news too that guerilla bands in Perak had more or less taken over and that lawlessness prevailed. I'm sure I was not the only one to look sideways at Goon Swee and wish that he and his men were not Communists. What his thoughts were we couldn't tell, but luckily his intentions appeared to be to do nothing – perhaps he was waiting for orders.

Waiting seemed to be the only thing that any of us could do. It was a frustrating time.

48. REJECTION BY THE GLORIOUS GUERILLAS

Ramakrishnan

I will show them, I vowed.

It was not that I was wanting to take to the hills, you understand, but after leaving lowly occupation of rubber-tapper and entering salubrious occupation of schoolteacher on nearby estate, near small town of Rembang, I am hearing much of one, Mr Wong Foo, B.Sc. Honours, who is leading glorious guerillas in jungles nearby. Said Chinese guerillas are planning to take over government of Malaya after departure of Nipponese. For it is being said most openly in all market places and public bodies that soon our masters will be leaving shores of Malay States.

I have been telling myself many times that indeed it is world of disillusionment that I am living in and now it is utterly proven that said world is all topsy-turvy upside down. When I am going with open hand of friendship and am for throwing in lot with new cronies, what do I find? Not glorious guerillas led by Mr Wong Foo, B.Sc. Honours, but guerillas under thumbs of white pigs and all-bloody-mighty-educated Vanniasingham.

I am having shockings indeed to find him there; he who called me rabble-rouser and junior rabble-rouser. And when I am asking for Mr Wong, Vanniasingham and cronies are being most uncivil.

I will rouse rabble indeed, Mister; you will be rubble, not rabble, I am telling you. Ha, ha, ha, Mister! You are thinking I do not know these vile English words. I will show you.

I am feeling foolish fellow indeed and not wishing to reap further humiliations by returning to estate, after telling all and sundries I am off to join glorious guerillas, and so I am seeking humble employment in silk store owned by one Mister Ramasamy – no relation of my father – in Rembang town.

It is lucky chance that I am passing said store when ignorant and inglorious guerillas have taken me back to town – I am suggesting they blindfold me, for, I say, I am bound to be leading enemy to them, because of insolent treatment received, but they are only laughing at suggestion most sensible – so, as I am not remaining to be laughed at for one minute longer absolutely, I am entering shop of compatriot and when this fellow is offering me employment in store, I am accepting.

This Mr Ramasamy, no relation, is bad boss indeed. I am telling you, man, he and wife and many ripe daughters are living in luxury most splendiferous, having glorious dwelling-place above store, whereas we most lowly and humble slaves are sleeping on counter or floor.

Sleep is absolutely out of question during first night in store, for I am busy cogitating recently refused hand of friendship and am forming plan both most glorious and vile.

By day is much menial work to be done. Store is in situation most congenial, with street to front and behind much park and orchard land, where Mr Ramasamy is keeping herd of fine cows. I am indeed being surprised, on assuming duties of salesman in silk store, to be ordered to milk same. Then is one of Mr Ramasamy's daughters, Devi, who is laughing at my antics, watching me with all teeth glistening and hair-oil gleaming in sunlight, until I tell you, man, I am becoming so excited that it is indeed different cow that I am wanting to put in milk.

But I have learned strict lesson. All pleasurable thoughts of fornication must be putting asunder until I am taking legally wedded wife. Besides, the apothecary is telling me much disease in town, and who knows with whom said Devi is copulating? There are many bangles a-jingle on plump arms and ankles of ripe daughters and wife of Mr Ramasamy; maybe it is that he is selling same wife and daughters to conquerors for most pleasurable sports? So I am bidding loins be silent.

I am proving I am not milkman indeed when Mr Ramasamy is ordering sweepings of cowshed and stacking of manure.

'Mister,' I am saying, 'I am student and schoolteacher both. I am now helping compatriot in need of employee. Cloth salesman is lowly job, but verily I am not night soil collector, nor yet nursemaid to cows.'

'I have seen your eyes on my daughter, Miss Devi,' Mr Ramasamy is saying, 'and thoughts of fornication are clearly to be read. Miss Devi is most spotless and unsoiled girl, but for good work on part of employee, she might become wedded wife. If you are wishing food, you must work. I have chicken and egg and vegetable behind store; other employees are glad to clean cowshed in exchange for same. Return to teaching if you wish.'

Truly he is most insolent fellow, but there is not much cloth and no silk in silk store, so he is making monies in other manner. Selling vegetable and milk is mustering fortune in such times and I can see he is after husbands for ripe daughters, so I am holding trumping card.

After I have been working in silk store for one week and two days precisely, I am walking down street and being pushed by rough Chinese fellow off five-foot way.

Chinese are all most bountiful superior beings these days, and I am telling this fellow to watch who he is pushing when he is laughing at me. At me, Ramakrishnan, and then I am recognising this rough fellow as one of the inglorious guerillas who led me back from the camp.

At that exact instant idea is being born. I will take Nipponese soldiers to camp and all guerillas, white pigs and renegade Indians both, will be wiped off.

On arrival at police station I am being shown into office of bearded Bengali.

'Brother,' I say, 'I see that you in wisdom most wise have joined illustrious Nipponese masters and it is said you are swearing to wipe out guerillas in jungle hills.'

'That was true,' he says, 'but now it is too late.'

'Too late?'

This is very tall Bengali with beard and turban both and he looks like tired elephant. 'We are awaiting orders to surrender,' he says.

'Surrender?' I am not believing ears.

'Perhaps the British are returning,' he answers. 'I do not know.'

Verily, this is most terrible news. I am understanding that Chinese would be taking over government. Thoughts are somersaulting in my head.

'And what will you do, Brother?' I ask.

'I am member of police force and whether British or Japanese are in charge, we are still police.'

'But, Brother,' I remind him, 'think of our peoples who are being brought to this land in chains. Think of the humiliations of being called Klings by such inferior races as Malays and Chinese. Oh think!'

'We Sikhs never came in chains,' he is saying, and looking at me with most scornful gaze, the haughty fellow. 'We came as policemen, members of an honourable profession, not untouchables.'

Truly he is most prideful fellow and I am betting you constable only before Japanese raised him to present exalted rank.

'Everyone hears news, whether allowed or not,' he says. 'Did you not hear of the bomb that has been dropped on Japan?'

'What is one bomb? Many bombs dropped on London town and even city of Singapore. It is only one bomb they are dropping.'

'Two.'

'Who is caring about two bombs?' I am shouting, 'when I can't take you to wipe out guerillas in one felling swoop?'

'Come back to-morrow,' he says, 'I will speak to Sergeant Omahu.'

This Sergeant Omahu is most scholarly gentleman like myself; thin, with long hands and quiet manner and with thickest spectacles I have ever seen. He is listening to story I am unfolding, then asks, 'Did you not see the sentry when you came in?'

I nod, because of course I bowed to sentry, muttering, 'Malay pig,' as I did so.

'He is unarmed,' Sergeant Omahu is saying. 'We have laid down our arms. The war is over.'

'But – ' He waves me to be silent.

'Quite. For you and me the war is not over. I do not inquire into your reasons, but my home is, or was, Nagasaki. I would not heed you otherwise.' Everybody is talking about the magnitudiny of these bombs. 'I will give you six men,' he says. 'Do what damage you will. By the time you return the British may be here.'

'But, Master,' I am wailing, 'it is camp of great vastness. Sixty men at very least are needed.'

Sergeant Omahu is giving bitter laugh. 'Sixty men? I have never had sixty men since I have been here. Anyway, you Indians always exaggerate.' I am dismissed.

I am glad to see that six men allotted are all Nipponese, for I know Malay mata-mata, that is constable, would not go farther than jungle edge. By time it is daylight next morning, we are already having boots fitted and rice in bellies and I am leading men forth, glad that I am making marks of my own, besides heeding path to camp.

We are about half-way to camp when there is hullabaloo – voices chattering, and so forth.

'Quickly,' I say, 'we must place ourselves in positions concealing.'

But quite unheeding of my leadership, Japanese are dispersing, leaving me only in position to hide, as Sergeant Omahu has not allowed gun, for which I am most displeased. Soon along path is coming party of men. I see white pig in lead turn to speak to Malay toady, and behind them many Chinese. All are armed, but most obviously not expecting ambush, when we are opening fire.

Suddenly the white pig is lying on ground with Malay bending over him and Chinese shooting every which way.

Then Malay is standing up and shouting to us to stop firing.

Truly I am ashamed of Nipponese friends. When we hear what Malay is calling out, that war is over and they will be going home, they are terminating fire and walking into path to lay down arms, then turning back.

I scream at Malay that large force is coming behind, then follow inglorious comrades helter-skelter, for I cannot take gun and shoot single hands. When I am reaching small clearing I see all Nipponese are waiting for me. I bow and say thanks awfully, jolly good show to wait. But they are not waiting for jolly good show.

'You knew the war was ended,' one accused.

I say that I am not surely sure, only hearing rumourings of same, but I am understanding that Sergeant Omahu has not been dealing with his men with perfect clarity, fair and squareness. I am having relief when Nipponese get up to go and when we are free of all jungle trees, I tell them there is no need for accompaniment to police station.

They are not caring about yours truly and so I am slipping back to silk store. Mr Ramasamy is giving very sideways look and so I am telling him windy fable of cocks and bulls and how I must keep out of way of Japanese masters until leaving. He is not questioning, for which I am most glad, and that night I am having better sleep than previously in police station. True it is that in my dreams I am lusting after Devi, but I am not thinking of future until all present situations are being clarified and we are knowing on which foot to be standing.

49. THE TURNING POINT

Vincent Lee Chee Min

I've heard a lot of people say that the dropping of the atom bomb was the turning point, and it sure was a turning point in my life. Not that the bomb itself had anything to do with it – we haven't felt the war too much here, except for all the evacuees and we've been rationed a bit, but nothing compared with the Poms, and no blackout – but it was owing to the celebrations afterwards that I became decided on a career which I had never even thought of before.

The day the first bomb was dropped on Japan, the headmaster kept us back after assembly to explain what an atom bomb was, who'd dropped it and why. And what the consequences might be. Made me feel like I'd like to be a scientist, if I hadn't already had the job of accountant mapped out for me by my old man. It wasn't long, as you know, before the second bomb was dropped, then hotfoot came the news of the Jap surrender and the end of the war. School was closed and everyone was out on the streets shouting their heads off. Yippee! Did we have a ball that night? And it was more than a ball, it was the night I decided to become a policeman.

We were supposed to be back in school by 8 p.m., but me and a couple of fellows played hooky and went for a roll in the park. You'll probably guess I'm just trying to sound blasé, because, Jesus, I was real scared!

I had my baptism that night – girlwise, that is – and we were just slinking down a back street and discussing the best way to get back into the dorm when we saw a scuffle a couple of hundred yards ahead. The next moment there was the sound of breaking glass and something flashed in the dim light. There was a kind of strangled cry and a thud, and the next thing we knew, men were running hell for leather away from the scene of the crime – we were sure they were criminals – and a fourth was left lying in the road.

'Christ, it's a bobby.' One of my cobbers bent down and tried to turn the man over, but he gave such a groan that we were scared to move him.

He was quite unconscious. His cap lay a few yards away and a piece of lead piping lay beside him.

'Don't touch it,' I said – I don't know why I took charge, but I did. 'There might be fingerprints on it.'

'Strewth! Look at this.' There was a pretty lethal-looking knife lying a few yards away. 'That must have been the flash we saw. Lucky it missed him.'

We were all Scouts and, remembering our first-aid classes, felt over the injured man for broken bones. He appeared to be all right, so we moved him to a more comfortable position with his cap under his head and discussed the position *we* were in.

We could hardly leave him there, but we were already into the early hours of the morning and there was going to be hell to pay if we weren't back in school pretty soon. We hadn't reached a decision when the copper came to.

He looked a bit dazed, which wasn't surprising, then, when he'd looked at each of us in turn and presumably noted our youth and school uniform, he put a hand to his head and closed his eyes again.

'I suppose the bastards got away?' he asked. 'Christ, my head feels crook. Did they take much?'

It was only then that we noticed the shattered glass lying on the pavement a few feet away and the broken window of the jeweller's shop.

The window was full of those little velvet-covered stands and we saw at once that one of them was empty. Another had been knocked over and the contents littered the floor behind.

Our bobby was standing up by this time, but not for long. He soon collapsed with another groan and held his stomach.

'Buggers must've kicked me in the guts,' he moaned. 'Can't have been professionals; reckon they just grabbed a handful of stuff then took fright.'

He suddenly passed out again and we decided the only thing to do was to get him to the nearest police station. We took it in turns, two of us making a hand seat while the third supported him from behind. It took us hours – or so it seemed to me – but we got him there at last.

A sergeant was sitting at a desk on the far side of the counter, doing a crossword puzzle. He looked up as we entered, put down the newspaper and stood up.

'Here, what's this? Oh my, where'd you find him?'

We explained briefly while we laid our burden on a bench.

The sergeant felt his pulse, lifted an eyelid and walked back behind the counter.

'First thing is to get a doctor,' he said, 'then we'll have a full account.' He lifted the telephone receiver as he spoke.

We looked at each other; words were unnecessary. Then we dashed, heedless of the sergeant's call for us to wait, and ran until we all had the stitch. The sky was becoming grey as we clambered over the school wall and up the fire escape to our dormitory window.

It was three or four days after our VJ-night lark that our stomachs had cause to sink.

Assembly over, the head told us to wait and beckoned to someone standing at the side of the hall. And who should walk on to the dais but the police sergeant.

Well, you can guess what happened. The only Chinese in the school, there was little point in hoping that I wouldn't be identified, so I came clean and my cobbers followed suit.

When Sergeant Williamson had gone out with the head, our housemaster stepped on to the dais and fixed us with a very beady gaze. He was not as enthusiastic as the police had been and it was only after a session in his study, when we were all feeling that we'd be happy to crawl back under our stones, that he told us that we'd been invited to tea in the police canteen the following Saturday. 'Six o'clock sharp, and don't be late. And now I don't want to hear any more about it.' Neither did we.

Well, that was the beginning of a friendship that was to alter the whole of my life.

Mum and Rosalie were pretty proud of me and it was all I could do to prevent Mum from framing the Commissioner's letter – that had been handed to each of us at the tea party – and hanging it on the wall of her flat. I took Rosalie to see Bill White – that was the bloke who had been clobbered – and once he was out of hospital he asked us round to his home.

'You know, Mum, I wouldn't mind being a policeman,' I told her. I'd been thinking about it ever since we'd lugged Bill into the station that night.

She gave me a funny, sideways look, and said rather tartly, 'That will be for your father to decide, and I am quite sure that is *not* what he has in mind for you.'

Too bloody right!

50. LORD LOUIS ACCEPTS

Jogindar Singh

The date is 12th September, 1945, and this morning Lord Louis Mountbatten, British Commander-in-Chief, accepted the formal surrender of all Japanese forces in South-East Asia and the East Indies.

I say formal, because, in fact, they surrendered last month, only it took the British a little time to arrive.

I cannot state that all my charges are in good order and ready for inspection. Many died but, thanks be to the Great Sahib, many are still alive. Unrecognisable in many cases, but alive nonetheless. Saved by the bomb.

I will never mourn for those families who perished in Hiroshima and Nagasaki; I have seen what they have done to others. Less than six weeks before the bombs were dropped, we had orders to make the prisoners hack a deep cave into the hillside. No easy task for old men at starvation point.

The cave was the first stage. When it was large enough to accommodate all the diggers, the transport of kerosene began. Tin after tin was hauled and placed at strategic points within the cave. And no doubts were left in anyone's mind as to what was the purpose of all this sudden labour.

'The day the first Allied soldier sets foot on Malaya or Singapore will be your last,' they were told.

After suffering so much, you would have thought they would have been apathetic. But not a bit of it. Men, who a year before had felt that the future was so hopeless that to die a quick death would be the best way out, had gained new hope as soon as they heard of the Allied victory in Europe.

Men, whose families had gone to England or Australia, suddenly saw the bright prospect of a reunion they had never expected. I heard men praying that the Allies would not land, that some miracle would save them from that hellish cave.

393

And the miracle *had* saved them.

The prisoners are going now. Going home.

The day the first troops arrived at the prison gates there was silence at first and then such cheering as I have never heard. They brought food and news and some wives were brought over from the women's camp to be reunited with their husbands.

Not all the couples recognised each other, for the women had fared no better than the men and all were thin and barely clad. I saw one of my erstwhile charges embracing an old, white-haired woman and rejoiced in seeing him greet his memsahib. But then he called me over to introduce me – to his daughter.

There was so much emotion in these scenes that, on recounting them to my uncle and aunt, I felt my eyes grow wet and saw the tears shining in their eyes as well. Ai-ee. My aunt wiped her eyes on her head-scarf and we all said a prayer of thanksgiving for our deliverance.

Many of the warders have elected to remain at their posts and guard the Japanese – and even some of their own number who have been denounced.

But not I. I had never intended being a warder. My place, I hope, will be with the police in the future, and I said as much to one of my charges, who I knew was a police officer. He was one of the ones whose testimonials reposed with Arjan Singh.

'Good boy,' he said. 'I'll be back as soon as I'm fit – come and see me then.'

I am writing this in the house of Arjan Singh. The old couple are filled with a new life these days. Both have been promised false teeth by the Medical Department and my aunt is wearing her jewellery again.

Two sons, of whom my uncle never spoke, have come home. Both had been hiding in a remote part of the island throughout the occupation, fed by relatives living in a nearby village. One is eighteen now and the other twenty, and both escaped from labour gangs.

I marvel at Arjan Singh's secretiveness; never even mentioning his sons. 'What you don't know can't harm you,' he said, 'and also cannot be discussed.'

What a wise old bird is my uncle. I shall do well to continue following his counsel in all things.

51. PEACE COMES TO TANJONG MAS

Omar

We had grumbled enough about having to work for the Japanese, but it was better than starvation. At least while we were working there was always a small ration of rice at the end of the day. But one day the lorries did not arrive to take us to work and that evening there was no rice at all. The ration that I received, enough for one person, did not go very far with my large family, but at least it was better than no rice at all. Adohi! What is there worse to hear than the cry of a hungry child?

They did not come the next day, nor the next, and, in fact, we never saw another Japanese.

We thought at first that the lorries had broken down and then perhaps that there was no more work for us for a few days; but a few days grew into weeks and then months and we knew that work was ended. I never dreamed that the day would come when I would wake every morning *hoping* to hear the Japanese, but that is how it was.

Rumours were rife, but where they came from I do not know. We waited and waited and nothing happened.

Perhaps, if we had been in better condition, we might have ventured forth to find out for ourselves. But it is difficult to use either your brain or your limbs when you have fallen into the state of lethargy that long-term hunger produces.

I did not move away from my own house very much, and if I did it was only to see that every other house was the same. People lolling on their steps or verandahs, too tired to take an interest in anything. Nothing moved. Not a cat or dog scraped among the sand, but only the occasional human being.

And so we waited, hoping that something would happen. Anything. We knew that nothing could be worse than seeing the little children dying of starvation and being powerless to prevent it.

When a lorry-load of soldiers did arrive we were almost beyond caring and it did not register with us immediately that they were white instead of yellow. We just stood and looked and I doubt if any of us had any thoughts in our heads at all.

There were two officers with the trucks and about a dozen soldiers. After watching them for some minutes I think what struck me first was not their colour but that they were unarmed. We had grown so used to the sight of Japanese soldiers and their generous use of the rifle butt and bayonet that it seemed strange to see soldiers without any rifles at all.

One of the officers spoke Malay and carried a loudspeaker. Through this he addressed the kampong, telling us first that the war was over and that there was nothing more to fear and, secondly, that the other officer was a doctor who would examine all members of the kampong and issue medicine where necessary.

Many of my people are still not used to Western medicine and as soon as they heard this most of the women and children began to creep away. Remembering how often I had wished that there had been a doctor for Zaitun, I called to the women not to be so foolish.

Quite suddenly the terrible apathy fell away from me and the years of discipline and training came to my aid. I remembered who I was.

I would like to say that I marched smartly up to the officer and saluted, but that would not be true. It is difficult to look smart in a threadbare pair of shorts, patched with pieces from many sarongs and flour-bags, and it had been many months since I had owned any kind of shirt or shoes. I could not have saluted, as I no longer had a songkok or any head covering, and it is quite impossible to march at all when your legs are as swollen with beri-beri as mine were, let alone come to attention. I suppose I waddled over and stood as straight as I could, and at least my voice was still strong.

'428 Corporal Omar reporting, sir.'

There were several other police who had evaded the oath, or were deserters like myself, but I was the senior. It was my duty to take charge.

'Ah, good. Well, Corporal, will you explain that we are only here to help and try and get these people into some sort of line.'

He seemed quite unperturbed by my garb and, to be treated as an NCO again, made me feel I was still a man after all.

My colleagues were quick to follow my example and in no time we had an orderly queue of women, children and old men lined up before the doctor.

He was a very young man, and when I took Zaitun before him I felt too modest to explain what had been the cause of her affliction, especially when the other officer had to interpret. But I think he understood. He shook his head and I felt him to be sympathetic, but the other officer told me that, although a consultation with another doctor would be arranged, he doubted if anything could be done.

The soldiers meanwhile had off-loaded the truck and were busy doling out rice, salt, dried and tinned fish, milk, vitamin tablets, and, most blessed boon of all, cigarettes. When you have smoked grass, palm leaf, and even seaweed for three years, there is nothing more wonderful than that first inhalation of real tobacco.

The lorry came every day for a week, and after the second day the children would wait for it to turn off the main road and follow it, shouting and laughing and catching the bars of chocolate and fruit which the soldiers threw to them. What sound can give more pleasure than the happy laughter of little children?

On the third day a European woman came with the lorry. She wore a grey dress with a red cross on her arm. She was a nurse, but she gave us all clothes; shirts and shorts, sarongs and blankets. The children tore round the kampong, posturing and gesturing and dressing-up, as children love to do. It was like Hari Raya!

At the end of the week the Malay-speaking officer came again and told all of us, police and soldiers, that the next day a truck would collect us, to take us to the Central Police Station, where one of our own officers would interview us.

We were like children returning from the town.

The officer had been in army uniform, but with the police badge in his cap, and was as thin and undernourished as the rest of us. After he had taken down the particulars of each man and we had been photographed, fingerprinted and issued with the rudiments of uniform, we had all met in the police canteen for glasses of coffee.

Men had been brought in from villages all over the state; Malays, Sikhs, Punjabis, and a few Chinese. Wah! So much news to impart, so many stories to listen to. The officer, the only European there, had been a prisoner of war in Singapore and, as he was a bachelor, had volunteered to work for a few weeks before going on leave.

'You'll have to find a wife to feed you up, Tuan,' we told him – we were very bold!

'Your wives don't seem to have done much for you!' he retorted.

Rank and station were put aside. We were sorry when a sergeant came to tell us that we had all been granted fourteen days' leave with pay and now we would be transported back to our kampongs and must report for duty in a fortnight's time.

Wah! Was my wife impressed by the real money I laid on the table. But she laughed at my uniform, hanging on me like one of the dummies we used to place in the padi fields to scare off the birds.

All the children laughed and danced round me – they had energy to spare again these days, Tuan Allah be praised. Only little Zaitun, nearly fifteen now, sat smiling into space while she played with the petals of a moonflower.

Sharif Ahmat

It was the end of the year before we reached our kampong.

We had all suffered from the anticlimax immediately following the surrender. Being keyed up for the invasion for so long, trained and retrained to take part in the fighting and prepared to meet the British and partner them when they arrived, to help them harry the Japs from the peninsula, it was frustrating just to sit and wait. One by one the guerillas quietly faded away. We presumed that they were making for Pahang and Perak, where their colleagues had virtually taken over certain areas and declared their own government. It was an exasperating time all right, those few months between the surrender of the Japs and the British return.

I went down to Singapore with Hassan and the European officers after Lord Mountbatten had accepted the surrender. It was the first time I had been there and I felt a real country bumpkin, marvelling at the city, with its tall buildings and magnificent harbour.

After that we reported to our own headquarters in Kuala Lumpur; then for a long leave.

I cannot, even now, tell you what that homecoming was like without getting a lump in my throat and gooseflesh on my arms. Already there were animals again, cropping the grass that spread below the grove of chempaka trees for which the village is named. The scent wafted towards us and the breeze blew the white flowers down to form a fragrant carpet on the sward. It was beautiful.

But what is there more beautiful, more tender, than a mother's love? I had not seen my mother since that fateful day nearly three years ago and was shocked by her appearance. Always small, she seemed to have shrunk to doll size; the skin hung loosely on a body of skeletal thinness and her hair was streaked with grey.

But her eyes, those huge eyes, which I have seen filled with stern pride, laughter and sorrow. Those eyes, when she perceived her eldest son – he whom she had thought lost for the past five years, he who had been her first-born pride and joy, he who had always treated her with love more than respect – they seemed like great pools of soft brown velvet. Shining with a light of such rare happiness that everyone who had come forward when they saw Hassan and me approaching, turned their own eyes to her and smiled in sympathy.

Gone was my mother's dignified restraint. With a cry like a young girl, she dropped whatever it was she had been holding and flew to Hassan like a homing bird.

My brother is tall, taller than me, and he lifted her like a child;

398

patting and hugging her as one does a child. I saw her tears overflow and wet the shoulder of his shirt and watched as he pulled a handkerchief from his pocket and wiped those tears away.

Women went flying in every direction to prepare a meal; men pressed forward to ask question after question, and the children stood and gaped, fingers to mouths and eyes wide.

The terrible reprisals of 1943 had been accepted as part of the fortunes, or evils, of war, and my sister's wedding day became just one of many occupation memories, to be talked of, put aside and resurrected as the conversation ebbed and flowed in its endless circle.

Hassan was to march in the Victory Parade in London and he now became not only my mother's pride, but that of the entire kampong.

They were happy months, those of early 1946. For my mother, the first happiness after three years of sorrow, and for us, her ambitious sons, a new beginning.

53. BETTER LATE THAN NEVER

Jogindar Singh

I waited until the end of the year in Singapore. Long enough to terminate my employment with the prison and to be on the spot for news of my family. But when, after three months, no one had contacted my uncle, I set off for Kuala Lumpur.

I had never been to the Police Depot before, although I had often heard my father speak of it. It seemed that wherever one looked there were barrack blocks, offices, parade grounds, MT yards, games fields and officers' quarters. It was huge. People were everywhere and I felt that there must be someone here who would at least have known my father at one time, if not the present whereabouts of his dependants.

During the course of the day, I spoke to a Sikh officer, ASP Ram Singh, who had, I had been told, spent most of the war as an inspector in Batu Rimau, which was where my mother's family had lived. He could not help me as far as my family were concerned, but he did suggest that, if I intended enlisting, I should do so without delay, and certainly before I went north to make further inquiries.

'When so many men are enlisting or returning to the Force,' he advised, 'even a few weeks may make a great deal of difference to your seniority in the long run.'

I took his advice and, to my surprise, when I returned the next morning with my completed application forms, I was told that the Adjutant wanted to see me.

I was even more surprised when he shook hands and told me to sit down.

The Adjutant was a European ASP who had spent the war in the army and had only recently returned to Malaya – he told me this during the course of our conversation, but mostly it was about myself.

'We've been expecting you to appear,' he told me, 'and I gave orders that you were to be sent in to me when you did.'

I was not kept waiting long for an explanation. He pulled open a drawer and extracted a file of letters and soon had one smoothed out in front of him. It was one of those blue air mail sheets and I could see that it had an English stamp on it.

By this time I already had out my own letters – the ones that had been given to me in the prison more than a year before. I put them on the desk tentatively and the Adjutant looked up.

'What are those?' he asked.

I explained.

'Ah,' he leafed through them until he came to a name, Boswell, then he tapped the letter before him. 'One of the Assistant Commissioners, Mr Boswell, whom you knew in internment, had hoped to be back by this time, but he's not fit yet – if he ever will be – so he's written out a list, both black and white, of personalities with police connections with whom he came into contact during the war. I'm afraid that on the whole your compatriots did not show up too well, but there is a short list of praise-earners. I am pleased to say that your name is on it.'

We talked for a little longer while the Adjutant read through my testimonials; then he handed them back and got up.

'The Force is proud of men like your father and yourself,' he said. 'I wish you the best of luck in your future career.'

He shook hands again and I was soon back with ASP Ram Singh, completing formalities. My next move was northwards to Perak, and I spent several weeks going from place to place, following rumours and advice, in search of my family. But I never did discover what had happened to them, and now I suppose I never shall.

It was pointless to delay my training any longer, and when the next intake was admitted to the Depot, I was with them. I should have been a recruit five years ago; still, as my uncle says, better late than never.

54. AN IDYLL REPAIRED

James Weatherby

It was a wonderful day when James was finally able to leave the hospital. Wonderful for the staff too, I should think – it had been difficult enough for me, visiting him, but how they kept their tempers I shall never know. The Matron informed me that in all her years of nursing, she had never come across such an impossible man – she said it in front of him though and with a twinkle in her eyes, so I felt there was hope.

We were married very quietly early in the new year, just a year after his last flight. But I didn't marry an Air Commodore. James was bitter, and it was no use explaining to him that his prang had had nothing to do with it, it was just the end of the war. He didn't want to believe anything good at that time, and when Substantive Wing Commander, War Substantive Group Captain, Acting Air Commodore Weatherby left the hospital as plain Wing Commander, he could hardly bear to put on his uniform.

I suppose you can guess where we spent our wedding night? Yes, we went to the pub where we'd had that silly row. At first I had not been keen, afraid that it would fall flat, but I was wrong, thank God.

I'm not sure that the receptionist recognised him until he signed his name – and even that looked different now, signed with the other hand – but when she looked up he was waving our marriage certificate under her nose and there, for the first time in a year, was that old, wonderful, white grin.

'Married at last,' he told all and sundry, 'and if I still had two arms I'd carry her over the threshold – lump though she may be!'

I found it difficult not to cry. All the emotion that had been pent up for so long threatened to overflow. I said nothing; just looked at him, and I saw the old James shining through and knew that it would be all right. I took his arm and led him towards the stairs.

I wore the same dress too, but it was a shock, looking in the mirror, to see how much I had aged in only a year. I was only twenty-eight and James was under thirty still, but we both had grey in our hair. I had to fasten my own pearls this time and I saw him frown and bite his lip, but I did my best to pass it off.

I did not take a bag down to dinner that night.

I had met James's parents on several occasions, and knowing how they would love to have him at home for a time, I had suggested that we spent his leave there. A honeymoon could come later, I thought, and so did he.

401

We spent two days at our pub, then travelled down to Devon by train. Poor lamb; I watched him as he slept, head jolting with the motion of the carriage. I would have to forgive his tempers, I knew. It wasn't only losing his eye and his arm. He did not regret losing his wife, but he had also lost his son – Elsie claimed custody of the child and he did not contest it – but I knew he loved the little boy. It would be up to me to make up for some of the unhappiness he had had, to ease his loss and help him in his still so longed-for career.

It was six years since I had first taken Elsie home as my wife and four since I had first met Helen. We had been over storm-tossed seas. But when I looked at my adored wife, helping my adored mother, and as happy in the company of Nannie and my father as they were with her, for the first time in my adult life I didn't care a damn if I never saw the air force again.

We had three months with my parents and when, at the end of the second month, Helen felt sick one morning and told me she was pregnant, I slid down the banisters and shouted the glad tidings for all to hear.

'You'll come and look after us, won't you, Nannie?' I sang, and waltzed her round the kitchen, frying pan in hand. She pushed me away and carried on cooking the breakfast.

'She hasn't had it yet,' she said dryly, but I could see she was as pleased as I.

I groaned when my posting came through though. Air Ministry. Oh well, I suppose I could expect pen-pushing from now on. But AM, oh Gawd.

'Ever hear of a General who hadn't done a spell in War Office?' Helen asked, and my father backed her up. 'Well, be thankful they haven't thrown you out.'

She could be tart, my spouse.

Once our destination was known, Helen went off to London – which she knew far better than I – to house-hunt. She had luck too and rang me up the next evening with her news. She'd found a flat in Richmond – I nearly had a heart attack when I heard the rent, but I told her to take it just the same. A year of incarceration had not been hard on my bank balance and, after all, we weren't too badly off.

She came back, tired and hungry and full of plans. She talked while the three of us sat and listened, and my mother put an arm round her and told me that it would be worth losing both arms to gain a wife like her, but not both eyes. I agreed.

Taken by and large, I was, for the first time in many years, a very happy man.

Our daughter, Angela, was born in the winter of that year, 1946. Poor

Helen, it was the coldest winter in our memory and I fretted the whole way to the hospital, terrified that we would be stopped by snow.

I was glad it, she, was a girl. I had no desire ever to see Elsie again, but I did miss my son. But for all Elsie's faults, she had been a good mum, and it didn't seem right to upset the boy, so I made no attempt to see him.

I wanted another son, one day, but for the present I was glad to be able to love the tiny thing without feeling that I had abandoned Toby. And Helen? Helen wanted what I wanted. It was not selfishness on my part, we just wanted the same things. Helen is a wonderful wife.

55. WEALTHY AND NOTABLE LOVER GENTLEMAN

Ramakrishnan

It is for long time that I am lying low after re-entry of most hated British. I am glad when Bengali police chief is having transfer to more salubrious post, for who knows what this prideful fellow might pass on in way of informations, false or true?

Truly I am most disillusioned man; disappointed in behaviour of would-be Nipponese saviours and fellow-countrymen both. Everybody is welcoming back British pigs and forgetting state of slavery endured hithertofore. Mr Ramasamy, no relation, is forever rubbing fat hands and pronouncing satisfaction at future prospects when all white peoples are returning, gentlemen and ladies both, to do deals with him in silk store, and already new stocks are being received from countries far and near.

It is eleven months precisely that I am working for Mr Ramasamy, no relation, when said gentleman indicates ripe daughter Devi and again makes mention of fact that loyal workers can be expecting rewards.

When before I am holding trumping card, I am thinking it is because husbands of Tamil race are between few and far in district. But in new Colonial era this is no longer so. Many Indians of diverse races and dialects are travelling country length and breadth, so I am knowing that there is other reason afoot.

Aha! I am saying to myself one day after much careful watching and observation both. 'Mister,' I am saying, 'I am after knowing full well why it is that husband is required for Miss Devi. For it is very plain that she is big in belly.'

At that, said gentleman goes most ashen colour and wrings hands in supplication most humble, denying all such happenings and maintaining that Miss Devi is virgin most pure and unsoiled.

I am waiting for two weeks over when Mr Boss Ramasamy, no relation, is relating at last truthful and sordid facts regarding daughters.

'It is true,' he is telling me, 'that Devi is with child, and second daughter also. It is most shaming thing to happen to daughters who have become, alas, overripe. I will raise wages of you and Devan both if you will marry my daughters before their time.'

Devan is assistant next senior to self.

'I will be clerk,' I say.

'Very well, man. Clerk it is.'

For new status I am demanding three pairs each white drill trousers, three shirts of silk, and socks of various colourings. Also desk in back but prominent part of store, with pile of ledgers and trays for innings and outings.

'I have fulfilled my part of the bargain,' Mr Ramasamy, not yet relation, is saying after one more month, 'you are now clerk, with desk and ledgers and much face. What more do you want before marriage takes place?'

For reply I am asking, 'And what colour will child be, man?' Yellow, I am thinking.

'Oh no,' said gentleman is wringing hands, 'Nipponese had already left before. Child is black, man. Of that there is no doubt.'

And when I am not believing that such opinions can be proven, Mr Ramasamy, not yet relation, is telling me story most long-winded and specious.

'Father is married man,' he is saying, 'most distinguished and wealthy notable of own race. Only I am not having daughter taken as second wife or concubine. For that reason only I am wishing husbands for daughters both.'

If he is wealthy man, I am thinking, I can demand funds whatever, and am putting said proposition before Mr Ramasamy, boss.

He is wringing hands again and rolling eyes every which ways.

'He must not know that I have told you,' he says, 'he is most proud and haughty fellow. But I will raise wages by further five dollars *per mensum* and will recoup from this gentleman in due course.'

'Twenty dollars.'

'My God, man. Are you for bleeding me dry?'

'If he is wealthy man, you can ask favours for allowing fornication with said daughters,' I am saying.

'All right. Twenty dollars. But he will be angry, mind. And now will you give a date?'

'I am thinking about it,' I say.

Truly I am holding trumping card.

But that is now more than four months back and I am rich man now. How I am becoming rich man I will relate as follows:

I have been clerk for one month when door of most inglorious happenings is opened to me.

Every afternoon for as long as I have been undertaking lowly employment in silk store, I am seeing Devi or other of ripe daughters entering shed at far ending of orchard field.

Aha! I am thinking, this is where they are trysting with wealthy and notable lover gentleman. If I am recognising him, fifty dollars, or even one hundred and fifty, will not be too much rising in wages.

Also, sometimes I am seeing Mr Ramasamy, no relation, entering same hut and I am betting that he is receiving fat payments from wealthy lover gentleman. Truly he is man of many diverse leanings; silk store owner, cattle man, market gardener, and pimp both.

I am watching for several afternoons between two and four o'clock precisely from behind cattle shed. I am seeing Miss Devi and two sisters approach orchard shed and also Mr Ramasamy, no relation, but no lover gentleman. All are going higgledy-piggledy, at different times, towards shed and verily my head is being buzzed and muddling by all these comings and goings.

Next morning I am approaching said shed myself.

It is only small shed with sleeping platform taking up half of space, with bolsters and mats. Over high window above platform is pulled old faded sarong on strand of wire.

On instant I am having most clarified idea. I am standing on platform and drawing curtain to give inch of view to one side. Window is next to tree and concealment in foliage therefore is easy task. I can be peeping tom and, once recognition of wealthy lover gentleman has taken place, blackmail is forever possible.

Next afternoon I am already hiding in tree when Devi is coming to shed. Without ados she is taking off all garments and prostrating herself on sleeping mat. Truly I am finding it hard to remain in tree.

Miss Devi is of rounded proportions most goodly and of skin lighter in colour than Muriani, who was field worker and not spoilt daughter of most bountiful father and plaything of wealthy and notable lover gentleman.

I am still enjoying view of future bride when door is opening to admit white garbed gentleman, and Miss Devi is already rolling eyes, wriggling and giggling. Man, it is being difficult exceeding to remain in tree under such circumstances.

Gentleman is remaining with back turned – and why for should he look at wall or window when there is spectacle on sleeping mat most goodly to behold? I can see from motionings that he is lifting dhoti, then he too is prostrating himself and lifts head for me to see face first time.

Goodness gracious me! This is moment I am waiting for and indeed shock is being so great that I am tumbling topsy-turvy, upside down, and hugger-mugger from leafy bower and hitting head with most uncomfortable knock against roots of tree. Truly this Mr Ramasamy is of personality most wily and vexatious.

It is not taking me long to reach conclusion that only with observance most patient and catching of Mr Ramasamy in position of undeniable guilt can blackmail be maintained to fullest extent. And so I must be biding time for ripe moment.

I am taking up position on following afternoon in foliage most luxurious and concealing. But this time I am carrying notebook in which to record all details for future confrontation of Mr Ramasamy, no relation.

This afternoon, performance is with second daughter and I am pleased to note that shape and skin are of lesser quality than that of Miss Devi, having less shine and showing bony structures, which are not made for comfort and joy both.

Every afternoon I am peeping. Verily Mr Ramasamy's actions with Miss Devi are filling me with disgust most horrible and vile. I am hardly able to watch; and so I am going again to see next day and next.

After six days my notebook is nearly full of revolting details and at moment of conclusion I am breaking glass of window, shouting rightful abuse and waving notebook at Mr Ramasamy, no relation.

'Oh, perpetrator of most dastardly crime,' I am shouting, 'pimp most incestuously inclined and filthy swine both. I have seen and recorded every vile act of impurification. I am telling you, Mister, you are tossing on troublesome seas forthwith.'

Aha! Indeed I have caught rogue most red-handed and he is turning colour of greenish grey, like shed skin of grass snake or old cattle manure both. He is blubbering and wailing so that I cannot make out actual words.

'You had better see me in office, Mister,' I shout, and leave him in state of botheration most extreme.

When he is arriving at store, Mr Ramasamy is not being so flustered, but still very agitated man. There is no need to mention terms, because said future father-in-law is mentioning them for me.

'I can get you good job as estate clerk on Tanah Kuning Estate, where Chief Clerk is friend and brother,' he says, 'and I will pay you so much *per mensum* for the rest of my life if you will marry Devi now and take her away from here.'

'And what sum will you be paying each month?' I ask, striking the hot iron.

'Fifty dollars.'

'One hundred.'

'Seventy-five.'

'One hundred.'

'Eighty.'

406

'One hundred dollars,' I say, 'and that is final, Mister. One hundred dollars *per mensum*, each and all properties to be bequeathed in will and testament at time of death.'

Mr Ramasamy, future father-in-law, groans and is saying I am hard man and I am telling him that he is incestuous bastard and reminding that at present time only future son-in-law has knowledge of such acts.

So it is coming to pass that I am taking Miss Devi, daughter of Ramasamy, to wife and am taking up abode and most congenial position as clerk on Tanah Kuning Estate. With father-in-law Ramasamy's cash arriving each month on dot and wage more dignified than hitherto received, yours truly is beginning to find world less disillusioned place.

My wife is giving birth one month precisely after marriage. But child is of sickly disposition and within three months is succumbing to enteritis, with much vomiting and purging. I am not minding and have already made sure that wife's belly is large once more. No more chances are being taken and making sure that belly is full always is most efficacious method of preventing bastards arising therefrom. Also Devi is most rounded and goodly to look upon when pregnant, and it is therefore all round most congenial proceeding.

56. THE REUNION

Abdul Karim

It was several weeks after the war ended that the news seeped through to Pasir Perak. We had seen very little of the Japs, so it made little difference to us at first.

Then one day Inche Yacob, our headmaster, made the announcement to the whole school and declared a holiday. 'Not that your parents will bless me,' he said. He was always saying things like that!

Of course, the first thing my father did was to uncover his boat from where it had been hidden under the passion fruit vine for so long. Wah! What a state it was in. But we soon got to work and it wasn't long before he was off to sea again and we had as much fish to eat as we wanted for, of course, the seas were teeming, not having been fished for so long.

But it's August 1946 now and that was nearly a year ago. Nothing much happened in the kampong, except, of course, that there was food in the shops again, and cloth and tools. As far as I was concerned I still went to school every day and played with my friends or helped Pak in the afternoons. But the day I want to tell you about was when I was on holiday and he had agreed to take me, with Rokiah and

Noraini and Musah – my classmate, whom I disliked, but my father thought smart – on a turtle-egg collecting expedition. We do this sometimes during the holidays and usually stay out all night.

Pak was in a very good mood on that occasion and made jokes about Noraini's white face showing up in the moonlight and how we would have to blacken it first with the embers from the fire!

Noraini can be quite cheeky and told my father that, if he wanted his meal, he would have to be nice to her – imagine a real Malay girl saying that! Mak says there are some things which are in the blood and can never be changed and I'm beginning to think she's right.

We all collected driftwood for the fire, then the two girls prepared the meal, fresh fish which we had caught with our casting nets in the shallow water.

Every so often we would walk along the beach to see how the turtles were getting on, but you can't hurry a turtle, so we were able to enjoy our meal with plenty of time.

What better food is there than that caught fresh and eaten fresh from your own fire on the beach on a cool night? I hoped everything would go well and Pak would take us out again. It was more fun when we had the girls to cook for us than when we went out on our own.

Our turtles are protected. That means that they cannot be killed for meat, and during the mating season certain parts of the beach are reserved and no one is allowed to disturb them. Several of the turtles we watched that evening were over five feet long and nearly as wide. Wah! I'm sure that's where the idea of tanks came from!

They crawl slowly, slowly out of the sea, the tide touching them less and less each time, until they are on the sand, then they stop and rest for a while – it always seems ages to me.

Then comes the long passage up the beach. Adohi! They move so slowly that I would like to give one a good kick, but Pak says I would only break my toes. They groan and grunt as they heave their lumbering great bodies up the beach, leaving two tracks behind them, exactly like those I've seen in pictures of where tanks have been – you see, I was right. I don't know how much they weigh, but it must be a great effort to heave all that armour plating across the sand.

At last the turtle reaches what she considers a good spot to lay her eggs, then we're in for another long wait. Eventually she begins to dig – and you should see the sand fly when those flippers get to work. This is when we must start watching carefully, because once she's finished laying she will cover her eggs up and we may not be able to find them again.

There is a deep, deep hole, four feet or more, before the turtle is satisfied, then she places herself over it and begins to lay. Plop, pause, plop, pause. The eggs that look so like ping-pong balls fall into the hole.

We spread out and took one turtle each to watch. I must admit I grew a little bored – keeping still for so long is not much fun and Pak would have been furious if we had disturbed them.

When my turtle had finished laying and covered up her eggs, I marked the spot with a cairn of coconut husks and went back to the fire.

Noraini was already there, wide-eyed and bubbling with excitement. It was the first time she had seen the giant turtles so close to.

'When I grow up, I'm going to marry a turtle fisherman,' she announced, 'then I'll make him take me with him every time. I'd never get bored.'

'I would. I'm not going to be a turtle fisherman. It's all right going with Pak, for fun.'

The first green streaks of dawn were appearing in the sky and I was cold.

'Let us fetch more wood,' I suggested, 'and remake the fire.'

By the time it was really light, all the turtles had returned to the sea and it was easy to go back to the marked spots and dig up the eggs. The law only allowed us to take a certain number of eggs – the rest have to be allowed to hatch out – so when we had taken our lot, we covered each hole over again and smoothed the sand.

We had come some way from the kampong, so into the boat went the sacks of eggs, followed by us. Pak started up the outboard and we chugged home, tired and pleased with ourselves.

But our adventures were not over for the day.

Pak had counted the eggs, put some aside for sale and a number to keep ourselves, then the rest he had divided into two smaller sacks for Che Fatimah.

As we entered her garden, Pak and I, each with a sack over our shoulders, and Rokiah and Noraini walking just ahead, a voice called out, 'Hold it,' and there was the click of a camera.

We were all so surprised that none of us moved until Rokiah's mother and aunt came forward to greet us.

Two smiling, young Chinese came forward as well, both in white drill slacks and long-sleeved shirts and ties – I'd never seen anyone wearing a tie in our kampong before.

Both men wore gold wrist watches and pulled out packets of cigarettes, which they offered to my father. One of them had a camera slung round his neck from a leather strap and the other carried an open notebook and several propelling pencils of different colours in his shirt pocket.

'And what's your name, little girl?' The one with the notebook asked Noraini in English.

She just shook her head and giggled behind her hand.

After that they stuck to Malay, asking both Noraini and Che Fatimah question after question.

Che Fatimah repeated the story we had heard so often, then they asked Noraini how she liked school and a lot of other things which did not seem to have anything to do with having a white skin and freckles. Then they asked Rokiah and me some questions too.

They took some more photographs then; not of Pak and me, but of Che Fatimah and the two girls. My deadly hatred, Musah, had arrived and in the last picture he was standing between Rokiah and Noraini, holding a hand of each. He spoke to the reporters in their own dialect and looked so superior that I dug my nails into my palms with rage.

Just then four Europeans walked into the garden; three men and a woman. Two of the men, one of whom was a police officer, I had seen before, but the others were strangers. The woman had coppery-coloured hair, streaked with grey, and she walked slowly, with a funny look on her face, happy and worried at the same time, sort of excited, but scared.

I looked at Noraini then and my mouth fell open. I wished I had been listening, but I had heard Che Fatimah's story so many times that my mind had wandered. Pak told me afterwards that the Europeans – Noraini's parents, of course – had arrived much earlier and had gone for a walk while they were waiting.

By this time quite a crowd had gathered. Someone motioned the reporters to step aside and the woman advanced towards Noraini. No one else moved and the only sound was the surf frothing on the beach and the clack-clack of the palm fronds in the breeze. She went down on one knee before Noraini and put her arms round her waist. Noraini just stared. Then her mother leaned her forehead against her daughter's – she was a tall woman and Noraini is very small – and I saw tears falling on the sand between them. The heads matched.

A sigh went up from the crowd and Che Fatimah began to cry. Then the woman's husband lifted her up and stood with an arm around each pair of shoulders. The camera clicked again.

Poor Che Fatimah. Noraini has gone. Not at once; her parents visited her every day for a few days, to let her get used to them, then they took her away. Che Fatimah has a big sum of money now and a handsome coffee service, but she says it is not the same. I think Rokiah is lonely too.

Che Fatimah had not been too happy about the interviews with the reporters – whose paper was taking much of the credit for finding Noraini – but when she received a complimentary copy of the Malay edition of the newspaper, she swelled with pride.

Rokiah came running to our house with the paper for Pak to read. There we were, right on the front page, Pak and I looking like a couple of surprised monkeys, with our shoulders bent under the sacks, and the two girls, hand-in-hand, and all of us gaping wide mouthed.

'Wah!' said my father, 'it certainly looks as though Che Fatimah has a couple of village idiots for friends!'

'HUNT ENDS IN REMOTE EAST COAST KAMPONG' were the headlines.

Underneath, in slightly smaller letters: 'Malay woman defends European child against Japs.'

And below that: 'Thou good and faithful servant, well done.'

And then in ordinary print, first how the parents had spent a year trying to trace their daughter, then Che Fatimah's story – only it didn't sound quite the same as when she told it. Noraini seemed to have gone through a far more adventurous time once she had reached Pasir Perak than we had realised.

'Wah!' exclaimed my mother, listening as Pak read the article aloud, 'I didn't know that the Japanese had been here, and in and out of our houses, so often. And fancy never suspecting that Noraini had spent all those hours hidden up trees and under the floorboards!'

Of course Mak believes everything that is printed and my father got quite cross with her, calling her a stupid, ignorant woman, who could be taken in by fairy-tales just like the rest of them.

The whole article painted the courage and loyalty of Che Fatimah in such glowing terms that she was too pleased to deny some of the silly things that were said.

57. STRANGERS IN UNIFORM

Philip Morrison

Have you ever been afraid to meet your wife? It was ridiculous. I had moved heaven and earth to get myself posted home or to get Sally out and, now that the train was actually stopping and a porter was walking down the platform, calling, 'Victoria, Victoria,' I was terrified.

Of course, I had been stupid to stay on in Italy in the first place. When the Germans finally had capitulated and we had walked out to meet our own troops, I could have gone. But like a mug I had volunteered to stay on – mainly because I wanted to make sure that the Scum were not badly done by and to follow up on the notes I had left with the various people who had helped me escape. And then, of course, I was caught.

I had nothing to prove that I was married, and Sally – who can be extremely obstinate – would not send the certificate. She still has that bee in her bonnet that it will pay us in the long run to keep our marriage quiet until it suits us. You can't argue with her. She couldn't have got a posting to Italy anyway, because she's dug in in some Far East intelligence job, and she couldn't join me as my wife because she wouldn't admit to being one.

But that was past history now. I had left, and all the way through Europe on the MEDLOC train I had been filled with alternate waves of excitement at the thought of seeing her again and a terrible hope that perhaps she had not been able to get leave. And here we were.

Standing on the boat-train platform, waiting for Philip, I shivered. Partly because of the draught which always whistles round one's legs on railway stations and partly with apprehension. It was so long – more than eighteen months.

The train was late and I searched vainly for him as the carriages disgorged their load of khaki, and dark and light blue. Boots and gaiters swung past, kit-bags at ear level, subalterns and red hats, some scruffy erks, a couple of ATS.

And suddenly we were facing each other, puzzled, nervous and ill at ease. For an awful instant I panicked. Was this stranger the man I was married to? This madly good-looking creature in tartan trews and glengarry, peering down at me? 'Philip?' I asked.

And then his arms were round me and my cap went flying and I started to cry. Great dry sobs that I couldn't control. It was all so silly. I was cross with myself and cross with him for surprising me so. And yet it was all wonderful and he was here. With me. In the flesh.

I took his arm and hugged it, 'I'll never let you go,' I said.

I hadn't recognised her at first. And then, of course, it occurred to me that, although I knew she would be in uniform, I had visualised her in battledress, trousers tucked into boots and hatless – as she had been when I had seen her for the first time. I wasn't expecting the small figure in neat SD.

Poor little thing. She looked like a rabbit transfixed by a stoat. Was I that bad? I had travelled in battledress, keeping my best jacket and trews and Sam Browne to change into when we reached Dover, but perhaps it would have been better if I had changed into a pullover and a pair of old corduroys. I bent down and wrapped her in my arms.

We spent a wonderful evening – eating at an Italian restaurant, naturally. I shouldn't think the food was much good, but the waiters made a great fuss of us. Having commented on our good Italian, they asked us where we learned it, and when they heard – well! Dinner was on the house and out came bottles of wine vastly superior to those being imbibed by our neighbours. It was all great fun.

I had nothing very much to tell Philip – life had been intensely dull – but I was avid for his news. He had been to Gianna Maria's wedding and Tom had been there – he had been accepted back into his own army after all and was doing a liaison job with the British in Trieste – but there was no news of the Scum. Dougal had left the army apparently and just disappeared. Still, that is what we would both have expected of him.

We were the last to leave the restaurant, bowed off the premises with great éclat and promises to return. And so to bed.

Quite suddenly the months of separation and frustration slid away and we were back on the pine-needles, looking at the stars. Marrying as we had done could have been so wrong, such a tragedy – but for us it was going to be right and we both knew it. It was wonderful to enjoy a man so much and to know that he belonged to me, wonderful to know that we had made no mistake. Perhaps, because we both knew that under different circumstances we might have been different people, with little in common, but tied, and, as things had worked out, found ourselves happy to be tied, our union was that much stronger than it would have been had we met and married in a more normal way.

It seemed no time before the telephone rang and a voice reminded us that we had asked for an early call. Philip stretched and held out his arms and I went into them for a last five minutes' warmth, and lying there, looking at the light in his eyes, I knew that I was as much to him as he was to me. So much luck, so much happiness, seemed too fragile to hold.

My reception at the Depot was much as I had expected. The second battalion was about to go into suspended animation, I was told by the Adj, and I would be posted to the first. It was going to be hard, un-learning all that I had learned during the past few years and starting from scratch again. I said as much as he handed me my ration card and railway warrant. But he merely shrugged, 'You're not the only one – chaps like you coming in every day.'

With two weekends conveniently placed, Sally had managed to get twenty-one days' leave.

We spent a few days in Inverness and a few days farther north, idling in the glory of the autumn gold. I remember once in Italy, on a really beautiful day in the mountains, that I said I would not exchange it for the Highlands in the autumn and I had been right. It was cold, but, as we ate a picnic lunch, sitting on a rug spread on the grass of a meadow on the Black Isle and gazed over the deep blue inlet, with the purple heather and bracken on the turn stretching as far as the eye could see, it was the nearest we had been to our days with the group.

Then west to my home. I had had no qualms as far as taking Sally to meet my mother was concerned, because I was pretty sure that they would like each other. In fact, they had a lot in common and I soon realised that, in my mother's eyes, Sally could do no wrong. They talked about the East and the war, and Mama was genuinely upset when I told her that Sally wouldn't come to her when she heard that her father had died. Bravery was, in her opinion, the greatest virtue, and when I recounted a little of Sally's past, I could see the admiration positively shining from her eyes.

But our leave went fast and soon it was time for me to put Sally on the southbound train. I wanted to ask permission and then get married again, but she has a stubborn streak – as I already knew, only too well – and flatly refused to bow down to service etiquette.

'If your colonel would really hold our marriage against you – and I doubt if he would – then, frankly, I think you'd be better out of the battalion. Out of the army for that matter.' And that was all she would say.

If only she had not had that fixation about staying in the air force and following me around, I could have come clean in the first place and no complications would have existed. I felt it was her fault and that the least she could do was to stop being so bloody-minded and let me do it my way. Would it really upset her pride so much to ask permission to get married? Pig-headed little so-and-so. It was the cause of our first row – but not the last.

Eventually we agreed to compromise. If we were to remain at the Depot for long, Sally would try and get a posting north and, when I thought the time was ripe, I would announce the fact that I was a married man and produce my wife. Meanwhile we would let things slide; she had already been promised Christmas leave and it was not so far off.

'Coldest winter for more than a hundred years,' the headline of the newspaper on the seat beside me told us. But I didn't need to see it in print. We dawdled north on the so-called *Flying Scot* and never had I been so frozen in my life.

I tried to knit, but spent more time sitting on my hands than using them to hold the needles. It was nearly Christmas and I was in a hurry to get it done. I finished the baby's vest and started on a boot and an old lady sitting opposite smiled knowingly. I smiled back, but it wasn't my baby that I was knitting for, but Gianna Maria's, due at any time.

Philip was to meet me at Edinburgh, where we were to have a couple of days on our own before going north to spend Christmas with his mother. I looked forward to a shopping spree because, besides other things, I was desperately short of clothes and, if we were to stay in hotels and I was going to continue knitting Gianna's baby clothes, I really thought it time I had a wedding ring. Uniform had become second nature, but the war was over now and I couldn't live in slacks and jerseys – the only things I had needed on the only leave I had taken before Philip's return. I had gone to Ireland then to stay with Mary O'Connell – a widow for three years now – who lived on the outskirts of Dublin with her father and small son. Thinking of her made me realise once again how lucky we were.

Waverley Station arrived at last and there was Philip, pacing up and down the platform in kilt and SD jacket, not even a greatcoat. Scotland might be cold, he informed me, but nothing to three winters in the mountains of Piemonte – as if I didn't know.

He took my arm and hustled me out of the station, and I could sense at once that he was bubbling over with excitement. We were hardly out of the place before he enlightened me.

'Sally, I take it all back, all the things I said when we had that row last leave. You wrote once, when I was still in Naples, to say that you could get yourself posted to Hong Kong or Singapore, but not to Italy – does that still hold good?'

'I suppose so,' I said. 'I haven't tried.' He had caught me completely unawares. 'Why?'

'Because rumours are rife that the battalion will soon be on the move and everything points to it being the Far East. At the beginning, at any rate, we gather there will be no wives. If you could get anywhere out there it would be better than here.'

'I'll see when I get back,' I said, 'but now I'm on leave. And there's something you haven't noticed.' I jerked my shoulder with its stiff epaulette against him – we were sitting in a taxi by then.

'Good God. Same rank as me – I can't allow that!'

I had recently been promoted to Flight Officer, but kept it as a surprise.

'You're still too young to draw marriage allowance,' I pointed out, 'if we're living out, somewhere in the East, you'll be glad of the extra pay.' At that moment I had no idea what a profound truth I had just uttered.

Mrs Morrison was sweet. It was no hardship for me to spend Christmas with my mother-in-law. Just one more stroke of luck. There was a tiny parcel for me at the top of the Christmas tree and I knew it was from her by the way she watched me undo it, although the donor was not named. I could see her pleasure in my pleasure.

It was an old-fashioned ring, an emerald, square-cut, and surrounded with tiny diamonds.

I just kissed her. I couldn't put my thanks into words. Not only for the ring, but for the way she had accepted me, the clandestine wife of her only remaining son. Philip had told me of the tragedy of his family, how she had lost them, one by one, and although he said she moaned, she had not moaned with me.

I suppose that things do even out and that after all the frustrations while Philip was still in Italy, we did deserve our luck.

'What chance of a posting to the Far East?' I asked the Wing Commander on my return from leave.

'Good, I should think,' he said. 'There's nearly always a man who doesn't want to go and both units are short-staffed just now. Why? Do you want one?'

'I'm not sure yet,' I told him. But not for long. Within forty-eight hours Philip was on the phone.

'Sally,' he yelled, and I could only just hear him over the dreadful line, 'get cracking on that posting. Singapore. We're being sent to Malaya. I'll write.'

I sent a wire to him the next day and went off to buy my tropical kit.

58. THE WAR IS OVER

Sharif Ahmat

Assembling for the Inspectors' Training Course was not unlike being a recruit again. We all arrived at the Depot the evening before the course was due to commence and were allocated beds in a long, concrete barrack block.

There were already half a dozen or so candidates unpacking when I arrived, and imagine my chagrin and surprise when I found one of them to be Hasbullah.

I had not given him a thought since the night I evaded the Japs and joined Hassan.

A feeling, which I can only describe as a mixture of disgust and frustration, swept over me. To think that, Jap toady and collaborator as he had been, he still held the same potential future in the Force as I.

It was the same old Hasbullah. If I hadn't known him so well I might have been taken in by that wide smile and outstretched hand.

'Well, Mat. I haven't seen you for ages. How did things go after you left us so suddenly?'

I ignored the hand. My thoughts flew to my mother and how her face reflected the suffering she had endured. So many dead and maimed. What was the point of fighting, if people like Hasbullah were still to be on top at the end of it all?

I fingered the puckered scar above my elbow and looked him straight in the eye.

'This was caused by a Jap bullet and is the very least of the wounds my family has to show.'

Well. I had to hand it to him. He didn't blink an eyelid, but smiled the smile of a tolerant schoolteacher when one of his dimmer pupils is being fractious.

'As you say, it was a Jap bullet.'

'But the Japs were led by a Malay.'

'Oh, come off it, Mat. I was on duty that night; I couldn't avoid taking them round.'

'And yet you led them to me.'

Hasbullah sighed, a sigh of patience nearly exhausted, but I could see the smile muscles were becoming taut – and I was glad.

'Is it my fault that, just because the door opens, you leap from your bed and scramble through the window like a mad thing? Be reasonable. You can't really blame the Japs for shooting – talk about behaving in a suspicious manner. . . .'

'And if I had stayed quietly in bed?'

'They'd have carried on to the next hut. It was purely a routine inspection.'

'A likely story.'

'Come on, Mat. The war's over. If I ever gave you cause to doubt my integrity, I'm sorry. Shake hands, man. You know I hated the yellow bellies as much as you did.'

I said nothing, because I was finding it difficult to control my temper. But I pointedly put myself into the at-ease position and clasped my hands firmly behind my back.

Hasbullah's smile faded at the slight and I was aware of one of those moments when time seems suspended. He still stood with outstretched hand, I stood with hands behind my back, my expression as wooden as I could make it, and the other occupants of the room stood and watched us. The silence was intense.

'Best to shake.'

I swung round at the sound of a familiar voice.

It was Inspector Ram Singh – ASP Ram Singh now. He stood just inside the door and I wondered how much he had heard.

We all sprang to attention as he moved forward and signified with a wave of the hand that we could relax.

'Sharif Ahmat, isn't it?' He held out his own hand.

'Tuan.' I did shake *his* hand. He had been a good inspector when I served under him and decent enough to me.

'Hasbullah is right. The war is over. It is better to shake hands and forget.'

Still I did not move.

Ram Singh gave a very slight shrug and walked along the line of men, introducing himself and announcing that he would be the chief instructor for our course. Then he went back to the door and paused, looking straight at me.

'Some of you have not been long in the Force and others I know only from your records. But Ahmat I know well. It was I who advised you to sign the oath of allegiance to the Japs, was it not?'

I came to attention to indicate the affirmative. 'Tuan.'

'And I advised you rightly. Not that it helped your family much. Oh yes, I know all about the tragedy of your father and your brothers. Your eldest brother and I were gazetted at the same time and we attended the Police Training College together at Hendon. I hear he is now on a fingerprint course?'

'Tuan.'

'Three times in Britain already. Soon he will be turning white!' A polite titter passed over the room. He was deliberately softening the atmosphere. 'We often talked about the war years and many is the time I told him that it was all very well for a young bachelor to run off to the hills, but the older men like myself – ' he indicated a few grey streaks in his beard ' – had our wives and children to think of. Many is the time I have undertaken duties which I did not relish, so perhaps I too should be called a collaborator.'

There was dead silence throughout the room. Ram Singh stood like a rock, only his eyes moving to each of us in turn. He was a tall, handsome man, with ramrod military bearing. He had always been known as a hard disciplinarian, but just. His face had become very stern.

'I want no feuds on this course. And no talk of collaboration. The war is over. Is that clearly understood?'

There was a chorus of 'Tuan,' and the senior man present called the rest of us to attention.

After that we got on with our unpacking in silence, until unaffected, new arrivals began to stream in and the normal chatter of a barrack-room took over again.

I wrote to Hassan that evening and to my surprise, when I received his reply, he wrote:

'Ram Singh is right. There are so many Hasbullahs, they are not worth worrying about. The war *is* over. My advice to you is to forget it and concentrate on the future.'

He went on to tell me about the course he was attending and how he expected to be posted to CID Headquarters on his return.

I took the proffered advice and concentrated on the course and I'm pleased to say I passed out top – this was a fillip to my pride, as it is difficult for us to compete against the Chinese and Indians, who are usually far better educated. I never did shake hands with Hasbullah, but we were polite to each other and as far as possible kept out of each other's way.

To my delight, on completion of the course, I myself was posted to the CID HQ in Kuala Lumpur, and when Hassan returned from England we found ourselves working in the same building.

It was wonderful to renew the comradeship that we had found during the occupation, but I did not feel it could last for long, and I was right. The years in the jungle had taken their toll and it was not many months before he was admitted to the TB hospital.

Attention and care were unstinted, but every time I visited him he seemed more wan, more finely-drawn, until one day the surgeon took me aside and told me there was no hope.

I cannot say it came as a real surprise. And yet, when I looked at him and thought of my father dying in madness, my brothers killed and Mahmood becoming a fly-by-night playboy with heady ideas, it seemed so unfair that Hassan, so young still and with such a future before him, should die.

After a battle with the medical authorities and the police, and assurances from our mother that she would be the only person with whom Hassan would come in contact, they eventually allowed him to be removed to Daun Chempaka so that Mak could nurse him during his last days.

He came by ambulance as soon as I was able to get leave to accompany him, and we made him comfortable on a specially-acquired hospital bed. This we set on the verandah – on the very spot, although he did not know it, where my brother Ghazali had fallen under my father's maddened thrust – from where he could watch the changing faces of the mountain which he loved, and which had been partly responsible for the early termination of his life.

He lived for nearly a year and I believe that in those last months he was able to assuage much of my mother's loneliness. The bed on which he lay is still there, inhabited now by the little cat that kept him company until the end, and beneath a yellow song bird which still trills in its wicker cage.

We buried him near his brothers. I do not believe it will be long before my mother joins them. She is alone again now. My sisters married and far away, Mahmood disinterested, my father an unhappy ghost. She is still a proud woman, but life has not been kind.

59. HOGMANAY

Donald Thom

Everyone was drinking and quite a few people were already way into the wind – and I guess I was one of them. Well, what the hell? It was Hogmanay, wasn't it? Judas Priest, if a good Scot can't get drunk at Hogmanay, when the hell can he get drunk?

I'm not sure which year it was, is. 1946, I guess. I mean was. 1947 is. Who cares? Well, I do. At least, I care about it being the 1st of January – I don't care which year. I only know it's the wrong one. My mind sure travels back on 1st January – guess it always will. I tried looking at my watch, but there's something wrong with my eyes – won't focus. Not that I'm drunk, mind you – Thom never gets drunk, only drinks. Good chap, Thom.

'Wha's time?' The guy I asked was sitting bolt upright on the stairs beside me.

'Four o'clock.'

'How you know it's four o'clock? You din' look at your watch. I'm not drunk.'

'I don't know, but I know it's four o'clock.'

I was about to argue, but then I remembered, never argue with a drunk. I got away from that guy, because it looked to me as though he might be going to puke, and who wants to be spewed over? So I moved to a chair and had myself a good think.

Yeah, I know what we were doing at four o'clock. We were just getting up. We'd made love for the last time and then she'd gone. Why did she go back? If she hadn't, she'd be here now – Mrs Thom. Mrs Marijke Thom.

Mrs Thom – the other Mrs Thom, Mrs Monica Thom, well, she was Mrs something else now. She'd been keen on hurrying the divorce through on account of she was having a baby. Baby by that Frog. Well, she'd got her divorce – I wasn't going to hang on to any woman who didn't want me – and I'd agreed to her having custody of the child, my child. I had no idea where she was now – didn't care – Canada, or France maybe.

I hadn't returned to Canada myself, not at all. We hung around Europe for a year or so. I got out of going back to Holland, but I rejoined the battalion when they moved over to the Rhine Army. Once the war was over, I applied to get out, go back to university, but I didn't want to go back to Canada – too many memories of that college – and it wasn't so easy being accepted for a British university, too many limeys, I guess. Anyways, here I am. Edinburgh. Good old Bonny Scotland, land of my ancestors. I always told Monica my name would be a help one day – but she didn't want to keep it – rather be called by the name of that Frog.

I still have a couple of years to do – didn't have to do the full course, on account of my having done a year plus in Canada before I joined up. It's not a bad joint here – I'm not sure where I am, but I know the people who own it are friends of mine. Quite a party. Glad I stayed in Edinburgh for the winter vac.

Two more years. 'Yipppppeeeeeeeee!' Heh, heh! That sure put all those old world Highlanders to shame.

They think they're doing the Eightsome Reel over there. Do you know, I think I'm getting a little high? Too many people leaping and yelling; I wonder where they get their energy from? What'm I saying? Energy? I'll show 'em!

60. A TEMPORARY HOME

Stanislaus Olshewski

Would you believe it, I had to carry that hulking great Canadian all the way back to his digs? It was just about the other side of the city, the building where he lodged, and not a taxi in sight. Bloody cold too.

It was just as I was telling all and sundry that the Eightsome Reel was a Polish dance and the Scots had copied it, that this great hunk came hurtling into the circle, yelling as though all the demons of hell were after him. He sent both my partner and me flying and then someone felled him, screeching, 'Damned Yankee,' as he did so! Of course it was the wrong moment to tell the Scots that they couldn't drink either and, to cut a long story short, it ended up with one 'damned Yankee' and one 'damned foreigner' in a heap in one corner.

I can't remember much about the party actually. I was down from St Andrews with some of the other med. students who'd stayed behind, and how we became involved I don't know. Some people called Wallace asked us, I think. Better find out. Oh well, it seems that I have a temporary home for a few days. I don't even know this character's name, but when he emerged for a short while just now, he suggested I cook some breakfast and stay on. There're two beds, so why not? He's the first Canadian I've come across since leaving prison camp and it makes a change.

As you will have gathered by the date, I've finished my first year and, taken by and large, things aren't going too badly. Not that it's going to be all that easy from now on. Although I've spoken, and written, English for so long, I'm still apt to worry about putting down the wrong thing. But I wasn't wrong about one thing; I do have a vocation. Of course I have a lot of people to thank; most of all Colonel MacArthur, for getting me started on the right track – if it hadn't been for him I wonder if I would ever have got this far. Doing the first exam in camp put me a leap ahead straight away, and at my age that's something to be thankful for. So many other people were decent, helpful and encouraging, and, in a nebulous way, I have that little WAAF to thank too – it was her nightmares that first made me want to practise medicine. Sally – wonder what's happened to her?

Sooner or later I shall have to think about the future. Haven't given it much thought yet, but if I want to get my British nationality I shall have to stay in Britain for a while after I qualify, or go to a British colony.

Right at the moment I think I could do with some breakfast myself. Wonder where that chap said the bacon was?

61. THE FIRST FEATHERY ISLANDS

Philip Morrison

As soon as the battalion was disembarked and we were settled in to our new home in Singapore, I realised that life, as far as my personal problems were concerned, was not going to be plain sailing.

Only the CO and one senior major had their wives booked to follow them, and it was made perfectly clear that those were the only wives who could be expected out for some time. The colonel didn't care for wives at the best of times – rumour had it that his own was a bitch and he would have done without her as well. I hadn't met her, she'd been away the whole time I was at the Depot, but if his own home life was not happy, he was unlikely to be sympathetic towards one of his juniors whose wife came out under her own steam. And no hope of quarters, even if he should prove amenable in time. Quarters were few and far between and for another couple of months I wasn't even eligible to put my name on the waiting list, nor draw marriage allowance.

In the circumstances, I waited for news of the arrival of Sally's ship with mixed feelings. Oh, blast the colonel and his narrow-minded, dogmatic principles. Was it my fault that I was sent to the second battalion? The colonel had no time for any battalion but his own. Or that I'd fought an unorthodox war? I suppose he would have thought better of me if I had stayed meekly behind wire and made no attempt to escape. Stodgy old sod.

Oh well. The only consolation to date was that Sally was bound to be stationed at Changi, which was the only RAF Station with WAAF on it, and our barracks were only a stone's throw away. We'd manage somehow.

I sat silent amid the chattering group of naval and army officers in the main lounge of the Grand Oriental Hotel.

Outside, sounds of traffic – horns, brakes, and the cawing crows as they flew in from the harbour to make one of their furious assaults on some speck of garbage left lying in the street – were muffled.

Inside, the gentle whirring of long-stemmed fans, flowering from high-domed ceilings, and the soft-soled slap of the Sinhalese waiters as they padded between the tables and bar, took me back to my childhood. Tall, dignified and stately, these quiet-voiced old men with their tiny knots of hair and crescent-shaped tortoiseshell combs, had always spelt out homecoming for me. As the commuter in UK starts putting away the crossword and looks at his watch when the train draws in to the penultimate station, so, for me, Colombo has always been the end of Europe and the beginning of the East. Next stop home.

I had had little enough to do on board – beyond repelling the advances of the Ship's Adj – but dream. And dream I did, all along the familiar route: Port Said, Aden, Bombay, Colombo. And soon it would be Singapore. I had been ashore at every port, listening with one ear to the amused or incredulous remarks of my companions – 'Oh, do look at that heavenly hat!' 'What *is* that chap wearing – looks like a winding-sheet!' 'What an extraordinary vehicle!' 'Oh, do listen – isn't it priceless?' – and with the other ear hearing all the dear, familiar sounds that meant home. I was happy, saying little and smiling a lot – I must have been a very dull companion.

But we were soon on board again, adding our ebony and ivory elephants to the pouffes from Port Said, the cameras and make-up from Aden, and the silk we'd bought in Bombay.

After that it seemed no time before we were sailing through the Straits, Malaya so close on the port side that the urge to jump overboard and swim for it was almost uncontrollable. I had missed lunch, refused to go inside for tea, remaining glued to the rail in case there was some familiar landmark that I might miss.

It is impossible to convey the emotion which came over me as Singapore harbour came in sight. The excitement which had been surging through me ever since boarding the troopship at Liverpool reached fever pitch as we passed slowly, slowly, between the first feathery islands. The sea changed colour from deep ocean blue to the turquoise and eau-de-Nil of sheltered reefs. Sand and palm tree, coral and kelong. The very air smelt different. Home. It was almost home.

A vessel sailing through tropic seas has a sound all its own. How can I describe it? A gentle sound, windblown but serene, a lazy, swishing sound that you never hear in northern waters. I listened and felt and revelled in the familiar, homecoming melody of the warm sea.

Soon it would be evening. The engines slowed as the pilot manœuvred us through the myriad stationary vessels, to drop anchor in the inner roads. Multicoloured specks, seen leaving the shore, had not yet materialised into the launches they inevitably were. The rattling anchor chain had ceased; we were still, alone, at peace.

And then the most almighty explosion rent the air and for a terrible, shivering moment I was back five years. I closed my eyes, hearing the rattle and report, but knowing also that soon would come the crescendo, climax and, at last, silence. I opened them to meet the amused gaze of the first officer, at whose table I sat in the dining saloon.

'Chinese New Year,' he said, 'it's only the second time they've been able to let off fire crackers since the war. Noisy blighters, but you can't blame them – after all, we have Guy Fawkes's night.'

I laughed and he moved on down the deck.

The launches were now all around us, nipping in and out and buzzing like inquisitive bees. Medical, customs, immigration, police. But before the first occupant of the little boats had set foot on the gangway, the Tannoy crackled and the voice of the OC Troops announced that, owing to a holiday on shore, due to start the following day, we would not be disembarking for forty-eight hours.

There must have been many people with mixed emotions in that ship. Wives disappointed at further separation; wives glad to have a brief reprieve; men who groaned at having to spend two more days on the troopdeck, and old sweats who told them that things on shore would be even worse.

For myself, I didn't really mind. I was sure that Philip would have enough initiative to wangle himself on board somehow, and I was so entranced with the sights and sounds of Singapore harbour at last that I was happy just to watch it for a spell.

As the sun went down and the sky reddened all around us, I could have cried at its beauty – and the memory of that other glow that had bathed this harbour five years ago. For, coincidentally, this was again February the thirteenth, Friday the thirteenth too, five years to the day since I had left these waters, under such very different circumstances.

The dinner gong sounded and I tore myself away from the evening sky. There would be to-morrow and, before that, the night.

'Friday the thirteenth,' grumbled my neighbour in the saloon, as he surveyed the menu with a jaundiced eye, 'I take it that "prawn cocktail à la Penang" is the same as "Mediterranean prawn cocktail, prawn cocktail à la Barren Rocks, and prawn cocktail Indienne"? Oh well, nothing else to do but eat. Fat chance of seeing anything of Singapore.'

'It's my lucky day,' I said.

All the diners looked at me in surprise.

'You're a queer girl,' one said, 'coming to meet your husband – you couldn't get here fast enough a couple of days ago and, now that you're held up for another forty-eight hours, you say it's your lucky day!'

I just smiled. I didn't feel at that moment like recounting the events of half a decade ago.

And then I looked up and saw Philip entering the saloon. He hadn't changed and was still in daytime togs, khaki shirt with rolled-up sleeves, kilt and webbing belt. He looked healthy and alive, skin darkened by the sun and lighter streaks in his hair. I had the same feeling that I had had on Victoria Station on his return from Italy – was I really married to this madly attractive man?

I watched him pick his way between the stewards and tables, but did not get up to meet him; there was a vacant place at our table for eight, I wanted to have him here, to show him off.

'Look,' I prodded my neighbour, 'you see, it *is* my lucky day.'

I got up then and Philip was beside me. We smiled into each other's eyes, then I introduced him, and the first officer suggested that he should join us – as I had hoped he would – and soon he was munching away while being bombarded with questions by those who had reached their journey's end.

'You see,' I said later, as we stood by the railing and looked over the harbour lights, 'my hunch did prove right.'

But while he was gone, getting our drinks from the bar, I thought that after all this subterfuge had gone on long enough. I had made no secret of being a married woman on board – why should I? I knew the job I was to do; once dug in I thought it unlikely that the air force would care whether I was married or not; unlikely that they would post me home. And now, almost his first words when we had been alone, were to the effect that the colonel would have a fit if he knew that he was meeting his wife. Oh, bugger the colonel, I thought, this was something we must tackle soon. I knew I had been pig-headed, but why the hell should Philip ask for permission to marry at this stage, and go through all that nonsense? I wanted him to stand up for himself, to stop being so damned lily-livered with this man, who could not possibly be the ogre that he was made out to be, I was sure. But why spoil our first evening together? I smiled at him when I saw him returning and put my thoughts away for another day.

We stood in silence for a long time, looking out over the sea. Any harbour at any time has a fascination for me, and of course Singapore is one of the busiest in the world. There was activity everywhere. Ships employing Chinese labour frantically loading and unloading by

425

floodlight before the start of the holiday. Launches, sampans, lifeboats, koleks, junks – every conceivable type of craft plied between ships and shore. And the shore itself – more neon lights than ever, and Singapore had always been gay. It was a spectacle.

I had not told Philip until then about the coincidence of the date. And, come to think of it, there had been so many other excitements in our lives when we had first met that I doubt if I'd ever told him in detail what this harbour had been like five years before. It had been to Stan, my Polish boy-friend, that I had unburdened myself – I wonder what happened to him?

Philip listened as I pointed out the oil islands that had been ablaze and tried to describe the extraordinary black pall, mixed with scarlet and crimson, that had hung over the island. And the noise – no, better not to remember.

Suddenly I felt my cheeks wet and his arm tightening about my shoulders.

'I'm sorry,' I said, 'I was only just then thinking that my happiness would be complete if only my father were still alive. He is there, somewhere, buried in a common grave, I suppose. I thought of him this afternoon, but it is only now that the horror of that spell has come back. The Red Cross merely told me that he had died in internment, but I shall have to find out how he died – to lay his ghost.'

Philip said nothing, but I could feel the sympathy in his silence, in his fingers caressing my arm, and the chaste kiss that he planted on top of my head. How lucky I was to have him. My home had gone, my family, but I had him.

62. CHAIRBORNE

James Weatherby

'Helen, Helen.' The voice sounded cheerful and I dared to hope.

I had been watching from the window of the flat as James plodded up the hill – as I did at the same time every evening. In summer I could see him as he rounded the bend at the bottom of the rise, but in winter I had to wait for the light from the lamp-posts to fall on each figure as he or she passed under its beam. If he was in a good mood, I would see him marching up the hill as though on parade, and the first glimpse I would have would be of an outstretched arm swung shoulder-high in the lamplight. But if the mood were bad, the hand would be firmly tucked into a pocket, matching the empty sleeve on the other side. Then the first glimpse would be of a shoulder, or hat brim, pulled well down.

It had been difficult to ascertain his mood this time. His figure had been erect, but slow, idling in the still mild October twilight. And so I had been unprepared for the exuberance in his voice.

'Helen – where are you, woman? Damn you. I've got important news.'

I stepped from the shadow of the curtain and switched on the standard-lamp. I had wanted to watch him for a moment unobserved, to see his expression, but the tone of voice was enough. And so I smiled.

'What are you doing, skulking in the dark?' His right arm had become incredibly strong, I thought, as he circled my shoulders and hugged. 'Honey, guess what? I've got a chance to get out of that blasted chair at last.'

I released myself and took his hat and gloves.

'Get yourself comfy first, while I get us a drink, then you can tell me all about it.'

I closed the kitchen door quietly and stood with my back to it, praying that this was not another false hope. Ever since James had dropped back to his substantive rank and been stuck behind that wretched Air Ministry desk, he had fretted and cursed and made life hell for everyone around him.

He had been in his present job for more than eighteen months and surely it must have become apparent to the powers that be by now that pen-pushing was not his métier? If only he could have got back to a station. Meanwhile he continued to fume about his ill-luck and I stood in the window each day to speculate on what sort of evening lay ahead for me with this unpredictable man.

Next door the sound of gurgling bathwater broke in on my thoughts and I realised that I must have been standing there for at least ten minutes.

I went over to the drink cupboard to see what we had. Half a bottle of whisky, three-quarters of gin. Perhaps this time it would really be good news – I reached for the whisky bottle.

I hurried through to the living-room and by the time he emerged, clad in shapeless grey flannel bags and sweater, I had the drinks poured out, the curtains drawn and a pile of chestnuts ready for roasting in the newly-lit fire.

I had never been one to linger in the bath, but to-night I wanted to soak in the hot water and go over the day's events. I'd had my hopes dashed before, but this time I really did think it would come to something. Helen had been marvellously patient with me this past year, but I knew I was being a bastard, both to her and to my staff. Every day I made new resolutions and every day I broke them. God knows, it wasn't Helen's fault that I was cooped up in that dreary office, nor the poor sods under me for that matter, but one frustration after another was driving me round the bend. I had quite given up any hope of advancement in the air force – and with the present government cutting down the armed services on all sides I was not just being a pessimist – but even the civilian channels I had explored had come to nothing. Either the service wouldn't consider release, or there was little chance of being accepted with any physical disability, or I just couldn't see myself in the job offered.

I lay in the bath, listening to the clink of glass as Helen organised our drinks in the kitchen on one side and Angela hummed herself to sleep on the other. Good heavens, I had been so engrossed in my own thoughts that I had neglected to go and say good night to her.

Funny little thing. Button-brown eyes and bright red hair, she didn't look like either of us. 'You're going to be a *femme fatale*,' I told her. It would be fun when she could talk back, instead of gurgling. I pulled the blanket up to her chin and closed the door.

My God, it was good to come home to a wife and child like mine. I looked at Helen, perched on the chair by the fire and pricking chestnuts. She was beginning to look large, must be seven months by now. She was still a beautiful girl, even when she was pregnant. I took in the scene and her alert face and brought out the sheaf of papers which I had held concealed behind my back.

'Take a gander at these,' I said, and held them out to her.

'Colonial Administrative Service? You mean leave the RAF?'

'Would you mind?'

She looked thoughtfully at the forms but shook her head. 'Not in the least – if you are going to be happier in another job. Do you think you'd get in?'

'With these you mean?' I inclined my head on the sightless side and flipped my pinned-up sleeve. A feeling of triumph had been saturating me ever since I left the MO; I'm sure she must have seen it in my face. 'Listen, honey – I heard about this job from another chap who applied. He gave me all the gen a week or so ago – I didn't mention it before because I didn't want you to be disappointed if it didn't come to anything – but to-day I went to see a fellow in the Colonial Office, who gave me these forms to fill in. It wasn't exactly an official interview, but he told me all the pros and cons and gave me a good idea of what the work would consist of. Apparently they're crying out for bodies, so, if they accept me – and he seemed pretty sure that they will – and I pass the medical and get out of the air force, I'm in.' I recalled with some bitterness how he had waved my flying experience and wartime rank aside as being of little consequence. 'It seems that a year or so behind an Air Ministry desk is worth more than all my years of flying.'

She asked quickly, 'Where would we go?'

428

'Africa, most likely, or possibly the Far East. Would you like that, darling?'

'I loved my trip to India during the war,' she said cautiously.

'I went over to see old Doc Matthews after I got these forms,' I went on, 'he gave me a thorough going-over and sees no reason why I shouldn't pass the medical. Organically I'm sound and, if I can push a pen in AM minus an eye and an arm, what's to prevent me doing the same in some secretariat in Kenya or Swaziland?'

I watched her, this woman whom I knew so well, and knew that she too believed that this time it would be all right. I bent over to kiss her neck and she smiled round at me.

'Let's have another drink,' she said, 'and then I'll go and cook the supper.'

'No. I'll cook the supper and you fill in these forms. I'm bound to make a smudge.'

I stood up, and as I did so a sudden kick reminded me that I was not all that far off from producing our second child.

'I was forgetting John,' I said, patting my middle. 'I'd like to have him here and I doubt if I'd be allowed to travel this size anyway.'

'Don't worry, darling, it wouldn't be as soon as that.'

He went out of the room and a few minutes later I smelled the right smells issuing from the kitchen. I listened for the blasphemy that invariably accompanied most of James's culinary feats and heard him singing instead. His voice was flat as a pancake, but it was better than an operatic aria to me, and I realised with a pang that the last time I had heard him sing like that had been when he first knew that I was to have Angela.

63. LINKED BY A PALE SCARF

Jogindar Singh

Sergeant Gurdial Singh did not recognise me, but I recognised him.

That is the crux of this episode, but neither the beginning nor the end.

When my training was completed, I went on leave to Singapore and to take my part in the marriage which had been arranged for me by my uncle, Arjan Singh.

I had not seen my bride before the ceremony, and as we walked round the Holy Book, linked by a pale scarf, I wondered what lay in store for me behind that heavy veil. She was tall and slender, that I could see, and from the skin of her hands and feet, fair.

I had not given marriage much thought until my uncle wrote to

429

remind me that I would soon be twenty-four and that it was high time I did. I left it in his hands and it was not until we reached the temple that I saw even the form of my bride to be.

Suvindar Kaur was her name and my uncle had chosen well.

When the ceremony was over and her veil removed, I beheld a demure, docile face of great charm; the eyes large, deep and liquid; her mouth full, and nose long and straight. She was young still, only eighteen, and the daughter of one of my father's friends.

I thanked my uncle and aunt for their solicitude and for the hospitality that they accorded us during my leave. Our bridal chamber, a room in my uncle's house, was decked with silk hangings and paper flowers, and the sweet scents of jasmine and incense intermingled on the air.

I had not had a woman before, but I was aware from the start that our union would be satisfactory. She lay on the couch face down, covered by a silken sheet, but when I pulled this away and placed my hand on her buttocks, I saw that she was as slim and lithe as a boy. She giggled and hid her face, but I could see her watching me from the pointed corner of one eye. I rolled her over then with one hand and removed her own hands with the other.

This was the beginning of my marriage; a marriage I was never to regret.

On return from leave I found myself posted to the Traffic Branch and, regrettably, serving under one Gurdial Singh, Sergeant.

I was but a beardless youth when my father had been led away to lose his head. I was full bearded now and mature in build, reaching the mark of six foot three inches. But those men who had chosen to join the enemy at the outset, who had been spat upon by my father, had already been mature then and had not changed. Gurdial Singh was one of them.

There are no doubt others in the Force by the name of Jogindar Singh, and Pritam, my father's name, is one of the most common of our clan. But Gurdial Singh knew who I was, seeking to ingratiate himself with me from the start; fearful, no doubt, that I might choose to bring to light scenes that were best forgotten.

After only a few months in Traffic, a vacancy occurred and I was promoted corporal – Sergeant Gurdial Singh being careful to point out that it was his doing, his recommendation that had got me my stripes. Perhaps it was.

My conscience was uneasy during these months. I had sworn to avenge my father and yet I knew that to denounce Gurdial Singh and stir up past mud would do nobody any good. Too many of my compatriots were involved, too many arguing that the government in power at the time was the one to be served, thus covering their defects and making for a smoother life. But every time I looked into his pock-marked, snake-like face, I saw my father's head leave his body and heard the final, eliminating 'thwack'. I had to leave.

After much deliberation, and remembering the interest he had shown in me when I first enlisted, next time I had reason to go out to the Depot, I asked to see the Adjutant.

'I wish for a posting,' I explained. 'For reasons which I cannot divulge, it is not possible for me to remain where I am.'

After a few minutes of evasive question and answer, I could see the Adjutant was becoming irritated with me. At length he said, rather sharply, 'I don't know what the trouble is, Corporal, but if you wish to be moved for personal reasons you must go through the proper channels which, as you very well know, is through your own Commanding Officer, and no one else. But as you've taken the trouble to come and see me, you presumably have your reasons. The very least you can do is to be honest with me. You may say what you wish in confidence.'

I cast my mind back then to the terrible day when my father, marching at the head of a column of men, had seen the PCs-turned-warders with their white charges. His words still rang clearly in my brain, as clearly as the intoned prayers of the elders and my mother's beseeching, 'Go!'

'You are, I presume, referring to Sergeant Gurdial Singh,' the Adjutant paused and gave me a piercing look. 'Is it your wish to denounce this man? I doubt if it would be wise.'

'Oh no, Sahib. With respect, you have not understood me at all. I do *not* wish to denounce him – as you have said yourself, many of my compatriots did not shine with a clear, pure light – but only to be removed from his presence, which contaminates my soul and my vow to see my father avenged.'

He was sympathetic, but not prepared to deviate.

'You will still have to go through your CO,' he said, 'but if it will help, I'll give him a ring and explain the circumstances, without mentioning any names.'

'Sahib,' I said, 'I am truly grateful.'

I returned then to barracks and wrote out my application for an interview with the OC Traffic Branch. Now we shall await events.

It will soon be the New Year. I wonder if 1948 will be as eventful as 1947 has been for me.

BOOK II

IN WHICH THE STREAMS JOIN
THE RIVER

'A State of Emergency has been declared'

64. THE LUCRATIVE CAREER OF
MR S. KANDIAH

Ramakrishnan

I am working for more than one year as clerk on Tanah Kuning Estate when my eyes are being opened to potential far beyond realms of clerking.

There are many things I am learning since leaving Mr Ramasamy's silk store. Typing, filing and general routines of office for one thing, and great improvement of English for second.

My wife, Devi, is bringing forth bouncing boy after one year of marriage precisely and I am already making sure that she is pregnant again – which is not difficult seeing that she is still most frolicsome maiden who is greatly enjoying embracings of yours truly.

Mr Ramasamy, father-in-law and father of wife Devi, is paying up monthly without hitch, thereby enabling purchase of radio, sewing-machine and motor bicycle. Verily it was good fortune most that allowed me to become aware of incestuous behaviour of said Mr Ramasamy.

In fact, eyes are being opened in two ways.

Firstly is coming several Chinese to estate and I am being given to understand that they are members of once glorious guerilla band during most clandestine wartime. They are telling all workers that white pigs are exploiting them most foul – in this I am heartily concurring – and that soon great liberation movement will be afoot and all above-mentioned white pigs will be killed or dispatched to own country.

It is time of Chinese New Year and these erstwhile guerillas are handing out ang pows, red paper packets in value one dollar each, to all Chinese workers on estate, at same time requesting support from Indians and Javanese workers likewise.

CC – Chief Clerk – is not believing this and is shaking head, whilst telling workers to remember Japanese times so previously past and stick only to letter of law and order. I am thinking that he is truly old stick-in-the-mud who is too drunken and lazy to remember chains of our people, but I am saying nothing, having learned tact and diplomacy both. But I am being much encouraged by these magnificent hopings and pledge my support without more ados.

In June 1948 great and glorious happenings are taking place. To wit: one European planter killed on first day and all erstwhile glorious guerillas are hiding in jungles again before stupid police are knowing. From hills and valleys they will be harassing enemy as needing.

Truly it is great day when most glorious State of Emergency is being declared.

I am not forgetting humiliations suffered at hands of said guerillas, mind, but am nevertheless approving of all plans and principles.

But not all labour force are understanding actions of said guerillas – now called bandits or Communist terrorists. It is like wartime; there are many stupid fellows who are preferring to continue falling into steps of white pigs rather than join great liberation movement.

I am growing up muchly in six years and am now holding tongue instead of giving vent to feelings true and valorous. Indeed, I am becoming veritable clam and expert in tact and diplomacy both. As soon as I am realising that many workers are not on side of glorious Communist liberating terrorists, I am keeping trap most securely shut.

It is not long before police are coming to estate and explaining to workers about not helping said Communists and soon there are Malay Special Constables living on estate, to guard installations and suchlike. I spit whenever I pass their post.

But second happening, although I am not fully understanding at time, is more important than declaration of glorious Emergency, because it is of great financial benefits.

One day I am checking list of labourers' pay when shadow is falling over shoulder and I am beholding one Mr Menon.

Truly he is most well-dressed gentleman indeed, with many fine gold teeth, rings, wrist watch, etcetera, etcetera.

'I am Secretary of Rubber and Tin Workers' Union,' he is informing me.

I can see at once that this is most worthy and important gentleman and am therefore giving him my chair and begging him to be seated forthwith. He is most graciously accepting my humble offer and when I have brought forward other chair for self, is explaining his business.

'It is to collect the quarterly subscriptions,' he is telling me, 'and to explain to Union members how their money is being spent.'

Truly he is most pleasant and plausible fellow. All the time I am looking at his clean and well-pressed suitings and brown and white correspondent shoes and thinking that indeed Mr Menon is in post most lucrative. Nylon socks he is wearing, of purple hue, and also purple nylon shirt and yellow tie and purple silk handkerchief is appearing in breast pocket of jacket.

Mr Menon is undoubtedly fine orator and holds all labour bound in spell for long period. I am listening to speech and learning for future reference what is most appealing to labourers' simple minds – for I am hatching plan most devious and bold – but also I am wondering if Mr Menon is indeed *bona fide* trade union official. It would be easy, I am thinking, to hoodwink simple labourers like these – trade

435

unions being in infancy only and many people still unaccustomed to such – and collect subscriptions from all and sundry.

When Mr Menon has finished speaking and is answering questions, his assistant is collecting subscriptions and ticking off names of subscribers in notebook.

Two men lend confidence, I am thinking; where one man is for arousing suspicions, two men are not. Also arrival in limousine most spruce and shining.

I myself am now joining union for first time and paying subscription, for purpose of checking on Mr Menon and also seeing how it is run and what benefits workers are receiving.

I am finding out that Mr Menon is indeed official secretary of Rubber and Tin Workers' Union and no hocus-pocus abounds. But I am wondering nevertheless if correct amounts are always being shown in notebook against subscribers' names and coming to timely conclusion that here indeed is way of making money most beneficial to yours truly, if not to workers.

I am brooding on above-mentioned happenings for several weeks, and then am taking motor bicycle to friend on neighbouring estate, one Mr K. P. Samuel, who is also clerk, to have discussion with him of great import to both.

K.P. is not knowing of my extra monthly earnings and because he is only poor man in unwell paid position is therefore also most cautious. I am not persuading him at first reasoning, I can see, but am suggesting that he is giving idea most serious and formulative thought forthwith.

It is taking K.P. two months over to make up mind and, when he does, I am having to show him that I am in possession of trumping card.

Money received monthly from Mr Ramasamy, father-in-law, is being put away carefully for future use. Now time is come and I am deciding that learning to drive is first essential, so that motor car can be purchased. It is fitting that delegates from powerful union should arrive at estates in motor car, which is in keeping with official dignity. Also stupid Malay police are not so often questioning drivers of motor cars as of motor bicycles. I am therefore, as first step, spending every Saturday afternoon in nearby town, learning to drive said limousine.

Once licence is acquired, I am purchasing discreet but dignified motor car of dark maroon colour. Also suitings of white drill for K. P. Samuel and self; nylon shirts, socks and handkerchiefs of gorgeous hues. Only it is remaining to obtain correspondent shoes, dark glasses and to have gold teeth fitted by Chinese dentist, who are most clever at such work. This last is being done by specialist in far town, as local fellow is most questioning chap.

When all organisations are ready and shipshape, I am asking for two days off to attend wedding of brother, which is being granted by most sleep-laden, toddy-drinking CC without trouble.

Then K.P. and I are driving pell-mell and helter-skelter to distant estate, to approach labour. We are choosing estate where manager is only visiting and name of clerk is available.

K.P. is nervous and all way to estate I am noticing that pink palms are clammy with much perspiration.

'Go faster, Krishnan,' he is urging. 'This is bad bandit area, man. No point in going to all these troubles if we are to be killed getting there.'

'You are not understanding those who you are calling bandits,' I am saying.

Nevertheless I am putting on spurt, for how are bandits, I mean glorious guerillas, to know that I am sympathetic without asking, and it might be that they will shoot first.

Malay Special Constable is stopping us on roadside before we are reaching estate buildings and I am seeing K.P. bursting out in such perspirations that truly I am becoming nervous myself.

'I am Mr S. Kandiah,' I tell this white man's stooge, with smile to show both gold teeth, 'and this is my friend Mr K. P. John. We are coming to see Chief Clerk, Mr Tetrasamy.'

I too am perspiring now, because I am suddenly remembering that decision to use false name was taken without consideration of National Registration Identity Card. But luckily he is dull fellow and waves us through.

'Thank you, most gracious friend.' I give SC widest smile and hiss at K.P., 'Control yourself, man. All will be going well if we are using bluffings sufficiently.'

I am striding into estate office and holding out hand to Mr Tetrasamy, making sure that gold teeth, rings and wristwatch are all visible.

'Good afternoon, sir. I am Mr S. Kandiah and this is my assistant Mr K. P. John. We are coming from Estate and Mine Workers' Union to gain members for valuable union support.'

Mr Tetrasamy is looking puzzled and before answering pulls list from drawer of desk.

'I know of no such union,' he is shaking head and looking at us with suspicious frown. 'All labour force here are members of Plantation Workers' Union.'

'You are right, my friend,' I say reassuringly, and sit down on ready chair, exposing nylon socks and correspondent shoes to make correct impression. 'Mr Aru, secretary of that union, is very good friend of mine. But this is new union, offering protection of workers against Communist Terrorist upsets; compensations to relatives when worker is deceased, etcetera.'

'But Plantation Workers' Union is also offering compensations.' Mr Tetrasamy is most cautious and suspicious fellow and is not being convinced, so I can see that it is time for me to be playing trumping card.

'My good friend Mr T. S. Aru is telling me that in future his union will only be looking after estates to north of Kuala Lumpur; our union will be looking after estates south of this city.'

I mention a few names to impress this most doubting Thomas, then I am looking at gold wristwatch importantly and turning to K.P., who is pulling out list as previously arranged.

'Well, Mister,' I am saying to Mr Tetrasamy, 'I must thank you for your time and courtesy, but wasting no more time. We have already listed members from five estates to-day and still have four to visit. It is not good to be out after dark with such dastardly terrorists in vicinity and accommodation is already arranged on one of estates to be visited this day. We are not wishing to force anyone to join our union, but only asking to be allowed to say few words to workers and, if anyone is wishing to join, he can do so at entrance fee of one dollar and annual subscription of fifty cents.'

I hold out my hand, and K.P. is putting lists back into most important-looking briefing-case when Mr Tetrasamy, as I am expecting, is stopping us.

'I have no wish to stop you, friend,' he is saying, 'nor to interfere with honest intentions. You can speak to labour force if you are so wishing. It is only surprise that Plantation Workers' Union is handing over southern areas to other union.'

After that he goes outside and soon small boy is bearing glasses of coffee and we are having chat most friendly and amiable about state of country, etcetera, etcetera.

I am not being student and schoolteacher both for nothing. I am explaining to workers all benefits to be obtained from joining Southern Estate and Mine Workers' Union and K.P. is already pulling out receipt book and official black tin box for money.

'I am not asking any worker to join who does not wish to,' I am telling them at end of most eloquent harangue, 'but for those who wish to join, one dollar entrance fee and fifty cents annual subscription.'

I walk away then and soon K.P. is coping with long queue of workers.

It is already getting dark when we leave and we are driving helter-skelter for state capital.

It is only when we are inside cubicle of Indian lodging-house that we are counting benefits. Four hundred and fifty dollars over. K.P. and I are having most sumptuous meal in town and next day returning to humdrum life of clerking.

'This is only food of chicken,' I am telling him. 'If four hundred and fifty dollars over is being obtained from one small estate, think how much it is we are getting from big estates, man.'

Truly this is most beneficial ruse and soon I am buying wife many gold ornaments, as becomes wife of Very Important Person. For verily, Mr S. Kandiah and Mr K. P. John will be going long ways I am telling you.

65. THE ODDITY

Vincent Lee Chee Min

I had more than two years in Aussie after the VJ-night incident, and it wasn't until June 1948, when the Emergency had been declared in Malaya, that I was able to persuade Dad to let me come home and do as I wished. Dad's a tough nut – he'd survived the war without a scratch – with some pretty definite ideas.

Mum and Rosalie returned to Malaya on the first ship they could get a passage in and I had settled down to swot for my school leaving certificate. But barely a week-end went by without my hot footing it down to the police station, and soon they were making jokes about their latest recruit, and sometimes, when I was hanging around, waiting for my friend Bill to come off duty, Sergeant Williamson would take me into his office and, without him realising it, I'm sure, I was learning a heap.

Sergeant Williamson introduced me to an old retired couple who lived up in the hills, who'd been with the Malayan police pre-war. A real dinkum couple they were, who made me feel at home in their house and encouraged my enthusiasm to join the force.

But it took the Emergency to budge Dad. No good telling him I was an oddity – a Chinese whose *métier* was not maths – it was something he just would not tolerate. So I set to on the accountancy course, hating every minute of it, and then, wham! The headlines announcing that the first planter had been killed were my saving grace. I reckoned it was the time to make Dad change his mind. I pointed out that a son in the police would surely be an asset in these new circumstances. I was now eighteen and, with my education, was bound to get direct entry into the Inspectorate and gazetted rank in time.

To my surprise there was dead silence for a few weeks, then his reply was of a very different tone from usual. He would give his consent after all, he said, provided I was accepted into Special Branch.

This may sound as though Dad were planning his own intelligence network – not that I'd put that past him, if he doesn't already have one – but there is something abhorrent about a uniform to most Chinese. It would not have worried me, but Dad is still China born in his ways, and in China, right through the centuries, there has been no lower standing than that of soldier or policeman. No doubt things have changed with Communism, but, as far as he was concerned, uniforms were out. He said he would be getting in touch with a friend of his, a senior Chinese officer in Special Branch Headquarters, and meanwhile I had better knuckle down and qualify; who knew when I might need a second string to my bow? It never occurred to him, I am sure, that I would get beyond the first interview for the police.

66. THE SHERIFF

Sharif Ahmat

After Hassan's death I had applied for a posting to Negri Sembilan, so that I could be nearer my mother. To my surprise it was refused because, I was told, I had been selected for a course at a Police Training College in England.

Selfish as it may sound, I was glad to go. Hassan had told me so much about Europe and I was eager to see for myself. Besides, it had been a harrowing year, for me as well as my mother, and I looked forward to having something other than family affairs to concentrate on.

I enjoyed the course. I should have been there eight months and I had arranged to take my accumulated leave at the end of it when, with two of my friends, I intended exploring the Continent. But that was not to be.

Imagine my amazement when I heard over the BBC news that a State of Emergency had been declared in Malaya. It seemed dreadful that, only three years after hostilities had ended, my country should once again be plunged into unrest.

As soon as they mentioned Communists, I knew that it was all our old friends of the MPAJA, who had taken to the hills and forests again, as they had said they would if they did not get their own way. This was no secret and I wondered what Special Branch were doing, to let them get away. But how can one understand these things eight thousand miles away?

I had never really gone into Communist doctrine – although Kassim had tried often enough to explain the whys and wherefores to me – and did not know what it was that they wanted. During the war

440

we had been fighting a common enemy. After the war I found their aims difficult to follow, so mixed up in flowery language and jargon. To be honest, I had forgotten all about them, but the news brought them vividly to mind.

It was obvious that with the declaration of the Emergency, every police officer would be needed at home, so I was not surprised when I found myself recalled before the end of the course.

Imagine my surprise, on return to Police Headquarters, to find myself seconded to the army for a year, not to do police work at all.

The life did not seem strange at all. Of course I had to put up with a lot of banter, such as the soldiers asking me what I had done with my four wives and where did I keep my prayer mat! I didn't mind. They were a good natured lot and, once I got used to their lack of dignity, I enjoyed their company.

The three officers were always meticulous in their address, calling me by my full rank and name. But Inspector Sharif Ahmat was too much for the men and within a couple of days the combination of my name and silver star cap badge caused some wit to dub me 'the Sheriff'. And the Sheriff I remained for a happy year.

The unit I was attached to dealt mainly with air photographs. It was interesting and exciting work and I really felt that I was doing something worthwhile. I have never forgotten Hassan's comment on my early wartime 'see nothing, hear nothing, do nothing' policy. 'Well, you were hardly a ball of fire, were you?' I could hear him in my mind as plainly as though he were there. I had smarted then and I still felt a mite ashamed every time I recalled it.

Perhaps you don't believe in ghosts, but most of us Malays do, and I had a strong feeling that Hassan was close by, watching over me. I remembered being shown an air photograph of our clearing and Hassan explaining why they had moved a hut after receiving the prints. I told the CO about it one day and he immediately wrote down the details of the area and sent a clerk to see if there were any photographs covering that map reference. He chatted to me in a very friendly manner while we were waiting for the prints, and I soon found myself telling him about our life during the occupation and Hassan's exploits and sad end. (I did not tell him about my sister's wedding, because running amok and suicide are things which anyone would prefer to forget.)

Imagine my joy when the photographs arrived! Not the ones I'd seen before, of course, but taken on a fairly recent sortie. Captain Jones took his stereoscope and started searching the prints for a camp and, as soon as he turned up the print with the huge Sakai clearing on it, I knew it was our clearing straight away. Allah, how my mind leaped back!

I showed Captain Jones exactly where the huts had been – and probably still were – and he searched again. After a while he remarked that our camouflage must have been pretty good, as he could see no sign of it, nor of any path leading to the camp. I thrilled with pride; although, of course, it had had nothing to do with me.

It was terrible to think that Dick Richardson and Hassan were both dead and the Chinese whom I had known were now our enemies.

Only the officers actually interpreted the photographs. I worked with the other ranks who plotted them and made maps and traces and sometimes mosaics of the required areas. But after that session with Captain Jones he often called me in to look at certain photographs and ask me questions concerning them.

I suppose one takes one's own country for granted and, although I had often been half asleep on beat duty, I found that my local knowledge was greater than I had realised.

It was during this time that I met Azizah.

There is quite a famous amusement park in KL, the Bintang Kilat, which means Shining Star. Part of it was out of bounds to the British troops, so, of course, that made it all the more attractive, and for some time the boys had been urging me to take them there.

It was nothing special really. I had been there a few times, but it wasn't one of my haunts. A good old jumble of noisy entertainment. Besides the shooting-galleries and the carnival side, there were a couple of cabarets – these were the main attraction for the BORs – where pretty little Chinese taxi dancers sat two to a table round the floor. You bought a book of tickets and each ticket was worth a dance with the girl of your choice. By rights a girl couldn't refuse, but occasionally they did – and who could blame them when you saw some of the sweaty, beer-sodden drunks looming over them? Then, of course, there would be a brawl and that was one of the reasons why several of these cabarets were out of bounds. The other was because many of the girls were also prostitutes, and there was insufficient control over disease.

There was also Cantonese opera, which is colourful enough if you can bear the noise; various juggling and conjuring acts; the Siamese *ramvong* and the Malay *ronggeng* stages.

It was to one of these last that I led my companions one Saturday night.

The Malay *ronggeng* is our national dance, although I believe it has its origins with the Portuguese. Only professional female dancers take part, and in this case four of them were sitting at one end of a raised platform beside a three-piece Malay orchestra, consisting of a drummer and two violinists.

I remember that evening very well, because it was the first time I saw Azizah.

She sat at the end nearest to where we were standing and she was the tallest, slimmest and fairest of the four. She was dressed in a sarong and kebaya all of one material; both the long-sleeved, tight-fitting bodice and even tighter skirt, of apple green, shot with a silvery thread. She wore high-heeled, red, Western-style shoes, and a silver anklet peeped out of the slit in her skirt. Her hair was thick and glossy and naturally wavy, and it fell in a heavy fold on her shoulders, glistening and swaying with every movement.

She was the most beautiful creature I had ever seen and I couldn't take my eyes off her. I have seen her in many different outfits and with many different backgrounds since, but it is always as I saw her on that first occasion that I remember her best.

We do not touch our partners in the ronggeng, and most often it is now just a shuffle backwards and forwards, with an occasional turn or sideways movement, but little more. A lot of it is called joget modern these days, and that is just what it is – a sort of aimless jog to samba rhythm, which anyone can do. But there are intricate steps and movements to the real ronggeng, and my father, being quite an expert himself, had taught us all as boys.

I realised with a sudden shock that I was getting on for twenty-seven and still unmarried and that women had played a very small part in my life. My mother was always pleading with me to be allowed to arrange a marriage and I had accepted the fact that I could not remain a bachelor much longer, but I had not given it serious thought.

But now, looking at this glorious girl, I knew quite definitely that I was going to choose my own wife and not be matched off with some boring frump from the right family.

'Go on, Sheriff – take your eyes off that girl and dance with her!'

All of a sudden I wanted to show off. I bought a beer all round for the band and asked the leader if he would play the intricate handker-chief dance.

At the first drum beat I was on the floor and whirling into the extravagant solo request that is the prerogative of the first dancer on the floor, but more often than not missed out nowadays, especially in public places.

Recognising the introductory strains, the girls began pulling out brightly-coloured chiffon handkerchiefs and a sigh of approval went up from the Malays in the crowd.

I continued my gyrations, every so often approaching the partner of my choice with bent knees and outstretched hands, until such time as three other men had joined me on the platform. My partner re-mained seated, looking bored and blank, as custom demands, until the band went into the rhythm proper, when all four girls rose.

Luckily I had a rather super white silk handkerchief with my initials embroidered in one corner, which I had bought in England, and I was able to pull this languidly from my sleeve and face my partner with the required air of nonchalance which I was far from feeling.

The footwork in this dance is precise and there are several moments when one goes down close to the ground with bent knees and ankles, dancing round each other in movements not unlike those of a Cossack dance. This is not easy to perform, especially when rising with slow grace and without losing the rhythm. Each time we went down there were cries of 'Good old Sheriff' from my friends, and applause from the crowd. Every time the band reached the final passage, the crowd roared for them not to stop and they struck up again.

My partner remained as cool and graceful as a swan, but I could feel the sweat trickling down my back and chest and was thankful when the last chord was finally played.

The beautiful girl actually smiled at me and I gave her a curt bow.

I knew that this was the moment to leave, so, jumping from the platform and mopping my brow, I cried out, 'Come on, I'll buy you all a beer. Allah knows, I need one!'

We went on to the cabaret after that but I didn't dance. I never have been able to get used to the Western style of dancing. I had been to many dances in England, but it still seemed slightly shameful to me to clutch a strange woman – or, even worse, one you knew – close like that.

I sat and dreamed dreams of my ronggeng girl.

It became a regular Saturday night routine for a whole gang of us, some of them soldiers from my own unit and two or three of the Malay NCOs, to visit the amusement park and end up with a meal.

After a while I began slipping off on my own on the odd night during the week, and soon I noticed that Azizah's face would light up when I arrived.

She had delicate features; a thinnish, bridged nose, which betrayed a portion of Arab or Turkish blood, and a wide mouth with the most perfect teeth I had ever seen. I never grew tired of looking at her, and when she smiled I felt desire leap in my loins like a shoal of fish.

There was an extra girl, who relieved the others in turn for a couple of dances throughout the night, and it was during one of these breaks that I asked Azizah to have a cup of coffee with me at a nearby stall.

It was the first time I had heard her speak. She had a clear voice, a trifle high, but melodious, with a terrible Pahang accent, but I felt sure I could eradicate that in time.

She seemed impressed when I told her I was a police inspector and, to her credit, made no bones about her own social standing. Her mother, she told me, had also been a ronggeng girl, who died during the occupation. She had no idea who her father was. At first I was shocked by this candid statement, but later I came to respect her for her complete honesty.

After a couple of months I ventured to ask Azizah if she would come to the cinema with me one Sunday, and imagine my delight when she assented.

It was a ghastly film, highly emotional and badly overacted. Something about a pontianak – you know, a woman who dies in childbirth and comes back to haunt the place. They are always portrayed as skinny hags with staring eyes, long fangs and claws, and hair like a bale of straw which has come unravelled. Ridiculous, of course, but Azizah was terrified and on several occasions clutched my arm with fright and buried her face in my shoulder. It was wonderful! I made a mental note always to take her to horror films!

Afterwards we went and had a meal of satay and chicken curry; it was one of the best evenings I can remember.

I had told Azizah a little about my family and during the meal she asked if my mother would not be shocked to think of my taking out a girl on her own, unchaperoned.

In truth my mother would have been more than shocked, had she known. But I had taken out girls in England and could see nothing wrong in what seemed to me a pleasant Western custom.

Soon we were spending every Sunday together. I had acquired a second-hand scooter, one of those Italian jobs, and I would pick her up at midday from the room she rented with a couple of other girls in the Malay reserve part of town, and off we'd go.

Mostly we would stroll round the Lake Gardens and have an open-air meal, but we usually ended up in the cinema.

Azizah wanted to go to Port Dickson and swim, but I could not contemplate seeing her in a bathing suit before we were married.

From this you will gather that I had thoughts of marriage on my mind, although I had said nothing as yet to her – nor to my mother. When finally I did mention it, she just laughed and said that as my mother would never permit our union, why even think about it.

I believe Azizah would have given herself to me had I asked – in fact, she almost hinted as much – and this worried me. I wanted her enough, my blood is as hot as the next man's, but loose conduct is something which I have been brought up to abhor and, when I married, I wanted my wife to be a virgin.

I tried to explain all this to her, but I couldn't. Europeans seem to find it so easy to discuss these things – I used to listen aghast sometimes to my English colleagues at the Police Training College when they talked about their love life with such frankness – but, modern as I am, it goes against all my upbringing.

I am sure that Azizah is a pure girl and I have told her that I would not soil that purity – she gave me a funny look, but I think she understands.

67. OF THOSE WHO SURVIVED

Jogindar Singh

I got my posting – traffic branch at Perangor Contingent Headquarters – and no more questions asked. I wanted to write a letter to thank the Depot Adjutant, but I am not very good at writing, so my wife made a fan of gold and silver paper on a bamboo frame and covered it with a mesh of lace and embroidery, which I presented to him for his little daughter. Suvindar is clever with her hands and it was a pretty thing.

It was during the first quarter of 1949 that we boarded the north-bound train from Kuala Lumpur, my wife already with child and suffering from dizzy spells, and our barang, that is, all our belongings, taking up half the railway carriage. It was a relief to arrive at our destination.

Wales is the Chief Police Officer of my new contingent. I didn't recognise him, but I never forget a name and his was on one of my sheaf of letters. I made it my business, therefore, to put myself where he might see me.

My chance came about a week after our arrival. The CPO was already in his car, with the driver walking round to the front seat, when he saw me and leaned out of the window, a puzzled look on his face.

'Just a minute,' he said to the driver, and to me, 'Corporal.'

'Sahib.'

I marched over to the open window and saluted.

He peered short-sightedly at me for a moment, then, 'It *is* Jogindar, isn't it?'

I smiled. 'Sahib.'

He smiled too and held out his hand through the window. 'I can't stop now, I'm on my way to a meeting. Come and see me in my office this afternoon.'

'Sahib.' I crashed my heels again and the staff car drove away.

'Come in, Jogindar, and sit down.'

I hesitated, but the CPO motioned me to bring up a chair.

We talked of the war years, of those who survived and those who had not, of the Japs and of the food, of the tragedies and some of the funny episodes, all the time being interrupted by the telephone and the entry and exit of clerks.

'It's a bit like being on a railway platform,' he laughed, 'I don't get much time these days.' Before I left, he asked me how I liked my job and then advised, 'Traffic's all right, but like most specialist jobs, it's a bit of a dead end. If you want to get on you have to be GD – if I can see an opening for you in a General Duties post I'll let you know.'

That first interview had taken place in June, soon after the Emergency had broken out, and since then the CPO had been busier than ever. He was not young and the years in prison camp had not made him any younger. He looked small and grey as he darted in and out, and there were many lines on his face. It was September when he sent for me again.

'I hear you've become a father *and* done well in your exams since I last saw you. I'm pleased to hear it. And now I have some good news for you. I'm putting you in charge of the police station at Batu Lima. It's a sergeant's post with a corporal and ten men. Only a small station, but it's in a bad area and it's a chance to prove your worth. If you do well, there will be larger stations to follow. No one wants an Emergency, but it opens up endless opportunities for young men like yourself.'

It seemed a long time since Uncle Arjan had mapped out a course for me.

I was thinking about this as I took off my boots outside my barrack-room and tiptoed inside. Suspended from a hook in the ceiling was a spring, which in turn held a sarong and inside the sarong reposed my infant son, not yet two months old.

'Ranjit,' I whispered, gently pulling on the spring, 'Ranjit Singh, son of Jogindar Singh, grandson of Pritam Singh.'

I was still rocking the child and crooning an ancient Punjabi lullaby when my wife came down the verandah from the communal kitchen, bearing our midday meal.

I watched her as she laid out plates and saucers, took the hot chapatties from a cloth and spread them liberally with *ghee*. Soon my meal was ready and she took the child from his swinging crib, to sit and suckle him while I ate.

'You are a good wife, Suvindar,' I said, 'a good wife, a good mother and a good cook. I am a lucky man.'

She lowered her eyes, with the shy smile which she had never lost, and hugged the child to her.

'I also,' she murmured. 'You are a good husband to me.'

I ate in silence for a while, enjoying my meal and the picture of my wife and son.

'The curry is good,' I said, as I folded a chapattie and dipped it in

447

the sauce. 'How would you like to have your own kitchen, instead of having to wait your turn with everybody else?'

'Of course I would like it.'

'You will have one soon – perhaps next week.'

At that her enormous eyes flew open wide and stared into mine, questioning, hopeful.

'A sergeant's quarters has its own kitchen,' I said.

Her brow furrowed and she put the child away from her. 'A sergeant's quarters?'

'Within a short time from now you will be the wife of the OCPS, Batu Lima.'

She smiled then and her eyes shone. She put Ranjit back inside the sarong and moved to replenish my plate.

There was no need to explain to her the meaning of OCPS; she was a police daughter. But for those of you who are unfamiliar with the police formation, I will explain.

At the top is the Commissioner, at Federal Headquarters, then each State has its own HQ – Contingents, the State formations are called – under a Chief Police Officer. Our Contingent was divided into four Circles, each one under an Officer Superintending Police Circle; and the Circles divided again into Districts, each one under an Officer-in-Charge Police District. The circle that I was posted to comprised three Districts, Kuala Jelang, Merbau and Kemuning. Batu Lima was one of the stations in Kemuning District and I was to be Officer-in-Charge Police Station. Of course we never use all these long-winded titles, but refer to the officers concerned as the CPO, OSPC, OCPD and OCPS respectively. There are several jobs that we refer to by initials, and I will tell you about these, then, if anyone in the police is telling you his story, you will understand what he is talking about. First, let me say that using initials as we do is not laziness, but for ease and clarity; whether we are speaking Urdu, Malay, Chinese, English, or any of the other languages used in Malaya, we always use the same initials. All the uniformed members of the force are General Duties, or GD; the plain-clothes ones are members either of Special Branch, SB, or the Criminal Investigation Department, CID. The lowest rank in either is Police Constable, or PC, and, if he is one of the latter branches, he puts a D in front of it for Detective. Every police station has a Charge Room Officer always on duty and he is referred to as the CRO. Of course there are many others and, now that the Emergency is on, you are always hearing references to CTs, or Communist Terrorists – often called bandits as well – the MCP, or Malayan Communist Party, SEPs, or Surrendered Enemy Personnel – those are the informers – nearly all the estates and mines have Special Constables guarding them, and they are always known as SCs.

I hope I have not muddled you, but you can see from the formation

448

I have explained that I would, in the future, be far removed from the CPO, under whose eyes I had worked for the past few months, but he will still have the last word on my promotion or demotion, depending on how I make out in my first sergeant's post.

I could see at a glance that there would be much to do in my new station. The men, all Malays, were undisciplined, lazy and frightened. My predecessor was a lily-livered Malay of the worst type. Scared of his own shadow, he had let the very thought of the terrorists get the whole station down. Who cared about a handful of Chinese bandits? I'd seen worse than that during the war. I told the men just that, and it was not too long before I had instilled some discipline and pride into them again and generally tidied the place up.

The OCPD had his hands full and only visited infrequently, but when he did he was quite complimentary and said he was glad to have me. He was very young and rather remote. I would never know him as well as I knew the CPO.

I enjoyed my new responsibility. The CPO had been right; traffic was a dead end. I was grateful for his help but, as I did so frequently, I had to think back and be grateful for the first help, the first guidance, that I had received from my uncle, Arjan Singh.

68. A MATTER OF LANGUAGE

Vincent Lee Chee Min

Dad had given his consent to my joining the police soon after the beginning of the Emergency, in the middle of 1948, and by the end of the year I was in Singapore, with him.

It had certainly looked as though he intended to kill the fatted calf when he wired me that a room was booked for me in the Cathay Hotel and I was to wait for him there.

Instead, he was at the airport to meet me and, if it hadn't been for the letter that I'd received from Mum in the meantime, I would have thought he was afraid I might give him the slip.

Mum had written to tell me that Rosalie was married and that the union had suited everyone. Two of my elder brothers were already back in Malaya, but the doctor, Anthony, had stayed on in Melbourne to do a post-graduate course. Apparently a friend of his, recently qualified from the same university, had called on Mum and Dad on his return to Malaya and fallen hook, line and sinker for little Rosalie. It was mutual and, as he was the son of one of Dad's important business associates, everything in the garden was lovely. Then, just a month ago, Anthony had written to say he was married too – and would soon be bringing home his Australian bride.

I gather from Mum the old man nearly threw a fit. That was *not* why he had sent us all to Aussie and he immediately panicked in case I should do the same thing. Hence the sudden summons home. Marriage, as far as Dad is concerned, is for one reason only, to unite businesses and to produce heirs to inherit them. The thought of marrying someone merely because you wanted to live with them was, in my father's eyes, sheer lunacy. Marriage was a business contract; you could always find secondary wives for pleasure.

I was thinking about all this while I waited for my bags to be cleared through Customs and responded to Dad's effusive gestures through the iron grille.

'Hi, Dad,' I was able to say at last, 'you look great. I thought you'd be white-haired by now!' I hadn't seen him for more than seven years.

'You look great yourself, son.'

He beamed and patted me on the back, but once we were inside his chauffeur-driven car he said, 'Let's not use a foreign tongue between ourselves,' and addressed me in our own dialect.

I was at a loss.

I could vaguely comprehend what he was saying, but I could not for the life of me reply.

My father looked hard at me and grew stern. 'Don't you choose to speak your own language any more – or can't you?' I shook my head, mute. 'Your brothers did not forget. And how about your mother – didn't you speak with her at week-ends?'

It was true that Mum had spoken a little Cantonese with us when she had first arrived, but she had soon got into the habit of speaking only English herself. She was better educated than Dad and I guess this was a sore point. But Dad is Fukien and we had always spoken his dialect at home.

'I was only eleven when you sent me to Aussie, Dad,' I reminded him. I didn't want to let Mum down.

'Hm.' He sat in silence for the rest of the drive into town. He had made an effort to learn English himself during the past few years, but it didn't come naturally and it was not a language he enjoyed.

That evening he took me to a businessmen's dinner and excused me, saying that I had almost forgotten my own dialect, let alone Hokkien, but I could see he was ashamed of me. I picked up my chopsticks and my fingers felt stiff too; I would have given a lot for a fork – oh Mum!

It was good to see Mum again, but I only stayed a few days at home. I had always thought of our house as being fairly vast, but it was even larger than I remembered and I had got out of the habit of being

450

waited on hand and foot. It seemed to me that the luxury was a little oppressive and, for the first time, I really understood why Mum had loved her little apartment, where she could do what she liked when she liked and in privacy.

Rosalie's husband was already practising in Kuala Lumpur and I was glad to stay with them while I looked up Dad's influential friend in the police.

My, it was good to be back to informality. I was already beginning to pick up my Chinese again, but those two spoke English at home from choice and had only one maidservant to attend to their needs.

We spent a happy evening talking about old times and then I was up early to see to my career.

Dad's friend at Police Headquarters was an austere, scholarly type, who greeted me without much enthusiasm. I don't know what rank he was, because he wore plain clothes, but by the deference he was treated with, I'd say pretty high.

'We should not have any trouble getting you into the Inspectorate,' he said, after he'd written down my particulars. 'We badly need more Chinese inspectors in Special Branch. You have a good background and education, and languages are all-important now.'

We had used English throughout the interview.

'We like at least three Chinese dialects if possible,' he went on, 'but two will suffice, and of course Malay and English. What's your Malay like?'

'Hopeless,' I told him, 'I haven't used it for eight years.'

He waved that away. 'Not important; you'll pick it up. You've got English. I'd better just make a note of your Chinese dialects though.'

He held his pencil poised and waited. Then he looked expectantly at me.

'None,' I said at last.

'Don't try to be too clever because you've become so Europeanised,' he sounded cross. 'You must have two dialects – and most educated Chinese of your age have Mandarin as well these days.'

'I'm sorry,' I said, 'I shall no doubt relearn them, but at present I have none.'

'Then it seems that you are wasting my time.'

It was obvious that he thought Dad had made a fool of him and his eyes and mouth were hard slits when I stood up to say good-bye.

He barely touched my hand and was already immersed in some report by the time I reached the door.

'Well, good on you,' I said sarcastically to my reflection in the office door; 'so much for Commissioner Lee!'

But I could still join the force; I didn't *have* to go through the

451

back door – although for Dad and his ilk that was the only way to go. I marched straight down the hill, along the road and the main street, until I came to the first police station. I went in.

'I wish to enlist as a police constable,' I said.

Bugger the old man!

69. AN ILL-CONSTRUCTED TRIANGLE

The first stream joins the river
Donald Thom

'How did it go?'

'All right, I think. When, and if, I graduate.'

Cautious Thom, they call me. Well, I didn't want to sound too cocky, but I was pretty sure it was going to be all right.

A chorus of groans greeted my last remark. Affectation really, because almost all those guys were just one hundred per cent certain they were going to graduate. Only I was afraid of not getting through – because I wanted to so much.

We'd all been through the war, none of us all that young, but they just didn't seem to care whether they passed or failed. There's always next time, they said. Judas Priest, was I ever that carefree?

The interview was for selection into the Colonial Forestry Service and just about every doggone one of us had applied. Sure hope there are plenty of vacancies.

Well, I graduated okay and that sure was a relief plus. The day those results came through we had some shindig and then it was a case of getting down to work.

The Board was as good as its word and I didn't have long to wait before a short, dry letter arrived from the Colonial Office, offering me a post in the Forestry Department of the Federation of Malaya, subject to my being found medically fit.

I had no worries on the latter score. It was a long time since I'd broken my legs and I'd been playing rugger and ice hockey since then, so the medical was a mere formality.

Three of us were on the same posting and I guess our faces must have looked like shining Edam cheeses when we left the Colonial Office, armed with lists of what to take and what not to. Then off to get our tropical kit and we were all set for the boat.

I guess I was labelled a wet blanket from the outset. I enjoyed the voyage okay, but hell, once bitten twice shy, damned if I was going chasing the girls, and honestly, the conversation every morning in the bar about who had been caught with whom and in whose cabin became just plain boring after a while. Judas Priest, you'd think those guys had nothing better to think about.

Well, I spent my time sun-bathing and doing PT, doing as much swimming as one can do in those pint-sized ponds they call pools on ships, playing deck tennis, and the rest. I disgusted my companions, but who cares? Probably never see each other again once we've reached Singapore.

I sure feel the heat, though. Gee whiz, this humidity! I thought my home state at harvest time was pretty near furnace heat, but that was easier to take than this. Seems like I change my shirt every half-hour and I'm still wet through. But I reckon if I can keep up this exercise now, actual work shouldn't be too bad when we start.

Well, we're here. That Singapore is quite a place. Noisier than any-wheres else I've ever been, and who says the Chinese are a quiet, dignified bunch? Mystic East, my eye – vulgar and ostentatious we'd call them back home, but I guess the old folks are different. Mind you, we only spent the week-end there, then the Monday shopping, and the night mail train to Kuala Lumpur.

We'd heard some about the Malayan Emergency on the boat, but I don't quite know what I'd expected. Certainly not the train with its armour-plated pilot engine, and so many troops and police swarming all over the place. Still, I gather there've been too many derailments for them to take chances. Mind you, the troops guarding the train that night – Jocks they were – were so darned high that they had to be taken off before we were half-way through the State of Johore, the most southern state, and replaced by Malay police. I sure wasn't so proud of my Scottish ancestry that night, but it seems like the Jocks were on the last lap of their tour and they were celebrating the thought of going home.

Jesus, you should see the railway station in Kuala Lumpur! Like something out of the *Arabian Nights*! I guess they built it to look like a Sultan's palace or something, and they sure did succeed. Marble columns and domes and all those little minarets and things. Certainly is quite different from anywhere else I've been. I reckon I'm going to enjoy it here.

And now I'm posted to Kuala Jelang and my head's sure in a whirl. The blurb tells me that it is a district comprising hilly rain forest – isn't all Malaya? – rubber plantations, one oil palm plantation, one tin mine, a rice-growing area, and the rest coastal swamp.

What it didn't tell me was that I was going to receive my baptism of fire on my very first day there. And in the darndest way.

Would you believe it? During the month we'd spent becoming

453

familiarised we'd spent some time on forestry stations in pretty dangerous areas and some on the rifle range at the Police Depot – after all, the forests are where most of the terrorists live. I'd got myself a carbine and been enrolled as an honorary inspector in the Special Constabulary, so what more natural than when seeing a coupla SCs standing by the roadside I should stop to say how do – try out my two words of Malay?

It's a red road from the state capital to Kuala Jelang and I'd been tense as a cricket the whole way down, expecting an ambush at every turn. Then, just a coupla miles out of KJ itself, I see these two guys, so I stop.

One of the bastards loosed off at me before I was even half-ways out of the car, and before I could aim myself they were away.

And so was I. That car sure became a hot rod and I kept my foot right down for the rest of the journey, and to hell with the tyres.

Did I feel a bloody fool, arriving in my first station with a bloodied shirt and my arm feeling a thousand hornets were having a go at it – yeah, the blighters had nicked me, just above the elbow, but I was so doggone mad I hadn't noticed it at the time.

Scant sympathy from the police. Laughed their silly heads off at my being so green – they sent out a patrol nevertheless. Seems a couple of SCs were killed in that area last week and those guys must've had their uniforms – I learned the bandits usually stripped them.

Well, Thom. Lesson number one: this is another war; you're not playing at Boy Scouts.

Kuala Jelang was not at all what I had expected and neither was, or is, the job. I'm not complaining. But I'll sure feel a fish out of water until I get a hold of this language, though, and in a minute you'll see why.

I was pretty glad when I'd been told that once I'd taken over it would be an all-bachelor station, but now I'm not so sure. My pre-decessor, a middle-aged guy named Leslie, with a young and pretty wife, threw a luncheon party for me when I first arrived, for me and the rest of the European community. That is to say, the District Officer and the OC Police – or DO and OCPD as I've learned to call them – the other two bachelors. Leslie spent most of the time telling me how he sure hoped for a town posting when he returned from leave, because his wife was going nuts here; and the other two kept telling me how they were going to miss having a woman around the place to stop them talking shop the whole time.

I don't reckon the three of us are going to have much in common. The DO's one of those maidenly old bachelors – you know the type, petit point pictures on the walls and a Malay youth in the servants' quarters. The OCPD, on the other hand, is a womaniser, a great one for the ladies. So where do I fall? I ask you, what an ill-constructed triangle – a stallion, a queer and a celibate monk!

I'd put both Monica and Marijke firmly out of my mind the minute I set foot on that boat, and that's where they were going to stay – I wasn't going to be haunted by any more ghosts. I'd come here to throw myself into my work and, Judas Priest, that's what I'm going to do.

It had been easy while I lived in the Rest House, but once the Leslies had gone and I moved into my own quarters, it was difficult to imagine how I'd cope on my own. And I nearly didn't have to. I said I needed to get a hold of the language, and if I had done so by then I would not have become the laughing-stock that I did – not that I knew what they were laughing at at the time.

Derek King – that's the OCPD – had helped me move. I'd assembled a fair amount of clobber already and my quarters are down by the Forest Station, some distance from the Rest House and the other two bungalows.

We were just standing in the main room and King was voicing out loud what I'd been trying not to think about, that the place sure needed a woman, when in glided Salmah.

Now Salmah was something for which I quite definitely had not bargained. Hell, no. She was Malay, pretty, graceful and of indeterminate age. King laughed when she arrived, seems he'd been expecting her. As I've said, he's a great womaniser that boy. He quite casually slaps her on the bottom and announces to me that she's always good for a roll. How do you like that?

'But I won't touch her, old man,' he says, 'she's all yours!'

I guess I must have looked pretty nonplussed, especially as it looked to me as though he'd already touched her quite a lot. It was all I could think of and I asked, 'But you?'

He laughed again – irritating laugh that guy has – and then said cheekily, 'No thanks, old man, I like them white!'

I was just about to tell this gal that I could dispense with her services thank you very much, when King caught my arm and shook his head.

'Don't be a bloody fool, old man. She can cook – and that's something that doesn't grow on trees in Kuala Jelang – the other thing does.'

Honestly, I hadn't even thought about eating and having my clothes washed, and all the other necessities which had just happened in the hotels and Rest Houses where I'd been living. So I engaged her, albeit reluctantly, and asked Derek King, my friend, I hoped, to make it quite clear that I required her to cook and nothing else. I didn't quite trust that guy, and with reason.

Well, they went into a long confab and came out of it in peals of merriment. God damn this language! How the hell did I know what he said to her?

'Will you please tell her,' I said, in my most sedate voice, 'that I shall spend my evenings learning Malay and shall require no other entertainment.'

The translation of that brought forth another gust of laughter.

Well, I never did discover exactly what that rotter had said that day, but when I returned from work – and I was pretty shagged after that first day on my own, I can tell you – Salmah quickly filled the tin bath with hot water, laid out my clean clothes, and by the time I was out of it had a drink poured out for me. Never did a Scotch go down so well.

Well, this sure enough is service, I thought, perhaps King was my friend after all. I knew he looked after his own creature comforts pretty well – he was a bit of a sybarite for all his outer veneer of toughness. I leaned back to enjoy my drink, and when Salmah was at my elbow I didn't refuse a refill.

With the aid of sign language and the dictionary, I managed to tell her what time I wanted to eat. Not bad, it was, either. Fish, I remember, with a coconut dessert and local fruit to follow; and properly made coffee. Better than any Rest House fare without doubt. I complimented her – and myself for not being as pig-headed as I nearly was – and settled down to my work while she cleared the table, asked me if there was anything else I wanted, and quietly disappeared.

I worked for about an hour, I guess, and when the print started to blur and I was yawning as often as breathing, I reckoned it was time for bed.

I told you that that King was a double-crossing rotter. She was there all right. I heard a small sound from the bed as soon as I opened the door. No need to turn up the light, but I did, and there I beheld my cook, a flowery sarong rolled up under her arms and long golden legs and arms bare – I hadn't become so celibate that I didn't look. She was all right, all right.

'Please go,' I said; I could manage that much in Malay. 'I thought I made it quite clear.'

'You learn Malay, no?' Her voice was high-pitched and staccato. 'I teach.' She held up her arms and smiled.

'Yeah,' I groaned. 'I've heard all about those dictionaries that always open at the same page. Now off you go.'

It was pretty obvious that Salmah wouldn't, or couldn't, believe it. I reckoned she had every reason to be surprised that her advances were being refused; I bet that son of a bitch had told her I'd take her on.

'You shy,' she said. 'Look, I make like cinema.' She pouted her lips into a grotesque reproduction of what she'd no doubt seen on many a silver screen and held up those gorgeous arms again. If I hadn't been so cross, I might have weakened.

'Now come on, git.' I lifted the mosquito net, but she just pouted prettily.

What does a guy do? Okay, okay, don't tell me. Well, I didn't. I picked up my pyjamas and went back to the verandah. I didn't want her to lose too much face for what I had a shrewd suspicion was not her fault, and I had already realised that I would lose a good cook.

I spent as uncomfortable a night as I've spent since the war – and if you've ever tried sleeping on one of those government issue settees, you'll understand – until the dawn came and I heard her creep out through the bathroom door. What a relief. I sank on to my still warm bed and caught an hour's sleep.

At breakfast Salmah was all demure eyes and she never troubled me again. *What* a relief! I still had my cook too.

It was not many days before the OCPD heard on the grapevine that the new Forestry Officer was, unfortunately, impotent!

70. THE WILL OF GOD

Omar

Is it possible that I have done some terrible act during my life without knowing it? In what way have I offended Tuan Allah, that I should be visited by tragedy yet again?

We had had two uneventful years in Singapore; years of blessed tranquillity after the horrors and privations of the occupation, and I had been promoted to the rank of sergeant-major, with a pleasant little house.

These thoughts go through my head as I stand in that little house and look at my wife's neatly folded clothes and the children's toys which I still cannot bear to part with.

It had been good to be back in uniform. I had been promoted to sergeant almost at once and we had spent a happy year in Malacca. Politics had never concerned the likes of me, or so I had thought, but when the Straits Settlements and the Federated Malay States ceased to be and became first the Malayan Union, then Singapore and the Federation of Malaya, it threw many of us into turmoil. Malacca became part of the Federation and I had the choice of remaining there

457

or joining the Singapore force, where so many of the old Straits Settlements police were going. I went too.

It took us some time to become accustomed to the life of a big city after the rural areas to which we were used, but once inside the police compound there was little difference. My wife had brought the cats and chickens with her; coconuts and a lime tree to plant – wah! what didn't she bring? It was all I could do to stop her putting a sack of dried fish on the top of the taxi that had taken us to the railway station! There were nine of us on the move. I shall never forget it. Bedding rolls, pots and pans, suitcases, plastic buckets, children's toys – my wife was sure that none of these things would be obtainable in Singapore. Adohi! She was a simple woman, my wife.

We were so happy. Even the plight of Zaitun could not mar our contentment.

The medical authorities did everything they could, but it was no use. Then one day a smart young Chinese lady called on us in our quarter.

'It is about Zaitun,' she said at once. 'I am from the Social Welfare Department and we have decided, after what the doctors have said, that it would be best if you let her come to one of our homes, where she can be properly cared for.'

Allahumma! You should have seen my wife burst with indignation! Of course the young lady meant well, but my wife would not calm down until she had been chased from our door. Adohi, I was hot with shame.

So the matter of Zaitun was closed and we went on living as we had since the end of the war, a peaceful family, accepting the will of God and praying that no more bad times would come our way.

But the will of God is difficult to understand.

We had returned to Tanjong Mas for my first long leave, and the three months were nearly up when I was recalled to Singapore to be a witness in a court case. There was less than a week of my leave left anyway, so, when the case was over, I did not return to collect my family, but left them to join me on their own.

They were coming by bus, as we had arranged, and I was already at the bus terminal to meet the express when the awful news was imparted to those of us who were waiting. The bus would not arrive; there had been an accident.

The office could only tell me that it had taken place on one of the ferries, crossing a wide river in Johore, and could not say what casualties there were, or if all were safe.

Without waiting, or seeking permission from my superiors, I hailed the first taxi I saw and asked him to drive me to the scene. The driver was a family man like myself and, may Allah bless him, took me post-haste, refusing to accept my fare.

We arrived at the river after about two hours' driving and it was not difficult to see where the accident had taken place.

I went first to the small office, where normally one pays to board the ferry, to make inquiries. Only one survivor, I was told. Of the forty passengers and the driver, only one survivor.

Next I pushed my way through the crowd which surrounded the place on the river-bank where the vehicle should have mounted the ramp to the shore.

Even now I am not clear exactly what happened. Whether the driver misjudged the narrow ramp, or the ferry had swayed out of line from the wash of a passing boat, is still uncertain to me. What matter? All I or anyone could see was the bonnet and front wheels of the bus. The rest of the vehicle was well under water at an angle of about forty-five degrees.

I stood, silent as the rest of the crowd, thinking of my poor wife and children, trapped in their seats, unable to fight the pressure of the water, until it was too late, and now they would be laid out on some mortuary slab. And I knew too, without being told, who would be the one survivor.

Sometimes I wonder if Tuan Allah plays tricks on us human beings.

On the river-bank, swinging her legs and humming a tuneless dirge, sat Zaitun, as unconcerned as though she were waiting for some small, routine event.

How she came to be the chosen one, I shall never know.

She turned to me without recognition and allowed me to help her down from the parapet on which she sat. I left her in the care of the kind taxi-driver while I went to identify the bodies of my wife and other children.

I had hoped that perhaps there had been a miscount of passengers, that perhaps some member of my family might be missing from the pathetic, white-sheeted line. But they were all there. Poor drowned things. I have seen many corpses as a policeman, but when I saw those of my own, I could only wish that Tuan Allah had seen fit to take me as well.

I took Zaitun back to Singapore and cared for her as best I could. It was not long before the Social Welfare worker arrived, the same Chinese lady who had visited us before, but once again I persuaded her to let Zaitun remain with me. I had friends, kind friends, who would care for her while I was on duty and, when I was off, in a way it was a help to have the girl there, albeit silent and remote.

It was some three months before the welfare worker came again, and that time I let her take Zaitun. I was so empty already, what was one more emptiness?

She trotted down the path behind the Chinese lady without giving me a single glance. Smiling, and twirling the inevitable bloom in her

459

hands, she walked out of my life as unconscious of me as when I had first picked her up, a parcel thrown from a passing car, seventeen years before.

And I? I turned to face a life so bleak that I daily committed the sin of asking Tuan Allah in my prayers not to leave me long in this world of suffering and torment, but to take me too, so that I might join my wife and little ones. Purgatory cannot be worse.

71. THE BATTALION GOES HOME

Philip Morrison

In January 1949 the battalion went home, but it went without me. So much had happened in the two years since we had first arrived in Singapore and yet it had flown. Not everything had gone right; far from it, but when the opportunity arose we both opted to stay in Malaya for another year.

To begin with there was the baby. Sally had been in Singapore about ten months when she became pregnant and, although it had been a mistake in the first place, once she became used to the idea it became an absolute obsession. The air force created merry hell when they discovered she had been married the whole time, but there was nothing much they could do about it, so she had resigned her commission and started making baby clothes. It was a good thing, as it happened, because not long afterwards we were posted up country and she would not have been able to follow me under her own steam.

The colonel had proved to be not such a bad old bastard after all. He liked Sally, which was the main thing, and he'd been pretty decent about giving me HQ jobs when the birth was imminent. We had moved straight into married quarters and I had got my majority, so things would have been rosy if it hadn't been for the baby. It was stillborn, and if you've ever seen the look on the face of a wounded bird, that's how Sally looked and she scarcely said a word the whole time she was in hospital. To make matters worse, the gynaecologist told me that I would be a very selfish man if I ever let her have another – I didn't understand all the technical details, but he made it quite plain that it had been a matter of my wife or the child and that the same thing could happen again.

If only she had taken it better. Sally's always been so full of guts, but it floored her completely; I've never seen her so down. I put all the things she had made for the infant in a top cupboard before she came home and she never once mentioned them.

The only blessing was that just at that time a vacancy for an IO's job arose; it was the type of work which Sally had been doing quite recently in the RAF, so it didn't need much persuasion to have her taken on. I had been worried about what she would do with herself, because, after all, I was a Company Commander and had to get back on the ground. I left with an easier mind, knowing that she had something to occupy hers.

Philip was right, the job was a blessing. Not particularly arduous, but it gave me something to do. I had tried so hard not to let him see how much I cared about losing the baby, but I don't think I was very successful. Of course he isn't fooling anyone – at least, not me. All this hooey about not wanting to risk my having a child in case he's killed. I know that doddering old quack told him there was something wrong with me, but there jolly well isn't and I'll prove it, one day.

I missed him terribly when he went back on ops, but I couldn't expect him to be away any longer. After all, he is a soldier, not a midwife.

1948 was a boring time for wives. Once we moved up country, all the wives, officers' and ORs' alike, were bundled in HQ quarters, while our men lived under canvas and visited us when they could. Sometimes they were only away for a few days, but at other times for more than a month – it was nerve-racking too, not being in the know and hearing odd snippets of information that such and such a company had been in action. Philip never said very much when he came home; he would want to go out to dinner and dance, or a flick perhaps.

A platoon sergeant was killed within forty-eight hours of my return, and two Jocks bought it the day before – a hand-grenade hurled into a coffee-shop – and only one bandit to our credit. As a mere soldier, it's difficult to understand how the civil authorities let all those bastards – known Communists – just scarper off as they did. Extraordinary. One of the police chaps, whose area my company were operating in, told us that they knew all along about it too but were powerless to act. Proves the old theory that the law is an ass.

In fact, we did have a few successes later on, but by that time the battalion was almost due to leave. A pity really; we'd all like to have chalked up a decent score.

A few jobs on the staff came up at that time and Bill Matheson, whom I had been with at the beginning, and I applied and landed two of them. I had never been a headquarters type, but it meant another year here and I knew Sally would be pleased. I was right.

And so there we were. Philip got his job, I was able to keep mine, and we stayed on in the same quarters. What could be cushier? I was all for having a husband on the staff.

I was sorry to see many of our friends go, but a few Inverness-shires remained and, as Philip so often said, he had started in the wrong battalion, so being ERE for a spell was unlikely to do him much harm. There didn't seem much future in the army anyway.

As soon as he decently could, Philip put in for some leave and insisted on taking me down to see my old home. Why, I don't know, but I had always put off going there – it would have been easy enough from Singapore – but this time he made the decision and booked us a room in a nearby holiday bungalow.

As soon as we were over the border I was glad that he had taken the initiative. What a goose I'd been not to go before. As the first familiar landmarks came in sight my excitement rose and I kept stopping him to point things out. He was looking smug as anything, and if he hadn't been driving I'd have given him a big hug.

The old house still looked wonderful; timbusu trees bordering the drive and the lawns even greener than I remembered. We had rung up the present occupant, who had invited us to stay. I declined, but it was marvellous having someone so nice to take us round.

We didn't stay long, though, and next morning drove to the kampong where our servants used to live. They still did. Daddy had built a house for them before the war and, except for the trees that had grown up round about, I had no difficulty in recognising it.

Ja'afar and Siti, looking very much the same as when I had last seen them, were leaning over the railing of their small verandah, talking to someone below. They looked up as the car stopped, surprised to see Europeans, no doubt, but without a flicker of recognition on their faces.

They, of course, had already been middle-aged when we had left during the shambles of 1942, but I had only been sixteen.

Both came down the steps, their expressions of surprise changing first to puzzlement, then wonder and incredulity.

'Missy Sally? It *is* Missy Sally.'

Then they were all wide grins and Siti wrapped her arms around me and shook hands demurely with Philip, and a small boy was dispatched for cakes and bottles of orange crush.

'But why didn't you let us know you were back? We would have come to work for you.'

We were sitting on the verandah by that time, Philip feeling a bit of a lemon, I could see, because I'd made him take his shoes off! I made some feeble excuse about moving around, but they were not to be put off.

'We shall come now!' Ja'afar was quite firm. 'Next month. That will give you time to give notice to whoever you are employing at present.'

I was amused by their arrogant self-assurance and translated for Philip.

'Why not?' he asked. 'It would be nice for you. But you must tell them it will only be for a year.'

I did.

Ja'afar was unimpressed. 'Time he found another job then,' he snorted. 'Fancy not speaking Malay and leaving the country after such a short time. Whatever would the Old Tuan have said?'

Irrespective of what Sally's father might have said, there was no doubt who was going to be boss in the house in future, and it wasn't going to be me – it wasn't going to be Sally either!

I was amused to see her meekly doing what she was told by the two elderly Malays – I say elderly because they were both wrinkled and inclined towards toothlessness, but Sally said they could not be much over forty-five.

To cut a long story short, Ja'afar returned to Kuala Lumpur with us at the end of my leave and within ten days we were being thoroughly organised and I found myself having to start understanding Malay. Not a bad thing, as events proved, but I didn't know that then.

72. TO BE A HERO

Abdul Karim

The time came for me to leave school and one morning the headmaster asked me what I wanted to do.

'I want to be a mechanic,' I told him.

'A mechanic?' Inche Yacob, our headmaster, raised his eyebrows. 'Lucky all the boats have sails, because you would put paid to their outboards in no time!' He was always saying things like that.

'A mechanic?' my father asked. 'And where could you be a mechanic here?' It was true. There were no real roads, only a few tracks that jeeps and Land-Rovers could use in dry weather. No garages, no workshops. 'And what do you expect to learn on, your mother's sewing-machine? You'd better put such notions out of your head and become a fisherman like me.'

But I didn't want to be a fisherman.

I did go to sea, however, and, quite the opposite from Inche Yacob's prediction, I kept most of the outboards in good running order; the inboards too.

'It seems that the boy has a bent for engines,' I heard Inche Yacob remark to my father one day, as they sipped coffee on our verandah. I was supposed to be mending nets, but of course I stopped and strained my ears to hear what else he might have to say. 'Have you thought of putting him into the police? There's a big recruiting drive going on – here, let me see, I think I have the dates of the team's visit to this district in my pocket.'

The police? I had time to think while Inche Yacob went through one pocket after another and then said he must have left it on his desk. What would I want to join the police for? No one from Pasir Perak had ever joined the police that I knew of. I wanted to be a mechanic, not a policeman.

Pak made no mention of the conversation and I had almost forgotten it until the next time the OCPD visited our kampong. It just so happened that his Land-Rover drew up outside the police post as I was passing. I looked at the driver with new interest. Of course he was a policeman, although he was a driver – I'd not thought of that.

When the officer had gone inside the post, I approached him, suddenly feeling that he was rather grand.

'Excuse me,' I asked politely, 'but are you a mechanic as well as a driver?'

'Why do you ask? Want some old outboard mended?' He was rather a cheerful fellow, with a mouthful of gold teeth and a Kedah accent that I could hardly understand.

'Could you mend an outboard?' I asked.

'Of course.' He grinned, but at that moment the officer called to him from the doorway and we were unable to converse further.

It made me think, though.

By the time the recruiting team arrived in our area I was seventeen and a half years old and had been out of school and messing around with the fishing fleet for more than a year.

'Could I be a mechanic?' I asked the Recruiting Officer.

'If you show aptitude and a vacancy exists,' he replied. I wasn't quite sure what he meant, but at least he hadn't said no.

The team were to be there all day. I would think about it, I said, and went home to talk it over with my father.

'Karim, wait for me,' I turned as I heard Rokiah's voice behind me. 'Oh, Karim, is it true? Are you really going to join the police?'

'I want to be a mechanic,' I told her, 'as you well know.'

'But the police, Karim – you might get killed. I know the Emergency hasn't touched us here yet, but hundreds of police are being killed on the other side.'

Musah had left the kampong, and it was generally thought that he was making his fortune in Singapore. I had been jealous of Rokiah's admiration for him.

Quite suddenly I wanted to be a hero in Rokiah's eyes.

'Men are needed,' I said shortly. 'It is better that I should serve

464

my country rather than mess around here as I'm doing now – besides, I'm bored.'

'Oh, Karim, I do hope you won't get killed.'

She took my hand and we walked together down the road to my house, as we had walked nearly every day since she was nine and I was ten years old.

73. A COMMISSIONER'S COMMENDATION

The second stream joins the river

Jogindar Singh

It was in May 1949 that we moved again.

I had had seven months as OCPS Batu Lima when, one day in April, the OCPD visited the station. He had inspected everything, the books, the barracks, the arms and ammunition, before he told me that I was posted.

'You've done a good job here, Dato,' he said, 'and if I were not moving myself I would probably jib at your posting – except that it's on promotion, so I couldn't.'

I should explain here that sergeants and sergeant-majors are called 'Dato' in the force; it means 'Grandfather'. In the same way, inspectors are called 'Inche' and officers 'Tuan', which mean 'Mister' and 'Sir' – although many of us have kept the terms of respect from our own language and still call European officers 'Sahib'. It is just one of our customs.

'Sahib?' I now inquired, and to be polite, although I was burning with curiosity regarding my own future. 'The district will be sorry that you are leaving.'

He laughed then, and looking at him closely I saw that he was not, after all, so young.

'Jungle training school for me. It'll be a rest cure after a district. But aren't you interested in your own posting?'

'Sahib.'

'Well, you're only moving next door – OCPS Kuala Jelang. It's district headquarters, so it'll be promotion to sergeant-major for you. Both the OSPC and I have been very pleased with your work here and there'll be a Commissioner's Commendation for that amok case last month. Congratulations.'

The episode he referred to was an unpleasant one, when a Javanese in one of the nearby kampongs had run amok. Two of the man's immediate relatives were already dead and a third one near-fatally slashed when we were called. I had seen him coming at me like a crazed bull, parang raised, and put up my rifle to take the blow, in the same way as we use our staves as weapons of defence. It had not been difficult then to disarm him with one hand and drive my free fist into his jaw. He had gone down as though dead – and indeed I was afraid that I might have hit him too hard – but he regained consciousness soon after we had him locked in the police station cell. It had been an incident in the normal line of duty and did not to my mind merit a commendation, but I was pleased to have it.

So once again we were on the move. Only a matter of some 40 miles to the coast and the OCPD let me use a troop-carrier to transport my family and belongings. Once more my wife was near her time and I was glad that she was able to ride in front of the van with little Ranjit, now eleven months old. The back was piled high with our bedding rolls, pots and pans, and furniture that we had acquired, and I followed in a hired lorry, carrying the fruit trees in pots that were nearly ready for planting out, and our three cows. These last I had purchased when first coming to Batu Lima, in order to obtain fresh milk for my wife and child. The Health Sister, who comes round with the Mobile Clinic, insists that it is unhygienic and has done her best to dissuade Suvindar from drinking it, but some of these young women are very ill-informed. I had travelled to Kuala Jelang on the first day off after being informed of my transfer and made sure that there would indeed be sufficient grazing ground in the vicinity of the police station for the cattle.

It had been a business, pulling the unwilling beasts up the ramp and on to the lorry, but at last we were under way, with instructions to the driver to keep an even, steady pace and not to go too fast – he might worry about ambushes, but I did not want to risk any broken legs.

Kuala Jelang was not unlike the coastal station where my father had ended his days as OCPS, only on the opposite side of the peninsula.

I was pleased to see that the police compound was well out of the town and away from the other government quarters. This made for both privacy and security and I believe that the police should always remain aloof from the civilian departments.

First I saw to the off-loading of the cows, then I saw my wife and child installed, changed into uniform, and reported to the OCPD.

On my recent visit I had come to an arrangement with a Chinese *towkay*, who owned a strip of grassland not far from the barracks, to let me graze my cattle there and provide him with milk in return. I knew I would never have to give him the milk – which he would not have touched anyway – but the offer had been made and he in his turn was pleased to be in favour with the police.

Poor things, they were badly scared and would undoubtedly not yield much milk for the next few days. I patted their rumps and noses and spoke gently to them until they were soothed and their great eyes were questing the juiciest grass, instead of staring in panic at the confining walls of the lorry.

Although still OCPS, I would no longer be my own master in the way that I had been at Batu Lima. Being a District Headquarters, the OCPD had his office in the station and there were a couple of Malay inspectors. Nevertheless, I was sergeant-major now, probably one of the youngest in the force; I could not complain.

The OCPS's quarter was a small wooden house, raised on concrete pillars and standing alone to one side of the parade ground. My predecessor had planted many flowers in kerosene tins and Suvindar was already adding ours. I was glad that we would be installed before the second child was born. I hoped it would be another son.

74. KUALA JELANG – A BACKGROUND

Until the outbreak of the Emergency in June 1948, Kuala Jelang had been a veritable sleepy hollow.

The remains of the Portuguese fort slept on the top of the hill, the grave of Rajah Adnan, the last inhabitant of royal blood, reposed under its soft mantle of grey-green moss and the tide slid gently in and out of the mangrove swamps.

Sometimes at high tide the steamers of a local steamship company could be seen alongside the riverside wharf, loading bales of rubber and sacks of copra and pumping the liquid latex and palm oil into their tanks. Machinery would be off-loaded and stores for the local shops and estates, and occasionally a few deck passengers would disembark. Irrespective of what the ship was doing or having done to her, there would always be a crowd, because the weekly visits were an event.

On Sundays, the planters and miners would come into town to play cricket on the padang, and to foregather afterwards at the atap and timber shack that was the local club. There were no other amusements and the club was the focal point of entertainment for all around, government servants, those living on the nearby estates and mines, the shopkeepers and anyone else who felt inclined to pay the modest entrance fee. Once a fortnight a film show was held and then all those inhabitants of Kuala Jelang who were not members of the club would crowd around the open windows, standing on orange boxes and home-made stilts, and sometimes taking it in turns to stand on each other's shoulders! The films were in Malay, Chinese, English, Hindi or Tamil – it made no difference, as the soundtrack could seldom be heard above the din.

Into this peaceful and somnolent way of life the Emergency had swept overnight, like some evil tidal wave.

Incidents erupted on the surface of the district like boils, while below, the pus of fear seeped steadily and mercilessly from estate to mine, to market garden and *padi* field, controlled by the pulsing head inside the jungle itself.

First a planter was shot at point-blank range as he walked from his office to the factory; none of the labourers saw or heard a thing, despite the fact that it was a busy time of day. Then the bodies of two Tamil tappers were found, their hands nailed to the trees on which they had been working; they had been hacked to death. Fastened to one of the latex cups was a note warning their friends to expect similar treatment if they continued to tap the white man's rubber. Once again, there were no witnesses.

While King was out investigating these murders, a Javanese padi planter brought news of strangers in the rice fields; Chinese, some of whom were armed. They were demanding monthly subscriptions, clothing and food, and had issued a warning enjoining silence on the part of the subscribers. The Javanese, brave enough to inform the police in the first place, bravely returned to his land and was never seen again.

From the other side of the district came information of an illegal still and the inspector who went out, to investigate what he considered to be a routine crime, was shot in the stomach as he approached.

It was no use King, or any other OCPD, urgently demanding reinforcements from their circle or contingent HQs; there were not the men, and almost every district was in a similar plight. It was soon clear that what had appeared to be isolated incidents were, in fact, part of a well-organised pattern of violence, intended to disrupt the government and industry of the country as a whole.

After four incidents in as many days, a planter and his clerk were ambushed as they returned from the bank. On this occasion, through skilful driving, a good deal of luck, and the swift action on the part of the Tamil clerk, who threw the payroll out of the window, they escaped unscathed, but shaken.

'What are you going to do about it?' the planter demanded, crashing his fist down on the OCPD's desk. 'Sit there and take my statement?'

King was almost too tired to hear the sarcasm. He was, in fact, at his desk for the first time since the initial shooting had taken place, and then only to use the telephone.

'What the hell do you expect me to do?' He had not been to bed for three nights; had not even had time to attend his inspector's funeral. He was at his wits' end, and his superiors could not help.

'Come and see my car.'

Wearily King had followed the planter outside, noted the shattered windscreen and the bullet-scarred bodywork. 'Lucky they didn't get the tyres,' he observed, and returned to his office to flop, head in hands, until his call came through.

The planter drove off in a fury.

Next day King himself was ambushed on the main road as he drove towards Circle HQ, but this time he and his escort debussed and fought back from the ditch. There had been a yell and a body fell from an overhanging tree, and moments later a wounded man emerged, hands on head. He was their first SEP (Surrendered Enemy Personnel), prepared to turn King's evidence in return for his life. The man had been well treated, clothed and fed, and as soon as he was fit, led King and a police party to his camp. Only the sentry and one man had been killed, the remainder getting away, but it was a beginning. These were the first corpses to be put on show to the public outside the police station and they marked the turning point in the utter helplessness that had previously prevailed.

During these weeks, terrorist incidents had continued; a young Chinese squatter had been nailed to his own wall, the nail passing through his head; two PCs were burned alive in their jeep; and a woman and child were killed when a hand-grenade was hurled into a coffee-shop. Feelings ran high, and the police bore the brunt of it.

And then there had been a sudden lull. The ambushed planter had apologised to King, who in turn had gone to his estate to supervise the erection of defences. Wire mesh, with a barbed wire vee on top, went up round the police compound and various installations; round estate managers' bungalows, factories and labour lines. Planters beseeched their principals for funds for wire, guns and generators.

Although caught out so badly in the first instance, it had not taken long for the wheels to turn and soon there was action everywhere. Special Constables were recruited to guard estates, a call for recruits into the regular police went out, and European officers and sergeants came from Palestine to help. More army battalions were posted out to boost the civil power, but it was still the police who bore the brunt and in the early days stood it almost alone.

There was action and there were men, but the danger did not lessen. Every day came news of ambushes, intimidation, thefts of arms and identity cards, and killings among the labour. The Chinese who did not co-operate suffered worst, but any European was automatically a target and an armed man a definite aim.

It was into this atmosphere of tension and intense activity that

469

Donald Thom and, a few months later, Jogindar Singh, were propelled.

At first Thom was peeved to find that his movements were curtailed and he was hampered from visiting most of his area. The police on their side had no men to spare for escorting a new government officer round his domain. It worked itself out in time, but for the first few months he had to be content to concentrate on the Forest Research Station and stay near home, only going into the jungle when the police were going anyway and were prepared to take him with them.

Meanwhile, a District War Executive Committee had been set up with the DO as chairman, and Thom found himself, along with the OCPD and others, a member. He had intended appealing to this committee until he realised, long before the first session was over, just what the police were faced with and the task in hand and then, being by nature of a reasonable disposition, he gave them his whole-hearted co-operation instead.

It had not taken the police station long to feel the hand of Sergeant-major Jogindar Singh. His predecessor had succumbed to the general flap, but the unrufflable Jogindar had seen the OCPD and two inspectors going to and fro and decided, once again, that his job was to clean things up. It suited him that his seniors were sufficiently occupied with the Emergency to leave him with a free hand and he set to with a will.

Barrack-rooms were scrubbed – mud coming in on jungle boots of tired men was no excuse; equipment cleaned – wearing jungle green without any brass was no excuse either; everything polishable was polished. And woe betide the man who was seen playing the fool in a public place, whether in uniform or not.

The men groaned, but some of the older hands were pleased to have this rock standing so firmly in their midst. He anchored them to the peaceful world of discipline, drill and parades – seeing the sergeant-major, never anything but smart himself, watching with scornful eye the sloppy figures of jungle-green-clad PCs padding softly in their high jungle boots, they felt that it would take more than the bandits to dispatch *him*.

Suvindar Kaur had given birth to another boy within a month of their arrival and, when her husband marched across the compound with stern countenance and ramrod back, she would see his eyes soften as he beheld his sons. The OCPS was a different man from the husband and father that she and the children knew. They were content.

Donald Thom too had settled down. He had had no cause to worry about his privacy being disturbed. Perkins, the DO, was already looking at the calendar and sighing. His leave was only four months away and there was more than the district from which he had to tear himself. He had little interest in the self-imposed solitude of the young Canadian. And as for King, although the Emergency had now been going on for a year and he had his district under control, he was still too busy, despite his nonsensical talk of living on one long blind, to worry overmuch about the personal feelings of a man whom he considered quite old enough to take care of himself.

75. AN AMBITION ACHIEVED

Stanislaus Olshewski

Take deep breaths! It seemed that I never entered a ward without hearing a nurse telling a patient, for one reason or another, to take deep breaths. And that is just what I was doing myself.

For the first time in my life I stood at the railing of an ocean liner and listened to the seagulls fighting and screaming, as we eased our way down the Thames estuary from Tilbury.

It was a wonderful feeling to have come to a decision at last and to be looking forward to the future with no regrets. The DP camp – where I had intended working – was behind me and soon the whole of Europe would be. It was a sick continent, I thought, and needing more than doctors to cure it.

I spread my hands on the railing, thinking back, and as I looked at them a clear, high, Glaswegian voice interrupted my reverie.

'A penny for them, Doctor?'

It was Kathy MacKinnon, the little round-eyed, curly-haired Scottish nurse, who was one of my table companions in the dining-saloon. A pleasant companion in a coquettish way, no doubt, but I had no wish to become involved, especially as we were bound for the same destination.

I had been thinking about that destination, and of the person who had first mentioned it, when Miss MacKinnon joined me. But the occasion demanded flippancy.

'I was thinking of a wee Scots lassie, no less!'

'Och, Doctor, you've got it just right! But I'll bet the lassie was no' Kathy MacKinnon?'

She positively bridled with coyness, but I was in too good a mood to retort.

'The same tribe, I imagine. Sarah Catriona MacCallum Gunn, to be exact.'

Not bad, remembering that mouthful after all these years. I doubt if I'd given much thought to my future when Sally Gunn had remarked that I had hands like a Malay. But here I was, on my way to Malaya and, thinking back, trying to remember all she had told me of her home.

'We all know what you medical students used to get up to; I'll bet ye've known many a lassie, Doctor!'

'Och aye! But never one more difficult than her – nor one as pretty as you!' I might as well give it up and resign myself to nonsensical small talk. 'What would you like to drink? I'll bring them out here.'

'A wee cherry brandy would do fine.'

She was part of the scene. The brightly-lit deck – hardly necessary that clear June evening – the old hands already reclining in deckchairs, the bridge fours in the smoking-room – partners from many voyages, no doubt – the crowded, noisy lounge behind.

By the time I returned with the drinks, the Thames had begun to spew itself into the open sea and the rolling and pitching that I had heard so much about began.

It was difficult to talk with the increasing wind, and I enjoyed the silence as the day died and the long dusk blew softly into night. The motion changed and, with my eye on a distant light, I felt us turn, leaving the North Sea to enter the Channel. How intimately I knew that sleeve of water.

After four years of hard work, indecision and a good deal of soul-searching, it was easy to relax in the holiday atmosphere of the big ship and the easy companionship of Kathy MacKinnon.

We ate and drank, played deck games, danced and made love – after a lot of coy refusing, naturally. Of course I realised that I was getting myself into deeper and deeper waters, but I was lazy, and by the time we left the Red Sea and entered the Indian Ocean, Kathy and I were unofficially engaged.

I took her ashore at Aden and went out to the RAF Station, where I had landed so often during the war. I took her ashore at Bombay and we went out to the beach where I had swum so often during the war. But it had all changed. I hadn't thought of Helen for years and, when we passed the block of flats where we had spent that leave, it was difficult to believe that that other world and its inhabitants had ever existed. Kathy was a great chatterer and I was able to sit back and dream most of the time and let her prattle on.

Don't get the idea that I was wallowing in a morass of nostalgia. Far from it. As far as I was concerned, the war was a world I had escaped from and nothing would induce me to return to it. I'd achieved my ambition career-wise; it was unlikely that I would ever pilot an aircraft again – wouldn't even go up in one if I had my way;

what was wrong with the sea? I had concentrated too hard on qualifying to worry much about the future beyond that goal, but I wasn't going back.

I had never tried to visit Poland – had no desire to do so – but I had spent two of my long vacs working in camps for displaced persons in Germany and that was enough to put anyone but a sadist off war, I can tell you.

After a short spell in a London hospital, I explored several possibilities and, just as I had almost finalised acceptance as junior partner in a general practice, I saw an advert of vacancies in the Colonial Medical Service. Well, I made sure that it would cause no hold up in my naturalisation and applied. It would appear that they were short of doctors at the time!

'Och, it would be fine if we were to work in the same hospital.' Kathy had expressed these sentiments at frequent intervals throughout the voyage.

But it was not to be. Our posting orders awaited us in Colombo; she was to disembark at Penang for a northern post and I was to continue to Singapore, for a hospital in the south of the Federation.

I had been as disappointed as she at the time but, once settled into my new job, there was much to do, to see, to learn. Hard work and a new language to tackle soon drove Kathy from my mind.

The wards of the hospital to which I was posted in Johore were a perpetual fascination. Heaven alone knows I'd seen enough shapes, sizes and colours in London, but I'd never visualised being called upon to perform the tasks which were soon to become everyday routine. And in London everything had been too efficient, too clinical, to enjoy the human side.

'I'm sorry, Doctor, it happens all the time.'

The sister, who was escorting me round male medical, drew my attention to a small Chinese nurse who was trying in vain to chase a brood of chickens from under a patient's bed before I arrived.

I laughed outright.

The ward was broad and long with open doors on both sides, opening on to a covered concrete surround, which in turn opened on to grass. Cobwebs festooned an inaccessible, gaping hole in the ceiling and many of the supports were wafer thin from the onslaught of white ants.

I had been thinking back a few months to the London ward; the starched sister; starched, make-upless nurses, the spotless patients, general cleanliness and strict visiting hours. The comparison had already been making it difficult enough to keep a straight face, but the chickens were the last straw.

'It's wonderful,' I said, 'I only wish I could sketch.'

'It has its frustrations. But I laugh too when I think back to my training days.'

The sister was a pretty girl, with starched veil pushed well back on her ginger hair, and showed a good deal of sun-tanned arm and leg. I could not visualise her in a London hospital either.

But we had arrived at the first bed.

I listened while my escort translated the old man's complaints, pleased that I could already understand the gist of what she said, then prescribed a stringent diet.

As soon as I turned away I saw an old Indian woman, presumably the patient's wife, who squatted on the concrete flange, fanning the charcoal under a batch of chappaties.

'Oh really,' I said, and it was impossible to keep the exasperation from my voice, 'that's going a bit too far. What's the use of putting the old fool on a diet if he's going to stuff himself with those the minute my back is turned?'

The old man must have understood my tone and let forth a veritable torrent of thick, fast Malay.

'He says his wife is only cooking for herself and the children who will come at lunchtime from school. They are not for him.'

'And do you believe that?'

The sister shrugged. 'If you frighten him enough, perhaps. We have an occasional blitz on relatives, but everything's so open here it's almost impossible to prevent them, and honestly, when you see how some of these people pine, I think in the long run the relatives do more good than harm. As I told you just now, it has its frustrations.'

We continued down the ward then, my companion telling me the race and religion as well as the case-history of each man.

I shook my head in amazement. 'I had no idea this country was so diverse.'

'Wait until you're in a district,' she laughed, 'you'll probably have cows and goats in the ward as well!'

I raised my eyebrows. 'I should have become a vet!'

But there was no chance for further levity. At that moment a young Chinese dresser came hurrying towards us.

'You are wanted urgently in Outpatients', Doctor,' he said, and we followed him out.

A Gurkha soldier was being carried in as I arrived. He was swathed in various cloths, but the blood still seeped through. He clutched his abdomen as though afraid to let go, but there was no fear in his face, only mild surprise.

A Naik who was escorting him crashed to attention.

'At least one bullet has entered stomach, Sahib.'

A senior hospital assistant came out, hypodermic poised, and gave the man a cursory glance.

'The theatre is being prepared, sir,' he said to me as he bent to swab the man's arm.

'Where is Mr Lawrence?' I asked, a tingle of apprehension already shooting through my brain.

'He is attending the surgical conference in Singapore, sir. He will be back at 3 p.m.'

'You'll have to operate, Doctor.' It was the soft voice of the sister, who had followed from the ward. She smiled. 'It'll be all right.'

76. TO HELL WITH FRIENDS AND NEIGHBOURS

The third stream reaches the river

James Weatherby

God, was I glad to get on that bloody boat – and off it.

The voyage out was gruesome. Of all the unkind things the Crown Agents could have done, they had to go and book us on a troopship. I shared a cabin with an elderly major in the Education Corps who never uttered, and a couple of infantile pilot officers who never stopped. Two good reasons for leaving the service if nothing else – what types are they commissioning these days? I could have forgiven them a lot if they hadn't whistled at Helen, but at that I blew my top.

Then eight equally gruesome months in a boarding-house in Kuala Lumpur – woman who ran it ought to be strung up if there's any justice. Not that it worried me much, I was seldom there, but I felt for Helen with the two kids. No need for her to have panicked about having the baby in England; John was eleven months old by the time their airships finally released me and spent his first birthday being sick in the Indian Ocean.

As a matter of fact, I became quite nicely dug in in the Secretariat and would not have asked for a district if it hadn't been for the fact that Helen was so damned miserable in those digs. I wasn't too happy about going out-station either – wouldn't have minded if I'd been a bachelor, but hell, people are being shot up every day and I didn't much like the thought of my family living under those conditions. Not that Helen could have cared less; all she wants is a house, but when I used to see all those grim-faced planters coming into town, armed and looking as though they belonged to a different world, it made me uneasy.

Anyway, in October '49 my posting came through and we set off for our new station.

Kuala Jelang was not everybody's cup of tea, I had been told, and I could see their point without having to delve too deeply.

My predecessor was a neat, finicky type, ten years my senior at the very least, I should say, and odd, to put it mildly. Wouldn't hand a thing over in the office and talked in a whisper, looking over his shoulder half the time. They might have warned me about him. 'Secretive type, old Perkins,' was all I had been told, 'but you'll find everything in apple-pie order.' Well, I suppose that was true.

Oh James, James, please be happy here. I closed my eyes and said a silent prayer before opening them again to look at the house. *Our* house. We'd been married for three and a half years and now, at last, for the first time, a real house.

The man James was taking over from was a precise old woman with a great air of 'hush, keep it dark' about him who had insisted on handing over his confidential files in the seclusion of the house instead of the office. So I had been banished and I can't say that I minded.

Everything was still. We had spent the night in a neighbouring district, having been advised not to travel after dark and, I don't mind admitting it, I've never been so scared in my life as I was on that journey; it didn't need much imagination to see a terrorist behind every tree. We arrived in Kuala Jelang while the morning was still cool; now it was afternoon and John was blessedly asleep. I took Angela by the hand and we wandered away from the men's murmurous voices and surveyed our future domain.

The two government quarters, ours and the one belonging to the OCPD, James's counterpart in the police, shared the summit of a highish hill between the river and the sea with a formidable lighthouse, the design of which had specifically been drawn for the Outer Hebrides! In contrast with this monstrous structure, the two wooden bungalows looked flimsy in the extreme.

At the back of the hill there was a Rest House, also of ancient origin, and a road leading a couple of miles to the Forest Research Station, where the Forestry Officer had his house.

On the river side of the hill nestled the town – one main street of Chinese and Indian shops, bordered with magnificent flame trees, and two smaller streets leading off at right angles to the main road. At the seaward end, immediately below the hill and unseen from the town, the police station squatted, surrounded by its barracks, parade-ground, canteen and games field. At the other end of the town a small hill was crowned by the District Office, and between the two, bordered by the town on one side and the river on the other, lay the padang, that open space found in every Malayan town, no doubt laid out by the first Britons, homesick for their village greens. It serves as football field, cricket pitch, meeting place, market place, the home of the annual county fair – in fact, not only does it resemble, but also serves the purpose of a village green.

Perkins was a bachelor and, being ready for leave, had packed up and moved into the Rest House before we arrived. I sighed with pleasure as we reached the top of the hill again and sat on a garden seat to look at the dilapidated old bungalow that was to be our home.

The dank smell from the mangrove swamp, the enormous scorpion I had found in the kitchen sink, and the myriad cockroaches; nothing was going to put me off. Even the oil-lamps would be fun; the mangrove shapes were quaint and the fact that the house looked liable to collapse at a puff of wind merely seemed to make life more exciting! James might be worried about the Emergency and the danger that surrounded us, but I was not at all.

'What does the European population consist of?' I asked.

'Actually resident, only the OCPD and the Forestry Officer besides yourselves. PWD and Agriculture visit once a week from the next district, Kemuning, and a doctor comes when he can. Socially, of course, there are a fair number of planters and miners around, but few people move around after dark unless they have to, even when the curfew isn't on. It'll be a bit lonely for your wife, I'm afraid.'

'That's what I was thinking.'

At that moment I saw Helen's face, eyes shining and lips pursed with suppressed laughter, peering at me round one of the verandah screens. Her expression had been enough to tell me that having a house was going to be more important than company and I turned back to Perkins with an easy mind. I could concentrate on taking over; domestic problems, thank God, did not exist.

I lay in bed, listening to James prowling round the garden and wishing he would come to bed. This job was not going to be easy for him, I knew. He had never been a 'hail fellow, well met' type; never a good mixer at the best of times, he'd become increasingly intolerant of his associates during the past few years and I could see he would have very little in common with our two bachelors.

But now I wanted to forget everything else, everything beyond ourselves. I wanted him to come and take possession of me as I had taken possession of the house; to love me and want me and be as happy as I intended that he should be, instead of growling about outside like an angry bear.

My thoughts were interrupted by an overwhelming smell of burning oil and I could see the silhouette of smoke against the open door.

'James,' I called, 'please turn down the light. I don't want to get out of bed in the dark with bare feet.'

I had left the light on the verandah; there were too many creepy-crawlies, and besides, I had nothing on.

Helen's voice forced me inside. I hadn't noticed the lamp going up, although I'd been watching its glow from the garden in a vague sort of way. Christ, if we set fire to the house it really would be the last straw.

The filthy thing was black and stinking, and by the time I reached it there was already an oily, discoloured mark on the ceiling. I looked at it with distaste; the last oil-lamp I had had to cope with had been in Libya.

'Better turn it right out,' Helen called, 'there's enough moonlight for you to see to undress by.'

I sighed and stood with closed eyes for a few moments, letting myself become accustomed to the gloom.

It had been an utterly bloody evening, spent in the company of people whom I could quite frankly do without. If leching at my wife was going to be a favourite pastime, I would have to ask for a posting; I just wasn't going to put up with it.

I suppose the Forestry chap is all right – looks pretty solid and doesn't say much – and I needn't worry about the few days we shall have with Perkins – that's another thing I don't go for overmuch. Helen seemed to think her discovery of a harem of flowery young men wildly funny, but I was disgusted. Yes, disgusted. God knows I'm no prude, but Christ, at least I'm normal. What must the locals think? How are they going to react to me, expect me to behave?

And as for that Brylcreem boy. I never could abide his type – typical Fighter, all dash and no sense of responsibility. He'd be better placed selling something on the Edgware Road than the job he's doing here. Whoever put a creature like that in charge of a district this size and with that number of men needs his head examined. And the infuriating thing is that Helen seems to find him amusing. Well I don't, and that's flat.

'Do stop rumbling, James, and come to bed.'

'I'm not rumbling.' But I was.

Then quite suddenly the moon crept round the edge of the bedroom window and a shaft of light fell on the mosquito net, suspended in the middle of the room from invisible wires and moving slightly in the faint breeze that was breathing through the wide open windows. It brought me into the intimacy of our home and away from outside thoughts.

I dropped my clothes on the bare floor and watched the moonbeam

478

picking out the hideous, heavy black furniture and sombre walls. It was all bare and impersonal, but it would not always be so. Helen was right. We had ourselves, the children and, at long last, a house. To hell with friends and neighbours – we didn't *have* to see them once the offices were closed.

I felt as though I were parting the wings of some great hovering white moth as I drew aside the mosquito net. And there, naked, lying on borrowed white sheets, was my wife, as white as the moonlight and as beautiful. My madonna lily. She held out her arms and I went into them gratefully.

77. JEALOUSY UNFOUNDED

It did not take James Weatherby long, after all, to get the hang of the job, despite his wife's fears. The crops and buildings, strange at first to one from the West, were now familiar, and he had broken the back of his first struggles with Malay.

As far as Helen was concerned, after the dreary months in a boarding-house, Kuala Jelang was sheer bliss. At most times it was hot and humid, and at low tide the mud-flats steamed and the sand flies rose in their swarms, but when the tide was high and the wind blew in from the sea, it more than compensated for the bad spells.

The only real fly in the ointment, it appeared, was the young OCPD. As James said, they had to work hand-in-glove and he just could not take to the chap.

After only a few weeks James marched in to lunch one day, his face alight with the arrogance which Helen remembered so well. It had made his juniors dislike him in the days when he had first been promoted Air Commodore and had nearly driven the hospital staff mad. It bode no good and she was wary.

He sat down with a thud and glared at his still empty plate.

'I shall report him to his superiors,' he fumed.

'Who?'

'Young King. I won't *have* that chap around.'

'What has he done?' Helen was aghast, terrified that her husband was going to make a fool of himself because, despite what else he might have to say, she knew in her heart what was the real cause of this outburst.

'It's his manner,' James muttered. 'He's out to sabotage me in every way.'

'James, you have no right. He may be younger than you and in the despised part of the RAF as far as you were concerned, but that was

479

years ago. He's been in Malaya ever since the end of the war, speaks fluent Malay and is considerably senior to you, even if he isn't in the same job.'

He looked stunned. He had expected sympathy, not an attack.

But his wife had not finished. 'His superiors would laugh at you,' she sneered.

She had to hurt. She knew very well what was at the bottom of all this and the sudden explosion merely served to confirm a suspicion which had been growing lately in her mind.

It all went back to their first night in the district when she, never dreaming that there were still places without electricity, had come to Kuala Jelang unprepared. They were to inherit the Chinese servants with the house, but they had gone on a fortnight's leave. Having no lights and unable to cope with the wood range, she had called on Derek King for help. He had lent them a lamp and insisted that they eat with him.

He was a bit smooth, it was true, but Helen was amused by his over-obvious charm and played him at his own game – until she had noticed her husband's sullen face.

Derek had seen it too and, to make matters worse, had deliberately picked up her hand and said, 'Ma'am, you don't know what a differ-ence it's going to make to Kuala Jelang, having a woman around – even if we do have to have her husband as well!'

She had laughed and drawn her hand away, but James had glowered and remained silent until they started for home.

'No need to come,' he had said icily to their host, 'I am quite capable of lighting my wife home.'

He had taken the light and stalked off without a single word of thanks.

The next morning she had written a short note to Derek King, thanking him and apologising for her husband's mood, saying that he had not been feeling well. But King, insensitive and typical of his breed, cared not a jot for what James thought or felt and, besides paying obvious and exaggerated court to his wife whenever the chance arose, took every opportunity to aggravate him in other ways. He was, by most people's standards, an infuriating young man. Happy-go-lucky, couldn't care less, he always managed to be at the right place at the right time and always fell on his feet.

Why, James asked himself, seething with irritation, should King always manage to reach his goal without any apparent effort, when he had to slog? Popular among the locals; respected by his men; and somewhat grudgingly reported well on by his superior officers. If it came to open conflict between the two of them, there was very little doubt as to who would win.

In his own mind James knew all this – which made it so much worse

– and was aware too of his own jealous nature and how unfounded all his suspicions were.

Sometimes when walking along the tow-path at Richmond, he had imagined that they were being followed, or that some man on the farther bank was eyeing Helen as he had no right to do. He would hurry her home and spend the rest of the day sulking, knowing within himself that there was no foundation for his rage.

He felt like that now. He knew Helen was right. 'His superiors would laugh at you,' she had said. What the hell did she see in the man? She must see something, or she would not have made a remark like that. He knew that she really didn't see anything at all, but he could not bring himself to admit it.

'Can't you stop those bloody kids from making such a row?' he snarled. 'I don't want any lunch.'

And with that he walked out of the front door and got into the car.

Helen sighed. She had been patient enough, God knew, but this time she rebelled – but only mentally. Her hands were tingling with rage and it was only with the greatest self-control that she prevented herself from picking up the nearest object and hurling it at the retreating car.

Back in his office, James sulked. Putting his head in his hand, he sank forward on to the desk. His head began to ache, as it always did on these occasions. It was a long time before he heard the sounds of exhausts and bicycle bells, heralding the return to work of the clerks. He sat up then and hit his head with his clenched fist, telling himself, as he invariably did, not to be such a bloody fool.

If he had had his way there would have been no more social contact with young King, but Helen, as soon as their china was unpacked, had insisted on inviting him back. Thom, the FO, had come too – thank God he could feel no jealousy there. A dour chap, he thought. He hadn't been in the district all that long and did not speak very much Malay either – *how* that young King liked to show off his knowledge of the language; cracking jokes at every opportunity, knowing full well that he could understand neither the speed nor the idiom. He ground his knuckles into his eyes; Helen apart, he could not like the man.

'What is it?' he called wearily, as he heard a respectful knock on the half open door.

It was Balasingham, his Jaffna Tamil Chief Clerk, carrying a pagoda-like pile of files. James watched him carefully off-load them on to the desk. Nothing for it but to forget King and lose himself in work, he thought with resignation.

Philip Morrison

'It could be that I have an early Christmas present for you,' I told Sally one lunch hour, 'it all depends.'

I held out the copy of Part II orders that had been floating round the unit for weeks, and waited until she'd read them through.

'As you see, the army is allowing transfers to the Colonial Service. Anyone who is accepted may retire.'

She said nothing for a minute, but turned them over and looked at the date.

'But these aren't new.'

'No. I wanted to find out all the pros and cons first.'

That was the understatement of the year. There were so many of us becoming fed up with the army that the whole subject had been gone into and thrashed out in almost every office – I was surprised that she hadn't heard it. Perhaps they were all contented Labourites or National Service in her section. It wasn't only the lack of prospects, it was the whole attitude. Even the RSM had admitted he could no longer keep proper control. As far as I was concerned, my mind had been made up the week before. It was a very small incident; I had kept the unit working late on an extremely urgent job and I vaguely remembered one of the sapper draughtsmen moaning that he had a cold – most of us had, there was one going the rounds. I thought nothing of it at the time but, before I knew what had hit me, I was on the mat, answering questions by post from the man's MP. Well. When the army reached that stage, I'd had enough, and I wasn't the only one.

'What job would you do?' Sally asked.

'Admin and police are the only ones I'm qualified for. From what I can gather, admin would mean Africa; but they want police here – so, police it is – if you agree.'

I could see that I had taken her completely by surprise.

After a while, she asked, 'But you're always so rude about the civil government; would you really want to join them?'

'We've had quite a lot to do with the police,' I told her, 'it's a para-military set up and I'm hardly complimentary about the army either these days.'

'What's the pay like?'

'Considerably lower than ours, I'm afraid.' The pension would be better, but I wanted to paint only the black side at this stage.

'Oh God!'

'And I'd go in as a cadet – two pips.'

'Oh God, again. What a come down.'

'I don't think you can really compare ranks; their responsibilities are quite different. In the district where we were operating last year, the OCPD only had two pips up, but he had more than a thousand men under his command, all told.'

'It's up to you, Philip. I've never thought of you having any career other than the army.'

'Career? With this ruddy Labour government cutting down the whole time? Times have changed since Father commanded a battalion. Think about it, Sally. The applications have to be in by the end of the year – you've got a month.'

I had been surprised to hear the bitterness in Philip's voice.

It was difficult to work that afternoon. For the first time I realised that other people were talking about the merits and disadvantages of transferring – I suppose they had been talking about it for some time; I just hadn't listened before.

The largest item in favour was, of course, the fact that we would be able to live together without the continual threat of separation. The battalion was on temporary duty in Berlin at that time, without wives, and I knew it was something I would have to face sooner or later. I knew nothing about the police – except that few days went by without some reference in the newspapers to an ambush or patrol where someone had been killed, and they were usually Europeans.

I hardly spoke for a week, so busy was I with my thoughts.

'You could keep Ja'afar and the animals,' Philip said one day.

Of course that was the second major point in favour. We had adopted three stray cats, whom I loved dearly and dreaded having to leave behind, and the past months, with Ja'afar and Siti in charge, had been very pleasant. Undomesticated creature that I am, it suited me down to the ground to go off to work knowing that the house would be well run; and Ja'afar was a superb cook. And, when and if I ever did have a child, they would be there to help me care for it, just the same as they had cared for me. I had a feeling that Philip was trying to prod me into giving an affirmative answer.

But I didn't want to leave army life. I had grown up in uniform myself and I was very happy being spoon-fed. I didn't want to be thrown out into the great, wide, open world.

I had just reached a stage when I was going to say 'no' to the idea when Philip rushed into my office one morning, looking very bright.

'Bill Matheson's applied and been accepted,' he said, 'he's retiring next month.'

I couldn't care less about Bill Matheson, or what he did. He was a contemporary of Philip's, in fact, they had been commissioned to-gether and bosom pals until Philip had been taken prisoner, then they had met up again after the war, both moaning about the colonel and the first battalion. He was a bachelor still and lived in the main mess; he came in for the odd meal and occasionally invited us out, but we didn't see all that much of him.

But what I did see was that Philip really did want to transfer and was using every subtle argument to persuade me. I sighed.

'All right,' I said, 'we'll go too.'

79. LIKE THE EDGE OF THE OUTBACK

The fourth stream enters the river
Vincent Lee Chee Min

A full year passed before I saw Dad again.

He had been furious when I joined up, but I think that secretly he was glad I had chosen to stand on my own feet and not gone crawling back to him.

In fact, I haven't done too badly for myself.

The recruits' course at the Depot was shortened because of the Emergency and I was already earmarked for Special Branch before it was over. My Chinese is still pretty stilted, but it's coming back and, when I went on leave after the course, I made a point of not speaking a word of English to the old man.

Actually I enjoyed my leave. There's a lot of good in Dad. He made quite sure that I understood what I was missing by choosing not to join one of his business concerns, the whole time with an amused glint in his jet-black eyes. But I wasn't taking the bait.

He's in far more than just tin now. Rubber, cars, hotels, import/export, and messing around on the stock exchange. You name it. He still lives in the same house, but he has offices in Ipoh and KL now; plush, air-conditioned jobs. Like his air-conditioned cars.

We only had one clash of wills and that was on the last day. The evening before he'd become positively benign over his XO – no three-star brandy for Dad – and announced that he was making me an allowance of two hundred bucks a month. My first impulse was to refuse it, but Mum had shaken her head and told me afterwards that he was giving the same to all his sons – even the one with the Aussie wife – and that I'd only make him lose face by refusing. The clash came the next morning when I was going to Ipoh to board the train. Dad had insisted that I be driven to the railway station in state, but not in my PC's uniform! So I said I'd walk, or go by bus.

Perhaps, although he was loath to admit it, he was glad that I too could be a chip off the same block and he partly relented, ordering the driver to drop me outside the station precincts – he wasn't going to have anyone seeing an ordinary PC alighting from *his* car! In fact, the driver took me the whole way – he's a Malay, there's nothing wrong with wearing a uniform for him.

I filled a sergeant's post, with acting rank, at one of the main police stations in KL for a few months, but it was soon apparent to me that if I were really going to get my teeth into Malay and Chinese I would have to be in a smaller station, where I would be using them the whole time, instead of spending half my day sitting behind a desk. Of course, I did go out a good deal, but too much of my time was spent on observation. I needed more interrogation and mixing with the local people.

After some thought, I asked the Deputy Superintendent if I could be sent to an out-station and explained why.

Kuala Jelang came my way just at the right time. It was a new post. To date, the SB officer from Circle HQ at Kemuning had visited the district a couple of times a week, but it had been decided to post a sergeant there permanently, who could get in touch with the officer when needed.

'Just the thing for you,' the DSP told me. 'It will give you a chance to prove your admin ability as well as being right on the ground. Stroke of luck for you that it became available just now; normally they would have sent someone more experienced.'

So Kuala Jelang it was, or is. My, it's a little hack town all right! About the size of some of the ones you find way out in Aussie; like the edge of the Outback. Real sleepy colonial, I should say, until the Emergency woke it up.

The OCPD seems quite a good bloke, but a bit leave-happy. Can't say I blame him, reckon the bright lights will call me too after three years in this joint. I can see the job will be all right though, once I get my teeth into it.

I settled down straight away to write and tell Dad the news. I don't think I've done too badly for myself one way and another. Fourteen months only since I arrived in Singapore and now I'm a sergeant with my own office and a fair whack of responsibility – and I've got here without anyone else's help.

I must write to Sergeant Williamson too, back in Aussie – his remarks on my becoming an acting sergeant in next to no time were pretty caustic, wonder what he'll say to this lark?

Chee Min was nervous. Infiltrate yourself into the squatter areas, King had instructed him, and glean what information you can. And now he was on his way, in a borrowed private car, an elderly Chinese detective sitting beside him. But soon he would be on his own.

The OCPD had given him a couple of days to settle in, lending him his own annotated map of the area to study. Chee Min had studied it and it had not taken him long to put his finger on the obvious trouble spots.

Kuala Jelang was a large, pear-shaped district, with the river, the Sungei Jelang, running east to west along the approximate core, cutting it in two. Roads ran parallel with the river on both sides, with turnings off both north and south, and meeting on the one bridge some ten miles upstream. A ferry served to connect the two coastal halves of the district, which contained most of the cultivated land and population. There were several rubber estates in both halves, and one tin mine towards the eastern boundary. The remainder of the district was jungle.

The township of Kuala Jelang itself nestled on the south side of the mouth of the river and, owing to the rock formation and an inlet which curved round the hill, was almost on a peninsula.

But it was neither the rubber estates nor the town that worried Chee Min. There were two squatter settlements, one on the same side of the river as the town and covering a roughly triangular area of low-lying ground, a moderately compact formation if he deciphered the OCPD's hieroglyphics correctly, and another on the far side of the river which was far from compact. Chinagraph dots speckled the talc and straggled on both sides of the road for more than a mile, terminating at the forest edge. He was not surprised when King stubbed his finger on that portion of the map and announced, 'That's the area I don't like. There are three main sources of supply to the Communists: squatter areas, timber *kongsis*, and estates. I want you to take them in that order of priority.'

Until the squatters could be controlled and their help and food denied to the terrorists, government was waging a battle already lost. From his father and his few months in Special Branch, Chee Min knew that these people, China-born for the most part, and owing allegiance to no one beyond their immediate kin, had no intention of co-operating. How many actually had Communist leanings and how many gave their support under duress, it was impossible to say. Riddled with secret societies and protection groups, they had lived since time immemorial in fear of losing what little they had. Small chance then that they would be prepared to betray the greatest secret society of them all, Communism, and risk the consequences.

Thankful that he had dropped Mandarin as his third dialect and studied Hakka instead, Chee Min questioned the detective at his side. He had taken the precaution of providing himself with a civilian identity card to enable him to travel by bus – too often they were burned and the passengers' belongings and identity cards scrutinised and stolen – but first DPC Chin was showing him the ground.

Chin, jealous possibly of the rank of the young man behind the steering wheel, took pains to point out the dangers of moving unescorted among the squatters. A quick cord round the throat, a knife; no one would see, no one would hear. And if he were taken alive? Who more hated by the CTs than a Chinese member of Special Branch?

'If we stop here, you can walk back to the bus stop we've just passed,' he told Sergeant Lee. 'Ask for Ulu Pandanus; the fare will be twenty-five cents. I'll take the car back.'

Chee Min stopped, got out and walked straight back. He could feel the cold sweat trickling between his shoulder-blades and his hands were clammy. Never before had he been so conscious of quiet. They were in open scrub country, flat, with stunted bushes. In the distance a kite was flying.

The road remained deserted although he waited nearly half an hour. Not a vehicle passed. He saw the bus approaching at such speed that he was afraid it would not stop. He stepped into the road and held up his hand, and with a screech of brakes the vehicle halted just long enough to allow him to cling on to the first step, then took off again, throwing him into a vacant seat. None of the few passengers seemed surprised.

For more than a week Chee Min walked through the vegetable gardens and orchards, asking questions about the crops and the soil and attempting in every way to get himself accepted.

Not that the squatters welcomed him with open arms. Far from it. They knew what he was about and told him nothing. He only had to be seen entering or leaving the police station once, he knew, for everyone to know exactly what he was and what his job. He knew too that he remained unmolested because the CTs might be hatching plans to use *him*.

He made no attempt to overcome the squatters' suspicions, but while he was amongst them he was able to listen and observe. The sideways glance, the lifted eyebrow or quietly closing door; all signs of furtiveness or guilt were noted mentally, to be committed to paper at the end of the day.

King studied his report, queried one or two observations, and knew that it confirmed his own conclusions. He had not told Chee Min that a police lieutenant and four jungle squad PCs had been killed there during the past month; that they were sure the area was being used as a rest camp and supply depot; he had wanted him to find out for himself. Resettlement of the squatters was the only solution, he was sure. He had said so at the last meeting of DWEC, the District War Executive Committee, but met with little response. The trouble was the head-on clash of personalities between himself and the DO and, although the police were responsible for security, the DO was chairman of the committee and as such held an excellent weapon for impeding progress. The planters' representative had been heard to remark that the only time the committee reached agreement was when either Weatherby or King was absent.

King tapped Chee Min's report with irritation. He despised Weatherby and did not bother to disguise his feelings; that they were mutual was equally apparent. Who cares? he thought. He was due for leave; it would be his successor's problem. To Chee Min he said, 'I'll take it up with the Special Branch officer next time I go to Circle HQ. Now for the timber-cutters.'

The timber-cutters were a different kettle of fish. Known providers, and whether voluntarily or not mattered little to the police.

King asked the Forestry Officer to come round to his office that afternoon and introduced Chee Min. Donald Thom was in an affable mood and delighted to have the chance to spend some time in the timber camps. Of course he would accompany the new detective-sergeant. Only too glad.

'Say, you sound kinda Australian,' he remarked, after a few minutes of conversation. 'Howcome you've picked up an accent like that?' Chee Min explained and Thom held out his hand. 'Shake, pardner, we're colonials together in this Imperialist set-up!'

They had all laughed and Jogindar Singh, looking in as he made some excuse to walk past the OCPD's open door, made a mental note that he would have to tell Sergeant Lee to have a little more respect for his superiors. He strongly disapproved of the way the young Chinese was leaning on the desk and talking in such familiar tones. Upstart!

They set off the next day, and the reception from the first timber kongsi they reached was cool, to put it mildly. All questions were dealt with in a masterfully evasive manner, and Chee Min noticed considerable surreptitious coming and going.

It was the same all along the line, and as they penetrated deeper and deeper into the forest Chee Min was glad of their strong, armed escort.

In fact they were safe, he was pretty sure, because the death or disappearance of a policeman and a government officer would almost certainly spell closure to the timber *kongsis* and cut off a valuable Communist supply line. He said as much to his companion.

Thom looked wistfully at the great trees surrounding them. He knew the police were keen to close the deep camps and in his heart he knew they should. It was only the revenue they provided for a government already overtaxed by the financial commitment of the Emergency that had allowed them to operate for so long. It was just his luck that he should have arrived in Malaya when he did. He would have so loved to spend long periods in the forests, free to go where he wished, unescorted and without fear.

He sighed. 'I suppose you'll recommend they be closed down?' They had visited seven camps and were on their journey back.

Chee Min shrugged. 'That'll be up to the OCPD, but it's certainly what I'd do.'

Chee Min's third assignment, the estates, had been the easiest of the lot but, as he sat drinking a beer with Snowy White – no relation of his friend Bill White, but from the same place – he was still smarting.

He had been warned not to expect much co-operation from the police lieutenants, but he had not been prepared for the rebuff he received on the first estate. He had jumped out of the police jeep and advanced with outstretched hand towards the uniformed European standing with the SCs.

'I'm from the police station,' he announced, smiling broadly. 'I'm the new SB sergeant, Vincent Lee Chee Min.'

Police Lieutenant Moriarty had looked him up and down, ignoring the hand. 'Bugger off,' he said, and turned away.

Chee Min's hide had not been toughened sufficiently by his Australian schooling. He had returned to the jeep, quivering with rage and humiliation, and gone straight to the managers' offices after that. But, coming out of the office on the fourth estate, he found a police lieutenant standing by the jeep. He stiffened and walked warily towards him.

'Hey, cobber, could you give me a lift into town?'

This one had held out *his* hand, and after finishing his business with the OCPD had invited Chee Min to join him in a beer.

'You don't want to take too much notice of Paddy,' he remarked when he had heard about the clash with Moriarty. 'He can be as mean as hell, but you know he's got the George Medal for gallantry? He's a bastard, all right, but a good man to have on your side in a fight. The best.'

'I hope I never need his help.'

'Aw, trouble with you Asians is you're too touchy. Never heard the old saying, "sticks and stones can break my bones, but words can never hurt me"? You see,' he explained, 'we're such a mixed bunch.

Most of the lieutenants are the ex-sergeants from Palestine, then when they needed more they advertised. A lot of applicants were attracted by the rank and were disappointed when they got here and found it was non-commissioned – bloody silly, misleading rank anyway, if you ask me – then there are the ones like me. I took the job for the money – make no bones about it – besides, suits me better than the desk job I had in Sydney. So there we are, the professional thugs, the disappointed hopefuls, and the ordinary mercenaries, like me!'

'I'm glad there are some like you,' Chee Min murmured, and meant it.

'Wal,' Snowy looked at his watch, 'you'll get along all right. I've got to get back to the estate. See yer, Vin.'

Snowy White had, in fact, summed up his colleagues very well. In Kuala Jelang district there were eight police lieutenants, all but one lodged on various estates, in charge of the Special Constables on their own estates and those within a certain radius. The odd man out, O'Brien, looked after the jungle squads. Some of them were first-class, responsible and reliable men; others were just plain bolshie. But almost all of them were fiercely loyal to their own men and although the bolshies were a permanent thorn in the flesh of the OCPD and the regular police, even they would stick up for them if it came to a fight with outsiders. King frequently remarked that there were several of them whom he could have done without, but, in fact, without replacements, he could not have done without a single one of them.

81. A UNION REPRESENTATIVE MEETS HIS MATCH

Ramakrishnan

For the whole of 1949, K. P. Samuel and I are representing Estate and Mine Workers' Union at estates far and wide and collecting subscriptions most satisfactory.

I now have rented garage in nearby town, where car is kept most secretively, and forged identity cards in names of S. Kandiah and K. P. John. It is not being difficult to leave estates for toddy-soaked CC is spending all days, except when manager is visiting, drinking with equally sodden cronies. I am therefore in charging of office duties and giving self time off whenever conveniently required.

Truly my brethren are individuals most cretinous and sheeplike, which is lucky for us. On each estate I am visiting it is only necessary to be obtaining one follower and all rest of stupid fellows pay up,

490

although most are already paying to real union. Truly I am despising them for being doltish fools – I was telling my father this always, but he was not believing me.

I am telling you, K.P. and I have milked all estates in area conveniently far from Tanah Kuning and far enough apart not to be having new union discussed. Fellows on our own estate are not asking questions as we are always returning by nightfall and wife Devi is most lazy and lustful still, and only accepting gold ornaments and marital caresses without using brains at all.

All is going well until we are collecting subscriptions for 1950.

Now we are going to fields farther and looking after area to the north.

We are no longer bothering about managers, for I am soon finding out that if chief clerk can be won over and is telling manager that genuine union official is visiting estate, manager becomes like putty.

Only I am not being given correct information regarding one estate and I am standing on forty-four-gallon oil drum, delivering honest and usual harangue to workers when manager arrives.

This is first time that manager has attended such speaking to workers and I am waxing eloquent most when he is interrupting most rudely.

'Get off that drum and off my estate,' he shouts.

Now is the time to show workers that I am not being intimidated.

'I am telling you, Mister,' I am shouting back, 'you do not have right to throw me off estate. Law is forever on my side also. I shall take civil suit and criminal suit against you for causing grievous bodily harm if you are for throwing me anywhere.'

At that, said manager is coming towards me with look most unpleasant upon face.

'Speak your own language so that all can understand,' he is saying in Tamil, 'or I shall have to teach you to speak proper English.'

At these insulting words many of the workers are laughing and I am quickly seeing that my audience is attending to this white pig more than they are to me.

'Take no notice of this white slave driver,' I yell at them, 'he is oppressor of the workers, like all his kind.'

From the corner of my eye I am seeing K.P. sneaking towards car. Lucky he cannot drive, I am thinking, or he would be leaving me in veritable lurch.

'Get off this estate without further nonsense, or I *shall* throw you off.'

'Yes,' I am jeering, 'you will be calling toadies to do dirty work, I bet.'

I see then that there are no SCs with manager and he is advancing towards me on own, but with manner menacing most.

'Shoot,' I call out, 'you will be using pistols on poor defenceless

491

representative of workers, I bet. You are big man, I see, ready to fire at inferior being.'

'Get off that drum,' he is saying, and quietly now, 'I have never yet hit a man smaller than myself.'

I am getting down then, to avoid humiliating indignities which appear to be impending. I see at once that manager is only small man of height like mine much of muchness. He looks at me with expression most scornful which I do not like and is undoing belt which holds pistol in holster and is removing stainless steel watch and spectacles.

'I am telling you once more, and for the last time, get off this estate.'

Manager is wearing khaki shorts and shirt and jungle boots. He is already dirty and will not be minding dirt more, but I am looking at my clean white suitings and correspondent shoes and recalling time most humilitous after affair with Muriani and state of clothes thereafter.

'You will be sorry, Mister, for such high-handed actions,' I shout, but already half-way to where car is parked and relieved that no one is following.

'Thank your lucky stars that you are being allowed to go scot-free,' he calls out and laughs, 'but justice will no doubt catch up with you in due course; it always does.'

I am making no further reply when sudden pain on side of head is making me aware that several labourers have picked up stones and I am target. Truly I am ashamed of my fellow-countrymen.

Next stone is cutting cheek. K.P. is lying in long grass beside car with face pressed to ground and hands over ears. I can see at once that his suiting is already stained and I give him feelingful kick in ribs.

'Get up,' I say, 'fair weathering friend.'

Then I am starting car and proceeding at leisurely and dignified pace along estate road until out of sight of jeering workers.

'What is happening to you?' Devi is asking when she sees my cheek already swollen and with blood caked higgledy-piggledy on side of face.

For answer I am saying nothing, but at once seizing her bangles from her and earrings and pendant which is suspended round neck.

'Quick, Devi,' I say, 'give me your nose ring and your anklets and all other jewels. There is bad rumouring that Communist terrorists are in vicinity and all such trinkets gold and silver will be taken. I am hiding these in place secure and you are not to be telling anyone that I have taken same.'

Devi hands over remaining jewellery and I add my rings, wristwatch, cigarette case and lighter, and am wishing I could remove gold teeth also. All these things I am stowing in powdered milk tins and burying behind quarter. Then I am burning identity card of Mr S. Kandiah and coming to unfortunate conclusion that it is necessary to return to life of clerk most ordinary and that S. Kandiah and K. P. John can no longer be existing.

82. THE BETROTHAL

Abdul Karim

Once I had done my six months' basic training at the Depot, I was allowed to go on leave. Of course I had not yet realised my dream of becoming a driver/mechanic, because so far we had only square-bashed, but there would still be a lot to tell them back home.

There was Kuala Lumpur for a start. Wah! I wondered if they would believe me when I told them about the tall buildings and wide streets and the traffic. I wish they could see us in our walking-out dress going on Mosque Parade on Fridays; wah, that was something! All the traffic held up while we passed, the inspectors marching in front in their black and silver and us behind in our blue and white.

It was a long journey home and it made me realise why we had been left alone so much, during the occupation and since. Wah! When we had had discussions about our kampongs, I had felt like an orang-utan compared with some of the sophisticated recruits from the western and central states. I might have boasted that my picture had appeared on the front page of the leading newspaper if I hadn't looked so like an orang-utan in it, but I kept quiet about that one!

I felt quite sophisticated myself, though, when I walked into the Police District Headquarters and asked if there would be any transport to Pasir Perak in the near future. I was in luck, because the OCPD was visiting the next door kampong that very same afternoon and would drop me off.

When I went outside and looked around I wondered why I had ever felt ashamed of coming from the ulu, the back of beyond. The sight of my home, the boats drawn up on to the wide beach and the nets laid out to dry, the tall coconut palms and the feel of sand between my toes were better by far than anything to be had in the city. It was wonderful to see my parents' familiar faces and to touch the familiar objects in the home. For the first time I appreciated how my mother must have felt when we first came back from Kelantan at the beginning of the war.

493

After I had told them all my news, I went to see Inche Yacob and then to find Rokiah.

Rokiah was like a stranger. She who was as familiar to me as my own parents. My companion in so many scrapes and adventures, who had romped with me in the surf, climbed trees and pelted me with jambus, stood by the hibiscus bush at the foot of her steps, smiling shyly.

All of a sudden I felt shy too.

I always pictured Rokiah in her patched and faded old blue and white school uniform, but of course she had left school now and it was a young lady who stood waiting quietly for me to approach. The old Rokiah would have rushed forward, heedless of dignity or decorum, but this one, clad in a flowered sarong and kebaya, remained modestly at the foot of the steps.

Perhaps I looked different too. Six months of uniform and drill had given me a new deportment and the Depot barber had seen to my unruly hair.

I went forward and held out my hand. She put hers into mine, but her eyes looked demurely at her feet.

'Rokiah, you *are* pretty.'

I said it on impulse and knew at once that it was true. I had never really noticed girls before going to Kuala Lumpur and I had never thought much about Rokiah being a girl!

She giggled and put her hand shyly before her face. I caught her eyes for a second but she dropped them at once and would not look at me.

Was it Musah? I wondered. Rokiah had always been my special friend, but I had been the stay-at-home while he had ventured into city life.

I clenched my fists at the thought of his large pale face – surely Rokiah couldn't find it attractive? – and quick brain. He'd been back to the kampong recently, Inche Yacob had told me, talking very big. My old headmaster had spoken to me as a man for the first time. A smart Alick, he had called Musah, and not to be trusted. He had been sly and spread ideas among the kampong folk that Inche Yacob did not like. Surely Rokiah could not care for a chap like that?

My thoughts were interrupted by a tactful cough and Che Fatimah joined us. We sat and chatted till the sun went down.

I went home then; my thoughts with Rokiah, my tomboy friend who had so suddenly blossomed into a woman.

Her face was powdered now and her pigtails coiled up into two heavy buns, one behind each ear. She would be considered old-fashioned in KL, where nearly all the girls wore their hair short, but I liked it that way. I'll never let her cut it, I thought, then wondered

494

at my own impertinence. What right had I to let her do or not do anything? I was no longer the elder brother of our schooldays, but a man. Welcome as a casual friend, no doubt, until such time as she was betrothed.

At that thought my stomach did a flip. Rokiah must be almost seventeen. It had not been mentioned, but without doubt she would be married soon. She had admired Musah; did she admire him still?

For the first time since joining the police, I sighed for my schooldays; days that I had not realised until now had been so happy and carefree.

There was a good meal at home that night, but not the feast with all our friends and relations present that I would have expected on my first day home. But I was soon to understand the reason.

My parents looked at each other, then my father nodded and my mother spoke.

'There is no kenduri for you to-night, Karim, because one is already prepared for three days' time,' she said. Then she looked at Pak again, as though expecting him to take over, but he signalled to her to continue. 'We wanted to speak to you before you went to see Rokiah, to save you both embarrassment, but we saw you crossing over from the school and it was too late.'

My heart was thumping. What had happened that this should be necessary? What had happened to account for Rokiah's downcast eyes? My earlier thoughts returned and I felt sick with apprehension.

My thoughts must have shown too, because my mother frowned and put a hand on mine.

'Karim, please don't be so upset. It is only right that we should arrange a marriage for you, and the kenduri will be a feast to celebrate both your betrothal and your homecoming.'

Then my heart really sank. The betrothal would not be a hundred per cent binding – people had opted out before – but in a conservative community like ours it simply wasn't done. I was still only eighteen and the wedding probably would not take place for a few years yet, but I knew that I must be content with whatever arrangements my parents had made.

It seemed that among the urban Malays they could pick and choose for themselves these days. It was a subject often discussed and I knew that if my parents had chosen someone whom I knew but could not stand, I could refuse – but they would not do that anyway. I cast around in my mind for the possible girls from amongst whom my betrothed would have been chosen.

The meal continued in silence until my mother said, in a disappointed voice, 'You don't seem very interested in the celebrations, Karim.' I smiled politely but said nothing. 'I know you are young still, but Rokiah will soon be seventeen and as Che Fatimah was willing, your father and I – '

'Rokiah?' I jumped up, rudely interrupting my mother, who looked up at me, a puzzled frown clouding her face.

'Of course. Who else? It has always been understood that you and Rokiah. . . .'

I sat down again then, cut my mother short with a big hug, and burst out laughing with relief.

Both my parents looked so upset that I told them what had been on my mind. We all laughed then and as soon as we had finished eating, Pak slapped me on the back and said, 'Come on, son. We men will celebrate now – we'll go to the coffee-shop.'

Wah! *What* a relief!

I had only been back at the Depot for a month or so, this time training to be a driver/mechanic, as I had so ardently desired, when I had the surprise of my life.

We were walking down the main street of Kuala Lumpur one Saturday afternoon when I saw a newsvendor holding out a copy of the *Malayan Times* and there, on the front page, were enormous headlines: STUDENT RIOTS IN SINGAPORE. That wasn't so surprising in itself; it was not the first riot of students – I think they were avoiding call-up, but I'm not sure – and I wouldn't have taken much notice if it hadn't been for the photograph below.

It was a terrible picture. A man and a woman lay dead beside the wreckage of a car, and standing over them, a large stone in his hand, was Musah.

I looked again to make quite sure. There were several young men, some who looked like boys only, and the print was a bit blurred, but there was no mistaking that face – hadn't I sat next to it for long enough to know?

That someone from my kampong should be involved – although he had been neither my friend nor even Malay – made me feel quite sick.

'Are you feeling all right, Karim?' It was my friend, Hashim, who spoke a little English, so I bought a copy of the newspaper and asked him to translate it for me. We took it to a bench on the padang and while he read the article to us, very slowly, it went through my mind that I had always hated Musah and that I had not been such a bad judge of character after all.

We looked at the other pictures. Not all the rioters appeared to be Chinese. I hope I never have to fire on a mob, I thought, even if it did mean the end of men like Musah.

'Which vehicles do you think we'll be working on on Monday?' I asked.

496

83. THE LITTLE CHILDREN

Omar

'Fire!'

The word echoed dully through my brain and then the same imperative voice, a note of irritability and slight undertone of panic in it this time.

'Sergeant-major, order your squad to fire.'

But all I could see were the little children. I was told in court that there had been no children; small men maybe, men crawling through legs to reach the front of the crowd, but no children.

I had been upset all day – it always upset me, the anniversary of Zaitun's ordeal. Eight years ago, and so many others gone, but I can never forget.

I do not understand what started the riots. They say it was students. But why should students riot? They should be in school, studying. But then I am a simple man; I do not understand half of what goes on amongst the young these days.

I was told there had been no children. But they had been young people – all children to me.

'Sergeant-major, give the order, damn you. Fire!'

Three waves of riot police had charged, wielding batons and rotan shields, but still the mob came on. I saw the grey-blue shoulders of one of my colleagues go down, his steel helmet rolling in the dust and baton flung wide as he sprawled before the oncoming surge. But still I could not act.

It was the children. We were in the normally crowded shopping district. The alert had been given as soon as the mob had been sighted, marching from the junction of the two main streets, and we had hastened there in our trucks, sirens blaring and tyres squealing, in order to prevent catastrophe.

But it was no use. The crowd was armed. My own cheek had been opened by a sliver of flying glass and blood mingled freely with the sweat on shoulders, legs and arms of my companions and on those of bystanders who had not been quick enough in entering shop doors.

And then, in the forefront of the men, as they marched down the empty street, small figures, running, crawling, and when we, the police, had taken up our positions, they were there, in the front. The children – or those whom I thought were children.

There should have been tear gas. Something had gone wrong. The rioters did not give before the charging men. Baton fell on head and shoulder and the mob did not falter.

497

The cries for holy war flew hysterically above us. Slogans that made the blood run hot – or cold. I heard them, but the court said there had been no cries for holy war.

And then, heedless of warning, a small car turned in at the opposite end of the street. Two Europeans sat in the front seats, a man and a woman. I could see their horror-struck, unbelieving faces as they swung into the kerb, even from where I stood, more than a chain away.

Motioning the woman to remain where she was, the man opened his door and got out. As he did so a flying rock hit him on the side of the head and he fell, like a stunned bullock, into the road. This seemed to be the signal for all sanity to disappear and the mob surged forward, over the man's prostrate form, to attack. I saw the woman's eyes widen with fear as the crowd began to rock the car.

'Fire!'

The car seemed to roll over in slow motion and the mob were upon the woman, hauling her out, tearing at her clothes and hair.

I saw her go down, blood scarlet against her white skin, and heard the mob's triumphant roar.

My command had been superseded; my men had fired, obeying the orders of that imperative voice. Whether they had fired into the crowd or over their heads, I cannot say.

The sight of the children, the woman's torn body and the mangled mass of metal that had once been a car, sickened me. The strap of my steel helmet bit into my chin and my mouth was dry. I had had enough.

Laying down my rifle, I turned away and walked through the ranks of my men.

'Where the bloody hell do you think you're going?'

I looked at the red, angry face and the massive shoulders towering above me and they were part of a dream; hovering, unreal.

A brown hand, a Malay hand, fell on my shoulder and spun me round and Red Face ordered, 'Put that thing down.'

I looked down at the broken bottle in my hand. How I came by it I do not know – the court didn't believe that, and how could I expect them to? – I must have picked it up when I put my rifle down, but I don't remember doing so. Bewildered and puzzled, I raised my hand to see what I held and at that moment a fist crashed into my jaw.

498

The fifth stream flows into the river

Philip Morrison

We drove out of Kuala Lumpur in the chilly grey dawn, Philip and I in our own car with Siti and the animals, and Ja'afar following in a hired lorry with all our goods and chattels.

Neither of us spoke much, we had a long drive ahead and too many thoughts behind.

Once I had resigned myself to the idea of Philip leaving the army, I had done my best to see all the benefits, and luckily, being a born optimist, it was not long before I began to share his enthusiasm.

'As a matter of fact,' I said, 'I might be able to help. Daddy had quite a lot of government friends; he was a member of Legco for years and was director of hordes of things – he was quite a bigwig, you know.'

'If I hadn't realised that before, I would have done when I saw the house,' he replied.

'Oh, that wasn't ours; it just went with the job.'

'That's what I mean. But I don't need any help, Sally; if other people have been accepted, I don't see why I shouldn't be.'

He did however accept my help in teaching him Malay, and Ja'afar and I pounded it into him at every available moment. Two and a half months did not get him very far though and, by the time we left the army, it was still hopelessly inadequate.

Out of the army one day and into the police the next. We had twenty-eight days' leave, but Philip wanted to take the plunge and start his new job at once, and I suppose he was right. We weren't given much chance to linger anyway; the new occupants of our quarters started moving in even before we were out and, remembering our days in boarding-houses, I couldn't really blame them, but I would have enjoyed a more graceful exit. And so we were off.

It had been difficult to gauge Sally's thoughts. I had done this really because of her, knowing how she hated living in England, hated the cold, hated the separations – and there would have been plenty of those ahead of us.

'Ever heard of Kuala Jelang?' I had asked her a few days before. She had shaken her head. 'Well, you have now; I'm its new OCPD!'

What I was letting myself in for I dreaded to think. Happily motoring out into the blue, with my immediate family beside me and everything else in the ancient lorry trundling along behind. Bill Matheson had been posted to a staff job at a Contingent HQ and was learning the easy way; it had never occurred to me that I might find myself put in charge of a district straight away, but I suppose that with the Emergency getting steadily worse they were becoming a bit short of bods.

I was growing tired and wished I could put on a spurt, but I didn't want to lose the lorry. Sally had offered to take over, but I couldn't bear being driven and she knew it, so I plodded on. She was going to be tired before the end of the tour. We had already done our three years in Malaya and Singapore that the army allowed, and now we were starting on another three. Six years without leave would be a long time. Sally's only comment was that her father had once done an eight-year tour. She's a good kid. I hope I've done the right thing.

There was very little difference between Kuala Jelang and a score of other little Malayan towns. A long drive in through the usual government quarters, an avenue of flame trees here and another of jacarandas there; sleepy old government offices on the one hill and ancient government bungalows on the other – I'd seen it all a hundred times before. One row of shophouses and lagastroemas surrounding the padang.

The one thing that made it different was the deep river mouth, where quite large steamers were able to load and unload. I brightened up at that, it was more like home – I have always loved ships and I was born by the sea.

The police set-up looked terrifying. PCs – or mata-matas as I had always known them – crashing to attention all over the place, and literally millions of wives peering at me from the barracks' verandahs; we had already gathered that it had been a bachelor station for some years. I sat in the car while Philip went in to meet the man he was to take over from. Derek King, his name was, and I hoped he was nice, because we should have been there the evening before. We'd not reckoned with a curfew.

It was a relief to see them come out, Philip and a bright-faced cocky little man who, even at a distance, reminded me of a cheeky sparrow. He was smiling and made a wry face at the police wives. 'All the monkeys aren't in the zoo,' he said, when Philip had introduced him, 'as you've no doubt already discovered. May I hop in and I'll take you up to the house.'

We made room for him in front and began to climb the hill.

'You've certainly picked an opportune moment to arrive,' King commented. We were in his office, having dropped Sally and the servants at the house. 'Take a look at this.'

He pushed a signal across the desk, the gist of which was a warning to expect a spread of the Singapore student riots to the Federation.

'They're terrified of being called-up,' he explained. 'Personally, I'm all for letting them go – put them on the first boat to China, which is what they want, and good riddance. Provided we don't let the little buggers in again.'

'How does it affect us?'

'We've only one Chinese school in the town, but it's a hotbed of Communism – those bastards sure know how to corrupt the young. A fortnight ago two boys disappeared for a couple of days and the last bandit leaflet to be found was printed on the school press. Some of the pupils come in from the squatter areas and there's altogether too much coming and going. That's one of the reasons for the curfew; that and the fact that a contractor's lorry was ambushed the day before yesterday, just outside the town limit. Driver and escort killed, everything stolen – a month's supply of rice for one of the estates and a hell of a lot of tinned stuff – and the vehicle set on fire. It was still smouldering when we got there and – of all the damned cheek – nailed on a tree nearby was a bloody great red star; made, incidentally, from materials from the school art-room.'

I chewed this over while King answered a phone call.

It was a long call and appeared to be mainly one-sided. During the course of it he dug a file from a drawer and passed it over to me. It contained his handing-over notes. Pinned to the cover was a square of paper marked 'most urgent' and listing: squatters, timber-cutters, estate defences, army – lack of. I began to read.

'Old windbag!' King put down the receiver at last. 'Wotherspoon, of Bukit Merah Estate. Never stops complaining about the SCs on his estate – I scarcely listen any more; he'll be on to the DO now. Hang on to those notes and we'll go through them as soon as we can. And now you'd better see the set-up and meet the staff.'

As we walked across the parade-ground he remarked, 'You must have been driving pretty slowly – there was such a long gap between two police posts reporting your passage that I almost took out a patrol to look for you!'

I blinked. I doubt if either Sally or I had given the Emergency a moment's thought; there had been so many other things on our minds. A year on the staff had lulled me into a false sense of security.

By the time we returned to his office, my head was in a complete whirl.

There were two Malay inspectors, the elder, Zainal Abidin, due for retirement, and the younger, Zukifli, just recently posted there – there should be three apparently, we were under strength – a Sikh sergeant-major, Jogindar Singh, and a Chinese Special Branch sergeant, Vincent Lee Chee Min – this last I felt I would find myself leaning on; language was going to be a terrible problem. There were also two clerks, both Indians, the chief clerk called Maniam; I didn't get the name of the second one – must ask.

Derek had arranged a lunch party for us at the Rest House, to meet the other Europeans, and that evening, having apologised because he was committed to a stag party, we were having dinner with the DO and his wife. Frankly, I wish we had not been so organised.

In my giddier and more ignorant moments I had said how much I was going to enjoy living in an old colonial-style bungalow.

The huge, rambling, barn-like house was painted throughout in a heavy, margariney shade of cream, picked out wherever it could be in chocolate. It really was rather nauseating. Things were a bit bleak.

Ja'afar too was regarding the house with disgust when a really rather beautiful woman arrived.

'I'm Helen Weatherby,' she introduced herself, and laughed – she told me afterwards that the expression on my face was a real picture. 'We took over from a bachelor too, but after a boarding-house in KL it was sheer bliss – I just couldn't find anything wrong with it. I'm sure you'll be able to do something with the house.'

I liked her immediately.

'I won't waste your time now,' she said, 'I can see your husband leaving the police station; I expect he'll want to change. We'll be meeting at lunch anyway quite soon, but I just wanted to pop in to say hallo and to ask you to have a meal with us to-night.'

She was gone almost before I had time to thank her, and I turned my attention to my heavy-faced husband, slowly ascending the long flight of winding steps up to our house.

I cursed myself all the way up those bloody steps. We had had Ja'afar for over a year and if only I'd started learning Malay when he'd first come to work for us, instead of leaving it until I had to, I wouldn't be in such a predicament.

Of course I had only seen the operational side of the police in the army; perhaps if I'd had an overall picture I might have had second thoughts about transferring. I shuddered when I thought of the responsibility – imagine a brand new two-pipper in the army being put in charge of an area this size, and with all these men – it was ridiculous. I wasn't worried about the operational side; anyway, there are eight police lieutenants, Europeans, in charge of the Special Constables. But everything's so strange. I know nothing about law and it's all very well King showing me through this ledger and that register – how can I possibly have a clue what he's talking about?

I did my best to muster a grin when I saw Sally's worried face, but it was no use, I'm afraid. She's such an optimist – thinks I can get the hang of things in two minutes flat. I know she'll help me with the language, but I can hardly keep her chained to my side as my unpaid interpreter.

I enjoyed our lunch. The DO and his wife are a charming couple, a little older than us. I'm sure we'll get on famously. Derek and the Forestry Officer, a rather gauche, blundery sort of person whom I'm sure I've met before somewhere, excused themselves to go to a meeting, and we had our coffee and fruit on our own with the Weatherbys.

It was really too funny watching those men. Sniffing around each other like a couple of suspicious dogs! Then they discovered that they were both thwarted regulars, who had joined the Colonial Service for similar reasons, and it was Helen and I who had to break up the party and remind them of the time.

Helen raised her eyebrows as she left. 'Thank God you've come,' she said. I don't know why, but no doubt I shall find out. It was fairly obvious, I thought, that there was not much love lost between her husband and Philip's predecessor, so I suppose that's what she meant.

Philip was in much better spirits after lunch and drove off to the office in quite a light-hearted manner.

How I blessed Ja'afar and Siti. By the time Philip brought Derek King up for a beer that evening we were actually able to produce beer mugs! Of course the whole place would be shambolic for days, but they had already unpacked three crates and our pictures were stacked along one wall, waiting for me to hang.

'How goes it?' I asked. Philip, I thought, looked all in.

'So-so. A bit 'ard, I reckon, asking anyone new to take over in three days. Ah well, here's to my boat. *I'm* all right!' Derek lifted his mug.

Philip grinned wanly. All my maternal instinct was aroused and I longed to cradle his head and stroke his hair. I wasn't sorry when Derek got up to go.

'Well, hope you enjoy yourself with the nobs as much as I intend enjoying my Chinese chow.'

He was obviously as smart as a cartload of monkeys, but I thought a little of him would go a long way. As soon as he had gone, Philip slumped forward with his head in his hands and I thought for a dreadful moment that he was going to cry.

'How *am* I going to cope?' he asked at length. 'King admits the senior inspector's an old dead-beat, and the young one's too new to help much. There's no one to whom I can turn.'

'You'll manage,' I said, and I was stroking his hair by then. I certainly hoped I was right.

While the Morrisons and the outgoing OCPD were discussing the district, the Weatherbys, on the other side of the hill, were discussing the newcomers.

Helen had been bubbling ever since lunchtime and James could not remember seeing her so frivolously excited before. She remarked, for the umpteenth time, that it would be nice to have another woman around, what a pity they didn't have any children and what fun it would be helping Sally to unpack and move in.

James sat on the edge of his bed, listening to her with one ear while she splashed around in the bath and chattered on. The other ear, as usual, was on his job.

'Brush my hair for me, James.'

She seated herself on the stool before the dressing-table in bra and pants and handed him the brush. With no one locally to cut her hair it had grown quite long. James picked it up and looked at it before wielding the brush; still as blonde as ever and her skin as white, despite the sun. He took up a firm stance and began to brush with long, sweeping, rhythmic strokes, smiling at her in the mirror as he did so.

It was ages since he had brushed her hair. He seldom suffered pangs of conscience, but it suddenly occurred to him that she must have been bored to death these past six months, and lonely too. What company there was had largely been barred – by him. He knew that he had nothing to be jealous about, and yet he could not bear another man looking at his wife and unfortunately, when you looked like Helen, people did look at you, especially men. He was proud of her and yet he hated it, sometimes wishing that she were ordinary and plain. And then there was his work; he was so bound up in it that even the odd evening in the local estate club seemed a waste of precious time and he made sure that they gave the weekly club night in town a miss if they possibly could. It could not have been much fun for her though. As far as he was concerned the Morrisons could only be an improvement, and first impressions had been good. Thank God he was married, if she and Sally got on it would make all the difference for Helen.

'I'm glad I asked them for supper on their own,' for an awful moment James wondered if she had only just spoken, or if he had been miles away while she had been talking, 'I suppose I should have asked Donald as well, but he's such heavy going and I thought it would be fun just the four of us.'

He made some non-committal sound.

'I'm sure we're going to have lots in common – isn't it strange that you and Sally should have been in the air force and Philip and I in the army?'

'Not really. Most people of our age were in one uniform or another. You're going to be late.'

'Oh James, you can be a wet blanket. You know you liked them – even if you never will admit to liking anybody.'

He slapped her on the bottom with the hairbrush and muttered something about tying his tie – something he had never managed to cope with one-handed.

In fact, they did find plenty in common and were still talking when the clock struck midnight. By that time they had all had a synopsis of each others' careers, moaned about the lousy pay of government servants, the disgusting colours that the PWD chose to paint their houses, and argued hotly about service matters. What a pleasant change it will be, James thought, to have someone here who knows even less about the district than I do.

The next morning Derek King was up at the house before Philip had even finished shaving.

'Anyone awake yet?' he yelled. And when Philip emerged, 'I didn't want to use the phone, but I've got an informer in the office. Came in from one of the timber camps. I'm taking a patrol out in half an hour; are you fit?'

'Never fitter.' It was a relief to tackle a job with which he was already *au fait*. 'I hope Ja'afar's unearthed my jungle-green. Have a cup of coffee?'

'Thanks.' While they drank, he outlined the plan.

An hour later they were walking in single file down a narrow-gauge light railway, running into the jungle from a roadside timber camp. The informer led, a sack with eye slits over his head and shoulders, police issue jungle-green below. Immediately to his side and behind came two jungle squad PCs, stens at the ready, then Morrison and King and some fifteen men.

They had walked for nearly three miles before the high-pitched whine of an electric saw reverberated through the forest. The informer stopped dead and held up his hand.

'He says we are now less than half a mile from the cutting area,' one of the PCs whispered to King. 'The men will be with the first trolley coming down.'

'As good a place to ambush as any,' King said to Philip. 'With any luck we'll get them as they come round that bend.' He waved his carbine in front of the sack and said to the Chinese-speaking PC, 'Tell him no nonsense or he'll be the first to die.'

It was eerie waiting in the intense gloom, Philip thought, the only sounds besides the insects the heavy breathing of his unseen companions and the occasional distant whine of the saw.

From where he lay the rails were above him and immediately in front. Quite suddenly they began to hum, and a moment later to shake. A trolley had started on its way.

A twig fell on the line; signal from a PC high in a tree that the trolley was within fifty yards. Philip licked his lips and counted.

The firing was practically instantaneous. Three men fell dead, and with a high-pitched shriek of rage the fourth person, a woman by the voice, attempting to use the trolley as a shield, flung her weapon on to it and pulled a hand-grenade from her shirt. With one movement two PCs grabbed her and she fell with them, kicking wildly and tearing at them with her hands. The trolley hurtled down a slight incline and the grenade rolled harmlessly along the line.

A third PC caught the woman's hands and tied them, but she was not beaten; she twisted round and spat, full in his face. The man hit her across the mouth and she started up a screeching that must have lasted five minutes, all the time thrusting her chin in the direction of her hooded compatriot, before King shouted, 'For Christ's sake, gag the bitch.'

When she was firmly bound and loaded on to the trolley with the three corpses and their weapons, the party started back.

Later that afternoon the woman's screeched invective could be heard all over the police compound. Chee Min came out of his office, mopping sweat from his brow and grinned at Philip. 'She could teach an Aussie truck driver a few words!'

'What did you get out of her?'

'That men may turn informer, but a woman never. We can gaol her, torture her, offer her cash, and string her up, but she'll never split. I believe her. Incidentally, she's accusing the two PCs who grabbed her of rape!'

When the men were told, their remarks would have shamed an Aussie truck driver too!

Sally had turned away, sickened, when she saw the three corpses being laid out on the grass verge outside the police station, but as soon as Philip came home she sensed that he had found his confidence. The first blood had done the trick.

The next day King handed over; they attended a stupendous farewell party for him and the day after that Philip was on his own.

Within days of taking over, and bearing the priorities in mind, Philip

Morrison visited the Ulu Pandanus settlement with Detective-Sergeant Lee Chee Min. He looked with interest as they moved slowly along the raised, flat road, with squatter huts and market gardens on either side.

'They seem well established,' he observed, pointing at the sizeable coffee bushes and fruit trees.

'I believe they've been here ever since the end of the war.'

At that moment a middle-aged man wearing a large topi and pushing a bicycle with a heavy-looking sack on the carrier emerged from one of the orchards and attempted to push his overloaded cycle up a makeshift ramp and on to the road. He looked at them with an expressionless face and called out to a boy, whom Philip judged to be about twelve years of age, to help him push.

The police vehicle continued to crawl through the settlement, until they were past the last house and already within the confines of the jungle.

Philip told the driver to turn round and stop. They all sat in the stationary jeep for a couple of minutes while he asked a number of questions, then said they would return the way they had come.

'Drive slowly,' he ordered, 'I want to have another good look at the area.'

Back they went until they reached the man and the boy, still heaving and pushing the heavy bicycle with much high-pitched abuse at each other, but little success.

Philip laughed. 'Go and give them a hand,' he said to the two PCs sitting at the back, who immediately jumped off the vehicle and ran towards the quarrelling couple.

As soon as they saw the police coming both man and boy abandoned the bike and fled down the path, past a couple of houses, through the market gardens and into the jungle fringe.

The PCs needed no orders to give chase and, picking up their rifles, dashed after the fleeing pair, closely followed by Philip and Chee Min.

At the jungle edge the man turned, pulling a revolver from his waist band as he did so, and fired, hitting one of the constables in the shoulder.

Philip and the other PC fired at the same time and the man fell.

'Get the boy,' he called to Chee Min, and went to the body lying on the path.

The man was dead, with two bullet wounds in the chest, and Philip stood up from examining the corpse to find the boy, with Chee Min holding his arm, looking down at it with a look utterly devoid of any emotion other than curiosity.

'Ask him who the man is.'

Chee Min interpreted.

'My uncle.' The boy shrugged. 'Can I have a cigarette?'

'No,' Philip stifled the impulse to hit the youngster, 'you're too young.'

Then he turned his attention to the wounded constable, who was sitting by the side of the track holding the blood-sodden sleeve of his shirt.

'Nothing much, Tuan, only a small wound.' The man grinned but he was obviously in pain.

'Where's the nearest doctor?' Philip asked Chee Min.

'Kemuning. But I expect the dresser will cope – he's removed bullets before.' He turned to the wounded man and spoke in Malay, 'Can you walk, Ismail?'

The man rose, unaided. Incredibly nimbly, Philip thought, and marvelled at his stoicism. 'I'll take your rifle,' he said, and turning to the other PC, 'yours too; you carry the body.'

They walked in single file back to the jeep, Chee Min leading with the boy, then the wounded PC, the PC carrying the corpse, and Philip bringing up the rear.

Not a soul was to be seen. Every house appeared to be empty, every garden deserted. But they could feel the eyes watching as they made their silent way back.

The body was thrown into the rear of the jeep with scant ceremony and the boy seated beside it under the guard of the able-bodied PC, while Philip and Chee Min examined the contents of the sack.

Rice and dried fish, tins of bully beef, pilchards, sardines, jars of chicken essence by the score and several well-packed bottles emerged. Philip carefully unwrapped one.

'Good God, look at this,' he held up a bottle of Benedictine. 'Whoever would have thought they had such sophisticated tastes?'

'It is a powerful body-builder and most strengthening to the constitution,' Chee Min remarked and, just in time, Philip realised with amazement that he was serious.

Back at the police station, Chee Min and a Chinese detective interrogated the boy.

There was no question of his trying to run away; escape was far from his mind. He looked around him, picked things up and showed no emotion whatsoever. After half an hour, Chee Min went into Philip's office to report.

'The boy's father is with the bandits proper in the jungle. The deceased, his uncle, was only Min Yuen, who kept that particular supply line going.' He paused for a moment, not knowing how *au fait* the new OCPD was with the local Communist organisation. 'You understand, sir? The Min Yuen who don't wear uniform, but keep the fighting terrorists supplied. They are the ones who collect food and money and act as contacts; the men in the jungle couldn't survive without them.'

'Sort of combined RASC and Ordnance Corps,' Philip murmured.

It was Chee Min's turn not to understand. He gave Philip a slightly puzzled look but went on, 'I cannot make out where they were actually heading when we happened to pass. But the boy will tell.'

'You can't beat him up,' Philip said hastily.

Chee Min gave a mirthless laugh, 'Not necessary, sir. He will lead us to his father's camp – depending on the amount of the reward money involved.'

'I don't believe it. No child would lead the police in – why, his father might be killed.'

'This one will. He's a hard little bugger, make no mistake.'

'We'll have to be on the alert for a trap.'

Inspector Zainal Abidin, the elderly senior inspector, who had been with Philip when Chee Min came in, murmured, 'Europeans find this mentality difficult to understand.'

'By God I do. It's horrifying.'

Both inspector and sergeant shrugged their shoulders and Philip told Chee Min to get what details he could to enable them to plan a raid.

By the following evening all plans were completed and a little before midnight two troop-carriers and a jeep, carrying the OCPD, Chee Min, the boy, Police Lieutenant O'Brien, and fifteen members of his jungle squad, set off from the police station in the direction of Ulu Pandanus.

Still incredulous that any child could be sufficiently callous to engineer the possible death of his own father for a cash reward, Philip had come well prepared to be led into a trap.

The vehicles separated before reaching the squatter huts, passing through the inhabited area at intervals, to rendezvous on the jungle-enclosed road beyond.

After a quarter of an hour's travelling, the boy called a halt and announced that a track began from behind a tall Ipoh tree a couple of chains farther on.

Philip held a sheet of paper on his knees in the front of the jeep and, beckoning the police lieutenant and Chee Min to his side, he flashed his torch on to it. The boy had drawn the plan in the police station that afternoon and Philip still marvelled that one so young could be so sure.

'We're here,' the child stabbed the map with a grubby forefinger, 'and this is the beginning of the track, here.'

509

There was one main track, the one they would be starting on, used by the Min Yuen and terrorists making direct for the camp, the boy had told them, but there were many hidden tracks, branching off and surrounding the camp, which the bandits used as escape routes. The only sentry was posted on the main track.

O'Brien, ex-Commando and Palestine policeman, had volunteered to take one of his men and deal with the sentry but, if the boy could be trusted, Philip's plans were otherwise.

If as many hidden tracks existed as marked, he intended that they should branch off the main one long before reaching the sentry and half encircle the camp from the opposite side. The moon was in the last quarter, giving them a glimmer of light by which to travel. A two-hour walk to the camp, the boy had said, and Philip allowed three, to enable them to be in position and ready to attack at dawn.

They had been moving in silence and in single file for about an hour when the boy suddenly stopped. He pointed to a large, moss-covered boulder and whispered to Chee Min.

'He says that one hidden track begins the other side of this rock; it goes to the left. A few yards farther on there is a rotting log, on the right side of the path, and another hidden track starts there. Which one do you want to take?'

Philip fought down his exasperation and said, 'Tell him the easiest one to get *behind* the camp.' He was still not altogether happy about their guide.

Without any hesitation the boy scrambled under a bush by the side of the rock, stood upright on the other side, asked for a torch – which was reluctantly passed – flickered it around the ground at his feet, gave an exclamation of satisfaction when he found a largish stone with a fern growing out of it, and parted the bushes immediately above it. On the other side was a well-used path.

'Oh for some aerial photographs,' Philip remarked, almost inaudibly. 'We'd never have found this in a month of Sundays.'

Trap or no trap, it was clear that the boy knew his way. After half an hour's fairly swift moving, he stopped again and pointed. In the remains of the moonlight it was possible to see the jungle thinning into secondary growth, and a few minutes later they were able to see the clearing itself.

Philip and O'Brien edged forward until they could make out the boundaries of the clearing and the outline of a long atap hut, nestling on the edge and sheltered by overhanging trees.

'Whole area must have been a Sakai clearing,' O'Brien whispered. 'Look, you can still see the remains of their tapioca over there.'

After a few more moments of examination of the area, they returned to the main body of the party.

'You stay here with the boy,' Philip instructed Chee Min and ordered that the rest of the men, led by the police lieutenant, should take up positions a short distance apart in a half moon round the back of the hut. He drew his whistle on its lanyard from his top left-hand pocket and held it up, the pale moonlight glinting on the shiny metal. 'This will be the signal to attack. When you hear me whistle, open up. If what the boy says is true and we are on one of their escape routes, at least some of the terrorists should run from the hut in our direction – that is the time to pick them off.'

The men began to spread out and Philip concealed himself in the fork of a low tree some twenty-five yards from the hut. There would be about half an hour to wait.

Dawn came very suddenly, and as soon as it was light enough to aim, Philip blew his whistle and the men of the jungle squad opened fire.

Bandits came popping from the huts like peas from a ripe pod. A few ran through the door and down the steps, but mostly bodies came hurtling through the flimsy atap walls, dropped through trap doors in the floor and on to the ground, and Philip dropped one man who thrust a ladder through the roof and tried to swing into a tree.

The firing lasted for about a minute, by which time it was daylight and, calling to a man near him to give him cover, Philip walked warily into the camp.

Nothing stirred. Complete silence reigned. The camp was deserted except for the dead.

Soon a great pile of weapons, uniforms, food and documents was being divided into portable loads and six corpses were laid out on the ground.

Three separate blood trails had been followed up and soon two PCs walked into the clearing carrying a wounded man, whose groaning rose above the excited chatter of the other men. They laid him on the ground, telling the OCPD that they had first come across his rifle, then, a few yards farther on, the man himself. The boy walked over and looked at him. No sign of guilt, recognition or accusation was expressed on either face.

'Is he your father?'

He shook his head and pointed to one of the six corpses. 'No. My father is over there.' He showed complete disinterest. Then, brightening up, 'Do I get the reward money now?'

Sally dashed to the verandah railing when she heard the vehicles grinding along the road. Watching townsfolk had seen the gruesome cargo of the last troop carrier and were already flocking to the police station in droves.

'Oh my God, how horrible.'

She turned away as she saw the six bodies being off-loaded and laid out in a row on the side of the road. Ja'afar was at her elbow, grinning.

'It is good luck for the Tuan,' he said. 'Nine bodies in as many days.' He started towards the front steps.

'I will not have any ghouls in this house,' Sally commanded, 'just you go and organise the Tuan's breakfast and leave the spectacle to the town.' Nevertheless, she knew he would go down as soon as her back was turned.

Ja'afar grimaced, said nothing, and continued to watch. So did Sally herself, but keeping her gaze averted from the gory sight. The morning air was crystal clear. She could even see the white smile in the beard of Jogindar Singh as he greeted Philip, and his clicking heels and call of attention to the Charge Room cracked up like pistol shots.

Then at last Philip himself was leaving the police station and ascending the steps to the house.

He dropped his muddy jungle-boots at the front door and padded across the room in blood-soaked socks.

'Philip, you're wounded,' Sally hurried towards him, and only then did he look down at his gory feet.

'Leeches,' he said. 'Bloody place was full of them.'

'Ugh!' They were one of the few things that she never learned to take in her stride.

Standing by the front door with Philip's bloody boots in her hand, Sally glanced over the heads of the milling crowd below and at the river, then raised her eyes to the blue hills; the hills where Philip would spend so much of his time.

Because she was so close to her husband, she was able to visualise the long night vigils and slow, weary, plodding through undergrowth and hampering vines that had to be cut, inch by inch, before success could be achieved. She understood the furtive rustle or sudden bird-screech that sent the adrenalin coursing through the blood. She knew the tense moments of apprehension that caused the throat to go dry and the palms to sweat; the terrible heartbeats that thumped in rhythm to the stranger's step; the moment of fire and the fleeting question, Will it be them or us?

She looked down at the boots in her hand and there, wriggling obscenely on the blood-soaked canvas, lay a satiated leech; pinkish, grey-white, bloated on blood. It was so like a segment of the entrails that had once been spewed over her lap that her memory betrayed her and she had to dash for the drain.

A minute later Ja'afar was relieving her of the boots and pushing back her hair. 'She must be pregnant,' he told his wife, and they both smiled with pleasure.

Sally washed and rinsed out her mouth in the spare bedroom, pulled herself together and turned her attention to the breakfast-table.

The plates and coffee-pot were squeezed to one end and she sighed as she looked at the great pyramid of files cluttering the major part. Philip was slowly wading through them whenever he had a break and she was doing her best to précis the long reports for him, but how could anyone be expected to spend hours and days in the jungle yet still cope with the weighty routine work? And yet scores of OCPDs must be doing just that.

Philip was singing under the shower. Will he still be singing in a year? she wondered.

'Aren't you going to get some sleep?' she asked when he emerged from the bedroom, looking a new man in clean shorts and shirt.

'Can't. The mail's in already and there's a pile in my tray I haven't looked at yet. I'll go to bed early though; we're going out again before dawn to-morrow.'

'Another camp?'

'No. We brought in a wounded man; he's told us where the escapees were heading. Also where there's a lot of equipment to be found. Chee Min was keen to go straight away, but if we give them time there should be a better haul.'

He ate a couple of slices of toast, swallowed only half his coffee and was gone.

Sally took another piece of toast – she's hungry, a good sign, Ja'afar thought, as he cleared the used crockery away – and thought how important it was to keep one's mind on mundane things. She spoke to Ja'afar on a number of household matters, but her thoughts kept wandering.

She had never appreciated how far removed from reality she had been as an army wife – and she had thought it nerve-racking at the time; nor how much worse it would be, being married to a policeman instead of a soldier. How much more down to earth. It wasn't only that as a police wife she herself was living in the danger zone, but that she knew too much. When Philip had gone out on ops with his company she had not known what was going on, or the area, and when he returned to their quarters he was always clean and shaved and neatly dressed. Reality was much closer when you saw your husband lacing his jungle-boots and picking up his carbine. Then the roaring of trucks away down the road and, once the sound had died away, the awful waiting. Not going to bed until the small hours, in case he should come home, and the ever-listening ear for voices or vehicles on the road below. And when they did return, sometimes wounded men were lifted from the trucks and sometimes corpses.

She took her coffee to the verandah rail. The crowd had dispersed; only the corpses remained, mangled, torn and bloody. She could almost hear the buzzing of the flies.

The information led them, needless to say, to the Ulu Pandanus squatter area.

Philip's whole body tingled with apprehension. They crept through dense, white, pre-dawn mist and arrived at the first houses as the first cockerel crowed. There was something sinister in the sound.

Faint and fleeting above the mist rose a kite.

'White,' Chee Min whispered. 'I haven't worked out their signals yet, but I think it means they have info to pass.'

The stillness was uncanny. The houses looked blind in the pale grey light, the mist sweeping them in ribbons, passing, circling, swishing on. Eyes seemed to be watching, narrowed, in every swathe of vapour. Suddenly a nightjar rose, squawking, in a flurry of feathers, at their feet, its crimson eyes glaring through the gloom. Philip caught his breath, Chee Min gave a faint, nervous giggle, and the man beside him swore.

And then, as though the curtain had been lifted on a stage, it was light. The cockerels crowed in unison and the search began.

Uniforms, material, sewing-machines, flags, arms and ammunition: all came from under floorboards, in tins tied to beams and to branches of trees. Babies were found lying on bundles of money; curtains weighted down with ammunition and pieces of dismantled weapons in every conceivable nook and cranny of the apparently poverty-stricken huts.

But of the escaped CTs there was no trace. Not a young man was to be seen. Chee Min looked reproachfully at his superior.

Philip, too, was furious with himself. The boy had said that about twenty men normally occupied the camp. They had accounted for seven. What had happened to the other thirteen?

On first entering the squatter settlement he had noticed something unnatural about one of the gardens, but could not pinpoint what it was. The house had been searched along with all the others and yielded nothing, but he was still not satisfied. While one of the other houses was being gone through he had walked back to take another look, and while he was doing so Chee Min joined him.

'What's different about this garden?' Philip asked.

Chee Min looked, then he walked to another garden and came back, shaking his head.

'I thought perhaps that it was that they are growing flowers instead of vegetables,' he said, 'but in fact most of the huts have a few flowers as well.'

It was the zinnia bed that stood out so startlingly, Philip realised, and then, quite suddenly, he saw what was wrong.

It was still early morning and the zinnias were growing in the shade of the hut. Standing like guardsmen, straight and bright, they bloomed, row upon row.

'No green,' he pointed out, 'no leaves.'

He strode forward and plucked one of the heads from the bed. It came straight out at the first tug, its stem cut clean about a foot down.

'Have it dug up,' he ordered.

The elderly occupants of the hut came out while the police dug and stood there watching, quiet, expressionless, flat-eyed.

The body was not more than eighteen inches down. Still in uniform and with a gash across the neck, he must have been one of the wounded terrorists who had come so far only to die on arrival.

'Do you know this man?' Chee Min asked the old couple.

'He was our son.' The disinterment continued and Philip was wondering at the humility of the old people when the man spoke again, a wistful note in his voice, 'His politics were not our politics, but he was our son.'

86. THE PRIORITIES

Donald Thom looked thoughtfully into his Scotch and listened to Philip laying down the law. This was no ordinary dinner-party; the Morrisons had asked him for a reason.

'I don't see how we can achieve anything until we get the supply lines under control.' Philip, the only person standing, emphasised his point with a cutting gesture. 'Cut them off. Get the squatters resettled and the timber camps closed down.'

'Steady on,' Donald interrupted. 'Regrouping was the intention, not closing down.' He drained his drink and Sally rose to refill his glass. He smiled at her. 'Taking the forward camps out of the deep forest and regrouping the various kongsis, sawmills and all, in an area where they can be guarded – '

'Guarded by whom?'

'You.'

Philip sat down with a loud humph and asked, 'And where, do you suppose, the men are coming from?'

'Gee, I dunno; guess that's a police problem. Thanks, Sal,' as she handed him his replenished glass, 'I can see your predicament, Phil, but it was all gone into before you arrived; the same throughout the state. The idea is to have these regrouped camps and then the cutters go into the jungle each day, having been searched – by the police – for supplies, then escorted – by the police, of course!'

Philip grinned then. 'Okay, Don. I'm not really being obstructive, but I want to have my facts and figures clear before the CPO comes down. We're hopelessly under strength anyway. I wanted to talk this over, amicably, with you and James, somewhere where we wouldn't have the phone ringing the whole time – '

The phone rang.

'Sorry,' Philip said, a minute later 'Scare on Belimbing Estate. I'll have to go. God, how I wish we had some troops here. James, can we discuss the squatter problem to-morrow? CPO'll be down in a few days.'

Sally spread her hands in a gesture of resignation as they heard Philip's jeep drive away. 'And to think I *wanted* to stay in Malaya.'

Philip tackled the DO on the resettlement problem the next day.

'It has been brought up with DWEC,' James admitted, 'but the trouble is finding land.'

He knew in his own heart that he had disliked Philip's predecessor so much that he had done very little to co-operate with him. King had been going on about resettling the squatters for some time and, not without malice, James had always found some other matter to take priority. On the other hand, land was a genuine problem. There was no Crown land available in a suitable area; it would mean buying land – funds would be forthcoming, but who was prepared to sell?

'To date it only appears to be those isolated squatters across the river at Ulu Pandanus that we can pin anything on,' Philip continued, 'but I suppose the Pasir Hitam crowd are helping too – although we have no evidence as yet.'

Pasir Hitam was the settlement to the south of the river.

'Obviously it must become number one priority,' James agreed. 'We'll have to have another go at finding a site.'

'And then, my next task will be to lay down the law a bit over defences.'

'Making yourself popular with the planting fraternity?' James raised an eyebrow.

'Well, perhaps it's my army mind, but it strikes me that if you're going to have SCs on the estates, paid by Government, then there must be reasonable defences to help them do the defending. Don't you agree?'

'On the whole I do.'

'Oh well, better get back to the grindstone. I have a new inspector arriving, I hope, on the bus and I'm going out on an overnight patrol. At least it can't be said that we lead idle lives.'

James sat for a while after Philip had left. It was a relief to be able to work with someone he liked for a change. Sally was company for Helen too. If only his eye wasn't giving him such hell he would really enjoy this job. His arm too.

He rolled up his empty sleeve and examined the stump. A mass of small ulcers covered it, that would not heal whatever he tried. This bloody climate, he thought. It had been all right in Kuala Lumpur, where he had had an air-conditioned office, but here there was not even a fan. He glanced up at the ceiling, where two hooks showed where a punkah had once hung. He had been amused to see on one of the old account books that had survived the war what the wages of a pre-war punkah wallah had been – everything was so penny-pinched he doubted if they would pay *that* now.

He called his clerk and asked for a file, then looked at his watch. He would have to go across the river to settle a dispute between two headmen after lunch; what a bore. He would have preferred to be going with Philip; he didn't feel like talking all afternoon.

Philip did not return to his own office at once, but went to the Forestry Station instead.

'I'm going to take out patrols and penetrate every cutting area and the surrounding jungle,' he told Donald, ' – having read the riot act to the towkays first – and hope we have the odd encounter at the same time. Do you want to come?'

'You bet!'

As Philip left the office he rubbed his hands. Action at last. Then he realised that he was aiding and abetting his own redundancy.

87. NO DENIAL

Sharif Ahmat

My year with the army came to an end and although I was sorry in many ways to leave them, I was still ambitious, and sensible to the fact that being out of sight was out of mind.

I was posted to Special Branch and it seemed that Hassan had been right about the inspectorate being a mere stepping-stone for me. Of course I was no keener than the next man to see my country plunged into virtual war again, but, as any regular soldier will tell you, there is nothing like a war for personal advancement – always providing that one survives.

These sentiments were echoed by the senior SB officer who interviewed me on arrival at my new post. I must say he was extremely friendly and told me that, with the sudden expansion of the force, I stood a better than ever chance of early promotion to gazetted rank. He also told me that my wartime background, knowledge of the Communist guerillas and my recent experience with the army, would hold me in good stead.

I can tell you, I walked out of that interview already mentally buckling on my Sam Browne and considering myself Tuan Allah's gift to the force!

My ego did not remain inflated for long though. I was to share an office for a week or two with a Chinese inspector, to learn the routine of filing, classification, etcetera, before going on an SB course. This man was my senior in both years and service and it was clear from the start that, as far as I was concerned, he was not impressed.

I suppose I was a mite cocky. I repeated the gist of the interview while he sat, picking his nose and jogging a knee – in that infuriating manner of many Chinese. Then he asked me just one damping question.

'Just exactly how long *were* you with the guerillas?'

The army had helped me to believe that I was one hell of a fellow, but when I stopped to think about it, I had to admit that I had spent far more time as an ordinary PC, maintaining a negative 'no see, no hear' policy than I had either as a go-between or in the jungle.

I felt my ears growing hot and I suppose I stammered some sort of reply. I can't remember now. I never did learn to like that particular colleague of mine, but I had one thing to thank him for – he taught me to stand on my own feet and not rely on Hassan's reputation.

I cannot tell you much about my work with Special Branch, partly because I had signed the Official Secrets Act and partly because it would be difficult to explain – I was, after all, a pretty small cog in a large wheel and my job was only a part of the whole, dovetailing in with other people's.

I went on seeing Azizah as much as I could, but I no longer worked regular office hours and was unable to maintain the weekly dates each Sunday.

We talked about marriage quite often and I finally won her over, but there was still the stumbling-block of my mother.

I think Azizah was quite looking forward to the status of being an inspector's wife – for I had made up my mind to marry her, whether my mother gave her consent or not.

And then the blow fell.

I must have been working in SB for about a year when I was summoned to the presence of my immediate boss.

I could see it was going to be a painful session as soon as I opened the door, and I was right.

He was a bluff, burly man, rather a jovial character normally, but now he was frowning and tapping a pencil agitatedly on his blotter.

'Sit down, Ahmat. I'll come straight to the point.'

He handed me a cigarette and lit his own.

'There has been an anonymous letter written about you. I abhor these things at any time, and even more so when it concerns one of my own men. But we can't be too careful with this confounded Emergency on and the Head wants your comments before it goes any further.'

Of course my mind leaped to Azizah, but I could not have been wider from the mark.

'The letter accuses you of being a Communist.'

'But – '

'No, wait. Let me finish first.'

'But, sir, I'm not a Communist.'

'It accuses you of having deliberately set fire to a police station in 1945 in order to facilitate the escape of a wanted Communist. Now what have you to say to that?'

What was there to say?

'Well?'

'I have nothing to say.'

'You don't deny having set fire to the police station?' The incredulity made his voice rise.

'No.'

'I never, for one moment, expected to hear that reply from you. In the circumstances, you can hardly expect to remain in Special Branch.'

'I am not a Communist, sir. Nor have I ever been one.'

'And yet you helped them.' It was a statement, flat.

There was a long silence before he spoke again.

'To say that I'm upset and disappointed in you would be putting it very mildly. Both the Head and I had taken your denial for granted – the letter seemed utterly ridiculous. Now I have no alternative but to suspend you from duty until such time as the Head decides what action to take. Inspector Nordin will take over from you temporarily. That's all.'

I returned to my own office and buried my head in my hands and nearly wept with the bitterness and injustice of it all. Hasbullah was behind it without a doubt – but how could I prove that he wrote the letter, or caused it to be written? And anyway, what it said was true. The escape of Ah Keow seemed a hundred years ago and even

Hasbullah had not been in my thoughts since the inspectors' course.

I must have been sitting like that when my office mate, Shau Lee, came in, and it was a relief to pour out my troubles to him.

'But my goodness, man, that was during the occupation. Plenty of people went into the jungle with the guerillas who weren't Communists. Didn't you tell him that?'

'How could I prove it? Hassan is dead, Richardson is dead, and I've no idea what happened to the army officers who were with us. There is only Kassim, and I don't know where he is. Everyone else *was* a Communist.'

'I don't believe that. There must have been others who weren't Communists.' I shrugged. 'But who could have written such a monstrous letter?'

'Oh, I know who wrote it all right. But even if I could prove it, it would be his word against mine.'

'But why didn't you explain? Old Hopper would have listened to you.'

I shrugged again. 'What could I say?'

'Oh, you Malays. When you get proud and stubborn like this it just makes me lose my patience.'

He slammed out of the office and I was left alone once more with my very uncomfortable thoughts. If it came to interdiction, I supposed I would have to fight, but if it were merely a posting it could be worse. The thought of leaving SB did not upset me much – in fact, I would prefer a more active job – but I saw all hopes of reaching gazetted rank receding from my grasp, and the unfairness of it all hit me all over again.

Soon afterwards Nordin arrived to take over. I went straight to the Bintang Kilat that evening, but I didn't dance. I did my best to smile at Azizah, but she was no fool and I could see her ill-concealed look of puzzled concern. At the first break she came over to where I sat.

'Whatever's wrong, Mat? You look awful.'

'I feel awful. Azizah, please come with me for a walk or something after you've finished – I've got to talk to you.'

'We're not busy to-night; Munah will take over for me. I'll come now.'

I didn't even buy her a cup of coffee. We went straight to the Lake Gardens and there, sitting on a bench in the kind, velvety darkness, I told her what had happened.

'You know, Mat, I'll marry you even if you are disgraced. After all, being the wife of an inspector isn't everything.'

'But even if I'm not disgraced, I'm bound to be posted out-station.'

'Oh yes,' she replied shrewdly, 'that's inevitable.'

I cannot tell you what a surge of joy and relief swept over me. I suppose at the back of my mind there had lurked a nagging, insidious little thought, that Azizah's interest was in my rank and position rather than in me myself. And of course I knew she liked the bright lights.

What a wonderful girl she was. I jumped up and hugged her and when I felt the softness of her cheek against mine and the scent of her hair so close to my nostrils, it was all I could do not to make love to her there and then.

After that we walked, hand-in-hand, over to the open-air restaurant.

'Are you a Communist, Mat?'

I stopped, open-mouthed in astonishment. I could not see her expression in the dark, but she had sounded casual, as though it were not at all important.

'Of course not.'

I had never told her about my war days, but when we had reached the restaurant and were settled at an isolated table with glasses of iced coffee before us, I told her the whole story from beginning to end.

She listened carefully and at length made a pertinent remark. 'If you can't find Kassim, don't you think the Ceylonese dresser might still be alive?'

Old Ratna. Of course. Why hadn't I thought of him? I had been so busy all afternoon hating Hasbullah that I had let my feelings cloud my judgment. There were several Jaffna Tamil clerks of his age in HQ; someone there might know him. I would make inquiries the very next day.

When the restaurant closed, we strolled again out into the black night and lay on the soft warm turf under a laburnum tree. You could see the carpet of bright yellow petals showing grey against the darker ground. Azizah sat with her back propped against the tree, gathering the petals into her lap and soon we were talking of other things.

I suppose I must have fallen asleep, for the next thing I knew was Azizah shaking me and seeing the first pale streaks of dawn reflected in the lake.

'Oh Mat, we're soaked with dew and my shoulder's bruised from cushioning your heavy great head all night!'

I could just see a glint of light on her eyes and teeth. She smelt good. I leaned down and touched her lips with mine, Western style, as we had seen on the movies. Then I pulled her up and brushed her down. She was right, we were wet.

'Come on, hurry. I'd better get you home before daylight.'

The noise of the scooter sounded vibrant and alive in the cool morning air. There was no traffic to speak of and I brpt-brpted up the middle of the road to reach her lodgings in record time.

Then I went and showered and changed into a clean uniform – the first time I'd worn uniform for more than a year – happy to face whatever the day might bring. Man, I felt good.

In fact, it brought nothing and I had to wait for nearly a week before a clerk told me that I was posted to Kuala Jelang as senior inspector.

During this time I had had several interviews with officers of varying seniority. I just kept quiet most of the time; I could not see any point in trying to explain myself. And anyway, I didn't care. I had Azizah behind me and in my heart I knew I had done nothing wrong. Tuan Allah knew that my conscience was clear, so why should I worry?

If my punishment was merely to be returned to general duties, and with what appeared to be promotion to boot, it was no great tragedy. But when the clerk also told me that the Chief Police Officer of Perangor, the state to which I was posted, wanted to see me first, my heart sank. Normally I would have gone straight to the station and reported to the OCPD. It was most unusual.

The next morning I set off to report to my new contingent, and find out the worst.

Berembang, my destination, was only a morning's journey from Kuala Lumpur, and as I hung around the railway station, waiting for the day mail to start, my head was full of memories.

Allah knows, I've been on KL railway station often enough during the past few years, but I never go there without remembering the sight of Mahmood walking down the platform the day after my father ran amok.

Mahmood. Allahumma! If only he had remained a little more stable, a little more conventional, life would be easier for me. He had never had much interest in the police, and when the RAF Regiment (Malaya) was formed, he left the force and went straight off to Singapore to join it. He had had a few months in Singapore, then a session up-country, where he'd been involved in a few skirmishes with the bandits – which was more than I had – and then his squadron had been posted to Hong Kong. Nothing much wrong with that; the pill was that in next to no time he had written to say he had married a Chinese taxi dancer and hoped to make his home in Hong Kong when his time was up. I gather he had not even insisted on her becoming a Muslim.

Needless to say, I had not imparted all Mahmood's news to my mother. Marrying taxi dancers was altogether too close to home and in my numerous requests for permission to marry I had not dared mention Azizah's profession. I bet Mak knows though – there's nothing she doesn't find out, whether she's told or not.

It was no good hoping that when she met Azizah she would change her opinion. She wouldn't consider one of the Sultan's daughters once she'd made up her mind that I was going to marry a girl of her choosing. I believe women of all races can be obstinate and stubborn, but there's nothing to touch a Malay woman once she digs her heels in. And my mother is the arch stub! We have a very good word in Malay – dĕgil; the e is almost an English i and you pronounce it with a very hard g. You can really get your jaw muscles round that one – I know, I use it in connection with my mother frequently!

While these thoughts were running through my head, the train was making ready to depart. It was almost like the beginning of the war again to see all those soldiers boarding it. First the armoured pilot engine got itself into position, filled with Gurkha soldiers and Malay police, and then the ordinary engine shunted behind it and a platoon of Scottish soldiers, our escort, took up their places in various parts of the train. I thought I'd try and find a seat near one of them – by the time I'd finished my year's army attachment I'd learned their jargon pretty well and it always amused me to see the astonished expression on a BOR's face when I addressed him in his own language.

The CPO was a dapper little man with grey hair and piercing blue eyes.

'Sharif Ahmat? Welcome to my contingent. I knew your brother well. Glad to have you. Sit down, won't you?'

The CPO did not smoke but gave me permission to do so if I wished. In fact, I was dying for a drag but thought it politic to decline. I read his approval and knew I had done the right thing.

'Now, Ahmat. I've asked for you especially, because the senior inspector in Kuala Jelang is due for retirement shortly and you're just the man to take his place.' This was a lie, of course. Perhaps he didn't know I'd been thrown out of SB, or maybe he thought I didn't know. 'The OCPD Kuala Jelang is just out of the army and he's having a tough time, learning both police work and Malay from scratch. Your English will be an immense help to him and, by taking a lot of the routine work off his hands, it will leave him freer to concentrate on the operational side.'

He looked as though he was expecting me to say something. I was a bit rusty on routine police work myself, but he must know that, so there seemed no point in commenting.

'Inspector Zainal Abidin isn't due to leave for another month and there's no point in both of you hanging around the station all that time. I see you have a lot of leave due to you, so I suggest you go down to Kuala Jelang to-morrow – make your number with the OCPD; then off you go on fourteen days' leave – unless he has other ideas – and report straight back there at the end of it. How's that?'

I made no attempt to conceal my grin of pleasure. I couldn't have done so anyway.

'That's fine, sir. Thank you very much.'

'Good. I'll write a note to the OCPD; you can take it with you.' He stood up and we shook hands, the interview was over. 'I hope you enjoy your new post. Send the clerk in when you go out, will you?'

Just as I was opening the door he spoke again.

'By the by. You should get on well with your new OCPD, you have something in common – he was with the partisans as well – not here though, Italy. Believe his wife was too.'

So he did know. I saluted and shut the door.

As the door shut the CPO lifted the telephone and put through a call to Kuala Jelang. The conversation was brief.

'I'm sending you a replacement for Zainal Abidin – Inspector Sharif Ahmat. I suggest he reports to you, then takes fourteen days' leave. He'll be on the bus to-morrow morning – if it's not burnt. Sorry I can't let you have any transport – we're too short.'

Turning to the clerk, he said, 'Prepare an envelope for the OCPD Kuala Jelang; Personal and Confidential. The new inspector will take it with him.'

Then, with a sigh, he set to to write a difficult and careful letter.

My dear Morrison,

Re our telephone conversation this afternoon.

This inspector has been removed from Special Branch because of suspected Communist leanings. I should tell you to watch them, but I have no intention of doing so, because I do not believe they exist.

I have agreed to have him in my contingent, partly because there seems to me to be a smell of injustice somewhere, and partly because I had the greatest respect for his brother – a GO who died a few years ago of TB. He comes from one of the oldest police families in the Force, his father being Chief Inspector at the Depot pre-war. He himself is, or was, earmarked for gazetted rank and, if he puts up a good show in your district, I see no reason why his promotion should be retarded.

I met Sharif Ahmat myself for the first time this afternoon and liked what I saw. He has a bright, open face and is obviously intelligent. I am sending him to you for two good reasons. Firstly, because, as a newcomer to the force, you will be better able to judge him with impartiality and, secondly, because his English is excellent. He is well educated and young, and I feel sure will be of great help to you. His police work may not be up-to-date, as he has spent the past two and a half years with the army and SB, but I am sure that a fortnight with his predecessor will enable him to catch up.

I shall look forward to hearing your opinion when I next visit your district.

Yours sincerely,
P. R. Wales.

I boarded the Berembang–Kemuning bus early the next day and, after a short wait, the one for Kuala Jelang.

Perangor was a new state for me, but little different from the ones I already knew. We passed first through tin tailings, rubber, then a stretch of jungle, climbing, with some nasty hairpin bends – I didn't much care for that and nor did the driver. He went as fast as he could, but I doubt if he got out of second gear for at least a couple of miles. Just my luck to be ambushed to-day, I thought, then we were travelling through rubber again and I heaved a sigh of relief.

Too soon. Almost before I realised what was happening, we were entering a cloud of black smoke and the stench of burning diesel oil was overpowering. We all started coughing as the suffocating waves rolled in through the open windows. But mercifully the driver had the presence of mind to keep going, murk or no, and we were soon through the pall.

I drew my pistol and prayed that the bandits had gone. I'd be a sitting target anyway and in uniform – it didn't bear thinking about. I slipped the safety catch as the driver stopped.

A pathetic group, all Chinese, stood by the roadside, looking lost and bewildered, and three women wailed over the bodies of an older woman and a boy lying in the ditch. Empty suitcases and cardboard cartons littered the verge and one old man was rooting through them.

It was apparent, thank God, that the CTs had left and I got down to question the occupants of the burned-out bus; the earlier one from Kemuning.

It did not take long to ascertain that all identity cards and clothing had been stolen and I was just taking a statement from the most responsible-seeming passenger when a police troop-carrier arrived on the scene.

A police lieutenant and half a dozen men jumped from the vehicle. I introduced myself.

'Looks as though the bastards have got away again.' The police lieutenant was clearly disappointed, but on this occasion I was grateful.

There had been too long a delay to make a follow-up worthwhile, so we crammed the unfortunates into the second bus and I climbed into the troop-carrier with the police.

Bus-burnings were so common at that time that I soon put the episode out of my mind.

I am not a creature of change. I never move voluntarily and, when I do, usually like to take some part of my previous station with me.

But in Kuala Jelang it was different. I don't know why. It was no different from a number of semi-coastal towns situated between Muar and the Dindings. I say semi-coastal because there was no beach, but only mangrove and bakau swamps along the coast itself and, although it is shown on the map as a port, in fact the life of the small town centred around the river. From the police station, although we were almost on it, we couldn't see the sea.

The town itself was similar to most small Malayan towns, with a few rows of Chinese and Indian shophouses, a padang, a few jetties, and a wide avenue of flame of the forest trees leading to most of the government offices, and a tiny hospital.

The police station was at the far end of the town, away from the other government buildings, and was flanked on one side by a highish hill, which boasted the remains of a Portuguese fort, a lighthouse and two senior government quarters. The OCPD had one of these houses and the DO the other. All this I learned from Zainal Abidin, the elderly inspector whose job I would inherit in a month's time.

Perhaps it was sun after rain, giving the grass that vivid green look, or the flame trees being in flower, or the lively river traffic. I just don't know. But there was something light and airy about Kuala Jelang, and before I had even alighted from the troop-carrier I was beginning to look forward to being stationed there. I was glad to have shaken the unhealthy atmosphere of Special Branch from my shoulders; I felt I was coming home.

I arrived just as the sentry slung his rifle and stepped forward to hammer out the hour on a curve of old railway sleeper – a custom I had forgotten in HQ. The sergeant stood up behind the counter and called the Charge Room to attention, and at that moment a smooth-looking Chinese in white shirt, black trousers and dark glasses came out of an office and passed through. No mistaking *his* job. He gave me a quick look up and down but made no attempt to come to attention, so I presumed he, too, was an inspector. On inquiry I found that he was Detective-Sergeant Lee. Detective-sergeant indeed. I made a mental note of at least one change which would take place in due course.

The station was standard pattern; a squarish, white building with the main part of the police station, Charge Room, cells, etcetera, in the front, and the remainder, consisting of offices for the OCPD,

Station Inspector, OCPS, CID, SB and a general office for the clerical staff. The compound was surrounded by a hibiscus hedge and high mesh fence and had raised barracks on three sides. One side was bordered by the road and the others by open ground, mangrove and the river. In the middle there was a large parade-ground, which doubled as a games field and football pitch. At one end of this stood one small house on its own, facing the river and surrounded by its own hedge of many-hued hibiscus and several creepers. This was the Station Inspector's quarter and I realised with a quickening heart that it was to be mine.

The house was, in fact, pretty shabby. Zainal Abidin had been waiting to retire for some time and had lost interest. I would be prepared to paint it myself and, if PWD would only change some of the battered furniture – I could already see it with gay curtains fluttering in the windows and gay cushion covers on the chairs, a home that Azizah would cherish.

As I waited in the Charge Room for the OCPD to be free, I heard a few sentences of stumbling Malay coming from his office and knew that the CPO had not lied in one respect – he certainly needed help language-wise! It appeared I would have my uses.

I had quite a short interview. The OCPD seemed pleasant enough, but a little harassed. He kept looking at his watch and told me not to think him rude, but he was shortly leaving on a patrol. He seemed interested in hearing about my year with the army; he knew my Captain Jones and told me that he himself had asked for aerial cover on a couple of occasions.

He asked me where I came from and if I were married.

'No, sir,' I replied, 'not yet. But the main reason for my being keen to go on leave now is to try and obtain my mother's permission.'

'Your mother's? I thought the men ruled in Asia.'

'Not in my state, sir.' And I told him a little about our matriarchal laws.

'Good heavens,' he laughed; 'better not tell my wife that. She was born in Negri Sembilan – might give her ideas.'

'In which case, sir,' I pointed out, 'she most probably knows.'

He gave me a shrewd look and we said nothing for a moment or two. We were summing each other up. I felt that I was going to get on with this man and I believe he was thinking the same. I hope so.

At that moment there was a knock on the door and Zainal Abidin came in to tell him that all was ready.

'Right, Bidin. By the way – ' he turned back to me, ' – what do I call you? I'm not yet *au fait* with Malay names – it took me a full week to discover that Inspector Bidin and Zainal Abidin were the same person!'

'Ahmat, sir, or just Mat. I used to be called the Sheriff in the army.'

'Were you? Yes, obvious, I suppose – especially with those star cap badges you used to wear. Well, Mat, see you in two weeks' time.'

I spent the rest of the afternoon wandering round the compound and the town, and in the evening had a meal in the canteen with the bachelor inspector, Zukifli.

The next morning I returned direct to Kuala Lumpur, and when the Bintang Kilat opened I was there.

Azizah was not quite as enthusiastic about life in Kuala Jelang as I was, but then she hadn't seen it.

'And anyway,' I told her, 'it won't be for ever. Just getting back to an ordinary police district was like a breath of fresh air for me. I realise now that I was never cut out for dark glasses and tight black pants – the operational police is my background and, thank God, I'm returning to it. You know, Azizah, the future looks better than ever. I'm sure I'll be gazetted soon and then you'll be an officer's wife. That means you can be a member of all the clubs and go into the Officers' Mess on Ladies' Night – how will you like that?'

She just smiled.

The next day I caught the southbound train on leave.

88. A TALE OF TWO FATHERS

It was on one of the evenings when he was trying to catch up with the mail and cursing the flickering oil lamp that Philip opened the letter which the inspector he had interviewed briefly the previous day had handed to him.

'Good God, Sally,' he passed the letter to her, 'look at this. Do you know, I must be going ga-ga or something – the CPO rang me up and told me he was sending a replacement for Bidin and then this chap arrived yesterday and I didn't really take it in. What do you make of the old man's letter?'

'Fair. Could be a blessing, or could be a problem child. What did you think of him?'

'Seemed pleasant enough. Tall, good-looking chap – spoke beautiful English certainly, what little I heard of it. He was in my office for less than ten minutes and I must admit I had my mind on a number of other things.'

'Oh darling, I do so hope he's going to be a success.'

'You're not the only one. Lucky I opened this this evening though – look at the last paragraph: "I shall look forward to hearing your

528

opinion when I next visit your district." He said he might be down in a couple of days.'

He worked on in silence for a while, until Sally interrupted him to say, 'There seems to be a light in your office, Phil. Don't you usually lock it when you leave?'

'I do, but the key's kept in the Charge Room – I suppose it's the CRO.'

'Whoever it is, he appears to be having a good snoop around. The shadow's moving all over the place.'

'I think I'll go down. I wanted another file anyway.'

To avoid having the Charge Room called to attention, Philip waited until the sentry was busy sounding the hour and could not slap his rifle-butt, then slipped into the station by a side door.

The door of his office was slightly ajar and he could see the shadow of a turbanned head on the far wall.

'What are you doing, Sergeant-major?'

Jogindar Singh whipped round and Philip heard the slap of something falling on to the desk.

'Just checking, sahib.'

Both top drawers of the desk were open and then Philip saw that the slap had been made by a passport. He looked inquiringly at Jogindar, who smiled sheepishly in his beard, nodding his head slightly from side to side and showing his empty hands.

'Just curiosity, sahib.'

Jogindar was telling the truth. It would never have entered his head to take anything, but, in the same way that he liked to know everything about the men who served under him, so he also liked to know about those in command. All sorts of interesting snippets could be gained from the odd letter left around, even if it was only the occasional word that he could understand. He had found something of interest too.

Philip suppressed the desire to tell him to get the hell out of his office. He was finding the job hard enough without alienating one of his senior NCOs.

'I appreciate your diligence, Sergeant-major, but I would not wish to put you in a position where you might be held responsible for any missing document.'

'Sahib.' Despite the fact that he was in civilian clothes, Jogindar came rigidly to attention. The OCPD had got his mark; he looked at him with a new respect. He was young and not long in the police, but he knew how to handle men. So did he.

'I'll lock up; I just want to collect a file. Good night, Sergeant-major.'

Philip picked up the passport and proceeded to close the drawers. Jogindar did not move.

'Sahib?'

'Yes. What is it?'

Jogindar pointed to the still open drawer, where the passports now lay.

'The Memsahib's passport, sahib – I see that the Mem was born in Malaya and that her own name was Gunn.'

'Well?'

'I knew her father. He was a fine man, sahib.' Philip was surprised to see the sergeant-major's face working with emotion. 'I was with him the day they led him away. It was a terrible day. Ten men they beheaded that morning. Please, sahib, will you wait here for a moment? There is something I want to show you.'

He left the office, but was back straight away, clutching a bulging wallet. He leafed through it excitedly and chose a scrap of paper which he held out to Philip, who took it and read:

'To whom it may concern. This is to certify that Warder Jogindar Singh has done everything in his power to help the internees for the past two years. If I am unable to testify to his courage and loyalty in person, I shall be grateful to any of my fellow-countrymen who will help him in turn.'

The hand was spidery and weak and it was signed 'George Gunn, Member of the Legislative Council.' It was Sally's father without a doubt. There was no date on the note, but it must have been written while they were with the partisans.

'There are many more, sahib.'

Philip glanced through the sheaf of papers on the desk before him. Torn scraps of brown paper, tissue paper, newspaper, the odd leaf from an exercise book, a couple of opened cigarette packets. All bore the same testimonial: loyal, trustworthy, prepared to risk his life, helpful, kind.

Thank God I didn't tear a strip off him, he thought. He held on to the note written by George Gunn and passed the others back.

'May I show this to my wife?' he asked. 'She will be very interested. It was quite a long time before she knew how her father died.'

'Sahib.'

'I have been a prisoner myself. I know very well how much help a friendly warder can give.'

'Thank you, sahib.'

'Good night, Jogindar Singh.'

'Good night, sahib. Please tell the Memsahib her father went bravely to his death. He was a fine man. I had the greatest respect for him.'

'He appears to have had the greatest respect for you too.'

'Thank you, sahib. My own father was beheaded by the Japanese – he was a sergeant-major also.'

'I'm sorry. Terrible things happen during wars. I'll tell the Mem.'

'Don't forget the CPO's coming down to-morrow, Sally. I've invited him to lunch.'

'Oh hell. I wish he could bring something with him. Unless there's some fish in the market, we'll have to have curried bully beef again.'

'I don't expect he'll mind.'

'Well, *I* mind. It's ridiculous not being allowed to keep anything in the house when, here we are, a stone's throw from the police station.'

'We're still outside the specified area.'

'Specified area my bloody foot! If the Big White Chiefs worried a little more about the squatters and less about a handful of Europeans, just because our hill isn't surrounded by barbed wire – '

'Squatters. That reminds me. Sorry for interrupting, but Chee Min has something on his mind that he wants to tell me this morning and I have to be at a meeting by nine. Better hurry.'

'Sir, the squatter settlement at Pasir Hitam. . . .' Lee Chee Min paused to let his words sink in.

'What about it?'

'I'm sure they're supplying the CTs.'

That was that conglomeration of huts and vegetables on the Sungei Belimbing road, where the people turned away as cars went past and went furtively about their work in silence.

'I've had men watching for the past three nights. The Min Yuen have visited them twice.'

'You're sure?'

'Quite sure, sir.'

'We'll go and take a look at it this afternoon.'

As soon as they were seated in Philip's car, Chee Min began to tell him how his suspicions had been aroused in the first place and how the visitors had been recognised as known Min Yuen.

'And if we guarded the settlement?' Philip suggested.

Chee Min shrugged. 'Useless, sir. They would just take the stuff out during the working day – most of them work as casual labour on the nearby estates.'

'We've *got* to resettle them,' Philip muttered, half to himself, 'not only this bunch, but all those stragglers across the river and all the isolated houses. The DO's looking for land, but it doesn't appear easy to find.'

The squatters were settled on a low-lying stretch of land between two roads which eventually met. The area was roughly triangular. After they had driven to the fork in the road, down the other side and back, Philip stopped the car and thought for a minute.

'We could wire it in as a temporary measure,' he said, 'at least until we get a proper resettlement area organised. What do you think?'

'It would give them protection, sir, if we guarded the wire. I do not believe many of these people really *want* to help the bandits – they are just afraid.'

'We would have to have a small police post and search the people as they go to work each day. I'll discuss it with the DO.'

That evening Philip drove James over the same ground as they had covered in the morning and told him what he had found out.

'I'll have to get the CPO to agree first though,' he said, 'because, unguarded, the whole idea would be pointless and the station's under strength as it is – I just haven't the men for even the tiniest police post.'

'If we can get government to cough up the necessary funds,' James mused, 'it would seem the best solution for the time being. If he agrees, perhaps you could get the CPO to put some pressure on at his level.'

'I'll try.'

The guard having been inspected and the customary courtesies with the senior NCOs exchanged, the CPO settled himself behind a large glass of sweet, milky coffee and, remarking that, after thirty years in Asia he still could not get used to having the spoon in the glass and most of the coffee in the saucer, they got down to business.

'Now, Philip, tell me, what did you think of that inspector I sent you, Sharif Ahmat?'

'I only saw him for about ten minutes, sir. He seemed all right. A trifle arrogant, I thought.'

Philip could see he was het up and wondered why.

'There was so much I wanted to tell you about him before you met him, but I couldn't put it in a letter. By the by, have you had SB's report on him?'

Philip coloured. 'To be honest, sir, I have, but I haven't read it yet.' He extracted a sealed envelope from a drawer and put it on the desk in front of him. 'It's not that I make a habit of leaving mail unread, but I've been so busy the past few days and, as the chap is still on leave anyway, I thought it would keep.' It sounded a lame excuse.

'May I read it?'

'Of course.' Philip passed it over.

With meticulous care, the older man polished his reading-glasses and went through the letter with ever-tightening lips.

532

'Do me a favour, my boy. Don't read this until you have had Ahmat under you for a week or two.'

'Certainly, sir, if you so wish.' He returned the letter to the drawer.

'Special Branch would have you believe he's an arsonist, a murderer – and after all, weren't our commandos? – and, worst of all, a Communist. You see, the whole trouble is that he won't deny anything. You know what those cloak and dagger merchants are like – tape everything they hear. Well, they taped all his interviews and, I must admit, were good enough to let me hear them. They reminded me of some of the Moscow spy trials. He could have cleared himself so easily, but would he? Would he hell – didn't say a damned thing. Just the occasional "Tuan" or "Sir," but most of the time he remained silent. Well, if you're assuming that a non-denial is an admission, then he's guilty. If it hadn't been for the intervention of one senior SB officer who, thank God, thinks like I do, he'd have been interdicted. Then I was called in and, between the two of us, we managed to persuade the Commissioner to give him a trial.'

'What do you want me to do, sir?'

'Just that – give him a fair trial. You know, my boy, many people in the force consider me to be an old dead-beat, and perhaps I am; I don't pretend to know much about cloak and daggery, but I do pride myself on knowing the Malays. You know, they're proud people, stubborn people, and if they think they've been done an injustice, they just close up like clams and remain silent. Not like your vociferous Chinese and Indians – and a lot of Europeans for that matter – who clamour for sympathy and call in lawyers at the drop of a hat. No, the Malay just bottles it up and then, one day, if he's an unstable type and things become too much for him, he runs amok. By the by, one thing you had better know, that won't appear on Ahmat's record, and that is that his father ran amok – with the greatest provocation, I believe.'

'I'm beginning to wonder what you're letting me in for, sir.' The CPO, however, was not amused.

'I'm letting you in for a damned good man – and I'll stake my reputation on it. I do so hate injustice. Nearly all those chaps who interviewed him may have been experts at their jobs in Palestine or Scotland Yard, or wherever they've come from, but only one understood the mentality he was dealing with here and to him young Sharif Ahmat has a lot to be thankful for.'

'He seemed pretty cheerful, I thought.'

'He was all right with me too, but then it was an absolutely straightforward interview. I'm hoping that sooner or later you may win his confidence – you were with the partisans, try and get him to talk about the war. Chap obviously needs a safety valve. Pity he's a bachelor;

'I'd have gone stark raving mad years ago if I hadn't had my wife to pour out my troubles to.'

'Me too.'

'Ah yes. I'm looking forward to meeting your wife – if you hadn't asked me to lunch first, I was going to ask you both to come to the Rest House with me. I don't mind telling you, Philip, that I'm probably talking to you like this because I had the greatest affection and respect for your wife's father.'

'You knew Sally's father, sir? She never told me.'

'She doesn't know – yet. We were cell mates. And by the by, that brings me to someone else I wanted to mention. That sergeant-major of yours, Jogindar Singh; he was one of our warders. I've only had him under my direct command for a few months as a policeman, but during the war he was a first-class *man*. Pity he's so poorly educated; might make inspector if he learns a bit more English, but he won't go any higher.'

'He always seems a bit smarmy to me, but I've seen a sheaf of glowing testimonials from ex-POWs. I gather his own father was killed by the Japs.'

'So he was. But Jogindar's all right; your predecessor had a lot of time for him. I shall never forget his description of Jogindar's arrival here. The driver was a nervous wreck! He only transferred from Kemuning, but, as you know, that road has always been bad. However, that didn't worry our sergeant-major one jot; along he came, troop-carrier with wife and barang in front and he himself following in a lorry with those blessed cows on the back and doing about five miles per hour all the way! King said he looked like a scruffy old bullock-cart driver, turban askew and torn shorts, but within minutes of his arrival and getting his cattle organised – before wife and child, mark you – he was reporting in uniform, bandbox fresh. As King said at the time, from that moment on he felt he was leaving the station in the hands of a most able administrator!'

Philip laughed with the older man and thought once again how glad he was that he had not handled Jogindar Singh differently.

'Well, so much for personalities. Now, let's have your problems – you mentioned something about a squatter settlement – and perhaps there will be time for a drink before lunch.'

'What did you think of Grandpa Wales?' Philip asked Sally later that evening.

'Bit of an old fuddy-duddy, but rather nice.'

'He's certainly worked himself into a state over this new inspector. Only hope he's as good as he thinks he will be.'

534

The sixth stream flows into the river

Sharif Ahmat

Whatever feelings I had had about this leave and confronting my mother, I was glad to see her again.

I fingered the carving on the verandah railing which my father had started on his leaves and Hassan had finished; played with the cats and sniffed the roses.

I sniffed at the good smells issuing from the kitchen too – my favourite chicken curry, with plenty of coconut, belachan and pine-apple sambal. My mouth watered and Mak smiled – she still thought of me as a schoolboy, as all mothers do.

Normally the men eat alone, but my mother ate with me and we were served by one of the women. Azizah and I would eat together like this, Western style, and I would buy her plastic flowers for the table. I smiled across at my mother, picking delicately at shreds of meat.

I did not mention Azizah for a couple of days. I spent the first day in the house and the second visiting my friends and relations and hearing all the gossip.

'Did you visit your Uncle Jalil?' Mak asked.

'Yes, I did. We went to the coffee-shop together.'

'And did you see his daughter, Maimounah?'

'I think I did.' There had been a couple of girls feeding the chickens and giggling a lot.

'Maimounah is nearly eighteen now. She has grown into a lovely girl. An obedient girl, too.'

'Has she?' I was not particularly interested in my plump, girly, second cousin. But, of course, I should have guessed where the conversation was leading.

'Maimounah will make you an excellent wife. I have already approached her parents and a marriage contract is being drawn up.'

'But, Mak, I do not wish to marry Maimounah.'

'Nonsense. Of course you will be very happy with her. Young men seldom know what they want.'

I was no longer all that young. 'I am not going to marry her,' I said.

My mother sighed. 'You are tired, Ahmat. We shall talk about it later.'

I went to bed fuming and the next morning I told her that I wished her permission once and for all to marry Azizah.

'She does not sound a very suitable person,' Puan Sharifa, my mother, remarked, very much on her dignity, 'I do not think I wish to meet her.'

Before leaving Kuala Lumpur I had insisted that Azizah have her photograph taken and the photographer had done her proud. It was an excellent likeness and the portrait showed her delicate features, gleaming hair and beautiful teeth to perfection. I passed it to my mother, who put on her glasses and gazed at it for some time with pursed lips and dead straight back.

'You must admit that she is beautiful,' I ventured.

'Skinny. I doubt if she would give you many children.'

'I don't want many children.'

'Nonsense. Every man wants plenty of children.'

She folded her glasses away carefully and announced that it was time for her rest.

What can you do with a woman like that? Etiquette did not allow me to talk things over with my Uncle Jalil and I spent a miserable few days. Every time I broached the subject of Azizah, my mother would either find some excuse for cutting short the conversation or retaliate by extolling the virtues of my cousin Maimounah.

It was impossible.

I had made up my mind that I was going to marry Azizah, permission or no, and towards the end of my leave I pinned my mother down and asked her to terminate any and all arrangements for my betrothal to Maimounah.

She was rather pathetic in a way and looked up at me imploringly with her great eyes, rheumy now, although she can't have been all that old.

'Give me a grandson, Mat,' she pleaded, 'I am an old woman and I have lost all my men but you. I do not wish you to be unhappy and I can see from her photograph that Azizah is very comely, but I want a grandson.'

'She will give you grandsons, Mother. Azizah is strong and healthy and will make me a good wife.'

'That type of woman seldom has children – but many miscarriages.'

'She is a ronggeng dancer, Mak, not a prostitute.'

'Yes. Well.' She didn't say it was the same thing, but the implication was there.

She remained quiet for a long time and I began to think she had fallen asleep, then she raised her eyes, a smile of sweet content lighting her face, and announced, 'I have decided. We must make cakes and prepare a kenduri. We shall celebrate your betrothal the day after to-morrow – I must send a message at once to your Uncle Jalil. As I have said, Sharifa Maimounah will make you an excellent wife.'

It was then that I lost my temper.

'I am twenty-eight years of age,' I banged the table with my fist and shouted at her, 'and you cannot stop me from marrying whom I want.'

Puan Sharifa rose to her feet with great dignity and looked down upon me, an expression of scorn in every wrinkle.

'It is true,' she said, 'you are twenty-eight years old and I cannot stop you.'

And with that she beckoned to one of her women and left the room.

It is unpardonable for any son to speak to his mother as I had, but in my case it was worse than unpardonable; it was a sin for which I would have to beg forgiveness.

I avoided her the next day, the penultimate of my leave, but when the time for my departure came I had to swallow my pride. I knelt before her and touched her folded hands with my forehead.

All the time she sat there, still as a statue and seeming more than ever like an angry old tortoise.

There were always a great many women hanging around my mother, near and distant relations, and some just hangers-on. She spoke not a word to me, but said to one of them, 'Tell my son that I wish him a safe journey.'

I was dismissed.

But the old lady was not going to be shamed by having me marry outside the kampong. She might have met her match in stubbornness – and, after all, I am her son – but she was going to have the last word. Azizah was an orphan, so there could be no case of my being carried to the bride's house. A week or so later, just as I was taking over in Kuala Jelang, I received a letter from my Uncle Jalil which read:

'Your mother instructs me to tell you that, should you still persist on going ahead with this highly undesirable union, she will make the necessary arrangements for the marriage.'

Allahumma! What an ordeal that is going to be!

90. A SUCCESSFUL DAY

'How's the new inspector, darling? And how's the famous English?'

Sally had worried about Philip, seeing him grow thinner and thinner and more harassed, and was afraid, too late, that after four years without a proper break, a new job and a new language were too much in one go. If Sharif Ahmat lived up to the CPO's expectations, it could make all the difference.

'Well, he can't be anything but an improvement, that's for sure. He's a bit piano at the moment – mother trouble, I gather. The old bag apparently won't give her consent to his marriage, so he says he'll marry the girl anyway.'

'Good for him.'

'Agreed – depending on the girl. As to the English – well! Of course I only heard a little of it before and it's certainly very fluent, but I'm not sure that it's benefited from a year of British Army influence!'

'Fruity?'

'Well, yes, but that's not quite the adjective I'd use. There was a hell of a rumpus going on outside my office this morning – whole gang of Tamils, all yelling at once in the Charge Room – and Ahmat went to sort them out. He's a very stately person, you know, and when he returned he said, with the most serene dignity, "I instructed the complainant to make his statement quietly and told the other buggers to shit off"!'

In fact, Ahmat was not only 'piano' because of his mother, but also because of the rustiness of his police work.

He still had more than a fortnight's leave due to him and had hoped that he could apply for it as soon as his marriage was arranged. But Azizah and police work did not go together and he put her firmly out of his mind for the time being and concentrated on learning all he could from Bidin, while he was still there.

The Sikh sergeant-major seemed a tower of strength, he thought, thanks be to Allah that *he* was OCPS – the station was clearly in capable hands. He didn't think much of that Special Branch sergeant; a smooth type and too familiar by half. Still, he was junior enough to be kept in his place and he need not have too many dealings with him. He liked the OCPD.

Philip, in his ignorance, had thought that Ahmat and Chee Min were bound to hit it off. They had so much in common, he had remarked to Sally, a good education, they'd both been overseas and both were ambitious men. For his part it was a tremendous relief to be able to hold a three-sided conversation in his own language and know that everything that was said would be understood. He looked forward to smoother waters, once Mat had settled down, and said so to Chee Min. But for the moment they were concentrating on squatters.

In fact, Chee Min thought Ahmat a proud, stuck-up Malay and longed to trip him up, but he was sensible enough to keep his feelings to himself.

DWEC had agreed that fencing in the squatters was a sound plan, and in due course much hammering was to be heard around the huts of Pasir Hitam, as the wire went up.

The squatters looked at each other and said nothing. The wire might protect them or it might present new problems. Each family was quietly paying subscriptions to the terrorists and keeping mum. The police were continually snooping round for information, but the squatters saw no one, said nothing, and minded their own business. Informing to the police was a profitable game if you could get away with it, but it was safer in the long run to keep quiet and produce when the Min Yuen demanded.

The squatters worked, ate, slept and paid, and the fence went up around them. Now the Min Yuen were asking questions. Who was putting up the fence? Why? Who had squealed to the police? Woe betide the family who had.

Each family looked at its neighbours and wondered if they had received informer's money. Signs of wealth were dangerous, and if anyone had suddenly become rich they were unlikely to broadcast the fact.

The day came when the fence was complete and a small police post was erected by the only gate. Several Chinese-speaking government officials explained to the squatters that the fence was there for their protection and that now they need no longer hand over clothing, food and funds to the bandits. Their days of extortion were over.

The squatters heard all this but their faces remained blank. There were many ways of getting money out of a man, in case the government officials did not know.

The first morning after the completion of the fence, Philip went with Chee Min to supervise the searching of the workers.

Each man or woman stopped at the gate, hands held above their heads, while the searchers ran their hands over their bodies and examined their bicycles, tools and bags. The supply denial operation was in full swing.

'Tell them we're sorry, but they will not be able to eat or drink anything but water until they return from work,' Philip said.

Chee Min walked over to where a man was arguing volubly with a Malay special constable, who had just removed his billycan of rice. Behind him stood a young girl with an impish smile and Chee Min was immediately attracted by her face.

She was covered from head to toe against the sun and carried only a tapper's knife. Her head was swathed in a nun-like coif and she laughed openly as Chee Min peered round the edge.

He smiled at her and went on to pacify the man. She was soon out of sight, cycling down the road, her narrow back trim and erect on the old-fashioned bicycle.

Philip followed the sergeant's glance and was amused, but said nothing.

When everyone who was going to work that day had gone, the gate was closed and they drove back to the station to start their routine work.

'I think I had better check again,' Chee Min said the next morning, 'once they get into the routine there will be no need, but until they get used to the idea . . .'

'Of course.' Philip smiled and thought to himself, I bet you'll go every day yourself, you fox.

That morning Chee Min asked for names, pretending to tick them off on a list. It was not long before the girl came along.

Rose Cheng, aged seventeen, occupation rubber-tapper.

'Find out which house that girl comes from,' Chee Min ordered one of the SCs. He had already made a rough plan of the squatter area and numbered all the houses, in preparation for this opportunity.

A few days later a kite was reported flying over Pasir Hitam. Chee Min was delighted; it gave him an excuse. He said to the OCPD, 'I think we should carry out a search of Pasir Hitam, sir, to make sure there are no arms or documents in those squatter huts.'

'Right. Go ahead – you know the correct procedure.'

The Chengs' house was small but neat, with curtains at the windows and flowers by the door. It was surrounded by raised vegetable beds and a few yards away an old man was hoeing.

Chee Min wanted to search the house. He produced his warrant card, but the man waved it away. 'I can't read foreign characters,' he said. 'My wife's inside – don't scare her.'

Chee Min and the constable took off their shoes and entered the house. At the back there were sounds of clothes being slapped on stone. A round table, covered with a pea-green velvet cloth with bobbled fringes, took up most of the space in what was obviously their living-room. There were schoolbooks on the table, English and Maths; on one wall a vivid print of the Bleeding Heart and on the other a crucifix.

'Old Aunt,' he called, and the washing noises ceased abruptly, 'may we look round your house?'

A middle-aged woman in blue samfoo, the pyjama-type clothes worn by many Chinese women, appeared in the doorway. Her eyes were round with fright and her mouth opened and shut, but emitted no sound. She had soapsuds to the elbow and was rubbing her wet hands up and down the sides of her trousers with nervousness.

'Don't be scared. We are police,' Chee Min told her. 'We are helping you; you must try and understand.'

The woman nodded but still made no sound.

'Whose are the books?' he asked, and a voice from the outer door answered him.

'They are our daughter's books.' It was the old man who spoke. 'You must forgive my wife. Our son was killed by the terrorists less than a year ago – they came here, just as you come now, and when he refused to join them they drove a six-inch nail through his head.'

The woman gave a wailing moan and rushed from the room.

'Please explain we mean no harm and not to be frightened if she sees us again,' he called, and left the house.

So it had been their son. Well, they were hardly likely to be Communist sympathisers, but no doubt paid up to the Min Yuen, just like everybody else.

The next morning Chee Min stopped Rose Cheng as she came out of the gate and asked how her mother was.

He asked her about the books. Yes, they were hers. She had been to the convent in Kuala Lumpur but had had to leave when her father's shop was burned down. They were not insured and had lost everything.

'This is very fertile land,' she told him, 'so now my father grows vegetables to sell and I earn good wages as a tapper. Perhaps one day we shall move back, but meanwhile I'm trying to continue my studies in the evenings.'

'The convent?' Chee Min was surprised. 'You must speak English then?'

'A little,' she said in clipped, staccato syllables, 'but I get no practice now.'

'I'm Vincent Lee,' he introduced himself, also in English, 'I could help you sometimes, if you liked.'

The girl smiled shyly and said that if she did not hurry she would be late for work. He moved aside to let her pass, happy in the knowledge that contact had been established.

Back in the police station the OCPD was happy too. But for a different reason. The army had arrived.

Chee Min had only just left for Pasir Hitam, and Philip was blessing the sudden lull and hoping to catch up on some routine work, when the sound of a jeep drawing up outside had made him groan. But it had contained a most welcome visitor.

'Mike Harrington,' and a thin, wiry little major of the Gurkhas had thrust out his hand. 'We're moving a company down from Berembang; hope to be here next week. I wondered if we might discuss a site for a camp.'

Philip blinked. 'Well, it's nice to know what's going on in one's district,' he remarked dryly, 'but I shan't take um – too pleased to see you.' He spread out a map of the area. 'When I asked, some months ago, if there was any chance of having troops stationed here, I had this piece of land at Sungei Belimbing in mind as a possible site for a camp. It's central and not too far from the bridge, you see, which would give you easy access to both sides of the river.'

'Could we go and see it?'

'Of course. I'll just give my wife a ring – you'll stay to lunch?'

Later that day Philip and Sally stood on their verandah, the dying sun in their eyes, waving as Mike drove away.

'Nice chap,' Philip remarked. 'I'm glad he accepted the offer of our spare room. I shall be happier knowing that at least sometimes, when I have to be out for several days, you won't be alone. Not that I imagine he'll use it much.'

Mike had approved the camp site, where he would have his Company HQ, and there would be a platoon under a Gurkha sub-altern under canvas in the police compound in Kuala Jelang itself. It had been a successful day.

Willing hands helped or hindered as the Gurkhas put up their tents – the Gurks were popular with everyone – and the police compound was a hive of activity.

Sally had asked the other Europeans to lunch.

'I suppose you'll be starting patrols soon,' James said.

'To-morrow, with luck,' Mike replied.

'Good God!'

To Philip it put the Gurkhas in a nutshell. 'If I hadn't been an Inverness-shire, I'd have liked to have been a Gurkha,' he had often said.

As he had predicted, although Mike had gratefully accepted the offer of their spare room as a *pied à terre* and a place to dump some kit, he was seldom there. But always the round, brown, smiling Mongolian faces were around.

91. TO TIMBUKTU

The seventh stream meets the river

Omar

In due course a Court of Inquiry was held, but it was not until some months after the riots that my fate was decided.

Dismissed.

A sergeant-major with twenty years' unblemished service. Unblemished until that terrible day, the day when I could not fire.

Dismissed.

Dismissed for believing that little children were in the forefront of the rioters. There had been few Malays amongst the rioters, I was told, and the leaders were known agitators, Chinese, Indonesian and Indian Communists. Perhaps if I had known that at the time I would have ordered the squad to open fire. But would I? To me it had had the appearance of an ordinary crowd of young people, angry perhaps, but ordinary. Youths, women – and children. There had been no women or children, I was told. Only men, a mob of uncontrolled, fanatically-led men, who had murdered without motive a helpless woman and her husband.

I had entered the court a sergeant-major still, ashamed, contrite and regretful, but prepared to plead my case. I left a civilian, disgraced, unwanted; a pariah.

I hung up my uniform for the last time, fingering the crown that had been my ambition and achievement, while my head buzzed with the dreadful words that had preceded my dismissal. Words of scorn and derision. Cowardice, treachery, unfitness to hold such rank, ignominious conduct. I had listened to the defending officer pleading instability; I had heard again the sad history of Zaitun and the untimely demise of my family, but it had meant nothing to me. What had those events to do with cowardice and treachery? Better to have kept my wounds to myself; I was still dismissed.

But they were in my thoughts, those little ones. As I lay down to sleep for the last time in the quarters which I had entered so jubilantly with my wife and children by my side, I wondered why our lives are planned as they are and why a man like me, who loved his fellow-beings, should be left so alone.

I was given a railway warrant back to my kampong, but when the train stopped at Tampin station I didn't get down.

I couldn't go back to Tanjong Mas.

It was not only the disgrace, but the thought of the empty house that was too much to bear. If my wife and children had still been there, perhaps it would have been different. But at least they were not there to witness my disgrace.

Dismissed with ignominy.

The tears rolled down my cheeks as I gazed at the dear, familiar sights. A young Chinese girl walked up and down beside the stationary train, hawking peanuts, langsats and bananas, and I thought tenderly of my dear, departed ones. How often I had given in to those clamouring hands. How many peanuts I had bought at so many station platforms.

The train gave a jolt and I sighed. A couple of Indians flung open the door and climbed into the carriage just as we began to move.

543

They jabbered excitedly and took no notice of me, the only other occupant. I hastily wiped my eyes and stared out of the window as the scenery changed from buildings to countryside and the fresh green of the foot-high padi came into view.

Where I was going, or what I was going to do, I had no idea.

I shut my eyes and prayed that the all-merciful Tuan Allah would show me the way, and then I must have fallen asleep.

'Kuala Lumpur. Kuala Lumpur.'

I must have slept right through Seremban and all the intermediate stops. I could not remember whether this train went on to Ipoh and Prai, or if this was the end of its journey.

Without thinking, I scrambled up and dragged my two suitcases from under the seat. To my surprise, besides the two Indians, there were several Malays and Chinese getting down, all of whom must have joined the train while I had been asleep. I waited for everyone else to leave the carriage, then I walked slowly to one of the platform benches, to sit and think out what I must do.

I had a friend, a sergeant from the same kampong, who was stationed in Kuala Lumpur. His wife was my second cousin. Perhaps I could stay with them for a night or two and discuss my problems with them.

Leaving my suitcases at the station, I walked the short distance to the main police station and inquired if Sergeant Othman was still stationed there.

Never before had I entered a Charge Room feeling like a fugitive. Of course I wore civilian clothes and, as has always been my habit, was neatly dressed, but I felt that every person there must have known that I was an NCO dismissed from Singapore. I looked at the 'wanted' posters on the walls, almost expecting to see my face amongst them.

The young constable on duty was very polite. He called me 'Father' and came to the door to point out my friend's quarters to me.

He would be off duty now, so, thanking the young man, I walked across the compound and called softly at the foot of the steps.

Malay hospitality would not allow Othman to turn me away, but he could have been chilly. But he was quite unperturbed and invited me in as though he had been expecting me.

I was still stiff from my long sleep in the train and took some time untying my shoe-laces. While I was bending down, Othman's wife, my cousin Saloma, came chattering out of the doorway, helped me with my shoes, shook hands, and pushed me into a chair almost in one movement.

I had forgotten what a great chatterbox and gossip she was. She went to fetch cold drinks and cakes, keeping up an incessant flow of small talk the whole time.

544

'Poor Omar,' she piped, 'we were so sorry to hear of your trouble. Fancy dismissing you after all those years. They ought to be ashamed of themselves. Ai-ee, there's very little justice, I sometimes think.'

She took a deep breath and held out the plate of cakes.

I shook my head. I was too filled with emotion at this sudden burst of friendliness to either eat or remember my manners.

I had seen Othman frown at his wife and had wondered how they already knew about me. Then I understood.

'Abubakar told us everything.' Of course. Abubakar was a taxi-driver from Tanjong Mas who plied between Kuala Lumpur, Malacca and Singapore. He was a well-known gossip and carrier of messages. I should have known.

I found myself having to wipe my eyes again.

Othman gave my shoulder a gentle shake. 'Come on, man, eat something. You know Saloma's cakes – better than those you can buy in a coffee-shop.'

I smiled at them both and took the proffered cake this time. Adohi, it's good to have friends.

'When you've rested we'll go to the station and pick up your things, then this evening we'll discuss plans.'

'You know you are welcome to stay here as long as you like,' Saloma chipped in. 'It's an honour to put up a man like you.' She gave an indignant snort, just like my wife. In fact, she was very like my wife; perhaps she was her cousin and not mine – I always get mixed up with relationships.

Othman was still in uniform and begged to be excused while he bathed and changed. 'We'll go to a coffee-shop before we fetch your cases,' he suggested. 'The children will be home from school soon and we shan't be able to talk in peace here. Besides, if I know my wife, she will want time to prepare a really good meal for you to-night.'

We spent several evenings discussing my future and, as I could already drive, had come to the conclusion that if I could get myself accepted into one of the kongsis, or partnerships, perhaps I could become a taxi-driver.

This was almost decided upon and we were awaiting a visit from Abubakar for his advice, when Othman came home one lunch hour full of a new idea.

'Wouldn't you rather have remained in the police than become a taxi-driver?' he asked me.

'Of course, but – '

'Forgive my interrupting. A tremendous recruiting drive is about to start – with the Emergency getting worse we need all the men we can get and men who are already trained will be doubly useful. Weren't you a marksman in your younger days?'

I puffed with pride, my disgrace quite forgotten. 'I still am.'

'So much the better. I've spoken about you to my inspector and he thinks you stand a good chance of being taken on by the Federation Police – no rank though, it would be as a PC.'

I thought about this for some time. It was twelve years since I had been a PC; it would be difficult, especially when it came to taking orders from men in every way my junior. Still – it was a way to acquit myself and, on the practical side, free board and lodging. Allah knew where I would live as a taxi-driver; I could not sponge on Othman for ever.

I felt very old compared with most of the young men waiting to enlist, and when a PC from my kampong saw me and asked in surprise, 'Hallo, Dato, what are you doing here?' I felt hot with shame. 'Dato' means 'Grandfather,' but it is a courtesy title we use for senior NCOs in the police. He could not have known and addressed me in ignorance, but I saw the officer's head lift with interest and I tried to pretend I wasn't there.

Of course, when it came to my turn it appeared so odd that a man of my age should be joining up for the first time that I had to explain. 'Sergeant-major, eh?' The Admin Officer had a very pink skin and ginger hair; he looked at me shrewdly and I stared through the ginger hair to a thin spot on his scalp. 'Are you prepared to serve as a PC, realising that your previous rank can have no influence on promotion in this force?'

'Tuan.'

'Very well. If you're prepared to serve, we're prepared to have you.' It was as simple as that.

After a short spell at the Depot I was posted to Alor Hijau. I had not wanted to work in my home state, but there was nothing I could do. Thank goodness it was some way from my kampong.

It was good to be in uniform again and fall into the orderly life of station routine. This was a quiet area and all went well until one day when there was a bandit scare.

The inspector was rushing round, getting all off-duty men into jungle green, and soon had us all lined up for roll-call by the main gate. Just as my name was called the OCPD emerged, slinging his carbine and pulling on his floppy, jungle-green hat.

'I won't have that man,' he called to the inspector. 'No one comes on a patrol with me who doesn't shoot when he's ordered to.'

There was a terrible silence. My colleagues stood as though turned to stone and the inspector looked most unhappy. I felt hot with humiliation; I felt I must faint with mortification. No one moved.

'Get that man off parade, Inche. We haven't got all day.'

I hated the OCPD. The whole station had heard him make me lose face.

I was still sitting on my bed, brooding over the incident, when the patrol returned, several hours later. It had been abortive and the men were hot, tired and ill-tempered. I could hear the OCPD shouting as soon as he got down from his jeep.

'Don't take any notice of him,' the first man to enter the room remarked. 'He's the most uncouth European I've come across – but he's brave.'

'Trouble is, he's a Chink-lover,' put in another. 'Makes it quite plain that he thinks little or nothing of Malays. Unfortunately for him the few Chinese in the force are nearly all detectives or in Special Branch – the only ones who go jungle-bashing are on the wrong side!'

Everyone laughed. Everyone except me. I was still too humiliated to find it funny.

I couldn't sleep that night and at the first opportunity next morning I got hold of the inspector and asked for an interview with the OCPD.

'Do you think it wise?' he cautioned. 'He'll only say something to upset you more. He can be a cruel bastard, you know.'

But I was determined, and by the time I heard a bellow of 'Send in our brave sergeant-major then,' I was quite unafraid.

The OCPD spoke very fluent Malay, but he didn't bother with any formalities.

'So you wanted to see me, did you? Why?'

'I wish to explain, Tuan, that when I disobeyed an order, it was not because of fear or cowardice, but because I could not – '

'I am not interested.'

'But Tuan, if I may – '

'You may not.'

He pointed to a livid scar which ran down one side of his face, ending in a cavity a little below the ear.

'You see that?' I remained silent. 'And that?' He opened his shirt to reveal another scar. 'I have two more which I do not propose to show you. Do you know how I got these?'

'A bullet?' I ventured.

'*A* bullet my foot. A whole bloody magazine. And do you know why?'

I shook my head. My mouth was dry.

'Because my patrol, consisting of a bunch of bloody useless, cowardly Malays, ran. That's why. Just one man, a Sikh, stayed with me and he was killed. So I was left to fight it out on my own.'

I wanted to say that I would not have run, but who knows, perhaps I would. I stood there, silent.

'Now do you wonder that I won't have a man behind me who's been *proved* untrustworthy?'

547

'But Tuan –

'Get out of my sight and keep out of it. If I'd been the recruiting officer I wouldn't have taken you on. You've been sent here, so I have to keep you, but the less I see of you the better it'll be for both of us.'

'Perhaps it would be better if the Tuan transferred me to one of the other stations in his district.'

'You can go to Timbuktu for all I care.'

The interview was over. I saluted, but he was already writing a letter.

I spent a most unhappy couple of months. Just when I was bitterly regretting having joined the Malayan Police and was passing the open door of the OCPD's office one morning, I was amazed to hear a cheery hail.

'Good news for you, Sergeant-major. It seems that the powers that be have decided that I have too many men for such a quiet place – I'm to lose six and you will be one of them.'

'And to which of the Tuan's stations is he sending me?'

'None of them. Right out of my district; right out of this contingent, in fact. Can't remember which state you're posted to – Perangor, I think – the inspector will tell you. One of the trouble spots – that should suit you.'

'Tuan.'

I was so pleased to be leaving Alor Hijau that I did not care where I was sent, and for once I had been able to ignore the sarcasm in the OCPD's voice.

All six of us were posted to stations farther north and were told to pack our kit and be ready to catch the northbound mail train that evening. I could not get away quick enough.

My posting was to Kuala Jelang – I don't think I had ever heard of it.

92. AN ORCHID FOR SALLY

Jogindar Singh lifted his third son in his arms and smiled.

The small boys, Ranjit and Ojagar, looked on and at their mother, swathed in many scarves and shawls, lying on the wooden sleeping-platform.

Suvindar Kaur had put on a lot of weight since her marriage three and a half years ago, but her face was still the face of a girl and her eyes shone with pride.

'Those are your brothers and that is your mother,' Jogindar told the infant, and gently laid him down beside his wife. He stooped then to push the sweat-sodden hair back from her forehead and gently wiped her brow with a towel.

'So many sons,' he murmured, 'so many sons.' Then, turning to his first-born, 'Ranjit, go and fetch Puron Kaur and ask her to mind the baby while your mother sleeps; I have to go to work now.'

He was late on duty for the first time in his life. Through the open door of the OCPD's office he could hear Philip Morrison talking to the clerk, and the Special Branch sergeant was on the telephone. The elderly PC on duty in the Charge Room rose to attention and smiled at Jogindar's radiant face.

'Good morning, Dato,' he said, 'I hear your wife has safely given birth.'

'A son.' He looked keenly at the old man who, rumour had it, had once been a sergeant-major himself. It would have been indelicate to ask. The man had only been in the station a week, but it was apparent that he knew his way around the books and registers in a way not expected from a PC with only two months' station experience behind him.

'Dato,' the call came from the OCPD's office, and both men rose.

So it was true. Omar quickly sat down again and Jogindar called, 'Coming, sahib.'

'Dato, will you find Inche Mat and tell him I want to take a few men out this afternoon.'

'Sahib.'

From the Charge Room, Omar had heard. He rose to intercept the OCPS on his return.

'Dato, if the Tuan is taking a patrol, I would like to go.'

Jogindar shrugged. 'If you wish. I will give the inspector your name.'

It was after they had returned from the patrol, late the following afternoon, that Omar appeared at the OCPD's house, bearing an orchid for Sally.

'Oh, what a beautiful thing,' she gasped with genuine pleasure. 'Wherever did you find it?'

Omar's grin spread wide. He was still muddy from the jungle and he pointed at his eyes. 'The Tuan sent me up a tree to scout. My eyes did not see any terrorists, but they did see this. It was in another tree, so I climbed up and got it down.'

He handed the little plant with its lush green leaves and long white bloom to Sally. Poor old man, she thought, he looks much too old to be a PC, and so tired and hot.

'Sit down,' she said, indicating the front step, near where she was

549

working, 'I must go and hang this in the shade, then I'll get you a cold drink.'

Omar was shy; he had not had much contact with European women, although he noted with relief that her Malay was good. He ran his tongue over dry lips – a drink would be welcome – but he did not sit down.

Sally returned with two long glasses of orange squash. 'I'm thirsty too,' she said, and sat down on the grass.

After hesitating for a moment longer, Omar too sat, and asked her how she came to speak Malay already when the Tuan was still learning.

Sally told him about her childhood and how she had left Malaya in 1942. In fact, he already knew from the servants, but it made a good excuse to talk.

To her surprise, the old man suddenly shot to attention, nearly spilling his drink as he put it down in haste. Shoulders squared, feet at an angle of 45 degrees, thumbs to the front and down the trouser seams. Good heavens, she thought, he's exactly like the flight-sergeant drill instructor at OCTU! His face stared woodenly into space and in a moment she saw the reason for all this show, as Philip's shoulders appeared at the top of the steps. She had not heard him on his rubber-soled boots, but Omar, who was sitting on a higher level, had been watching him ascend.

He looked surprised and Sally explained, 'I've just been given an orchid – do you see it hanging over there? Isn't it a beauty?'

Ah, Philip thought, this was the old boy who has obviously been trying to get me on my own ever since he arrived. The orchid and holding Sally in conversation were a good excuse. The station had recently been brought up to strength and this was one of the new arrivals, but damned if he could place them all yet – which one was this?

He sighed to himself. His hair under his beret was wet with sweat and he longed to have a shower. Best to get it over with.

'That was very kind,' he said, and smiled at the old man, motioning him to relax. 'I'll just get myself a drink and then I'll join you.'

Sally rose to get it for him, but he frowned at her and slightly shook his head. As he brushed past he whispered, 'Try and find out his name.'

Omar stood first on one foot and then the other until Sally asked him outright if he wanted to speak to her husband.

He nodded eagerly. 'Yes, but please, Mem, stay. The Tuan must think I am very stupid, still to be a PC at my age – I used to be a sergeant-major – I want the chance to explain. Please, Mem, I don't speak any English, would you help?'

Sally's eyes popped wide. 'Oh,' was all she said, and they remained silent until Philip returned. 'Omar has been in the police for many years – he wants to tell you about it.'

Oh God, now? Philip thought, I shall be having my bath at midnight. He sat down.

'The Singapore Police,' Omar began, 'but I want you to understand, Tuan, that I am not a Singapore Malay. I come from Malacca, which is only a small state, with not enough land for everyone to cultivate – it produces many soldiers and sailors and police. Before the war, as the Mem knows, Malacca was part of the Straits Settlements, with Singapore and Penang – I was in the Straits Settlements Police then. Then, after the war, when the Federation was formed, I found myself in Singapore.'

He looked up to see if the OCPD had taken it in. The latter nodded and he went on to tell his story, hoping that this time it would not fall on deaf ears. Philip groaned silently.

Omar was terribly long-winded and, although both his listeners were sympathetic and Philip assured him several times that he quite understood his reluctance to shoot, he still repeated himself *ad nauseam*, until they both began to wonder if he was ever going to go home.

'It seems a pity that you are here in barracks on your own,' Sally remarked, getting up from her chair and hoping that he would follow suit. 'Have you no family to join you?'

'Only one daughter left, Mem, but she is in a mental home.'

'Oh, how sad. Was she born mental?'

Omar gave a great gulp and his eyes filled with tears. And then out it all came, the whole tragic story of Zaitun and how he lost the rest of his family.

Sally sat down again abruptly and Philip lit a cigarette, which he placed in the old man's trembling hands.

There was no question of their attention wandering this time. Omar was more eloquent than he knew and the rape of Zaitun became as vivid in its horror as the night it was committed.

When he had finished, he hastily wiped his eyes and looked at his watch, embarrassed by his own emotion.

'I am deeply grateful, Tuan and Mem, for listening to me. Now I must go.'

'Don't you think that perhaps a drink of something stronger than orange squash might do you good?'

'No, thank you, Tuan. It is forbidden.'

'Yes, I know, but – '

'I have never touched alcohol, Tuan, and if I had before, I never would again after I saw what it did to the Japanese.'

They were silent for a long time after Omar had left; his presence still very much with them, like a sad ghost.

'Well, there's one Malay who doesn't bottle things up,' Philip remarked at last, 'and luckily, I should say.'

'How *can* life be so unkind to one man? And to think how I've fretted and pined over losing one baby whom I never even knew.'

93. TRULY THERE IS NO JUSTICE
The eighth stream reaches the river
Ramakrishnan

I am sorry most that it has not been possible to continue in lucrative role of Mr S. Kandiah, but with large nest-egg now put aside and monthly remuneration still being received from Mr Ramasamy, father-in-law, I am not poor man and have much dignity in being.

I am now father of three children and wife Devi is rounding nicely with fourth.

One evening, after long and tiresome afternoon spent in company of visiting manager, I am returning home to find one strange man with Devi, and my wife is beating breast and wailing and tears are running through ashes which she has smeared on cheeks and forehead.

At first I am suspecting bad doings of this stranger, before seeing said ashes, but Devi beckons me and says, 'Oh, Krishnan, my father has died, seemingly of a stroke or heart attack.'

For me this is good news, for my bargain with Mr Ramasamy, no relation at that time, was to be left all in last will and testament.

'I must go to Rembang at once,' I say.

Rembang is much changed since days when I am lowly employee in silk store and I am wondering now why I ever thought it grand town indeed.

Mr Ramasamy's wife, all other ripe daughters and many friends and relations both, are weeping and wailing and all and making din most terrible to hear. Body of Mr Ramasamy, deceased, is already being cremated and male relatives are just now returning to abode.

'What is content of late deceased's last willing and testament?' I am asking, and am surprised to see widow's puzzled face.

Then Mr Ramasamy's brother, Nathan, whom I am not knowing existed, but turns out to be most notable attorney, speaks.

'There is no will and testament.'

'But what of me, Ramakrishnan, also son of Ramasamy, although no blood relation, but son-in-law?' I am asking. 'Deceased is promising me great beneficiaries when time is coming for him to pass away.'

'I am sorry, man,' lawyer brother is saying. 'This lady here is sole beneficiary under the law. And if it is not too impolite to ask, why should he leave anything to you?'

'For services rendered,' I reply, 'for great number of services rendered.'

Lawyer brother Nathan is again shaking head. I can see that he is not believing me.

My God, man, after all such work and careful planning, truly there is no justice in this world. I am telling you, I could easily kill both widow lady, ripe daughters and all brothers and sisters both.

Instead I return to estate and beat my wife.

'Your incestuous and evil-living father was not man of good word,' I am shouting, 'but you will pay for sins of father instead. Every dollar which your mother is receiving you will take and hand to me, or I shall tell all most foul happenings that are taking place before marriage.'

But Devi is truly stubborn. 'I shall give you nothing,' she is yelling, 'nothing, you hear? I know you have been bleeding my father all these years, but no longer. I am glad he is dead now and can pay you no more.'

Truly then I am losing my temper most incredibly and hit Devi across face, breasts and abdomen.

'You will do as I say,' I hiss, 'or I shall tell secrets most vile.'

'Tell them,' she screams, 'I do not care,' and runs from quarters to outside.

Already many labourers and their wives have gathered to investigate sounds of quarrel most shrill. Devi runs into middle of them, hands clutching belly and hair falling over eyes.

'Tell them,' she is screaming again, 'no, I will tell them. You are not going to blackmail me.' Pushing hair from face, she stands upright in light from many windows and doors and shouts, 'Because my father was first man to enter me, Krishnan here has been receiving money all these years. I am not ashamed; I don't care; I am not first daughter to be entered by father before husband. When sacred bull mates with cow who is daughter, is there so much fuss, man?'

I am hitting Devi then, again and again, and soon I feel hands pulling me away and face of chief clerk is peering into mine.

'So it was you,' he is hissing at me like most malevolent snake, 'it is you who has been bleeding my friend Ramasamy. I should have known. All these golden ornaments you are buying, while my friend is selling cattle and dispensing with services of assistants in silk store.'

This is truth, for I have been putting veritable screw on Ramasamy, ex-father-in-law, until one hundred dollars is becoming one hundred and fifty, two hundred, etcetera, until now three hundred and fifty dollars each month I have been receiving. I am rich man, with many cachings of money put away in secretive hiding-places on estate, but I am afraid to leave job in case foul white pig of planter who is threatening me has reported said incident to police.

All this time CC is shaking me like dog with rat. 'If it were not for Devi, I would be making sure you are being given sack,' CC is saying, 'but because she is daughter of old friend and I am not wishing to see her without roof over head of her and children, you shall retain employment of clerk without report of such incident being made to manager. But, on condition, man, that you apologise to your wife, understand, and be causing no more trouble on this estate.'

He is shaking me until teeth are rattling in head and I am knowing that I have to go with him when he is marching me off to apologise to wife, otherwise I am most undone. Verily there is no justice. Why am I apologising to girl who has enjoyed overtures of father most vile?

But Devi is not to be found and quarter is only full of wailing children and remains of rough housing and uneaten dinner both.

'I am calling midwife.' It is neighbour's wife who is speaking. 'You kicked your wife in belly, and now she is in travail. Your fault, Mister, if mother or baby dies.'

At that moment I am being glad if everybody dies, but CC is again shaking me in manner most threatening and unfriendly and hissing again in ear.

'You will take care of your wife now, Krishnan. If she dies in childbed, it will be murder, man, and it will be pleasure taking you to police station.'

But Devi does not die. She is being delivered of seven months' child most frail and premature, but who lives also.

She is cooking my food and washing my clothes, but truly she is now most sullen and unattaching wife. Submitting to marital rights without pleasure or lust, she is for driving me away from job, I know. But I cannot leave.

When I have been putting up with said situation for three or four months and Devi is once more pregnant, suddenly there is coming to estate one Tamil police inspector with two Malay constables in uniform and one Tamil constable in plain clothes – I know he is constable because he is showing warrant card and saying he is detective from Criminal Investigation Department.

First inspector is asking to see lists of labour, payrolls, etcetera, etcetera, then he is asking if anyone is knowing Mr S. Kandiah.

I am telling you, man, truly I am quaking in shoes and glad now that CC and wife are being under impression that all monetary rewards have been coming only from Mr Ramasamy, ex-father-in-law.

Everyone is showing ignorance of Mr S. Kandiah and then inspector is saying, 'On information received, car has been discovered belonging to S. Kandiah, garaged in rented shed in nearby town. That is why we are making inquiries from all estates in vicinity.'

'And what has this Kandiah done that inquiries are necessary?' I am asking.

'Impersonating official of non-existent union and thereby receiving money under false pretences from labourers.'

'How is it a crime to impersonate man who does not exist then?' I am asking, but realising too late that it is indeed stupid fellow to be smart with police. Inspector is turning cross eye on me and next words are making perspiration break out all over body.

'Kandiah's assistant, known as K. P. John, has turned King's evidence and confessed all,' he says.

I am trying hard to stand still and not to run, and then inspector is asking if anyone has seen this man and reads out official description. I am listening carefully then, but description could fit at least one-third of labour on Tanah Kuning, let alone other estates, and I am most thankful of having taken precaution of having gold teeth covering removed after last act as S. Kandiah and doubly thankful that K. P. Samuel is in ignorance of said precaution.

Next, inspector is reading out description of car. 'Registration number is BA – ' But I am not waiting to hear more, but sliding away from crowd and hot-footing it for K.P.'s estate on motor bicycle.

I stop only to pick up identity card and driving licence, but it is long enough to see Devi, who has been listening at window without emerging from room, give cunning smile.

As I am leaving quarters, she is calling out in voice most provocative, 'I can tell them who is Mr S. Kandiah,' and, as I move towards her, 'No, don't hit me, Krishnan – I don't *have* to tell them, but I can. It will go the worse for you if you turn on me again.'

'Verily thou art stupid daughter of a she-goat,' I say, and lose no more time in prattle.

But when I am arriving at K.P.'s estate, he is not there.

No one is knowing where he is gone, but only that he is left estate one week ago. Wife, children, bag and baggage also.

Indeed, then it is panicking that I am. How do I know if K.P. has in fact divulged true identity of S. Kandiah? Maybe it is that inspector is playing cat and mouse game, already being in possession of relevant facts and evidences. But if he is knowing already, then surely he would have been arresting me outright, not giving chance to escape?

With such thoughts giving me much needed hope, I am riding as hard as motor bicycle will speed me back to own estate.

Devi must be forgiving and protecting both when she understands that I have money and many golden articles and that she will have nothing if I am being denounced. Thus reasoning, I am relieved to reach estate and find no further sign of police party.

But Devi has gone. Neighbour's wife, the same who helped deliver Devi of last child, is standing by doorway, smiling. Verily I could have kicked said smile from face.

'She has gone, Mister; children and all belongings,' she says.

I cannot afford to be arousing suspicions, so I ask civilly, 'Where? And when?'

'She telephoned for taxi to come to estate,' I am being informed, 'and left about one hour ago. She said she had important information to give to police, too important to wait until morning.'

'They are coming back, then?' I am asking, and trying to sound most casual.

'Inspector said to-morrow morning they would be returning for sure.'

There is no time to lose. I am throwing clothes, towel, etcetera, into case, all the time under direct gaze of neighbour's wife.

All the time I am thinking that if Devi left one hour ago and is being believed straight away by police, then they could be back here in less than one hour more, or even less. I am thinking too of the many cachings on estate where I am secretively hoarding funds and knowing there is no time to reach them. I am having one cache in fireplace, but how can I dig up bricks with woman watching? Truly it is most frustrating time I am going through.

'I must follow Devi,' I am saying, by way of excuse for unnatural rush, 'she will have gone to her mother's house in Rembang for sure.'

Still woman does not move, watching me like mongoose watching snake, and I am unable to retrieve money or any golden articles. Only one milk tin which is conveniently near case under sleeping-platform am I able to take, this containing about two hundred and fifty dollars over.

Soon time limit is up and I must travel at top speed, only hoping that Devi is calling bluff and giving such sayings to neighbour's wife to cause my unease. I have been dropping many hints to get rid of woman, including leaving her to relieve nature outside, but on return she is still there. Now I cannot delay if I am to be avoiding police and so all money and golden articles both must be left behind.

Soon I am out of estate wire and speeding northwards on motor bicycle, with heart in mouth and only two hundred and fifty dollars over in pocket. Verily there is no justice.

I am lying low in railway lines in Kuala Lumpur for one month over before hearing of vacancy as clerk in District Office, Kuala Jelang. Many police stations are displaying among 'wanted' posters one

556

showing face of S. Kandiah. Picture is taken from group photograph, showing self and K.P. in places of honour. I am being fat at that time and now thin, also picture shows me smiling to show gold teeth – verily I am grateful that precaution was taken to remove said teeth.

No one in railway is recognising me, so I am hoping all is safe. Kuala Jelang is in Perangor state, well away from former residence of yours truly, so I am applying for said vacancy. First, for one hundred dollars, I am obtaining certificate of leaving from Railway School and changing date of birth thereon, to give impression of younger man, luckily being of stature small.

It is now just new year of 1951 and I am resolving to turn over new leaves and trying to forget many cachings of money and golden articles rotting on Tanah Kuning Estate. I am now becoming plain Ramakrishnan, son of Ramasamy, respectable government clerk. I am travelling by train and omnibus to said district and making straight for office of Mr Balasingham, chief clerk of District Office, whose name I am careful to learn, presenting credentials and making first good impression most necessary for future employment.

94. A CLERK FOR THE DISTRICT OFFICE

'Sir, there is coming a young man who is after wanting a job.'

The DO stopped writing and asked his clerk to repeat what he had said. Pausing just inside the door, Bala did so.

There was a vacancy for a junior clerk, it was true.

'What's he like?' James asked.

'He is a youngish man, sir, only just leaving school, he says. He has a bright face, sir.'

James tried to sound more interested than he was. 'If you think he's all right, I'll take your word for it,' he said, 'but now the Emergency's on, he'll have to be vetted by the police before we can take him on. What's his name?'

'Ramakrishnan, sir. I am already asking the police to vet him, sir.'

'Good. Well, I'd better see him, I suppose.'

Ramakrishnan, who had been listening behind the half-open door, came in. He was bowing and smiling and washing his hands with invisible soap, but his thoughts were flying like pigeons suddenly released from a loft. Police vetting was something he had not bargained for. To date nobody had connected S. Kandiah with Ramakrishnan, and if either Devi, K. P. Samuel or the chief clerk of Tanah Kuning had informed the police, he would have been arrested by now.

It would appear that they had not informed. His only worry was if they had taken fingerprints from the car – it was something he had not thought of when he'd been driving along so happily with K.P. beside him and another haul of subscriptions in the brief-case on the back seat. The whole populace had been fingerprinted at the outset of the Emergency, when identity cards were first issued. In time, no doubt, if the police were diligent enough, they could find out that the prints of S. Kandiah also belonged to him, Ramakrishnan. But surely fingerprinting was only connected with murder and theft? He was worrying too much. Bluff had always been the best way; it was unlikely that they had bothered about fingerprints. He swallowed and gave the DO his most toothsome smile.

He was a small man, quite unlike Balasingham; a Tamil from south India, James supposed.

'Have you been a clerk before?' he asked, as a matter of routine.

'I have only just left school, sir, as I heard my good friend Mr Balasingham here telling you, sir.'

Bala winced. James was not much taken; he seemed an oily little man, but Bala had assured him that they were desperate for a clerk.

'All right,' he said, 'if the police clear you, we'll take you on.'

Krishnan's head rolled and his hands spread, 'I am forever your most humble servant, sir.'

Bala too spread his hands; a gesture in his case of resignation. James laughed. Bala was a good egg.

But the mixed-up mind of Ramakrishnan could not settle to the disciplined routine of a junior government clerk. Thoughts of all that beautiful money going to waste on Tanah Kuning Estate were too much for his peace of mind. Within a few weeks he was casting round for a diversion.

As usual, bitterness and hatred played their part and he decided that here, in a district with three European government officers, a perfect opportunity to get even with the hated white pigs must present itself.

It did not take him long to find a victim. Although not particularly intelligent, Krishnan was gifted with more than his share of low cunning and he discarded at once the DO, his immediate boss. Nor would he be so foolish as to risk entanglement with the police. The OCPD therefore was also out, and the Forestry Officer was too infrequently in Kuala Jelang itself. There remained only the wives.

He soon found out that, whereas the DO's wife had come from England with her husband and was in Malaya for the first time, the OCPD's was not only Malayan born and bred, but the daughter of a planter to boot – the most hated of all breeds in Krishnan's mind.

So Sally Morrison forthwith became his target.

Satisfied with his knowledge, Krishnan waited for a suitable occasion to pounce – and he did not have to wait long.

From the office window he had a clear view of the main road out of the town, and within twenty-four hours of selecting his victim he saw the largest of the police vehicles, a three-tonner, wending its way slowly along the road with the OCPD seated next to the driver. Standing at the back were several men. Undoubtedly they were going on an operation.

Making some excuse to leave the office, he went at once to the post office and ensconced himself inside the public telephone booth.

The OCPD's wife answered his call.

Speaking through his handkerchief, Krishnan said, 'Your husband is on way to certain death. He is recently leaving here with many men on way to dangerous area, where Communist terrorists are already setting ambush. He will be killed, man, and nothing you can do.'

He was sweating when he returned the receiver to its hook and wiped his face and hands before hurrying back to his desk.

Sally put down the receiver with feelings composed of a mixture of incredulity, unease, puzzlement and a sense of having touched something dirty.

The voice had been Indian without a doubt, despite the attempt to disguise it. Obviously someone who wished her or Philip ill. A PC with a grievance perhaps, but who? She thought quickly; the Pakistani driver was on leave – Philip had mentioned it, because he always drove his jeep – and also the junior Tamil clerk. That left only three possibles in the police station: Jogindar and another Sikh – who had only just arrived – and the civilian clerk, Maniam. The new man was too new; it was hardly likely to be Jogindar, which left Maniam. Unlikely, but Philip might have upset him in some way.

Taking the bull by the horns, she went straight down to the police station, hoping to tell by the expression on the clerk's face whether or not he was responsible.

To Sally's relief, Maniam showed neither surprise nor guilt on her arrival in the office and, rising to greet her, said in his usual voice, 'There are some letters for you on the OCPD's desk, Mem.'

'Thank you,' she lied, 'that's what I came down for.'

She continued on into Philip's office, picked up the mail and was just leaving the room when the telephone rang. Maniam came through to answer it and, as she went back through the main office, she saw the open door into the SB section. Sergeant Lee was writing with bent head; the opportunity seemed too good to miss. Quickly she slipped inside and closed the door.

559

'Hi, Ma'am,' Chee Min rose, and Sally thought, not for the first time, what an attractive smile he had, 'anything I can do for you?'

'Well, yes and no. Only please, what I want to ask you must remain absolutely confidential.' Chee Min nodded and pulled out a chair for her. 'I have just had a rather horrid phone call and I was doing my own bit of detective work.'

She told him what had been said and of her suspicions, but he firmly shook his head.

'Not Maniam, Ma'am. My door's been open all morning; I haven't moved and nor has he.'

'I'm glad.'

'And don't you worry, Ma'am, the OCPD's only gone to the Forest Office. He should be back any minute now. Do you want me to look into it?'

'No, thanks. But what did he mean by going out with "many men"?'

'Just hang on a minute; I'll ask the OCPS.'

Sally heard the brief voices of Chee Min and Jogindar Singh, then he was back.

'The "many men" were those who went on board that Indonesian ship that was in – they're now on their way to the hospital for cholera jabs in consequence; I expect he was dropping them off *en route*. He usually takes his own car, but it's being serviced.'

'I'm so relieved,' she said, 'and please don't tell my husband, I don't want him to make a fuss.'

'Okay. Just as you wish.'

Sally went out then, smiled at Maniam and returned home. She was only half-way up the steps when the police truck returned. She saw Philip jump out, say something to the driver, and walk towards his office. Thank God, she thought, and resolved to put the incident out of her mind.

Three days later an anonymous letter arrived. Written on lined paper torn from an exercise book and in thick pencil, the capital letters read: 'YOUR HUSBAND WILL BE KILLED TO-DAY. IT IS YOUR FAULT. YOUR PAST AND THE PAST OF THOSE LIKE YOU IS YOUR UNDOING.'

Philip had, in fact, gone to a particularly dangerous part of the district that day and told her that he was unlikely to be back before evening. If Ramakrishnan could have seen her, he would no doubt have danced with glee. Poor Sally, it was pointless telling anyone; there was nothing she or anyone else could do, only wait.

When Krishnan had overheard the DO and OCPD discussing a visit to this area, he had written the note with much care and posted it on the crucial day. But Sally stayed at home; he did not have the pleasure of gloating over her strained face.

On the rare occasions when Krishnan did see Sally, he gnashed his teeth at her calm manner – as though he had expected her to turn grey overnight – and decided to try new tactics. Obviously she did not care whether her husband lived or died. Something more drastic was needed.

The first opportunity came at the annual Agricultural Show.

As Sally and the wife of one of the Malay schoolmasters entered a marquee to judge the handcraft exhibits, a sudden commotion at the entrance caused them to pause.

'It is your father and his kind who are being responsible for dilemma of yours truly. Chained we are and chained forever shall be. But you, lady, will shortly be paying just price.'

Sally swung round at the extraordinary words. Behind her were a bunch of giggling schoolchildren, a couple of Boy Scouts and a neat, well-dressed little Tamil, whom she took to be a shop assistant or a clerk. Surely none of them had spoken?

'Did you hear anyone speak just now?' she asked her companion, but the woman shook her head. She had, in fact, been several feet away and the voice was only a whisper.

Unaccountably, Sally did not connect the mysterious voice with either the phone call or the letter. This time she did tell Philip.

'Imagination,' he shrugged, 'why should anyone want to say anything like that to you?'

And there the matter rested. Both had plenty of other things to occupy their minds and gave it no more thought.

It was nearly a month before Sally received another telephone call. Krishnan, in his warped way, was determined to make her sweat. So far she appeared to have kept her troubles to herself, but this time he would send her running to her husband, whose work would go to pot in consequence – the possibilities were endless – and he would exult in the mental torture of those hated Europeans.

With memories of Muriani, Devi, his ex-father-in-law and many estate stories in mind, he rehearsed his speech once more and asked the exchange for the OCPD's house.

Sally listened, almost hypnotised, and when she put the receiver down she was not only white and trembling but very near to tears.

It was in this state that Helen found her. Amazed that her normally cheerful friend should so give way, she hunted in the Morrisons' medicine chest for some aspirin and refused to hear a thing until Sally had swallowed them and a glass of water. Then she asked Ja'afar to make some coffee and sat down.

'Now tell all,' she commanded.

Sally shook her head. 'I can't. It was too horrible. Oh, Helen, I've never heard any man say things like that before. He must be sexually deranged, a pervert. It was revolting, obscene.'

'We'd better ring Philip.'

'He's out. He'll be away for two or three days. It always happens when he's away.'

'Always?'

Sally told her then of the previous call, the note, and the voice outside the marquee which, to her own surprise, she now connected for the first time.

'Well, if anything else happens and you don't want to involve Philip, at least tell me. It's always better to get it off your chest to someone, even if they can't do anything.'

Sally promised that she would and, Ja'afar having arrived with the coffee, they talked of this and that until Helen brought out the purpose of her visit, a dress that required the hem putting up.

Although she did her best to concentrate, first with helping Helen do her dress and then gardening and a pile of letters she had to write, the obscene words kept floating back into her mind, disgusting her again and again. She slept little, jumping at every sound, and finally woke late, feeling tired and heavy.

The office orderly brought up the mail. There was only one letter; an ordinary buff-coloured business envelope with a local postmark, probably a bill.

But it was not a bill. Sally turned the letter over, put it down and picked it up again. Before she finally opened it, her heart began to thump and her guess was not wrong.

'I AM COMING TO GET YOU,' was written in the same pencilled capitals as before, 'YOU KNOW WHAT FOR.'

In a moment of sheer, panic-stricken terror, she rushed for the telephone and called Sergeant Lee.

Chee Min sensed her agitation before the first sentence was completely out and interrupted her, 'Now hold on, Ma'am. I'll come up.'

He gave her a few minutes on purpose and, as he had expected, she had herself under control by the time he arrived at the house. She thrust the offending letter at him without preamble.

At Chee Min's look of inquiry, she told him all that had happened since she had first sought his aid, only asking to be allowed to gloss over the actual wording of the phone call. He did not press her.

'Would you be happier if a PC slept in the house while your husband is away?' he asked.

'No, I don't want to make a fuss. I'm sorry I troubled you – you must have so much work to do – I'm afraid I panicked.' She was feeling embarrassed by then and genuinely wishing that she had kept her head.

'A lot of OCPDs have a guard posted on their houses when they're away. It wouldn't be anything unusual, you know.' Sally still shook her head. 'And I'm sorry, Ma'am, but this time we shall *have* to tell the boss.'

'Oh no, please not. I don't want to worry him. He has such a lot on his plate just now; all this resettlement and the Malay language exams next week. No, please don't tell him.'

Chee Min smiled. 'Me and the OCPD have something in common – struggling over languages. I have a couple of Chinese ones ahead of me.'

'Chinese? You're joking!'

'I'm not.' And he went on to tell her of the ludicrous position he had found himself in.

'What a lot of nonsense, especially after such a good education.'

'Too right!'

'Gosh,' Sally laughed, 'that takes me back. I was at school in Australia too, you know – not for long though, less than a year in fact, thanks to the Japs.'

They had parted with Sally in a more normal frame of mind, but Chee Min still told Inspector Zukifli, who in turn told the sergeant-major, and Jogindar himself made sure that the house and grounds were patrolled each night until Philip's return.

Sally was grateful but embarrassed, and Ramakrishnan, who watched the steps to the house from a coffee-shop near the end of the town, hugged himself with delight at the thought that he was responsible for upsetting the police station routine.

But then he had a sobering thought. He had already sailed close to the wind with the police on more than one occasion. Here he was, watching the house; but what if someone were watching him?

He looked round the coffee-shop hastily. He recognised no one. Any one of them could be a PC in plain clothes. Or perhaps two, or three, waiting to pounce as he left the shop.

And what if they had checked the fingerprints on the car and had married them up with his? Or they might still be checking; he had no police record – as yet – and there would be a lot of prints to wade through if they relied on identity cards. There might still be time.

At that moment a young Chinese whom he *knew* was a detective-sergeant came in and Krishnan nearly sent the table, with his half-finished cup of coffee, flying, as he jumped up to leave in such a hurry.

Several customers looked at him curiously and he sat down again, trying to muster some self-control.

'Your mosquitoes are bad, towkay,' he tried to laugh the incident away as the coffee-shop proprietor brought him the cake which he had ordered. 'One bit me so hard, I nearly upset my coffee just now.'

The man made no reply and Krishnan settled back to drink his coffee and try to appear nonchalant.

Chee Min had wanted to help Sally, but he was quite unaware that he had done so by the simple act of walking into a coffee-shop that evening.

He noted the incident of the nervous little Tamil, but was quite oblivious of the fact that he was the cause and that one spilled cup of coffee and a barked shin had spelt 'finis' to the anonymous phone calls and letters.

95. A FRUSTRATING INTERVIEW

Chee Min had waited a week or two after his 'search' of the Cheng house and then dropped by casually one day and asked if he might come in.

This time he received a very different reception. The family were all smiles and invited him to drink some tea with them.

Rose shyly produced an exercise book and asked him to correct her English, which he did without much difficulty, but was better pleased with himself for being able to chat to her parents in their own dialect.

Mr Cheng was delighted on both counts.

'A teacher *and* a sergeant,' he exclaimed, and mother and daughter beamed.

Chee Min beamed too, but soon he got up to leave – no point in outstaying his welcome. He left, satisfied that they were genuinely sorry to see him depart, thus ensuring a welcome in future.

In fact, this was the first of many pleasant social interludes, and it was not long before he began spending most of his off-duty time in the Cheng household.

It was not long either before the friendship blossomed into something more – as everyone except Chee Min himself, or Vincent, as he was called by the Chengs – could have foreseen.

She would make me a good wife, he thought, and once the idea had taken hold in his mind, he was convinced that he could not marry anyone else.

He was still only twenty and sparks would fly at home, he had no doubt, but that was something he was confident he could overcome.

Meanwhile he confided in Sally and asked if she would meet Rose.

'Of course,' she said, 'bring her along any time you like. I'd love to meet her.'

But not so Rose. She was quite overcome with shyness at the thought. Chee Min did not press her; after all, it might not work.

Sally was kind, but she was blunt. He was used to bluntness, heaven knew, but Rose was not.

Sally shrugged when he told her; she was not upset. 'Only one bit of advice I would proffer,' she said, 'which, of course, you can ignore, and that is, if you haven't already proposed to her, don't until after Chinese New Year.'

She could well imagine the set-up at Chee Min's home and had no doubt that his father would already have a prospective daughter-in-law in mind. If Chee Min burned his boats before talking to 'Dad,' she could see him being hurt on both sides.

He pondered her advice, chewed on it, and found it sound.

Chee Min had learned sufficient tact not to approach his father during the holiday and for that reason he had asked for an extra day. But he did tell Mum.

She merely raised her eyes to heaven and said, 'God help you when the explosion comes! I've been waiting for this. And you'll have your way, no doubt – you're as pig-headed as your father!'

The festivities over and everyone in genial mood, he bearded his father in his office the following day, but realised within five minutes that it was a mistake.

Lee Chee Onn sat with his hand on one telephone while he spoke into another, at the same time motioning with his head to his son to sit down.

Chee Min shivered slightly in the cold air-conditioning and hoped he would not have to stay in there too long. He wondered how much money his father had to pay the Communists to be allowed to remain in an office like this.

'Nice to see you here, son,' Mr Lee put down one receiver and picked up the other. 'Be with you in a minute.'

This time it was only a short conversation, then, with a surreptitious glance at his watch, he leaned back and smiled at his youngest son.

'Now, what can I do for you, Chee Min? How much leave have you got?'

'I have only to-day, Dad, and I had to see you urgently. I want to get married.'

'Married? Nonsense. You're far too young – ' A telephone rang.

'Dad, I'll be twenty-one in five months' time.' He got it in quickly, as soon as the phone was down and before his father could start another conversation.

'Maybe, but I have plans for you. Anyway, who is it you want to marry?'

'A girl I've met in Kuala Jelang. Her name's Rose Cheng.'

'Cheng? Do I know her?'

'I think it most unlikely.' The phone rang again before he could go on – he was beginning to feel very frustrated. He stood up and, as soon as his father was free, asked, 'Please, Dad, could we discuss this at home this evening?'

'Sorry, boy; got a business dinner to-night. You'd better tell me now.'

Chee Min sat down and prayed that the phone would not ring again, but his prayer went unanswered.

'Now,' his father seemed settled for a spell, 'this Rose Cheng. Where does she come from? What does her father do?'

Chee Min took a deep breath; he had reached the tricky part.

'Her family came originally from Kuala Lumpur, where her father owned a shop. She now lives in a squatter settlement, where her father market gardens.'

No point in beating about the bush. He sat still and waited for the fireworks display to commence.

But not as still as his father. He sat so quiet and so still and for so long that his son began to wonder if he had had a stroke. Then he came to life and began roaring like a wounded tiger.

'*Squatter* settlement, did you say?' Before Chee Min could get a word in edgeways, his father made a gesture of finality with both hands and shook his head so violently that his chops wobbled. '*No!* I don't want to hear another word – not one. D'you hear me?'

Chee Min heard but, as his mother had so recently remarked, he could be as pig-headed as his father.

'I intend to marry her whether I have your permission or not – I shall soon be twenty-one.'

Something in his tone made his father give up his blustering for a short while.

'Now, Chee Min,' he pleaded, 'think. I have let you have your own way over joining the police – the last career *I* would have chosen for you – and you will go far. To-day you are only a sergeant, but to-morrow an inspector; you'll be gazetted in no time. Think what a handicap it will be then to have an illiterate wife, however pretty she may be. Besides,' he added as a last resort – which was sheer hypocrisy for him – 'we are Christians.'

His son grinned; this was one of the things he had been keeping up his sleeve.

'She is a Christian too,' he said, scarcely able to conceal the triumph in his voice, 'she is convent-educated and speaks English – they have only been driven into their present environment through hard times – and no doubt lack of business acumen. At least her father could read and write before Rose was born!'

He should have resisted the temptation to make that last quip, he knew, but he couldn't. His father still only signed his name to dictated

566

letters, never putting pen to paper if it could be avoided, and certainly not when anyone else was around. Chee Min had probed a sensitive spot. As a younger man, Chee Onn would tell people proudly that his father had come from China as a coolie and that he himself could neither read nor write for many years. But times had changed – and he with them. To be a well-educated, rich tycoon, with secretaries, mistresses and an air-conditioned car was one thing, but to be an illiterate tycoon was to be the laughing-stock of the younger genera- tion and that was something which Lee Chee Onn could not have stood. His face went a deep plum red and he stood up and shouted at his son.

'Make her your mistress if you like – if she's pregnant, I'll pay – but if you marry her I'll cut you off. No more allowance, no car for your twenty-first. If you marry her you can expect no further help from me. Do you understand?'

Perhaps it was Chee Min's police training that came to his aid, or maybe his natural control, but whatever it was, he handled himself with admirable restraint and dignity. He had no intention of shouting back.

'Very well, Dad,' he said in an even voice, 'I am sorry that I have earned your displeasure and not gained your consent. However, your threats will in no way alter my intentions – as soon as I am twenty-one I shall marry Rose.'

He gave his father a slight, old-fashioned bow and left the room.

He had intended spending the evening with his mother, but now he was no longer in the mood to stay at home. If he left at once, he could still make Kuala Jelang that night.

As he eased himself behind the wheel of the borrowed car, he had a momentary pang that now he would not soon have his own, but it did nothing to lessen his determination. He would propose to Rose as soon as he returned; his mind was made up.

96. TO LIVE IN PEACE

James had just about given up hope of finding a suitable site for a resettlement area, without requisitioning or forcing someone to sell, when he received an unexpected visit from one of the planters.

It was Wotherspoon, manager of Bukit Merah Estate. An elderly bachelor, he was always making complaints about government, and the police in particular. James was wary.

Extraordinary, he thought, as they shook hands and the older man seated himself, how many people seem to find pleasure in playing one government servant off against another. With King it had rankled, and he had been too new at the time to know it was just a local pastime. With Philip it was different; they were able to compare notes and laugh about it.

'What can I do for you?' he asked.

'I understand you are looking for some land.' Wotherspoon had a high-pitched, rather querulous voice.

'Indeed I am.'

'My company has about twenty-five acres that they want to get rid of, possibly more. Any use to you?'

It seemed too good to be true. In wartime, James had climbed partly through efficiency and partly through luck, but a good deal through ruthlessness. He had often been criticised for being too high-handed; it was strange that he should now be the very opposite. The police seemed to requisition things left, right and centre, and DWEC, or its state equivalent, SWEC, had powers that could so easily be misused. All along he had been determined to avoid requisitioning, shunning the power that could put it into effect. He looked steadily at Wotherspoon, still warily, but with hope.

'Can you show me where it is exactly?' He walked over to the map of the district which hung on the opposite wall, below the photograph of the King.

The area was part jungle and part disused rubber. It adjoined Bukit Merah Estate.

'No use to me,' the old man said, 'estate's already too large for me to cope with single-handed – be glad for government to take it off my hands.'

'I'll have to have the police opinion first, then we'll raise it in DWEC.'

'The police,' Wotherspoon sneered. 'All that Morrison's interested in is making me spend more money. Do you know, the blighter had the cheek to threaten to withdraw my SCs if I didn't improve the defences?'

'That's up to him,' James said quickly; he had no intention of becoming involved. In fact, he did think Philip was antagonising the planters rather unnecessarily, but they were his men.

As soon as Wotherspoon had gone he rang Philip up. 'Let's go and have a look at it this afternoon,' he suggested.

'Well? What do you think of it?'

Philip leaned against the jeep and stroked his chin. Ahead and behind them men of the jungle squad stood, weapons at the ready, alert against the ever-present menace. It was not the most salubrious of areas. He did not, in fact, think very much of it at all, but James was so het up about this wretched land that he was not prepared to make matters worse by saying so.

568

'I could wish it were in a better area as far as security is concerned,' he said at last.

James sighed. 'Well, we've got to find something and this seems the best bet so far.'

Reluctantly Philip agreed.

It was true. They had no hope of clearing the CTs from even part of the district as long as they continued to prey on the squatters, forcing food, funds and information out of them. To resettle all the squatters in the area, where they could be guarded, was the only possible solution. Communal kitchens would be set up and the workers searched every morning when they left the area, to ensure they were not carrying food for the bandits. Information was another problem, but at least cutting off their material needs would be half the battle. It had worked in other districts, it must work here.

He turned to the back of the jeep where his detective-sergeant and an SC were already installed.

'What do you think, Chee Min – you spend enough time with the squatters?'

Chee Min lowered his eyes and gave Philip a slight smile. He would not be happy with Rose in this area, so he must let that be his guide.

'I think it is a dangerous area, sir.'

James slapped at the side of the vehicle impatiently. 'Special Branch,' he spat out, making it sound like a curse.

Chee Min was not going to be rude, but his opinion had been asked. He coloured slightly, but his voice was steady.

'Until we can be sure there are no bandits living on Bukit Merah Estate,' he said, 'I do not think it will be safe.'

It was exactly Philip's own opinion, but it was one of the few matters on which he and James did not see eye to eye.

'Who says there are bandits on Bukit Merah?' James snapped. He was looking very hot and cross and kept dashing the sweat from his forehead with his one good hand. 'Christ, it's hot,' he added in a less belligerent tone of voice.

They all agreed.

'Wotherspoon –' Philip began, but was cut off in mid-sentence by a frown and an impatient gesture from the DO.

'Can't discuss it here,' he interrupted, meaning not before Other Ranks. 'I've got a bloody meeting at five o'clock. Come and have some grub to-night, Phil – pot luck; I'll ring Helen as soon as we get back – we can discuss it in the cool of the evening while the women talk about their knitting – or whatever they do talk about.'

Over coffee and as soon as the servants had left the room, James turned to Philip without preamble.

'I know the police have had it in for old Wotherspoon ever since he refused to spend any more money on his defences,' he said, 'but have you any proof that there are bandits living on his estate?'

'When we moved in after that last ambush and caught the CTs on the hop, amongst other things that they left behind was a typewriter. The fact that all the recent propaganda leaflets had originated from that machine was not difficult to prove.'

Philip looked James straight in the eye, who in turn stared back at him.

'Go on.'

'Wotherspoon denied ever having seen that typewriter before and even made a statement to the effect that nothing had been stolen from his estate. On the bottom of the machine there was a label – stuck on by the agents in KL, who certified that it had been repaired and serviced on such and such a date. Of course we checked to see who had taken it in – Wotherspoon.' James opened his mouth, obviously to protest, but Philip shook his head. 'Let me finish first. I went into the office myself when I was last in KL. There is a very efficient Eurasian girl running that side – she remembered Wotherspoon coming in and described him very well. There is absolutely no doubt that that typewriter belonged to him, or to the estate, but he slipped up – if he had admitted that a typewriter had been stolen, we should probably not have given it a second thought.'

'Is that conclusive proof?'

'No, it's not. But don't most managers deal with one shop for the bulk of their estate supplies?'

'I should imagine so.'

'Wotherspoon runs three accounts at three shops – one in his own name, one in the name of the agents, and one in the name of the estate. The combined amount of rice he draws each month would feed more than twice the strength of his labour force.'

James was now sitting up very straight and staring not at Philip but out into the night.

'I wish you'd told me this before,' he said.

'I should have done so soon, but we're still investigating – I'll let you have the whole story as soon as I can.'

'Do you consider your Special Branch to be infallible?'

'Far from it, but in this particular instance I agree with them. In fact, I'd go so far as to say they are merely confirming my own suspicions.'

The two women had been listening intently.

'You don't think he's actually "in" with the bandits, do you, Philip?' Sally now asked.

'A Communist?' ventured Helen.

James stood up. His head was aching. 'Convince the girls, Philip,' he said, 'I'm going to get us a drink.' He hated the whole business and women could be such ghouls.

'He's old,' Philip told them, 'old, a bachelor and alone and, like most old men, he's selfish. Anything to be left in peace – you leave me alone and I shan't see you. Do you agree, James?'

James was behind a screen, where they had a small bar. Four splashes of soda were heard before he replied, and then he sounded tired.

'I suppose so. It's the only charitable view we can take. What do you propose to do?'

'Let him know that we know. Suggest politely that he mends his ways – at least that is how I would like to handle it, but the CPO is coming down in a few days; I shall ask his advice.'

'Hm. Old Wotherspoon wouldn't take it kindly from you – he'd say you were too young to know what you were talking about, too new in the country, too new in the police. I think he could be difficult.'

Philip's face went hard. 'We've had too many police killed,' he said, 'and planters, to put up with any nonsense. I feel sorry for the old boy, all on his own up there, and I'll handle it in the kindest way I can, but I'm not prepared to risk men's lives so that Wotherspoon can live in peace.'

'Hear, hear.'

Philip gave a mock bow to the wives. 'And having said my piece,' he grinned, 'let's let the CPO sort it out.'

'And the land?' pressed James.

'I suppose it will be all right, if we can clear sufficient space around it.'

'By the way,' asked Helen, 'on a lighter theme, is it true that we're getting a quack?'

'Well, how the devil did you know?' James looked at her in surprise. 'I haven't mentioned it to a soul yet, because if we can't find anywhere for him to live, he won't be posted here after all.'

'The servants know,' Helen looked smug, 'they always do. Do you think he will come? It would make such a difference, not having to worry when the children are ill.'

'If they can find a bachelor, I'm hoping to persuade Donald to let him share his bungalow. I've just written to the Medical Department to find out.'

'I hope he does come,' Sally put in, 'then we can have six for dinner instead of always the four of us, and Donald the odd man out.'

'Our social Sal,' James smiled at her. 'I'd be glad to have a doctor in the district, period.'

'I'm not an easy man to live with,' Donald was saying.

He was horrified at being asked to share his bungalow and yet, at

571

the back of his mind, a little sneaking thought insinuated itself: perhaps company would be, could be, pleasant. Someone to talk to in the evenings, someone to drink with, perhaps someone with whom he could play chess. But supposing he got a TT or a God-botherer? He might even be a queer. He looked across the desk at the DO.

'I'm not too keen,' he said.

James was becoming exasperated. 'I can't force you, Don,' he said, 'but you'd be doing the whole district a favour and it would only be temporary – until we can find somewhere else for him.'

Then there was Salmah. She had been mistress to at least one of his predecessors and he remembered well how she had expected him to take her on – what a rat that King had been! He had only kept her on because she could cook, but it had taken a long time to convince her that that was all he wanted of her. Well, she probably thought *he* was queer – or impotent, more likely – he'd heard the rumours. Supposing this new chap should accept her advances and take her on? It could be damned embarrassing.

'I understand that he's not an Englishman,' James's dry voice cut through Don's thoughts.

Oh boy, these bloody, superior British! That did it.

'I'll share,' he said abruptly, and stood up to go.

James smiled at his retreating back. Helen said he was hard, but in his air force days he'd always been able to handle his crew. He picked up the telephone and asked for his house.

'Helen, can you water down the soup? Don's coming to lunch!'

Donald swung round just as he reached the door. The two men grinned broadly at each other.

'Well, you old bastard!' was all Don said.

97. THE GRASS GROWS GREENER
The ninth stream enters the river
Stanislaus Olshewski

A lot of water had flowed under the bridge since the day when I removed my first bullet from my first Gurkha rifleman.

I had removed a lot of bits and pieces since then. I'm not quite sure what I had expected my job to be; leisurely encounters with Malay, Chinese and Indian civilians during office hours? And learning Malay in the evening? I suppose so. Well, it certainly didn't take me long to find out that that was just part of it. The Emergency had already been on for more than a year when I arrived in Johore, and we were hardly in the healthiest of areas. We were, in fact, a good deal nearer most of the fighting troops than any military hospital, and I soon found myself, at all hours of the day and night, treating wounded British, Gurkhas and Malays, soldiers and police.

After I'd been working flat out for more than a year, I took some local leave and visited Penang. Kathy and I were still engaged and she had written to me every week since leaving the ship, but I noticed she wasn't wearing the ring I'd bought her in Colombo. Her eyes followed mine as I looked at her empty hand.

'I didn't think you wanted to be tied, Stan. I thought you'd consider it just a shipboard romance and I'm not one to force myself on any man.'

I really felt a heel then – I think I had written to her twice. The Emergency had doubled the work at the hospital, but not the staff. And I really had devoted every spare moment to learning the language. Not that languages ever presented a problem to me, but I was determined to know it thoroughly and not get by with the bazaar Malay that half the Europeans considered sufficient. But there was no need to make excuses to Kathy; she waved my explanations away with an impatient shake of her head.

'It's enough that you're here, Stan. You wouldn't have come if you hadn't wanted to.'

It was true; I had looked forward to seeing her – when I'd thought about her at all. I enjoyed Penang and I enjoyed her company, but after a week I was fretting to get home.

'You want to get back, don't you, Stan?' Kathy knew me; I hadn't said a word. 'I love Penang, but I wish I could come with you.'

Well, why couldn't she? I only had to say the word. I would have liked to have had her with me, and yet I was jealous of my solitude, my privacy. That, I suppose, is what happens when you're still a bachelor at thirty-five. I pressed her hand, but said nothing.

Back in my bachelor bungalow, which boasted no luxuries, no adornment whatsoever, I missed her intolerably. It would be pleasant to come home to a civilised house, have someone to discuss my problems with. We were so short-staffed, she could help out in the hospital too; she'd not be bored.

But it was equally pleasant to sit in dirty shirt, unchanged, unbathed, and unnagged at. To sit in the velvet thrum of the Malayan night, for company cicadas and the toc-toc bird.

What happened, of course, was that I just let things slide. And then my mind was made up for me. I was posted. And posted to Berembang, up in Perangor, to a bachelor mess, so that a married couple could have my bungalow in Johore. Accommodation was such a problem at that time that it influenced postings a good deal.

I accepted my transfer with a fatalistic shrug, but once there I was

573

miserable. Work and responsibility had been the very savour of life and suddenly they were removed. I was one of a number of junior MOs and every case of interest I had to pass on.

The Emergency seemed a hundred miles away – although, in fact, it was just around the corner – and the mess was foul. No privacy, lousy food, and no kindred spirits.

And then Kathy was posted to Kuala Lumpur. It was only a few hours' drive and I thought things would perk up. We saw each other perhaps a couple of times a week and still I made no move. Then, one Sunday morning, when we were sitting by the Lake Club pool, she pushed a letter over.

It was a love letter and I didn't want to read it, but she read it out to me anyway. It was from a doctor in Penang.

'I didn't think you were interested in him.' I couldn't even feel jealous. She had said she was thirty and as things were going would end up on the shelf if I didn't make up my mind. 'Are you in love with him?'

'Are you in love with me, Stan?' I'd asked for that.

'I don't know, Kathy. I just don't know.'

'So what do I tell him?'

I was silent a long time then, not knowing what to say. On impulse I nearly said to hell with him, marry me, but a terrible lethargy was descending on me.

'It's all my fault – I just seem to have lost interest in everything. Most of all myself.' I must have sounded like one of those ads for vitamin pills; night starvation or something. By God, I wasn't even interested in that any more.

'Which means I tell him "yes".'

I said nothing. She rose from the grass and I saw the tears filling her eyes. There have been many times in my life when I've hated myself; that was one of the worst.

'Kathy, I'm sorry.'

She shook her head violently. 'Please don't say any more, Stan. Just try not to see me again, that's all.' And she walked away, a small dignified figure, straight-backed and proud.

The next morning I approached the CMO for an out-station posting. I had done so before, but there had been no go.

'There is a district that's badly in need of an MO,' he told me. 'But the trouble, as usual, is lack of accommodation. There's already a small hospital there, run by a senior dresser, but now that the Emergency has made it so dangerous to send patients by ambulance for any distance, a doctor is badly needed on the spot. The post has been approved and the Director is keen to fill it as soon as possible, 'but . . .' he spread his hands in a helpless gesture; hell, I could happily have lived in a tent.

'Isn't there a Rest House?' I asked.

'There is, but you couldn't live there for ever – only two rooms and they're nearly always in use. The DO is trying to organise something and, as it will have to be a bachelor posting, I'll keep you in mind.'

Whether it was the prospect of leaving Berembang or having made the final break with Kathy – severing a connection which I never should have made – I don't know, but quite suddenly the lights shone brighter, the grass grew greener and my patients, if it were possible, less drab.

I celebrated the arrival of the New Year with a surge of hope and a thick head. One thing was for sure, no year could be as dreary as 1950.

Kathy had been a Christmas bride; my conscience was clear. And if the photo of her wedding in the local rag was anything to go by, she looked a lot better off without me.

Time went fast after that, and it seemed no time at all before I was back in front of the CMO. My posting had come through at last.

'It'll mean sharing a house, I'm afraid,' he said, 'but it may not be for long.'

I was as excited as a schoolboy and couldn't have cared less where I was going to live, just as long as there was a decent job of work to go with it. The thought of being my own boss again was exhilarating. I said as much to the CMO and was just about to thank him and go when it occurred to me that I didn't know where I was being sent!

We both laughed at the absurdity of the omission and the CMO duly enlightened me.

'Kuala Jelang,' he said. 'Not a bad little place.'

It would not have worried me had I been posted to the moon, so pleased was I to get away from urban life. Piling my belongings into the old second-hand Ford I'd bought in Johore, I set off, singing at the top of my voice and generally behaving in a manner unbecoming. I had been advised not to travel alone and to get myself a gun, but I had the feeling my time was not yet up and I'm afraid I politely ignored the well-meant counsel. I cocked a snook at every high bank and concealing tree and thought, to hell, you can shoot at me another day.

Kuala Jelang was on the coast and for the last few miles of the journey I was travelling along a raised road, the ridge down the centre of a narrow peninsula, hemmed in on both sides by mangrove swamp. It was my first encounter with mangrove and there seemed something infinitely evil about its devious, intertwining roots and the black oozing mud in which they lived. It was a relief when the swamp opened out and the first buildings came into view.

There's one thing about British colonial town-planning – you can never lose yourself! Once inside the Town Board limit notice, everything began to fall into place. A wooden building on my left bore the sign Forest Checking Station, and stretching out behind was what appeared to be a forest nursery. Behind that again, built on a low hill and with a long, winding drive, stood an old-fashioned bungalow almost entirely grown over by bougainvillaea of varying shades. A typical old government house; the Forestry Officer's quarters presumably, and if so, my temporary home.

Within a couple of minutes a ramshackle conglomeration of low, whitewashed buildings appeared and I slowed down, knowing that they could only be the hospital.

Resisting the temptation to go in – it would be unfair, when I was not expected before the next morning – I stopped the car on the opposite side of the road and looked at it with satisfaction. I saw at a glance that most of the buildings could do with a coat of paint, the grass needed cutting and a few well-kept flower-beds would not come amiss. A couple of young nurses, who looked smart and cheerful enough, flitted between the buildings like trim, starched butterflies, and an elderly Chinese in a white gown, whom I took to be the Senior Hospital Assistant, emerged from an office and went into a ward. At that moment I noticed that some of the mobile patients were clustered on a verandah and watching me watching them, so I decided it was time to make a move. Brief though the glimpse had been of my future domain, it had been enough to fill me with plans of pleasurable anticipation and I started the engine with spirits soaring.

Through a suburban area of junior government quarters, like so many flower-surrounded boxes in dotted rows on either side of the road, until I came to a fork with a two-armed signpost pointing to 'The Town' in one direction and 'Government Offices' in the other. Taking the latter turn, I came across just exactly what I had expected – an avenue of flowering trees ascending a small hill, crowned by what could only be what they were, the government offices.

It was so similar to so many of the districts I had visited in Johore and passed through on my way down that it was like coming home. I smiled to myself as I read the boards: District Office, Treasury, Public Works Department, Survey Office, Agriculture and, slightly on its own, Post Office.

At that moment I heard a familiar sound as well, the clanging of metal against metal as the police sentry struck the hour. Judging by the sound, the police station must be some distance away; the other side of the town apparently.

There was a great commotion as doors and windows were shut and clerks began hurrying from all directions, Chinese and Indians mostly, with a couple of Malays and one tall, thin Eurasian. Only then did I realise that it was five o'clock. I had been driving all day and forgotten about the time. Smiling at the curious stares that I received from the home-going clerks, I ran up the steps and knocked at the wooden swing doors marked 'District Officer'.

The DO was on the phone and motioned me to a chair. I was glad of the chance to size him up and also to relax for a moment, for I had suddenly become very tired.

He was a short, squat man, with one arm, a glaringly obvious glass eye and a lot of brown crinkly hair, which I suspected he tried unsuccessfully to subdue, as I did my own. He grunted monosyllabically at intervals into the receiver, which he held between shoulder and neck while doodling on the blotter with his one good hand. There was a hint of ill-humour in the face and more than a hint of pain. He must have a bloody temper, I was thinking, when he suddenly put the receiver down and smiled.

I looked at him with fascination as he walked round the desk with outstretched hand, amazed at the transformation of his face. There are smiles and smiles. This one lit the whole face and I wondered how many women it had enslaved.

'I'm Weatherby,' he said, 'and you, I take it, are the new quack. As you will no doubt find out when you see the amount of work awaiting you, you are a very welcome addition to the district.'

'Thank you. I hope I shall fulfil your expectations. My name is Stanislaus Olshewski.'

'So you really are Polish? My God, your English is bloody good.'

'Thank you again.'

'I suppose you know you're sharing a bungalow with the FO, Thom – only a temporary arrangement, I hope. I'll take you round.' He looked back at his desk and sighed then and said, rather wistfully, 'On second thoughts, I don't suppose you could find your own way there? I've got such a pile here –' he indicated the laden desk ' – and once I leave it, I find it so hard to start concentrating again. This is the only time one has any peace. You've already passed the house –'

'On the hill behind the Forest Checking Station?' I interrupted, 'I'll find my way.'

'Good man. Glad you've arrived before the week-end; the police band is coming down to beat the retreat on Saturday. The whole district will be coming to town. You'll be able to meet everyone in one go; most convenient.'

Right at that moment all I wanted was a shower and my bed. It had been a tiring drive and the grit and sweat were causing my shirt to stick to my back and chest, a feeling I detested. But I said it was indeed most opportune and turned to go.

A small Austin was parked beneath and through the porch, leaving room for my car. A considerate character, I thought, thank God.

And then I saw him.

Large, gingery and familiar. His name meant nothing, but as soon as I heard his New World voice, the tantalising buzz in my brain increased. He was unlikely to be an American, so the accent must be Canadian, but where? He looked at me without a flicker of recognition at first, then a puzzled cloud descended over his face as well.

'Wait a minute,' he said, large paw still pumping mine, 'we've met before.'

'I know we have.'

'Judas Priest, my doggone memory's gone. Were you in the army?'

'No,' I replied, 'air force.'

'Pole? I never met no Poles. Holland?'

'No. UK, Middle East, East Africa, India,' he shook his head at each one, 'and finally Germany. Were you a POW?'

'No. You a partisan?'

'No.'

We both stopped and thought. Then, 'Were you at Edinburgh?' he asked.

'St Andrews.'

'I've got it! That Hogmanay party at the Wallaces'. I got blind drunk and when I woke up we were in a huddle on the floor – if I remember rightly, I was holding your head!'

'I was poleaxed by one of those kilted fiends!'

'We have one here, the OCPD – dances round like a dervish on tribal festivals! You were bragging about vodka if I recall aright!'

'I carried you home – and cooked the breakfast!'

'Well, Judas Priest! Talk about a small world. Glad to have you share my home for a second time, Doc! Say, how's about a shower and a drink and then I'll drive you round the rest of the metropolis before it gets dark. We get quite a spectacular sunset this time of year from the top of Nobs' Hill.'

As expected, Kuala Jelang continued to follow the usual pattern.

Hedged in by mangrove, I had been unaware when driving down that such a broad river ran so close to the road. I had been told it was a peninsula, but I hadn't appreciated that the water on one side was not sea.

Thom drove on, beyond the government offices and along the river bank. Two quite sizeable steamers were loading rubber and beyond them I could see several boats of the fishing fleet chug-chugging out of the river mouth to the open sea.

'Good fish here,' he remarked, 'you want to see the rest?'

I nodded. It was wonderful to be away from the big town and the shower and a beer had momentarily banished fatigue.

Conforming, the town was centred round the padang. Good old traditional English village green. It was all so right.

'Do they play cricket on Sundays?' I asked, a trifle maliciously, not expecting to evoke a rush of enthusiasm.

'Sure thing. Some of the Indians are first-class. One of your sports, Stan?'

'Not too keen,' I murmured. 'I imagine I'll have a fair amount of work to do.'

'Oh well, we can't all have the same interests, I suppose.'

He was clearly disappointed and I was sorry I had brought the subject up. He wasn't the first overgrown schoolboy I'd met.

The usual Chinese shophouses bordered two sides of the padang and at the end of the main street stood a war memorial and to the left of it a mosque. After that the road curved round the base of a sudden hill and we began to climb.

Immediately the jungle noises of the night rose around us with the gathering dusk, bullfrogs and cicadas taking up the chorus where, for me, they had left off a year before.

'OCPD's house on the right, DO's on the left, Rest House straight ahead.'

We were at the top of the hill now and lights were beginning to come on in windows seen vaguely at the end of the tree-shrouded drives. The road was terrible and I felt for the little car as we lurched in and out of potholes and ruts. It was a relief when we were past the Rest House and he stopped.

'We'll walk from here. You should see this road when it's rained – sometimes you can't take a car up here for weeks, then they all have to walk. Does 'em good, I say, they none of them get enough exercise.'

God preserve me from professional keep-fitters! I knew one subject to avoid!

As though to prove his point, Thom set off with great strides to cover the short distance to the lighthouse, a solid grey stone tower that looked as though it would be more at home in northern seas than the tropics. Perched on the very edge of the escarpment, it afforded an excellent view of the seaward side of the town. He beckoned me to follow him on to the parapet and pointed down.

Immediately below us a fringe of mangrove ended abruptly at a bund, beyond which nestled the police compound. Station and barracks and a few individual houses bordered a central parade-ground and, to the left, a line of khaki tents.

'Army contingent,' Thom explained, 'we have a few Gurks stationed here.'

'Good.' Things were getting better all the time.

Figures moved like ants down below and the hum and throb of a myriad radios mingled with the engines of the fishing boats leaving port and the insect life above.

'The silent and inscrutable East,' I laughed. 'I never thought that so many people could own radios and find so many different stations to tune them in to!'

'Yeah, they're a noisy bunch. But look at those clouds.'

I raised my eyes to one of the most beautiful sunsets I had ever imagined, let alone seen.

A shoal of fishlike, silvery clouds, reflecting lilac, turquoise and soft green, sailed into a salmon and crimson patch, arched round by cerulean blue with purple depths. The sun itself, crimson, orange, gold, majestic, hung like a god amidst the splendorous shafts of pagan light. Then to sink, slowly at first, then faster, faster, faster into the brazen sea. And suddenly, with that heart-pulling stab of sadness which so often follows beauty, I looked out at the now black, empty sea and shivered.

Neither of us spoke as we walked quickly back to the car and drove in silence to a silent meal.

'Sorry I'm such poor company,' I excused myself. 'Fact is, I'm dead beat.'

He nodded and I went to bed.

The DO was as good as his word and arrived at the bungalow while we were still having breakfast.

He frowned, and with a glance of manifest displeasure at Thom's unshaven face, remarked curtly that he was a busy man and if I didn't mind – I got the message and, picking up my bag, joined him in the car.

I myself had noticed the empty bottle and overflowing ashtray where I'd left Thom sitting the night before. The few words he had spoken at breakfast had been truculent and aggressive, and confirmed my suspicions that he was a soak.

Weatherby introduced the Senior Hospital Assistant, handed over a few files and left.

My day was spent between alternating periods of satisfaction and dismay. The staff seemed fair and eager to please, but the equipment, or lack of, presented an impossible situation.

'Perhaps, now that Doctor is here, he could request these.' The dresser laid a list before me of indents which had, he told me, been consistently ignored.

I groaned as I went down the list; items of the most elementary necessity, I would have thought. The hospital, which had appeared so promising from the outside, was merely a shell. I did my rounds grimly, making copious notes, then I went over to the District Office to try and borrow a clerk and a typewriter.

I gave lunch a miss and, by the time I returned to the bungalow, my voice was hoarse from shouting down the telephone over impossible long-distance connections and my arm stiff from writer's cramp.

At least I returned to find my stable companion in a different frame of mind. It appeared that once his hangover was past, he was all right until the next morning.

'How did it go?' he asked, and I was glad that there was someone there to whom I could moan. 'Pretty frustrating, eh?'

'That would be the understatement of the year.'

'Wal, you can't blame them not putting too much in the hands of these guys. Having seen what our driver can do to an engine, can you imagine some of your blokes playing with a microscope or an X-ray machine?'

'I suppose so.'

'Aw, come on, Doc, don't be so low. It'll all change now that you're here; it'll sort itself out, but you can't expect the whole caboodle to fall into place and spring up over night, now can you? Bring your letters over to me until you get a proper clerk and my girl will do them.'

'Well, thanks, Thom, Don, that would be a help. I was wondering how to cope.'

Our conversation was cut short by the entrance of a stunning Malay girl. Plump and pretty, her sarong was so tight and her slippers so high-heeled that she could hardly walk, but minced in with tiny steps and swaying hips. I reckoned her kebaya was even tighter than the sarong – if that were possible – and as she insinuated herself into the room and past my chair, my eyes practically left their sockets.

'Wow!' I exclaimed, 'falsies, I bet!'

I was aware of the fact that Donald had been eyeing us in turn, tight-lipped and dour, and when he spoke he sounded positively prim.

'I really couldn't tell you,' he said.

'You mean you have no claims?'

'No claims at all.' I didn't know then that he was falling back on someone else's remark, 'I like them white!'

'We-ll. Purely for research, of course!'

581

'Of course.'

The girl swayed so far that she almost overbalanced and I laughed. However, she recovered herself and tottered out with a fair semblance of dignity. To my relief, Don laughed too, and I had the impression that, after all, he couldn't care less whether I slept with her or not.

'Let's have a drink,' he said. 'No vodka, I'm afraid.'

98. THE PAST CATCHES UP

'You haven't forgotten the band's coming down this afternoon, have you, Sally?' Philip called, as he left the house after breakfast. 'Hat and gloves and all that?'

'No, darling, I hadn't forgotten.'

Half-way down the hill he turned, thought for a moment and went back.

'I forgot to tell you, Donald's bringing the new doctor along this afternoon – do you think we should ask them to dinner? We shall have Mike and the bandmaster anyway.'

'Oh yes, that'll be fun. I'll ask Helen and James as well. Better pray that the bus doesn't get burnt to-day though, or heaven alone knows what we'll give them to eat.'

Ja'afar stood by the linen cupboard, waiting to make up the band-master's bed, amused by the antics of his charge – as he still thought of her – as she alternately sang and muttered to herself.

'I like to be a Clerk SD and make controllers cups of tea,
   And then I'll get my LAC,
   It's crafty, but it's done.'

Sally sang, high and slightly flat, as she pulled clean sheets from the cupboard and hunted unsuccessfully for a towel without a darn.

Parades were fun – and the band in full dress too. What ages since I was on a parade, she mused.

'I like to be a Clerk SD and sit on the controller's knee,
   And then I'll get tapes, one, two, three

It's crafty, but it's done. Oh damn, where *did* I put those new pillow-cases?'

'You sound happy, Mem,' Ja'afar murmured, as he took the sheets.

'It's just a silly wartime song – I don't think I can translate it. I love parades – didn't even mind going on them myself – I'm looking forward to this afternoon. Do you know, Ja'afar, the last parade I took, I open-order marched the rear rank over the edge of a bank and they all went for six!'

'Yes, Mem.' He hadn't the foggiest notion what she was talking about, but she was the Old Tuan's only child and he was pleased to see her happy. A pity that her father was not alive to see her married and settled down – even more of a pity that she had no children of her own.

He stood aside to let the DO's wife come through the open door and smiled to see Missy Sally strike an operatic pose and sing even louder.

'*Squadron Leaders and Wing COs are easy ways to wealth,*
I'll work on them from morn till night, although I'll
wreck my health.
In my off times to bed I go,
I've found out all I need to know,
I'm bound to get my ASO,
It's crafty, but it's done!'

Helen sat down on the edge of the bed and shook her head, laughing.

'How you take me back, Sally. They were good times, weren't they?'

'Luckily it's usually the good times that we remember.' She paused to close the cupboard doors, then turned to face her friend. 'But do you know, Helen, it's an extraordinary thing, but the air force keeps coming to mind to-day and for some unknown reason I'm really excited – the parade this afternoon, I expect – but although I was only in the ranks for less than a year, it's that time that I keep thinking of. I can see the Ops room and the plotting-table as clearly as though they were just next door – keep thinking I ought to be getting ready to go on watch!'

'I try not to think back too often – James was so different then.' She changed the subject abruptly, but Sally had caught the momentary wistfulness and wondered. 'But that's not what I came over about and I must hurry back – I just wondered if you wanted any help this afternoon; teas or anything.'

'Not to worry, thanks all the same. The men are having theirs in the canteen; I doubt if I'll even have the bandmaster to cope with. But I'm glad you came because I wanted to ask if you'll have dinner with us. Don's bringing the new doctor over, so there'll be eight of us. One odd glass and two plates, and I'll have to borrow a couple of knives if I may, but I don't suppose anyone will mind.'

Helen's face clouded. She was too loyal to James to dream of discussing him. She had nearly made a slip only a few moments ago, and anyway, would Sally ever believe it if she told her that, when they got home, James would undoubtedly accuse her of flirting with Philip, or say that he hadn't liked the way Don looked at her, or suspect her of having an affair with the bandmaster? There was no rhyme nor reason for his dark moods; nothing that anyone as un-complicated as Sally could be expected to understand. He lost more than his eye and his arm in that crash, she thought bitterly.

She raised her head to meet Sally's compassionate eyes.

'I'd rather not,' she said bleakly, 'I'd love to accept, but. . . .'

'James?'

'He's not well. It's difficult to explain, but things upset him – little things. He was never like this before that last crash – it did something to him.'

'Maybe, but I think it goes deeper than that.' Helen looked at her friend in surprise and listened intently as she went on, 'You know, I used to have nightmares early on in the war – awful dreams about leaving Singapore.' She paused for a time, looking out of the window, and Helen began to wonder what was relevant to her and James in Sally's thoughts. 'When I have nightmares now, they are different; now it is because I once attracted a man's attention so that another man could strangle him. I was proud of myself at the time, but I'm not now, so many years later. He was a German soldier.'

'But that doesn't seem so terrible – after all, it was war and thousands of people were being killed the whole time.'

'No, it's not very terrible in itself, just a tiny pinprick in a great hole of destruction. But it's terrible to *me*. I can't even bear to kill a centipede these days. I remember once a boy friend of mine suddenly getting cold feet – he wept on my shoulder, literally, because he had strafed a railway platform with women on it. I thought he was rather wet at the time – now I'd be more sympathetic. It's a pity that we only learn tolerance so gradually. But he was a fighter pilot – don't you think a bomber pilot must wonder sometimes how much of the destruction, how many lives lost, were due to him? Why have so many turned to religion or good works of one sort or another?'

Helen stirred uneasily. Sally was becoming too intense and she wasn't sure what she was getting at. James had been no worse than anyone else during the war.

'Don't you see,' Sally persisted, 'we all have our quirks? I don't believe that any of our generation have been left completely unscathed by the war; only some of us were affected more than others. You've told me often enough that James was on some of the largest raids and you've implied – though never said – that he was pretty hard and ruthless in his job. I've no doubt he had to be and I'm sure it's telling now. All this bitterness – it must stem from something. Oh dear,' she grinned suddenly, 'I'm becoming involved and I'm not going to spoil my day worrying about a war that's already past history. Come on, Helen, stay and have a cup of coffee while I polish Philip's medals; I'm sure you have time.'

Helen rooted around in the cardboard box from which Sally had taken the medals, while waiting for her coffee to cool.

'We're a magpie race, aren't we?' She smiled as she picked up a square of tartan and fitted a badge to it. 'What did that go on?'

'Philip's balmoral. Can't think why we keep all this junk really.'

'This looks familiar.' Helen was holding up a brass button, its heraldic eagle looking strangely medieval beside the simple thistles and albatrosses. 'American?'

'Polish. I swopped it with a boy friend's, years ago. Oh, damn these corners – whoever designed campaign stars never thought of the person who'd have to clean them. I'd leave them to Ja'afar, but he will polish the oak leaf and clasps as well.'

Helen looked wistfully at the medals. 'That's another thing,' she said, 'medals. James can't bear them. I put his out to wear on our first Armistice Day here and he was furious – flung them into the WPB and said he never wanted to see them again.'

'It all adds up, doesn't it?'

Helen finished her coffee and walked slowly home. She was seeing Sally in a new light and realising that, after all, there was someone on whom she could lean, someone who did not condemn James, but who sympathised. She sighed with something near satisfaction; it had been a good day for them when the Morrisons arrived.

It's as good as Ascot, Sally was thinking. The padang was looking as green as it could and the late afternoon sun slanted out of a cloudless sky. A warm breeze stirred the bunting with which the area had been squared off, and a gay crowd milled in all directions.

Two or three rows of folding chairs faced the band and she noticed that a sprinkling of European women, Helen and some of the planters' and miners' wives who had come in for the occasion, were already seated.

If you closed your eyes to the fact that the road was lined with armoured vehicles, jeeps, and large American Ford V8s with armoured protection, if you considered the number of SCs in town to be normal, and if you did not know of the piles of serviceable clothing littering the two rooms of the Rest House, you really could believe it was a normal, peaceful, social gathering.

The women, who seldom met or left their estates these days, were dressed to the nines, all with hats and gloves and some with the odd parasol as well. Helen sat in the front row, alone except for the two children, looking strangely cut off, and the men were gathered in groups behind the chairs. With the exception of Mike Harrington, all were dressed in Palm Beach suits and might have been discussing the prospects of the forthcoming race; but in fact they were discussing their defences, the merits of various types of wire, and the latest gun to be imported from Australia.

A planter's daughter herself, Sally had found it easier to fit into this setting than Philip had done, although he was sure of himself now.

'Ah, you are all most bountiful lady. But how about the oppressed slaves, I am asking you? Is it that you are seeking to chain us for ever then?'

Sally whipped round at the whispered, venomous, hissing words. A small Tamil confronted her, face and hands ebony against his white, long-sleeved shirt and trousers. Huge eyes rolling and accusing finger pointing, he darted in her direction again, only to fall over a large police boot.

Joginder Singh, standing on the fringe of the crowd, had seen the incident and stepped forward to trip the man.

The Tamil was shorter than Sally and Joginder was a very large Sikh. He picked the little man up by the collar of his shirt and held him, struggling, as a mother cat holds a recalcitrant kitten.

'Oh please, Dato, put him down!' The last thing she wanted was a scene on a day like this.

'He was annoying you, Memsahib. What did he do? What did he say?'

'Well – nothing really. Nothing that means anything. I think he's a bit tiga suku – not all there.'

'I should take him to the police station.'

'Please, no.'

'If it is the Memsahib's wish, I will let him go then.'

Clearly thwarted, Joginder strode off with great dignity, head and shoulders above most of the crowd, while Ramakrishnan retreated, muttering threats against all comers and Sikhs in particular.

Sally glanced round to see if the incident had been noticed, but it seemed that only the immediate onlookers had paid any attention and the seated spectators were oblivious of what had occurred. Relieved, she greeted the assembled women, gave a casual wave to the men and sat down beside the DO's wife.

'Thank God you've arrived,' Helen whispered, 'I seem to have been here for hours. Government servants' privileges are all very well, but sometimes I feel such a dreadful snob.'

James and Philip, from the far side of the padang, had, in fact, seen Ramakrishnan dart up to Sally – appearing like a diminutive fighting cock from that distance – and the latter had been about to intervene when he saw that the sergeant-major had the matter in hand.

'I'll swear that's the clerk I've just sacked,' James remarked, 'but I thought he'd left the district.'

'Why did you sack him?'

'Bala said he was a trouble-maker and was keen to get rid of him and I'd always accept his word. He was only employed on a monthly basis anyway.'

Sally settled into her chair and looked around.

'We were just saying, Sally, dear, that your Philip is really a very handsome man.' It was one of the elderly planter's wives who spoke, leaning forward to tap Sally's shoulder as she did so.

She turned, childlishly pleased. 'Oh, do you think so?' Then she looked towards the band, who were seated in a crescent, playing light music. Philip and James stood chatting to the bandmaster a little distance away from them. She was so used to him in uniform that she took it for granted, but I suppose he does look good, she thought; still, I wish he were in full dress. Because of the Emergency, the local police were in everyday khaki; only the band was on parade. In their blue and silver sarongs, white shirts and trousers, white webbing and black velvet songkoks, they were a pleasure to the eye. She turned again, 'I don't think he's too bad myself!'

As the two men walked across the padang towards the knot of Europeans, the newly-arrived doctor looked around him as though in a dream. Was it possible that this could be the 1950s and in the midst of an Emergency?

It was the first time he had been stationed in a small district and the atmosphere was so exactly as he had imagined a pre-war district *en fête* to be that it hardly seemed true. The women all decked out in garden-party hats and gloves, those of the correct seniority sitting in the prescribed seats, the men standing behind, more uniformly clad than the one man in uniform.

It amused him to note the two solitary occupants of the front row; government wives, no doubt, who would be joined by their husbands in due course. Two children, offspring of one of them, he supposed, climbed on and over the chairs until their mother scolded and they sat down primly beside her. Stan smiled. Then he saw the other woman and, as she turned, he caught his breath and stopped.

Was it possible? They were within fifty yards of the seats now and there was no mistaking the identities of the two European women who sat together and apart.

'Something wrong?' Don turned, puzzled, to his companion.

'No. I just wanted to digest the scenery, all this colour, before I became involved in polite conversation.'

God, what were the next ten minutes going to be like? Bumping into a casual acquaintance, as he had with Don, had been a welcome surprise, but meeting up with two of the women with whom he had been on such intimate terms as these was a bit shattering. Of course, there had always been the possibility of meeting Sally, ever since he came to Malaya – although he had no idea that she had returned – but to be confronted with a double slice of one's past so unexpectedly was enough to take the wind out of anyone's sails! Helen would probably be all right, but Sally – oh Christ! She might well refuse his hand or make some crushing remark, such as colonial ladies were always supposed to make.

'Say, you sure you're all right? You look quite queer.'

The twangy voice was a welcome intrusion into his thoughts and Stan shook himself, both mentally and physically, before he laughed.

'That's one thing I am not!'

'Yeah. No fear of that. Thought you were going to burst a blood vessel when Salmah came in last night! There was a real beauty when I first came here though. Judas Priest, what a guy!'

'I suppose that is the OCPD, the one in khaki talking to Weatherby?'

'Yeah. Philip Morrison.'

'What's he like?'

'Okay. A bit too good to be true sometimes, but okay. But Jesus, you should have seen the previous bunch – can't complain about these two guys. DO gets a bit "English" on occasions, if you know what I mean.'

'He was very pleasant, but I had the impression he didn't like me much.'

'Foreigners and colonials – bad as each other in his eyes, I guess; that's what I mean.'

'Wonder when he lost his arm.'

'During the war, I guess. He never talks about it.'

'Which one was the bomber pilot?'

Don looked surprised. 'Why, the DO. But how did you know one was?'

'I guessed.'

Stan looked at the two women again and decided that he had procrastinated long enough. Better get it over with. He took a deep breath.

'I suppose we should make a move,' he said.

'Yeah. The men'll start sitting down as soon as the band begins to move.'

Helen drew Sally's attention to the two lounge-suited figures approaching across the grass.

'That must be the new doctor,' she said, 'James said that he'd moved in with Don.'

Sally looked up. The sun was in her eyes; it was difficult to tell whether the newcomer was grey or fair. Then she heard Helen gasp and turned to see the colour drain from her friend's face.

'Oh no,' she whispered. Then, quickly busying herself with Angela's dress, 'The children shouldn't be occupying these seats; I'd better take them back and leave them with Ah Ling.'

Sally was puzzled. True, the men would be sitting down soon, but

588

there were still plenty of empty chairs. Helen had already moved when she heard Donald's voice close by.

'Sally, can I introduce our new MO? Dr Ol – '

'Stan!' Sally, eyes and mouth wide with amazement, stood up abruptly, handbag and gloves falling to the ground. He bent to retrieve them, and by the time he straightened up she had recovered her composure; her face split in an incredulous smile. 'Stan! I don't believe it!'

Stan felt the sweat of relief break out on his forehead, and as he bent over her hand he whispered, 'I hope you have tropical weight PKs for this climate!' Aloud he said, 'Charmed, Mrs Morrison.'

'Oh, Stan, you haven't improved!' Sally felt the hot colour spreading up her neck and put her hands up to her face. So I can still blush, she thought. Good grief, after all these years.

Stan was regarding her with an amused grin and she turned away, embarrassed that she should be the focal point of so many eyes and wished that someone would say something.

Donald came to the rescue. 'Say, do you two know each other?' he asked. 'You know, it's the darndest thing – first I meet this guy and recall getting drunk with him in Edinburgh, and now you too. Who next?'

Who next indeed? Stan looked up to meet the eyes of Helen as she rounded the rows of chairs. James was coming towards them. She gave a little frown and tried to mouth a warning without being seen as she put her hands up to adjust her hat. Bless him, he had understood.

No sign of recognition passed between them as she held out her hand, and Donald continued with the introductions.

'Mrs Weatherby?'

'How do you do?'

James had arrived. No ruddy foreigner was going to kiss *his* wife's hand. He quickly held out his own.

'Ah, Ol –, Ol –, old man. Nice to see you here. I can see that Thom is doing the necessary, but they're about to begin the *Retreat*, you'll have to meet the others after the parade.'

Stan looked at him keenly. Was this *the* famous bomber pilot? The bastard who had given Helen such a bad time? She had never mentioned him losing an eye, nor an arm.

'My first name is Stanislaus,' he said, 'but most people call me Stan, they find it easier.'

'Well, er, Stan, as I remarked before, your English is perfect.'

'Thank you,' Stan inclined his head in a gesture which was not English at all. 'I spent much of the war in England.'

James's eyes narrowed. If he had only been there a minute sooner he would have heard how Helen greeted him.

Stan had turned away and, seating himself beside Sally, asked, 'Is that your husband over there?'

She nodded. 'Yes. Don't you think he's good-looking?'

Stan shrugged. 'What does it matter, Sally, as long as he's kind?'

James stiffened. Sally already. Not backward in coming forward. He looked at Helen, but her eyes were intent on the band, who were stacking their chairs at the edge of the padang, preparatory to beginning the *Retreat*.

The men formed up, the bandmaster took his stand, and Philip walked over towards the chairs.

Sally leaned across Stan to where her husband stood. 'Philip, this is – '

He nodded and motioned her to stand as the band struck up 'The King.'

The band played and the crowd clapped. Marching in intricate patterns, back and forth, in and out, the flash of blue and silver weaving through their own shadows on the grass, they were the only moving things. Soon the last of the sun was glinting across the sea and the bunting waved briskly in the sudden evening breeze.

As Philip marched across the padang and the flag came down, Sally smiled a small, secret smile to herself. How lucky I am, she thought, her mind flowing back to the turbulent affair with Stan and the trials and tribulations before, how lucky I am to have married the man I did. Stan was right; it's more comfortable remaining within one's own race and creed. Not that everything had been perfect; they had their rows – tempests, one of Philip's colleagues had called them – and they were both stubborn, but they had a lot else as well. I'm proud of him, she thought, and, taking his arm as soon as he returned, completed the introduction she had attempted at the beginning of the parade.

There was general upheaval as soon as the *Retreat* was over. Most of the planters wanted to return to their estates before it became too dark, the band were putting away their instruments and the crowd drifting away. With a feeling of anticlimax, Sally looked up at the flags hanging sadly down and watched the backviews of the few club-bound Europeans. But Philip was soon tugging at her sleeve.

'Sally, is the room ready for old Jones? I want to settle the band.'

Driving back to the house he asked her about the incident with the Tamil.

She told him. 'It's the same man who spoke to me before. Do you remember? You thought I was imagining it. I suppose he must have been one of Daddy's clerks or something. But he looked too young, and anyway, Daddy was always so good with the labour.'

'James thought it was a clerk he had just sacked.'

'Maybe. Oh well, the world's full of cranks. Let's forget about him. I'll have to hurry if dinner is going to be anything like organised.'

'I think I'll look into it, just the same.'

Helen and James drove home in silence and it was not until they were on the last half-mile that James, who had been staring moodily ahead, asked in a grumpy voice, 'Why didn't you marry him?'

Helen did not take her eyes off the road.

'Marry whom?' she asked.

'That Pole, of course. He is the one, isn't he?'

Could he know? How long had he studied that photograph for, before tearing it into shreds? Not long enough to recall the face, surely? It must just be intuition. She thanked Providence that firstly she was driving and, secondly, that a buffalo should choose that moment to wallow out of the ditch and on to the road. She had to swerve and it gave her a moment's respite.

'Of course not,' she lied firmly, once they were beyond the lumbering beast. 'Don't be so ridiculous, darling.'

Clearly James was not convinced. 'He looked at you as though he knew you,' he grumbled.

'I don't think so.'

'What was the name of your Polish boy friend, anyway?'

Helen said the first name that came into her head, 'Paderewski.'

James raised his eyebrows in disbelief and she went on quickly, before he should comment, 'You can imagine what he had to put up with, with a name like that. Everyone reacted in the same way as you've just done, whenever he tried to reserve a table or anything.'

At last he seemed satisfied and said no more until she changed down to take the hill.

'He seemed pretty familiar with Sally, I thought; actually whispered in her ear when they were introduced, and she went as pink as anything. Funny chap, Philip, he must have seen, but he didn't appear to mind at all.'

'Why should he?'

'Well, I can tell you, if it had been you I'd have been bloody furious.'

Helen sighed. 'You would have had no reason to be. Anyway, as he was RAF, Sally possibly knew him during the war – she was a WAAF, don't forget.'

'Who said he was RAF?'

Oh God, she thought, now I've done it. Aloud she bluffed, 'You did, didn't you? I know someone said he'd been in the RAF.'

Thank God, they were home and there were John and Angela rushing down the steps to meet them.

591

James was soon fussing over the children, who were cross because they had been sent home for supper before the end of the parade. Helen went into the bedroom to remove her hat and have a quick think. When she emerged she stopped to watch as James, his blind side towards her, swung the children in turn between his legs and over his head. Why can't he be like this always, she wished, and put his futile doubts and jealousies away. If I'd ever given him cause. A great wave of fondness swept over her, but it was tinged with fear.

'That's enough; off you go.'

He clapped each child on the behind and straightened up.

'More, Daddy, more, more,' they chanted.

'That's enough, I said. You'll be sick. Off you go.'

He turned to Helen and smiled. 'Whew, I could do with a drink after that.'

She smiled too, but mainly with relief.

'I got a bottle of wine in the last cold storage order,' she said, 'shall we have it with supper?'

'Good idea; I'll go and decant it now.'

Thank God, she thought, that I refused Sally's invitation.

'Do we dress up?' Philip called from the bath.

'Just ties, I think. I shall wear a long skirt. Thank God the food turned up; I want this to be a nice party to-night.'

'Weatherbys coming?'

'No.'

'James, I suppose.' He stood dripping on the bathroom steps. 'He can be a cussed devil all right. I wonder what gets into him?'

Sally finished putting on her lipstick before she said slowly, 'Helen came nearer to-day to discussing him than she ever has before – I rather imagine she has a pretty sticky time. Of course, he's frantically jealous – did you see how he dashed in to prevent Stan from kissing her hand? Still, I think we should be very tolerant of our James – I'm sure that, besides everything else, he has a lot of pain.'

'You're probably right. Nice chap, that Pole. Stroke of luck your knowing him already; he won't be so shy.'

'My dear,' Sally had started brushing her hair, 'you don't know the half of it – he's one of my old boy-friends.'

'Oh, indeed?'

'Indeed! Poor man. I was beastly to him and he was such good fun – kind too. He tried to rape me once.'

'And did he succeed?'

'You know he didn't.' She turned to him, her eyes soft in the lamp-light, 'You were the first – and I'm glad.'

He came over to put his hands on her bare shoulders and kiss the top of her head as they looked at each other in the mirror.

592

'It's a long time ago. Watching you brush your hair just now took me straight back to the night Enrico cut it off. From the pine-woods of Piedmont to the mangroves of Jelang – that sounds rather good, I'm sure one could make something out of it.' He looked at his watch. 'Hurry up, old girl, we're going to be late.'

It was some hours later, long after they had finished the wine, that James rolled over and gently stroked his wife's neck. Outside the rain poured down, but inside they were snug and secret behind their white mesh of fragile security. There is nothing more intimate than a mosquito net, he thought, and pulled Helen towards him.

'I'm terribly glad that Pole isn't the one,' he said softly. 'He's probably a very nice fellow and I've no doubt we shall get on. Thank God he isn't Paderewski though – if he had been, I should have had to request a transfer. Oh Helen, I've been eaten up with jealousy all afternoon – hating him, hating myself – you've no idea what an awful day it's been.'

He buried his face in her neck and Helen stroked his hair some time before replying.

'You never have any reason to be jealous, darling,' she said at last. 'You know that.'

She kissed him and caressed him and drew him to her, but at the same time she was thinking that she must get hold of Stan before he and James met again, to explain the lie of the land.

What an extraordinary day it had been.

Stan lay in bed, listening to the rain, and going over in his mind the events of the past twenty-four hours.

The parade to start with: the colour and provincialism – just exactly as he had imagined it. The women's clothes and the small talk – although, to give them their due, much of that covered deeper subjects. He was a stranger amongst them, an unknown quantity still, not to be admitted without reservations to their inner circles. He'd know them in time. But the quite incredible, the extraordinary coincidence of meeting up with two of his old flames in one day! It was strange, thinking back, that of all the affairs he had had in his lifetime, some casual and some not so casual, the two women involved in the least casual of all should be those he had re-encountered that afternoon. Sally had been part of the most emotional phase of his life; Helen of a more tranquil period, a time when his collapse was over and he had been finding himself. He and Helen had never been in love; completely in accord, but never in love. His feelings for Sally had bordered on hysteria. He felt the thin, slightly-ridged scar on the back of his hand and frowned in the dark as he remembered with shame the degrading culmination of that love. He would never show her the scar. He was

593

grateful to her for her reception – he was sure he had detected genuine pleasure in her greeting and the evening had gone smoothly enough. The only reference that had been made to the past had been when the Malay boy was handing him a dish. As he was helping himself, Sally had remarked, 'Do you remember I once said you had Malay hands, Stan? Now you know what I meant.' It was true. He had looked at his hands, then at those of the man serving him, and his hostess had made a remark to Ja'afar. He had been irritated by the arrogant way in which she had taken it for granted that he would not understand and had retaliated by making a quip himself. Donald had grumbled that he seemed to be the only person who had never caught on to the language, and Sally's husband had made some comment on his murky past and everyone had laughed. He and Mike Harrington had discussed mutual acquaintances in Johore, while Sally questioned the bandmaster on various aspects of the police, and Philip and Don had talked shop for a few minutes, but otherwise the conversation had been general throughout – he would have to catch up on Sally's history another time. She had been seventeen – and only just seventeen at that – what was she now? Twenty-five, twenty-six? She had grown up – and so had he.

But what of Helen? That was odd. Obviously her husband was a jealous type, but surely, behaving as she had, was carrying it too far? He tried to recall the name on the newspaper announcement that had upset her that morning, so long ago, in Bombay – he had not heard anyone use his Christian name. Was this the famous bomber pilot? She hadn't talked about him very much, but he remembered him as James. Oh well, perhaps one day soon she would explain and, until then, he would play it her way and pretend they had never met.

The rain had stopped and, putting his thoughts aside, he stretched out and listened for the first onslaught of the bullfrogs to begin and the high whine of the mosquitoes after rain. He was content. Content to be away from urban life, back to a district where the jungle was nearer, the problems smaller – but greater by comparison – it was like becoming a name again after an age as just a number. Ah, there was the first frog; there should be a chorus soon and it would be cooler after the downpour.

Whilst listening for the amphibian choir to get up steam, he heard another sound, a light scratching on his bedroom door.

He smiled – and Sally would have remembered well the cynical down-turned corners of his mouth. He had no doubt but that it was Salmah. She had been eyeing him ever since his arrival. Not a dish had been handed nor drink poured out without a coquettish glance and giggling withdrawal; playing hard to get. Well, she could go on playing as far as he was concerned, he was not bent on any chasing

594

game. But, of course, if she were to come to him outright, he'd think about it, give it his due consideration.

The scratching continued. He feigned a groan, a 'just woken up' noise.

'Masok,' he called, in his most sleepy voice.

Salmah came in. She carried a small lamp and there was jasmine in her hair. A short sarong was pulled tight across her breasts, ending above the knees.

Stan's eyes opened with interest and appreciation. The soft light showed her flawless, pale-brown skin, the lovely limbs; she held it with good effect to highlight the gleam of her long, black hair.

She stood for a moment, motionless, saying nothing; then she lifted the net and, sitting on the edge of the bed, put out a tentative hand to touch him.

Why not? he thought, and aloud he said, 'Tuck in that net, you're letting the mosquitoes in.'

99. A BUSY DAY FOR THE NEW MO

More than a week had passed since the advent of Stanislaus Olshewski on the Kuala Jelang scene and Helen was growing desperate.

She dared not ring him up, because the telephone exchange listened to all personal conversations and gossip had a nasty habit of reaching the wrong ears.

She thought of confiding in Sally and asking her to speak to Stan, but it seemed too disloyal to James.

What extraordinary twist of fate had brought Stan, of all people, to Kuala Jelang, God alone knew, and He was not being particularly helpful just now.

But in fact it was only a few minutes after these thoughts had been running through her head that she was able to quote the proverb of the ill wind silently to herself.

She had been sitting at the desk, trying hard to write letters, when a high-pitched screech announced the arrival of Ah Ling, the Chinese amah whom they had inherited with the house.

'Look, Mem, look – ' Ah Ling dragged her bleeding son in front of her and thrust him forward at Helen. 'Your dog bite my boy.'

It was useless, with her limited vocabulary in Malay and Ah Ling's English, to go into the subject of provocation, but she had seen the little brat throwing stones at Mollie, their young Alsatian bitch, and on two occasions the dog had yelped and the child had been seen running away. Helen had warned Ah Ling that it would be the sack for her and her husband if she caught them or the child maltreating any animal, but this time it suited her to be merciful.

'All right,' she said, 'I take you by car to hospital – doctor inject.' She made the appropriate mime – muttering, 'And I hope it hurts,' to herself – and the child yelled twice as loudly.

Ah Ling looked smug. 'Your dog him bite.' No doubt there would be a great exaggeration of the incident told to all and sundry when they arrived at the hospital.

'She doesn't bite my children,' Helen retorted. 'Go and get ready; I'll ask Tuan for the car.'

It was a God-sent opportunity. Even if she did not have the chance of seeing Stan, she could pass a message to him. She sat down to write a note.

> Stan,
> Please don't ever let on that we knew each other before. I will try to explain when I can. And please, please, whatever you do, *don't* mention having been in Transport Command.
>
> H.
>
> ps Don't reply.

She rang up James, explained what had happened and waited for the car.

Helen left the boy with his mother in the small dispensary to have his anti-tetanus jab and went in search of Stan.

Seeing the queue of people waiting to see him, she soon gave it up as a bad job, but in answer to her query a dresser told her, 'The doctor is examining a patient now, but I can ask him to see you next.'

'No, don't bother,' she replied, 'but perhaps you would give him this note.'

The dresser took it and she waited until he came out of the office again and, through the open door, saw Stan smile and hold up a hand in acknowledgment.

Her heart felt light with relief. Now that he had been warned it would not matter what James said to him. Really, this jealousy was ridiculous, but she had come to the conclusion that there was little she could do about it other than try to prevent any incidents.

Stan glanced at the note between patients. So he had guessed right, it was a jealous husband. Whatever did she mean about not mentioning Transport Command? Why did women have to be so melodramatic? Still, he had to admit that Helen had been one of the more sensible ones he had known.

His mind was drifting back briefly, but with pleasure, to that happy fourteen days in Bombay, when the nurse announced the next

596

patient. He looked up to see a Malay PC being wheeled in, blood oozing from a sketchily bandaged wound in his chest. Immediately his thoughts returned to the present.

'Emergency, Doctor,' said the nurse, 'he's just been brought in. The OCPD is here; he says it is a gunshot wound.'

'Ask the OCPD to come in.'

Philip strode in, his jungle green shirt filthy with blood and sweat. His hair was matted and there were deep scratches on his face and arms, but he was cheerful. A good man in a fight, Stan thought.

'Hi, Doc,' he said, 'I'm group O if he needs any blood.'

Stan nodded. 'How did it happen?'

'We flushed a camp – cheeky bastards, not more than half a mile from the main road. We killed three – ' his teeth grinned white in his dirty face and Stan thought how long it had been since he too had been able to smile about killing, ' – and none of ours.'

He gripped the Malay's shoulder. 'Tahan, Omar, you'll be all right. You have some of my blood, that'll put strength into you!' He imitated the growl of a lion and Omar managed the glimmer of a smile.

While they were talking, Stan and the nurse had been carefully uncovering the wound.

'How did you get him out?' Stan asked.

'Carried him piggy-back.'

'You deserve the VC.'

'Nonsense. He'd have done the same for me. As a matter of fact, my sergeant-major carried me out like that after Tobruk. I only had to get him to the road anyway – I sent a couple of bods ahead to organise some transport.'

Philip watched in silence for a few minutes, then whispered behind his hand, 'Is he going to be okay?'

'I hope so,' Stan replied. The man's face had turned a deathly grey and he saw that he was not as young as he had first thought. 'I may well need that blood though, will you stand by?' Philip nodded. 'Perhaps you'd like a wash – there's a bathroom through there.'

'Thanks, I would. And I'll use your phone too if I may. Don't want Sally to get some garbled message.'

Sally's not done so badly for herself, Stan thought, as he heard Philip ask the telephone operator for his house.

'Nurse, call the senior dresser, please. We'll do the rest under anaesthetic.' He turned to Omar, whose great spaniel eyes were moving from one face to another. 'We're going to put you to sleep,' he explained, 'we have to dig the bullet out and then perhaps we'll give you some blood – make you strong, like the OCPD says.'

Omar smiled.

Hot and dirty as he was, Philip went straight to his office from the small hospital. There he took a sheet of paper and sat for some time staring into space and fingering the square of plaster on his arm.

He went back over the events of the morning, trying to fix them clearly and accurately in his mind. He could not, with any honesty, go as far as to say that Omar had actually saved his life, but he had shown, quite definitely, that he was no coward.

He always found it difficult to put facts of this type on paper. That's what comes of generations of regular soldiers, he thought ruefully, no good at waffle.

The element of surprise was the most difficult to convey. It had not been a planned raid; none of them had expected to stumble on a bandit camp so near civilisation and, for a split second, as they had entered the clearing and taken in the small thatched huts and knot of men sitting down, cleaning their weapons, no one had moved. They, of course, had had the advantage, because their weapons were already in their hands and ready for firing and they had put their fire-power to good use. But it was Omar who had pushed forward and received the only wounds inflicted by the terrorist sentry.

He had not had Omar under him long enough to put in a confidential report on him, but he would very much like to put him up for promotion – not only because of that morning's work, but because of his conduct generally. If he had had a good report from his previous OCPD it would not have been so bad, but when Philip opened his personal file he was horrified to read that he had been labelled cowardly, lazy, untrustworthy, and unfit for promotion.

The official report was easy enough, but it was Omar who was on Philip's mind. You cannot write 'his previous CO appears to have been lousy at handling men,' even if that is your opinion.

He concocted a short synopsis of the incident but was soon stuck. He was still staring at the sheet of paper when Sally came in.

'Don't you think it's time you came home for a wash and something to eat?' she asked gently. 'It's ages since you left the hospital.'

He looked up at her with gratitude. She had been so much part of every aspect of his life, his work, for so long. He rose from his chair and sat her down in it.

'Here, Sally, have a go at this, will you? I'm flaked.'

She read through what he had written, asked a few questions about the incident and about Omar generally. Then she wrote a couple of concise sentences and ended with, 'when a vacancy exists, I recommend that this constable be considered for promotion.'

He had not mentioned promotion to her, although he knew that she too had a soft spot for Omar.

'You read my mind,' he said. He showed her Omar's file then and added, 'Better seek the CPO's advice in the circumstances, but know-

598

ing the old man's penchant for justice, he should be sympathetic. I think I'll ring him now.'

When Philip had finished speaking, the CPO remained silent for a moment and then said thoughtfully, 'I'm sorry. I hadn't realised you'd been sent another problem child. I don't know this man's case, but I do know the OCPD Alor Hijau – hard and intolerant in many ways, but he's a first-class officer. Got the CPM for gallantry in Pahang. Probably been shot up once too often – people become biased, you know. Anyway, put your chap up, with all the details, and I'll see what I can do.'

If he had sounded only faintly interested and somewhat non-committal to Philip, it was a good act. In fact, old Wales was delighted.

He had taken a chance with Sharif Ahmat and been proved right. That young man's doing well, he thought, it's time I paid him another visit.

Stan thought he had seen his last patient and was preparing to leave his office when the nurse announced that Detective-Sergeant Lee was outside.

He groaned inwardly. 'If it's about that PC, tell him he's all right.'

But the nurse held her ground. 'I've already told him that, sir, but he says he's come on a personal matter.'

Stan groaned again. In his comparatively short experience, he had found out that, when someone sought him out after office hours, it was usually, in the case of a woman, an unwanted pregnancy and, in the case of a man, VD.

'Send him in then.'

He got back into his white coat and began to wash his hands. He was not sure if he had met Sergeant Lee, but he seemed to have had half the police on his hands to-day. He was surprised when the good-looking young man, neatly dressed in civilian clothes, was ushered in.

Chee Min sat on the edge of the indicated chair and smiled shyly. He was not sure how to start.

The doctor looked at him inquiringly. 'Well, Sergeant, what's your trouble?'

Chee Min cleared his throat and straightened his tie, which was already as straight as it could be. Strangely enough, he had not felt half as nervous when he had approached his father.

'I am not coming to you because you are a doctor and I a policeman,' he began, 'but because we are both Catholics.' He paused. 'Please, Doctor, I want your advice.'

Oh God, what is he going to ask? Stan wondered. He looked over Chee Min's shoulder at the blank wall, and in his mind's eye saw the tall, foaming glass of Tiger beer which he had been looking forward to for the past half-hour.

On the spur of the moment, he asked, 'Is it something that must be discussed in the consulting-room, or could we talk about it over a glass of beer?'

He had glanced briefly at his watch; Donald was playing tennis this evening, he would not yet be home.

Chee Min's face relaxed. 'I'd be happy to talk over a beer, sir,' he said.

'Good man. I thought you would with that accent!'

Stan hung up his coat again, told the nurse to lock up, and they both got into his car.

'Ahhh!' Stan smacked his lips as he put down the empty glass. 'Nothing like a cold beer when you're really hot and thirsty. Now, when I get myself a refill, you shall tell me all your troubles.'

He held out a hand, but Chee Min shook his head; he still had more than half a glass left and did not want to become cloudy.

After Stan had heard all about Rose, he counselled, 'Don't be too impatient with your father. You are young. On the other hand, if you are quite sure that she is the girl for you, then I'd go ahead and marry her. But I reserve judgment until I've met the young lady myself – when may I have the pleasure?'

Chee Min noted the time. 'She will just be returning from work – in about half an hour would be a good time.'

'This evening?' Stan had not been quite that enthusiastic. 'Well, why not? Make yourself at home while I have a shower.'

Chee Min listened to the doctor singing while he showered. It sounded sad and in a strange language. It must be awful for him, Chee Min thought, not to have anyone to speak his own language with. In fact, Stan had not spoken a word of Polish for more than a year and would have been surprised to learn the sergeant's thoughts – it did not worry him in the least!

At the main entrance of the squatter settlement the guard came to attention and opened the gate for them to pass.

Chee Min led the way to the Chengs' house. It was the first time Stan had been inside a squatter area and he looked around him with interest. The industry of the Chinese never failed to impress him, and wherever his gaze wandered there was someone, man or woman, hoeing or digging, tending chickens or pigs.

'This is the house, Doctor.'

Stan had almost forgotten the reason for their visit until Chee Min's voice cut into his thoughts. They stopped outside the front door and, in answer to Chee Min's call, Rose came out and Stan noticed how her eyes lit up when she saw who it was.

'Hallo, Vincent,' she greeted him, 'I am glad you have come.'

She looked shyly at Stan and held out her hand, lowering her lids as she did so, and gave a little bow when he was introduced as 'my friend the doctor, who happened to be with me.'

She looked freshly scrubbed and wore a flowered samfoo. Stan liked what he saw. Rose was petite and pretty, but it was not a doll-like prettiness. She had a ready smile and her eyes were lively and intelligent, shining black in a clear, pale skin. Her face, he thought, was unusually strong for her age.

Briefly she introduced her parents, who exchanged polite nods and smiles and retreated into an inner room. Rose dismissed them with a youthfully intolerant, 'They speak neither English nor Malay,' and sat down.

'Vincent has been helping me with my English,' she explained.

'I didn't know that you were called Vincent,' Stan remarked, for want of anything better to say. The visit showed all the signs of becoming sticky.

Chee Min shrugged, 'Sometimes I am called Vincent, sometimes by my Chinese name, Chee Min – it makes no difference, I answer to both.'

Stan listened obediently while Rose read out a passage from *Jane Eyre* and asked for correction of her pronunciation afterwards. Chee Min immediately opened his mouth to speak, but Rose held up her hand, 'No, no. The doctor must correct me,' she said.

'He's not English either,' Chee Min remarked a trifle sulkily, 'but of course he speaks it very well.'

'Thank you,' Stan was amused at the condescension in his tone.

After an hour had passed, Stan said that he must go. It was a genuine excuse; he wanted to see how Omar was getting on. Calling good-bye to the unseen parents and promising to come again, he walked out into the warm night.

'I like your Rose,' he told Chee Min. 'If your father doesn't relent after a month or two, I should marry her anyway – but try and persuade him or your mother to meet her first.'

Chee Min asked to be dropped off at the hospital; picked up his borrowed car and drove back to barracks feeling well pleased with himself.

'Anyone at home?'

'Damn,' Sally muttered, straightening up from the flower-bed where she was working. She wiped her earthy hands on the grass and calling, 'Coming,' walked round to the front of the house.

'Oh, Stan, it's you.' She was both surprised and relieved; glad that it was not anyone with whom making conversation would be an effort. 'Come in; I'll just wash my hands.'

He's aged, she thought, as she brushed her hair and put on some lipstick; there were streaks of grey in his fair hair and the habitual expression of cynicism had left his face.

'I came to see if you and your husband would come and have a drink with me at the club.'

'Philip's off on a five-day patrol,' she told him, 'otherwise we would have loved to.'

'He should not have gone out so soon after giving blood.'

Sally shrugged. 'He's tough; pig-headed too.' In fact, she had tried to persuade him not to go.

'And foolish it seems. A pity he's not here though, I wanted to tell him that that PC he brought in, Omar, is making good progress.'

'Is he? Good. Philip's put him up for corporal; it would be awful if he died now. He was a sergeant-major once – did you know?'

'No. But I thought him a little old to be a PC still – he doesn't appear dim.'

Stan was interested and Sally told him Omar's story.

Afterwards he looked at the sky; it was beginning to get dark. 'Well, Sally, how about you coming to the club?' he suggested.

'All right, I'd like to. Give me half an hour to wash and change.'

An hour soon passed while they caught up on each other's news. So much had happened in the years between. For Sally, her time in Italy, her wedding, the baby, and the years since. For Stan, his transfer to Transport Command, D-Day, and the prison camp, then St Andrews and Kathy. He made no mention of his breakdown, nor of Helen.

When she said it was time she left, he urged her to return with him to supper.

'Do Don good,' he said, 'he's such a morose bird – he'd enjoy the company, honestly he would.'

Donald stood awkwardly as Sally came up the steps. He was still in shorts and a rather sweaty shirt, a towel round his neck.

'I hope you don't mind, Don,' she said, for she too felt awkward, 'Stan insisted that I come. Philip's away.'

It was the first time that she had been inside the Forestry bungalow. Her glance took in a typical bachelor establishment. Nondescript curtains and cushion covers, chairs set squarely round the table, the lot resting on a much-weathered coir mat. Odd calendars were tacked up at random and the table was littered with an untidy mass of magazines.

A curtained screen partitioned the verandah from the dining-room and, before she had even sat down, this was pulled aside and Sally was aware of being inspected from head to foot by a pretty Malay girl. She began to wish she had not come. It was a relief when Stan returned with the drinks.

'Well, if you'll excuse me. . . .' Donald indicated his attire and made to leave.

'Please don't bother on my account.'

'Nonsense,' he looked suddenly brighter and took a gulp of his drink, 'I was just about to change anyway.'

'Do you know,' Sally turned to Stan as soon as Donald had left the room, 'ever since we came to Kuala Jelang, I've been trying to place Don, and it's suddenly come to me where I've seen him before.'

'Another boy-friend?'

'No. It was in Piccadilly on VE-Night. He was very drunk and insisted on having yet another with me. Kept muttering about his wife and someone who had been killed.'

Stan looked thoughtful and unconsciously fingered the note that he had received from Helen, which was still in his trouser pocket.

'I wouldn't mention it unless you're absolutely sure he won't be upset,' he said, 'not everyone leads such straightforward lives as you and Philip, you know.'

Further discussion was cut short by Donald's return. 'Surprise,' he called, and disappeared in the direction of the kitchen.

There were raised voices at the back of the bungalow and a few moments later the Malay girl flounced in and banged down a third plate on the dining-room table – it remained for Donald to add a knife and fork – glared at Sally, pouted at the men and swept out again.

Donald was grinning from ear to ear. 'Don't know if we'll get anything to eat,' he said, 'but we have this to drink.' He held up a bottle of claret and very studiously drew the cork.

'I don't know which one of you she belongs to,' Sally murmured, 'but I do wish you'd tell her that I already have a husband, or she might put arsenic in my soup!'

'Oh, Salmah – don't take any notice of her; she goes with the house. She's always the same when we bring in an unexpected guest. God

603

alone knows why, it only means frying another egg and opening a larger can of baked beans. I must admit she usually glides though, in a sulky sort of way; this is the first time she's banged and crashed so much, but then it's the first time the guest has been a lady. Say, Sal, can you eat baked beans?'

'I went through the war too, you know!'

'So you did.'

Sally smiled at Salmah and thanked her politely as she was served, but received a corn cob in the lap and a bruise on the ear from the water jug for her pains. Both men glowered and Stan jumped up to fetch a sponge for Sally's dress. Salmah snorted and Sally found it hard not to laugh. She was eaten up with curiosity – the girl was so obviously the mistress of one of them, if not both, but she could hardly ask. She was not, however, left in doubt for long. Going through Stan's bedroom to use the bathroom, she almost tripped over a pair of tiny, high-heeled slippers. A gauze scarf was thrown carelessly over the back of a chair and a flowered sarong, neatly folded, reposed on the pillow next to Stan's checked one. Had they been put there deliberately during the meal, she wondered, or had Stan merely made no attempt to remove them?

The two men rose on her return. Sally looked thoughtfully at Stan, who was pouring out the coffee. There was no sign of Salmah.

'Sally has black, I know,' he remarked, and passed her cup with an intimate smile.

But Sally had just seen the slippers and the scarf; she had no intention of being coy. 'I see you use your eyelashes to as good effect as ever,' she remarked dryly.

'*Touché!*'

They both laughed.

'What's going on?' Don shook his head in a fuddled way. 'All this is lost on me.'

'Just getting my own back,' Sally explained. 'Stan caught me on the hop with a most unfair crack when we first met at the parade – I couldn't think up a suitable retort at the time – although I've thought of several since!'

'So you two really did know each other before?' he looked from one to the other. 'I've a good mind to open the other bottle.'

'As a matter of fact, we've met before too,' Sally chirped; it seemed a good thing to mention it after all, 'but it was only just now that I remembered where and when.'

'Go on!'

'Piccadilly on VE-Night. I supported you to a bar, where you proceeded to become even more drunk than you already were – if that were possible! Not that everyone wasn't pretty high.'

'Go on!' Don said again. He peered at her quizzically, then stood up. 'I remember you now – you were in uniform. Only time I was guilty of fratting with the RAF!' A cunning smile touched his face fleetingly and was gone. 'Yeah, I remember you – wasn't as drunk as you thought I was. Stop me if I'm wrong – and Scout's honour I won't blackmail you – but didn't you tell me a rather odd story about getting married in a Swiss mountain village or something?'

'That's right,' Sally grinned, and he looked relieved.

'Well, I'll be darned! I don't remember a word I said to you though.'

'Nor do I,' she lied, 'you were far too incoherent.'

'Was that Philip who was still with the partisans?'

'It was.'

'Judas Priest! I *will* get the second bottle.'

'You see?' Sally laughed happily when Donald was out of earshot, 'it was all right.'

'I've yet to see him in such a good mood,' Stan replied, 'it only needs – ' he was about to say Helen, but checked himself in time, 'Philip, and you'd be able to tie up all your men!'

Plop!

'Ah,' murmured Donald with satisfaction, 'that came out beautifully. Now I shall sit back and drink myself into a stupor and you two can tell me how the air force won the war.'

'But what did you do during the war, Don?' Sally asked.

'Me? What did I do? Well, let me see now. I was trained as a commando, then I went on a super-duper assault course, I was commissioned, I was a mountain warfare expert and a parachutist, but I'm not sure that I actually *did* anything.'

'Oh, don't be so silly,' Sally teased. If she had known him better she would have heard the underlying bitterness in his voice and stopped. As it was, she merely thought he was being modest. Stan heard it, but made no attempt to stop her; he was hoping that Donald might talk. 'You were with the partisans too – you told me so.'

'I was *with* the partisans certainly.' He appeared to have forgotten what she had said before, or at least did not take her up on it. Stan leaned forward with interest.

'And you had both your legs broken – you told me that too.'

Don nodded assent and refilled his glass.

'Where were the breaks?' Stan asked. It looked as though they might be getting somewhere at last. Broken legs were unlikely to be the cause of his mental attitude, but they might be tied up with it. 'Were you injured on impact?'

Don nodded again and, with a guillotine-like motion of his forearm across the thighs, indicated the approximate place. 'I was very well looked after.'

'Bet you had a jolly pretty nurse!'

He looked at Sally and raised his glass. 'Hm. Here's to her.' Then quite suddenly his expression changed. She thought she had never seen such a look of pain in a human face. 'Can we change the subject, please?'

'I'm sorry, Don. I didn't mean to pry.'

' 'S'all right.' He drained his glass, refilled it and drained it again, and was now holding the empty bottle upside down with an expression of disgust. He went to the cupboard, filled his glass with something else, then, sitting down again, began to hum a maudlin dirge.

Sally glanced at Stan who nodded, and they both got up.

'Good night, Don. Thanks for the supper.'

But he did not hear her. He still gazed straight ahead, his eyes glassing hastily, and continued to hum.

'You see how it is?' Stan remarked, as he helped Sally into the car. 'If only he'd talk, get it off his chest. I'm a good listener, I might be able to help him – I helped you once, you know. I cured your nightmares, didn't I?' She nodded in the dark. 'Only through listening, making you talk about them. If only I could do the same for him. Beyond the fact that he's divorced – and I heard that from my dresser – I know nothing about his private life. He said more to-night than he's ever said before. I was hoping you'd go on – either drag it out of him in the way that women do, or make him lose his temper or something.'

'Thanks!'

He smiled ruefully and gave her arm a slight pinch. 'It wouldn't have hurt you and it might have helped Don. He's terribly bitter about the war – perhaps he was passed over for promotion or something, who knows? Perhaps I'll get to the bottom of it if I'm here long enough. Pity he didn't take on Salmah – a woman might make him relax. As it is, he just gets drunk, night after night, and his staff bear the brunt of it next day.'

Sally made no comment and they drove the rest of the way in silence, each busy with their own thoughts.

Stan stopped the car at the police station. 'Hope you don't mind walking up the steps,' he said, 'after that rain I daren't take the top road – might get stuck.'

'Not at all.' She got out and was starting to say good night when he interrupted her.

'I'll come up,' he said, 'see you to the door. I've got a torch somewhere.'

'Will you? Thanks. I'm terrified of snakes.'

They climbed the long, winding path to the house and stood panting a moment by the front door.

'Philip must be fit,' Stan commented as they reached the top step, 'going up and down all these so many times a day.'

'Yes, he is. Good night, Stan. I did enjoy the evening, although I'm sorry old Donald was upset. Despite your psychology, I'd prefer not to be the cause of his breaking down.'

He made no answer to that, but putting his hands lightly on her shoulders asked, 'May I kiss you good night, Sally? Just for old times' sake?'

'We-ell. I suppose so. Oh, all right.' Demurely she held up a cheek.

Stan's hands slid down from her shoulders and his arms encircled her. Then moving her face with his head, his mouth came down on hers, gentle at first, lingering, then searching, forceful and strong. It was no use, she had to respond. He was kissing her as he had first kissed her nearly ten years before and, like then, she clung, her whole body crying out for him.

For a fleeting second, the temptation of the empty house behind them crept into Sally's mind, to be instantly dismissed. She pushed him away.

'You wicked, sinful creature,' she said, as much to herself as to him, 'go away. And never do that again.'

'I shan't,' he said, 'I never meddle with other men's wives – besides, I like your husband. But I had to, once – I had to know. Good night, Sally.'

'Good night.'

She watched his back view, silhouetted against the shifting torch, descend. With breasts taut and her stomach turning somersaults, she saw the light throw back the pale outline of his blond head, cream slacks, and shirt, as he wended his way through the ferns and under the rain trees, but in her mind she saw him again in blue, walking through the beech trees and fields of Devon. I was a fool, she thought, a prude and a fool; I did neither of us any good and now I shall never know what I missed.

Turning, she pushed the ill-fitting door and went into the house.

Strange, she thought, that the servants did not leave a light for me, then seeing the glow under the bedroom door, presumed that they had put one in there instead. She went in, running her hand through the hair that Stan had just run his hands through and stopped in surprise. Philip was lying in bed, reading.

'Darling,' she gasped, 'you gave me a fright. But I'm glad you're home,' and was pleased to realise that she was. 'But how come?'

'One of the boys went sick – malaria, I think – and sending a couple of men back with him would have left the patrol too short. So we all came back. I had covered the area I most wanted to anyway. Where were you?'

She told him. 'But I rang Ja'afar from the club; he never told me that you were home. Have you had anything to eat?'

'The servants had already gone to bed when I came in, so I had some mee with the boys in the canteen.'

'Good.'

He had already put his book down when she came out of the bathroom, but Sally was not deceived. She lowered the light and crawled under the net and into his arms.

'Love me, Philip,' she demanded, 'love me hard.'

Was it imagination or did she detect a glint of amusement in his eyes?

'Of course, my darling, always ready to oblige! But why so earnest?'

For answer she lowered her mouth hard on his. You do not tell your husband when another man's kiss has set you on fire – you let him reap the benefit.

She leaned across him and turned the lamp right out.

As soon as he was clear of the town, Stan stopped the car and lit a cigarette.

He had not meant to kiss Sally like that. He had only intended it to be a friendly peck; but then he could not resist it. The spark was still there all right, in both of them, and it would not take much to ignite it. He looked up at the starlit sky, listening to the frogs croaking in the swamp and the chorus of cicadas in the trees that lined the road, mixing the present with the past. She had not changed much. A little older, perhaps, a little wiser – she should be – but physically much the same.

He sat for a long time, recalling the summer of 1942. Sally singing, Sally crawling under the wire, Sally with headset and plotting-rod, Sally in the punt. He smiled.

A passing car brought him back to the present with a jolt. He looked at his watch. Good God, it was after midnight and there would be the usual stream of patients to cope with from crack of dawn onwards. Well, I've achieved my ambition, he thought with satisfaction, it's the life I wanted. He lit another cigarette and started the engine.

His room was dark, but he knew that Salmah was there.

'Off you go,' he said, 'I'm not in the mood.'

He heard her stir, but there was no reply. Possessive women were something he could not stand, and in these circumstances he was not prepared to put up with it.

'I know you're jealous,' he sighed, 'but you are also stupid, and if you ever behave again as you did this evening, you will have to go. Tuan Thom has no interest in you and we can always find another cook.' Silence. 'Mem Morrison is an old friend of mine and you insulted her. It will serve you right if she complains about you to her husband, the OCPD.'

She was silent as a cat, but he heard the floorboards creak once and a slit of lighter grey appeared as she disappeared through the bathroom door.

He undressed and lay down, noting with irritation the hot patch that she had left. What a bore to have a woman always sharing your bed; thank God he had never married, he thought.

101. FROM EAST TO WEST

The tenth and final stream joins the river

Abdul Karim

It was near the end of 1950 before I returned home again, and then I was there for a long stay.

After completing my training as a driver, I was posted to Batu Tukul, a station in Johore, and had my first real taste of the Emergency.

It was so bad there that the bandits had even captured one of the stations in our area and held it for several hours. Wah! There were a lot of police killed and I was glad I was a driver and not with a jungle company – not that I was all that safe, as you will see.

I had been taught to drive several different types of vehicle at the Depot, but the whole time I was at Batu Tukul I drove only a jeep. It was quite exciting – better than the war, because then I had been too young and now I can only remember feeling hungry. When the OCPD asked me if I was frightened one day and I said no, he laughed and said that was because I was excited, which was a good thing.

Most of the roads round us were 'red' roads – that meant that there must always be at least two vehicles – and the day I caught it, the second one had broken down and we had just been back to fetch the fifteen-hundredweight to tow it in.

It was on the return journey and, going round a bend that we'd already passed twice that day, that we were ambushed.

'Put your foot down, Karim,' the OCPD, who was sitting beside me, ordered, as he opened up with his carbine and the two PCs in the back with their stens.

As I did so there was a ghastly scream and a body came hurtling down the bank.

'That's one bastard less,' remarked the OCPD, 'get the one that's running, Zainal.' Another burst from behind me and a satisfied, 'Good shooting, man,' as the OCPD fired again himself, told me that Zainal had found his mark.

I don't know how many there were but, just as I thought we were out of it and on to the straight and I was changing back into top, the sound of automatic fire spurted from all around us – or so it seemed – and I skidded furiously into the ditch.

'Christ, they've got the tyres. Out and run, all of you.'

There was no need to repeat that order. We were out in a flash and running towards the shelter of a pile of timber stacked, waiting for collection, on the side of the road. I shouted as I saw a figure leap to the top of the bank with raised arm.

The next moment the grenade hurtled through the air and I felt the most agonising, burning pain along my right side.

'I've been hit,' I yelled. And yelled again as one of the other PCs flung himself on top of me.

'Try and be quiet; I think they've gone.'

We waited in absolute silence for what seemed an eternity, then the OCPD took off his hat and stuck it on the end of his carbine. 'We'll try the age-old trick,' he said, and raised the hat slowly to the top of the wood pile.

Nothing happened and he motioned Zainal to do the same a little farther along.

All was quiet, and after a short while the OCPD got up and came over to me.

'Now, young Karim, we'd better see how much lead you've stopped.' He began to move me and, hard though I tried not to, I yelled again. 'Good God, it's not a bullet at all; you're impaled.'

The blast from the grenade must have flung me against the pile of logs and a protruding splinter had passed right through the flesh between hip-bone and rib cage.

I looked down at the jagged wood emerging from my shirt and the OCPD drew a penknife from his pocket and began cutting the cloth away. By this time my companions were all standing over me and discussing what to do. I felt sick.

'My God, you've been bloody lucky. If only we can get you off it. Grit your teeth and we'll try.'

I did grit my teeth, but the pain was awful. Searing, white-hot, I'd never known such pain.

'Stop, Tuan,' I begged, 'I can't stand it.'

They stood back and the OCPD said, 'The only thing to do is to cut the wood from behind and get you to hospital as you are. It'll be hell, but not as bad as trying to extract it.'

There was an axe in the jeep and Zainal set to work, but the wood was several inches thick at the point where he would have to cut and he was unlikely to manage it in one blow. I shut my eyes and clenched my fists and waited for the worst.

He did it though. The OCPD and Ramli held me as Zainal took one terrific swipe, and the next thing I knew I was being held by four men and we were in the back of the fifteen hundredweight.

'He's come to, Tuan.'

Through a haze of pain, I saw the OCPD turn round from the front seat.

'Thank God for that. You'll soon be home, Karim.'

We had had more than our share of luck it seemed. Two terrorists killed and no casualties ourselves, bar me. Both the broken down vehicle and the fifteen hundredweight coming up behind had heard the shooting and the latter had sped to our aid.

It was not long before we drew up at the hospital and the Indian dresser was pushing up my sleeve.

A prick, and heavenly oblivion.

That explains why I was at home for a long stay. The splinter had not done any vital damage, but it had earned me some sick leave.

My father had written while I was in hospital and asked if they should arrange my wedding for my next leave and I had replied 'Yes.' It was all right living in the bachelor barracks and eating in the canteen, but I missed my family, and it would be a better life having Rokiah with me.

The preparations for the wedding appeared to have been going on for some weeks before I arrived home. Carpenters were busy in Che Fatimah's house, putting up partitions to provide a separate bedroom and extending the verandah to accommodate the many guests.

It was always the same couple of carpenters who did this job and they knew exactly how much space to leave for the ceremonial bed that went the rounds from one house to another – we usually sleep on mats, which are rolled away during the day-time, but of course this was a special occasion and no wedding would have been complete without the presence of the well-known bed.

I was supposed not to see Rokiah during this time, but we didn't take too much notice of these formalities. She was excited at the thought of leaving the kampong and pestered me for hours on end with questions about station life and what it would be like where we were going. Of course I couldn't tell her, because I had no idea where we would be posted when my leave was up.

The day came when we sat to have our nails hennaed, the contract was signed, and only those parts of the ceremony to be witnessed by the guests remained.

I had been carried to Che Fatimah's house on the shoulders of my bachelor friends and now Rokiah, my bride, and I were seated in state for the long and exhausting bersanding ceremony – the dais and ornate chairs were passed from house to house too, by the way.

I had only had a fleeting glimpse of Rokiah before we were led to our thrones, but I would not have known who it was under so much finery. She was dressed from head to toe in heavy, stiff, purple cloth, interwoven with gold and silver thread, and carried a head-dress of gold filigree, jewels and flowers. Her hands, with their stained finger-tips, were hidden under a wealth of rings and bangles, and ears and throat were similarly adorned.

Poor Rokiah. I could not look at her, not even out of the corner of my eye, but I knew she must be wilting. The heat, made worse by the heavy curtains behind, above and to our sides, was suffocating.

When we had discussed adat, our customs, at the Depot, one of the other drivers had once called our marriage ceremony barbarous and I had disagreed with him. After all, there were no difficult rites to perform, no tests of endurance, as I believe they have in some countries. But now I was not so sure. Sitting absolutely motionless for hour upon hour, spread fingers on knees and eyes staring straight ahead, was bad enough for the groom, but for the bride, under her weighty head-dress – no wonder they sometimes fainted and had to be carried out. In the more emancipated communities, the bersanding was being cut to a mere token half-hour or so, but we were still old-fashioned in Pasir Perak and must sit while the wedding guests assembled, chatted, stared at us and tried to make us smile, and then sat down to eat a long and leisurely feast. This could last for hours and usually did.

It seemed an eternity before the guests were being handed the coloured eggs and paper flowers, symbols of fertility, and we were being escorted to our marriage bed.

The bed was decked throughout with yellow silk – colour of royalty – and yellow hangings covered the rough wooden partitions and yellow curtains screened the only window.

I looked at Rokiah, shorn now of her heavy outer garments, as she sat, dazed, on the edge of the bed. Her hair was wet through with perspiration and her skin under its tan was pale with fatigue. Outside, the guests laughed and joked and my bachelor friends shook their tambourines and made ribald jests. How many marriages were consummated on the first night, I wondered, under these conditions?

I loosened Rokiah's tightly coiled hair, then taking her hand, I pushed her gently back on to the yellow pillows and lay down beside her, waiting for the din to cease.

We remained at the house of Che Fatimah until my leave was up, and then I made my way to the district headquarters for a medical check and to find out where I was to be posted.

'Kuala Jelang,' I told Rokiah when I got back. 'The sergeant showed me on the map; it's on the west coast, almost exactly opposite us here.' I showed her the steamer tickets I had been issued with for the journey and her eyes lit up, for Rokiah loves the sea. We felt sad at leaving Che Fatimah, alone now but for her younger sister, but once we were on board it was difficult to remain downhearted for long.

A stiff breeze made the waves race and the small ship rocked as we headed for the open sea. We were travelling 'deck' and everywhere there were huddles of moaning, seasick men and women, spread out on their sleeping-mats and groaning as though their last moments had come.

Not so Rokiah. She stood, laughing into the wind, at the ship's side, her hair coming adrift and clothes whipping against her. She hardly stopped to eat or sleep during the ten days it took us to reach our destination. Dashing ashore the minute the vessel tied up in each port and when at sea plaguing the sailors with endless questions, to say nothing of wanting to dive overboard for a swim each time the ship slowed down. Everything was new, everything exciting. The state capital had impressed her, for she had never been farther than our own district headquarters since she was a baby, but Singapore reduced her to awe-inspired silence.

This was the old Rokiah, the best friend of my childhood, and my heart rejoiced that Fate had been kind and given her to me for my wife.

Kuala Jelang was quite a large station, District Headquarters, with a European OCPD, two Malay inspectors and a Sikh sergeant-major. There were also several European police lieutenants and numerous other NCOs it seemed, but I was told that I need only worry about those four.

Rokiah became modest and shy again in the presence of so many older married couples and was wont to hide her hands, from which the stain had not yet worn off, whenever she could. I did not have time to worry about these things, because I had to concentrate on learning to drive an unfamiliar vehicle, five tons of it. But I knew that she was homesick. She longed for a beach, she said, on which she could walk and swim and get away on her own – she was unused to barrack life.

We were on the coast, but it was all mangrove swamp and river mud. Quite different from the beautiful beaches and fast-running surf to which we were accustomed. But soon there was a different kind of sickness for her to think about, because, although I didn't know it at the time, Rokiah was already carrying our first child.

BOOK III

IN WHICH THE RIVER FLOWS
DOWN TO THE SEA

Kuala Jelang

'So you're the new driver?' It was a statement rather than a question, but Philip had to say something to the young man standing rigidly before him.

'Tuan.'

'Have you driven a GMT before?'

'Not since I left the Depot, Tuan.'

'It hasn't arrived yet, but it should be here within the week. Perhaps the driver who brings it down can take you out in it a few times to get your hand in.'

'Tuan.'

It would be a change driving a vehicle so much larger than a jeep, Karim thought, and went to report to the MT corporal.

Philip watched Karim's retreating back and thought how things had both improved and deteriorated since his own arrival in the district, fourteen months before. On his personal credit side, his Malay was now pretty fluent and he had already passed the first of the prescribed exams; as far as the station was concerned, they were up to strength bar one inspector, they had the army to call upon – and they never had to call the Gurkhas twice – and now, at last, they were to have an armoured vehicle.

It was the thought of the GMT that brought his thoughts back to the debit side of the page. Seventeen PCs killed – all but three of them in ambushes – and one police lieutenant, the rough-mouthed Moriarty.

Moriarty's death had been a useless tragedy and one that might have been avoided. Suspecting that there were bandits on his estate one night, he had gone out, on his own, to investigate. Why the bloody hell didn't he take some SCs, Philip thought with irritation, certainly not for the first time, or call on us for help. But no, he had to go it alone. And gone he had, with a magazine full in the stomach. Philip had only just dispatched the small parcel containing his George Medal to his mother in Ireland. He was too honest to pretend, even to himself, that he had ever liked the man, but nevertheless, what a bloody waste.

He was still musing on this theme, while he opened the mail, when he heard a car arrive and the guard presenting arms. Oh God, he thought, the CPO's arrived. He grabbed his cap and was at the main entrance by the time the senior officer alighted from his staff car.

'Well, Philip, how goes it? I haven't been down here for months.'

'All right, thank you, sir.'

Grandpa Wales settled into the proffered chair and for the first time Philip thought he looked not only old, but sick.

The Emergency was telling on everyone. Work, work, and more work. Dashing out at a moment's notice, eating and sleeping when one could, always on the alert, never being able to relax. Their social life consisted of dinner-parties in each others' houses and an occasional film at the club, but there was little real relaxation. When the planters and their wives came in they enjoyed themselves, but there was always the thought of the journey home along dark, narrow, lonely roads, eyes glued to the headlamps' beams, hand on the door handle or a gun. Never being able to move in freedom, always escorted. It had become second nature to appreciate the potential hazards of every inch of the road ahead – to such an extent that one planter, on leave, had accelerated and shouted 'Ambush' coming out of Tunbridge Wells! They joked about it, but the menace was always there. For Philip, such dinner dates were an added strain; he fretted if he was away from the station for long and Sally complained that they were always interrupted anyway. She had been stranded on so many estates when he had been called out during the evening, that she had taken to keeping an overnight bag in the car.

'Time you had some local leave, Philip.'

Philip raised his tired eyes to the tired old face before him and smiled. 'I imagine the same goes for you, sir.'

There was no hope of leave and both knew it.

'Let's have your problems then. First?'

'Still the squatters. Pasir Hitam's more or less under control; at least they're guarded and wired in. But we're no further ahead with resettling the Ulu Pandanus crowd and that's where the real trouble lies.'

In fact, Wotherspoon's land had been accepted for the resettlement scheme and plans for wiring and building had been drawn up, but, when members of the Resettlement Committee had come down from Berembang, and James and Philip had thought everything fixed, they had been told there would not be a Resettlement Officer available for another six months. It was frustrating, but only one of the thorns in the police flesh.

The biggest thorn was Wotherspoon himself. He did everything he could to sabotage the police, never dealing with either Philip or the OCPS direct, nor even the CPO, but sneaking up to Kuala Lumpur and going through the back door at HQ level. And when it came to accusations, the planters massed behind him in a solid block. Detestable old man, Philip thought, and yet he felt sorry for him as well. He suspected the other planters – most of whom he got on pretty well with – did not care for him either but, as in most professions, they were not prepared to brook criticism of one of their kind from an outsider.

While the CPO was talking, Philip glanced at the slip of paper, the priorities listed by King, which still remained under a paper weight on his desk. Squatters were still a problem. The timber *kongsis* had been regrouped – he could have become a rich man on the bribes offered by the *towkays* to leave them alone – and poor Donald Thom was confined to his nurseries and the forest edge. The estate defences were under control; some planters co-operating wholeheartedly, and others, like Wotherspoon, a permanent pill. He smiled at the last item on the list, army – lack of, and crossed off the last two words.

'Now for my good news.' Philip looked up at the change of voice. 'I'm sending you another police lieutenant, besides the replacement for Moriarty. A rather staid, elderly type, a bit old for jungle-bashing – you can use him as your assistant if you like.'

'Empire-building, sir?'

'Not really. I shouldn't think you've had much time off during this past year, have you?'

Philip thought. He could not remember when he had last had a day off. His home had become a place where he could dash in for a quick snack and occasionally sleep, Sally his anchorage. It was true that his operational burden had been eased considerably since the arrival of the Gurkhas and Ahmat had become his right-hand man, but a little extra help would not come amiss. He replied, 'No, I haven't. Thank you, sir.'

It was only when they were in the CPO's car, on their way up to the house for lunch, that the older man asked, 'Now what's all this I hear about some Tamil intimidating your wife?'

Now how in Hades could the old man know about that? Jogindar Singh, of course. How strong are wartime ties, Philip reflected, not for the first time. However well he might get to know his OCPS, there would never be the affinity that existed between the sergeant-major and the CPO.

'I wanted to investigate it, but Sally wasn't keen. Still, I did get Lee to make a few inquiries. He'd been one of the district office clerks.'

'Her father was on the Indian Immigration Committee many years ago, you know, the body responsible for bringing the first Tamil and Telegu labour to this country. It could be something to do with that. The originals were untouchables who found a far better life here than in India, but now it's the fashion to decry the previous generation and so many of their children are spouting a lot of nonsense about freedom and chains. It's a pity, because on the whole the Tamils are such a good crowd.'

'She thought it must be something like that. We were going to call him in for questioning, but he seems to have disappeared. Left the district, I hope.'

As far as the rest of the district was concerned, life went on. Emergency or not, personal problems, passions, worries and hates could not be placed in any 'pending' file. Some were busy, some bored, but on all the lives of others impinged.

For James, the Emergency was one long slog and if he did not have the operational commitments of Philip and the police, he was equally overworked, hampered and frustrated on the administrative side.

The Weatherbys took little part in any but duty social functions. Helen would have liked to have had more contact with the outside world and was quite prepared to entertain, but James remained aloof and became so blunt that she was always afraid of what he might say. Only the Morrisons remained real friends, and James actually sought their company.

'Go and ask Sally if she has enough for four,' he would say, 'and we'll provide the booze.' Or, 'What about seeing if Sally and Philip can come and have pot luck to-night?'

'If I were the jealous member of the family, you know I'd be seriously worried about you!' Helen remarked to her friend on one of these occasions.

And indeed Sally did seem to possess the ability to draw James out and make him laugh.

'Thank God I never had to serve under you,' she would often say to him, 'you must have been an absolute bastard!'

James would grin. 'I was – particularly to the WAAF!'

On rare occasions Stan would join them, but then James shut up like the proverbial clam, a surly one at that, and Sally took to inviting him only when the Weatherbys were not going to be present.

Donald had gone on leave and, with the intention that he should return to the same station, had not been replaced. Stan now had the bungalow to himself and Mike Harrington had moved his belongings from the Morrisons' house to his.

Stan had reverted to the habits of his happy days in Johore. He worked hard and spent his evenings studying, reading or occasionally going down to the club. Having mastered Malay, he was now intent on Hakka and enjoyed trying it out whenever he could. The Chinese laughed at him, but they had taken him to their hearts.

Jogindar Singh stood like the rock of Gibraltar, with the tides of the Emergency and police comings and goings washing around him. His wife was pregnant again and he had begun to seek solace elsewhere.

There were one or two young bachelor PCs on whom Jogindar had his eye, but the one who attracted him most was the new driver of the

GMT. Karim had fallen into the sergeant-major's web by borrowing money from him shortly after his arrival and Jogindar had intimated that there were other ways to pay his debts. But Karim was terrified and had shied away so violently that Jogindar had laid off, laughing into his beard and increasing the rate of interest at the same time.

Karim had now completely mastered the idiosyncrasies of the GMT and even Philip, who normally had very little good to say for the average police driver, admitted grudgingly that he was pretty good.

The vehicle had arrived one morning, lumbering down the road like some gigantic, prehistoric monster, and all the townsfolk had turned out to stare. And not only the town. Sally had watched from the verandah with Ja'afar, who could say nothing but 'Wah!'

Every off-duty man had followed the OCPD out of the police station to view the monster, and Karim had been the first after Philip to go inside. The driver from Contingent Headquarters had spent half a day refreshing his memory, turning this way and that, going uphill and down. It had been pleasant to be the focal point of attention and he had smiled proudly at Rokiah, standing outside their barrack-room, watching him.

Rokiah too had settled down to barrack life and, if she still had thoughts of home, she kept them to herself.

Omar had mended well. He followed Philip around with soft, adoring, spaniel eyes, and fingered the scar on his chest and his corporal's chevrons with more pride than he had ever fingered his sergeant-major's crown.

He had been accepted. No one asked him for an explanation of his actions in Singapore – if indeed they were interested – no one shunned him.

Jogindar Singh, despite their difference in present rank, began to treat him as an equal and it was not long before Omar mentioned something that had long been on his mind.

'It is indeed strange, Dato, that I should serve under you in the same rank as I served under your father when he was a sergeant-major.' Jogindar looked perplexed. 'Yes, Dato. You would not remember me, and I would not recognise you now, but I was there that day when your father was executed. I saw you walk out to face the Japanese officer. It was a brave act; one that I never could have performed.'

'You were stationed at Mering?' Jogindar asked.

They soon knew each other's histories well and the young Sikh and the elderly Malay not only treated each other with a new respect in their jobs, but became off-duty friends.

Jogindar did not, in fact, look young. Many in the police station would have been amazed if they had known his true age. With his full figure and strong beard, he looked well beyond his years. Only Omar had known him as a boy of nineteen.

Had he but known it, Omar had done some good. Sally, who had pined for so long, had ceased to fret. Omar's sad story had touched her so much that she had felt ashamed of herself and turned her energy to helping other people's babies instead.

A clinic for police families had recently been opened and here, once a week, Sally, with the help of a young nurse on loan from the hospital and occasionally Stan himself, reigned supreme. It was not long before Philip declared that she knew far more about the goings-on amongst the rank and file than he did himself. Sally just smiled, but she knew it was true. Many of the men, as well as their wives, finding her a sympathetic listener, and hoping that what they said would get back to her husband, poured out their problems to her. What they did not know was that she sifted everything that she heard very carefully and only passed on those items which she thought Philip ought to hear.

Ramakrishnan had disappeared. Sally was glad, but both Jogindar and Chee Min were piqued; the former because he felt he had lost face and the latter because he had been thwarted. It was only after the last incident on the padang, which had been witnessed by the OCPD, that he had felt able to come into the open and take some action, but it seemed that Krishnan had done him out of it. And for Chee Min there were other matters weighing on his mind.

Rose had consented to become his wife and now, without the help of his family, he had to arrange everything himself.

It was a pity that he and the Malay inspector had never become friends, for Ahmat too had marriage very much upon his mind and they had far more in common than they knew.

103. AHMAT TAKES A WIFE

Ahmat's wedding was indeed the ordeal he had prophesied.

It was a back-to-front wedding in every sense. Che Puan Sharifa was acting as the bride's mother instead of the bridegroom's, which would have been less incongruous had she already known her future daughter-in-law, and had she approved.

Not that everything was not absolutely correct. Far be it from Ahmat's mother to upset custom by one jot. When Azizah arrived, she treated her with the utmost courtesy and even the chill could be put down to her immense dignity.

Poor Azizah. Ahmat's heart went out to his sophisticated, urban

621

bride when she alighted from the station taxi and was led to his mother's house. She could not have looked more out of place in this rural setting, swaying across the grass in her tight sarong and high-heeled shoes, the sunlight shining down on her lustrous hair. The girls of Daun Chempaka covered their heads when they went out, or at least wore a token selendang thrown casually across their shoulders, but Azizah's head was bare.

Ahmat was too far away to see his mother's expression, but he could imagine it – there would be no expression at all, just a porcelain glaze. But he was not too far away to see that Azizah wore more make-up than usual. He winced. Was she doing it in deliberate defiance of his mother? he wondered.

Uncle Jalil, who stood with him at the entrance to the coffee-shop, barely suppressed a whistle.

'I don't blame you, boy, for not being interested in your cousin Maimounah when that one was around! She's a silly girl anyway,' he dismissed his daughter with a wave of the hand, 'nearly drove me mad, giggling all the time.'

Maimounah had since married; honour was saved and his uncle could afford to be magnanimous, but Ahmat was nonetheless grateful for the easy way in which he had accepted facts.

All the regalia, which had not been used since the wedding of his elder sister a year before the war, had been brought out. Puan Sharifa would not have it said that she considered Azizah second-rate and no trouble was spared.

Ahmat could not criticise his mother, but he was still smarting from her final action the night before.

When their meal was over, she had brought out her jewellery box and laid each item carefully on the table, making two piles. One she had said would be for Ahmat's sisters, in due course; the other would be for his bride, now.

'She will have trumpery stuff no doubt,' she said, 'but only real jewels are worn in this family. I shall instruct her properly before the ceremonies begin.'

Ahmat had thanked her and watched as each item was carefully put away and the lid of the box closed.

Then his mother had put her hands up to her own ears, where the gold filigree pendants had hung for as long as he could remember. 'Nah!' she said, pulling them off and laying them before him on the table. 'She's having you, all I have, she'd better have these as well. And these.' She pulled the rings from her fingers and unfastened a brooch from her kebaya. 'Nah! Take them!'

Ahmat had protested. He could not bear to see the empty holes in his mother's ears, and the kebaya gaping open to show her withered breasts.

'Take them,' she said again and left the room, returning a minute later with her kebaya held together by a large safety pin.

It was the final humiliation.

Somehow Ahmat survived the ceremonies, hardly aware of the girl at his side.

He was relieved to see his mother appearing dressed in her finery and wearing jewellery which he recognised as coming from his sisters' share. He should have known better. Whatever faults she might have, the last thing Puan Sharifa would have done would have been to cause a scene.

He did not speak to Azizah until it was all over and they were aboard the northbound train. He had pleaded the Emergency as an excuse to leave immediately after the bersanding, saying that he had to be on duty the following day.

This was true. He had fixed it before leaving Kuala Jelang. He had gone through what had to be gone through, but he could not have stood the ceremonial putting to bed. Not with his mother looking on.

Thank God for the CTs, he thought, as he stretched out on his sleeper bunk, fully dressed.

In the bunk below Azizah lay, wide-eyed and far from sleep. She was grateful to Mat for sparing her the last ordeal, but she knew already that she was going to miss her urban surroundings.

They arrived at Kuala Lumpur in the early morning, quickly collected her belongings from the left luggage office, where she had deposited them a week before, and boarded the next train north.

They spent that night in Kemuning Rest House, unable to share a room owing to the number of guests. Ahmat was not sorry; he looked forward to spending the first night with his wife under their own roof.

At the police station a tea party had been laid on for them, he knew, to welcome him back with his bride. The OCPD's wife had defied Malay custom and refused to attend herself unless Azizah was there as well.

'I will not come to a party, the only woman among all you men, if the guest of honour can't be there. Really, some of these kampong traditions are too archaic for words – this is 1951,' she had said, and Ahmat realised that his mother was not the only woman who could dig her heels in.

And so it had been arranged. Secretly, he was grateful to Sally, although he had pretended to glower at the time. He told Azizah while they were on the last lap of their journey by bus.

Tables had been laid out on the police station padang and Philip and Sally went forward to meet the bridal pair.

It was all rather embarrassing, Ahmat thought, but he enjoyed the admiring looks that were being bestowed upon his wife. A momentary shaft of passion shot through him, as he looked at the sweet cakes and orange crush, at the thought that she was his; the givers of the glances could but admire from a distance, she was his to possess.

'Better put you two women together,' Philip had said, while they were waiting for the newly-weds to arrive. 'We can't impose our customs too much.'

Sally did her best to draw Azizah into conversation, but it was hard going and very much a case of question and answer, the latter usually monosyllabic. She was grateful for the presence of Chee Min on her other side.

'Your turn next,' she said. 'When is it to be?'

'Next month. I have to wait until I'm twenty-one.'

'Gosh!' Sally exclaimed, 'so young and thinking of getting married already. Heavens!'

She, in fact, had been only nineteen and Philip twenty-three when they were married, but one tends to forget these things.

'Will you come to the wedding, Ma'am?'

'Of course. Where will it be?'

'At Kemuning, I think – that's the nearest church – but I haven't spoken to the priest yet.'

'Of course we'd love to come – now that my husband has an assistant, I can afford to make these promises, unless something drastic happens. Let us know if there's anything we can do to help.'

At that moment Philip stood up and a great banging of spoons against teacups brought everyone's attention to him.

How his Malay has improved, Sally thought, as she listened to his speech. I would never have thought it possible a year ago.

The tea-party over, Ahmat led Azizah to their house.

He looked happily at it as the new paint caught the last rays of the setting sun and the crimson hibiscus flamed.

The house was raised some four feet from the ground. They climbed the steps and kicked off their shoes at the top. Azizah was already across the narrow verandah and about to enter the front door when Ahmat called to her to stop.

'Azizah, wait.' He looked around quickly, but they appeared to be unobserved. He picked her up. 'This is a Western custom; it's supposed to bring good luck.'

Once across the threshold he put her down, but held her close.

'There will be many Western customs for us, Azizah,' he said. 'I do not want you only as a piece of furniture, to cook my meals and bear my children. I want you to be my companion in all things, wholly my wife.'

She said nothing, but released herself and looked around.

'Wait,' Mat said again.

The light was fading, but he had already placed matches beside the lamp. He drew the curtains and lit up. Immediately the room sprang to life. He grinned at her triumphantly; this scene had been rehearsed several times, but without the principal actress.

'How do you like it?' he asked.

It was on the tip of his tongue to tell her that Sally had helped him choose the curtains and cushion covers, but he thought better of it. In fact, he had already painted the house when he had plucked up courage to ask her advice in decorating it. They had been shopping together and then he had had the material made up. It had been fun and all the time he had had this moment in mind.

'Not bad,' she said, 'a bit dull.'

Then she burst into tears.

No one could know what mixed emotions were going through Azizah's head.

An orphan, who could hardly remember her mother and had never even known who her father was, she had never known any home except the room in the Malay Reserve of Kuala Lumpur where she and two other dancers had lodged.

Suddenly she had been parted from all that was familiar; thrown into a kind of life of which she knew nothing. She had had to put up with the icy courtesy of a mother-in-law by whom she knew she was despised; been the focus of attention amongst a crowd of strangers, and now she was alone with this man.

At that moment she would have given anything to be waiting on stage at the Bintang Kilat amusement park.

And yet she was being given a home – something she had never had before. She was wanted, loved, respected, and all by this man whom she thought she had known, but now seemed as strange as the rest.

It was all too much for her.

She sobbed and sobbed, leaving poor Ahmat quite nonplussed, trying to calm her down. A light was weaving across the compound in the direction of the house; unless he succeeded, he was in for an embarrassing few minutes.

'Don't cry any more, Azizah, please,' he begged, looking over her shoulder and through the open door, 'a boy from the canteen will be here in a moment.'

At last she stopped and wiped her eyes. 'I'm sorry, Mat,' she said, 'it's just – '

'I know,' he interrupted. If the wedding had been an ordeal for him, what must it have been for her?

He led her into the tiny kitchen and lit another lamp.

'I haven't bought any pots and pans yet; I thought you'd rather choose your own, so I ordered a meal to be sent over for us from the canteen to-night.'

He rejoiced in her look of pleasure as she fingered a rose-patterned cup.

'These are pretty.' She took down one plate after another and looked at each in turn. 'Did you buy these for me?'

His heart gave a great leap and he would have put his arms round her again if he had not heard the boy at the door. The china too was Sally's choice, but no need to tell Azizah that. She was smiling up at him with her large, adoring eyes, and he would have bought the world for her had he been able to.

'Masok,' he called to the timid knock and watched the boy lay the contents of his tray on the table. He must tip the canteen cook to-morrow, he thought, he had done well.

As soon as the boy had gone, Ahmat pulled a chair out for his wife as he had seen European men do.

'Come,' he said, 'sit down. I'm famished.'

They ate in silence for a while.

'We may have to follow our own customs in public,' he said at length, 'but when we're alone we'll be on equal terms. No waiting on me, you understand? We eat together.'

Azizah only smiled. She was overwhelmed and had not realised until she began to eat how hungry she was.

'You know, Azizah, there are many Western customs for which I do not care; many that to us seem coarse and ill-bred, but there are also many that I admire. I have often been up in the OCPD's house and there the Mem is so free and easy – she is her husband's equal in every way, and yet he still treats her with the courtesy that she deserves. We will be like that when we are on our own. By the way, what did you think of the Mem?'

'All right.'

'You didn't say much to her.'

'I have never spoken to a European woman before.'

Perhaps it was the first warning of the great gulf between them, but Mat paid it no heed, only thinking that she still had much to learn and that he would be her teacher.

He stretched and yawned. The OCPD had said he would not be expected on duty for another couple of days, for which he was thankful. To-morrow they would buy those items still lacking in the house – but that was to-morrow.

'Azizah,' he asked, 'shall we go to bed?'

'What did you think of her?' Philip asked.

'She's the most beautiful thing I've ever seen; I only hope she isn't as dumb as she appears though.'

626

'Perhaps she was only shy.'

'I hope so. I'm so fond of Mat, I'd hate to see him hurt.'

'Me too. Oh well, they should be well away by now. I hope he finds he's the first.' And so saying, Philip lifted his glass, mentally wishing his inspector and friend all the best, and doubting that he had it.

'Do you think he is?'

'I doubt it.'

But as a matter of fact Mat was.

'Oh Azizah, my darling, my love.' He nuzzled into her neck as the first streaks of dawn were drawn across the sky.

He thought his heart would burst. It was all he had ever hoped for. She had been so expert – the second time as though learning by instinct as they went along.

'Azizah.'

She turned towards him then and smiled. He pulled her head on to his chest, stroking the shining hair and admiring the smooth, pale skin. So peerless, so beautiful, so – he ran out of words and sighed instead.

'Azizah. My wife – at last.'

104. JAMES MAKES A DECISION

It was about this time that James received a letter. The writing was unfamiliar and yet vaguely remembered, as though from someone he had known long ago. There was no address on the back.

He turned to the last page and the signature first. Good God, it wasn't possible. Norman Parkes. He hadn't given him a thought for years. It couldn't be. But it was.

'I hear that you've ditched both the service and the tart,' the letter began. Good old Norman; never one to mince his words.

What was most surprising was that Norman had bought himself a farm – James looked at the address: Mittagong, New South Wales. He laughed out loud to think of the urbane Norman wallowing in cow dung, or whatever it was one was supposed to wallow in on a farm.

He read on. 'I am looking for someone to share my venture and it occurred to me that if this colonial service lark is not long term, you might be interested.'

Now how the hell had Norman traced him? He looked at the envelope again. Air Commodore J. M. Weatherby, DSO, DFC, care of the Colonial Office, London. Old Norman really was out of date. Then he looked at the postmark. Penny-pinching bunch, he thought, they would forward it by surface mail. He would most probably have given him up by now and found someone else.

He returned to the letter itself. There was a lot more, mostly details about the farm itself and the amount of capital required.

Me farm? James thought; then thought again. His family had never farmed, but they had always lived in the heart of farming country; it would not really be such an alien life. He had been thinking more and more recently of asking for a transfer to a less humid territory when his tour was up. But he did not have to stay on in the colonial service at all; he was not yet committed. At the end of the first three years, either he or government could terminate his service; once confirmed it could not be so easily accomplished, unless he were invalided out. Now would be the time to go – if he wanted to.

He picked up the telephone. 'Helen,' he began, 'you'll never guess – oh hell, it's no use over the phone; I'll tell you when I come up.'

For once he did not stay late at the office, but hurried home on the stroke of five.

He waved the letter at Helen but did not give it to her to read. He was still a little sensitive and he'd never told her much about Elsie. The most talented tart in East Anglia, Norman had called her, and been proved right – no man liked to be taken for the ride that he had been.

'An old friend of mine, Norman Parkes, has asked me to go part shares in a farm in Australia. You've never met him – long before your time. He wasn't particularly enamoured with my first wife and, of course, he thinks I'm a lone wolf now. Don't know if he'd have asked me if he knew I had a family in tow.'

'But I have met him,' Helen said quietly, 'on the ship from Capetown. He was one of the ones who warned me off you – I was under the impression that, on the contrary, he was rather pro your wife.'

It was so long ago and she had won in the end, but the hurt and frustration that she had felt at the time reached out over the years.

'Good God. I'd forgotten that. Good old Norman; I expect he was just protecting me. See for yourself.'

He did show her the letter then, tossing it over in a too-casual manner, which did not deceive her for one moment. She smiled as she read.

'What do you think, honey? Would you like to farm?'

'I honestly don't know,' she said slowly, 'and, as you say, the offer might not stand with me and the kids having to be taken into account.'

'I know what you're thinking – that I'm becoming a rolling stone.

It's not that, Helen. I like this job well enough; I have had every intention of making it my career, but I don't think I can stand this climate for ever. Australia would be dry.'

'Why don't you write and see if he would still want you, with us as well? Then you can decide.'

That will give us time to hash it out, she thought, disappointed that James should want to change his job again so soon. But it was true about the climate; try as he might, he could not always keep his ulcerated stump away from her view and he had refused to go to Stan to see if anything could be done.

He walked over to the desk and started at once.

'I am married again,' he wrote, 'with two kids – the ATS beauty from the boat – '

He stopped and looked at his wife. She was beautiful still, but her face was becoming lined and the brightness of her hair fading – little wonder that grey streaks were on the increase, it must be hell for her half the time, living with him. She can't have had the happiness she must have expected – and it was his fault, always his fault. He rose quietly, so as not to disturb her, and went to stand behind her.

He stooped to kiss the top of her bent head. 'Do you know, woman, that I love you more than anything else in the world?'

Helen put down her sewing and smiled a sad little smile. When she lifted her eyes to his and spoke, her voice was husky.

'Yes,' she said, 'I believe you do.'

To their surprise, a reply came by return of post.

'Delighted to hear you're happily married at last,' Norman wrote. 'We would have to build a house for you anyway and, taking the best sites, the homesteads would be nearly a mile apart, so our domestic arrangements need not overlap. As a matter of fact, I'm thinking of getting married myself.' And, farther down the page, 'Perhaps your Helen could cope with the bookwork, if you can find someone to look after the kids.'

'What do you think, darling? Even if we don't go, I think I should have to apply for a transfer to another colony – somewhere with a better climate than this.' Before Helen had time to reply, he played his trump card. 'It would mean not being separated from the kids when they reach school age.'

It was the only thing she had against the colonial service as a job; the knowledge that sooner or later the children would have to go home to boarding-school. She dreaded the inevitable separation and he knew it – he dreaded it himself. The fact that he had brought out this apparently casual remark so pat, showed that he must have been thinking out arguments to win her over in advance. Perhaps it would be a good thing, branching out on something quite different from government or service life, and perhaps James would be easier to live with if his health improved.

'When would you have to decide?' she asked at length.

'I'm not sure; I'll have to find out. I should be due for leave any time after the New Year. I presume I would have to give notice during the next two or three months.'

'I don't see how I could cope with the bookwork side though – although I'd like to have an interest in the place other than being just a wife. Angela could, I suppose, start school next year, but John is only three still. I could hardly leave him and I imagine it would mean working in the office.'

'Darling, I've just had the most wonderful – no, the most *bonzer* idea – how about asking old Nannie to come out? She's on her own now; she'd love it.'

Both James's parents had died during the past year and Nannie was indeed on her own. By the time both children had reached school age, she would be getting too old to cope anyway and, if his memory was correct, she had a married sister in Australia somewhere. It really could work out.

'How about it, Helen?'

She had not heard him enthuse so for years.

'All right, darling,' she said, 'if Nannie will come, let's go. We'll make her reply the deciding factor.'

105. A NUPTIAL MASS FOR VINCENT LEE

'How much longer is this going to last?'

'Catholic weddings always take ages. It's only the mixed ones where they whisk the heretics out in a hurry in case they pollute the sacred surroundings!'

The very sophisticated Chinese lady sitting in front of them turned her head slightly in its tall, tight collar and smiled.

Ever since they had driven over to Kemuning for the wedding of Rose and Vincent Lee Chee Min, Sally had wondered who the small woman in the elegant cheongsam could be.

The church was pathetically empty. Mrs Cheng sat in the front pew of the left-hand side, with a very few Chinese scattered behind her, and the bridegroom's side was worse. When Sally and Philip had arrived only the one woman sat in the front pew and a couple of detectives some way behind. They sat in the second row and wished they could have been farther back.

630

There was no music, and only a scraping of feet as the few guests rose announced the arrival of the bride.

'She looks perfectly sweet,' Sally remarked.

In her white, Western-style wedding dress, hired, no doubt, from some professional photographer, Rose did look pretty as, smiling nervously, she came down the aisle on her father's arm.

But the surprise came when the best man, who must have been standing behind a pillar, emerged.

'Philip, do look – it's Stan.'

'Good God! Now wherever did Chee Min get to know him?' Philip was beginning to think his detective-sergeant was something of a dark horse.

Then the service began and went on and on and on, and Philip grew bored. He kept looking at his watch until Sally nudged him and shook her head.

'I had no idea it was going to take such hours. I don't like leaving the district for so long.'

'Oh Philip, don't fash! Ahmat's there and you have Cameron now.'

Her remark and the thought of Cameron made him smile and gave him something to think about. The nuptial mass droned on and he sank into a pleasant doze. Cameron was the police lieutenant he had been promised as his assistant, who had arrived a couple of weeks before. He was small, grey and clear of eye and the minute Philip had heard his soft Highland voice, he had accepted him.

Cameron did not hold with what he termed 'larking about in the jungle,' which he considered a job for soldiers. He was a policeman through and through. Philip was still a soldier and it had not taken him more than a couple of days to find out just how ignorant he was! Running a district in the Emergency with his army background was fine, but what would happen when he had to tackle the other side of police work – dealing with crime? Cameron had asked. The Circuit Magistrate visited at regular intervals to hear all cases in the district and he had insisted that Philip should prosecute at the next session.

'It's no use being a soldier, sir; you'll have to pass your law exams before you can be confirmed,' he said. 'I'll teach you as we go along.'

Philip was learning.

A shaft of sunlight piercing a stained-glass window caught his glance and quite suddenly he was overcome with a feeling of immense gratitude to what he called his team.

I have some splendid chaps around me, he thought, how lucky I am with my subordinates. There were one or two police lieutenants whom he would rather not have had, and his second inspector, Zukifli, was pretty useless, but the others – Ahmat and Chee Min, more than mere subordinates, more than just reliable workers; they were friends, people on whom he could count. The sturdy rocks, Cameron and

Jogindar; even the old corporal who never left his side, Omar, and Karim, the first decent driver he'd come across in the police, who now drove his jeep when he was not on duty with the GMT.

Perhaps, after all, I should be giving thanks, he thought, instead of fretting about the waste of time. He bowed his head and his wife looked at him in amazement.

'Philip, do you feel all right?'

At that moment, and before he had had time to answer, their attention was arrested by a well-dressed Chinese girl, followed by a young man in a thick, dark suit, who slid into the pew in front of them. She grimaced at the lone occupant and pecked her on the cheek.

'Sorry we're late, Mum.' There was no mistaking the Australian twang.

'Oh Rosalie, I thought you'd never come.'

At last the service was at an end and the bridal pair moved solemnly towards the aisle.

'Hey, Mum, Vin's got himself a doll,' the girl in front remarked, not bothering to lower her voice, 'a living doll!'

At the sound of her voice, Chee Min's head shot up and an expression of such radiant happiness lit his face that Sally felt tears coming into her eyes.

'How ridiculous,' she laughed at herself. 'It's true though, people do cry at weddings.' And looking around, 'I say, Philip, do you realise that, bar Stan, we're the only Europeans here? How awful! I do think that at least the SB type might have come – after all, Kemuning is Circle Headquarters, it isn't as if they had to travel to get here.'

'Both he and the OPCS declined to come to the church, but said they'd be at the reception. Clever bastards!'

'*I* think it's plain bad manners,' she remarked primly.

The reception was held in Kemuning's only hotel, a crumby place, but the best available. We did better with the mayor's house, Sally was thinking, even if it was a far cry from the traditional white wedding.

Chee Min had borrowed Philip's sword to cut the cake and, by the difficulty he was having, it looked as though he should have borrowed an axe. He had just about given up the battle when an agitated little Chinese, wearing a tall chef's cap, dashed in and indicated that they were trying to cut the wrong tier. Only the bottom layer was actually cake, he pointed out, and showed everybody, as he removed the second and third tiers, that they were only cardboard.

Sally began to giggle. The Chinese were taking it very solemnly, congratulating the cook on his ingenuity, and Philip threw his wife a cross glance as she turned to look out of the window. But the girl

632

called Rosalie caught her eye as she turned and walked over to where she stood, trying to control herself.

'It is comic, isn't it?' she remarked. 'I take it you're Sally.'

Sally at once looked put out and Philip smirked in turn. For all her apparently easy-going ways, she could be on her dignity, as he well knew. Nevertheless, he came to her rescue.

'And you can only be Chee Min's sister,' he said.

'Yeah. We call him Vincent. I'm Rosalie Tan and that's my husband and Mum over there.'

'Chee Min – I mean Vincent – didn't tell us you'd be here. I'm so glad that you are.'

'We sneaked over behind Dad's back, I'm afraid. Mum's supposed to be staying with me in KL, but she came straight here, it's nearer. What do *you* think of this match, Sal?'

Philip had to turn away that time to hide his smile; he could almost feel her wince. But when she spoke her voice was natural enough.

'I honestly don't know. He's very keen on her and she sounds bright. She's certainly a very pretty girl. I hope it works out; I'd like them to be happy.'

'Aw, it'll be okay. Vin's too stubborn – just like Dad. If he'd waited, Dad would have come round in time. Anyway, he's lost his allowance so he'll have to live on his pay now,' she grimaced across the room at her brother, who smiled back; 'that'll teach him!'

'What a relief to kick off my shoes.'

Sally threw them on to the back seat and stretched her toes. It was a relief to be driving home too.

'I hope Chee Min's done the right thing,' Philip remarked, 'you can see his family are upper crust.'

'Doesn't mean a thing,' Sally said tartly. 'Half the rich Chinese here were coolies one generation back. I doubt if their blood is any bluer than the Chengs'.'

'On your dignity still?'

'Not at all. I thought both his mother and sister were extremely nice. Although I must admit, Australian familiarity does take one back a bit – I'm no longer used to it.'

'Tell me, Sal,' he mimicked, 'what did you call your officers' wives behind their backs, when you were in the ranks?'

'Our immediate officers didn't have wives – they were women!' She put out her tongue in a gesture that twenty years earlier would have been accompanied by a 'So there.'

'Well? What did you call them?'

'Some we were quite polite about,' she grinned, remembering, 'we had a couple of beauties though – Lezzy Lizzy and Bugger Blight!'

'What charming girls you must have been!'

'We were.'

With the police clinic going full swing, Sally got to know the other ranks' wives far better than she would have done otherwise. And when the clinic session was over each week, she would make a point of calling on Rose Lee, Azizah or Suvindar Kaur.

It did not take her long to come to the conclusion that Chee Min had done well for himself and she became very fond of Rose. Not so Azizah though; try as she would, she could make no headway there.

'I had so hoped to bring her and Rose together,' she complained to Philip. 'Two new brides should have so much in common, especially as in their cases neither was acceptable to the husband's family. But I'm afraid it's hopeless; they're poles apart.'

'Give it up,' Philip advised. 'I've not succeeded with the husbands either. Here am I, doing my best to instil team spirit and yet I know that if I don't tell them both something, the one I haven't spoken to will never find out. Don't Asians ever tell each other anything?'

'I don't think they do, unless they're asked.'

'Well, I find it one of their most infuriating traits.'

Sally shrugged her shoulders; she was used to it from childhood. One morning, as she was leaving the clinic, Rose called to her from where she was sitting on her verandah, sewing.

'That's pretty,' Sally remarked, picking up the embroidered baby coat, then looked at Rose with interest. 'Not already?'

Rose went into peals of mirth, showing an attractive dimple on either side of her mouth. 'No, Mem, not yet. But one day I shall have a son. I embroider for pleasure. In the evening I sew while Vincent studies. He wants so much to have money enough to buy a car, so I am making him stay in and save. I have persuaded him to buy a motor cycle instead.'

'Good for you.' Sally picked up the tiny jacket again. 'It's beautifully done. That's a convent education for you. I'm sure you could make some money with embroidery like that – not baby clothes, but tablecloths and mats and things.' She was thinking; she could ask around the planters' wives. She would certainly buy something herself, and Helen would. 'Oh, here's your husband coming home. I hadn't realised it was so late.'

'Hello, ma'am.'

'Hello, Vincent. I've just been trying to persuade Rose to have a go at embroidering for money.'

'Say, Rosie, that's a great idea. Hadn't appreciated my allowance till Dad stopped it!'

'According to your sister, it was your own fault!'

'Aw, Rosalie. Still, Dad'll come round one of these days. Especially when we give him a grandson, eh, Rose?'

Once again Rose subsided into a fit of giggles, hand before mouth.
'I must go,' Sally said. 'My husband will be waiting for his lunch.'
'He's still in the office, ma'am.'

'She's nice,' Rose said to Sally's retreating back. 'Just like the European ladies who taught at the convent.'

'Yeah, she's all right. Phil's all right too.'

'Oh, Vincent, you are so familiar,' Rose reproached in her high, staccato tones.

'Who cares? As Snowy White says, sticks and stones may break my bones – that won't do him any harm. Got any grub fixed?'

106. RAMAKRISHNAN'S NEW JOB

Ramakrishnan had not left the district.

After the humiliating scene on the padang when he had been shaken like a rat in the jaws of a terrier by that proud and treacherous Sikh, he had lain low and sulked.

It had been bad enough getting the sack – an action which he still considered unfair. After all, was it not his duty to point out to the District Office staff that they were being exploited by the white pigs? Was it not his duty to advise them to ignore government rules and regulations and strike for better wages and less working hours?

That old fool Balasingham had complained. He knew it. A white man's toady if ever there was one. He spat.

It was Maniam, the police CC, who had mentioned that the manager of Bukit Merah Estate was looking for a clerk. But that had been several weeks ago. He had made no friends in Kuala Jelang, there was no one to whom he could turn, no one who was prepared to help. Only one Tamil family had offered him lodging until such time as he could find work, but even they were only doing it for the money he brought in; they would not be sorry to see him go. He knew it.

The only thing he could do was to go to Bukit Merah and find out for himself.

Having made this decision, he took to hanging around the store where most of the estates purchased their supplies. It was a bad road to Bukit Merah, he knew, no vehicles other than estate lorries and the police went along it unless they had to. An estate lorry was therefore his only means of reaching it.

In due course a lorry arrived and Krishnan hitched a ride.

Old Wotherspoon looked at him quizzically. 'How did you know I needed a clerk?' he asked.

Instinctively Krishnan knew better than to say he had heard it from a police clerk. Instead he said, 'I heard it in the store.'

'Why do you want the job?'

'I am after leaving government service, sir, which I could not stand, wishing to revert to former status of estate clerk.'

'Oh?' Wotherspoon's eyebrows rose, 'so you've been an estate clerk before, have you? Which estate?'

Krishnan thought quickly. If he said Tanah Kuning he was trapped. It didn't matter; there were so many estates with similar names.

'Tanah Puteh,' he lied. 'It is in South Johore.'

'Never heard of it.' Which was hardly surprising.

He looked Krishnan keenly up and down, until the latter began to feel uncomfortable.

'Before I say whether there is a job or not,' he said at length, 'I want you to understand one thing. What goes on on this estate is the business of this estate only and concerns no one outside it. Do you get me?'

The quick brain of Ramakrishnan worked at the double. So the grapevine rumours were true. It was to his advantage.

'You can be trusting me, sir. My mouth is sealed like veritable clam.'

'All right. When can you start?'

'Sir, I am here.'

Krishnan was as good as his word. He kept his mouth shut, but his eyes were everywhere.

The work was simple, but there was one big difference between his work on this estate and that of Tanah Kuning. Here he kept two sets of books. The list of labourers on the payroll was nearly double the number who were actually paid. Similiarly with rations; and the indent for office equipment bore no relation to that actually used.

He had been working for less than a month when he had occasion to return to the office one evening. All estate lights were put on and off by a master switch in the manager's bungalow, so he was not surprised to see the lights blazing out from the uncurtained office windows.

He had already started to open the door when he heard the sound of a clacking typewriter and paused.

The sight that met his eyes, as he peeped through the inch-wide crack, caused his hair to stand on end.

A uniformed man sat with his back to the door, typing a stencil on his, Krishnan's, typewriter. There was no mistaking the uniform – Krishnan shivered – the pentagonal cloth cap was set firmly on the

636

man's head, and one leg which stuck out from the side of the desk was bound with the type of puttee that only the Chinese wore.

Krishnan began to back and slowly close the door, but as he moved a hand shot out and grabbed his wrist, forcing him inside.

He knew better than to make a sound. He stood, silent, his eyes rolling madly with fright as he observed the second man, who had been watching him but whom he had not seen.

The man sitting at the desk made some remark in Chinese, but the typing never ceased and he did not turn round.

The second man released his grip on Krishnan, but moved to stand with his back against the door. He swung a pistol loosely in his hand.

'Are you the new clerk?'

Krishnan only nodded. He was incapable of speech.

'You have not seen us here to-night. Understand?'

He nodded again.

'We come here often to write our news bulletins. You will never see us.'

This time Krishnan found his tongue.

'But I am your friend,' he said. Then, seeing that the man was unimpressed, 'As far back as 1945 I am trying to join most glorious guerillas in jungle hills.'

The man at the typewriter swung round.

'Which company?' he asked, 'and where?'

'I am not after knowing which company,' Krishnan began to whine. He knew he could not fool with these hard-faced, ruthless men. 'It was in Rembang, Negri-side.'

Why had he said that? He could have bitten off his tongue. Suppose one of them had been at that camp? Suppose one of them had heard him accused of being a Japanese collaborator? Suppose . . .? But neither of the men looked in the least interested. They spoke together briefly in their own dialect.

Then they looked at him, very straight. 'We shall see whether you are our friend or not,' the man by the door said in Malay. 'Good night.'

He opened the door and pushed Ramakrishnan through it. It was quickly and silently closed again.

Krishnan stood in the blackness, trembling, feeling that there were eyes all about him and wishing he was not wearing his habitual white trousers and shirt.

He had quite forgotten what it was that he had gone to fetch.

Donald had made a bad mistake. Thinking that he was cured, he had paid sentimental visits to all his wartime haunts. But he was not cured.

The camp in Surrey was still there, used by the TA for their weekly parades. It had not altered much. He walked past the building that had once housed the headquarters of the Canadian Red Cross and had dinner in the small restaurant a stone's throw away that had been one of his favourites. He went up to Scotland and he went to Holland. And all the time he was alone.

How alone he had not realised before. He made no attempt to seek out old friends and acquaintances, just visited the places where he had known them and looked about.

It was absolutely fatal.

He stood in Piccadilly Circus and gazed at Eros, jostled and pushed by the unheeding crowd. He had been jostled and pushed before – and picked up. It was here that Sally said she remembered him toppling over and she had supported him. That was his friend. Yeah, those were his real friends: Sally and Phil, Stan, James and Helen. He thought with equal affection of his forest rangers, his typist and the clerks, even Salmah.

'Yeah,' he said out loud, 'that's where I belong. Not in this goddam, phoney hub of civilisation.'

I'll think about it over lunch, he thought, weigh the pros and cons.

He ate and thought and put down several beers and by two o'clock he was at the Crown Agents, requesting them to book his passage home.

'Home?' inquired the disinterested clerk.

'Yeah, home,' he had worked himself into a fine, belligerent mood. He spelt it out, 'H-o-m-e. Kuala Jelang, Perangor, Malaya, South-East Asia. Got it?' Then in a more reasonable tone, 'I'm not due back for a couple of months, but I want to be home for Christmas. Okay?'

'As you wish,' the clerk shrugged, 'we're only agents. What address? We'll let you know when we have a booking.'

'I'll be back to-morrow. Save time.' He ignored the raised eyebrow. 'Come on, man, be a pal, you can do it if you want to. Use the phone.'

He went back to his hotel with a lighter heart and settled down to write to Stan.

Strangely enough Stan was pleased. It was not that he was lonely or that he missed Don, but he would be pleased to have him back nevertheless.

'Looks as though you'll have to move back to the Morrisons',' he told Mike Harrington. Not that Mike spent much time there, only the occasional night or two.

'I doubt if it'll be necessary,' he replied. 'I haven't mentioned it, because it's only rumour so far, but I've heard on the grapevine that they may be sending a British company here. We're due for a rest and with any luck we may be relieving the battalion presently in Hong Kong.'

'We'll be sorry to see you go. Does Philip know?'

'Not yet – and neither do the Gurks. Keep it under your hat.'

Stan nodded. Indiscretion had never been one of his vices. 'Let's go down to the club and have a drink. I have a couple of new phrases that I want to try out on my Chinese friends.'

Mike groaned. 'Count me out. Anyway, I have to be off at crack.'

Stan had taken to spending more and more of his free time at the local club. He no longer needed an interpreter when dealing with most of his Chinese patients and frequently told Chee Min that he would be the first to pass his Hakka exams.

'Just as you like,' he said to Mike. 'I won't be late.'

Salmah was waiting for him just inside his bedroom door. She could understand a fair amount of English when she wanted to.

'You going out?' She pouted. 'Always out with Chinese friend.'

'What about it?'

'One day I kill her.'

'Well, you'll find yourself confronting several men! Good night.'

Salmah was becoming a bit of a bore and he often wished that he had never taken her on. Possessiveness was something which had made him avoid marriage – a possessive mistress was too much. He slammed the car door with irritation, forgot it was in gear, choked, and stalled.

'God damn the bloody woman!' he muttered as he restarted the engine. 'Why doesn't Mike have a fling? Take her off my hands now and then?' At that moment he noticed Salmah's shadow advancing along the verandah. He smirked, sat watching for a moment, then said aloud, as he drove off, 'Perhaps he will, perhaps he will.'

The rumour was true. Everyone was sorry to see the Gurkhas go, and the police more than anyone. It was sad seeing the large khaki tents coming down, not to be replaced.

Sally and Helen watched from the verandah of the OCPD's house as the little brown men scurried to and fro, removing every trace of their sojourn there.

A tremendous farewell party had been thrown the night before in the police canteen, and for once the laudatory speeches had been sincere.

Their replacements belonged to an English county regiment and their company commander had decided not to split his men, but to have them all in the one camp at Sungei Belimbing.

'It's his command,' Philip said to Cameron, as they watched the Gurkhas pack, 'but I shall miss not having the army here.'

In fact, they were to miss more than the tents and the presence of the men who had slept in them. Both the new company commander and his second-in-command had quarters at Headquarters and naturally hurried home whenever they could.

'Can't see this new mob ever fitting into the district like the Gurks,' James remarked. He had come to join Philip in saying a last farewell.

The last truck left the police station, full of grinning, smooth-faced little toughs, followed by Mike in his jeep. Both men sighed and, on the hillside above, their wives sighed too. From the door of the hospital office Stan waved as they passed, and turned to watch as the last vehicle sped on its way to a well-earned rest and the bright lights of Hong Kong.

Soon everyone was back at work, but a sad, empty feeling of anti-climax had set in.

108. THE PRICE OF PEACE

'Helen, we're in luck – she's going to come.' James read out the letter from Nannie over the phone.

So now all that remained was to write to Norman and tell him all was set. He put down the receiver and stretched back in his chair, smiling with satisfaction. He had proved to himself that he did not have to stay in a rut; the air force was well out of his system now; he'd mastered another job. In many ways he'd be sorry to leave. There were some good chaps in the colonial service and he had enjoyed his work on the whole. Still, the thought of a dry climate and feeling well for a change was something to look forward to.

He pushed a heap of files to one side and wrote his letter advising the powers that be that he did not wish to be confirmed; then he rang for his clerk.

'Please type it out yourself,' he asked, 'I would not wish the staff to feel that I did not like it here. It's just this,' he indicated his arm and his eye, 'and Bala, would you send round to the shop and see if they have any champagne – two bottles, please – and have it put in my car?'

Balasingham picked up the letter without comment. 'Yes, sir. The OCPD is just arriving, sir.'

'Good. Just the man I want to see.'

He would ask them to supper and the four would celebrate, drink a toast to his and Helen's future.

But Philip was not in a celebrating mood.

'We've got to get a move on with shifting those squatters,' he said without preamble, not giving James a chance to mention his news. 'Has Wotherspoon agreed to the government price yet?'

'He's just hedging,' James admitted, 'although, to be honest, I've had so many other items on my mind, I'd rather shelved it until there was definite news of the Resettlement Officer.'

'We want to have the place cleared and built upon before he arrives,' Philip was terse. 'Take a look at these.'

He threw four photographs on to the desk. Chee Min had taken them the day before and the subject was gruesome.

Five men lay face down, wrists and ankles bound. Each body was horribly mutilated, and even in the black and white prints bruises and bloodstains were clear. Fingers, ears, one hand and two feet could be seen lying separately on the ground.

'Not a pretty sight, are they?'

'Who were they?'

'Residents of Ulu Pandanus who wouldn't, or couldn't, pay their dues.'

James said nothing more, but lifting the telephone receiver asked the operator for Bukit Merah Estate.

After some time a voice told him that the manager was sick.

'Did you tell him it was the DO calling?' he asked the voice. 'Please tell him it's a matter of some urgency.'

There was a long pause before the voice came back. The manager was too sick to speak.

James put the receiver down and looked across at Philip. 'What now?'

'I don't believe he's sick. Stan was there yesterday, dealing with an accidentally wounded SC who couldn't be brought in. Let's ask him.'

James put out his hand to the phone again.

'Do you have Philip with you?' Stan's voice was cautious.

'Yes.'

'In my opinion, the whole trouble is that Wotherspoon's so terribly anti-police. He feels that, with a Resettlement Area on his doorstep, there'll be too many of them around – I'm sure that's why he's farting around.'

'Well, why did he make the original offer then?'

'God alone knows.'

James covered the mouthpiece with his hand and repeated the gist to his visitor, who, he could see, was becoming very cross. Then into it, 'Thank you, Stan.'

'He's the only bloody manager who does absolutely nothing for his SCs and goes out of his way to sabotage me. He even wrote a complaint to the CPO, because the SCs had been playing badminton in their off-duty time and had made a mess of the grass. Can you credit it? If there's any more nonsense we'll have to requisition the land, that's all.'

'We can't do that.'

'Why not? Two Gurkhas killed near Ulu Pandanus only last month and now these.' He tapped the photographs. 'Give me one good reason why not.'

'Well, we can, if we *have* to – it's just that I don't like doing things that way.'

'Balls!'

The two men glared at each other across the desk, then Philip turned to go.

James sat down and put his head in his hands. He did not want to ride roughshod over an old man, but he knew he could not put it off any longer. When the Resettlement Committee had gone over the area it had been taken for granted that the land was theirs, and then, quite suddenly, Wotherspoon had jibbed at the government price. It was a fair price; what had happened to make him change his mind?

'Philip,' he called in a quiet voice. The latter turned just as he reached the door. 'I'll go and see him to-morrow. Try and find out what's going on. We may have to requisition, but I'd prefer not if it can be avoided. I think it would be better if you don't come. I'll go alone.'

'Good. I'll give you a police escort.'

He strode out and, as the door swung wildly on its hinges, Bala-singham went in.

'Sorry, sir. No champagne in shop.'

James sighed; he'd forgotten all about his request. 'Perhaps it's just as well.'

The DO made little progress with Wotherspoon. The manager in-vited him to lunch, plied him with drink and talked about every subject under the sun except land. No mention was made of his sick-ness of the previous day.

By sheer determination, James succeeded finally in turning the conversation round to the Emergency.

Wotherspoon began to whine. The police, he said, were bleeding him white. Didn't they realise the cost of lighting and wire? The labour needed to erect the defences they demanded and the cost of main-tenance?

James pointed out gently that other estates had complied.

'Why don't they leave me alone?' The old man moaned in a high-pitched, plaintive voice. 'Why don't they leave me alone?'

'Who?'

Wotherspoon's head jerked up. 'Everybody,' he snarled; 'the whole bloody lot.'

James had done his best to think kindly of the elderly planter; had alienated his fellow-government servants to do so. Now he knew that the police were right. And yet he still felt sorry for him. The old man was so clearly frightened; perhaps he was being intimidated, threatened with the loss of his life or property.

'If you have anything to be uneasy about – after all, this is rather a remote estate – why don't you tell the police? You could seek their protection.' It was a shot in the dark.

The old man's eyes blazed.

'I wouldn't touch them with a barge-pole.' His mouth curled in scorn and he spat on the floor. 'That's what I think of them. That.' He spat again.

James controlled himself with difficulty. He would never have credited the old man with such a gesture.

'We shall have to have that land, Mr Wotherspoon,' he said coldly. 'I'd be grateful if you would finalise the sale now, without further delay.'

'It's out of my hands.' He was looking both triumphant and crafty now. 'It's up to Head Office to make up their minds. Look, I'll show you the file.'

He called into the outer office and Ramakrishnan contrived to slip the file on to his desk without being seen – he knew James had only one eye.

It was true that Wotherspoon had written to say he felt unable to complete the sale without confirmation by his principals. James passed the letter back. Playing for time, he thought; I should like to know why.

'I shall be glad if you will write to your Head Office, advising them that the land is needed urgently and that we can brook no further delay.'

'Oh, they'll answer soon enough. No hurry. Will you stay to tea?'

James ignored the invitation.

'You do understand, don't you, that under the Emergency Regulations, we have the power to requisition land?'

'You can't do that.'

They were the exact words that he himself had used.

'On the contrary, Mr Wotherspoon, we can.' He got up to go then. 'Please let me have your answer as soon as possible. Thank you for an excellent lunch. Good afternoon.'

There was no reply.

All the way back to Kuala Jelang the problem went round and round in James's mind. It was Wotherspoon who had initiated the sale. Why?

Perhaps, he mused, he did it because, to begin with, he *wanted* to have the police near at hand. The bandits – if indeed he *was* in touch with them – would undoubtedly have found out and maybe they had ordered him to cancel it, or else. Maybe.

It must be grim to be as scared as that. Involuntarily his sympathy went back again to the old man.

'There is someone wishing to see you.'

Ramakrishnan turned to face the labourer who had entered the office on soundless bare feet. His nerves were bad these days. Always the expected hand on the shoulder, the shot in the night.

'Tell him to come in, then.'

'No,' the man looked unhappy, 'he is waiting for you over there.'

Krishnan joined him at the window and the man pointed to the edge of the rubber. The late afternoon shadows made it difficult to see through the trees. But he knew someone was there. He said nothing to the labourer and went out.

As he had expected, it was the man who had been using his type-writer a couple of months before. He had heard it clacking away many times since then, but had kept away.

He felt sick and his legs were quaking, but by the time he confronted the man, he had succeeded in mustering a bright smile.

'You are sending for yours truly to benefit from my services?' he asked with a small bow.

'The District Officer was here to-day. Why?'

'He was taking luncheon in manager's house and discussing matters of land during afternoon time.'

'What land?' The man took Krishnan by the shoulder and shook him. 'Details.'

Krishnan's eyes rolled frantically. Luckily he had heard the conversation. He repeated it word for word.

'Your information had better be correct.'

The man turned away without another word.

Krishnan could still feel where the fingers had dug into his flesh. He rubbed himself thoughtfully and made his way cautiously back to the office.

The bandits had appeared within a couple of hours of the DO leaving. That meant they must have spies around. Labourers who reported every move, no doubt. Krishnan tried to remember if he had ever said anything detrimental about the terrorists to the tapper

644

who had summoned him; he was a man to whom he had spoken once or twice. He was sure he had not, but he must be careful. They were ruthless men. Perhaps it would be wise to volunteer a little information of his own accord now and then, instead of waiting to be called. Yes, that was a good plan. It should not be difficult. He would see what items of interest he could pick up.

Wotherspoon had finished his solitary evening meal and was still sitting at the dinner-table, reading a book, when the bandits arrived.

It was not the first time, but they still never failed to take him by surprise. He hardened his jaw and waited. He knew what they had come about.

But they were in no hurry.

One man picked up a banana from the table, peeled it and stuffed it, whole, into his mouth. Wotherspoon watched, fascinated, like a rabbit cornered by a stoat. The other man took a long swig from a bottle of brandy on the sideboard, then walked round, hands in pockets, looking at the pictures on the walls. A third man guarded the door. A fourth would be on the open verandah behind him, he knew.

For several minutes not a word was spoken.

'What did he want?' came at last from the man scrutinising the prints.

Wotherspoon knew better than to hedge. 'He came about the land,' he said.

'What did you tell him?'

'That it was out of my hands. That I could do nothing before I had Head Office's reply. After he had gone, I rang Head Office and asked a friend of mine to make sure the letter was delayed – I made a personal excuse.'

'That was stupid of you. The telephone operator might repeat the conversation.'

'I doubt it. We spoke in French.'

'You expect us to believe that?'

Wotherspoon was tired, but it was the price he paid for peace. He sighed.

'All Englishmen learn French at school,' he said.

The man walked over to the table then and, picking up the bowl of fruit that was the centrepiece, held it at arm's length whilst looking the manager straight in the eye. Then, quite deliberately, he dropped it.

The impact of the china bowl on the tiled floor caused it to break into smithereens. The harder fruit rolled across the tiles, but a slice of ripe papaya splashed and spattered as it hit the hard surface with a most sickening sound. The bandit ground what remained beneath his rubber boot.

'That also can happen to men's bodies,' he said, and his companions laughed.

For many minutes after the terrorists had gone, Wotherspoon remained motionless, apparently reading his book, but he did not turn a page.

He should retire, he told himself, he was well past retiring age. But why the hell should he retire? He had no home; he'd torn his roots out of English soil some thirty years before. *This* was his home, the life he loved. Why the bloody hell should he retire? It was all the fault of the police. Officious young men. First King and now this creature Morrison. Just as bad. Young enough to be his sons. Less than half his age. That had been the trouble in the first place – that bouncy young man, typical product of a grammar school, he supposed, had had the cheek to order him, yes, *order* him, to do this and that. And this one was worse. Wire here, lights there, kubus somewhere else. The SCs had to be mollycoddled, nursed. He wasn't going to put up with that and so he had refused to co-operate on principal.

And then had come the terrorists. Not uniformed men; well dressed, smooth. He was not on the side of the government, so he must be on theirs. They had spouted a lot of Communist propaganda, straight from Peking, and he had told them politely that he wasn't interested.

The murder of the Kangani was the next step and the realisation that most of the labour had been intimidated to such an extent that they were helping the bandits whether they liked it or not.

Then they had come again. The same men, but this time they were wearing uniform.

All they asked was a little co-operation, they said, a little rice, the occasional use of a typewriter. He need not see. All he need do was ignore them and he would be left in peace.

The temptation was too great and he had agreed.

That had been the first stage, then came the requests – requests? Don't be such a bloody fool, he told himself. Demands. Demands for more rice, more tinned food, office equipment, clothing, medicines.

When he thought he would no longer be under observation, he got up and poured himself a large tot. He swallowed three sleeping pills and turned out the light.

'Forgive me, Sally, for bursting in like this.' It was James, coming through the back way, torch in hand.

'That's all right. It's early yet, not ten o'clock.'

He smiled and squeezed her arm. 'Do you think I might have just five minutes with Philip, on my own?'

'Of course.'

646

James knew, or suspected, that Philip had no secrets from his wife, but he could not bring himself to admit to being wrong with a third person present.

'Philip, I'm sorry. I only got back from Bukit Merah at six o'clock and I've been thinking about it ever since. You were right.'

'I'll get you a drink.'

When they were both sitting down, he repeated the conversation of the afternoon.

'I think I was pretty blunt,' he said, 'let's give him until the end of the month, then we'll take it up with the DWEC if necessary.'

109. DOMESTIC STRIFE

Ahmat was having a bad time.

Azizah could hardly be bothered to conceal her boredom and, after a while, made no effort at all.

What really infuriated him was that she would not try to amuse herself or even keep herself occupied. The food that was thrown at him, on plates none too clean, was almost inedible. He had eaten far better as a bachelor in the canteen.

'Why don't you ask one of the other wives to teach you how to cook?' he asked, but Azizah only shrugged her shoulders and left the room. It was always the same. He had given up trying.

The house, the little house that he had taken so much trouble to beautify for her, was a mess. Dust accumulated, nothing was ever put away. Glass rings appeared on the furniture which he had polished so carefully, stains on the floor and cushion covers, and chips in cups and plates.

The greatest disappointment of all, though, was her complete lack of interest in his work.

That night they had lain in the Lake Gardens, talking about the future, all Azizah's comments had been constructive and intelligent. They had given him false hope. He had tried telling her where he was going, what he was doing and repeating the more amusing items of station gossip, but she paid no attention, often walking away while he was still speaking.

Religiously, he took her to every film at the club, but on one occasion, when he had been leaving on an operation at first light on the Monday morning, he had cried off, saying that he would be too tired. The scene that followed was the first of many and something that he came to dread.

He had returned in the afternoon to find her sitting on the verandah, staring into space – her usual attitude these days. The house had not been touched and the saucepan that she had thrown at him the night before was on the floor where it had fallen, its contents hardened and caked on the wall behind.

He looked at her with disgust.

'It's time you grew up,' he scolded, 'I'll give you anything I can, but it's up to you at least to feed me and keep my home in some semblance of order.'

She still sat, clothes rumpled and hair awry, and he saw the tears welling up in her eyes.

At once he was cross with himself, regretting his words.

'Azizah, please don't cry. I only meant . . .'

She turned her huge, great eyes on him then, the tears slowly trickling down her cheeks, and held up her arms to him in a gesture of appeal.

He was tired and hot, but he led her to their bed and she had pulled him down.

'You've no more duty to-day, Mat,' she pleaded. 'Stay with me.'

He had stayed, and after they had finished making love he cleaned up the house and took her into the town for a meal. But he was worried.

There was only the one thing that he could not complain about – Azizah in bed. Whatever the day had been like, however awful the food and slovenly-looking the house, whatever scene there had been or reception he had received, when he sank into her perfumed, smooth embrace, he was lost.

But lost only until the daylight came.

Since the arrival of Cameron, he had been going out with the OCPD more and more and this Azizah seemed to resent.

'You give him more time than me,' she pouted, 'you never used to be away so much.'

'But, Azizah, be reasonable. He's my boss. I'm only doing my job. His wife is left alone too – I'm sure she isn't always complaining.'

'Who cares about her? She has servants, she doesn't have to cook or clean the house. What does she do all day?'

'And what do *you* do? You can't cook and you won't learn. The house is filthy and you no longer keep yourself as you did – you're becoming a slut.'

A bottle of orange crush had narrowly missed his ear, breaking on the wall behind and saturating a chair in a fizzing orange cascade.

Ahmat jumped up, temper aroused.

'Look what you've done. It'll stain,' he cried. It was still his beloved house. 'Fetch a cloth and some water, quick.' Azizah did not move. 'Do as you're told.'

648

'You can't order me about. I'm not one of your PCs,' she screamed at him.

Mat took the dripping cover to the sink and did his best, but it was a woman's job. His hands were clumsy and he made, if possible, a worse mess. Frustration welled up in him like a cork and he flung the sticky cloth to the floor and strode out.

Azizah was already weeping, the usual routine, but this time his patience was exhausted. He went off to the canteen for a meal and, ignoring her open arms on his return, slept on a mat in the living-room. He had very nearly had enough.

In the morning she was contrite and when he returned at midday she had a passable meal waiting. She did not apologise and nor did he, but they were at peace with each other. Perhaps it is the turning point, he hoped; perhaps at last she has settled down, seen sense.

That evening the house was clean and she greeted him in a newly-pressed sarong and kebaya and freshly-done hair. A jasmine blossom was pinned a little above her ear and he smelt the scent as soon as he entered the house. This was the Azizah that he used to know.

He hurried under the shower and changed; white slacks, white shirt and police tie.

She noticed the tie at once. 'Oh Mat,' she said, 'I'm glad you haven't forgotten there's a film show at the club to-night.'

'Of course I hadn't. I'm dressed up to escort my beautiful wife.'

Azizah preened. 'I thought we might eat out first.'

It was near the end of the month. Mat frowned.

'I'm afraid my pay won't stretch to always eating out. I'm sorry, Azizah, I haven't enough this month; we'll have to eat at home.'

Immediately her face assumed sulky lines and it was at that moment that he saw the one bare cushion, standing out starkly from the rest.

'What happened to the cushion cover?' he asked. 'Wouldn't the stain come out?'

'I don't know.' She shrugged and adjusted the flower in her hair. 'I threw it away.'

'Threw it away?' He could hardly believe his ears. His family had never been poor, but there had never been any waste either. 'Why?'

She shrugged again and he had to stifle an impulse to hit her.

'I don't care for them much anyway.'

'When I think of all the trouble I took and the help from the Mem,' Mat flared, 'it makes my blood boil. What do you want? Would you have preferred to end your days as a raddled prostitute on the rong-geng stage? That's what you would have become.' She raised her arm to hit him, but he caught her wrist in mid air. 'Where did you throw it? Fetch it back. I'm sick and tired of all this waste.'

649

For answer Azizah hissed at him, 'What do you mean by help from the Mem?'

'She spent a lot of time helping me choose things, in getting the house spick and span – and all for you. She was prepared to be your friend. I believe she still is.'

'Stuck-up bitch. I don't want her for a friend.'

She seized the nearest cushion and ripped the cover off, then, picking up a pair of scissors from the table in front of her and looking her husband straight in the eye, she proceeded to cut it systematically into shreds.

For a moment Ahmat was so astounded that he could not stop her, and by the time he came to his senses she was in the kitchen.

'Did she choose these too?'

She held up one of the rose-patterned plates. One glance at his face was enough. The plate crashed to the floor, then another and another.

He was through the kitchen door in one stride and Azizah began to scream.

Jogindar Singh walked outside his quarters nearby and smiled to himself.

The crashing crockery had been heard all over the compound and heads were popping out of every barrack-room.

Serves him right, Jogindar thought – and he was not the only one – for being so soft. He should have dealt firmly with her from the start.

There was not a person in the whole of the barracks who did not hope that Ahmat was beating his wife. But they would have been disappointed. After a few minutes the screaming stopped and Ahmat walked down his front steps. Heads retreated and doors quickly closed.

'One meal needed for Inche Mat,' called the canteen boy to the cook.

The motley crowd surged in and out of and around the club and soon the weekly film show was ready to begin.

Philip had wanted to speak to Mat and had been sure, so he thought, of finding him there. But the lights were already being dowsed and he had not turned up. Before complete darkness descended, he walked over to where Rose and Chee Min were sitting.

'Where's Inche Mat?' he asked. 'He never misses a film.'

Both faces went as blank as only Chinese faces can and Chee Min's eyes were quite opaque.

'Having a little wife trouble, I believe, sir,' he said. He could not help sounding a mite smug.

Philip snorted. Was Ahmat really under the impression that no one knew? He must be.

'Again?'

At that moment something was hurled through one of the side windows and bounced on a shoulder. Chee Min was facing that way.

'Hand-grenade!' he yelled. But the warning was superfluous; the Emergency had been on long enough for everyone present to know quite well what it was.

Bodies hurtled through windows and doors and more people were crushed and injured in the ensuing stampede than by the explosion which followed.

It seemed to James that every woman in the building must have screamed. He jumped on to a chair in front of the screen and shouted, 'Stay put. Give the doctor some space.'

But if anyone heard him they took no notice. Only the police and a couple of planters remained calm, trying to prevent worse tragedy.

Stan was already examining the wounded and soon the ambulance arrived. 'Help me,' he called to Sally, as he lifted a young woman from the floor and passed Helen her child. 'I don't know what damage there is, but try and keep her still.' He left her with the writhing woman, but was soon back with a syringe. Once she was out they lifted her on to a stretcher, then he straightened up. A gruesome pile lay to the side, but the last of the injured was being carried out. 'Well, that's the last. It'll be a full ward to-night.' Then he followed the ambulance.

James, Helen and Sally looked at each other and at the mess.

Besides the actual damage caused by the grenade, chairs had been overturned and smashed, empty bottles rolled in every direction and a mass of broken glass and peanuts littered the floor.

'It could have been worse,' James said. 'Only three dead. Bloody lucky Lee saw it bounce.'

Chee Min had gone off with Philip to give chase, although the culprit would almost certainly have disappeared amongst the milling throng outside. Rose stood nearby, white-faced and looking very young.

'This is Mrs Lee,' Sally said. 'I think I'll take her home.'

'Take Helen too,' James suggested. 'I'll stay here and supervise some clearing up.'

The three women left him and climbed into the Morrisons' car. Perhaps it would have made Azizah happy to know they had not seen the film.

Having once made up his mind to co-operate with the terrorists, Ramakrishnan lost no time.

On the first occasion that he saw the tapper who had summoned him to the presence of the bandit that day, he beckoned him over and told him that he wanted to meet the same man again.

It was not until the following afternoon that the labourer told him the man was in the same place and to hurry, they did not like to be kept waiting. There was something insolent and familiar in the man's manner that Krishnan did not like.

There were two men waiting in the rubber, both in uniform.

'Well?' asked the one whom Krishnan already knew. 'Why have you sought us out?'

'Master, I have been giving matter much urgent thought and am coming to conclusion that I can render much valuable aid to Communist cause.'

'Such as?'

'I am listening to all telephone conversations in office. I can tell you when arrangements are being made for police or other running dogs to visit estate. You will know then when to set ambushes on road.'

The bandits appeared to ignore him and spoke together in Chinese for a good ten minutes.

Then, 'Why do you do this?'

'Master, I have always been holding most deadly hatred of white pigs and most especially the police I am not liking at all. Only a few months ago, one bearded Bengali policeman shook me in most humiliating manner in public place, causing much loss of face and honour both.'

Again they spoke together.

'We haven't enough men free to man an ambush position the whole time, only on certain days. We would require the information in advance. Here, take this.' It was a small red square of cloth. 'Stick it in your office window when you have information to impart; then come and wait here.'

'But the manager might – '

'The manager . . .' Both men laughed scornfully.

It was then that Krishnan made the mistake of showing off.

'I have been clerk in District Office, remember,' he said. 'I am knowing that District Officer keeps engagement pad on desk, telling of all visits and items of importance for following month. I have seen him writing in it often.'

At that some interest was shown.

'Do all government officers keep such a pad?'

'Oh, most verily,' Krishnan stated, without having the faintest idea, 'it is of a certainty.'

The terrorists spoke together again, then, with a sign of dismissal, they walked away.

It was a fortnight before Krishnan stuck the red square in the window and went off to the plantation edge to wait. He was well pleased with himself.

'I have news of informations most advanced,' he announced proudly. 'To-day I am hearing invitement of doctor by manager to come and stay. At Hari Raya he is coming, two months over from now.' He beamed. 'Ambush positions can be arranged in most plentiful time.'

The bandits were not impressed.

'No point in ambushing the doctor, he travels unarmed,' they said. 'You had better do better than that.'

Crestfallen, Krishnan watched them saunter away. He thought he had done very well.

Wotherspoon had asked Stan to come and spend a few days with him on impulse. Nice chap, he thought, and he had said that he had never spent more than a few hours on a rubber estate.

'Come for Hari Raya,' the planter had suggested. 'My Javanese labour usually put on quite a show.'

That was bait, of course; most of his labour was Tamil, but he did have a few Javanese and he might persuade them to dance a bit.

He would have to square his khaki-clad friends, of course, but that should not be difficult, if they could be persuaded to listen to sense. It would look more normal, he would point out, if he were to have a guest to stay. If friends were kept away from the estate, people would become suspicious.

Not that he had many friends. He had always been a lone wolf, seldom mingling with the crowd.

But he was lonely sometimes. He admitted that. Yes, it would be pleasant to have European company for a few days.

He wandered out of his office and up the drive to his bungalow. It was a good house; he had supervised the building himself before the war and he had been one of the lucky ones; very little stuff had been touched.

He had been happy enough until this confounded Emergency broke out. If he had wanted company he could always go down to the club, or to Kemuning, even to Berembang or Kuala Lumpur; he was very much his own boss. His so-called Head Office were really only agents; they left him alone. But he had not sought company often; he was content with his pictures and his books and his garden. His hobby for many years had been trying to raise rare plants. He had taken immense pleasure in growing flowers and trees that, according to all the experts, could not be grown in the Malayan climate.

He walked round the garden once before going inside.

The mango tree was in full foliage; he looked up at it with pride – it had come over from the Philippines some twenty years before and produced the most delicious fruit.

Then his eyes narrowed. Those damned SCs. They were throwing sticks up into the tree, trying to knock down the still green fruit.

'Stop that,' he yelled. 'Get out of my garden, damn you. Stick to your own quarters; I won't have you here.'

By the time he reached the house his whole body was shaking with fury.

They had come, ruining his grounds and taking away his privacy. A bush had to be cut down because it would give access over the wire, a flower-bed was trampled on, marked as being a good place for a light. Well, the bush had not been cut down, nor had the wire gone up – it was there, in rolls still, in the store, but it had not gone up. Nor had the light. He had lived amongst Asians long enough to know that, if you hedge long enough, people turn their attention elsewhere – or so he hoped.

All he asked was to be left alone. To plant what he liked where he liked and to have his privacy undisturbed.

His attitude might cost lives, he had been told. Well, so what? No one worried about *his* life. He had had the SCs thrust upon him; he didn't want them, hadn't asked for them. They were a confounded nuisance. Let them ambush all the government wallahs who came up his road. Who cared? Wish they'd kill that bloody OCPD, and the police lieutenant who kept snooping round the SCs. Well, one *had* been killed fairly recently and not so far away at that. Served him right.

He had a good mind to forbid government servants from entering the estate. Put up a barricade – get the bandits to do it for him. Why not?

That Pole was government. He had a good mind to cancel his invitation. Well, he'd see. He'd think about it.

654

Donald arrived back from leave in good time and announced that the seasonal festivities could now begin!

Sally took a lot of trouble with their Christmas dinner that year. The previous year it had been the Weatherbys' do, this year it was their turn. Ja'afar had done his best to persuade her to make it a big party; to ask as many of the planters and their wives as the house would hold, but she was determined to keep it small and have only what she called 'the hill.' Don and Stan they might meet again, but even if they were posted back to the same district after leave, which was unlikely, they would not see the Weatherbys again, unless they too should end up in Australia.

'I congratulate you on achieving an oasis of civilisation in the wilderness,' Stan said, as he bowed over Sally's hand.

You're still very smooth, she thought, but in fact he meant it. He and Donald stood admiring the table, waiting for the Weatherbys to arrive. The silver and glass had been polished that day and gleamed softly in the pale candlelight. Pink and white Honolulu creeper cascaded out of a central bowl to mingle with tinsel and touch the lace table-mats.

Truth to tell, Sally herself was pleased with the effect, but apprehensive. 'If only we're allowed to enjoy the evening in peace,' she said wistfully. 'We've never yet been left alone on Christmas Day.'

Later she was to say, 'Well, at least they let us reach the coffee stage this year.'

The turkey and plum pudding had been well washed down and they were just making room amongst the debris of nuts and spent crackers for their coffee cups when the telephone rang.

Philip got up. 'Right,' he said, after the voice at the other end had crackled for a time, 'I'll come now.'

'I knew it was too good to last.' Sally tried not to sound plaintive but was unsuccessful. She had started to get up, but Philip motioned her to sit down again.

'I don't want to break up the party,' he said, 'and there's no great rush; it'll take a few minutes to root out the ferryman.'

He went into the bedroom, followed by Ja'afar with a hissing pressure lamp.

'I hate those things,' Helen remarked, 'but there's no denying that they do give a good light.'

No one could think of anything else to say and Sally suggested that they should take their coffee and liqueurs over to the more comfortable chairs. Philip joined them in a moment, sitting to gulp down his coffee while he laced his jungle boots.

'Rather a garbled message,' he told them. 'Two Europeans reported killed on the other side of the river. I can't think who they can be. There's only one estate there and the manager's on leave. There should be only one police lieutenant in the area – I'll have to go and find out.'

'But couldn't the army – ' Sally began. But he shook his head.

'Both the company commander and his two i/c are spending Christmas with their families. There must be a duty officer, but it's quicker to go myself.'

'Well, I do think – '

'I used to come home to you when I was in the army,' Philip interrupted, and Sally looked squashed.

He picked up his beret and torch, pecked his wife on the cheek, and ran down the steps.

'Well, if that isn't the most tolerant guy,' Don remarked. 'He sure settled your hash, Sal!'

Sally made an effort to laugh. 'I do try not to mind, but it's reached the state where, if the phone doesn't ring for a couple of hours, I begin to think there's something wrong! Half the time it's false alarms, but of course the time he doesn't go it won't be – I can see his point really. You know, one evening, about this time last year, a rather panicky planter rang up to say he was surrounded; that his wire was being charged. Philip and Mike both turned out with every available man, only to find it was a herd of cows!'

The night drew on; they were all tired. Carols from the radio had long since ceased. Sally persuaded Helen and James to go home; she knew that Helen had a children's party on her hands the following day.

Stan and Don had already said that they intended staying.

James actually kissed Sally on the cheek and everyone let out such a whoop of surprise that the tension was broken at last. Conversation between the three became easier and it was not long afterwards that lights were seen on the river.

The sound of the ferry chugging across was quite clear in the still night and soon an engine started up below and a jeep drove off in the direction of the pier.

'Shouldn't be long now – ' before Sally had finished her sentence the phone rang. It was Philip.

'I'm back, Sally. Two soldiers, I'm afraid. If Stan's still there, would you ask him if he'd come down?'

Sally and Don watched from the verandah as the jeep and troop-carrier drew up. Then she turned away and sat down.

'I'm sorry, Don. I can't bear to watch. I'm too afraid that one day it might be Philip's body being lifted from that van.'

Donald gave her a sympathetic look, but he was too engrossed with what was going on down below to pay her much attention. Two blanket-covered forms were being carried from the troop-carrier and into the police station, followed by Philip and Stan. Soon a number of men had clustered round and he could see no more. Perhaps it *was* rather sickening.

'May I take the liberty, Sal?'

Without waiting for her reply, he crossed to where the decanters stood on the sideboard and poured them both a healthy tot of Scotch.

'Drink up,' he said. 'Perdition to the Communists.' He finished his at a gulp.

Sally had still only sipped her drink when the other two men returned.

'Two BORs,' Philip told them. 'Apparently they were trying to capture the Christmas spirit in one of the coffee-shops, when a couple of masked men walked in and shot them at point blank range. God alone knows what they were doing so far from the army camp – they didn't appear to have any transport – unless they were going to pay a Christmas call on Stubbs, the police lieutenant who's stationed nearby. Anyway, if the bill the towkay presented me with is correct, they must have been roaring fu' – they can't have known what hit them. I wanted Stan to dig the bullets out to find out what weapon was used.'

'Weren't there any witnesses?'

'Hordes. But none of them will admit to having seen a thing. It's the usual story.'

'And only the other day,' Sally said quietly, 'I was saying what a gay time we had to look forward to – Christmas, New Year, Chinese New Year and Hari Raya, all within a couple of months. Let's hope we don't have a repeat performance each time.'

Luckily Sally's fears were unfounded. At least the Christmas tragedy was not repeated at New Year.

'It only seems to happen when people come to our house,' she remarked as they walked up the Weatherbys' drive. 'It's almost an excuse not to entertain.'

They had reached the steps and she paused to look back. It was a brilliant moonlit night and the sound of the sea could be heard faintly, as the tide flowed into the tangle of mangroves below them. In the other world, a few yards away, voices could be heard coming from the verandah, and Helen's remark that the Morrisons were late floated out to them.

'Come on,' Philip tugged at her hand, 'we're always the last to arrive.'

As they neared the top of the steps, a concerted yell halted them momentarily and Donald and Stan advanced towards them.

'Do you see what I see?' Donald was grinning like a Cheshire cat. Philip was wearing the kilt. 'Doesn't this remind you of another Hogmanay?'

With one leap they were upon him, but he was ready for them. 'Duck,' he ordered Sally, and moving forward with outstretched arms, he met them as they charged and banged their heads together.

The Christmas decorations were still up. 'Observe tradition,' Philip cried, 'you're under the mistletoe!'

The three onlookers guffawed.

'I'd never have guessed it of old Don,' Helen laughed. 'He's certainly been in incredible form ever since he came back from leave.'

It was true. Donald had burst on the district like a firework. 'He's almost becoming the professional life and soul of the party,' Stan had been heard to remark, somewhat gloomily.

'Hi, Jim! Hi, Phil! What's cookin', Doc?' had been his greeting at the small welcome-back party that had been arranged for him at the club on his return. And that had been his tone ever since. It was not altogether surprising, therefore, that he should be the one to remind them when midnight was almost due. And James had hardly popped the cork before Don was grabbing hands and starting up with 'Auld Lang Syne'.

'Happy New Year. Happy New Year.'

When everyone had drunk and their glasses were refilled, he called out, 'Now everyone, our own private toasts, our hopes for the coming year.'

The Weatherbys drank to their new life in Australia; the Morrisons to their leave. Don drank to Kuala Jelang and Stan, after being prodded, raised his glass with a whimsical expression and drank to 'Heaven – or hell.'

Still holding his glass high and looking through the champagne as he watched the others, Stan stood aloof. They seemed to be gradually fading out, as actors fade into the wings. He had a fleeting impression that he was above a stage, where each person spoke a part. He looked down on them and saw their mime, but he could not hear their voices any more.

'Stan. Stan, are you all right?'

He saw the top of a brown head below his glass and felt Sally's hand on his arm.

He lowered his glass then and their eyes met. He saw the sadness in hers.

658

'Stan,' she whispered, 'I do believe – for a moment – we shared the same thought.'

He smiled then and kissed her upturned face.

'Happy New Year, my dear,' he said.

112. CHINESE NEW YEAR

Broomph-broooom! It was Saturday afternoon. Chee Min rode up to the police station on his new motor bike and stopped with a flourish.

Omar, who was on duty in the Charge Room, walked outside to see who had arrived and exclaimed in admiration.

'Wah!'

Chee Min beamed proudly. He had saved for this, he and Rose – it was partly what she had earned from her embroidery that had paid for the bike. He had been going backwards and forwards to the cycle shop for weeks, trying to make up his mind between a Norton and a BSA, and here it was, a Norton, *his* Norton, 500 cc.

Omar ran his hands lovingly over the powerful machine and nodded his approval.

Karim walked over from the MT yard and admired it from several yards' distance. Now that, he thought, is something I would like to have. Perhaps, one day. Rokiah would enjoy it too. Speed. The whistling of the wind as it whipped past one's ears. Wah!

Ahmat looked out of his office window to see what was going on, and his lip curled in disdain. *Nouveau riche*, he thought, just what one would expect. He closed the window and went back to his work.

Jogindar Singh watched from the main door of the police station. Now, if I had a little money to spare, he thought, I'd buy the odd acre of land, or maybe a few more cows. Strange how we all hanker after different things – luckily. The machine did not interest him at all.

All this time, Rose had been standing by the main gate, but Chee Min was so busy explaining the finer points of the bike to its admirers that he had not noticed her until she moved towards him.

'Isn't she a beaut?' he called. And then, 'Hey, Rosie, what's this?'

Rose sometimes wore European clothes and sometimes a *samfoo*, but she was dressed quite differently now and in something he had never seen her in before. A red and white gingham smock topped a straight white skirt – maternity clothes?

'Rose!'

The clothes had been given to her by Sally, who had kept them hopefully all this time. And then, one day not long before, when Stan had been examining a police baby in the clinic, she had remarked that she still hoped to have one herself one day.

He had been very stern.

'You'll be extremely selfish if you do,' he had said. And, to Sally's surprise, 'Philip told me exactly what the obstetrician said. It's not an uncommon deformity that you have, but you'll never produce a live child and there's a good chance of you popping off yourself. Think of Philip instead of yourself for a change.'

She had been cross with him at the time and indignant at his accusation of selfishness, but when finally she admitted the truth to herself, she knew that he was right.

Hence the clothes. As soon as Rose had mentioned that she thought she was pregnant, Sally had passed all her maternity clothes on to her.

'Rose! Rose?'

Rose giggled, blushed and turned away. It would be months before she showed, but she wanted to wear the smock, just to give Vincent a surprise.

'Crikey! What a Chinese New Year present. Come and look at her, Rosie.'

Rose climbed on to the pillion seat and soon they were off, up the hill and through the town and back again. A new set of admirers awaited them and a cross face at the window put hands over ears.

Chee Min mentally cocked a snook at Ahmat, working late. It was a good world all right; who wanted to be cooped up in a stuffy office on a day like this?

He grabbed Rose's hand. 'Let's go and tell old Stan.'

'Oh, Vincent, you must *not* be so familiar!'

'Why not?'

Brooomph, roomph-rmph!

'Well, Rose, do I see what I think I see?'

'Oh, Doctor, not for ages yet.'

Chee Min was a little bit peeved that Stan had noticed Rose before the bike. But not for long. Rose frowned and tried to indicate the machine with her eyes. Stan twigged.

'Good heavens, Vincent, what a magnificent machine. A Norton, eh? Something I always wanted but never had.' Which was quite untrue.

They went into technical details then and Rose wandered away into the garden, picking up frangipani blossoms from the grass.

'That sergeant of yours is a blooming menace,' James complained. 'Damned nearly ran me down.'

'The novelty will wear off in a few days, then you'll be safe again!'

660

'I thought he came from such a wealthy family; couldn't he afford something a little more sedate?'

'It's his own private revolution,' Philip explained. 'Thumbing his nose at his old man and saying, "I'll marry whom I like, thank you." He's got a lot of guts, Chee Min.'

'Well, I wish they'd come out in some other guise!'

'It was last Chinese New Year that I had that row with Dad,' Chee Min remarked. 'Do you think we should try and make it up? Just appear and say, "*Kong hee fatt choy*," and see what his reaction is?'

Rose shook her head. 'I'll give him a grandson first, a real living *ang pow*. None of your brothers or sisters have had children yet, have they?' Chee Min shook his head in turn. 'Well, then, we have a good chance. Let's let things work themselves out.'

'Dear Rose, you are so prudent and so wise,' he said. 'I must write and tell Mum though.'

113. NOTHING IS SIMPLE

Before Ramakrishnan had reason to stick the red square in the window again, the terrorists sent for him.

'This diary, this engagement pad that you spoke of. You said all government officers keep such pads?'

Krishnan sensed a trap, but he could not, dare not, deny what he had already told them. He merely nodded.

'Then the OCPD must have one.'

'Oh, of a certainty, Masters.'

'Get it for us.'

Krishnan gasped. The clammy sweat sprang out on the palms of his hands and his eyes rolled.

'That is not possible. I am thinking that police station routine is not being understood. Always there is someone on duty, day and night. It is not like other government departments, which maintain office hours pure and simple. Always the police station is awake.'

'We know that.' The speaker regarded him with scorn. 'You were a government clerk, weren't you?'

'Yes, Master.'

'So you must know the police clerks.'

'I am knowing them only slightly, Master.'

'What are their names?'

'Maniam I am knowing, Master. Names of secondary clerks I am not knowing.'

'Maniam will get this pad for you.'

'But Master, I am only working for short time as government clerk of most junior capacity. Maniam is chief clerk, man. I am hardly knowing him, Master.'

The three uniformed men stood silently regarding the little Tamil, as he wagged his head, rolled his eyes and fidgeted generally. They were very still.

'You will get it,' the leader said and, as usual, turned and walked away without another word.

All night Krishnan tossed and turned in despair. It was true that the District Officer did keep an engagement pad, but what he wrote on it Krishnan had no idea.

Why had he pretended to know more than he did? Oh, truly I am being hoisted with own petard, he groaned; for foolishness I am taking much to beat.

How could he gain access to the OCPD's office to find out if indeed he did keep such a pad? Maniam had never even spoken to him, except in a general way when he had visited the District Office. He had no friends in Kuala Jelang to help in such a venture, let alone the police clerk.

Eyes seemed to be watching him from behind every tree and bush. Voices whispered and he lived in constant fear of the dreaded summons.

After three days he could bear it no longer. He would ring up Maniam, pretending the manager of some mythical estate wanted to see the OCPD. He would ask him to make a note of the time and date on the OCPD's engagement pad and see what the answer would be.

As soon as he had thought of this brilliant plan, Krishnan began to bounce. If such a pad did indeed exist, then he would have to think again but, for the time being, he could always tell the bandits that the OCPD had stopped writing his engagements down.

Oh, it was easy. Why had he been such a fool? To be afraid of three men not much larger than himself. They were only men.

The idea had come to him in the middle of the night, and as soon as the office opened the following day, he put through a call to Kuala Jelang Police Station.

Ten minutes later he was leaning back in his chair, laughing to himself and sweating with relief. He went over to the window to affix the red square.

'Maniam is on leave for two weeks,' Ramakrishnan informed his listeners, 'and then two more days. He will not be returning until the end of the Hari Raya holiday.'

He faced them triumphantly this time, hands thrust into trouser pockets and a smile upon his face. But his cockiness was short-lived.

'Liar!' He felt the blood spurt as the man standing opposite leaned forward and struck him across the mouth.

'Oh, most honestly, Masters, I am not lying. Verily I am not. It is easily found out that it is only the truth I am telling. Only one half-hour ago I am ringing police station and being informed that Chief Clerk Maniam is on leave two weeks and two days precisely.'

'You will go to the police station then yourself.'

'I cannot.'

The police! Oh, what had he done? To go to the police station would mean certain disaster for him. In a flash his mind sped back over the past years; outwitting the police at every turn, only to fall into their hands now.

'You will go with the next lorry that goes into town.'

'To the police station I cannot go, Masters.'

'A lorry goes down on the last day of every month, as you well know. You will be on it at the end of this month.'

'Oh, Masters.' Krishnan fell on his knees, hands clasped in an attitude half of pain and half of supplication.

He received a kick in the jaw for his pains.

This time the bandits did not melt silently away – they were laughing as they tramped through the rubber.

About a week had passed when both manager and clerk looked up on hearing a tap on the office window.

Outside stood one of the terrorists, his face as impassive as stone.

Krishnan's heart began to turn somersaults. Oh my goodness gracious, he thought, they have come for me.

'The audacity,' Wotherspoon muttered, half under his breath. To come to the office in broad daylight, and in uniform too. 'Better open the window,' he said to the clerk.

Krishnan did as he was told.

The terrorist smiled. 'Just to remind you not to forget,' he said. 'The police.'

He walked casually away, leaving Wotherspoon red with fury and Krishnan grey with fright.

The man had spoken to Krishnan, but Wotherspoon had not known that. To him, it was a warning about the land. Such boldness could only mean one thing – he was entirely at their mercy and had to play their game.

Without a word he left the office, got into his Land-Rover and drove off to Kuala Jelang.

'Aren't you coming to our Hari Raya party, Stan?' Sally asked. 'The police always have a tremendous binge – kenduri, ronggeng girls, the lot. It's fun.'

'No. I'm going to Bukit Merah Estate for the holiday and part of my local leave.'

'Old Wotherspoon's estate? Oh Stan, you traitor!' she cried. 'He's terribly anti-police.'

'But I am nothing to do with the police, my dear,' he said, with the cynical smirk that took her straight back to the war. She was infuriated. 'I've always wanted to know what it's like living on a remote rubber estate during the Emergency, and this is my chance to find out.'

What he did not add was that he had dreaded the thought of spending the holiday in the bungalow alone with Don. His good spirits had been short-lived and he was back to his maudlin state, only worse than ever; drinking himself to death, as Stan had already told him on several occasions. He was becoming so argumentative and belligerent after only a very few drinks that Stan was doing his best to keep out of his way.

These thoughts were going through his head as he stood and smiled at Sally. But she had the last word anyway.

'Better take Salmah with you for protection then,' she said. 'By all accounts he's very odd!'

Philip had been listening with one ear to the conversation between his wife and Stan and was amused by Sally's pique.

'Just because he was a boy-friend ten years ago,' he said, when they were walking up to the house for lunch, 'gives you no proprietary claim. Besides, I don't think you're the only one.'

'That Malay girl? I know all about her – practically knocked me out with a corn cob that evening I had supper with them!'

'No, not Salmah. Helen.'

'Helen? Don't be ridiculous. Honestly, Philip, you do imagine things.'

'Do I? I wonder. I don't believe she's nearly as chilly as she appears.'

'But how could she possibly have known Stan?'

'How could you?'

'That's different. We were in the same service.'

'So was James.'

'Well, anyway, I think you're talking rot.'

'Why is she so careful to avoid him then?'

'I don't think she is.'

'Oh no? You watch.'

If Helen had heard this conversation she would have had fifty fits.

James had been so much easier of late; ever since their Australian plans had been settled. But she was still on edge whenever Stan was

664

around, terrified that one of them would make some thoughtless reference to the past which, if heard by James, might start an avalanche.

In fact, she would have loved to have had a chat with Stan about old times, but as it was she had never had a chance even to explain fully the reason for her pretence. Once, when Angela had had a fever and he had come up to the house to see her during working hours, she had begun, but, within five minutes of his arrival, James was there too. Why? Because he was worried about his daughter, or because he had seen the doctor's car turn up towards their house? She never knew and gave up trying to catch Stan on his own after that.

But Stan's interests were purely in the present. He enjoyed Sally's company, although he found her irritating at times, and Helen was altogether too aloof. Besides, he not only liked at least one of their husbands, but had to work with them. He was not going to stir up any hornets' nests. The Weatherbys would be on leave in six weeks' time and the Morrisons a few months after that.

Helen would be sorry to go, but James could not get away fast enough. It was always the same with him; once a decision had been made he had to get on with it; it was hopeless hanging around.

Norman had organised a caravan for them – a trailer he called it – large enough to accommodate the whole family while their house was being built. There had been a letter that morning, telling them that the last details had been fixed. Next week would be the holiday; if he could clear up his outstanding work before then, James thought, he and Helen could spend the few days putting their heads together over passages, getting their clothes sorted out, and suchlike. Nannie would be arriving within the month.

He had just put Norman's letter away and was getting down to some routine work when the telephone rang. It was Helen.

'Mr Wotherspoon's here,' she said. 'He wants to see you urgently, but not in your office. Can you come up?'

James stifled an oath. 'I suppose I'll have to. Tell him he'll have to wait a little while.'

It was always the same. It seemed inevitable that good news should be countered with bad.

He rang Philip to tell him and to ask if he had any idea what it might be about. He did not. 'I'll let you know what ensues,' James said.

Wotherspoon was clearly in a state.

'I can't sell,' his voice rose to a high-pitched note, 'I won't.'

'I think you'd better have a drink,' James said, and poured him a stiff brandy and ginger-ale.

It disappeared in a couple of gulps, but it was no use. Nothing would calm him down. His eyes were shifty and his hands shook. He told a long-winded and completely incoherent story about the reasons why Head Office would not permit him to sell.

James wished he had a tape-recorder, but he had asked Helen to listen from behind the bedroom door.

Wotherspoon did not stay long.

'I've given you my reasons,' he said, 'and they're final.' And then, rather pathetically, 'I don't know where we go from here.'

Helen's shorthand was rusty, but she had taken sufficient notes for them to go over the conversation again. Little of it made sense. James jotted down the gist and went down to the police station.

'It's quite incomprehensible,' Philip remarked after he had read it through. 'What did you tell him?'

'That the matter would now rest with DWEC. There's a meeting to-morrow, don't forget.'

'I hadn't. Good.'

After much discussion, the members of DWEC came to the unanimous conclusion that they had given Wotherspoon more than sufficient leeway; the land should be requisitioned.

But the matter did not rest there. It was not that simple.

Only a very few days after the meeting, the Special Branch officer from Circle Headquarters, Bill Young, was on the blower to Philip.

'I've got the minutes of your last DWEC meeting here,' he said. 'Hold everything. Tell the DO not to go ahead. I can't tell you anything more over the phone. I'm coming down. If I may, I'll spend the night with you.'

'Don't force Wotherspoon's hand just yet,' they were told. 'It might result in open killing – probably of him – and the bandits going to ground. I'm as sure as you are that they're there, although that typewriter is still the only proof we have, and he might wriggle out of that – a good defence lawyer would get him out of it at any rate.'

'Do you mean he'd be taken to court?' James felt sick.

'Not if it can be avoided – he's one of us, after all, regrettably – but I want to have a snoop round that estate myself and perhaps post a few men there. Later, we might be able to mount a raid – a lot will depend on what information we can glean and whether the CTs are living in the labour lines or in a camp in the vicinity. In any event, we'll get the old boy removed from the state.'

'You police are very harsh.'

'There haven't been any DOs killed to date.'

James raised his hand in a gesture of resignation. 'I give up,' he said, and he sounded very tired. 'Heaven alone knows I've done my

666

best for Wotherspoon, but one can't go on farting against thunder for ever.'

'I would suggest, James,' Philip said, 'that you and I go and see him together and argue it out. Not by arrangement though; take him by surprise. And it must be soon.'

'I'm absolutely snowed under until the holiday.'

'So am I. Let's make it the first day after, then.'

'All right. But let's give him the benefit of the doubt just once more, for the last time,' pleaded James, going back on his resolution. 'There might be something on that land, timber or something, that his Head Office don't wish to lose. Let's have a better look at the land itself before we tackle him. I'd like to take Don along.'

'Why not? I shall certainly take Ahmat and Chee Min.'

114. HARI RAYA PUASA

The thud and thump of the mosque drum reverberated through the small town and the Malay police streamed out of the station compound, dressed in their best, to answer the call to prayer.

It was Hari Raya Puasa, the end of the fasting month of Ramadan, or Puasa. Police on active service were given a special dispensation, but many of them were strong-minded and, particularly the older men, still held their fast throughout the daylight hours, obeying the rhythmic command of the drum as the sun rose and set.

Sally looked on with a feeling of relief. Puasa was always a trying time, even for those who did not fast. Tempers were high for the first few days and Ja'afar was quite unapproachable. As their throats and stomachs grew accustomed to the new routine they gradually settled down, but she hated asking anyone to cook or pour out a drink, knowing that they could touch nothing themselves.

Ja'afar himself was quite philosophic, invariably apologising for his bouts of ill-humour at the outset and laughing when he saw his employers surreptitiously sneaking food and drink from the refrigerator.

From where they stood on their verandah, high on the hill, the men leaving the station looked like so many butterflies winging their way across the green grass. Purple, royal blue, maroon, and bottle-green sarongs, many worked with gold or silver thread, were girt about marching hips. Arms and legs swung in silks of pink and blue, salmon and mauve, white, green or grey; every colour except the royal yellow. Black velvet songkoks topped almost every head, with here and there a contrasting deep blue, green or crimson.

'Selamat Hari Raya, Tuan. Selamat Hari Raya, Mem.'

They turned to see Ja'afar and Siti, looking quite gorgeous, on their way out.

'Selamat Hari Raya.'

Ja'afar was dressed in pale blue silk and gold embroidered purple. His open leather sandals clacked on the steep stone steps, and Siti, in a flowing, flowered baju kurong, floated behind, her head and shoulders encased in a film of delicate gauze.

'Glad we stayed here?' Philip asked, and put an arm about Sally's shoulders. 'Glad that you were able to take them on?'

She smiled and snuggled into his arm. Of all the festivals, Hari Raya was the one she liked the best.

'It's always a salutary jolt for me,' she said. 'It's only when the servants are off for a few days that I appreciate how much work they do!'

Better tidy the house up now, she thought. Ahmat and Azizah and Zukifli and the most recently arrived inspector, Ismail, would be coming up later on, followed by the Malay NCOs and their wives. Bottles of Coca-Cola, sarsaparilla and orange crush were already nestling in tin baths of ice and the small eats had been prepared.

The sun shone out of a cloudless sky and a gentle breeze stirred the leaves of the rain trees. Fragile pink blossoms shivered and shook, but sprang to meet the sunlight. It was a happy day.

But for Ramakrishnan it was not a happy day. It had been bad enough knowing that Maniam would be back in a few days and that the end of the month was drawing near. But that was not all.

He had been got out of bed by a labourer early that morning, telling him that he was wanted.

No need to ask by whom.

He had dressed hurriedly, shivering in the dawn damp, and gone at once to the usual meeting-place under the rubber trees.

This time there were four men and Krishnan felt sick as he approached them.

'Why did you not go to Kuala Jelang with the lorry yesterday?'

Krishnan hedged. 'But, Masters, you said the end of the month, and it was not the lorry, but the Land-Rover, that went.'

They looked at him with distaste.

'I did not know it was going,' he pleaded. He knew better now than to go on his knees to them. 'It was not scheduled to go.'

'You told us yourself that the doctor would be coming to stay. You told us more than two months ago.'

'But how am I for knowing that manager would send estate Land-Rover for him? I am expecting doctor to arrive by own car.'

668

There was a terrible, pregnant silence, while the terrorists looked at Krishnan and Krishnan looked at the trees.

'We are supported by all the labour on this estate,' the leader said at last. 'Do you know why they co-operate?'

'Of course, because they are hating white pigs like I, and are forever looking forward to times of democracy when colonialism is at an end.'

One of the younger bandits laughed.

'When we first came to this estate, more than three years ago,' the leader went on, 'the labour were not co-operative. So we took the kangani and hacked him to death – just where you are standing now.'

Involuntarily Krishnan took a step back and looked at the ground and the young bandit laughed again.

'He died very slowly. We took a piece at a time, until his cries had attracted all the labour force. They stood around; they saw him die.'

There was another silence while all five men stood still and Krishnan felt the vomit rise in his throat. He swallowed, but no words would come out.

'And that is what will happen to you, if you do not do as you are told. If you are not on the next vehicle to leave this estate, you will die – here. And do not think, my friend, that you can escape us. We can get you as easily in Kuala Jelang, or anywhere else, as here. You will return by that same lorry and in your possession will be the OCPD's engagement pad, or it will be the worse for you. Go.'

Krishnan turned. His legs were shaking so much that his knees knocked and his head felt unsteady on his neck. Before he had left the shelter of the rubber, the terrorists called him back.

'Hacking can be a slow death,' the leader said. 'I can hear the screams of that kangani now. Yes, he took a long time to die. There was much blood and many parts of him falling out. I remember it well. You will do well to remember it too, my friend. We make no idle threats.'

One thing they did not do was make idle threats; there was plenty of proof of that. Krishnan crawled back into his bed, pulling the blanket over his head, and wept.

Suddenly, the thought of a police cell seemed a haven. The more he thought about it, the more he preferred the idea of arrest to the fate the bandits would mete out.

He would write a letter to Post Office Box 5000, the police PO Box where informers, who wished to remain anonymous, could post their information. There would be a raid then, no doubt – but what would happen to him? Suppose the raid were unsuccessful? Any terrorists left alive would know at whose door the blame lay.

669

Krishnan shivered under the scarlet blanket. No, there was only one thing that he could do. Go to the police, give his information in person and demand their protection. After all, he was a citizen; he had the right to protection, hadn't he? If only he did not have to wait. In his present state of mind he was afraid that the bandits might even be able to read his thoughts. He did not get up all day, but lay there under the blanket, stiff and silent, keeping his head covered and jumping at every sound.

Wotherspoon, too, was on edge. Ever since he had returned from the DO's house, he had expected the telephone to ring.

But there was a simple way of dealing with that. The phone in his house was on a ledge behind a potted palm, out of sight. He simply left the receiver off the hook. It was annoying having asked that doctor to stay, but unless he wanted to use the phone – and he was unlikely to do so without asking first – he need not know.

The Javanese wouldn't play ball. What was there to dance about? they asked. Labour was becoming more and more difficult these days. Bolshie. They knew that if they got the sack there were always jobs going on other estates. That was the trouble. A little unemployment would not do the country any harm.

Ever since the invitation to the doctor had been issued, he had wanted to withdraw it, but could not do so without arousing suspicion. So here he was, an inquisitive type, always wandering around. Wotherspoon didn't like it. These ruddy Communists were becoming so bold, they were as likely to walk in on him as not, guest or no guest. Perhaps when the Pole realised how boring life on an estate could be, he would return. That was his only hope. He had tried to sound surprised when Stan told him the receiver was off the hook and had put it back until the doctor was out of sight, but he would have to take care. Must make sure the one in his office was off too; the house phone was only an extension of the same line.

'Come into the garden,' he called to Stan. 'I have some interesting shrubs that I'd like you to see.'

In Kuala Jelang itself the holiday proceeded without mishap. Friends and relatives visited, prayers were said, a good deal of aimless wandering went on and far too much was eaten.

For the police, who were mainly Muslims, and mostly far away from home, the biggest event was without doubt the party on the last night of the festival.

A platform, some three feet from the ground, had been erected, large enough to accommodate four ronggeng girls and a three-piece band. Hours were spent plaiting palm fronds and forming intricate paper flowers with which to decorate it. Poles were stuck up at intervals round the parade-ground, on which were tacked tins holding candles, and the police station itself, the canteen and the part where the onlookers would be sitting, were festooned with coloured lights.

'It all seems so much work for just one night,' Sally murmured, but she enjoyed it as much as the men.

Certainly more than one man. If it were possible to kill by telepathy, Sally would have fallen dead at that very moment.

'I suppose *she* will be there,' Azizah remarked sulkily.

'If you mean the Mem, yes.'

'And the wife of the DO?'

'Yes.'

Ahmat had done his best to make the holiday a success. He had taken Azizah out on every day and for once the terrorists had done nothing to mar the few days off. Open-air film shows had taken place on the padang every night. They had gone to these, eaten at the only Muslim restaurant and played tombola at the club.

He had never changed his mind about the equal part that his wife should play in their private lives, but he was too disciplined and came from too old a family to do anything which went against custom in his public life. Hence he had vetoed the kenduri and the dancing that would follow that evening. The European women were expected to be there, but Malay women simply did not attend such functions with their men. Times, no doubt, would change, but at the moment it was not done.

It was no use Azizah sulking and stamping her foot and breaking his favourite glass; nothing would change his mind.

No one seeing Ahmat on the night of the final Hari Raya party would have guessed that all was not well with him.

Dignified and handsome in their inspectors' evening dress of black satin with black and silver embroidered sarongs, he, Zukifli and Ismail dominated the feast.

Tables had been set on the grass and Philip sat at the head with an inspector on either side. Sally and James sat on Ahmat's right and Helen and Don on Zukifli's left; it was all very correct.

'Couldn't Azizah join us?' Sally asked before the meal began. It would take but a moment to set another place and fetch a chair.

Ahmat frowned. 'Our customs are different from yours, Mem,' he said. No doubt but that it was a polite rebuke, but she remained deliberately unperturbed.

'Oh, I know,' she said impatiently, 'but times are changing. This is 1952. You often see Malay wives with their husbands in the "Dog" in KL now.'

'Not my wife. Excuse me, Mem, I have to go and see about the band.'

'That's put you in your place,' James chuckled as Ahmat left. 'I'm all for keeping women in their place – enough of this emancipation nonsense!'

'I'm very fond of Mat,' Sally mused, 'but he can be a bit stuffy at times. It must be difficult for his wife.' Bitch as she is, she thought, but did not say so aloud.

Eventually the meal was over, the debris cleared away and the band was mounting the dancing dais followed by the four ronggeng girls.

Ahmat tried not to look in the direction of his house. He had moved a chair on to the verandah, taken Azizah a plate of curry and a bottle of orange crush and now had a painful bruise where the bottle had hit his head.

The first tune began and there were cries of, 'OCPD, OCPD, Tuan Morrison to dance,' from the assembled crowd.

Ahmat pleaded a strained ankle and Philip was tactful enough not to comment. He and Zukifli took the floor.

'Trust him to choose the prettiest girl,' Sally remarked as Ahmat rejoined them. He smiled faintly; it was a sore point.

Soon the first stint was over and others were urged on to the platform. James refused. He was always conscious of his defects when in the public eye; he hated it. Don got up with the young inspector and was joined by Jogindar Singh and the Malay CID sergeant. One after another, everyone took their turn.

'I think we should go now,' Philip whispered across to Sally. 'The girls are only hired until midnight. They'll have a better party once we're no longer in the way.'

'Come and have a glass or a cup of something with us,' Helen suggested. 'You'll never get any sleep in your house. Ronggeng girls or not, I should think that party'll go on all night.'

'Not for too long then,' Philip said, looking at James, 'we have a heavy day ahead of us to-morrow. Back to the grindstone.'

115. TO BUKIT MERAH ESTATE

Rokiah had been taken into hospital at the beginning of Hari Raya and Karim had spent the whole holiday by her bedside.

Most police wives were delivered in barracks, but at the outset the midwife had reported that it would not be an easy birth. She had been in labour for more than thirty hours already and now they had moved her out of the labour ward and back into her ordinary hospital bed.

The bed had been screened, but Rokiah asked that the screens should be removed. 'I don't want to be alone when you go back on duty,' she said to Karim, 'it is better when I can see the other women.'

Now the holiday was over and they were at the start of another working day.

'It is a Caesarean section that she is needing,' Mr Ponniah, the chief dresser, explained to Karim, 'but Doctor is not here. He is telling me to ring him at Bukit Merah Estate if any emergency should occur, but all yesterday I am trying, and again this morning early, but nobody answers. What to do? Telephone operator says the line is in order, but maybe receiver has been left off instrument. If by ten o'clock I cannot get through, I am ringing doctor at Kemuning for advice.'

Karim's face fell and Rokiah, seeing his consternation, smiled and put out her hand.

'Don't worry. I am young and strong, only too narrow. You wouldn't want a wide woman, would you?'

'There, my son,' kind Mr Ponniah laid his hand on Karim's shoulder, 'what your wife says is true.'

'I have to go out to-day,' Karim was miserably unhappy at the thought of having to leave Rokiah, but it never occurred to him to ask for time off, 'I am on duty.'

'I am hoping perhaps that police have ways of reaching Bukit Merah Estate,' Mr Ponniah said. 'Radio, walkie-talkie, or suchlike. I will write a note and you see if OCPD can help.'

He went into his office and Karim stood, dumb with misery, looking down at the girl who had been his childhood love.

Rokiah of the coconut palms and the pounding surf; of racing out to sea and collecting turtle eggs. Other men's wives might die in childbirth, but not his, not Rokiah.

'Rokiah,' he whispered at last, 'when the dresser returns, I will have to go. Don't be scared; Mr Ponniah is a good man, he will look after you and I will fetch the doctor for you somehow.'

But the elderly Tamil was already back.

'Go, boy,' he said. 'You can do no good here. If Doctor is unable to be found, I shall ring for Kemuning ambulance – ours is broken down – but by hook or crook we shall save your wife, if not baby also.'

Karim left the hospital with tears in his eyes, cramming the letter into his breast pocket as he went. In less than half an hour he would be sitting beside the OCPD; he would ask him if he could help.

Stan had seen the receiver left off the hook and quietly replaced it, saying nothing. He had done the same thing a second time, but after the third he mentioned it to Wotherspoon. He expressed surprise, but Stan was sure it was feigned and later, when he had been alone in the bungalow for a short time, he had lifted the receiver and tried to ring the hospital. The line was useless; clearly the instrument in the office was receiving similar treatment and there was little that he could do about that. It was the same this morning.

He had been on the estate for four days now and there were things going on that he neither liked nor understood. If only he could get hold of a vehicle, he would return to Kuala Jelang and take the remainder of his leave some other time.

In fact, this jaunt had been a bit of a dead loss. He had hoped to wander around and see the various aspects of estate life, but he was not given a chance. Every time he asked Wotherspoon if he could see this or that, some excuse was made as to why it was not convenient.

He had watched the tappers bringing in their latex to be weighed, and that was about all that he had seen. Having observed the same proceeding several times, he grew bored and went through a door into a nearby shed to see what went on inside. Immediately the manager materialised, from what appeared to be thin air, and barred his way.

Stan was irritated. 'It's only a store, isn't it?' he asked.

'Yes, but . . .' and he had been carefully led away.

Wotherspoon had given him free run of his extensive library, but as Stan had tried to point out, reading was not his reason for wanting to visit an estate; he could sit on his arse and do that in his own bungalow. Then there was the matter of the telephone.

It was all rather frustrating.

Ahmat had had a dreadful night. Azizah cursed and screamed and this morning they had had the worst scene to date.

Much as he hated to admit it, it looked as though his mother had been right after all. And yet? He thought back to the night at the Bintang Kilat when he had first seen his wife – in similar circumstances he would no doubt become infatuated all over again.

He felt a fool, drinking his morning coffee in the canteen, with men all around him who must have witnessed the humiliating scene. Impossible not to have done. Azizah's shrill voice must have been heard in the town. And the things she had said. Ahmat went hot under his collar at the thought of them. Language which no well-bred Malay girl could possibly be expected to know, let alone use. And the final insults and curses. 'I'll prepare the yellow rice,' she had screamed. The yellow rice that was for special occasions, the celebration meal on high days and holidays. For any wife to gloat, to threaten, as she had done; it was unspeakable.

He looked up at the canteen clock. Nine o'clock, the OCPD had said he wanted to leave. He was glad he was going out to-day. Allahumma! He could not have stayed in the police station this morning; he was humiliated enough as it was.

Jogindar Singh stood at the main door of the police station, picking his teeth.

It was always a difficult day, the first working day after a holiday. Everyone was lethargic and he himself did not feel like urging for once. Watching Omar cleaning the Bren gun on the GMT, he almost envied him. He would like to be going out to-day. One became stale, never moving out of such an enclosed area and he was in no mood for sitting at a desk.

Suvindar had thought that her first pains might be coming on. There was nothing he could do; best to keep out of her way until the time came. Even then, according to the midwife, husbands were nothing but a nuisance.

He spat out the toothpick and straightened up as he saw the OCPD coming down the steps.

'Good morning, Sahib.' He gave his most crashing salute.

'Good morning, Dato.'

Philip went straight through the Charge Room to his office. Jogindar Singh is getting fat, he thought.

'Ten-to-nine and I've done everything I can before we leave,' Philip told Cameron an hour later. 'Don't know when I'll get back, but you know where we'll be. I just want to have a look at the vehicle before we start.'

He picked up a file and left the office.

'Atten – shun!' The whole of the Charge Room sprang up with a resounding crash. Jogindar looked smug, he felt better, he liked to get a good noise out of them.

'Better have one more man for escort, Dato,' Philip said, and then, as though reading his thoughts, 'If you want a bit of fresh air for a change you can come yourself if you like.'

The sergeant-major needed no urging. His white smile split the heavy black beard.

'Thank you, Sahib.'

'Come as you are. No need to change; we're not going on a foot patrol.'

'Sahib. I'll just go and tell my wife.'

He handed over to the sergeant and proceeded to his quarters at the double.

Suvindar was still in the same state. 'Might be to-day,' she said, 'to-morrow, or the next. Who can tell? Better that you go out.'

'Ranjit,' her husband called, 'look after your mother, son. If you think she needs help, you are to run at once for Puron Kaur. You understand?'

'Yes, Father.'

Ranjit was growing into a tall, thin lad, all eyes and legs and top-knot. His steel bangle looked too big for his bony wrist. He is a good boy, Jogindar thought; already he has a sense of responsibility.

'Good morning, Karim. You a father yet?'

'Not yet, Tuan.'

'Everyone here?'

Philip peered into the back of the truck. Ahmat stood silent, looking out to sea; Omar was fondly polishing his Bren gun; Chee Min was waiting for the OCPD to move, so that he could climb inside; Jogindar was coming at the double across the parade-ground, hand held out to take his Sten gun from the PC waiting with it at the main entrance. Philip smiled.

'All set,' he told Karim, and climbed into the passenger seat.

'Tuan.' Karim shut the door and walked round to his own side.

'First stop District Office to pick up the DO, the Forest Checking Station to pick up the FO, Pokok Api Police Station, then Bukit Merah Estate.'

'Bukit Merah Estate, Tuan?' Philip turned in surprise at the driver's relieved tone. '*Nasib baik,*' Karim murmured, half to himself. 'Oh, Tuan, fate is kind.'

Then out it all came; his fears for his wife, the note for the doctor, the unanswered telephone.

'Good heavens, man,' Philip said, 'I don't want to take you away from your wife. You'd better turn back. We'll get another driver; it's only just after nine.'

'No, Tuan,' Karim shook his head resolutely, 'I'd rather go. Mr Ponniah said I could do nothing. I hope perhaps the doctor will come back with us. The road to Bukit Merah is a difficult one and – forgive my lack of modesty, Tuan – but I drive this vehicle better than anyone else.'

'You do indeed. Come along then, the sooner we see the doctor the better. I'll speak to him, but I'm sure he will need no persuading to return with us.'

As Karim started up, thoughts on both his wife and his job, it occurred to him suddenly that the heavy GMT was like one of his own giant Trengganu turtles. Just as slow, just as lumbering. It will be good to go home on leave, one day, he thought, he and Rokiah and the child. Then he swallowed and frowned; he must concentrate on the turtle of the present, not tempt providence by thinking of the future.

When they reached the District Office, Philip left the front cabin and climbed into the back.

'You'd better go in front, Dato,' he said to Jogindar Singh. 'You're the best-dressed person here. Good for public morale to see a smart policeman sitting in front!'

Chee Min and Omar laughed, because of course no one could see inside the vehicle anyway, and even Ahmat managed a sickly grin. Philip was in high spirits. He was glad things had finally come to a head; he wanted to get this resettlement area organised without further delay.

' 'Morning, James.' The DO was given a hand in.

'Good morning, all.' And aside to Philip, 'I'm not looking forward to this jaunt.'

'Oh, I don't know. It's a glorious day and I could do with the odd jolt – that curry is still lying heavy on my stomach from last night.'

'I thought you'd danced it off; you were active enough, heaven alone knows.'

Philip laughed. 'Malays aren't so different from Jocks,' he remarked. 'I never believe it does any harm to play the fool at the right time.'

'I envy you the ability.'

James was stating the truth. He had watched Philip clowning the evening before and wished that he could do the same. He used to be on such good terms with his crew; somewhere along the line he seemed to have lost contact with his fellow-beings.

They were at the Forest Checking Station.

Donald climbed in and the pleasantries of the day were exchanged again.

Karim did not bless the OCPD. Now he was going to have the big Sikh laughing at him all the way out and back. He was terrified of the sergeant-major.

But Jogindar's mind at that moment was on his wife; then he remembered Karim's.

'How is your wife?' he asked. 'Given birth yet, or is she still having trouble?'

'Still having trouble, Dato.'

Jogindar Singh approved of Rokiah. A natural, kampong girl, who didn't paint her face or wear clothes so tight that nothing was left to the imagination.

'Don't worry, lad, she's a healthy girl. She'll give you a fine son soon.'

'I rather hope she has a daughter,' Karim replied. 'I've always liked girls.'

Jogindar gave a great belly laugh and poor Karim felt his face burn.

'What's up?' James asked, as the truck began to slow down. They were at Pokok Api Police Station. He looked out and saw a European and a Tamil standing some distance away. 'I say, isn't that your Special Branch chap?'

'Yes.' Philip was waving to the waiting pair.

'I didn't know they were coming to-day. Why are we picking them up here?'

'I didn't want them to be seen leaving with us from the town. They're going to have a look round.'

The GMT stopped and Bill Young and the Indian climbed aboard. He was introduced to Donald Thom and, in turn, introduced, 'Detective-Corporal Pillai, who is accompanying me.'

'Good,' said Philip.

Soon they were on the winding road to the estate, which made further conversation impossible.

More than one person was listening to the rumble of the heavy vehicle as it approached the office buildings of Bukit Merah Estate.

Stan, standing on the upper verandah of the manager's bungalow, watched with interest as the monster heaved into sight and wondered what was up.

Ramakrishnan listened and hoped. Only the army or police could be coming in anything as heavy as that.

Krishnan was at his wits' end. His nails were bitten down to the quicks and he was sure his hair was turning grey. When the black, armoured vehicle appeared, he burst from the office door like a rocket going off. The police. He was saved. He would demand protection – *now*.

Men were vaulting from the back. Krishnan recognised the OCPD and went running straight to him.

'Sir, sir, oh, most esteemed sir! I have news of great import. Informations most vital to impart. I have composed letter lucid and true to PO Box 5000, but no chance to post. Oh, sir, I need protection; Communist terrorists are all around!'

Before Philip could take in what the excited little man was babbling, Jogindar Singh was at his side.

'That, Sahib, is the man who insulted the Memsahib. He is the one she would not let me arrest.'

'It is true, sir, it is true. It is I who wrote the letters to your lady wife; I who intimidated her on the telephone; I . . .'

Chee Min had drawn near. He recognised the Tamil as the man he had seen upset the table in the coffee-shop. So that was it.

Krishnan saw him too. His eyes rolled and his head wagged vigorously.

'Most honourable sir, I am understanding that you have come here to arrest me. Most bountiful lord, I am confessing, giving myself up to your lordship's mercy. Not only did I intimidate your lady wife. It is true that I collaborated with the Japanese. It is true also that I blackmailed Mr Ramasamy and that I am Mr S. Kandiah – you have no doubt taken fingerprints from car – '

'Hey, steady on,' Philip patted his shoulder, trying to calm him down. 'I don't know how many crimes you're confessing to, but this is neither the time nor the place. You had better come back to the police station with us.'

Krishnan fell on his knees for the second time in a matter of weeks. He felt that he would not be kicked this time.

'Oh, sir, lord, your Excellency, my gratitude is bounding unlimited.'

'For God's sake, get up, man,' Philip said.

'Oh, sir, I am in durance most vile. If I am staying in estate office I shall not be alive to accompany you. Please, oh kind sir, may I be climbing into truck forthwith?'

Philip was completely taken aback. His thoughts had been more on Stan and Karim's wife than anything else. He looked with distaste at the grovelling little man.

'Get into the front then,' he said. 'I don't know when we shall be going back.' And to Jogindar Singh, 'Better keep an eye on him, Dato.'

Karim had left the truck and made a beeline for the doctor, who was walking across the grass from the manager's house.

'Tuan, I am so relieved that you are here. There was no answer to the telephone.' He handed him the dresser's letter.

Stan read it in silence. He did not need any persuading to return with them to Kuala Jelang. In fact, he viewed the arrival of the GMT as a godsend and Ponniah's letter the perfect excuse to get away without offending Wotherspoon. He didn't much care for what he had read though. Ponniah was not given to exaggeration and if his fears were correct, the girl stood little chance. But no point in upsetting the husband now.

'I'll come,' he said. 'We'll do our best for your wife – you had better drive well and make sure you get me there, though!'

Karim smiled. He removed his beret and wiped over face and head with an enormous handkerchief. The doctor was already walking back in the direction of the bungalow, no doubt to pack his kit. He would soon be with Rokiah. What a relief!

At that moment Wotherspoon appeared on the scene from behind the office buildings. He had been told by the kangani that the police had arrived and had already worked himself into what he considered to be a fit state in which to greet them.

'How dare you enter my estate without permission,' he roared.

No one saw fit to comment. They let him rant on for a couple of minutes, then James stepped forward.

'We have decided that, before the matter of your land is taken through the final stages in DWEC, we should discuss it fully with everyone interested present.'

The manager ignored him.

'I saw my clerk climbing into your truck,' he said to Philip. 'You have arrested him. Why?'

'He asked to come of his own free will.'

At that Wotherspoon's eyes widened and he had to fight down a moment of rising panic. So Ramakrishnan had turned informer; no doubt of that. Well, if it came to the clerk's word against his, he would just deny everything. What was there to deny? The terrorist's face at the window. But he had got straight into his Land-Rover and driven off to Kuala Jelang, hadn't he? Plenty of witnesses to that. He had tried to inform the police, but there had been no one there. Then why hadn't he told the DO? No, that wouldn't wash. Better to deny even having seen the terrorist.

He looked at the ring of faces. It was difficult to gauge whether they were hostile or not. He'd bluff it out as best he could.

Bill Young was introduced. On hearing that he too was police, Wotherspoon declined to shake hands.

'As you have insisted on invading my privacy,' he said coldly, 'you had better come into the office.'

The four Europeans followed the manager. Ahmat went off to question the SCs and Chee Min to see the Chinese house-servants. Corporal Pillai had melted away as soon as the truck had stopped.

Everything was still. Jogindar and Omar kept up a desultory conversation and Karim stood by the front of his vehicle. Krishnan huddled inside, grateful for the protection both of the armour plating and the armed men about him.

More than half an hour passed. Then Karim saw the doctor emerge from the house with Chee Min; the sergeant was carrying his bag. Karim ran across the lawn to take it from him and he and Omar heaved it over the back of the GMT and stowed it inside.

'I hear that your wife's time is due as well,' Stan said to Jogindar

Singh. 'My God, you're a prolific lot – three of you here with pregnant wives. It's obvious the OCPD doesn't give you enough work to do!'

They all laughed. Stan had become a favourite with the police.

He walked over to peer in at the office window.

'I don't think they'll be long now,' he told the waiting men. 'They seem to be putting their papers away.'

A scraping of chairs soon confirmed his prediction and the door of the office opened.

It had not been a particularly successful meeting, but at least no one could say that Wotherspoon did not know exactly where he stood. The land would be used – whether he sold it or it was requisitioned was up to him.

'I think I'll stay on the estate for a day or two,' Bill Young announced. 'You don't have to put me up, sir, I can doss down with the SCs.'

Wotherspoon was furious but he kept his temper under control. 'Never let it be said,' he remarked icily, 'that I denied anyone the hospitality of my house. You can have the doctor's room; I see he intends to leave.'

'Yes,' said Stan. 'I'm sorry to go so soon, but the driver here has a very sick wife and the hospital have asked me to return. I am glad I was able to come. Thank you so much.'

The manager waved away his thanks and stood watching while Omar and Jogindar opened the heavy back doors of the truck.

Just as the last man climbed in, Ahmat appeared and quietly went over the top.

'I think I've picked up quite a lot,' he said to Philip.

'I'm not sorry to be leaving this estate,' Stan remarked to no one in particular. 'Place gave me the creeps. Sally was right, I should have stayed in Kuala Jelang for your Hari Raya party.'

Karim pushed home the heavy gear and they started off along the downward slope. Shouldn't take us long getting back, he thought. It was noon; they should be home by two o'clock. It was good to know the doctor was on board, that in a couple of hours he would be with his wife.

His throat was parched. How foolish; he had rushed off to the hospital as soon as it was light, missing his customary coffee and cake. He should have had a drink while they were on the estate. Now he would have to wait. He swallowed, trying to coax the saliva into his mouth.

James was relieved. Not that anything had changed; it was just that

681

he had felt some personal responsibility for Wotherspoon before – although there was no reason why he should – and now, having thrashed it out with nearly everyone concerned present, the air seemed to have been cleared. Let things take their course now; he had done his best.

On the whole it had been a satisfactory holiday. All their arrangements were worked out and Helen would have typed the necessary letters while he was out. Now they could start packing and soon, very soon now, Nannie would arrive and then they would be on their way.

Fancy old Norman Parkes turning up after all these years. He, certainly, had never been included in James's plans for the future. Well, one never knew.

Ahmat looked sullen. He had no wish to return home. Of course, he could divorce Azizah if he wished – but did he? Perhaps he should ask for a posting – the OCPD would understand and, anyway, he would be going on leave himself in six months' time; Kuala Jelang would change. Perhaps if they were in a larger place she might settle down. Somewhere where there was more to occupy her. Perhaps. But he wondered how it would be when he got back that afternoon, after the morning's disgraceful, humiliating scene.

'I'll prepare the yellow rice,' she had yelled. How *could* she? How could she be so cruel? 'Yellow rice, yellow rice,' went the wheels of the truck, 'I'll prepare the yellow rice, yellow rice, yellow rice.'

Wonder why people don't go in for timber more, Donald was wondering. There were some magnificent trees out there and he had already proved in his research work that there were many more species that would grow well here.

So much emphasis on rubber. Seemed like putting too many eggs in one basket, particularly with the threat of synthetics always just around the corner.

Jesus, I wish I hadn't had so much to drink last night, he thought; this motion is beginning to make me feel sick.

Omar kept his eyes on the jungle most of the time, but every so often he would turn and look at the OCPD with an expression almost of love.

With all the sadness of the past behind him, he was truly happy these days. His story was known to everyone in the police station now, but no one sneered at him any more; he was accepted. It was true, as he had said so often of late, that his corporal's stripes meant more to him now than his sergeant-major's crown had ever done. He would miss the Tuan when he went on leave. Oh well, why think about that – there were still a few more months.

The feeling of security that he had enjoyed whilst sitting in the stationary truck was beginning to desert Ramakrishnan.

He had no idea how the terrorists were deployed, or how many of them were actually living on the estate. They had said they needed advance information to stage an ambush in case there were insufficient men around. *In case* – that meant that sufficient men *might* be there.

Everyone in the vicinity of the estate office had seen the police arrive. The truck had stood for nearly an hour. Plenty of time for them to get organised.

Suddenly Krishnan began to shake. They had scorned his advice about the doctor because he would be unarmed. But what a target this would make. Eight men in the back of the truck and seven of them carried arms. He glanced at Karim. Even the driver had a pistol. Eight weapons at a minimum; uniforms, dead police. Could they resist this prize?

Suppose there *were* sufficient men at hand? Suppose they should choose to set an ambush for to-day? With him on board. If they had seen the truck at all, the chances were that they had also seen him in it – might even have seen him voluntarily going up to the OCPD.

'Is this the fastest you can go?' he asked.

Chee Min had not been able to glean much. There were no Chinese labourers on the estate; only the house-servants. And they were loyal. Hailams, who had worked for Wotherspoon for years. If they knew anything they were keeping it to themselves. They were genuinely fond of the old man, and within five minutes of questioning Chee Min had realised that he would get nowhere.

Oh well, who cared? That was a slap-up do last night. Hand it to Ahmat, he knew how to organise. Pity his wife was such a bitch. He was sorry when he had refused Sally's suggestion that she should join them, because then he might have brought Rose along as well. As it was, etiquette demanded that she stay put. Not that she minded, she had said, she was feeling sick. Poor Rose. Still, with the clinic and Stan at hand, she'd be well cared for when the time came.

His thoughts switched to his motor bike. Wow! What a beaut! Never thought he'd be so enthusiastic about anything less than a car. Just goes to show.

Jogindar Singh was feeling out of condition. His shorts were tight round his stomach and the webbing belt ate into his waist. Time I had a bit more exercise, he thought; sitting in an office all day, I'm becoming overweight. Suvindar was a good cook too. The journey out had been comfortable enough, sitting in the front, but standing at the back, with no protection against the midday sun, was far from comfortable.

Fancy having to give up his seat for a Tamil clerk. Like most northern Indians, Jogindar held his southern brethren in contempt. The Mem should not have hindered me, he thought, I should have dealt with him that day of the parade.

He wondered how his wife was getting on.

Stan was experiencing the same feeling that had come over him on New Year's Eve – or rather the beginning of New Year's Day.

He looked down on the truck as though he were floating above it and saw the occupants, like so many ants, each busy with their own thoughts. Fading away, fading out, all of them, even him.

He looked at each of them in turn. The kindly, wrinkled face of Omar; the dissipated face of Donald Thom. James, hot and sweating, the glass eye standing out bleakly against his sunken cheek. The happy face of Vincent; the shamed, unhappy face of Ahmat, and the hot and bulging face of the sergeant-major – that would teach him to eat less! The clear, tanned face of Philip – his first love's second love. And in the front, Wotherspoon's shifty clerk and the slim Malay youth, Karim, husband of the girl whom he very much doubted he would be able to save.

The thought of the girl in labour pulled him sharply back to earth. But even he, the doctor, was not indispensable – if the dresser has any initiative, he thought, he will have got the ambulance over from Kemuning by now. He could trust Ponniah; she was in good hands.

And so, he thought, there is no reason why I should not fade away as well.

Philip was thinking back to Chee Min's wedding; how he had said a prayer of gratitude for the men with whom he served. Omar, Karim, Jogindar Singh, Chee Min and Ahmat – it was Ahmat's doleful face that was giving him these thoughts. Poor bugger, he thought, what awaits him when he gets home? If it had been anyone with less pride it would not have been so bad. But Ahmat, with his serenity and grace – to have that foul-mouthed wench screaming at him in front of the whole station. The bitch. Something would have to be done about her, but what? Perhaps he should talk it over with the OCPS or CPO. Poor devil, it seemed certain at the moment that if one thing did not put paid to his career, another would.

There was something different about the road. Some alteration since this morning. Nonsense, he told himself, it's the shadows, a different angle of light. The trouble was that, ever since the CPO had told him that it would suit the leave roster if he were to go on leave after only two and a half years instead of three, he had been getting jumpy. Nevertheless, leave or not, this was a hell of a road. Incredible that there had never been an ambush on it. The jungle rose steeply on their left as the road unwound downhill. Below them was a ravine, covered with trees and bushes, but as steep as the other side. He peered down. He could not see the bottom, only the tops of the lower trees, many splotched with a vivid orange creeper.

Never an ambush? He thought he had caught a glimpse of something on the road, but at the next bend it wasn't there. Nor at the next. Must have been a trick of the light.

At the third bend he saw it again. So did everybody else. Christ, was it a log? Not worth taking a chance. He raised his hand to bang on the driver's cabin and was about to shout the order to debus when he saw that it was only a rotten bough.

The sweat sprang out on his temples like heavy dew and he wiped it away with relief, conscious that the other occupants of the truck were all doing the same thing. He grinned wryly, half to himself, and looked up on hearing Stan's laugh.

'People change,' the doctor remarked. 'Ten years ago I'd have been on my knees by now. Scared bloody stiff!'

He couldn't look less scared, Philip thought, ashamed of his own clammy palms. It had been a bad moment.

They were on a more even stretch of road, with the trees growing farther from the verge and the sun beating full upon them. Momentarily relaxed, the sound of voices rose above the engine, but Philip listened with only half an ear. He knew the road too well to be complacent. Little chance of an ambush for a mile or two, but then they would begin to climb again, there would be more hairpin bends and overhanging foliage. He took stock of their fire power.

Omar was on the Bren, Ahmat and Jogindar had Stens. He had a carbine; so had Don. James had a service revolver strapped to his belt – but count him out, he thought, he was finding it hard enough to remain upright with his one arm on the side of the swaying, jolting vehicle, let alone fire with it. Chee Min was pulling an automatic from his pocket – perhaps he was having similar thoughts – he and Ahmat had pistols too; also Karim.

Conversation, spasmodic as it had been, soon died. Each was busy with his own thoughts. The heat was intense and those who knew the road began to look forward to the shade to come, despite the danger the closer-growing trees would present.

Karim ran his tongue over the roof of his dry mouth as he changed down to negotiate the first of the hairpin bends. This was the worst part of the journey, almost a pass. Easy enough in a jeep, but driving the GMT for any length of time was always a strain. He should have had a drink when he could have done. Never mind, once on the straight he'd be able to put his foot down.

They were over the ridge and just beginning to descend when Karim saw the log. Placed strategically on the far side of one of the sharpest bends, they came upon it too suddenly to take evasive action. Instinctively he braked.

What the hell's he slowing down for? Philip's head jerked up. 'Keep going, Karim, don't stop,' he shouted.

At the same time James yelled, 'Who threw that stone?'

The object hit the side of the vehicle and bounced off.

'Hand-grenade.' As Philip spoke he opened fire at a movement in the undergrowth. He could see at a glance that it would be impossible to debus; with a steep wooded bank above them and a sheer drop to the ravine below, they could only jump on to the road itself. They would be sitting ducks anyway; better to stay where they were. Their only hope was that the weight of the vehicle would dislodge or surmount the obstacle – he could not see the log – and to make the most of their fire power. There was no turning back.

Ahmat pointed and fired almost simultaneously. 'There, Tuan.'

Philip followed his aim; both he and Donald fired at once. Omar rattled away, but he was firing blind, although he had a better chance of aiming than anyone else, with his weapon mounted on the cabin roof.

Jogindar Singh grinned as he fired. He had always been pretty useless on the range, but he doubted if it would matter now.

Philip dropped his empty carbine – no time to change the magazine – and drew his pistol. At that moment there was a cry of anguish from above. 'Seems we've got one,' he yelled. They all floundered as the truck hit the log, the impact sending a shudder through the heavy metal body. 'Don't stop, Karim. Whatever you do, don't stop. Oh Christ, this bloody thing's jammed.'

James tossed over his revolver and Philip let the useless automatic drop. As he took aim, a tremendous burst came from the bank above them. The vehicle lurched and began to go slowly over the side.

116. WHEN WIVES WAIT

'I couldn't stay at home.' Helen came quietly through the back door of the OCPD's bungalow, glancing at the two places still laid on the dining-room table as she passed. 'Sorry if I made you jump – one gets into the habit of creeping about at this time of the afternoon, when the children have just gone to sleep.'

'Do you feel like that too?' Sally asked. 'I don't know why I'm so jumpy; it's not yet two o'clock and Philip said he might not be back until three. Have you had lunch?'

'Yes. I had mine with the children. Are you going to have yours?'

'I don't think I want any. I was just about to make a cup of coffee though – would you like some?'

'Please, I would.'

Helen followed her out to the old-fashioned kitchen, placed well behind the house. Loud snores emanated from the servants' quarters nearby.

'One thing I've learned from them,' Sally gestured with her head in the direction of the snores, as she emptied half a bottle of kerosene over the wood, 'is how to light a fire. And to think I spent the whole war trying to learn!'

Helen looked on, aghast.

'Stand back,' Sally ordered, and tossed a lighted match on to the wood. Once the explosion had subsided she placed a large tin kettle on the roaring flames.

'I must admit that the one vestige of so-called civilisation that I do long for,' her friend remarked, 'is electricity. And with you around it's positively dangerous to be without it!'

'Oh well, we all have to die some time.'

The moment she made the thoughtless remark, Sally regretted it. Neither of them said anything more until the kettle had boiled and they were carrying their cups back to the verandah.

'I never really understood that quaint military term "suspended animation",' Helen said, 'but I'm sure this must be it. There's a terrible scent of destiny in the air.'

'Stan knew it at New Year's Eve – did you see his eyes? Dilated like a cat's – or perhaps I was just looking through the champagne.' She paused and Helen knew that her eyes saw farther than the point on which they were fixed, the rain tree with its dancing blooms. 'One day, not very long before we came here, one of my cats died. I was utterly miserable, because animals are no less precious than humans to me, and Philip had taken me away from the house. There was a tin mine not far from our quarter, and we sat on the hillside and watched the little men far below at work; ants, digging up the tin, day after day of heavy, sweated labour – and for what? To eke out a poverty-stricken existence, always too many children and seldom enough to eat, to die in the end. It is not the finality of death that is so shattering, I think, as the irretrievability. The unfairness. Why, I cried, did my little cat have to go? There must be cats down in that mine to whom death would be a happy release, and yet it was my cat, young still, much loved, a rescued stray with a happy life before her. She was gentle and sweet-natured; she'd never done anyone any harm. Why should she be the one to be taken? It was the same during the war – you must remember – why should a young man with everything before him be killed when others, possibly unhappy men with domestic burdens and troubled minds, be allowed to live? And all of a sudden, feeling bereft and alone – although Philip was beside me – I was no longer there, but away and above, looking down on the mineworkers and Philip and I watching them; looking down on myself. And I could imagine God, looking down too, and putting a finger on one man, one animal – you and you. Why should Fate decree that one life should be saved and another destroyed? And then I knew that it was no use fighting; that we have to accept God's will – as old Omar has accepted it – and resign ourselves to being the playthings of Fate.' Her eyes left the rain tree and turned to rest on her friend, giving her a sad little smile. 'Stan felt all that on New Year's Eve – I know, I felt it too.'

'It's a strange thing,' Helen mused, after they had been silent for a moment or two, 'how a knot of people can be drawn together on a small station like this and, whether we like it or not, we all become part of one another's lives. You and James might have met before; so might Philip and I. You and Stan had met.' She paused to take a deep drink and put her coffee cup down. 'I knew him before too, you know.'

Sally's interest immediately perked up.

'Philip thought so,' she said. 'I told him he was talking rot.'

'Philip? How on earth could *he* have known?'

'He didn't. Only guessed. He said it was something about the way you looked at him.'

'Oh God.' Helen's hand went to her throat in an uncharacteristically dramatic gesture. 'I only hope we can get away before James finds out.' She paused again and went slightly pink. 'You must think me an awful fool, Sally, but James is so terribly jealous – for no reason – it's just something in his nature that he can't help. We had a dreadful row before we were married over Stan – James had never met him, only knew he was a Pole – but he suspected it was him the day he arrived here. It's been a nagging worry ever since.'

Sally felt an involuntary stab of jealousy, because she knew instinctively that Helen and Stan had been lovers when she and Stan had not. She was so flabbergasted that she could not think what to say. So she said nothing and walked over to the verandah rail to watch as the sentry in the police station below marched forward to strike the hour. The length of bent railway sleeper was suspended from the eaves of the main building and the hammer lay on a ledge behind it. She watched every detail as the man transferred his rifle to his other shoulder, took the mallet from its shelf and struck the metal crescent twice. The sound of the strokes reached the listeners on the hilltop a fraction of a second after the PC's arm had swung back each time.

'Two o'clock,' Sally said, unnecessarily. 'Another cup?'

Hardly had she poured the coffee and sat down when a hoarse cry rose from the police station. Both women jumped to their feet and saw the sentry move towards the sleeper once again, this time at the double.

Clang, clang, clang, clang, clang, clang, clang, clang! The man had dropped his rifle and was beating the metal with all his might.

'Oh Christ! The general alarm!'

Men came running from every corner of the compound, those on standby in uniform and the rest in varying stages of dress and undress.

Before the sentry had finished sounding the alarm all the police vehicles were beginning to line up in front of the main gate, waiting with engines running. Cameron stepped into the road and stopped a PWD lorry; after a moment's talk the driver turned round and fell into line. Next a civilian Land-Rover was commandeered, but the driver jumped out and ran away; a police driver took his place and that too joined the queue.

The servants now came rushing in as well.

'Is it an ambush, Mem? Has the Tuan been ambushed?' they cried.

'Yes. It is an ambush.'

'Oh Sally, don't *say* that. You don't know. It might be a fire or something. It doesn't have to be an ambush.'

'Yes,' repeated Sally, and her voice was very quiet, 'it is an ambush. I knew before Philip left the house this morning. Ja'afar, go down and see what you can find out – but don't get in anybody's way.'

'Yes, Mem.' The old man sprinted down the steps and a minute later they saw him speaking to the driver of one of the stationary vehicles.

The men were pouring out of the Charge Room now, some still carrying shirts and boots, but each with a weapon in his hand, and began scrambling into the waiting transport.

'Couldn't we ring up now?' Helen asked.

Sally shook her head. 'Not until the flap is over.'

She noticed the eight white knuckles of Helen's hands clenched on the railing, then saw her own. Sixteen points of tension. I'll count twenty, she said to herself, before I make a move. But she did not have to. As Zukifli jumped into the front seat of the leading vehicle and the convoy moved off, the telephone rang.

Helen watched as Sally listened to the crackling voice on the other end for what seemed an eternity, then, 'Thank you,' Sally said in a quiet voice. 'Please let me know when you have some news. Good-bye.'

She turned to her friend. 'That was Cameron. Apparently the Special Branch chap, Bill Young, stayed behind – I knew that Philip was picking him up somewhere *en route* – a man from one of the outlying divisions came in to report that he had heard shooting; it was about half an hour after they had left the estate. It's taken him all this time to get through. Bill is trying to investigate, with a party of SCs from the estate, but, as usual, the only available transport has gone u/s. It doesn't *have* to be them, but Cameron is pretty certain it is. And so am I.'

The only unusual activity in the police compound now was small groups of wives talking together outside the barracks, during what would normally have been their sleeping-time.

Suddenly, a long drawn-out, keening wail rose from the compound and two women dashed into the station inspector's quarters. It was followed shortly by a high-pitched, hysterical scream, as Azizah raced into the middle of the grass, brandishing a cooking-pot over her head. The immediate cause of her actions was not apparent, but women started running towards her from all sides. It was not possible at that distance to distinguish between the many voices, but clearly above them floated the words 'yellow rice' and 'he's dying, he's dying, he's dead.'

Azizah went into a kind of drunken dance, flinging the pot in the air and catching it; laughing and screeching all the time. The women had stopped at a safe distance and formed a ring about her. The scene seemed set for a lynching, or a trial for witchcraft.

'I think I had better go and sort this out,' said Sally, and strode out of the house and down the steps. In a way it was a blessing to have something to do.

Nodding to the sentry in passing, she marched straight past the police station and through the milling throng of women, who gave way as they saw her approach. What had been in her mind when she left the house had been forgotten; without further thought she went straight up to Azizah and hit her a stinging blow across the left cheek, then with the back of her hand across the right.

There was a stunned silence throughout the compound. Azizah dropped the cooking-pot and gaped open-mouthed at the woman who had dared to hit her.

Neither said a word and Sally turned on her heel and walked away. One of the women plucked at her sleeve as she passed and pointed to the OCPS's quarters. From where Helen watched, she saw Sally pause and say something to the woman, then continue on her way. Azizah had walked slowly back to her own house, leaving the cooking-pot lying on the grass, and the crowd had begun to melt away. It had had the desired effect, but Helen had shuddered when Sally raised her arm, and Siti, standing beside her, had murmured, 'No, Mem, don't hit her,' and given a start when the hand met its target.

Helen saw the elderly police lieutenant leave the OCPD's office to intercept Sally; saw them speak for a moment, then he put an arm across her shoulders for an instant and they walked back to the police station together. Again they paused and soon Sally's footsteps were heard upon the steps.

Helen could not hear the words, but Cameron had said, 'Thank you, Mrs Morrison. I'd have shut that woman up myself if ye hadna' come along.' And, 'I'll let ye know the moment there's news of the boss.'

'Ought you to have done that?' she asked, as Sally re-entered the house.

'No, I ought not.' She slumped into the nearest chair, head in hands, and Helen wondered whether to go over to her or not. It was only a moment, however, before she regained her composure and, smiling at Siti, she said, 'The sergeant-major's wife has had another son; you predicted right – as usual.'

To Helen she said, 'You and I are not the only wives. That woman was mouthing the foulest obscenities about poor Mat, interspersed with shrieks of joy because she is so sure that he is dead. She's a bit off her rocker, I think, but I couldn't let it pass. There is Suvindar Kaur and Rokiah – the driver's wife, who has been taken to Kemuning, although old Ponniah doesn't think she'll survive the journey – and Rose Lee; we're not the only ones.'

'No,' Helen admitted. 'You were quite right; I shouldn't have questioned it.'

Sally picked up her cup of coffee; it was stone cold.

'Be a dear and make us some more,' she said to Siti, then walked across the room to fetch the box of cigarettes. 'I'd given up smoking, but there *are* times . . .'

Helen nodded.

As Sally held the match for her friend, their eyes met over the tiny flame, each seeking comfort and assurance from the other; each determined to mask despair.

Then they sat down in silence to wait.

EPILOGUE

Abdul Karim died with the first burst. Beside him Ramakrishnan screamed as he saw the blood-spattered body slump over the wheel and felt the heavy vehicle leave the road.

Stanislaus Olshewski smiled as he looked straight into the muzzle of a Bren gun, mounted on the bank at exactly the right height to mow down the occupants of the truck and camouflaged with branches and twigs. He took one of the first bullets straight between the eyes and continued to smile in death.

Omar bent over the doctor's body and never straightened up again. His head split open like a ripe fruit and spilt its contents over James Weatherby, who looked up with a start and, as he did so, clutched his stomach, tightly closing his eyes in pain.

The vehicle slid gently over the side of the precipice and, equally slowly, began to turn. For a fleeting second, those occupants who were still alive, had a horrifying view of the rock-strewn slope towards which they were now hurtling.

Philip Morrison and Vincent Lee Chee Min hung on to one side of the truck and each other, as it somersaulted, righted itself and careered down the hillside again.

On the opposite side Sharif Ahmat too hung on with both hands.

During the first roll Donald Thom was hurled out as though he were a rag doll and hit the slope a split second before the armoured truck arrived on top of him. His neck was broken and although he remained alive long enough to see Jogindar Singh flung out at the next turn, his eyes soon glazed over and within a matter of seconds he was dead.

The truck came to a slithering halt and, with a final jolt, spewed most of its remaining passengers on to the ground, before rolling on to its side.

Only Ahmat was thrown completely clear. Philip lay with his legs trapped under several tons of metal; Chee Min crouched close beside him and, from inside the cabin, Ramakrishnan screamed with fear and frustration as he tried, unsuccessfully, to open the jammed door.

Except for those high-pitched screams, everything was silent. Above them the road appeared deserted and around them not a twig moved.

'Shut up, you little bastard,' yelled Philip, 'or I'll come and slit your throat.'

The screams stopped abruptly and gave way to a low whining mumble.

Jogindar lay with his head against the bole of a tree. His turban had saved it from being bashed in, but his back was broken and he knew that he would never move again. He had inherited his father's spirit though, and even in such straits he was amused by the OCPD's threat, when his legs were pinned firmly under the GMT and his hands appeared to be useless, bloody stumps. He smiled, his teeth showing bright white in his full black beard.

Philip lay silent and still, taking stock of the situation. He himself was useless; he must have put out his hands to protect his face and hit something on the way out. Either his wrists were broken, or very badly sprained. His legs were only visible from above the knees. As yet he could feel no pain, but he dreaded to think what lay under that heavy mass of iron. To his left Chee Min squatted on his heels, holding one arm with the other and rocking backwards and forwards, obviously in pain.

Jogindar continued to smile and rolled his eyes, but there was something unnatural about his position.

'Can you move, Dato?' Philip called.

Jogindar lifted his arms and let them fall. He tried but could not shake his head.

'It must be my spine, Sahib,' he replied. 'Only my arms can move.'

At that moment James crawled from the vehicle, looking dazed and with blood pouring from a gash across his temples.

'Grenade hit me in the stomach,' he explained. 'Must have been a dud, but it creased me; I couldn't move before.'

He got to his feet and tested his limbs, while the others watched. He looked a dreadful sight, but much of the blood on him was Omar's.

James in turn looked at Philip and his mind at once flew back to a tail gunner, legs trapped, scrabbling in the flames. 'Thank God it didn't catch fire,' he murmured.

'Can you stand, Chee Min?' Philip asked. The sooner the able-bodied amongst them went for help the better.

'Bastards got me in the arm.'

The DO went to him and rolled up the sleeve of his shirt. The elbow was shattered; a bloody mess and Chee Min stifled a scream with his other hand as he touched it.

James was wearing a scarf tucked into his shirt; he pulled it off. 'If someone can tie this, it'll do as a sling.'

'I have a field dressing,' Ahmat said. He appeared to be the only one uninjured.

'Mat, you must go for help,' Philip said. 'If you can get to the main road, there's a Chinese kedai there that has a telephone. We'll need a stretcher for the sergeant-major.'

But Ahmat shook his head. 'No, Tuan. I won't leave you. The DO and Sergeant Lee can get there just as fast.'

'I'm giving you an order, Mat.' Philip knew that there was little hope for anyone who was left behind; better that everyone who could should go. 'See if you can fix Sergeant Lee's arm, then off you go. No delays.'

Ahmat tried to stand up, but one leg straight away collapsed under him. He gave a low moan of pain and sat down. Rolling up a leg of his jungle green trousers, he exposed a perfect compound fracture, the tip of bone gleaming white again the brown skin. Both Philip and Chee Min gasped and Ahmat himself went a sickly, greenish grey.

'You see, Tuan? Tuan Allah has taken it out of my hands. I have no choice but to stay.'

As he finished speaking, their attention was attracted by a sound from the road above. Philip held up his hand for silence.

'The only thing to do is to lie still and keep quiet. If they think we're all dead they may go away.' His voice was little more than a whisper.

'Loot.' The one word was spoken by Chee Min. 'They may take their time, but eventually they will come for our watches and our guns.'

Philip himself did not hold out much hope. He too knew that they would come to examine the bodies, strip them of their uniforms and take whatever there was to take. How they would kill whoever they found alive did not bear thinking about. Hacking to death with parangs was the most common method, but, not long after his arrival in the district, a police lieutenant and his men had been thrown on to their jeep and burned alive and Chee Min's brother-in-law had had a six-inch nail driven into his head. He shuddered involuntarily and quickly looked round to see if anyone had noticed. He of all people must not show fear. James stared up at the road; Jogindar and Ahmat both lay with their eyes closed and Chee Min was praying in a quiet voice, telling his beads by heart.

A cracking branch caused Philip's ears to strain and Ahmat's and Jogindar's eyes to fly wide open. Chee Min stopped his prayer. James continued to stare, unmoving.

There were several minutes of silence, then again the undeniable sounds of movement in the undergrowth.

From the cabin of the truck Ramakrishnan let out a wail. 'Oh Tuan, sir, please to shoot me! Shoot me quickly! Please, sir! I will be suffering most terrible death at hands of Communist terrorists. I would be better deserving death from the hands of you, whom I have betrayed also.'

And then, in fits and starts, spasms and long strings of words, sometimes moaned and sometimes screamed, out came the whole sordid story. All five listeners understood English well enough to get the portent. All were silent.

Again from the truck came the high-pitched, pleading wail. 'Have mercy on me, kind sir! Please to kill me, sir! Do not leave me for the bandits.'

'I would willingly kill you,' growled Jogindar Singh, 'if I could move. But it is justice that the terrorists should look after you.'

Krishnan moaned and the sergeant-major gave a maniacal laugh.

'Quiet, all of you,' commanded Philip, and listened.

The noises in the undergrowth had started again. Cautious, but getting nearer. Still, it was a long climb down and they did not know what reception lay at the bottom. He knew that they would not waste ammunition in finding out.

'Come one step further and we open fire,' he roared in Malay. All sounds ceased immediately and after a few minutes voices were to be heard, low but audible.

'What are they saying, Chee Min?' Philip asked in a whisper.

'They are arguing, sir.' Then they all kept quiet while he listened. The talk went on interminably and Philip succeeded in placing three different voices. They argued for nearly twenty minutes and could then be heard retracing their steps.

Jogindar Singh let out a most blood-curdling laugh and there were distinct sounds of hurrying at the top of the ravine.

'There were three men,' Chee Min told them. 'One wanted to throw a couple of hand-grenades down, but the others warned him of their strict orders that grenades and ammo must be conserved. Much of the talk was impressing on him that all three would be punished for his act. One of them wanted to come down and finish us off with his bayonet, but the other two were more cautious – they did not know what our fire power consisted of, nor how many of us were left alive. They knew that only one was dead. They have gone back to the estate for reinforcements, but they will be back later on.'

Donald Thom's body was the only one lying out in the open for the bandits to see. Those of Omar and Stan had, for some unknown reason, remained huddled at the bottom of the truck and Karim was still wedged behind the steering-wheel. There was no reason for them to know that only half the original number were still alive.

'Now is the time for you two to go,' Philip said. 'Your quickest route will be to follow the river – the road is all hairpin bends from here to the main road. You should hit Tukul Puteh Estate, but if you don't, you'll come out by the bridge and the Chinese shop-house is not far from it. Get through to the police station and Cameron will do the rest. Now. For heaven's sake get cracking while the going's good. Good luck.'

James bent to grip Philip's shoulder, his face working, but no words would come out. He touched the hands of Ahmat, and Jogindar and Chee Min did likewise.

'Good luck, good luck, good luck.'

The place seemed unutterably lonely when the two men had gone. Pushing their way slowly through the undergrowth, James limping and Chee Min hanging on to his arm, they could be heard for a long time after they had disappeared from view.

Philip calculated. It would take the CTs the best part of an hour to reach the estate – unless they met a party on the way – and then they would have to tell their story. He knew from experience that the leader would not believe one man straight away. Each would have to recount his version, then there would be question and answer, verification of facts; that should take at least another half-hour. Getting their numbers together would not take long, provided they were not otherwise employed, then the trek back. They should have at the least two, at the most three, hours. If anyone had heard the shooting and reported it without delay – and if it could be heard on the estate Bill Young was sure to act – so, help *could* arrive by then. James and Chee Min would not be able to move fast; it was a long way on foot to the main road – the time would be much the same. There was nothing they could do but wait and hope. He told them what he had been thinking.

'Anyone any arms?' he asked.

It appeared that all weapons but his had been lost in the descent. He had taken the revolver from James and stuffed it in his shirt as the truck began to fall. It was still there, cold against his skin.

'Mat,' he called, 'if you can get over to me, the DO's revolver is inside my shirt. I only remember firing once, there should still be five rounds.' He paused then, not wanting to sound melodramatic, but nevertheless to face facts. 'None of our religions tolerate the taking of human life, neither murder nor suicide, but knowing what the terrorists will do to us if help does not arrive in time, helpless as we are, I believe that God will understand and forgive.'

Ahmat dragged himself over to the OCPD, inch by painful inch, pausing several times on the way. At last he reached him and drew the revolver from his shirt.

'Look at me,' Philip said quietly, attempting unsuccessfully to grip his shoulder with one of his bloodied hands. 'This is the most difficult task that any man can be asked to perform. Normally it would fall to me, but now you are the only one who can carry it out. Understand that this is only as a last resort. With luck help may arrive in time, but if it doesn't, and we hear the bandits coming down the slope, you must act at once. The Tamil first, then the sergeant-major, myself, and then yourself. If you hesitate before shooting any man, think quickly what his fate may be if you don't.'

Ahmat had nodded several times during the exhortation and a succession of expressions had flitted across his face, but he had seemed unable to speak. Philip gave him time to think and was relieved to see his eyes harden and his jaw set.

'I will do it,' he answered, 'if I have to, but I pray that it will not be necessary.'

'I only remember firing once, but you had better count the rounds.'

Ahmat broke the revolver and jerked his head in the direction of the cabin. 'Surely you are not going to waste a round on that little tick,' he said, and Jogindar gave a great guffaw.

At that Krishnan burst into a new stream of lamentations.

'Shut up,' roared Philip, 'or we *will* leave you to the mercy of the terrorists. Not one more word.'

There was immediate silence.

If Ahmat had known that, besides his other crimes, Krishnan had also been responsible for the death of his friend, Dick Richardson, he would no doubt have refused point blank. But he had been ordered to shoot the Tamil and, if it came to it, he would.

Jogindar had actually seen Philip fire twice and he thought he had heard the DO fire as well, before passing the weapon over to the OCPD. He could not be sure of that, but he was sure that there could not be five rounds left in the chamber. He also knew that the bandits would be back – and sooner, he thought, than the OCPD had said. He tried once more to move his legs and head, without success. Even if help did arrive – which he thought most unlikely in the time – would life still be worth living? He had visited India often enough as a youth to know what cripples were. It would be the end of active service, the end of the police for him. And of what use would he be to his family? Nothing but a burden; if he lived at all.

Carefully, so as not to attract attention, he felt in the folds of his turban and extracted a razor blade, new and greasy sharp. He had kept the blade there, against emergencies, for many years, but never before had had cause to use it. While Ramakrishnan whined and the OCPD scolded, he drew the blade deeply across each wrist, then, burying it in the soil beside him, he folded his hands over his stomach so that the source of the blood should not be seen. He lay there quietly, the fingers of one hand gently caressing his steel bangle and thinking of his father.

'Sahib,' he called after a while, and forcing a smile, 'Sahib, no need to keep a bullet for me – I must have been hit in the belly without realising it before.'

A great dark patch was already spreading across his chest and abdomen, staining the khaki cloth. It was clear that he would not last long.

'Good-bye, old man. May you be as brave in the next world as you have been in this.'

697

In common with the rest of the police station, Philip always thought of Jogindar as old, though in fact he was younger than himself.

'There are three rounds,' Ahmat said abruptly. He had been holding the broken revolver in his hand all this time. He now clicked it shut and shoved it inside his own shirt.

Philip tried not to look at his watch too obviously although there was little point in subterfuge at this stage. They still had at least an hour to go. He thought of James and Chee Min and wondered what progress they had made. He was glad that James had not been killed – it would have been so unfair, only a few weeks away from a new life. If the journey took them long enough, he could pick up a little Australiana from Chee Min in advance! Better not to think about his own future; of Sally. He resisted the temptation to glance at his watch again and looked at his companions instead.

Jogindar Singh appeared to have fallen asleep; he had in fact been dead for half an hour. Ahmat lay on his back with his eyes wide open, staring up at the sky.

'What are you thinking about, Mat?' he asked after a while.

Ahmat slowly turned his head and surprised Philip with his peaceful smile.

'I was thinking of the day I met my wife. I was being very, eh, debonair – is that the right word?'

'Could be.'

'I don't usually drink much, but I'd had a few beers I suppose; at any rate I felt very bold – I wanted to show off. I had never danced in public before, but when one of my pals dared me to go on the floor, I went up with a great flourish to face Azizah, who was to become my wife. Did you know she had been a ronggeng girl?' He didn't wait for Philip's reply. 'I thought she was the most beautiful woman I had ever seen – I still do.'

His voice faded out and when Philip turned to look at him he saw that there were tears in his eyes. He said nothing and in a little while Ahmat frowned and spoke again.

'After this morning I do not believe that Tuan Allah means me to see her again.'

'Nonsense,' said Philip briskly. 'It will be all right. By this time she will be feeling sorry for all the things she said – you wait and see.'

'Where did you first see your wife, sir?' Ahmat asked, deliberately changing the subject. He in turn saw Philip's eyes go soft, and smiled.

'She was floating down from the sky in the moonlight,' Philip said softly. It was a different world; difficult to believe now that it had ever existed.

698

'The Mem – floating?'

Philip actually laughed. The incredulous tone of Ahmat's voice had quite taken his mind off the present for a fleeting moment.

'She's not all that heavy,' he said, 'and besides, she was at the end of a parachute.'

'A parachute? Wah!'

Before there was time for further explanation, the sound of movement on the road above drew their attention. So they were back sooner than expected. Must have been better organised than he had thought.

Philip counted ten. If it were the police they would call out, but there had been no sound of a vehicle approaching.

They were not left in doubt for long.

'Red devils, running dogs,' a high voice floated down from the road, 'we are coming. Muslim pigs. And you Indians – we shall defecate on your sacred cows when you are dead.'

'Ahmat, now. But don't hurry, take time to aim – you can't afford to miss.'

Ahmat dragged himself off while the voice from above continued its empty insults.

But it was not the voice that had caused Philip to act. The crashing in the undergrowth of many feet announced the departure of the terrorists from the top. It was impossible to estimate the number accurately, but the sound of violent movement was covering such an area that there could not be less than ten. He reckoned considerably more.

Ramakrishnan sat frozen with terror, his eyes rolling and his face grey. He did not move as Ahmat leaned through the opposite window and fired at point blank range.

Crawling back to where Philip lay trapped, he reached out to Jogindar to make sure that he was not still alive. It needed but a touch and, relieved, he crawled on.

Ahmat's mouth formed a hideous grimace as he felt the tears prick his eyes and he tried to control them. He looked at the OCPD; the terrorists were still a little way off, if only they could fight it out. But he, who had seen the guerillas at work during the war, knew better than anyone what the odds were.

'Don't waste time, Mat,' Philip's lips barely moved. 'You must not forget yourself.'

'Please, Tuan, turn your head; I cannot shoot when I can see your face.'

Philip smiled and turned his head.

Ahmat gave a great choking sob, as he pulled the trigger for the last time.

'Take that, you filthy, murdering swine,' he shouted, hurling the empty weapon in the direction of the oncoming men. Then, closing his eyes, he lay back to wait for them to come.

Long after the last alien sound had ceased, when the dust had settled and the leaves stopped their quivering, the insects resumed their song.

Below them, the beetle lay on its side, stripped clean; its armour dull and lifeless, untouched by the rays of the setting sun.

Deep in the ravine, already swathed in the shades of night, the Styx-like, yellow river roared, crashing its way towards the sea. And in the distance, disinterested in the foibles of humankind, the blue, eternal mountains slept on.

GLOSSARY

Adat custom
Adohi! Oh dear! Alas!
Allahumma! Oh God!
Alor place
Amok furious attack, while temporarily insane
Ang pow present, traditionally red packet containing money (Chinese)
Api fire
Atap palm thatch

Baju garment
Baju kurong long loose shirt, worn over sarong
Bakau type of mangrove
Barang things, stuff, 'clobber'
Batu stone, mile
Belachan strong prawn paste, eaten with curry
Belimbing a small fruit
Belukar secondary jungle
Bersanding 'sitting in state' part of Malay marriage ceremony
Betel small nutlike fruit, chewed like tobacco
Bintang star
Bukit hill

Changkol type of hoe
Che Mr, Mrs or Miss; used for women more often than men
Chempaka a sweet-smelling, flowering tree
Cheongsam sheathlike Chinese dress

Datin female of Dato
Dato grandfather, title (courtesy title for senior NCOs)
Daun leaf
Deepavali Hindu 'festival of lights'
Degil stubborn
Durian a large, strong-smelling fruit

Fukien southern Chinese race and dialect

Gunong mountain

Haj pilgrimage to Mecca
Haji man who has made the pilgrimage to Mecca, title

701

Hajjah female of Haji
Hakka southern Chinese race and dialect
Haram forbidden by Muslim law
Hari Raya Puasa holiday following the Muslim fasting month
Hijau green
Hitam black
Hokkien southern Chinese race and dialect

Inche Mr (courtesy title for police inspectors)

Jaga to watch, night watchman
Jakun aboriginal tribe from southern Malaya
Jambu guava
Joget modern Malay dance

Kampong village
Kangani overseer on rubber estate (Tamil)
Kaum Ibu womenfolk; in this case the women's section of a political
    party
Kebaya tight-fitting Malay blouse
Kedai shop
Keling, or *Kling* Malay for Tamils or Telegus (now considered
    derogatory)
Kelong a large fish trap
Kempeitai secret police, 'gestapo' (Japanese)
Kenduri feast
Keris long Malay dagger with wavy blade
Kilat shining, lightening
Kolek type of canoe
Kong Hee Fatt Choy Happy New Year (Chinese)
Kongsi communal business or association, usually Chinese
Kuala river mouth
Kubu fort
Kuning yellow

Langsat a small fruit, sweet white flesh with thin brown skin
Lima five

Mak Mother
Mangosteen a smallish round white fruit with thick purple skin
Maraiee Japanese name for Malaya
Mas gold
Masok to enter, 'Come in'
Mata-mata policeman (literally: eyes)
Mee ribbon-like noodles (Chinese)

Merah red
Min Yuen plain clothes terrorists, food and money collectors (Chinese)

Nah! Take that!
Nasib fate
Nasib baik good fortune, thank God for that!
Negri country, state

Orang utan large ape (literally: jungle person)

Padang field at centre of most Malayan towns, 'village green'
Padi rice, in growing state
Pak Father
Palong trough, on scaffolding used in tin mining
Pandanus type of palm, much used for weaving mats
Papaya a large melon type, marrow-shaped fruit
Parang long-bladed, all-purpose knife, both domestic and a weapon
Pasir sand
Penghulu headman, minor chief
Perak silver
Pokok tree
Pontianak ghost of a woman who died in childbirth (Malay folklore)
Puan courtesy title, extra polite form of Mrs or Miss
Puasa Muslim fasting month, Ramadan
Puteh white

Rambutan a small sweet fruit with hairy red skin
Ramvong a Siamese dance
Rei bow (Japanese)
Rimau tiger
Ronggeng a Malay dance

Sakai generic term for Malayan aborigines
Sambal side dishes with curry
Samfoo pyjama-type suit worn by Chinese women (Chinese)
Sampan general term for small boats
Sarong sheath, skirt-type garment worn by Malays of both sexes
Satay mutton or beef cooked on a skewer, similar to kebabs
Selamat Hari Raya Happy Hari Raya (literally: Peaceful Holiday)
Selamat jalan bon voyage (literally: peace on your going)
Selamat tinggal good-bye (literally: peace on your staying)
Sembilan nine
Selendang scarf worn round the head or shoulders by Malay women
Sharif man claiming descent from the Prophet Muhammad
Sharifa female of Sharif

Songkok velvet cap worn by Malay men, usually black
Sungei river
Syonan Japanese name for Singapore

Tahan hold on, bear up
Tanah earth, land
Tanjong cape, headland
Taukeh, or *Towkay* Chinese merchant
Tiga suku three-quarters, slang term for someone 'not all there'
Timbusu a tall, flowering tree
Toddy palm wine, mostly drunk by Tamils
Tukul hammer
Tuan Sir, or Mr in extra polite address

Ulu back of beyond, interior

Wah! exclamation of amazement or surprise
Wayang theatre, show